LONGING

By J. D. Landis

Lying in Bed

Longing

LONGING

J.D. LANDIS

HARCOURT, INC.

New York   San Diego   London

The line of verse in the book's dedication is from "The Seventh
Elegy" in *The Selected Poetry of Rainer Maria Rilke,* edited and
translated by Stephen Mitchell, copyright © 1982 by Stephen
Mitchell. Used by permission of Random House, Inc.

Library of Congress Cataloging-in-Publication Data
Landis, J. D.
Longing/J. D. Landis.—1st ed.
p. cm.
ISBN 0-15-100453-6
1. Schumann, Robert, 1810–1856—Fiction.
2. Schumann, Clara, 1819–1896—Fiction. 3. Composers—
Fiction. 4. Pianists—Fiction. 5. Germany—Fiction. I. Title.
PS3562.A4767 L66 2000
813'.54—dc21   00-035049

Text set in Monotype Garamond
Printed in the United States of America
First edition
A C E G I J H F D B

For Denise

("Nowhere, Beloved, will world be but within us")

and for Benjamin, Jacob, and Sara

and in memory of

Eve S. Landis

(October 29, 1910–February 9, 2000)

My first reader

I am grateful to
Walter Bode, Nicholas Delbanco,
Henry Dunow, and Leslie Gardner
for advice, support, reprieve.

AUTHOR'S NOTE

The epigraphs are archival. The characters are historical. The dates of events and correspondence are, when verifiable, authentic. The rest is fiction masquerading as fact, and the reverse.

LONGING

PROLOGUE

Endenich

JULY 23, 1856

*If you want to penetrate the mind of an artist,
you must visit him in his studio.*
Robert Schumann

He lies in bed, waiting for Clara.

Southeast, over the roofs and spires of Bonn and across the Rhine, his favorite river until it belched him back, the peaks of the Siebengebirge will not relinquish the sun. Each morning they grasp it at their back and tease him with it. Guess which hand.

He has played the same game with his children. Of them all—eight, when he counts the dead Emil—he misses most the one he's never seen. Felix. The mathematics of conception have proven sporadically diverting. Or what passes for diversion in an institution such as this, which, to give it its name despite the civilized beauty of its gardens and the willingness of his half-deaf doctor to engage in endless, intimate conversation, must be called a madhouse:

Felix Schumann, born June 11, 1854, three months, seven days after his father had been taken to Endenich. Had begged to be taken to Endenich, though it was the sort of place he feared above all others. (Probably because he'd always known he'd end up in one. He used to fear death, too.) Conceived, therefore, September 1853. Which was precisely the month there appeared at their door in Düsseldorf an angel, a demon, a child-voiced boy of the vaguely familiar name Johannes Brahms, with long blond hair and blue eyes and strong hands and a face merely beautiful until he played the piano, and then it was transfigured.

Were he to have another son, which seems out of the question considering the fact he hasn't even seen his wife in the nearly two and a half years since he was taken to Endenich, he would name him Johannes. A daughter: Clara.

And if Johannes Brahms were indeed the father of Felix, and therefore his wife's lover, he would be Robert's lover as well, for an absent husband resides as much within his wife as within Endenich, and her pleasure there-fore becomes his own and the possession of her, too, the possession of himself.

He longs for her. Cut off from her by mountain and valley, so much space and time between themselves and peace, happiness and suffering, he longs. That's what desire turns to over time: long-ing. It doesn't become merely protracted with the passage of the days and nights but intensifies into what seems an eternal cupidity. It becomes an emptiness unrelieved by either imagination or memory.

It's an emptiness he's fed, ironically, by refusing to eat. He stopped eating in order to die. Therefore, Dr. Richarz had him fed with a tube. And a tube down the throat or nose, no matter how thoughtfully it's been greased, oiled, waxed, or otherwise mollified, in and of itself ruins the appetite. To get him to eat, they destroyed his desire to eat. Where was the satisfaction in starvation after that?

What they've fed him since is some kind of soup whose consistency re-minds him of cold semen, washed down with wine because he still loves wine, almost as much as he still loves to smoke. And if there's any reason not to die it is to continue to be able to have the occasional cigar, preferably during every waking moment, while sitting by one's smoking stand with an atlas in one's lap, plotting elopement into the great book of the world.

Clara has sent him cigars now and then. When he smokes them, and draws the smoke as far down into his body as his weakened breath will per-mit, he imagines she had touched the cigar and that it is she who enters him, becomes the kind of vapor that invades him as she always has, carried by his blood to the very insides of his eyes.

But he knows he won't actually see her until he's dead, and then what sight he has will be the sight of the dead, which if it's anything is backward sight, memory alone. Death must kill the present, or otherwise it would be called not death but something else, like lapse or lull or interlude. But at least they would be reunited, not that a funeral makes for a particularly sat-isfying reunion when one of the parties is the deceased.

It's the opposite situation from that experienced by one of his literary he-roes, Harry Heine, the greatest poet of Germany, who died scarcely five months ago, this past February in exile in Paris, after eight years in bed. Eight years in one room! Eight years—drugged up on the friendly mor-phine moxased into the sores kept open along his spine—in what he called his "mattress tomb."

Mathilde Heine disappeared from Paris and did not attend the funeral. But she was there when Heine died. Better that than the opposite, better to have one's wife skip the wake but wake the skipper, as they say cunningly of a sailor finally home and docked between his wife's legs.

Schumann has set Heine's poems to music. But what he sings now to greet the new day are his own silly, unpoetic words, the song he's been composing in his head because he's been too weak to walk into his sitting room to work at his piano, his square piano used by his old friend Franz Liszt at the dedication of the Beethoven statue just down the road in Bonn on August 1, 1845:

> I'm ending it in Endenich.
> I'm ending it in Endenich.
> My body's shrunk, my mind is sick.
> I'm ending it in Endenich.

"What is that you're singing?"

The sun floats off like a wedding ring from the fingers of the Siebengebirge.

Day has broken. With the consequent dispersion of the night comes Dr. Richarz, as always.

"My song." He can scarcely hear his own voice, which is roupy less with sleep unslept than with death unattained. "The one you detest."

"I didn't hear it."

"That's because you're going deaf."

Dr. Richarz comes closer. "And because you're whispering, Herr Schumann."

"I don't have the strength to talk!"

The exertion makes him cough. Phlegm fills his throat like food.

"I've told you before—I don't detest your song. I merely disagree with it."

"We all end up ..." Schumann starts to sing, but the words stick within the mucus.

He tries to sit up against his pillows, but he can't lift his body with his back or arms or hands. He needs one of those machines that Heine had with ropes and pulleys, though he'd no doubt think of hanging himself with it, just as Heine had considered. But Heine had been opposed to self-starvation on principle, and to Schumann it is the most, which was to say the least, meaningful of deaths.

What's the use of losing so much weight if you can't even raise what's left of you? He motions for Dr. Richarz to come closer. Only when he can smell the daylight in Dr. Richarz's hair, and feel Dr. Richarz's breath give his face its morning wash, does he settle back peacefully onto his mattress.

Dr. Richarz pulls the sheets and blankets from Robert's body.

It always shames him to be exposed like this. He'd been getting rather fat before he came here, his features bloated, even the pupils of his eyes swelled large, to judge from the drawing done of him in 1853, not long before Endenich, by Jean-Bonaventure Laurens, whose sketch of Johannes's innocent face sits right here by his bed, and not a day goes by, nor a candle-lit night, when he does not gaze into it and try to see himself. And now, because he's starved himself, he is a skinny thing, almost fleshless, and what flesh remains hangs from his bones like laundry from a string.

But he's grown accustomed to the indignity of such exposure as well as to the evidence of an incontinence that even his two frisky attendants are unable to anticipate despite their bedpans and their clucking censure. He permits the doctor his examination.

"Edema."

"Who?"

"Edema," the doctor repeats.

"Beautiful name. Sounds Italian." He takes as deep a breath as he can, as if memory must be swallowed before it can be released. "I was in Italy once ... during a holiday from law school in Heidelberg ... eighteen twenty-nine ... paintings by Veronese ... Tintoretto ... a naked tour guide ... female. Is your Edema Italian ... and is Frau Richarz aware —"

"*Starvation* edema, Herr Schumann."

"So 'Edema' is her *surname*?"

Dr. Richarz shakes his head as he comes around from the foot of the bed. "You are suffering from starvation edema. It's evident from the swelling of your feet. Do you know what your feet are saying to you?"

"'Let's get out of here'?"

Dr. Richarz does not laugh. No wonder: "That you are dying."

Dr. Richarz reaches down to take his hand. This is not something he's done except to abstract the pulse. Schumann wonders if it is his standard gesture, performed at that moment when he finally gains in himself the courage to speak aloud what he and his patient have been speaking of silently for so long. How difficult it must be for him to lose someone, particularly a formerly robust if melancholy man barely forty-six years old. Endenich is, let it not be forgotten, an institution for those whose minds are sick. And while the health of the mind may, in Dr. Richarz's passionate belief, be intimately connected to the health of the body, a sick mind is not enough to destroy the body in which it resides. No wonder Dr. Richarz has shoved tubes down his throat.

"Have you nothing to say? Have I shocked you? You see, the reason I—"

"Forgive me."

"For what, Herr Schumann?"

"For wanting to die. Do you know the lines from Hölderlin?—'I remind myself of the terrible truth: I am a living corpse.' And that was only because he was insane and unable to write!"

"Can you truly want to die?"

"Would you not want to die if you were I?"

"Not until I'd seen my wife."

"Can you possibly be so cruel?"

"I've sent her a telegram. She's on her way here now."

"Alone?"

"With Herr Brahms."

"Yes. And what did your telegram say?"

"I'm afraid I can't..."

"Can't what—hear me? Will you force me to scream?—I can barely talk." He coughs, dramatically, the way his children would in presentation of embellished evidence.

"'The end is near.'"

"What?"

"My telegram. That's what it said. 'The end is near.'"

"I trust you're not speaking apocalyptically."

Dr. Richarz shakes his head and squeezes Robert's hand.

Schumann is overwhelmed with feeling. Whether it is for Dr. Richarz, Clara, Johannes, or himself he cannot tell. But it seems to want to express itself in song.

In his mind, whatever is left of it—and since it is his own, how can he tell?—he composes:

> I'll soon be leaving Endenich.
> The way I came, a lunatic.
> But first—I hope it's not a trick—
> My beloved comes to Endenich.

PART ONE

The Secret Listeners

Zwickau

JUNE 8, 1810
Between end and beginning there will be chaos.
Metternich

On the day Robert Schumann was born in this formerly peaceful, formerly populous Saxon town on the left bank of the River Mulde, the loudest cries were not those of his mother, Christiane, being delivered of her sixth child. Her screams were eclipsed by those of her remaining neighbors, some of whom lined the streets and some of whom stood in their windows and all of whom screamed with even more passion and certainly less pain than Christiane Schumann. For who should be riding through town on his way across sweet Saxony, which hung like a plumped penis from the groin of Prussia, but the Emperor Napoleon (who could be heard gaily singing the aria "*Gia il sol*" from Paisiello's *Nina*) and his brand-new, politically correct, lobster-and-sour-cream-ravening eighteen-year-old bride, Marie Louise of Austria, his second choice as a broodmare after he had been embarrassingly rejected by ripe Russian Anna, the fifteen-year-old sister of Czar Alexander. Napoleon had occupied Marie Louise's country, as he was soon to remove his Léger-tailored suit to occupy Marie Louise herself (with—finally!—an heir, the future King of Rome), and had installed the cunning, ruthless, altogether magnificent Metternich as Chief Minister and Marriage Broker at the same time he disinstalled his own creamily Creole Empress Josephine, though he would never, nor would he want to, banish from his memory the rammish, faithless smell of her.

As is the case whenever famous people pass through a town, they seem to come and go in an instant, even when their procession has been slow and stately. So it was with Napoleon and Marie Louise. Scarcely had their green carriage entered town from the west behind six Limousin horses than it seemed to disappear into the east, so that many people came to doubt by the end of the day and certainly by the end of the war that the imperial couple had been in their town at all.

But what no one doubted ever was the passage of Napoleon's army. Even those who hadn't seen it remembered it. Through Zwickau that day, and for several days thereafter, marched nearly two hundred thousand men—and a mere several hundred women, all virtuous laundresses and seamstresses, absent Pauline Fourès, the no-longer-exigent mistress Napoleon had taken in revenge either for Josephine's affair with Hippolyte Charles or for her having nearly ruined him by buying five hundred and twenty-four pairs of shoes in the previous year alone. With their ten-mile column of food supplies and their thirty-one million bottles of wine and cognac and their thousand big guns and four thousand ammunition wagons and several million lances, sabers, and smooth-bore muskets, and one hundred and fifty thousand horses and nearly as many cows and their massive bridging equipment and forges, they were on their way toward Silesia and Bohemia, to conquer and thereby bring freedom and the rights of man and Chambertin to eastern Europe. The apple cores and horse manure they left behind seemed to have been left behind for good—their clean and crapulous odors were said to mingle in the air for the next century at least, only to dissipate in 1914.

Robert's father, August, was one of the few townspeople who did not stand at his window. This is not to say he stood by his wife either. Her labor was a long one, and while August would now and then look in upon her, hold her hand and with the back of his other attempt to wipe the sweat from her brow on this hot day in early June, he spent most of it in his study, smoking his pipe and working. He had worked, as he recalled, during the births of all his children, though when Laura had been stillborn just the year before he had stopped working instantly and had not gone back to work that day, though he felt quite guilty for *wanting* to go back to work.

His work was book publishing. At the time, however, he was better known as a bookseller and so allowed that designation to be entered on Robert Alexander Schumann's baptism certificate in Zwickau's Church of Mary, into which even heathens ventured to see the retable done by Michael Wohlgemuth, whose reputation was based not so much on this work as on his having been the teacher of Albrecht Dürer.

As anyone who has ever been a book publisher, or lived with one, knows, there is no end to the work. For every manuscript you publish, you read, to put it modestly, a hundred; the ninety-nine unhappy authors demand an explanation for your rejection, and so you must dream up something preposterous to tell them so they will not hang themselves on the truth; then you must take that one-in-a-hundred manuscript and read it again so when its author asks you your favorite part you can name ten of them, though it's never enough; then you must correct the author's spelling if nothing else and set the book in type and read the proofs and correct the proofs and read the corrected proofs and finally print it and try to figure out a way to sell it; and no matter how you have figured out a way to sell it you discover either that you have printed too many copies or too few, so that either you or your author is guaranteed to have reason to despair.

But August Schumann had invented a way out of this quagmire of expense, complaint, and time-consumingness. At the time of the birth of his fourth son and last child, he was just beginning his new venture: the publication of pocket editions of European classics, something no one had ever done before in any country in any language! Not only would he publish German writers, like Goethe and Lessing* and Schiller, and Continental writers like Cervantes and Alfieri and Calderón, but he would also publish his beloved English writers, in particular Sir Walter Scott and George Gordon Lord Byron, and he would translate them himself, for he was as proficient in English as he was, like any worthy burgher, in Latin, Greek, and French.

Indeed, at the time he believed his son came yelping no differently from most babies into the world, he was sitting in his study humming some Scottish tunes by François Boïeldieu as he put the finishing touches on his translation of Scott's *Lay of the Last Minstrel,* which he trusted would right the wrong done by Scott himself when he so mangled his English translation of Goethe's *Götz von Berlichingen.* Hanging in those few spaces where the thousands of books opened their teeth to the walls were several of Alexander Tibrich's bucolic Saxon landscapes and a small but uncharacteristically violent painting (some years later to be of conventional prurient interest to the young Robert Schumann) by Januarius Zick of the murder of the men of Lemnos by the wives with whom they had refused to mate because, the men said, the women smelled bad.

"Herr Schumann, Herr Schumann, come!" cried the doctor's assistant.

He leapt from his seat and spilled tobacco embers on his pants, which he brushed off and crushed into the Turkish rug—the same country of origin as his splendid weed—with his shoes. "What is it?" he called.

"It's Napoleon!" cried the doctor's assistant.

"I meant, is it a boy or a girl?"

"Napoleon is male," he was informed.

---

*Gotthold Lessing was a distant relative of the Schumanns who had died some thirty years before Robert was born. What was to become Robert's favorite story about his famous ancestor concerned not his celebrated plays or the audacity of his political liberalism but an incident that occurred late one night when Lessing arrived home and found he had forgotten his key. He knocked on the door, awakening his servant, who called down from his window on the third floor, from which he did not recognize his master, "Professor Lessing is not at home." "Please tell him then," responded Lessing, "that I shall call at another time." With that, he walked off into the night.

By the time Robert was actually born, *The Lay of the Last Minstrel* was completed and August Schumann had succeeded in burning a hole in the crotch of his gabardines.

There had once been ten thousand people living in Zwickau. But by the end of the Thirty Years' War, which virtually coincided with the end of the thousand-year Holy Roman Empire,* there were half that number. A century later—the century that Friedrich Schiller said went out with a storm so that the air might be cleared for the new century to be opened with murder—the population was further shrunk when Napoleon (now barely whispering Leporello's lugubrious *"Tra fume e foco"* from *Don Giovanni*) and his troops returned. Defeated, diseased, and, because they had destroyed through the weight and drag of their caravan the alluvially fertile soil, famished, they subsisted, in the absence of sugar beets and alfalfa and coffee and even chicory, on roasted asparagus seed. They were on their doomed way to fight in Russia, where they'd end up sleeping in the steaming carcasses of disemboweled horses and bandaging their frightful wounds with paper ripped out of books from pillaged libraries (those urbane and foolish enough to stop to read bled to death but at least made their exits worthily occupied).** For every soldier who followed Napoleon to Russia, approximately one-sixth of a soldier returned, including the elite of the Dragoon, Chausseur, Polish Lancer, and Grenadier regiments of the Imperial Guard Cavalry. Here in Zwickau the civilians were victims of the very things that were killing the soldiers, except the townspeople were not being paid to die, and their survivors would receive no pensions, and the logic of death and therefore the meaning of life were absent: cannon balls, starvation, and typhus.

Robert's mother caught the typhus, which was carried by the waters of the lakes and rivers into which corpses of men and animals had fallen or

---

*Whose duration as the First Reich inspired the optimistic and/or pessimistic prediction that the Third would last precisely as long.

**Not lost upon some of these bibliothanatic veterans of the Napoleonic wars in Germany was the coincidence of its having been a matter involving a book that had united many Germans against them. In 1806, Johann Palm, a merchant in Nuremberg, was executed by the French for selling *Germany in Her Deepest Humiliation*. Herr Palm went to his death shouting, "But I didn't *write* it!" In fact, the book's author was anonymous, which caused the French to kill as many Germans as possible in the belief that sooner or later the writer would join the bookseller in hell.

been slipped for serous burial. So Robert, the baby in the family, was sent to live with the Ruppius family. There he remained for two and a half years.

He returned home in that sunny period between Napoleon's banishment to St. Helena in 1815 and the assassination in 1819 of the reactionary writer and spy for the Russians, August von Kotzebue. It was the latter that gave Metternich all the excuse he needed to begin censoring the press and oppressing all those demanding little university students who seemed to think that the only way to educate a mind was to open it first. The Emperor himself, Francis I, that veritable Justinian (whose closing of Athens's schools of philosophy in 529 was to most rulers a touchstone of inspired tyranny), offered an equal exchange of scholar for obedient subject, the latter to arise, if necessary, out of the ashes of the former. Metternich met during most of August of that year in Karlsbad with representatives from ten of the dozens of German states, and there they passed, unanimously, decrees allowing their governments to punish any teacher who "spread dangerous ideas that would undermine public order and weaken the foundation of the State." (In this, they were inspired by Louis de Saint-Just, the archangel of the French Revolution, who had succored all government when he said that even the Republic consisted in the extermination of everything that opposed it, and was himself relieved of the burden of his angelic face when it, along with the rest of his head, was guillotined from his less thoughtful parts in his twenty-seventh year.) They also created a Central Commission to coordinate and enforce censorship and through the unspeakable *Untersuchungsgesetz* installed the Federal Bureau of Investigation to uncover and punish "revolutionary agitation."

The demanding and occasionally quite agitating little Robert Schumann himself found the coast clear enough to go back home to his parents and his mother sufficiently recovered from the typhus to have rediscovered her singing voice, which to Robert was a revelation of the first order.

For all the love he had found in the Ruppius house, there had been no music. There was virtually no music in all of Zwickau. Yes, there was a great Thuringian musical tradition, and all those Bach boys, once they removed the embarrassment of their father into an unmarked grave, had gone on to no small success. But the only musician presently to be found in Zwickau was found in the Church of Mary, for most people worked as clothmakers and cloth dyers and linen weavers and tanners and, though they almost died out after their exploitation by Napoleon's army, blacksmiths.

But Christiane Schumann had sung. She had sung, she pretended, secretly, just the way her husband would sit in his study and pretend to be working on his publishing business or his translations when in fact—like so many publishers who fool themselves into believing that because they know how to read a book they will know how to write one, as if someone who has sat on the back of a horse were to believe he could now run as fast as a horse—he was writing. Under the seemingly unavoidable influences of Jean Paul Richter and E. T. A. Hoffmann and Hoffmann's late mentor who died while still almost a boy, the irreplaceable Wilhelm Wackenroder, and Edward Young, whose *Night Thoughts* had brought August "deliriously and deliciously near madness" at the same age that Robert was when August was to confess this to him, August Schumann was turning out poems and tales of medieval knights and monks and cavaliers.

And Christiane had been singing. It was not as easy to sing secretly as it was to write secretly. Besides, Christiane didn't want her singing to go unheard. She merely wanted anyone who heard it to love it. Here again the analogy can be made with her husband, the secret writer, who like any writer would happily display his work in progress to the eyes of others so long as it was understood that their criticism must consist entirely of praise.

Christiane, though she had been out of her sickbed for several weeks, went back to singing the day Robert returned from the Ruppius house. She did this not because she had any hint that Robert might be musical—he had been away for two and a half years and she didn't know if he was finally trained to make his ploppers in a pot let alone if he could carry a tune—but because she was so happy to have him back and she knew of no better way to express her happiness than to sing.

So that day, when Frau Ruppius brought Robert to the door of the Schumann house at the corner of the market square and, with tears in her eyes, knocked on the door, she was not answered immediately, because August Schumann, who had expected that his wife would attend first to the anticipated return of their son, was forced to come all the way out from his study.

His wife was in the parlor, its door open, playing the piano and, in her disease-diminished voice, singing her heart out.

She was singing an old Saxon love song, meant to express the happiness of a man whose betrothed (albeit a ghost) has returned to him after they had been separated by war. But it was just as beautiful in a woman's voice and its words just as appropriate sung by a mother to her long-lost son:

> Oh, now that you've returned to me
> My life has done the same.
> Without you I had lost my life,
> My soul, my face, my name.

Without you I cannot exist.
Let death come take me too.
My heart is cold and empty when
My arms cannot hold you.

Hearing his mother sing, Robert rushed to her. He threw himself into her arms. But in fact it was the music into which he was throwing himself, because he did not know this woman, though he knew who she was.

Frau Ruppius stood weeping at the front door. August Schumann at that moment fell in love with his son through her and, to supply what little comfort he could as a substitute for his beautiful little boy, took her carefully in his arms.

Robert and his mother sang together every day. She called herself "the living book of arias." She would play a song on a piano, they would sing it, and when they were done, he would play the same song on the piano. To her this was miraculous, as is a child's playing by ear to many people, who have no idea that it is hardly an uncommon talent and must not, if a life of agony is to be spared the child, be used to determine that the child be pushed in any serious way into the all-consuming embouchure of music.

What Christiane did not realize should have prompted her to let her son be eaten alive, as he was destined to be, was what he did with a song *after* he had played it by ear. For then he would begin to bang away at it, change it, vary it, minor it, major it, syncopate it, ruin it, revitalize it, tear it apart, not quite put it back together but close enough. "Stop it!" she would say and sometimes put her hands over her ears. She should have known better.

But she did know enough to arrange for him to take piano lessons with the one musician in town, Johann Kuntsch, the church organist, who was not much of a musician himself and not even much of a teacher but who loved music and introduced his pupil not only to the four-hand pieces by the likes of Hummel, Weber, and the inevitable Czerny, and not only to the piano arrangements of the overtures and even of the symphonies of Haydn and Mozart, but to sonatas by the virtually unknown Beethoven, including the second movement of *Les Adieux,* and only two years after it was written, when Robert was seven, to the piano part of Schubert's "Erlkönig," and then, brand-new, when Robert was eight, to Beethoven's *Hammerklavier,* Beethoven! who made Robert want to tell everybody else in the world about him, Beethoven! who everybody else in the world didn't seem to want to hear about, or hear, at least in Zwickau, for he was too hard on the ears, they said, and this was in 1818. Robert was playing Beethoven in 1818 and was sick at heart and angry when people told him to play Rossini, *Tancredi* if he must, but please stop playing Beethoven because Beethoven *hurt*.

Fortunately, there was always one's own work to which to turn in order to torture people.

Karlsbad

AUGUST 4, 1818

Nearly thirty years ago in Karlsbad I saved as a sacred relic
one of the concert programs you had touched.
Robert Schumann

It is an amazing thing when a young person first experiences an art in its transcendence. There is a good chance this experience will destroy him, whether it inspires him to attempt such transcendence himself or discourages him from even the most meager of efforts in its pursuit. But there is no doubt that whether ultimately destroyed or saved, he is at that moment reborn. He is taken from his parents and released from the grip of duty. He is both freed from and bound to the past. He is coupled intimately and irrevocably with death, and is quite happy with the relationship. He is borne away on the wings of beauty from our inconsolably wretched earth.

When Robert's father took him to hear the pianist Ignaz Moscheles, Robert was eight years old and Moscheles twenty-four, which is to say that as musicians the former was merely novitiate while the latter was stolidly, as he himself put it, *entre deux âges*.

Before Moscheles began to play, what most impressed Robert about him was his hair. It was curly and soft and fairly fluttered even in the still air of the salon, which was moist from the waters of the spa to which it was adjoined (architecturally and pecuniarily) and from which could be heard through the open double doors the splashing and gurgling and occasional sighing of people immersed in its waters and swathed in its steam and engulfed in its muds. On their way in to the salon, Robert and his father had passed by its patrons with their various afflictions: from what was then called dropsy, which caused swaying, saclike accumulations of fluid in their tissues; to sciatica, which caused its sufferers to walk as stiffly as the monster in *Frankenstein; or the Modern Prometheus,* which had been published in English earlier that year and that August was eager to translate and publish himself in German; to housemaid's knee, which swelled the bursa of its victims so that they walked with what looked like ripe, burstable fruits on their knees, an ailment that, for the mostly bourgeois women in attendance at the spa, always brought with it the suggestion of deviant sexual practice rather than the household drudgery that had provided the malady its name.

Robert's own hair was dark and thick and oily but had never been, until he saw Moscheles's hair, a source of dissatisfaction. And it was not so much even then that he did not want his own hair as that he wanted Moscheles's.

Moscheles was a bravura pianist, of the Viennese school, though he was known to straddle the Clementi convention, in which Robert himself had become interested when Herr Kuntsch had acquired a copy of Clementi's new instruction book, *Gradus ad Parnassum,* which Robert had enjoyed using for the few minutes each day he spent studying before flying off into improvisations. But whereas Clementi was a devoted employer of, and advocate for, English pianos, Moscheles walked out over the floor of the salon and sat down at a piano made by Anton Walter in Vienna and, it had been whispered among a group of young patrons who seemed to have curled their hair like Moscheles's, owned by Mozart before he'd had to sell it after his final, failed tour to Frankfurt in 1790, where his appearances had been grievously outdrawn by the coronation of Emperor Leopold II.

While he didn't play Clementi's personally endorsed brand of piano, Moscheles did play his music.

The moment he began, Robert stopped looking at the pianist's hair, resisted the temptation to look at his fingers, and simply closed his eyes.

It was Clementi's Sonata in B-flat, which Robert had never heard but now, hearing, felt he would never stop hearing. True, there was something familiar about its opening theme, with its three-bar repeated succession of six eighth notes that Robert recognized as B-flat/F/B-flat. But beyond that theme, the music was wholly new and, if not wholly original, thrilling.

What dazzled him most was the playing. He had never heard anyone play the piano like this. He had not known the piano could be played like this. And, had he not been sitting there, he would not have believed that a piano ever would be played like this. This was, to his experience of piano playing, what the flight of an eagle was to a roasted pigeon. It was a new language, being spoken by a new being, being performed in a new world, being heard by a new boy who felt he was hearing it in confidence. He was destroyed by it, and what a luxury that was. His knees shook, his fingers trembled, his heart burst absolutely open, and—he was sure of it as he sat there sweating in that humid, heavenly room—his hair curled.

After this grand opening, Moscheles moved on, as was the custom, to some smaller works, all eight of Dussek's boringly named *Eight Pieces,* which title made Robert wince when Moscheles announced it, though he recovered his admiration when he learned, also from Moscheles, that each of the eight pieces had its own name, Robert's favorite of which—the name, not the piece—was "Consolation."

Robert was surprised at first to hear Moscheles speak. It troubled him. He had not expected this man to have a voice. He did not want him to have a voice, or at least a voice that not only would he understand but that would be youthful and modest and altogether too human.

"Before Jan Dussek," Moscheles addressed his listeners, "the pianist might sit facing his honored audience, or even with his back to it, but no pianist sat sideways to the audience. And now we all do, which makes one wish one had a better profile!"

Better profile! No man had ever been more beautiful, more heroic-looking than this one.

Moscheles ended his recital, as was also the custom, with work of his own composition, much to the delight of those who seemed to know the piece when he played the first note and thus gasped audibly and then gazed about with undisguised hauteur: "Alexander's March." There seemed not one of his skills he left unexplored and unexploited in these variations, with their chords succeeding one another with such rapidity that Robert looked around to try to find the other, hidden piano. And while he was looking, he happened to be the first person in the audience to see a naked young man, dripping wet, come dancing wildly through the double doors at the back of the salon, his limbs jerking, his shoulders rolling grotesquely, and his face twisting weirdly as if a huge, invisible hand were squeezing it in rhythm to the music.

As the man danced his way down among the audience, people gasped yet again, and ladies either covered their eyes or used their hands to dry themselves when the man dripped spa water upon them.

When he reached Moscheles at the piano, the man stopped—his progress, not his dancing. In fact, now that he stood in one place, he danced more wildly than ever, quavering, wriggling, virtually convulsing right there at the side of Moscheles, who rather than seeming to be disturbed by this peculiar interruption played all the more wildly and passionately himself, glancing over at the man when he wasn't looking down at his fingers that moved so fast they appeared to be gloved.

Robert found himself both angry at the man and envious of him. Moscheles was smiling at him. Moscheles was playing for him. Moscheles was inspiring him. And the man was unafraid to display his passion for the virtuosity that seemed to be turning his body into the very music itself.

It was all Robert could do to sit there and not get up and dance himself.

He might have done just that had "Alexander's March" not reached its conclusion and Moscheles risen to bow first at the audience and then at the strange dancer, who, as the last note was echoing through the salon, seemed to quiver with it as it passed through him and then stood there completely still, turned sideways between Moscheles and the audience with his hands now resting modestly over his recently circumrotating private parts.

"I'm cured," whispered the young man, just loudly enough for Robert to hear.

"What did he say?" asked Robert's father, who had his arm around his shoulder.

"He's cured," Robert explained.

"As a shoulder of ham," said Robert's father, who was fond of wordplay.

It turned out that the young man had chorea, otherwise known as St. Vitus's dance. For all the good it had done him, he had been taking the waters when the sound of the music inspired him both to seizure and to dance, which in his case were the same. But perhaps inspiration had indeed proven cure. He now stood next to Moscheles wrapped in a towel that had been provided, thoughtfully, by some staff members of the spa who had been prepared to throw a net over him and had been deterred from this necessary maneuver only when his seizure had ended completely coincident with the completion of Moscheles's playing.

Robert was desperate to approach Moscheles, which his father had urged him to do and to tell him that he, too, was a pianist. Yet Robert was unsure of the etiquette. There were others hovering near Moscheles. But no one was close enough to him to speak except the young dancer, who was engaging the great pianist in a visibly passionate if one-sided discussion. All the others seemed to be waiting for him to finish before drawing closer.

While the young man spoke directly into Moscheles's ear, which required him to stand on tiptoe, Moscheles nodded not so much patiently as desperately. His kind eyes wandered along the decorative molding where the salon walls met its ceiling, until finally his gaze drifted slowly down through the room and landed right on Robert. There was no question about it! Herr Moscheles was looking at him! And in his look was entreaty.

Robert went to him.

"Thank God," whispered Moscheles.

"What did you say?" asked the young man, who stepped down from Moscheles's ear and looked at Robert as if to ask how dare he presume.

"I was saying," said Moscheles, "'thank God you have been cured.' And what brings you here?"

"St. Vitus's dance," said the young man. "As I was *telling* you."

"I was speaking to *this* young man."

Moscheles held out his hand to Robert. Robert looked at it as though it were made of glass.

"Don't worry," said Moscheles. "If you break it, I know plenty of pieces for the left hand."

Robert slid his hand into Moscheles's. He closed his eyes as he did so.

"It doesn't really work that way—generally, one has to practice," said Moscheles. Could he read minds as well as he played the piano? "And you must bear in mind that most pianists would rather cut off one another's hands than pass along inspiration through them, though you should feel free to hold mine for as long as you like."

"Let me hold the other one," said the young man in the towel.

"Are you a pianist too?" asked Moscheles.

"I'm a law student."

"Oh, my," said Moscheles. "In that case I think I'd best hide both my hands." He winked at Robert before withdrawing his right hand from Robert's grasp.

"I am a pianist," said Robert.

"I could tell," said Moscheles.

"From my hands?" asked Robert.

"No. I could feel you listening to me secretly as I played."

"You could?"

"Absolutely."

"Truly?" Robert could not believe he was doubting Moscheles. It was like telling a god you mistrusted his powers.

"What about the Clementi?" said Moscheles. "Did it not remind you of something else?"

"Yes!"

"Aha! And do you know what it was?"

Robert shook his head.

"Let me give you a hint." Moscheles put his hand on Robert's shoulder and drew him away from the young man in the towel, but the young man followed them step for step.

"Clementi played that same sonata—the B-flat—in a famous duel. Remember what I told you about pianists wanting to cut off one another's hands. It never goes quite that far, thank God, but we are always dueling with one another. We meet like gladiators, either in person, in someone's salon where the spectators scream for us to pour out our music like so much blood, or in the press, where we put our reputations in the hands of those whose hands can no more play the piano than they can dress a grouse. It is that way between Johann Nepomuk Hummel and me in Vienna. And if you know anything about Hummel, you know he thinks he has revolutionized the playing of the piano by insisting that trills be commenced on the primary note and not on the note half a step above, which, if you've ever tried it, has the same effect on music as ironing her hair does for a woman—it removes the *frisson,* as it were."

Frisson was perhaps the wrong word to use around the young man with the towel, though Robert had studied enough French, what with his dear father's insistence on the primacy of language, to appreciate the pun Moscheles was making. However, at the very pronunciation of the word *frisson,* the young man began to shudder once again. And it was not long before the shudders turned to twitches, the twitches to spasms, the spasms to ictuses, the ictuses to throes, until finally his entire body was once again involved in a disturbing convulsion that carried him dancing off back toward the double doors and the bubbling baths whence he had arrived.

Herr Moscheles shook his head sadly at his departing admirer and said, "So much for the curative powers of music. Or at least its lasting effects. Now, where were we?"

It was a moment before Robert could take his eyes from the poor dancing man, who was maintaining, Robert realized, the rhythm of the last of the "Alexander's March" variations. "Duels," he answered finally, as he realized that he and Moscheles were now surrounded by all the people who had apparently been afraid to approach so long as the St. Vitus dancer was in close attendance.

"Ah, yes," said Moscheles, ignoring the others and looking straight down at Robert. "I was about to ask you if you knew just who it was Clementi was dueling with when he played the B-flat Sonata. Answer that and you will be a long way toward knowing of what, indeed, that sonata reminds you. Here, I'll give you a hint: The duel took place in 1780."

"That's a hint?"

Moscheles put his chin in his hand, which struck Robert as a strange use for a hand so accomplished, and said, "Not much of one, I admit. How about this: Mozart!"

"The duel was with Mozart?"

"Absolutely."

"The Magic Flute!" exclaimed Robert, as at once Clementi's opening theme, with the rising repetition of eighth notes, echoed in his mind with the same theme from the Overture to that opera, which he had also attended with his father and had made him dream not of playing the piano but of conducting an orchestra, for he had never seen an orchestra before that.

Moscheles said not another word but settled his hand on Robert's hair, patted it twice, and then, without speaking to anyone else, walked modestly through the crowd, which honored him by standing out of his way.

All the bumpy, endlessly swift way home, Robert could feel that hand in his hair, curling it and otherwise passing on its magic.

Zwickau

MAY 12, 1824

The great object in life is sensation—to feel
that we exist—even though in pain.
Lord Byron

The new Streicher, a grand, had finally been delivered to the Lyceum from Vienna, and Robert was the first to play it publicly, for the whole school.

The headmaster, Karl Richter, fetched Robert from his Latin class the moment the piano arrived and took him into the theater where the workmen were consolidating it under the supervision of the tuner, who had come all the way from Leipzig.

"I want you to play the first note," said Herr Richter to Robert. "For me."

"What note would you like it to be?"

"You choose," answered Herr Richter.

Neither of them could wait, so even before the piano was tuned, Robert stood before it—its bench had not yet arrived, it was coming by land whereas the piano had been shipped by water—and played a B-flat.

"Very nice," said Herr Richter. "What is it?"

"B-flat," said Robert. "Listen."

He played an A and named it. He played a C and named it. He played now a B-natural and named it. Then he played a brief fugue on those four notes.

"Bravo," said Herr Richter.

"It's Bach," said Robert.

"I thought it sounded familiar."

Robert wasn't sure whether to smile but found himself smiling before discretion could be exercised. "Bach didn't write it," he explained. "It's Bach's name. I made it up."

"You could have fooled me," said Herr Richter.

Robert held his tongue this time.

"And you certainly did," Herr Richter supplied the rejoinder and threw his arm around Robert's shoulder.

Robert loved Herr Richter's school. It was, in the perfect adjunct to the education he received at home from his bookish, dreamy, but business-minded father and his father's library of nearly five thousand volumes, a means of exploding him into the world.

Herr Richter, in addition to his duties as headmaster of the Lyceum, edited a political review called *The Bee*,* which prompted the first real discussion father and son had about politics, when Robert learned that his father harbored for all humanity passions Robert had thought were reserved for himself. This made Robert begin to mistrust politics at nearly the same moment he had begun to embrace them. His father learned that his son was not nearly as interested in all humanity—in any humanity, for that matter—as he was in music, which even then he knew could serve no purpose but its own and that of its creator.

Actually, there was a part of humanity for which Robert harbored the utmost passion, but he did not feel he would be comfortable discussing this with his father, who, for all his love of Byron's work, seemed almost haughtily disdainful of the poet's vaunted love life, which any fool should realize, Robert knew, could not be separated from the popularity of his poetry, any more than you could skin a cat and expect people to hold their hand out to it, calling, "Pussy, pussy."**

The Bee was banned by the Central Bureau of Political Investigation (a more intemperate version of the aforementioned Federal Bureau of Investigation) in 1833, at the very time Robert was planning a revolutionary magazine of his own.

**What August Schumann admired most about Byron's life was in fact countererotic. Barely a month before Robert was born, August celebrated with the rest of Europe the news of Byron's swim across the Hellespont in his successful attempt to duplicate Leander's nightly journey into the arms of Hero. What Byron could not duplicate was Leander's notable potency. Indeed, Byron found the journey so enervating that he was led to question whether Leander's "conjugal powers must not have been exhausted in his passage to Paradise."

The previous winter when he went with a group of friends into the mountains, he saw Liddy Hempel riding on the sleigh before his own. As her body vibrated with the ruts in the path and bounced with the rocks and roots, he could see and feel himself grasp her from behind and lift her coat and skirts and slide beneath her and pull her down upon himself and join himself to her in a way that had inflamed his thoughts ever since.

What shamed him was not so much the imagining of it as the secrecy. No one knew but he. Yet when he discussed it with himself, it got only worse. Try to have a civilized discussion with yourself about your wholly fantastical love life and you end up less illuminated and more aroused than when you began. If you can't talk to yourself, to whom can you talk?

His best friend, Emil Flechsig, was away at school, which Robert thought might make confession easier, so he wrote Emil a letter and told him about his vision of Liddy Hempel and his belief that when the pleasures of the senses become dominant, "man becomes an animal, and that's exactly what I was."

Though Robert was not shameless enough to put this into the letter, when he wrote those words he found himself immediately thereafter whinnying like a horse as he sat there at his desk. And not only that, but in desiring Liddy Hempel, he was being unfaithful to Nanni Petsch! "It is Nanni Petsch with whom I was first secretly in love, Emil! I have all the symptoms—whenever I see her, my hands sweat and shake, my voice trembles, I get dizzy. And this is with the girl I *don't* picture taking from behind like the aforementioned horse!" Robert added, unaware that he had no more actually mentioned the horse in his letter than he had truly learned the nature of desire or even, in his innocence, how to dampen at least the edges of its fire when you are alone and frightened and paralyzed by inexperience. "Oh, Emil," Robert concluded, "on your chest, on your understanding bosom I must pour out my heart. I have no friend but you. I have no beloved but you. I have nothing and no one but you."

When Emil's response to this outpouring was not answers but questions—"Dear Robert: Have you lost your mind? Your friend, Emil Flechsig. P. S. Is not, as I recall, Liddy Hempel's backside big enough for the two of us?"—Robert realized he had best discuss this with a woman.

He thought of his mother first, but when he realized what he was suggesting to himself he was too ashamed to join the family for supper that night, which made matters worse because it brought his mother knocking on his door to find out what was the matter and interrupting him as he was precisely in the middle of the kinds of thoughts he was trying to protect her from by not discussing them with her in the first place.

This left his sister, Emilie.

She was fourteen years older than Robert but was of all the girls in the world the one to whom he felt the closest. He thought of her as a girl even though he knew that by the world's standards she was now a woman and even though he knew that when he was her age he would be far away from Zwickau, writing poems in a small hut in an utterly silent primeval forest or playing the piano on the top floor of a vast townhouse in a cacophonous, cosmopolitan city, one or the other he was sure, he just didn't yet know which.

Sometimes he daydreamed of taking Emilie with him. As it was, she rarely left her room, which had been converted out of the attic on the third floor when they'd moved to a bigger house at Number 2 Amtsgasse just off the market square, and never, any longer, left the house.

There was something wrong with her skin. Two minute, itchy spots— one on her forehead and one on the back of her right ankle — had appeared when she was not much younger than he was now. From these, an infection had grown, a plague had crept, a fire had spread down her body and up her body, reddening her skin and sometimes leaving her with an itch so bad that she begged him to take her by the wrists and not let go until the temptation to scratch had subsided.

"Come, little Robert," she would say. "Hold me hard. It will make your hands strong."

True enough. Emilie was a great advocate of his piano playing. He repaid her support and the hand-strengthening that came from his nursing her by performing for her whenever she wanted, whatever he might be doing, however much he might prefer to be reading or setting off for a hike into the forest with one of his friends. But there had come a time when she stopped asking him to perform, a time when the spread of her rash had made her isolate herself increasingly in her room. To get her out, Robert would play the piano, louder and louder, more and more to the understandable irritation of the rest of the family, for hour after hour if necessary, until finally Emilie would appear, dressed in the simple but pretty white dress she always wore whether in or out of her room, pulled into life by the music. He would see her through the parlor doors glide down the stairs with each foot turned daintily out like a princess at a ball, a ballerina come to Earth from Heaven, and she would give him an impish smile as she entered, as if to say, "All right, you sneak, you got me down here," as if *he* were a Siren and *she* were Odysseus, though he realized she really was Penelope, alone in her room while the very fabric of her body was undone.

With her arrival, then, he would play softly, some of Schubert's sinuous *Ländler* perhaps, and Emilie would dance around the room, holding an

{ 25 }

imaginary partner, who Robert wished could be himself if only he could be in two places at once. His brothers sometimes watched from outside the parlor door—never his father, whose emotions were always too close to his eyes, as he put it—but they did not ask her to dance, and Robert never inquired why, because he preferred to go on admiring them. And then, as he would change the dance through one of Beethoven's folksy *Ecossaises,* the tempo and volume of his playing would necessarily increase, as would the speed of her feet and the breadth of her movements and the dishevelment of her hair and the wideness of her eyes. She appeared to be living out the dictates of one of the philosophers they had read and discussed together, Johann Hamann, who said all of nature itself was a "wild dance" and those of us who are wild—the outlaws, the visionaries, the mad—hear more of the music of life than do the philosophers and the politicians and the bureaucrats. Robert never knew which brought in Emilie such a burgeoning of intensity to the other, the music or the dance. He knew only, as he improvised madly on themes he stopped drawing from any known source and created on the spot, and she leapt and turned and sometimes wrapped her arms about herself and twirled like lovers soon to love as one, that he could do no more for her than this, nor she for him.

But now he needed her to tell him about love. He knew she knew about love, but he didn't know how. Such knowledge, he believed, was not so much a matter of experience as a grasping of the essence of the heart. Emilie grasped the essence of the heart with as much strength as she grasped his wrists to keep from flaying herself. She knew with the knowledge of the dispossessed.

Thus, armed with his desire and his inability to have expressed it to anyone but Emil Flechsig, who seemed no more eager for Robert to leave him for these girls than Robert would have wanted Emil to desert him, he knocked on Emilie's door.

She knew it was he. Only her mother and Robert ever actually came to her door—the rest of the men in the family preferred to confront her at the supper table on those occasions when she wanted to leave the comforting blindness of her room in order to dine en famille, and besides Carl was now off living in Schneeberg and for all she knew Eduard and Julius, who had joined the family publishing business, bless their unimaginative hearts, had found homes of their own in Zwickau.

"Come in, my little pet," she called.

He entered. Her room always smelled good, fresh, of flowers and the earth, he didn't understand how or why, given her constant presence. Even the salves she used sometimes, unfruitfully, which inevitably either burned or irritated her skin and thus made her more vulnerable to the rash, and which always smelled of some corrupt herb, could not rob her room of its cleansed airiness. It was a sickroom, yes, but to him it was a place where life was renewed, not diminished. His sister was being eaten alive here, but as her body was consumed, her soul was expanding. To be with her here was to be blessed, as nowhere else, with anyone else.

She was lying on her bed, shadowed by its canopy, reading. It was the smallest bed imaginable, an angel's bed, so narrow that her thin body barely fit within it and her arms hung off the sides as if she'd tossed them out to sea. She used neither sheets nor blankets, because of how they found their way to her skin no matter what she might be wearing. She lay instead upon the thick, huge pelt made of the remains of what Robert guessed were nearly a hundred rabbits, which their mother had stitched together.

"Listen," she said before Robert could even greet her, and held up her hand until she found a certain page in her book: "'I often find surging up within me a wild, mad desire for something I seek outside myself, but with a never-satisfied passion, because that something is my own heart, an obscure mystery, a confused and enigmatic dream of paradise of utter peace.'"

"Yes," said Robert.

"You know it?" Emilie asked.

"Kreisler," Robert answered.

"I should have known," said Emilie.

Johannes Kreisler, the mad musician created by E. T. A. Hoffmann to be Hoffmann's own double, was the artist that all artists now wanted to be, slightly insane, wholly brilliant, completely mysterious, utterly desirable.

Hoffmann had died two years before. The youth of Germany was still in mourning.

"Now everybody wants to be an artist," said Robert, "instead of committing suicide like Werther."

"Did you ever know old Cousin Georg?"

Robert shook his head. He had always found it difficult to keep track of his relatives. There was in him a desire to have no relatives. Not that he didn't love his family. He simply wanted to be an Isolate, a free spirit born of no man and thus wholly of his own inheritance.

"He killed himself," said Emilie.

"How?" Robert wondered immediately why that was the first question he asked when he heard about a suicide and not Why?

"He ate himself to death," Emilie answered.

"You mean he deliberately ate so much that he exploded?"

Emilie smiled. She had a beautiful smile, though she seemed to have let her teeth go a bit. The rash was now so much part of her face that Robert didn't see it any longer; or perhaps it was simply part of his eyes. He knew, from having held her head against his chest some few times when she was overcome with sadness, that her scalp was as pink with the rash as her face. He lived in fear that she might shave her head and then he would not get to see her toss her hair into absolute anarchy as he played the piano and she danced her way into the oblivion of the music.

"No, I mean he *ate himself* to death. He began with his toes and eventually consumed himself all the way up to his mouth."

He watched her fight to level her lips so no smile would betray the extravagance of her story. "He must have had a very long neck," he said. "Indeed, that is what has always troubled me about the story of Erysichthon—he too was said to have begun his self-devourment with his legs. But how, I have always wondered," he added, like an old man inquiring into the preposterousnesses of myth, "did he accomplish this?"*

"Actually," said Emilie, "Cousin Georg hanged himself."

Now Robert knew how. He was determined not to ask why. "May I sit down?"

There was a chair next to her bed. He never sat on her bed, because it was too small. But when she was suffering, and needed him, she would point with her left hand, as she did now, to a spot on the floor where her rabbit-pad overflowed her bed to become a rug, and he would kneel there and blow gently on her skin if that's what she wanted or smooth an ointment on her or lock her wrists within his strong hands to keep her from clawing herself.

---

*Erysichthon, a Thessalian prince, made the mistake of cutting down some trees sacred to Demeter, who was as serious about trees as about eggplants. For punishment, Erysichthon was given so great a hunger that he devoured his own flesh, either the legs alone or, indeed, his whole body, depending upon which version of the myth one credits. In either case, his hunger proved fatal, which is why Erysichthon was often seen as an archetype of the artist, who also eats himself, though he usually starts with the heart or the brain, depending upon what sort of artist he is, or was before he got so hungry. (The artist also regurgitates what he has eaten, a fate spared both Erysichthon and any audience Erysichthon might have had.) Erysichthon is also renowned as the father of a beautiful daughter, Mestra, who gave herself to Poseidon, for which license she was granted the power to assume the shape of any animal she liked. Each animal Mestra became, her father sold at market; once arrived, zoöidalized, at the barnyard of her hapless owner, she would change herself back into a girl and run home, there to recommence the lucrative process. Mestra is known as a goddess of actresses.

He knelt beside her. "What's the matter?" he asked.

"You first."

"It's about love," he said.

Emilie's head flew back deep into her pillows and her mouth opened and flung straight up into the old attic beams an uproarious burst of laughter. Then she grasped his hand. "Tell me. Tell me now."

"When I'm with Nanni Petsch," he explained—"you know Nanni Petsch" (though he realized then that Emilie would not have seen Nanni Petsch since Nanni Petsch had been a little girl and would have to imagine what gifts Nature had bestowed upon her)—"I want to fall down on my knees and pray to her like the Madonna. But I can't say a word. She's the first one like that. I mean, the first one I truly desired. But then I found I desired Liddy Hempel even more. I asked her to dance at a ball, and she did. I could scarcely grasp what was happening to me. I remained unable to say a word. But her hand—it was in my hand. I could feel her thumb in my palm. It was all I'd ever dreamed of. I wanted nothing more out of life than this. And then a few days later at a party she didn't seem to know who I was. I mean, she knows who I am, Robert Schumann, but she didn't so much as acknowledge my existence. And she certainly didn't seem to know that she had moved into my being and was now as much part of me as I am part of myself. I didn't know what to do. I ran out to the tavern and drank so much Tokay I got drunk. I told her I loved her, but of course she wasn't there. I mean, her body wasn't there. *She* was there—*here!*" He put his hands against his chest. "She is always here. I tell her over and over that I love her. But can she hear me?"

"No," said Emilie.

"Then how am I going to tell her?"

"Don't."

"Not tell her at all? Why?"

"Because for you the agony is far more rewarding than any reply she might possibly make. Do you have fantasies about her?"

"No."

"Liar."

"Yes! I do!"

"Act upon them."

"What!"

"Make love to her."

"Make love to her! She probably won't even dance with me again."

"I'm sure you're right. But you're not going to ask her to dance, Robert. You're going to ask her to make love."

{ 29 }

"I'm fourteen years old!"

"Best get to it, then. Off with you, Robert."

"I'm not leaving." He held more tightly to her hand and with his other hand grasped the pelts of some of the poor little rabbits.

"Will you stay with me forever, then?"

"Yes," he said, relieved.

"Do you know what's happening to me?"

"Is the itch coming back?" Now he held out both hands to her so she might put her wrists in them. She did not.

"The itch is never gone."

"I mean the bad itch."

"They've met."

"Who's met?" He thought she might be changing the subject, as she sometimes did to try to distract herself.

"The rashes. The one that started here"—she touched her forehead—"and the one that started there"—she pointed toward her feet. "Each day they've moved toward each other, down my body, up my body. It isn't visible, day by day, but I can feel it on the skin, beneath the skin, I can tell when they've moved toward each other by a millimeter each. And now they've met, Robert. Last night they met. The poison has spread and can spread no more. Now it can only intensify. They've met. And the itch..." She brought her arms up beside her on the bed. The fingers of both hands clenched and unclenched in a steady rhythm. It was how she tried to keep from scratching.

"Bad?"

"It is indescribable. It is a desire so great I feel I would sell my soul to be permitted to give in to it."

"Act upon it," he said, as she had said to him.

She gave him a weak smile. "It *is* like love, Robert—do it, and the desire to do it grows. Do it, and you will be consumed by it."

"I would like to be consumed by something," he said.

"You have no idea what you're saying."

Her hands rose from beside her and stopped above the center of her body. They hovered, trembling, in the sweet air of her room like famished birds over the bounty of Paradise.

Once again he held out his hands to her.

She shook her head. "It will do no good." Her voice was a choked whisper, as if she were trying not to scream. "It's too strong."

"You underestimate me." He smiled and leaned forward on his knees and reached out to take her wrists in his hands. She acquiesced. She gave herself up to him. His large hands completely enveloped her small-boned wrists. His nails dug into his own palms around them. Half of each of her hands was trapped within his hands. He felt he could hold her till doomsday.

Then she began to struggle against his grip. He didn't intensify it immediately, because he knew this was just the beginning and that she would grow stronger in her desire to escape, and this was nothing compared with that, she was capable of taking him to the limits of his own strength. He was strong because she was strong.

"Let go," she said, as she often did.

"Never."

She tried to pull her wrists away. Down, up, to the side. He was too strong for her.

She raised her back from the bed. She brought her beautiful, veiled face up close to his. She looked sadly into his eyes and spit into his open mouth.

Still he did not let go. He swallowed what she'd given him and wondered if she thought he feared contamination. He feared nothing.

She flung her head at him as if to knock him senseless. He moved his head to the side and only their cheeks touched. Hers felt hot, from the exertion or the rash he couldn't tell.

"You *shave*," she announced.

"Yes," he said proudly and relaxed his grip and realized immediately she had tried to trick him with her flattery.

She swung her legs around and curled them back and pressed her feet against his shoulders and pushed him, and he nearly lost his grip upon her wrists and maintained it only by twisting his body to the side so that her feet slipped from him, tearing the buttons from his shirt.

Then she kicked him. She rained blows down upon his head with her heels. He had to lower his head to her mattress and his face into the fur of the rabbits and to cover the back of his head with his hands and thus with hers. She ended up kicking her own arms until the pain and the contortion of it and perhaps her exhaustion seemed to cause her to lie flat against the bed again with her hands still locked in his over the center of her body.

He had won. She had fought him more violently than ever before. But he had won.

"Is it over?" he asked.

She shook her head.

"Do you feel better?"

She did the same.

"What do you want?"

There were tears in her eyes. He had never seen her cry before. Emilie didn't cry. Her rage and grief were expressed on her skin itself. Her eyes had always been immune to her pain.

"I want it to stop."

"It will," he said, because he had always believed that someday she would be free of her affliction. Life was a series of trials, was it not? The universe was in flux. The self was in chaos, torn between joy and pain. But Nature was ultimately good, and Nature would not allow his sister to suffer forever.

"And I don't want it to stop."

He took a deep breath. Her wrists went limp in his hands, but he did not let go, he merely loosened his grip and began gently to massage her skin with his thumbs in case he had hurt her. "That's natural," he said. "We can love as well as hate our pain."

"You know nothing!" she screamed and tried to pull her hands from him and down upon her body.

He felt, though she had not yet succeeded in moving, that somehow she had grown stronger than he. He could feel her strength pass through his hands and into his arms and up through his shoulders into his back and down his back into his buttocks and legs and to his feet, the tops of which he pressed through his shoes against the floor to try to resist her. But it seemed no use. As she pulled her hands down toward the center of her body, he felt she could lift him right off the floor.

For the first time, he could not hold her back. He pressed his elbows into her bed and put his bottom lip between his teeth and placed the top of his head against his forearms for added leverage, but she was moving her hands toward her body and taking his hands with them.

As their hands descended, she raised her knees from the bed by bending her legs. He looked up. Her thin, white dress hung between her knees like a bridge. She pulled his hands down until he could feel her dress on the backs of both his hands and beneath it the inside of her thighs, which she pressed together as if to trap him there.

"Emilie!" he screamed as she pulled his hands farther down between her legs.

He let go. His hands flew off like starlings frightened from a treetop.

Her hands, free now, fell down between her legs and threw back the hem of her dress and seemed almost to fight with one another for position as they met where her legs met and her disease met, and she turned her hands upon herself and her fingers dug into her flesh and moved upon her, and when Robert could look no more he looked up at her face and saw upon it such ecstasy as he imagined he would never see again.

After the piano was tuned, and all the Lyceum students were finishing lunch, Herr Richter stood before them as he often did at this time of day. But instead of lecturing them on some aspect of political philosophy suitable for discussion over dessert, like whether whipped cream itself was counterrevolutionary, or announcing a student debate in which one side would be permitted to speak only Greek (ancient) and the other Latin (necessarily ancient), he told them that the first class after lunch would be canceled for all of them because the new piano had finally arrived from Vienna and their very own Robert Schumann had agreed to, as many students later recalled Herr Richter's exact words, "deflower it."

"And I am certain he will play," Herr Richter went on, "music worthy of an instrument that will become as much a part of the liberal tradition of this institution as the memory of your own dear selves within it. Perhaps some Beethoven, Herr Schumann, or even some Schubert."

"Or some Schumann," called Robert from his seat at one of the long tables in the dining room, where he sat with no more than a good view of each of the girls he desired when what he really wanted was to sit so close to each of them that he could taste their food even as they swallowed it.

"Or some Schumann," echoed Herr Richter enthusiastically. "Bravo!"

The entire school marched to the theater, to which Robert and Herr Richter had preceded them, so that when the students arrived, Robert was alone on the stage, seated at the piano on two boxes, because in tottering combination they best approximated the height of the missing piano bench.

Robert turned to his fellow students and said, "Who is this?"

Even as they whispered among themselves, "Who is *who*?" Robert began to play.

He played a complex tune, serious on the one hand and not so much frivolous as gentle on the other, moving between the keys of D minor and F major, a little piece full of generosity and hope but growing in tension until it ended in a kind of indefinable disillusion if definitely not sadness.

When he finished, his fellow students started to applaud, but Robert held up his hand for them to stop and repeated his question: "Who was that?"

After a few moments' silence, one brave soul ventured, "Herz?" and another "Hünten?" and Robert pretended shock at the names of these popular composers at the same time as he shook his head disparagingly but with a smile just as Herr Richter would when he meant to criticize without demeaning the student who had given so foolish an answer.

Now there was a longer silence, until finally Herr Richter himself ventured, "Was it I?"

"You pass with honors!" shouted Robert as he raised his hands over the piano and brought them down into a slow melody full of yearning that increased in tempo until it sounded like the sound of a horse rousingly pulling a sleigh through the snow as within it sat a girl whose slim, dark body rose and fell with the rhythm of the ride and whose skirts billowed high in the wind as she gave herself passionately to the music and to the musician himself, who bent ever closer to the keyboard until his lips were practically upon it as his own bottom left the boxes on which he sat so that just as he finished they toppled over and the uppermore came crashing to the floor.

The students laughed almost uproariously until one among them rose from her seat and was, in fact, forced to hold her skirt high up off the floor as she pushed her way down the row and then flung her skirt down again while nearly running up the aisle and out of the theater.

"It's Liddy Hempel!" said several voices together, and many other students sighed in recognition and agreement.

"Very good," said Robert as he rearranged the boxes and sat down again and began his next piece, which was trembly and dizzy like Robert himself until he moved his hands down the keys to produce chords that were lush and full and teasing in the lack of resolution in their progression and finally angry in their jealousy and yet haughty in their distance from the tonic.

"It's Nanni Petsch!" came the nearly universal cry.

Nanni, rather than rush from the theater, stood gamely and proudly at her place and, turning about so all could see her pretty face and full, lush figure, gave herself to the admiration of the crowd as she would never, despite his apprehension of her in his music, give herself to Robert.

Leipzig

MAY 12, 1824
The tree of knowledge has robbed us of the tree of life.
Johann Georg Hamann

All she heard was music. Music was all she heard. She wasn't deaf. She was mute. But she wasn't deaf. She could hear music.

Words, which is to say speech, meant nothing to her. She had no idea speech was made of words, any more than she knew, when she was four years old, that music was made of notes. But music spoke to her. It was speech that did not yet speak to her.

And so on this day that her mother took her and together they left her father, neither of them told her where she was going or why. But she knew why.

Her mother was music. Her mother sang. Her mother played the piano, as did her father, but her mother played the piano better while her father sold pianos and strange contraptions like finger stretchers and trill machines and dumb keyboards that he used to help his pupils learn the instrument, for her father was a piano teacher.

When her mother played the piano, or sang while accompanying herself or was accompanied by her own teacher, Herr Bargiel, whom Clara knew as the man who made her mother smile and put her hands to her face as if to stop her smile, Clara would listen.

Sometimes she would listen from her room, or from the rooms of her two little brothers, or secretly from the room where her older sister, Adelheid, had lived before she died and where nobody lived now because her mother could not bear to go into that room, though Clara didn't mind, in fact she liked Adelheid's room best of all. The music filled it when her mother played in the parlor right below, and Clara felt she was able to speak to Adelheid by passing the music on to her, her sister, who had died before Clara was born and yet was somehow the only person Clara felt could understand her when she spoke. She would climb into Adelheid's crib, which made her realize that Adelheid must have been younger than Clara was now, four, when she died, and sing to her baby sister with their mother's voice as it rose through the floor and filled both of them with joy.

Other times Clara would go down to the parlor and stand outside its doors and listen to her mother. She was never able to stand there for long. The sound of her mother singing and playing or just playing would draw her in. She would open the door and walk through the parlor right up to where her mother was sitting alone at the piano or with Herr Bargiel next to her on the piano bench, and she would sit down next to her mother or squeeze in next to Herr Bargiel and watch her mother's hands on the piano keys and think that this is how you learn to talk, you learn to move your fingers up and down upon yourself and something beautiful comes out.

Her mother never minded she was there. Her mother knew that the music made her happy. And Clara knew that her mother was never happier herself than when she was playing the piano and Herr Bargiel was there and he was making her smile and Clara walked in and her mother was able to show her how music and love could speak as one.

That is why, on this day when her mother took her and together they left her father and neither told her where she was going or why, she knew why.

Zwickau

NOVEMBER 15, 1825
Man is a footnote in the book of Nature.
Jean Paul Richter

Robert was in mourning. Jean Paul was dead. He had died the day before in Bayreuth.

Robert sat on the bank of the River Mulde, as he did nearly every day until the snow came. He was Robert of the Mulde and preserved that name for all eternity on his first volume of poems, *A Hodgepodge from the Pen of Robert of the Mulde,* to which he added at least one poem a day as he sat here writing and dreaming and imagining his poems being read by all the girls who appeared in them. As they could recognize themselves in his music, surely they would be able to recognize themselves in his poetry.

Robert was two people. But which was real and which was the double: the writer or the musician?

Man is not a footnote in the book of Nature, he realized, but a question mark for himself to answer.

Robert wished he had been born in 1796, the year Jean Paul Richter had created the double in *Siebenkäs.* Another reason he wished he had been born that year was because that would make him the twin of Emilie, whose double he also was, the male part of her, as she was the female part of him, mixed together within both of them, for we are neither male nor female but a combination of both, and those who recognize this and live by this truth are the only humans who are allowed to, and are able to, live as gods on Earth.

Now, just before he died, Jean Paul had written at least a volume of a new work with an irresistible title, *The Time of the Young.* In it he had created his own twins, Walt and Vult, and the two of them were exactly who Robert was singly within himself, the gentle poet who dreamed his life away and the passionate artist who lived his life away.

When Robert wrote a poem, a great calm settled over him, his blood seemed almost to stop flowing, and time was suspended.

When Robert wrote music, or improvised, his whole being became agitated, his blood literally beat out the rhythm in his groin and in his head, and time was destroyed.

No one understood this like Jean Paul. And now he was dead.

When Robert had been still in love with Liddy Hempel, he wrote a poem that began:

> I see you riding through the snow
> and dream of things you'll never know.
> If you're superior to me
> why can't you see the things I see?

But ever since Liddy had said that Jean Paul was corrupt in his thinking about doubles because God had made each of us unique and given each of us a destiny we could not alter, which was the reason she could not let Robert kiss her even if she had wanted to, and it didn't matter if he sent his double or his quadruple, she wouldn't kiss any of them—ever since such apostasy, Robert had disdained her and, miraculously, as his vision of her as an ideal vanished, no longer pictured himself stretched out beneath her.

But he couldn't forget her, and so, because he had already written so many poems to her and about her, he wrote another:

> The news has come—Jean Paul is dead!
> But you don't care, you dunderhead.
> No longer will you be my queen,
> For you've become a Philistine!

It was a strange feeling to have someone die. The only person who had ever died was his sister Laura, and she had died before he was born, which meant that while he had thought of her and dreamed of her and spoken to her and done everything he could to bring her to life inside himself—and had succeeded in this!—she had been unable to do the same with him. But Jean Paul, though he was not a Schumann and as a human being was more god than man, had been able to communicate more to Robert than had his own sister. Robert had spoken to Jean Paul, and Jean Paul had spoken to Robert. Was this not the sacred benefaction of art? And was not art the highest calling to which a man might summon himself? But when the artist died? When one voice was shut off and the other left giving off its lonely cries? It was sad, of course, but it was also somehow just.

Death was the greatest mystery of all. What better place to think about it than by a river? As in one of the mystical sixteenth-century landscapes by

Albrecht Altdorfer, whose work Herr Richter had asked the Lyceum art classes to practice duplicating, its waters flowed like time, never to return. And on its banks a young man could dream in the sweet breeze blowing through the box elders with their fingery leaves and through the hairy sumac and Norway maples with the milky juice ejaculated from their leaf stems when he snapped them and the juice ran down his fingers to their very webs.

Snipes chortled. Geese yawped in migratory diminuendo. Hawks cruised silently above the tree he leaned his head upon to hold the weight of all its poems. Detritus from the cold-killed meadowsweet lay scattered on the ground, its powers lost to make the drink his father read him of in Chaucer, save, a name that Robert joked belonged to wine because it was the only thing that to drown in was to be saved. He had picked toadflax in a field on his way to the river, because its yellow flowers still spent their color upon his skin and because he'd read that the plant could yield a salve that might cure the kind of rash his sister had.

He closed his eyes and thought of lines to add to his poem about Liddy and the death of Jean Paul. Perhaps it could become an elegy, for Jean Paul himself and for the death of his love for Liddy Hempel, a way to conjoin sex and death, as they were said to meet as the "little death" in the climax of the very making of love itself, which he had yet to experience with anyone but himself, alas.

The notion of the Philistine was a good one for such a poem, because it aroused a heroic image of the defense of fragile goodness against the brute and crushing force of ignorance. On the other hand, the word "dunder-head" was not sufficiently threnodic even when used to describe the enemy of art. And lines with four beats were really too short for an elegy, which needed the graceful elongation of the more extended line to represent both lamentation and testimonial.

He fell asleep under the influence of such rhetorical retrospection and dreamed the dreams that wakefulness did not provide. Liddy loved him then. He heard her scream and wondered at the sound, if women cried out thus in pleasure. It frightened him — the strident passion of the sound itself, and the monstrous chasm between desire and experience — and excited him. He saw her dressed in white, a pretty dress, adhering to her skin so that her body was before him unadorned. Her hair was wet, and on her eyelids glistened drops of dew or sweat or something unknown put forth by women in their ardor. She seemed exhausted now, wholly spent, floating by before his eyes before he'd chanced to touch her. It was not fair. Her leaving him without...

He opened his eyes. There, through the trees, he saw her, all in white, her dress so wet her skin showed through, her breasts, the sacred pyramid between her legs, her head thrown back so as she moved away from him, he saw her eyes, upside down, bounce open and look back at him from a maiden's radiant countenance. She was a phantom floating through the forest, suspended between the fallen autumn leaves and the unforthcoming Saxon sky.

Four men carried her. She seemed no burden, but they were downcast. He wondered had they had her; he'd heard tales of men within these very woods taking women brutally, which sickened him, though not as much as his mind's unwillingness to stop imagining the scene. Her arms and legs were casually tossed over the men's own arms as they carried her away from him and toward the town.

He gathered up his books and pens and flowers and leather cap, then hurried to his feet and off to follow her. Even moving, he felt contained in his dream, trailing this buoyant woman as she wafted through the spiny shadows of the nearly undressed autumn trees.

He heard his name. He heard it called with the same hoarse resonance in which he'd heard this woman scream her rapture.

It was his mother. She appeared before him suddenly, out of or into his dream, and for a moment he believed he was a small boy again, the night he'd come home from Frau Ruppius and had fallen asleep with the sound of his mother's singing and awakened in the dark from an unremembered dream to find her standing there, looking at him and saying his name as if she could not believe he was alive, or hers, come home, reality.

Now she said his name again and again, but without fondness, only anger. She took his arms within her hands and pressed her nails into his flesh and shook him. She was hurting him, and confusing him. Yet even as he tried to absorb what he knew was her suffering, he wanted to break from her grasp and follow the woman who was floating out of sight through the forest.

"She's dead," his mother said.

"Liddy?" Where was the despair? Why was he somehow either relieved or released, he could not quite locate the emotion?

His mother pushed him from her but did not dig out her fingers. She shook her head and showed him what was in her eyes.

"Emilie!" he cried and tried to break from his mother's grasp. But she held him and held to him so he could not desert her.

"Drowned," she said.

He could not picture it.

"Herself."

He took that to mean she had been alone.

"In the river."

He turned around to look at it. He hoped to see her as he might have, if only allowed by serpentine time, Madeleine au Bois d'Amour, alive on the bank of the Aven, painted by her brother who no more knew than Robert did that she, too, would soon be dead.

His mother, who would not let go of him, turned with him, as in a dance, so now she faced the receding procession in the midst of which her daughter floated dead.

Robert looked into the River Mulde and knew then what had happened. In the very moments when he had been sitting on its bank, lost within its influence on him, its inspiration, its assurances that through it he was the very questing hero in the book of Nature, his sister had been drowning down around the bend.

He and his mother followed the body home.

When his father came out of his study, pipe still lit and spectacles on, he rushed to his daughter and grasped her so hard she nearly fell from the arms of the men who had carried her from the river. Robert could hear some embers from his pipe hiss against the wetness of her dress. His father threw his pipe to the floor, where its stem flew off and bowl shattered, and put his face to his daughter's breast and locked his arms around her and wept in a way that Robert had never imagined a man might weep. He did not release her until the doctor arrived, and only then at the doctor's insistence.

The doctor shook his head sadly and said, "It is for the best."

Robert wondered whether the lie was contained within the doctor's gesture or his words. Angrily, he said, "Save her!"

The doctor looked at him as if he were mad, or just a child, and turned away and asked, "How did it happen?"

"I was sitting by the river—," began Robert.

"She drowned herself," said one of the men.

"Yes. I thought so," said the doctor. "I'm not surprised. But we mustn't judge her harshly," he added, to Robert's parents. "Her torment had become unbearable. The infection had spread to her vulva. The itch she had experienced periodically over the rest of her body became intensified when it reached the delicate tissues of the genitalia. To see her try to alleviate it..." The doctor shook his head. "Her efforts were as tragic and unsightly as the disease. And there was nothing to be done. I tried everything, as you know. There was nothing to be done."

"Try this!" screamed Robert as he threw the crumpled blossoms from the toadflax at the doctor and ran toward the stairs to escape from existence in the room where his sister had left her suffering to him.

Leipzig

JANUARY 22, 1826
*An angel-child floats down from on high,
Sits at the keys, and the songs sweep by.*
Robert Schumann

Friedrich Wieck celebrated the first anniversary of his divorce from Clara's mother by having a new Stein piano delivered for his daughter.

He could not believe she was his. It was not the possession of her, to which he was entitled by law, but the possession *of* her, precisely *her* being possessed by what he could not have given her himself. She was a genius at playing the piano. And he, while he might be a genius at teaching the piano, was not at playing it. And genius was not something to be taught, only nurtured. Therefore, she did not come to her genius through him. Therefore, he could not believe she was his.

But she was his. She was his by law, and she was his by love. It was even his love for her that had allowed him to let her, his firstborn after the death of little Adelheid, go off to Plauen with her faithless mother and her lover, Bargiel, for the summer of 'twenty-four. She was female, and she could neither speak nor hear (words only; he was convinced she could hear music), and he let her mother keep her for the few months until her fifth birthday. Then he sent for her. He didn't care whether she could talk to him or hear him talk to her. He wanted her for the music he knew was in her.

Her mother had no choice in the matter and did not try to keep her. By Saxon law, thank the good Lord, Clara was his property, to do with as he wished. And what he wished was to nurture her genius.

Marianne had begged him to allow her to deliver Clara personally. But he couldn't bear the sight of her, his beautiful wife, who had betrayed him with his own good friend and colleague. And he couldn't bear the idea that she might come back into this house where she had allowed herself to be courted by the man who had become her husband in place of him. So he had sent his maid to Altenburg, halfway between Leipzig and Plauen and thus a compromise in itself, to fetch Clara and bring her to him.

"Hello, Clara," he said when Fräulein Strobel appeared with his daughter. Her eyes, which had always seemed unnaturally large, perhaps in compensation for the apparent uselessness of her mouth, now appeared positively monstrous, perfect black eggs set in the pearl of her face.

She looked at him blankly.

Fräulein Strobel shook her head sadly.

He didn't care she could not speak. Or even that she could not hear—language, that is. In fact, he thought she might be all the better a pupil if she couldn't talk back to him or ask questions of him and if he didn't have to talk to her but merely demonstrate and play and thus guide her only by touch and the sound of the piano. Music and words were inimical.

He did not believe that instruction should begin before the pupil's sixth birthday. Never mind that Mozart had become celebrated overnight when he played publicly in Vienna at that very age in 1762. So he planned to wait a year before sitting Clara down at the piano.

He lasted a month.

On October 27, 1824, five years, one month, two weeks after her birth, he conducted her first lesson.

He did not believe that pupils so young should have more than three lessons a week. But Clara was not young musically. So he gave her a lesson every day, without fail.

But before he even put her at the piano for the first time, he took her to the table in the kitchen and, because the chair was low and could not be adjusted like the piano stool, sat her on his lap and placed her hands on the tabletop. Because she neither spoke nor heard words, he said nothing. He put his hands on top of hers and was prepared to cup and flex hers up into the proper position, when he felt the pressure of the back of her hands on his palms and realized that her hands were moving into position by themselves.

With her dark, sweet hair in his face, and her thin legs wrapped around his as if she knew she was about to be appropriated by powers greater than herself, she made music on the table by moving each finger discretely up and down, learning how familial they were, born together but destined to play apart.

Thus he began to train her physically. There was the hand, which encompassed for some pianists the wrist and the arm, though Wieck preferred the Clementi style of someone like Moscheles, on whose arm it was said one might successfully balance a full glass of water while he played the most strenuous piece. And there was the ear.

For the former, she continued to practice upon the kitchen table, even when she became tall enough to sit there by herself, and at the piano to play scales, which she enjoyed more than he'd ever seen anyone enjoy them, so that he had to limit them, as was his custom, to fifteen minutes a day, in all keys, fast and slow, loud and soft, staccato and legato. He gave her various exercises so that she might master the eternal passing under of the thumb and in the end, as he called it, "dethumb" her hand and turn the demon of the thumb into an angel (albeit never as graceful as the others in its shape) of a finger. (As it was, she very early on could easily take tenths in both hands; a tiny, skinny girl with big hands was like a little man with a huge zubrick, disproportionately admired, inequitably skilled.) He also had her play the scales with separate hands, so that the hands, like the fingers on each, would be forced to become independent of one another and thus not attempt to hide, like twins, one another's faults. "Hands alone," he called this, and while later it would prove a fine technique for her early forays into J. S. Bach's fugues, it was a phrase that always brought to her a feeling of loneliness, even estrangement—her hands from one another; her hands, together, from the rest of her being—and was also the first musical words that registered as words within her mind.

Within the practice of scales came the flowering of technique. Fingers were to be held close to the keys. The keys were to be squeezed, never struck; the sound of the finger on the key should be no sound at all, neither of the exertion of muscle nor the application of skin nor the click of finger-nail; the only sound to be heard should be musical sound.

In other words, you draw music from the piano, you do not make music upon it. The music is in there; it is your job to find it.

But technique went only so far. To try both to teach and amuse her, in case she might finally respond to speech, he made up a jingle:

> The first rule of the artist to defend
> Is "Technique's no more than a means to an end."
> When mere technique controls the day,
> Art will always waste away.

He thought it brilliant himself, but to judge from Clara's vacant expression at hearing it (if she could hear it at all), it was redundant. She seemed to know without having to be taught that she was training her hands to be able not simply to move them flawlessly upon the piano keys but to thrust them into the piano itself, without making a sound, and to hold the beating heart of that instrument within the opulence of her fingers.

As for the training of her ear, it was begun with her closing her eyes and her concentrating on the ears as organs of the body that could be exercised as much as could her fingers or her legs and lungs during the long, silent exercise-walks on which he took her to the wooded park at Zweinaundorf, east out of Leipzig. "The ear can be opened from within," he would tell her, unsure whether she could hear him but knowing from the increasing looks of pleasure on her face when she listened to him play that she understood and that she was teaching herself how to capture music through the strengthening of her ear.

In the beginning, he would permit her to play only by ear. This allowed him to gauge her grasp of sound, which was all music was before it was written down, and her to listen to music rather than read it and to close her eyes if she wished and pretend her body was the piano and no one was permitted to draw pleasure from it but herself.

Once she learned to distinguish all the keys, major and minor, by ear, and to locate and practice triads and dominant sevenths with inversions in all keys as well, and to find the subdominant and dominant chords in each key and to modulate when she wanted or when he demanded from major and minor keys through the diminished seventh, by using the leading note of the dominant, she still was not given music to read but instead was encouraged to improvise and to compose her own pieces, which he taught her to write down and in so doing taught her to read music. He considered it very important to excite a student's mind and let it develop, not degrade it into a mere machine. She learned more than sixty short pieces by ear, which she could play in any key, in any style, and with the myriad cadences appropriate to the pieces themselves.

When she was ready to play from music set before her, he started her on Karl Czerny's Toccata, which most of his students couldn't play until much farther into their studies. And for the improvement of her improvisation, which was expected of all pianists who performed in public, she studied Czerny's *Guide to the Art of Improvisation.*

And she sang.

He believed not so much that the human voice was the first great musical instrument, as the cliché had it, as that the piano was the first great voice created by humans, toward which all musical instruments had been striving since man first blew through a reed and banged together the bones of an enemy and the Greeks plucked kitharas and the Jews tongued trumps.

And nothing facilitated unaffected keyboard cantabile better than the singing voice itself. For him, the basis of all pianistic phrasing was song, with its natural rise and fall of tone, its breath points, its expressive accentuation. In each phrase, there was a center of gravity, to be located by the finger in the gut of the piano like a singer in her own belly.

Thus, the first sounds Friedrich Wieck heard his daughter make, from her body and not solely from the piano that she seemed to grip in her fingers like a hawk its prey, was in her imitating him in the simple E-flat major andantino duet that Pamina and Papageno sing about the blessing of love toward the end of the first act of *The Magic Flute*:

> In love abides life's greatest bliss.
> Love guards the heart from life's abyss.

"You sing beautifully," he said.

"Thank you, Papa," she sang, and laughed, because she had meant to speak, and the words had come out as music.

He laughed as well. "You've been listening all along?"

"Not listening," she managed to say with a bit less lilt in her voice. "Hearing."

"Why have you not spoken before this, my child?"

"I was listening," she answered.

"Sing," he said, because he thought she was confused.

Clara's new piano had been made by Andreas Stein in Vienna. Friedrich Wieck enjoyed a profitable relationship with Stein and had no hesitation in selling his pianos, but between the two dominant schools of piano execution, the Viennese and the English, he preferred the latter.

The "bravura" school of Vienna, championed by Czerny, demanded that its piano have light action, so that, in the words of Hummel, "it may be played upon with ease by the weakest hand"; which is not to say that Clara, as young as she was, was weak of hand. The Viennese damping was perhaps more efficient than the English, for while the hammers of both were covered with leather, the Viennese were mounted on the key and not on the frame and were sometimes hollow and were always lighter, which allowed the pianist greater velocity, delicacy and roundness of tone, lambency, elegance, and, as Hummel also said, "every conceivable degree of light and shade." It was no wonder that Mozart favored the Stein, which allowed his playing to "flow like oil," as he boasted, though Friedrich was forced, alas, to take such description on faith, since he had been only six years old when Mozart died in 1791, thirty-four years ago and seeming an eternity.

Why did it seem an eternity? Beethoven! Beethoven played the piano from the "singing" school of England, founded by Clementi upon the instruments fashioned by the Erard brothers in Paris and especially John

{ 45 }

Broadwood in England itself. The English piano was heavier and deeper in touch, slower, more difficult to play. But what rewards there were for the effort! Beethoven had transformed the piano from a toy to a veritable bomb from which exploded the expression of his torment. Its sonority was staggering, the brilliance of its sound almost unendurably profound. It was no longer merely a musical instrument. It was an expression of being.

Wieck had heard Beethoven play. Not in some salon or draughty hall but in Beethoven's own rooms on the fourth floor of Pasqualati House (named for the court physician of Maria Theresa, whose son was so thrilled to become Beethoven's landlord that he unwisely did not demand from him a security deposit) on the Mölker Bastei in Vienna. It was one of more than thirty flats in which Beethoven would live during his thirty-five years in that city. Wieck, who prided himself on the orderliness of his own home, if for no other reason than to demonstrate to his students that art and anarchy were not synonymous, found Beethoven's distressingly squalid and, given his admiration for the art of its tenant, disillusioning. Clouds of moisture threatened the cracked ceiling. Ink-scabbed pens lay strewn upon a walnut secretaire. Worst of all, the piano was defamed by scrolls of dust upon the top and a brimming chamber pot beneath. Friedrich had gained entrance through the pretense of being a specialist in diseases of the ear and a manufacturer of hearing-aid devices. But Beethoven proved so deaf that Friedrich was not sure the composer even heard what he was there for. He simply pointed Wieck toward the only caned chair untenanted by tossed-off clothes or half-finished plates of food, ordered him to sit, and, explaining that he needed to drink to subdue the torment of his colic and the anarchy of his diarrhea, poured them both glass after glass of red wine, which was too good to have been Austrian and filled in the pockmarks on Beethoven's face with tiny pools of florid incandescence. Seemingly under the influence of the wine, Beethoven talked incessantly of how his housekeeper was torturing him, and his brothers cheating him, and the Viennese public demeaning him, and Ignaz Schuppanzigh disgusting him by swallowing his violin within the folds of his many chins, and the Leipzig Gewandhaus ignoring him, and democracy disappointing him, and Italian opera diminishing him, while German opera was boring him (he even made up on the spot a ribald poem that ended, "Catalani, Lablache, and the splendid Rubini / Are the only ones worthy of holding my wienie"), all the while rolling his eyes and pulling at his hair and calling Wieck "my good man, whoever you are" when he was not calling him "my savior." Finally, Beethoven pushed himself out of his chair, spilling red wine all over his trousers, and sat down at his Broadwood, and with his eyes gazing heavenward improvised crystalline and charming melodies that to Wieck were all the more precious because he knew he was the only one in the room who could hear them.

He had come away from Beethoven both drunk and determined that the piano must be put back on the path Beethoven had forged and on which the world was afraid to tread. Through the piano, and the piano alone, came the voice of God to man, and the voice of man to God. And the music... the music had been changed forever by Beethoven. Yet no one but he had been able—no, others had been able, simply not willing—to hear it.

Clara, his precious daughter, his little genius, whom he possessed but who was possessed by more than he would ever possess himself, heard it. Her obliviousness to speech seemed to mask a passion for musical sound, as out of her own reticence grew an exquisite musical expressiveness. He did not expect her to be Beethoven. He did not *want* her to be Beethoven. One musician should influence another only up to the nearest boundary of the latter's singularity.

So let Beethoven have his Broadwood. Clara would have her Stein, because he had promised it to her once she learned all of Spohr's songs and Mozart's E-flat Major Concerto and because it suited her and because he knew that in the presence of such ability as hers he must be flexible. There is a natural conservatism among teachers of music, because music's rules require obedience. But music itself is a radical art and demands of its followers an insurrectionary bias. Therefore, he must be both tyrant and patron. It was not so much that his dreams for himself were wrapped up in his daughter—for he was a great success as a teacher if not entirely as a man—as his dreams for her were wrapped up in himself. He could only imagine what it must be like to be so gifted. He wanted her to experience her gift in its full flowering. He would be, thus, her gardener, no more, no less.

They sat together at the new piano.

"What would you like to play first?" he asked.

Without answering, she ran four octaves up and down of the B-flat minor scale, eschewing legato for the leap of her left ring finger off the G-flat.

He recited another of his verses:

> The artist's first rule
> Is "Technique is a tool."
> But your art suffers shame
> If technique is your aim.

"You're not a very good poet, Papa."

"Oh, really?"

"But you're a wonderful teacher."

"Oh, really."

"I love my new piano."

"And well you should. It cost a fortune."

"I'll pay you back someday."

"Not someday. Now."

She turned to him where he sat next to her at her new piano and put her hands on his knees and bunched up the cloth from his trousers within them.

"But I don't have any money."

"The money will come in time," he said. "What I want from you now, and why I bought you this new piano, is for you to begin to prepare to play for others."

"But I'm too young." She punctuated her words by hammering softly on his knees.

"Not young," he answered. "Only inexperienced. At your age Mozart was a great success in Vienna. Music is more the emperor in Vienna than the emperor himself, and in Vienna more than half the concert musicians are under fourteen. What you must understand, Clara, is that music does not choose or need as its vessel some ancient pot. There are children who can play their instruments as if they were limbs on their bodies."

She looked at the large, six-octaved piano before her and opened her huge eyes amusedly.

"You make me laugh," he said. "Very few people make me laugh."

"You make me make you laugh."

He thought for a moment and then asked, "How do I do that?"

"By only pretending to be stupid."

Now he didn't know whether to laugh or chasten her, and his very indecision forced him to laugh again.

"You see," she said.

He put his arm around her. "If I could keep you to myself, I would. But God would never forgive me."

"I'm not going to run off and get married that soon, Papa."

He removed his arm and took her by both shoulders. "Listen to me, Clara. Girls are playing music all over Europe. One can't go anywhere without hearing of what Leopoldine Blahetka is performing in Vienna or Anna de Belleville in London and especially Marie Moke in Paris, Marie Moke, to whose playing it is said people are deaf because they are blinded by her beauty, which is as nonsensical as it is heretical."

"No one will ever be blinded by my beauty," said Clara, wiggling her shoulders so that he released her.

"Thank goodness," said her father, celebrating the anniversary of his divorce with precisely the kind of insensitive remark that had sent his wife into the arms of another man. "What I'm telling you, Clara, is that these girls are older than you but started younger than you and that you are start-ing older than they but will be greater than they long before you are as old as they are now. They are not even your competition, though the world will judge them so at first. But your true competition will be the Moscheleses and Kalkbrenners of this world. Make no mistake about it—music itself may be pure, but the performance of it in public is always more duel than divertissement. And these girls ... these girls will disappear. They always do. They play until they can be judged wunderkinder no longer, and then they marry and become musicians to the court or teachers, because that allows them to stay at home and care for their husbands and children. That is not the life I choose for you. Do you understand? A woman need not succumb to the diminished expectations with which society pretends to alleviate her lot. You will be a woman one day, but this does not mean you must sacrifice your life and your genius to custom and to the pressures of the temperate. Do you understand?"

Without a moment's hesitation, she said, "No."

Once again, she'd made him laugh.

Zwickau

AUGUST 10, 1826
The specter of dead people appears to be pursuing me.
Robert Schumann

When August Schumann dropped dead at his desk at the age of fifty-three,* there was no one in the house but Robert and the ghost of Emilie. His brothers lived elsewhere. His sisters lived elsewhere too, wherever it was that whatever of us, if anything, survives, goes. His mother was in Karlsbad, taking the waters.

Robert was alone with his father, he playing the piano, his father working concurrently on his encyclopedia of Saxony** and his translation of Byron's

---

*Thus having lived longer, as it would have grieved him to know, than would any of his six children.

**Eventually completed by others and published in eighteen volumes in 1833.

Manfred and a novel about a woman poet forced to travel backward in time to confront the curse put upon her centuries before by an evil doctor who believed that eternal life was to be found in the dew that appeared on her skin when she was ecstatic.

Robert's amiable father, who had once written seven novels in eighteen months, was never so busy that he didn't welcome an interruption from his cherished son, who now decided to visit him in his study. Robert had lately been in torment over what he felt was the need to choose between music and literature. He wanted to be a musician and thus to live within what Hoffmann called the spirit realm, like Hoffmann's own Johannes Kreisler, about whom he could no longer think without thinking too of Emilie, asleep now in "the paradise of utter peace." Hoffmann—who had said that music's subject was the Infinite, the secret Sanskrit of Nature that fills the heart with endless longing. And what was life itself but endless longing? Yet Hoffmann himself was a writer, as was Jean Paul, and they were his heroes more than anyone else, more even than Ignaz Moscheles and Carl Maria von Weber.

Robert was forced to admit to himself, as he got up from the piano, that another reason he had decided to see his father was because of Weber himself. Weber had died in London not two months ago. Now Robert was attempting to learn Weber's Sonata in A-flat. He had taken this difficult task upon himself as a kind of memorial to the creator of *Der Freischütz,* perhaps the greatest German opera* (how the scene in the wolf's glen had frightened Robert and simultaneously aroused his desire!) and the Wertherian figure who at an age barely greater than Robert's now had swallowed some of his father's engraving acid and, while not succeeding in dying, had rotted out his voice into a sensuous rasp. But this sonata! There were chords in it that Robert simply couldn't stretch to play. There were chords in it that made him bang his overstrained hands upon the keyboard and then look down at them disdainfully as if they were disobedient students and think of slitting them at each digit's webbing so he could watch his blood drip down between the keys as finally he achieved the vagrant fingerings.

---

*The premiere of *Der Freischütz* in Berlin five years before—a key moment in the substantiation of romanticism, a signal victory over the newly appointed musical director to the court of Berlin, the spidery Spontini—had been attended by three of Robert's greatest influences, though they did not sit together: Heinrich Heine, E. T. A. Hoffmann, and Felix Mendelssohn.

When he could take no more of it, or of the doubts in which his failure stained his art, he went to seek the aid of the man he loved beyond all other men: affectionate father, passionate poet, sensitive observer of mankind's frailties, generous benefactor.

When he entered the study, what struck him first was how little it smelled of his father's cherished Turkish pipe tobacco. It was in his father's honor, not to mention his footsteps, that Robert had taken up the smoking of cigars, a pipe having proven too difficult to keep lit and a cigar much more in accordance with his image of the rakish artificer.

Then he was perplexed at how his father not only didn't greet his entrance with his usual "Ah, Robert" but seemed fast asleep upon his papers, books standing around his cradled head like so many tombstones. He had always worked too hard—his doctor and his wife had said as much. He'd claimed he couldn't rest nor since the death of Emilie even sleep at night, which Robert understood because the same was true of him. Her leaving them had left them both, of all the family, most bereft.

Now, as he stood before his father, afraid to touch him for fear he would not wake no matter how caressed, Robert felt upon himself the touch of Emilie. She grasped his wrists. He could not move his hands and felt she would not let him go until his desire to reach out to his father had subsided. And when he finally yielded to the overwhelming power of her grip, she loosed his hands and put her arms around him and danced him out the door.

They buried August Schumann in the summer heat. When his wife returned from Karlsbad, refreshed, indeed rejuvenated by the salutary baths, it fell to Robert, having chosen it himself, to tell his mother that her husband was no more. He told her of Bach, away with Buxtehude in Lübeck when his wife, Maria Barbara, had died in Cöthen, and when he had returned she too was buried in the earth. He could read his mother's thoughts: no good-byes, no final embrace, no vision to carry forever of her husband vulnerable upon his back and within his closed eyes the being he saw last, his sacred son come through the door with questions on his lips. Though he held his mother in his arms, he felt he was now, and would be forever, alone. Even Emilie had fled, aware that her own death had hastened her father's and aware more than any of them except perhaps Robert that death was, of all the curses visited upon man, the most malign.

Leipzig

MARCH 31, 1828

Whenever I tried to sing of love, it turned to pain. And
when I tried to sing of pain, it turned to love.
Franz Schubert

They arrived late at the home of the Caruses. Clara stood in the doorway
between her father and her stepmother-to-be, Clementine Fechner, who
was half her father's age and pretty and could no more carry a tune than she
could a cannon. Clara recognized the parquet floor of the foyer and the red
Persian runner that led to the steps that led to the hall that led down a vista
of infiladed drawing rooms, from the last of which, with its delicately mul-
lioned windows, issued, as it always did during a Carus soirée, music.

Her father took her regularly to the Caruses', as he did to the homes of
many of Leipzig's educated, musical, wealthy families, who were (often)
good customers for his pianos, whose children were (occasionally) adequate
candidates for his lessons, and whose tongues were (inevitably) good cata-
pults from which to launch her career as a pianist.

She came here, and to the others', not as a sweet little girl for whom there
might be no nanny to tend in her parent's absence but as a performer, expected sooner or later to sit at the piano and play something better than
anyone might imagine from observing her frail figure and wide eyes and reluctant speech. That was as it should be. Heaven forbid they might expect
her to play better than she looked as if she might. What she loved, almost as
much as the playing itself, was the shock of her playing. She loved how the
first few notes reduced the jabbering to silence and how the next few notes
interrupted the silence with an audible, universal intake of breath and then
a sibilant, surprised whispering that was hushed only by a sharp "*shhhh,*" always the product, and always right on delighted cue, of her father's munificently satisfied lips.

Even before she arrived at the drawing room, rushing ahead so as not to
be identified with Clementine, and lured by the prospect of performing, she
recognized both the song—Schubert's "Gretchen at the Spinning Wheel"—
and the voice of the singer. It was her hostess, Frau Agnes Carus, who was
scarcely older than Clementine but already a wife, a mother, quite a good
singer and pianist (if not as good as I, thought Clara), and the only truly

beautiful woman the sight of whom made Clara feel beautiful herself, rather than the opposite.

It was because of Agnes—and not the imposing Graf piano or the delectable wrapped sweets or Agnes's charming, fat baby who was allowed to crawl among the guests—that Clara preferred a Carus soirée to any other. Agnes was who Clara would like to be—her beauty, her grace, the charming whimsy of her irrepressible speech, the bosom that always seemed but an inhalation away from unbridled revelation—provided she could continue to play the piano as she did and not as Agnes did.

But it was not Agnes accompanying herself on the piano now. Clara could hear as much before she saw what she saw. This was a far more adventuresome pianist. As Gretchen sits with her wheel spinning and her head spinning, the former with cloth and the latter with covetous images of the very flesh and touch of the man who has taken her innocence, the pianist, like a lover, virtually infiltrates her song. He wraps his notes around her words and enfolds her thoughts within his music, which wanders key to key in endless speculation like the girl herself, who wonders if her lover will return, embracing death if he will not. The piano spins the agony of her desire.

This pianist seemed desire itself. He did not play cleanly, but to say there was passion in his execution would be to degrade even that cliché. The voice of the piano lurked beneath the voice of the singer, opening her words with its iniquitous tongue. Agnes Carus seemed inspired by this violation. Clara wanted to protect Agnes and herself.

She stepped into the drawing room and saw she had been right. It was a man, though he seemed more a boy, a big boy; but at least it was not another little girl, imported like some caviar to twiddle the gathered guests. His dark hair was thick and long and wild. She could see the engines of his shoulders grinding through the tight cloth of his fitted coat. Agnes's hand rested lightly on that muscle, her golden wedding band bobbing like a thing adrift.

Clara couldn't see his face, but she imagined it on fire, not simply from Agnes's untoward touch but from the smoke that rose and swept back along his hair. She made her way around the room to see it, behind the guests, who ate and drank and listened but seemed not to see what she saw or even hear what she heard.

Now she faced them both across the body of the piano. The smoke was from his cigar, if not from his wicked smile, which made the cigar swell upward from his lips and his blue eyes dance. He didn't need the music written out. He looked at nothing but his singer's face, which looked at him conspiratorially, the two of them against the song and all within the room and poor Dr. Carus himself, who would end up like Clara's own father if he weren't careful, his wife run off, the mother of his child, and he in search of someone new but someone who could never match the one he lost. This boy loved his Gretchen. But it seemed to be she who was seducing him. It was wrong, enviably wrong. Agnes was hers. Yet if Agnes won this boy, would he then belong to Clara too or would she belong to neither one of them?

The song ended. Agnes's hand remained on his shoulder but pressed into it more deeply as she leaned to take first one and then a second glass of champagne from a passing servant's tray. Hers she put on the piano. His she put into his hand. Clara pressed against the end of the piano to watch them, as if she might put herself between their faces, which came closer now as they touched their glasses and began to drink, Agnes having taken his cigar between her fingers, which became wet from his lips. But Clara was, she knew, invisible to them. She felt as she had when she could not hear—disconnected from some bond that lashed humans one to the other.

He drank down his champagne in a single series of swallows, which Clara could see squeezed through the muscles of his neck. Agnes merely sipped, made demure, it appeared, through admiration of this young man's utter passion for everything he did.

Clara reached behind her to a small table and took from it a half-finished glass of the same wine. She didn't care who had drunk from it. You couldn't get cholera from the rim of a glass. She wished it was his.

"Clärchen, have you lost your mind?"

Her father, from behind, removed the glass from her hand.

"Never drink before you play," he said and smiled at his joke, which softened her disappointment at being forbidden to drink at all.

Her father now looked at the boy at the piano. "Who is that?" he asked.

"Who knows," answered Clementine, before she realized from the impatient look on Friedrich's face that he had asked the question not of her.

Clara shook her head at her father, disguising from him whether it was in answer to his question or in disapproval over how he treated his fiancée, whom Clara felt it was her job to criticize. She didn't need another mother, but less did she need an unhappy marriage in the midst of which to live and to play music, the latter in particular, since she was not one of those fashionable souls who believed that art was improved by suffering.

"He plays the piano... atrociously," said her father, "but—"

"Passionately," Clara interrupted.

"I was going to say 'brilliantly,'" said her father.

"Atrociously and brilliantly both?"

"I was referring to his tone," he said. "Harsh."

"Perhaps it's his behavior that's harsh."

"You haven't even met him," he said. "What can be so harsh about his behavior?"

"It looks quite tender to me," said Clementine, which drew back to her the attention of her betrothed, who did not seem at all pleased to discover her quite wholly engrossed in the continued display of affection between Agnes Carus and her young pianist.

"Who is he?" Wieck asked again. This time neither of his ladies ventured a guess.

At that moment Agnes noticed them gathered at her piano and quite unashamedly gestured that they come around to join her. Clara was disappointed to see that Agnes's beautiful green eyes had sought out her father's and not her own, a feeling only somewhat mitigated by the fact that the blue eyes of the pianist settled within her own. Poor Clementine. Clara saw her quite deliberately take the arm of her intended as they walked from behind the piano toward their hostess.

Agnes had turned her attention back to the pianist, who had reciprocated in kind, so that by the time the trio reached them, the two were once again engrossed in the most obvious flirtation, she still sipping her champagne and he seeming to watch every bubble as it danced and died upon her bottom lip.

Agnes spoke to the boy: "Allow me to introduce Herr Friedrich Wieck, his bride-to-be, Fräulein Clementine Fechner, and his brilliant daughter, Clara. And this, my good friends, is"— she took the young man's arm so enthusiastically that her breasts came in intimate contact with one another— "my good friend also, Herr Robert Schumann, though I call him Fridolin."

"Ah, Schiller," said Wieck, clearly delighted to have caught the reference from the work of another Friedrich, who until the time of his death some twenty years before had been Goethe's sole rival as a playwright.

"It is only through beauty that man makes his way to freedom," Robert quoted with no acknowledgment to Schiller but more than enough to Agnes, to whose beauty he most obviously referred in what was clearly his attempt to flatter his way toward some as-yet-undeclared compass of freedom with its fleshly divulgence.

"Who is Fridolin?" asked Clementine.

Agnes looked at her gravely and answered, "Fridolin was a young page so utterly devoted to his mistress that she gave herself to him"—here Agnes broke into the most seductive laughter—"that is to say, she gave her *heart* to him. As I have mine to Robert." She laid her head upon Robert Schumann's shoulder, which looked both powerful and inviting in the snug sleeve of his coat.

Herr Schumann blushed and to cover his embarrassment drank from the glass of champagne on the piano.

"You see," said Agnes, "we even drink from the same glass."

Herr Schumann realized what he had done and, putting down the glass, blushed even more.

"What brings you to Leipzig, Herr Schumann?" asked Wieck, though Clara knew it was not the question foremost in her father's mind.

"I am a lowly *studiosus juris*," he answered, in a voice both shy and charming. "I have been here but two days. I enrolled at the law school and the next thing I did was to look up my old friends the Caruses in their Leipzig abode."

Law school! Clara thought he looked like a gymnasium student.

Agnes shook her head. "Law school! You have as much reason to be at law school as I have to be in a convent. It's his mother's doing," she explained, before addressing herself once again to her young page. "You may go to law school from now until you're eighty—by which time you will still not have passed your exams, I am sure—and you will remain a musician and not a lawyer. Fridolin and I have been singing and playing together for over a year now. He writes songs for me, you know. One of them was based on Ernst Schultze's 'Transformation,' the title of which speaks for itself, does it not, Fridolin? And another is to his own lovely poem, 'Light as Quivering Sylphs,' which describes both myself in his presence and the very trembling called for in the voice of the soprano. What you were just listening to, however, was by Schubert, not Schumann. You are familiar with Schubert, I am sure?"

"Of course," said Wieck.

Clara nodded.

Clementine also nodded, though unconvincingly.

"So it was music that brought you together?" asked Wieck, closing in on his prey.

"Not music," said Herr Schumann.

"No?" questioned Wieck.

"Illness," said Herr Schumann.

"Robert is a patient of my husband."

Her husband knew this man! Clara would have thought the two of them would go to any length to avoid her husband. She would have thought Agnes would deny being married (though she had let her wedding ring bob on her young man's back, where Clara was sure he could feel it through his coat and

{ 56 }

shirt). Poor Dr. Carus. He must be going through what her father had gone through. But her mother had never behaved like this. Her mother had shown her smile of joy in the presence of her lover only to her daughter, and even then she had always tried to hide it with her hands before her face.

"But you look so . . . robust," Clementine said to Herr Schumann.

"Madness," he responded.

"I beg your pardon." Clementine was immediately flustered. "How dare you . . . I meant only . . . Forgive me if . . ."

"No no no no no." Herr Schumann reached out his hand toward Clementine, only to have it grasped, though not withdrawn, by Agnes. "I didn't mean *you* are mad. I meant I went to see Dr. Carus for madness. *Mine,* Fräulein Fechner."

Agnes now took Herr Schumann's hand as far out of the vicinity of Clementine as possible, by pressing it to the chaste but ravishing landscape of freckle and shadow that lay naked between her throat and her bosom.

"My Fridolin isn't really mad," she said, though it was quite clear to Clara that if he was, it was Agnes who was making him so. "Not mad, but disturbed perhaps."

"What are your symptoms?" asked Clementine.

"Insomnia," he answered. "Dreams. Night sweats."

"Oh, my!" responded Clementine, who appeared unprepared for such specifics. Her eyes went in search of a new glass of champagne but found instead the far-less-bubbly countenance of her husband-to-be, who was concerned, Clara knew, that his fiancée's prying would deprive him of a potential paying, and in this case potentially brilliant, customer.

"Well, you'd have them too," said Herr Schumann, clearly trying to thaw poor Fräulein Fechner from the icy gaze of her paramour, "if you were to stay even one night with the Caruses in their castle in Colditz."*

It was all Clara could do to keep from shaking her head. Dr. Carus not only treated his wife's lover but invited him to stay—to sleep!—in one of their homes. Such intrigues made her wish to grow up as quickly as possible, not so she might emulate such behavior, she told herself, but that she might understand it. In the meantime, it was disturbingly enjoyable simply to observe it.

"Oh, castle," sighed Clementine.

"It's not what you might expect," countered Herr Schumann.

"Don't you make fun of our castle," chided Agnes, clearly inviting him to do so.

---

*To become in due course a concentration camp.

"How old is it?" asked Clementine. "I love old castles."

"Not so old," he said. He looked to Agnes for corroboration: "Perhaps four hundred years?"

She kissed his hand. "Precisely."

"And do you live in it all alone?" Clementine asked Agnes.

"Well, there's my husband and our baby."

Herr Schumann laughed.

"Do you live there too?" Clementine's desire for gossip seemed to have overcome her sense of propriety.

"Oh, not I. I lived in Zwickau until two days ago. Now I live here in Leipzig. But four hundred others do live in the Caruses' castle."

"Four hundred!" Clementine was aghast.

"Precisely." It was Herr Schumann who said it this time, though this did not keep Agnes from kissing his hand once again.

"Four hundred *servants*?"

"Not servants," answered Herr Schumann. "In——"

"Robert," cautioned Agnes, putting a finger to his lips.

"Inmates." Herr Schumann at once pronounced the word and kissed his mistress's finger.

"Inmates!" For Clementine this seemed to have gone beyond gossip into the repellent. "You live in a prison?"

"Asylum," answered Herr Schumann. "Dr. Carus is the medical director."

"We call them patients," said Agnes.

"They are inmates," said Herr Schumann forcefully, in a way that made him seem no longer quite such a boy. "It's not the Caruses' fault, but these 'patients' live in filth and squalor. They don't bathe in a month and, while they are not beaten, they are punished by being told that their suffering is itself a punishment for some defect in their souls. The soul! I believe in the soul as much as the next man . . . and I don't believe in the next man at all."

Clara laughed. No one else did.

"Thank you," Herr Schumann said to her. "At least somebody here has a sense of humor."

"I have a sense of humor," said Clementine.

"May the Lord spare us," said her husband-to-be.

"So you must picture it," continued Herr Schumann. "Frau Carus and her husband live surrounded by four hundred madmen—and soon to be many more, because the Sonnenstein asylum at Maxen is going to be transferring those it releases right to the castle in Colditz instead of to prison, as they have done heretofore. This is evidence to the American doctor Pliny

Earle of the rising of the morning sun of a new day in the treatment of insanity in Germany—sending people to Colditz instead of to prison!"

"You seem to know a great deal about this," said Clementine. "I should think you would be in doctor school and not lawyer school."

"It's because I am frightened, Fräulein Fechner."

"Of medical school?" she asked.

"Of madness," responded Herr Schumann.

"Oh, you don't seem mad to me," said Clementine.

"How would you know?" Clara's father apparently couldn't resist asking.

To Clara's relief, her stepmother-to-be smiled sweetly at her future husband and said, "Why, thank you, Friedrich."

Clara's father must have decided that the time was right to change the subject to music; specifically, to music lessons.

"You play the piano well," he said to Herr Schumann. "You are, I assume, self-taught?"

"No." Herr Schumann looked around for something. When he couldn't find it, he put his fingers to his lips and seemed to begin blowing kisses at Agnes. Clara wondered if Agnes would respond in kind until Agnes reached over to the edge of the piano and produced for her lover what was left of his cigar, which he put hungrily between his lips and upon which he began to suck, and upon which he continued to suck though the cigar was clearly extinguished and nothing was produced from its end but a few airborne flakes of dry gray ash.

Herr Schumann seemed quite content to smoke in this fashion, rather than talk, when Clara's father, as she had guessed he would, pushed stubbornly on. "Are you saying, Herr Schumann, that you do not play the piano well or that you are not self-taught?"

"Yes," he answered.

Her father had the sense not to ask which but to say simply, "Would you like me to teach you?"

"What a splendid idea," said Agnes.

"Why?" asked Herr Schumann.

Her father was confused. "I'm sorry. To which one of us are you speaking?"

"Neither," answered Herr Schumann.

"You really are quite mad," said Clementine.

"If I am, it's not because I ask the question 'Why?'"

"Are you asking it of the universe?" asked Clara's father.

"Now *that* would be mad!" Herr Schumann looked right at Clara and said, "I ask it of *you*—why have you not said a word?"

"She is not comfortable speaking," her father said.

"Is anyone?" asked Herr Schumann.

Is anyone? What a splendid question. Clara felt she spoke constantly. But rarely within hearing.

"Most people never stop talking," said Clementine.

"Exactly!" exclaimed Herr Schumann, who added, "That's the first intelligent thing you've said this evening."

"Thank you." Clementine actually appeared to curtsy.

"So you like Schubert?" asked Clara's father, as if to take attention from both his girls.

"Oh, yes."

"And Goethe?"

"Of course. But you know that Goethe does not like the songs Schubert has written to his verse. Or Beethoven. He prefers Zelter's settings."

Her father ignored that embarrassing information and said, "I am planning to take Clara to play for Goethe."

"How old are you?" Herr Schumann asked her.

"She is eight years old."

"Too late," said Herr Schumann sarcastically.

"What do you mean, 'too late'?" boomed her father, who did not like anyone to question anything having to do with his teaching her.

"Goethe saw Mozart when Mozart was seven," said Herr Schumann.

"Mozart!" said her father, leaving it unclear whether he meant to deify or demean his example.

"Goethe explained Mozart's genius by saying that music must be instinctive, innate. He said it requires almost nothing from the world, from experience, from life. So much for teaching," added Herr Schumann.

"I am the greatest teacher in the world, and Clara will become the world's greatest pianist! And when she does, it will be because of my teaching!"

Poor Herr Schumann. He had touched upon the one subject, along with money, that made her father grow loud and swollen and quite mad himself.

Clara saw Agnes catch her eye and start to gesture that she should sit down at the piano when Herr Schumann, apparently unmoved by her father's outburst, said, "I'm glad you liked the song we played. It was, you know, one of the first songs Schubert wrote. He wrote it for a girl named Theresa Grob. Her voice was as pretty as she was homely, for she was said to be one of the ugliest girls in Vienna. Her face was pitted and she was as wide as a cow. But he loved her more than he'd loved anyone else. So he asked her to marry him."

With that, Herr Schumann stopped talking and started to suck once more on his dry, dead cigar. He looked into her eyes again with his blue eyes. She knew what he wanted. She knew why he had stopped telling his story at its moment of greatest suspense. He wanted to hear her voice.

"For God's sake, how did Theresa reply?"

Clementine had spoken for her, in her vulgar way.

Herr Schumann answered without looking away from Clara. "She said she would marry him. His heart took flight. But he had no prospects—he was only a poor composer, only a genius whose work would therefore be appreciated by only a few, among whom I include ourselves. And so her family would not let her marry him and arranged for her to marry a rich baker, who has seen to it that she is now as wide as two cows. Yet Schubert loves her to this day, fifteen years since he saw her last."

"Is that a true story?" asked Clementine.

"As true as I can make it," answered Herr Schumann.

"How old were they—Schubert and Theresa?" Clementine pushed on.

"Seventeen."

"My Fridolin is seventeen." Agnes pushed her fingers into his hair.

Not even twice her own age, Clara figured. In ten years, he would be but a third older than she. In fifty years, no one would be able to tell them apart.

"If I can't hear you talk, I might as well hear you play," Herr Schumann said to her. "Play for us, Clara. Let us see just how good a teacher your father is."

"What a good idea!" said Agnes, leading Robert away by the arm.

"Clara," she whispered, saying her name to herself as he had said it to her, and to himself and to anyone who would listen, for the first time.

Leipzig

DECEMBER 28, 1828

The state should keep me. I have come into the world
for no purpose but to compose.

Franz Schubert

When news of Schubert's death reached Leipzig, he had been dead for one month, ten days. This delay was occasioned not by a paucity of technology capable of transmitting such news with greater speed—my God, a man might have walked on his hands from Vienna to Leipzig in that time!—but because such news was not, in essence, news at all. Robert would have been as likely to have been informed of the death of a Viennese pastry filler as of Schubert's. Schubert was just another impecunious artist (genius!) barely out of his twenties whose death was announced with the taciturnity reserved for the unknown and the unmourned.

Robert was living on Am Brühl* with Emil Flechsig, whom he'd followed from Zwickau to Leipzig University. Among its three courses of study—law, medicine, and theology—Robert had chosen the first, not because he was particularly interested in the law but because medicine would leave him no time for music or girls and theology was the refuge in Leipzig as everywhere else for the ambitious poor. It had been thus for poor Friedrich Hölderlin, who had been forced by his poverty to seek his education at the seminary in Tübingen, where he wrote in praise of revolution rather than of God, and then as tutor to a banker's children fell in love with the banker's wife, Susette, who became the Diotima of his great poems and the cause—more because she loved him in return than if she had not loved him at all—of the madness into which he had fallen five years before Robert was born. Every time he read Hölderlin's work—such inspiring words as, "He who steps upon his misery stands higher"—Robert could not help but think about the man who wrote them, who was at that very moment living outside his own mind, or so deeply within it that there was no difference.

What if this were to happen to him? What if Agnes loved him as he loved her and her husband sent him away, and Robert went mad and were locked up forever in a madhouse?

All because he'd gone to law school.

At least he didn't have to live at the school, as Hölderlin had been forced to live at the seminary. But he was no longer happy living with Emil. Emil had been the sort of hometown boy who, when he goes off to the big city, seems in one's mind to acquire all the virtues of the big city: worldliness, geniality, savoir vivre, profligacy, voluptuousness, and a superior haircut. But Emil in reality was no better-looking than he'd been in Zwickau and was as uncouth in his Bavarian temperament as he was pedantic, a strange combination that rendered him simultaneously crude and fussy.

Robert no longer loved Emil, which made living with him something of a nightmare, particularly since there were others he did love.

One of them was Gisbert Rosen, a Jew who had left him and transferred from Leipzig's law school to Heidelberg's because in the university at

---

*The street where Richard Wagner had been born some fifteen years earlier.

Leipzig the burgeoning of the *Burschenschäften* was threatening Gisbert both bodily and spiritually. The *Burschenschäften* were fraternities organized around principles of bumptious nationalism that had come to encompass a distaste for, if not yet an utter disgorging of, Jews, and held together by a celebration of the male body that had everything to do with its aggressiveness and nothing to do with its beauty. The *Burschenschäften* boys had betrayed one of their own heroes from the century before, Johann Winckelmann, who had loved the male form (equally in marble and in flesh) but had no idea it would end up being promoted as the German version of a living, breathing weapon, as physically perfect as it was morally corrupt.*

Robert missed Gisbert terribly. Immediately before Gisbert had settled in Heidelberg, the two of them had shared their love for Jean Paul by going off on vacation to Beyreuth to visit Jean Paul's grave. From there they made their way to Augsburg, where they stayed with Dr. Heinrich von Kurrer, who had years before lived in Zwickau and been August Schumann's best friend. The sadness Robert felt at seeing his late father through the eyes of someone who himself had seen the same man when he was not much older than Robert was now (and what man is a more beloved if confounding mystery to his son than his own youthful father?) was immediately transformed into a kind of passionate joy when Dr. Kurrer's daughter, Clara, appeared. Fortunately for the two boys, if more so for Clara herself, she was betrothed to another. But they left with something of greater value than either her virtue or the loss of their own: a letter of introduction from Dr. Kurrer to Heinrich Heine, in Munich.

The capital of Bavaria combined Leipzig's veneration of music and Dresden's of painting and sculpture. As Robert and Gisbert walked through the streets in search of Heine's house, everyone they observed seemed either to be singing a song to himself or viewing a work of art behind his eyes. They all seemed quite mad, or at least distracted. Never had the two youths been so bumped into and jostled by seemingly intelligent people who were not yet—the boys' coach had arrived early in the morning—drunk.

Robert had expected Heine to be moody and misanthropic but found instead a veritable Anacreon, at thirty-one nearly the same age as that great

---

*Winckelmann was succeeded in his naive innocence by Johann Lavater, the Swiss founder of physiognomics, who loved the preserved dead bodies (or at least their surviving representations) of ancient Greek boys and believed that the well-toned body is the outward manifestation of inner moral goodness. He also believed that we have all been magnetized by God and that to locate this magnetic force within ourselves is to put one's hand upon our divine organ, as it were.

poet was when he died and like him able to contain a reckless freedom in subject matter within a graceful and confining prosody that gave form to his raptures and made art of his passions.

He had also expected Heine to be surrounded by followers and sycophants, for he had recently become immensely popular with the publication of two volumes of *Travel-Sketches* and his *Book of Songs*. But Heine was alone when he answered their knock on his door and, when Robert mentioned Dr. Kurrer's name, shook hands warmly and immediately welcomed them in and engaged them in the kind of conversation Robert had always dreamed he might have with a great artist.

When Robert told Heine that he and Gisbert were in law school, Heine smiled with a kind of ironic bitterness and said, "I was sent off to study Roman law myself. I studied Roman law in Bonn. In Göttingen. In Berlin, of all places. But all the while I studied law, what I learned was literature. I memorized the law; I absorbed *Don Quixote*. So what do you think of Dr. Kurrer's daughter?"

"Don't ask," said Gisbert.

"She killed me and brought me back to life with a single glance," said Robert.

Heine's smile turned positively wistful. "I had a cousin like her. She won my heart and destroyed it, if not with a single glance then a single word."

"What word?" asked Robert.

"The worst word a woman can say to a man."

"*What* word?" insisted Robert.

"'No.'"

"Ah," said Robert.

"Ah, indeed," Heine amplified.

He asked Gisbert if he was Jewish, and when Gisbert said he was, Heine said, "They've recently excluded all Jews from academic positions in Prussia. With the departure of Napoleon, if you were a Jew and forwent a good dunk into the bloody river that flows from the fundament of Christian doctrine, you could scarcely find work at all. When I wrote for the newspaper in Augsburg they put a Jewish star next to my contributions. Presumably to signal both my corruption and the corruption that might envelop anyone who read my words. I hated it, but better that than a cross, no? The morbid little sect of Nazarenes that gave birth to Christianity also gave birth to the kind of asceticism that sets such limits upon its followers that it cuts off their balls and cuts out their hearts and then sends the poor, doubly emasculated souls out into the world with the injunction, 'Go forth, and be miserable.' I should know—I'm like you now," he said to Robert.

"I'm not like that!" Robert protested.

"Baptized, I mean," explained Heine with an expression that fused upon his lambent features a furious rage with an appalled contrition. "I was led to believe that the baptismal certificate was the price of admission to European culture. Some culture! It thrives on the detestation of the incompatible. When I was a Jew, only Christians hated me. What should have been a mark of distinction I was so immature as to take for a mark of Cain. Now *everybody* hates me. As well they should. I am an absurdity: Christian Johann Heinrich Heine, according to my baptism of June 28, 1825, at Heiligenstadt. But you, my friends, may call me Harry."

So Harry Heine fed them lunch in his garden and then took them that very afternoon for a walk through town and then for a tour of the Leuchtenburg Gallery, where he was approached, and they with him, by dozens of admirers, who seemed not to hate him at all but crowded around this small, trim, handsome man as if for no other purpose than to absorb some minute portion of his being into their own. This is what it meant to be an artist, Robert realized: to remain whole even as you fed yourself to others. What a glorious way to live. No one else — no emperor, no priest, no general, no physician, no courtesan, no streetsweeper, no seer — gave to mankind what the artist did. The artist, who created beauty out of the raw material of his self, was the only possible savior. Man without his politicians and police was at worst man disorganized; man without his artists was man erased.

Robert's joy at meeting Heine was tempered by his separation from Gisbert, who left Munich for Heidelberg while Robert made his slow way back to Leipzig behind a series of geldings whose very asses mocked his loneliness. There he found Emil waiting for him when he would much rather have found the man he had so recently left at the station in Munich, to whom he wrote, "I think of you most lovingly, though even while both asleep and awake I see sweet Clara's image perpetually before my eyes."

But there were others Robert loved and with whom he was able to replace Emil, in his heart if not actually in his dwelling. Chief among them was Wilhelm Götte, with whom he had lately been learning to get high, as he called it, in taverns and, while high, carrying on with Wilhelm an endless conversation about what Jean Paul called *Sehnsucht,* a longing for what was not there, which Robert had concluded was the essence of music, not merely in its creation, whether on paper or improvised, but in one's experience in listening to music, that great longing music brought forth in our beings for what had been lost and what had been forgotten and what had simply never been at all.

Robert compared Wilhelm not to a Greek poet or a Roman god but to

Napoleon in his twenty-fourth year, still noble, trim, distingué, superhuman. When not talking with Wilhelm, Robert wrote about him and how he felt for him the "nameless and infinite something that cannot be spoken, the overwhelming desire inspired in those of a lyrical nature like myself when the world of sounds breaks open or when the sky is rent by thunder or when the sun comes up from behind the mountains."

He also wrote for Wilhelm, and dedicated to him, an essay that he called a "Fantasie Scherzando" and entitled "On Geniality, Getting High, and Originality," in which he called love "the true sensorium of chaste sobriety" and intoxication—whether from alcohol, tobacco, black coffee, or women whose shape alone beneath gauzy gowns causes arousal—a means to inspiration.

He wrote poems as well to Wilhelm, finding words before music the accurate means for the expression of his feelings:

> And how madly one boy loves the other boy,
> And how he holds him, and how they weep together...

It was Wilhelm Götte who delivered the news of Schubert's death. He entered Robert and Emil's rooms without knocking and found the latter reading and the former composing at his ducat-a-month rental piano, his nearly black cigar pointing upward to keep the smoke from his eyes, his eyes squinting nearsightedly downward at his hands, his face contorted with the effort to see and smoke at the same time and also because he liked to whistle while he wrote and it was probably more difficult to whistle while smoking than it was to write music in the first place.

Robert was so happy to see Wilhelm and so eager to impress him that the moment he became aware of his presence he doubled the tempo of his playing and began to improvise, changing the key from F major to E-flat minor, so that his friend might see his fingers operate almost wholly upon the black keys.

Robert signaled with his head and the cigar that Wilhelm should approach him. But Wilhelm merely stood in the doorway with a stricken expression upon his perpetually suffering and therefore always striking face.

He had never seen Wilhelm like this. Robert sensed he had come as a messenger of doom. He did not want news of further death, but neither did he want Wilhelm to stop looking as he did. He was pale and hollow-eyed so that the only color in his face was upon his lips, which seemed to have been bitten into red. It was a mask of anguish, which, should he never take it off, would leave him singularly blessed with the gift of eternal comeliness. Suffering was always the midwife to beauty.

Robert ceased playing at the very instant Wilhelm began to speak. It was as if they had rehearsed and the singer was now beginning his unaccompanied lament.

"I have terrible news. Schubert died of typhus last month in Vienna. Schubert is dead, and with him all that was brightest and most beautiful in our life."*

Robert's hands went over his ears. Emil, discovering it was too late to drop his book in what might be taken as a spontaneous reaction, tossed it gently and safely, but with a simultaneous cursing of God, across the room. Wilhelm closed the door behind him, shutting up within this small room all of what was surely at this moment the most intense grief being experienced anywhere by anyone.

"We must drink," he said. "Where's the liquor?"

With his hands still over his ears, Robert said, "Dead?"

Robert did not wait for an answer before he put his hands down upon the keys of the piano and began to play Schubert's "Blessed World."

As Robert played, the room turned black with night. Emil sat uneasily next to Wilhelm on the couch in order that they might share the bottle of brandy. The darkness became so complete that they spilled as much as they drank. Wilhelm seemed not to mind, but Emil began to think more of the cost of cleaning the couch than of the pleasure of having such a perfect excuse to get drunk, so he rose finally and lighted the oil lamp.

Robert's face was so wet from weeping as to suggest a membrane of moiré. His tears had even soaked through his cigar, leaving its wrapper heavy and wrinkled like an old man's skin and its burned-out coal an extinguished black blind shrunken eye.

Both boys went to him. This was dejection as they had never before seen. They had no words for it or for him, as Robert had no words for them. He seemed incapable of speech, only of the music he continued to play and the whispering glissade of his tears.

They tried to lift his hands from the piano, at first competing for possession of them both, until finally Wilhelm took one and Emil the other. But Robert fought them, without seeming to put forth any effort. They knew he was strong—each, in fact, venerated his broad shoulders and barrel chest—but neither knew he could resist them thus. His hands went on playing even as his friends grasped a wrist apiece and tried to separate him

---

*Wilhelm Götte did not acknowledge that he was here quoting Schubert's friend Moritz von Schwind.

from the piece he was playing, which they recognized as "Der Erlkönig," becoming more and more impassioned as the music gave forth the terrible story of the boy in his father's arms who is at first tempted and then threatened by the king of the elves.

Finally, as they continued to hold him, he finished the piece, whispering the final words—"the child in his arms was dead"—and his hands seemed to float away from the piano and to take them with him.

He rose. He turned toward the door to his bedroom. His tears now fell directly from his eyes to the floor and left their trail as he walked between his two friends, each of whom put an arm around his waist.

In his room, he fell backward upon his bed, and the boys lay down with him, one on either side. Each curled up against him and eventually fell asleep, while Robert wept the whole night long and still failed to drown either his sorrow or himself.

Leipzig

OCTOBER 4, 1829

I have wept only three times in my entire life:
when my first opera failed; when a turkey stuffed with
truffles fell overboard; when I heard Paganini.
Gioacchino Rossini

Earlier that year, Niccolò Paganini, on his first tour of north Germany, had stopped in Leipzig on his way to Berlin. He was not booked to play Leipzig, but Friedrich Wieck, with Paganini's permission, tried to free up the Gewandhaus for a one-night stand. In this he failed. But when Paganini left for Berlin, he was followed by Wieck, who arranged for him to come back to Leipzig in the autumn and play not one but four concerts. "And by the way," said Wieck, upon taking leave of Paganini, "when you are in Leipzig in October I trust you will do me the honor of listening to my daughter." Paganini hooked one of his talon-like fingers into the bridge of his dark spectacles and pulled them down his nose so he could look at Wieck without the asylum of obscurity. "Violin?" he asked. "Piano," answered Wieck. "Well, then," said Paganini, shoving his glasses back up his nose and grinning in a bright and fetching way that Wieck would never have imagined his devilish features could align themselves, "since she is not competition and therefore will not rob me of my livelihood, the honor of listening to her will be mine."

At the time Paganini arrived back in Leipzig, Clara had been composing music of her own and playing in public for almost two years, mostly in private homes like that of the Caruses, although she had also traveled to Dresden to appear at two court soirées hosted by Princess Louise and at a fund-raiser for the Dresden Institute for the Blind, and had performed her first concerto, Hummel's G major, to a private audience. She had even appeared at the Leipzig Gewandhaus; not, however, in official debut but merely as primo in Kalkbrenner's four-hand Moses Variations.

She had never played for anyone like Paganini. He was, her father told her, perhaps the greatest virtuoso, if not musician, alive. More important than that, he was the most famous. And what fame did for a musician, aside from making him rich, was to give him the power to make other musicians famous. And therefore rich. There were dozens of great virtuosi playing all over Europe, hundreds of wunderkinder, her age and even younger. What separated one from the other was not so much a question of talent—for how many among even the cosmopolitan public could discern with any subtlety the nuances of technique and interpretation?—as of reputation. And reputation was made through the stated opinions of those already famous. Therefore, she must play for Paganini. Therefore, she must dazzle him.

She was not at all nervous about this. The important relationship in music was between her and her piano, not her and her audience. It was the piano that received her body and through her body the transubstantiated body of the composer.

Even hearing Paganini play did not shake her confidence in herself.

She and her father went to the first of his Leipzig concerts. They sat in the audience with all the rest of their expectant neighbors, few of whom had heard Paganini play but all of whom knew his reputation. It was said of Paganini, and was being whispered now within Clara's hearing, that he had been born of the Devil or was at the very least in league with the arch fiend. That he could raise the dead with his playing. That he had labored for, as both musical director and lover, Napoleon's sister, the Princess of Lucca. That he had been in a Naples prison for twenty years for having murdered another of his mistresses, solitarily confined for that entire time with nothing but a chamber pot and a one-stringed broken violin, and of the two he used only the violin in all that time. That the strings of his favorite violin had been fashioned from the intestines of that same mistress, whom he had murdered not because she had been unfaithful but because she had yawned when he was playing, and upon pushing his knife into her guts he had said, "Sorry to bore you."

As had been written of him, "You would as soon expect melody from a corpse," and that is what he looked like as he seemed to float into the hall simultaneously with the raising of the curtain, which revealed dozens of golden candelabras in which burned what seemed like thousands of black candles. Their flames twisted in terror as Paganini drifted past them to the center of the stage, which at least proved he was made of matter and was not what he appeared to be, a skeletal wraith, though neither was he the romantically arrogant, curly-haired artist represented by Jean Ingres in the portrait of which Clara's father had given her a copy for her recent birthday, painted ten years ago, at the very time of her birth.

He wore a coat and vest so tight she could not imagine he could scratch an itch, let alone raise both violin and bow, and pantaloons so loose she could not keep from envisaging his private parts swinging like a bell and its clapper. All his clothing was as black as the candles, blacker than the blue-black glass in his spectacles, which sat atop his huge hooked nose like the lashless, dispassionate eyes of an insect. His skin, however, was pale, more yellow than white, which is how Clara imagined the dead must look, sickly rather than pure, his cheeks hollow as if they had never been fed, and his black hair growing long down his back the way the hair of the dead was said to grow long after the rest of the body was left looking . . . well, exactly like Paganini.

In one hand he held his violin and bow, in the other a pair of scissors. Clara thought, "I knew his hair was too long!" and wondered if he was actually going to cut it and perhaps throw the strands out into the audience for souvenirs, as a young pianist in Paris named Franz Liszt was said to throw his cigar butts to certain women in attendance at his concerts. But Paganini did not use the scissors to cut his hair. Holding his violin out before him like a magician attempting to display the incorruptibility of his props, Paganini severed three of its four strings, each of which gave one sharp and final cry of wretched music before trembling to death. The audience gasped, Clara recoiled out of sympathy for the pain being suffered even now by his poor mistress, and Paganini began to play, on that one G string, the "Witches' Dance." Oh, what a trick it seemed, even the impossible production of what sounded like but could not be polyphony on that single string, as the severed strings whipped around his neck and head like long filaments of glass dipped in candlelight. If he went this far, she wondered, why did he not simply cut all four strings and then play?

But even that could not more have impressed the audience, which greeted the end of the "Witches' Dance" with an applause that would have been of greater suitability to a witnessing of the resurrection of the body of our Lord.

Paganini bowed. It was not a gracious bow, such as her father had taught her, a humble bow, and it did not appear directed to the audience so much as to his violin or to his own hands or to himself. He bowed the way she imagined a man with tight pants would upon lowering himself onto a chamber pot.

The audience might have applauded forever had it not been relieved of this effort by the arrival on the stage of a tiny, beautiful boy with golden hair who carried with him a properly stringed violin and exchanged it for the one Paganini had mutilated.

As he received the new violin from the small hands of the boy, Paganini smiled at him, smiled in such a way that Clara felt she had never been smiled at in her life, not by her father or her mothers or her brothers or by Herr Schumann himself, whose smile she most wanted to provoke. She envied that smile, and the man who was so at ease with his place in the world to be able to smile it, and the boy, whoever he might be, however lowly a servant or princely a prince, who was its recipient.

It was as if the boy had brought not only a violin but the beauty of music itself. For when Paganini played upon it, he played a rondo by Beethoven, and he played it with such feeling and with such control and with such knowledge of the music that Clara found herself weeping. From then until the end of the concert—despite Paganini's seeming inability to refrain from such tricks as dual-hand pizzicato and ricochet bowing and octave trills and double stops and the production of shimmering flageolet tones and what Clara could have sworn sounded like scordatura tuning, to say nothing of his getting his violin to bray and hoot and yelp like various animals and finally at the end of his encores to pronounce in what sounded like perfect Italian "buona sera," which of course had nearly everyone in the audience shouting back, "buona sera"—she had tears in her eyes. What he did, it seemed impossible to do: And that is why her tears were both of wonder and of anger.

She slept that night with the image of him in her mind. She was to play for him the next morning, and if she lost any sleep, it was the consequence not of nervousness but of enthusiasm. She felt his equal, not in style, certainly, but in value. He had taught her something, he had even inspired her. But she would teach him something, too. She would inspire him, too. At the very least, she would dazzle him.

It was only when she and her father were shown into Paganini's sitting room at the Hôtel de Pologne that she became concerned. At the center of the room was a piano, and it was a miserable specimen: old and scarred and lopsided and dirty-keyed. Her father went over to it and shook his head and actually pinched his nostrils together with his thumb and forefinger while scrutinizing its innards.

At that moment, Paganini's servant opened wide a double door at the rear of the sitting room, and there appeared Paganini himself, coming out of what was clearly his bedroom, which Clara was pleased to observe was disastrously untidy, with clothes and peculiarly high, narrow shoes thrown everywhere and, most shocking of all, piles ... heaps ... nearly mountains of stuffed animals, whose brilliant colors contrasted peculiarly with the blackness of the clothes and shoes and whose very presence in Paganini's bedroom made Clara feel much better about the wretched piano on which she was supposed to impress Signor Paganini so he would utter such words as would please her father insofar as they could be used to spread her fame.

Paganini was wearing a gigantic fur coat, which Clara thought might be appropriate in the chilly autumn air outside but was hardly necessary here. The room was not warm—there was so much energy expended in the concentration upon the playing of most instruments that musicians customarily preferred cool dwellings—but neither did it call for the donning of the piliferous epidermises of whatever herd of animals had been fashioned into Paganini's garment.

But the coat did, at least, make Paganini seem less cadaverous. He appeared, in fact, almost jollily roly-poly. And that, like his stuffed animals, helped to put her at ease.

From beneath the huge coat peeked out those same strange shoes she had glimpsed in his bedroom and the left one of which she now remembered beating time like a meat cleaver upon the floor of the stage as Paganini had played his violin. The shoes had a high heel for something a man would wear and such pointed toes that Clara thought the end of Paganini's feet must resemble nothing so much as his own nose.

He did not come over to shake hands with her father and to do whatever he might have done to greet her. Instead, he sat immediately down in the room's one large chair and sighed the way a fat man does when he sits. He folded his arms over the large belly that his coat created for him out of its countless pelts, then motioned for her father to sit down in a small chair farthest from the piano and with the least good view of it and for her to sit down at the piano.

She was about to announce the piece she would play when Paganini spoke his first words: "Please forgive the deplorable condition of the piano, young lady. Would one could use a scordatura tuning as easily on a piano as I do to cheat on the violin. It was abandoned here by a student who was either destitute or deaf, let us hope the former. You will have to be a far greater musician than I to get even a single note out of it."

Her heart leapt and stilled within the same moment. "Polonaise in E-flat," she announced softly and perched her hands over the keys.

Before she could lower them, Paganini asked, "*Whose* polonaise?"

"Mine," answered Clara, and played.

It was no more difficult than playing for her father at home; easier, in fact, because of how Paganini had made her father sit with as poor a view as he might have of her hands from anywhere in this bare, cavernous room. Paganini seemed to have known that she would not now, or ever, have as severe a critic as her own father, for whom her playing was an expression not merely of her own life but of his as well. Because Paganini had seated himself so much closer to her than he had her father, he had contrived to make her feel she were playing for him alone. This conspiracy between them more than overcame the fact that the piano sounded even worse than it looked. It was terribly out of key, and she wished only that she could have done with it what Paganini had done with his violin during his concert when he tuned up his A string by a semitone.

When she finished, she could not help looking first at her father, however, who she was shocked to see was looking not at her but at Paganini, as if he did not want to disagree with any judgment the maestro might make, not even when it came to his own daughter.

As for Paganini, he said, "Well, what did you think?" addressing that strange question at neither Clara nor her father but, she concluded, his own fur coat. She glanced over at her father, who had the stricken but halfway angry look he got when he was forced to deal with a madman (a not uncommon occurrence when one made a living in the field of music).

But then, of all things, the fur coat answered. "It was wonderful!" it said in a high, tiny voice with what Clara assumed must be an Italian accent.

Was it possible that Paganini possessed, aside from his phenomenal musical skills, the ability to throw his voice like those men with puppets who often appeared on programs with musicians?

That question in Clara's mind was answered negatively, but more shockingly than had it been answered in the affirmative, when out of the front of Paganini's fur coat popped the head of the golden-haired little boy who had carried Paganini's fully strung violin to him on the stage during his concert.

"Allow me to introduce my son, Achilles." Paganini unbuttoned his coat fully, revealing that he was wearing nothing beneath it but long flannel underwear, and kissed the boy several times as he emerged and placed himself on his father's lap and pulled his father's arms tightly about him. "He's my own worst critic, and so I thought he should be yours, mademoiselle. Please forgive the subterfuge. I don't know about you in your performances, but for me it is always most intimidating to play for children. Like dogs, they hear things the rest of us cannot. And like dogs, they do not hesitate to howl if what they hear does not please them. And you did not howl, did you, little man?"

"No, I did not, Papa."

"She plays wonderfully, does she not?"

"I said that already."

Paganini laughed and tightened his arms around his son. "So you did. So you did. And on that perfectly atrocious piano."

"Atrocious," repeated Achilles, who might be trying the word for the first time.

"Wonderful tone," said Paganini. "Would you not agree?"

"Good technique," said Achilles.

"He gets that from me," explained Paganini. "The concentration on technique."

"Out of tune," said Achilles.

"The piano," said Paganini.

"*You're* out of tune sometimes," his son clarified.

"Of course *I'm* out of tune sometimes. I'm a violinist. But we never speak of a pianist as being out of tune. Only a piano."

"Or you," said Achilles.

"Or me," said Paganini, smiling with the proud paternal smile that invites all those present to replicate it. Clara had always been embarrassed when her father did the same, but she was touched to observe it in Paganini, whom she could not have imagined as a father and now could not imagine otherwise.

"I know," he said to Achilles, "that you could not see Mademoiselle Wieck because you were hiding in my coat, but if—"

"You *made* me hide."

Paganini kissed the top of the boy's head, which Clara was sure other people aside from herself must be tempted to do. "That's true. I made you hide. But that's not my point. My point is only that you could not *see* Mademoiselle Wieck play, you could only hear her, and if you could have seen her you would most likely have told her that she has such a genuine sense of the beauty of music that she ought not to play so restlessly and with so much movement of the body."

"Ah, thank you, thank you," said Clara's father, as if he'd been paying for a lesson and wanted to get his money's worth.

"No," said Achilles to his father.

"No, what?"

"No, I would not have said that."

"Why not?"

"Because I would not say anything bad."

Paganini looked at his son with an exaggerated expression of shock. "But you do sometimes howl when you hear music played badly."

The boy put his head back against his father's thin chest and smiled the huge smile of a fat-faced angel and tried unsuccessfully to contain his laughter: "Like a dog."

Paganini invited Clara and her father to the remainder of his Leipzig concerts, where they sat on the stage as his special guests. Her father in turn arranged for a new piano to be delivered to Paganini's rooms at the Hôtel de Pologne, to which he invited them in order to ordain the instrument. This they did with a four-hand arrangement of a rondo on themes from Paganini himself, which brought him to tears and Achilles, witnessing his father's joy, to the same.

He told Clara she would be famous one day and must beware of fame's blandishments. "I refer not to money," he said, "for money is the least to be given to a person who can make other people pay for the privilege of hearing him create nothing more substantial or permanent than sound. I refer to those things that have nothing to do with music. There are Paganini canes and Paganini frocks and Paganini umbrellas shaped like violins and Paganini gloves, a pair of which I was offered myself in Paris, which led me to ask the saleswoman if she didn't by chance have a pair made from the leather of another animal. We musicians are not animals, mademoiselle, but we are not exactly human either, are we?"

Clara loved being spoken to like a fellow musician, worldly and accomplished. But she loved even more leaving Paganini and her father to talk about her while she went into the bedroom with Achilles and the two of them played with his stuffed animals.

On the day Paganini took Achilles and left Leipzig, she brought the boy two bunches of grapes, one white and one red, and Paganini asked for her journal and wrote in it some notes from one of his scherzos and a harmonization of the chromatic scale in contrary motion and signed it with his name to "*al merito singulare di Madamigella Clara Wieck.*"

Leipzig

SEPTEMBER 19, 1830
People find her very lovable.
Friedrich Wieck

Robert had barely turned twenty when Friedrich Wieck accepted him as a resident piano pupil in his home at Grimmaischestrasse Number 36.

Wieck wrote to Robert's mother, who remained not at all convinced that her son should be abandoning his legal studies: "I shall turn your son Robert into one of the finest pianists now living. He will play with greater feeling than Moscheles and finer technique than Hummel. As proof of this I offer you my eleven-year-old daughter, Clara, whom I am now beginning to present to the world."

Wieck had no intention of offering Clara to Robert—this was hardly his purpose in inviting Robert to live with him and his family. It was traditional for students of music to live with their teachers. Music was not something like cooking or equestrianism. It did not inhabit a particular time or place so much as it inhabited the beings of those who became its votaries. You might remove your hands from the piano, as you might your legs from the horse between them, but you could not remove the music from yourself or yourself from the music. There was no escape. You might as well, said Wieck, live with it, and thus with me.

"I want to have a house like Bach's," he explained. "I have a mere four children thus far, of course—you've met only the best of them, Clara, the others being boys, God help them—but Bach had what?—two dozen? three? Yet he had his students live in his house. They were with him all day long. Not studying the whole time, God forbid, but playing, yes, and tuning the instruments and repairing them if need be and tediously copying music and listening, listening, listening. Can you imagine, Robert? Bach himself once played through the whole of *The Well-Tempered Clavier* three times for Nikolaus Gerber, three times in succession, without so much as tugging his cuffs or taking a coffee. Gerber said afterward that he had learned more in those hours, which passed like mere moments, than he had in all the years of his life. Bach then told Gerber he must begin his studies not with these forty-eight preludes and fugues but with four months of finger exercises. And so it must be with you."

"But you are not Bach," said Robert.

"And you are not Clara," said Wieck.

Robert sometimes, in his Hoffmann-inspired love for nicknames and pseudonyms, called her Zilia, actually a nickname within a nickname, for Zilia was itself Robert's playful name for Cecilia, the patron saint of music.

She called him Herr Chumann, slightly mispronouncing his name not on purpose but because she had, in beginning to speak so relatively late in life, developed a bit of a speech impediment. Naturally, he found it appealing.

He also used with her the formal *Sie,* not, as he did with her brothers Alwin, Gustav, and half-brother, Clemens, the familiar *du.* This was not because he felt particularly formal with her—how could he be, when she was so spirited and playful and, in his presence if not her father's, wild? He wrote in his diary, "What a creature Clara is! Barely three hours old, her heart is evolved in a way that disturbs me. Moods and fits, crying and laughing, withdrawn then exuberant. Her father ought well be in bliss at having Zilia."

No, the formality of the pronoun with which he addressed her was occasioned by the respect he held for her musicianship. They were, after all, students together. But while she was merely a child and he was, he liked to think, a man of at least part of the world, she was so much more at ease with the piano than he, and so much more accomplished at it, that he sometimes felt he was in the presence of his master.

She intimidated him, though she inspired him as well. He practiced between six and seven hours a day, perpetually disoriented by Wieck's demands for both technique and beauty. Wieck accused him of believing that the entirety of piano playing consisted in pure technique and used Clara to show him what he called "a pure, precise, smooth, clear, elegant touch." But when Robert attempted to let the piano sing, as Clara did, Wieck pushed him to study dry, cold theory. Robert was willing to acknowledge that he lacked much more than a rudimentary knowledge of thoroughbass and counterpoint, but he rebelled against what he considered the rigid and abstract recapitulation of mere musical principles and refused to study theory and composition with Christian Weinlich, the St. Thomas's Church cantor to whom Clara went diligently without a single complaint and from whom she returned with ever greater fluency. He threatened to run off to Weimar and enroll with Johann Hummel, who after all, Robert told Wieck, had himself been a student of both Mozart and Clementi. "With all due respect to Mozart and Clementi," said Wieck, "I am the better teacher."

Wieck nicknamed Robert "the hothead," and in retaliation Robert refused to practice even his finger exercises. But he still played the piano for six or seven hours a day, as many of them for Clara as her crowded schedule allowed.

Just as she had her own room on the top floor of the house and had been allowed to decorate it with the soft and comfortable furniture and billowing drapery that both she and her destructive kittens found so inviting, so Robert had his own room on the ground floor overlooking Reichstrasse, and his own piano, and it was at this piano he was sure to be sitting whenever Clara came home from her classes. It was his way of enticing her to him. He had discovered it quite by accident one day soon after his arrival when, instead of practicing his exercises, he had been improvising, wildly as usual, laughing and crying, getting up and sitting down, cigar in mouth, eyes closed against the smoke and the music, ears themselves half-closed to the dissonant harmonics and contentious rhythms and aggressive changes of key he seemed destined to produce whenever he was playing freely, as if his music were literally his signature, which itself was notoriously unreliable, and represented the perceptible manifestation of his otherwise inscrutable being. Improvisation was, for him, the writing of his autobiography upon the parchment of the air. But it was not merely the story of what he had become; it was also the story of what he was becoming. To make music was to give birth to oneself. You were, at the same time, naked, in terrible pain, dissevered, ecstatic.

What a state in which a little girl should find him.

But there she had been, sitting in the bay window or next to him on the piano bench, so still as not to be breathing, so quiet as not to be alive. He might never have seen her—or not seen her until he had finished his playing, at which he sometimes continued for hours, long after his cigar had burned down to a wet stub and self-extinguished—had not some ashes fallen from it and begun to smolder in his lap, the woodsy smell of which caused him to stop playing and start slapping himself around the buttons of his trousers.

It was not her laughter that startled him so much as the mere fact of her presence. The music he'd been playing drenched the room, pushing at the walls, beclouding the windows, securing the door. There was no room in here for anyone else. She had invaded his being.

"Your pants are on fire," she said.

He tried to jump up, but his legs were so stiff from his having been seated for so long that he rose slowly and had to lean one hand against the piano for support while he slapped his backside with the other.

"Not *there!*" she said, and laughed even more.

He had not been trying to make her laugh. But aware now of the effect of his action, and captivated by this spontaneous expression of delight in a little girl whom he had known hitherto primarily through the often intimidating sound of her piano playing, he began to spank at himself with both hands.

She was reduced to incomprehensibility. She tried to speak but could not through her honks and giggles. He worried for a moment that she would be thrown into terror at this replication of her years of speechlessness, about which her father had told him rather proudly, as if it had been an augury of musical genius. But the levity in her huge eyes, which caused them to glow with tears and in their beaming elongation to drown his own in light, convinced him she was uncomplicatedly pleased with him.

She laughed long after he had stopped banging at his bottom. He had not known she was capable of being so amused, or himself of being so amusing. It made him cherish her for the very fun of this. The world was a gloomy place, after all, and there was little humor in it or in the way his favorite writers represented it, which is what he had always loved about them: their fatalism, their enveloping pessimism, the shrouds and veils and masks and shades with which they lent impermanent disguise to the tragedy of love and the implacable envelopment of all our dreams in death. Even when he went out to the taverns and drank himself into the shared hilarity that seemed to reach its utmost pitch in the moments before self-consciousness and the poison of the alcohol suddenly ground him coarsely down like a pestle into terror, he had experienced no such gaiety or airiness as this, which could hold no terrifying consequence, which was innocent and wholly blithe.

She had given back the bright, cheerful days of childhood to a man who had for years been preyed upon by the most horrible thoughts and who had a genius for uncovering the dark and terrible side of things and who had seemed capable of throwing away his life like a farthing.

He sat himself down and sought the refuge of communication not in speech but music. She sat there next to him for as long as he played, quiet, tiny, and, for the moment, altogether his.

Leipzig

NOVEMBER 8, 1830

At night when you were very small
I came bedecked as specter tall
And rattled at your door.
Robert Schumann

Clara had been scheduled to make her official debut at the Leipzig Gewand-haus on September 30, but what was somewhat grandiosely called the Revolution of 1830 intervened and effected the postponement of this much-anticipated event.

The revolution was said to have started two months earlier in France, where Clara, though barely two weeks beyond her eleventh birthday, was most eager to travel and perform, the name Paris having become synony-mous, as it had and would in the minds of many who had never actually vis-ited either place, with Paradise. But like most political events that convince people to take up arms and attempt to slaughter those of whose ideas, ac-tions, language, iconography, appanages, child-rearing, or baba-baking they disapprove, this revolution did not begin where or when it began but else-where and earlier. Which is to say, it began generally at the birth of man, whether at Eden or at what Germans liked to think was Heidelberg, and specifically at the Karlsburg Congress of 1819, the very year of Clara's birth. It was there that Metternich, so upset over student demonstrations in honor of Martin Luther (who had been hereticized by the Edict of Worms a mere 309 years before and been dead for only 273), compelled the universities to teach nothing of which he did not approve and ordered the press—for if Metternich believed anything, it was that what the public didn't know couldn't hurt him—to print nothing of which he did not approve. (And that of which he approved was "the monarchical principle.") Or better yet, print nothing at all. It was around this time that Metternich's secretary, Friedrich Gentz, defended his boss's proposition, as follows: "In order that the press not be abused, nothing whatever shall be printed. Period." Noth-ing. Shall. Be. Printed. Besides, who needed to read when they could be watching their eyes glaze over?

So it was too in France, where, during the White Terror after Waterloo, the French press was (how tedious becomes the catalog of repression) smothered, divorce outlawed (discontent is best left at home), and those with the most money were as if by divine fiat the most "conservative" and thus the most eager for a return to the fine old days of the Ancien Régime. But, like all ancien régimes, this one had to be paid for by those who had no stake in its recrudescence. In order to indemnify his aristocratic friends for their losses during the most recent revolution, King Charles X merely lowered the interest rate on national bonds, thus squeezing the lucre out of his subjects so he could spread it upon the *pain* of his people. When this was objected to, Charles stifled the press.

There were riots in Paris, and for good measure they expanded beyond the politics of power into the very politics of art and therefore life, out of the broken bones and taunts of philistinism of which emerged the nascent but wholly triumphant romanticism of Victor Hugo's *Hernani*. As for musicians, they were freed by the revolution from having to enter through the back door and leave through the back door. Now they might even find themselves invited to tea with the understanding that they be permitted to "leave their fingers at home."

July's *trois glorieuses* plucked Charles from his throne and placed upon it the cunning Louis Philippe, who chose to align himself with the contra-Metternich Lafayette and thus to fool all the folks who thought he might actually belittle and belie his own beloved Bourbonism.

Like the cholera that was spreading at the same time through Europe, the revolution seeped from country to country in its attempt to bring democracy to those who didn't know they wanted it until they heard it was coveted by the French.

In Germany, the unrest began in Dresden and moved soon to Leipzig, where the police created a Communal Guard to protect the city from the egalitarian impulses of its citizens, to say nothing of the rioting of locksmiths whose jobs were being given to out-of-towners and the vandalism of rowdies over perceived rudeness in the passport office.

Clara found her father concerned very much with the possibility that, because of the small-scale but persistent rioting in Leipzig, her Gewandhaus debut might have to be put off, but he seemed otherwise uninvolved.

Robert, however, would play and sing for her the song of the Strasbourg revolutionaries—*"Mort aux tyrans! Vengéance et liberté!"*—improvising madly between choruses. He also set to music the antimonarchist version of the Lord's Prayer—"Our ex-king, who art a knave, cursèd be thy name; thy kingdom never come; thy will be done neither in France nor anyplace else"—and then persuaded her to sing it along with him, which produced in her a tiny thrill of transgression that she attempted to deepen as she sat beside him at the piano feeling rebellious and well on her way to twelve.

He expressed to her his concern that he might be drafted come his own next birthday, as every unmarried man in town between the ages of twenty-one and fifty was required to enlist and bear arms. She was unable for some time to express to him her contradictory feelings about this: She did not want to lose him, her best friend, to the militia, yet she was eager to see him, so tall and broad and handsome, in uniform, defending her and her alone from the barbarians, whoever they might be and whatever they might want to force her to do that she did not want to do with anyone but him.

"They'll probably draft me despite my poor eyesight," he said.

"I didn't know you couldn't see well," she said, realizing at the same time that this and not his cigar smoke must be why he was always squinting his deep-set blue eyes, which, as when he smiled, caused tiny whirlpools of dimples to draw her eyes toward the corners of his lips.

"I can see nothing," he said. "And I can see everything," he added grandiloquently.

As if it might prove a weapon against the military, he purchased a lorgnette, which he would leave on the piano except when he had her hold it up to his eyes at such times as he actually read or wrote some piece of music instead of merely improvising. When her arm became tired, she would rest her hand against his right cheek and let the joint of her middle finger settle into the dimple there, which slowly moistened with the pressure, and allow the backs of her other fingers the luxury of being simultaneously tickled and prickled by his whiskers.

By now her time with Robert was not limited to their hours together at the piano in his room. He also climbed the stairs to her room on the top floor. There, every night he wasn't out drinking with his friends, or before he went out drinking with his friends, he entertained her and her little brothers.

Sometimes they would play games like charades or see who could stand on one leg for the longest time or he would clench his hand around some little surprise like candy or a piece of colored glass and try to trick them by saying, "Look!" when there was nothing to be seen and then saying, "Which hand?" so they could guess, though she suspected some kind of benevolent treachery on his part because no matter which hand she chose, there was always something in it for her. Sometimes he told them one riddle after another. But what she liked best was when, having earlier put a lamp on the floor, he would burst in dressed as the ghost of someone who had been killed in the riots outside. He moved grotesquely through the dusky shadows cast by the lamp, causing her brothers to flee to her arms and she to flee to his, so that all of them ended up being hugged together by the ghost himself. He would then sit them down and tell them scary stories, sometimes about brigands in the woods or jungle animals in the forest and sometimes — these were her favorites, which he seemed to save for her alone, when her brothers were busy elsewhere — about doppelgängers.

"I have a double," he told her. "You have a double. We all have doubles. But most of us don't know it. We go through life unaware that there is someone else who is also ourselves, exactly like us, except that our double is of the spirit only and we are of the flesh. We are visible and palpable. Our double is invisible and untouchable."

"And what does our double do?" she asked. "Do you think my double might sometimes practice the piano for me?"

She said this to amuse him. The last thing she might want a double to do would be to take away from her time at the piano. She lived in fear of not being allowed to play, rather than being forced to play too much. When her father wanted to punish her, he kept her from the piano.

Robert did laugh. "No, Zilia, your double can't play the piano for you. In your case, and yours alone, your double is not your exact replica, because there could be no one else in this world or any other who could play the piano as well as you."

She was not unaccustomed to such praise. She had played in enough salons to have become quite in demand, and when her father allowed her to accept invitations only to those homes at which there were likely to be in attendance people who could be of genuine use to her career, those who had been rejected sent her not only flattering entreaties but also accompanying gifts, from candies and cakes to earrings and rings and lockets and bracelets and in one case a slender gold chain about which she exclaimed, "They must think I have a neck the size of a cow's!" when she did not realize, until her stepmother told her, that it was meant to be worn around the waist, beneath her clothing, so that it was taken from her as indecent when it was the one gift she truly wanted.

Sometimes women, and their daughters with them, would, in their servants' places, deliver the gifts themselves, and it had become the custom for them to ask to fix her hair. People loved her hair. It was dark and soft and fine, and when it was pulled away from her face and piled atop her head or twisted behind in elaborate shapes, her eyes, like an actor's when the curtains are drawn apart, seemed to grow larger and become more alive. "Striking," they would say, looking at her. Never "beautiful"—always "striking." She thought she would play the piano for anyone who called her beautiful, and go anywhere to do it.

But there was no praise like Robert's. He was some kind of mad genius, the way he would sit at the piano and improvise for hours on end and produce unanticipated changes of key and strange chords she could not manage to find within her own fingers. She often felt a longing for his music. It was not altogether a pleasant longing. She felt the same thing when he was not there, as when his music was not. A missingness, she called it, a grief, like for her distant mother, or her dead sister, or even her own double, who she thought might take from her some of the burden of her life.

"I would like to meet my double," she told him.

"Oh, no!" he said. He seemed shocked. "Oh, no, you wouldn't! To meet your double is a sign you will soon die."

She thought for a moment of pretending to be frightened, so that he might hug her, but she preferred he see her strong. "I don't believe that," she said.

"Don't believe that? But you must. It is true. How can you not believe that?"

"For the very reason you gave me. My double cannot play the piano as well as I. You said so yourself. Therefore, it would have to be my double who died and not me, should we ever meet."

He hugged her anyway. "Has anyone ever had such faith in her art?"

It was he, not her art, in whom she had faith. It was he who spoke of art as if it were religion. So far as she was concerned, she simply played the piano. It was her purpose on earth. This was not religion but life.

But so was this, being held by her friend, who was indeed her only friend, and feeling it would be impossible for her to have a double because there was no room in the universe for such a feeling as this to be duplicated.

When Robert's mother in Zwickau sent him his birth certificate, which he was required to show to the military authorities, Clara asked to see it.

She smoothed it out with her hands and then read it. "'Robert Alexander Schumann,'" she said. "I don't believe it."

"You don't like my name?"

"I love your name. What I don't believe is that you actually exist."

He spoke of trying to get a medical deferment because of his eyesight and a tendency to vertigo, but he was convinced he would be drafted and spoke of escaping either to America or to Twer, in Russia, where he had an uncle.

She desperately wanted him not to go, and at the same time to go with him. She imagined an endless trip, with howling winds and blankets over their laps and all the untold stories he would tell her, and at the end of the trip, when she would be much older than she was now, a piano.

As it turned out, he was not drafted and he did not go away. The revolution was over quickly, at least in Germany, and from what she could tell in hearing her father discuss it with Robert and some of the older students, the freedoms that were being won by the people in England and Belgium and Portugal and Spain and Switzerland had been denied the people of Russia and Poland and Austria and of course Germany. Nothing had changed except for those who had died.

And for her, since she could now make her debut at the Gewandhaus.

The Gewandhaus itself was an old clothing hall, where Leipzig's linen merchants used to store and sometimes sell their cloth. It had been converted into a concert hall nearly fifty years before, and a local orchestra had been playing there—never very well—in the intervening time.

A Gewandhaus performance represented a significant change in the status of the solo musician. In the past, such artists, no matter the glory of their virtuosity, were primarily household servants who performed at the whim of their wealthy patrons; musicians were paraded out like so many jugglers and tumblers to impress invited guests or on occasion to perform privately for the patron himself, who might have a headache or want to play along upon his very own flute or, if he were truly enlightened, to take a small dose of the profound humility any sensible human being should—but so few do—experience with religious ferocity in the presence of a great musician.

"What shall I wear?" she asked Robert.

"You're asking *me*!"

The shock and amusement on his face simply amused her. "My mother is too far away, and my stepmother is too vulgar."

He considered for a moment. "A dress, I should think."

Having no idea whether he was serious, which made his remark all the funnier, she laughed again. "Of *course,* a dress! But what *color*?"

"Black," he said.

"You're impossible."

"I wear black. All the time. It's the only serious color."

"You're a man. And a most serious man at that. I'm just a little girl. I can't wear a black dress to my debut."

"Of course you can," he said.

She wore white. Until then, when she had played in public, her colors had indeed been those of a little girl, pastels in which she had always felt both shrunken and giddified, offered like a candy to a fat man. Lately, at home, she had been wearing darker clothes, almost, she realized, as dark as Robert's, though usually set off at the throat and wrists and sometimes even at the hem with lashings of white lace. But for her debut, she would wear white, silk, with some of the jewelry people had been sending her so she might show her appreciation for their acknowledgment of her superiority.

She was not nervous over her debut. Most important, the piano was to be one of her father's Grafs, familiar to her in its suppleness and vastly different from the tree trunk of an instrument whose unyieldingness had caused her the year before to interrupt the wild cheering of the audience at the end of her performance in Dresden with an apology for her tone and tears for their ignorance. She had by now played so often for an audience that she was more concerned with the grace of her movements onto the stage and the depth of her bows than with her musicianship. Perhaps this was because the major works she was to play—by Kalkbrenner and Herz and Czerny—were no longer difficult for her. They might be virtuoso pieces, meant precisely for the kind of show she was expected to provide, but, once mastered, they were reduced to a kind of animated simplicity. They were hell to practice, because without an audience to hear them, they had no meaning. But with the Gewandhaus filled—and her father had seen to it that there would be no empty seats—this music, and she, would be rapturously hosannaed.

She spent much of her performance trying to find Robert in the audience. It was not easy, and she never succeeded. Those seated down the long, narrow auditorium that extended from the stage to the back of the hall faced not the stage but the center corridor and thus one another across it, making it difficult for the soloist, whose back was to the audience when she was playing, to find anyone's eyes. So she imagined his on her, wide and blue, not squinting, able to see her hands, impressed with their strength and ridiculous speed in the Kalkbrenner rondo, dazzled by her dress, pleased with her hair as it sat motionless and undisturbed atop her head, as fond as he could possibly be of his little friend, especially when she was up here all alone, the orchestra departed, her father and his physharmonica departed, she by herself at the end of her recital with nothing to occupy her hands but her own variations on her own theme, such a relief to be playing, and nothing to occupy her heart but him.

She saw him finally after the first of her final bows, so that it was the only successful bow, the rest being much too quick.

Leipzig

MAY 13, 1831
Charitas came completely and was bleeding.
Robert Schumann

Christian Glock was looking at Robert's penis through a magnifying glass.

"Oh, my," said Glock. "Oh, my my my."

"I trust you're exclaiming over its magnitude," joked Robert, who wouldn't have minded a look at it himself in its enhancement but had been ordered to remain supine upon Glock's examination table.

Robert had turned to Glock, his medical muse and fellow Hoffmann worshipper, because he couldn't bear the thought of displaying to Dr. Ernst Carus the very organ he still dreamed of burying deep within the doctor's very own wife.

"What's her name?" asked Glock as he raised and lowered his face as if to bring the suffering beast into proper focus.

"I'd hardly call it a 'she,'" Robert answered.

"Then what is *his* name?" asked Glock.

"My penis doesn't have a name!"

Glock laughed. "I should hope not. It is my experience that men who name their penises are otherwise without friends. And I would have thought that you came to me with your problem precisely because we *are* friends."

"Precisely."

"Then as your friend, and also as, for the moment, your physician, I would like to know the name of your lover."

"Christel," Robert pronounced her name.

Glock looked disappointed. "Who?"

"Christel. Otherwise known as Charitas."

"Known to whom?"

"To me, of course."

"Well, I don't know her by either name. Who is she?"

"She studies with Wieck. I don't know her surname."

"From the condition of your prick, I should think she studies even harder with you."

"Thank you," said Robert proudly.

"Don't thank me. Thank her. Though I'm not sure it's gratitude you ought to be feeling. You must be in considerable pain from this."

"I am. But, oh, what pleasure has caused it!"

"I can imagine," said Glock.

"'Imagine'?" Robert teased him.

"Alas, yes. Imagine. I've not had a woman since I began my studies."

"Medical school?"

"Before medical school."

"Law school?"

"Before law school."

"Theology school?"

"Yes, before theology school. In fact, it was a woman who caused me to enroll in theology school in the first place."

"How so?"

"She left me. The pain was so great that I thought I would never understand it until I came to understand God."

"And did you?"

Glock shook his head. "I came to understand that the two things that can never be understood—*never understood!*—are the workings of a woman's heart and the pain that God allows us—*causes* us—to feel."

Sad at his friend's sadness, Robert whispered, "And so you . . ."

"And so I became both a lawyer and a doctor. This way I can at least understand the workings of man, if not of God. Man cheats. Man decays."

Robert sat up, to engage Glock more closely in his cynicism. "And that is your total view of man?"

"Man also engages in sexual intercourse," added Glock. "I may not, thank God, but Man does. Now this Christel, Robert, is she your first?"

"I don't know," he confessed.

"What do you mean, you don't know?"

"I mean, I don't know if she was my first. She may have been, she may not have been."

"With all due respect, Robert, and speaking out of experience that may be years in the past but lives within my memory as if it had happened not five minutes ago, one's first woman, whether she is merely one's first or is also one's only, is not someone to be forgotten, to say nothing of the first time she *is* gotten."

"I'm sorry, Christian, but I just don't know. She feels to me like my first, but there may have been a whore here and there. I simply can't remember."

"And why can't you remember, Robert?"

"Drink."

Robert confessed this somewhat shamefacedly, for while he had certainly drunk his share, and more, in the presence of Glock the friend and musician, who himself was known to take a glass of wine so long as it was not of German origin, he felt he was speaking now to Glock the physician, and all the physicians Robert had ever known found drink the easiest thing to tell a patient to forgo, as if they had no understanding of what an important function drink served in painting over the grim features of life with its own limpid tinctures.

"Ah, yes," said Glock, smiling leniently. "I recall one night this past winter when you came to the Hôtel de Pologne dressed as a woman, like some Berliner attending the Inverts Ball. We ended up carrying you home, and you woke up on the very threshold of the Wieck residence and said, 'Don't let Clara see me like this, she will think I am a ghost,' as if such a child might be awake at such an hour. And were those clothes you wore that night perhaps borrowed from this Christel of yours?"

Robert buried his face in his hands, though whether out of embarrassment or a memory of another of his terrible hangovers he did not know. "Believe me, if I had had Christel at that time, I would not have needed to go about in her clothes."

"So this relationship of yours is of more recent vintage," said Glock.

"Much more recent."

"Well, from the looks of your member there, I would say that the two of you must be going at it not only with ferocity but also with rather alarming frequency."

"You would not be wrong," said Robert with undisguised pride.

Glock's face suddenly lost its look of commodious remembrance and hardened into the physician's captious gaze.

"How can you be fucking someone in the home of your teacher? Right under his nose, as it were? And one of his own students? Does this not strike you as both indiscreet and degenerate?"

"But she doesn't board there, as I do," Robert excused himself lamely. "And I can't very well do it in her house, with her parents protecting what she takes absolute delight in describing as their utter belief in her virtue, which I can assure you was lost both to her and thus to me a long time before I came along. Besides," he confessed, "I can't get enough of her."

"Clearly," said Glock with an agreeable sympathy so rare in a physician and even rarer in a man not so much visited as tenanted by chastity. "Which means that you have, indeed, had quite enough of her. And I must order you to resist, for now and, if you truly want my advice, forever, whatever her charms may be that have caused you thus to lay bare, if you will forgive so lame a play on words, your poor, capricious, unrepentant penis. For you are, quite literally, wearing it away. You have a wound here on the frenulum that has been caused by one thing and one thing alone, and that can be cured by one thing and one thing alone."

"So it is not syphilis?" Robert asked warily.

"You may say as much to Christel."

"And the one cure is abstinence?"

"Did I say that?" Now Glock was smiling again.

"You did imply as much."

"Never trust a doctor who prescribes by implication. That's the lawyer's way."

"Then how am I to be cured?"

"Narcissus water," said Glock, who proceeded to dip his hands into his own bowl of soapy water, as if to signal that the examination was over and that he felt the need to cleanse himself of Robert's luxuriant sin. "Bathe your organ three times a day in a distillate of daffodil bulbs. And may I suggest you not have Christel do the honors."

"And yet the cure is not abstinence?"

"Not for your body, my friend."

Leipzig

MARCH 21, 1832
The whole house is like an apothecary's.
Robert Schumann

They had left him, and now he sat here with the middle finger of his right hand dipped in oxshit.

Christel slept in his bed across the room. So she had been sleeping since he had risen from her arms and gone out to the butcher to fetch this rather farfetched cure, which had been prescribed not only by the medical student Robert Herzfeld but also by numerous of his more established if also more expensive physicians, among them Raimund Brachman, the estimable Moritz Reuter, and even the always skeptical Christian Glock, though Glock had not even deigned to mention an animal dip until both the herb poultices and the brandy rinse, not to mention abstinence (from the piano, in this case), had failed.

It amused him to think, as he sat here with his nose closed against the smell and his eyes cloudy from the fecal steam joining his cigar smoke to veil his head in this room still chilly on the first day of spring, how Christel would react when she awakened and, if she followed her usual practice, called him back to bed in her sleep-soaked, sex-singed voice.

He had moved out of the Wieck house just days after Clara and her father had departed for her first extended European tour, which had long since landed her in their ultimate destination, Paris. There, according to her charming letters, she was frustrated in her art—despite the fact that Kalkbrenner himself, as prelude to his self-serving condemnation of German pianists in general, had kissed her and in the act whispered, *"C'est le plus grand talent"*—and miserable in her missing her home, her room, her brothers, *him*.

He missed her too, of course, that spirit in her being that brought him out of himself. He had thought he would stay on in the Wieck household during her absence but had soon fled for the anonymity of the suburbs and this little room, preferring to be alone for the first time in his life to the way he felt on Grimmaischestrasse, abandoned to the silence, bereft of her music. That Christel might seek him out for periodic visits he had not expected, and he found himself as flattered by her lust for him as he was disturbed by his lust for her. He did not love her. She did not fill him with the kind of desire for perfection in his life that little Clara did; Christel merely fulfilled his desire for her, as she was, not for himself as she might render him.

Clara and her father had been planning to leave in the very midst of the previous summer. But before their scheduled departure, Clara came down with measles, which gave Robert the opportunity to sit beside her on her bed and help her with her French. He even found the word for measles, of the German variety—*rubéole*—and pretended to be her doctor and asked her what was the matter, *"Qu'avez-vous?"* so that she might respond, *"J'ai rubéole,"* unless it were the French variety, in which case she should say, *"J'ai rougeole."* One day she surprised him by having learned, *"J'ai des frissons,"* and then throwing herself into his arms, pretending to shiver and then seeming to shiver for real, though he realized it was only her attempt to refrain from laughing that caused her to tremble. *"J'ai soif,"* she said, yet when he fetched her tea, she said, *"J'ai faim,"* and took his hand and dipped his fingers into the honey and then into the tea and only then satisfied her thirst or hunger or whatever it could possibly be by taking his fingers in her mouth, laughing almost too much to permit herself to swallow.

Once she was recovered, their trip had to be postponed once again because the Polish-Russian war of that year had augmented its spread of deliberate death with an unintended but even more efficient and democratic epidemic of cholera (unless it was true, as many said, that the disease had been caused by Jews poisoning the well water). It had wasted its way through Bavaria into Saxony and was well on its way to Leipzig, causing Robert to drink more beer than ever, as the only safe alternative to water, and to make out his will and to announce to Clara and her father as they ate lunch at the Wasserschenke that this might be the last time they would see one another because soon he was either going to be dead or on his way to live in Italy or Weimar. At this news, Clara grasped him by both arms and either pulled him to her or her to him and clung to him for the rest of the meal, while Wieck sat shaking his head after having pronounced, "Weimar is no safer than Leipzig, considering that both are on major roads. But Clara and I fear neither and in fact leave tomorrow ourselves for Weimar to seek the blessing of Goethe himself." At this news, Robert found himself as much clinging to his friend as clung to by her.

The next time he heard from her, she wrote about how they had been refused entrance to the great Goethe's preposterously yellow house on Weimar's Jungfrauenplan, so her father had found other homes for her to perform in, homes of enough "aristocratic pretension" to allow reports of her playing to reach Goethe, who insisted on being kept informed of all that was new and exciting though he himself had only just come around to appreciating Mozart, whom he had heard play when Mozart was only seven, and even now found Schubert's music incomprehensible.

Goethe invited Clara to perform for him, and for his grandchildren, and, as Clara wrote to Robert:

He went out of his way to rise from his chair—he is over eighty and none too swift of foot nor straight of spine—to find a pillow for me. He delivered it to me at the piano and pushed it under my fanny in such a way that his hand, which I could feel and later see had a ring on nearly every finger, was between the pillow and my fanny itself. And wouldn't you know that hand stayed right there, as if to arrange the pillow though it was my fanny he nearly rearranged and almost caused to close together upon his hand and trap it there. When indeed the piano bench was of sufficient height for me without either a pillow or his naughty hand. And yet once he withdrew his hand, I think his grandchildren heard me better than did he. I had wanted to play Chopin or Beethoven, as I had in other homes in Weimar, but Papa insisted I play Herz, because Herr Goethe made no secret of his distaste for Beethoven and his ignorance of Chopin. [Why is it, thought Robert upon reading this, that artists who were revolutionary in their youth become not merely indifferent but antithetical to artistic revolution in their age, as if to shut out the light in fear of the darkness soon to fall upon them?] So I played Herz, and the children bounced around in their seats appropriately—I could scarcely sit still on mine as I played the Bravura Variations—while Herr Goethe himself sat there staring off into space with one finger occasionally in his ear, which had a halo of little white hairs around its hole, and another finger even more occasionally in his nose, the hairiness of which I shall desist in describing to you in case you are eating while you are reading this letter. I can only imagine what was on his mind. (I shall put into these secret parentheses some gossip I heard: when Herr Goethe was in his seventies, he fell in love with a teenaged girl scarcely older than I, who in case you forgot turned twelve almost a month ago, and it was for her he wrote his *Trilogy of Passion* poems, which I'd never heard of but which of course I can't wait to read if I can do so in secret without Papa knowing. Can you imagine! A man like that in love with a mere girl.* I'll bet you can! This story at least went a long way toward explaining to me why he had put his hand upon my fanny, though of course I did not mention this to those who told it to me nor to Papa either but only to you, dear Herr Schumann. And lest you think you are so different from Goethe, though you are in terms of genius, yours being greater of course, you should realize that he too came to Leipzig to study, and he too left his friends behind in Leipzig to study law, though in Strasbourg, not Heidelberg, and he too traveled to Italy where he no doubt to judge from his hand on my fanny had acciacctura adventures to rival your own, mere grace notes before the true melody of love. And that's the end of the secret part of this letter.) While he may not have listened to me, old Goethe did exactly what Papa had wanted him to do. He wrote a letter about me and put it in a little box and gave me the box. Papa

---

*It would be interesting, if impossible, to learn whether Clara is referring to Ulrike von Levetzow or to Marianne von Willemer. The former was fifty-six years Goethe's junior, a difference in age that was of no concern to Goethe himself, who believed that the older a man became, the more women there were to love, not the fewer; it was for Ulrike that he wrote the *Marienbad Elegy,* convinced he had lost her because his passion was so vast, the accumulation of love in a man that toward the end of his life is simply, and tragically, too intense for any woman, no matter how youthful and acquiescent. Marianne, whom he had known earlier, was scarcely fifty years younger than he and still unable to match his ardor, not so much physically as in terms of an impetuous avidity for both experience and knowledge; it was for her he wrote the *Divan* lyrics.

took it away immediately. But I got to read the letter. In it, he said I was stronger than six boys put together—which made me picture whether he had perhaps wrestled with that girl he was in love with and seems in love with still. He told me if I would call him Herr Schönfuss,* he would give me candy; which I did, and he did. But the candy tasted quite old, more like his foot than a sweet, just the way a footnote is rarely as delectable as the text it hangs from.** And then he gave me a bronze medal with—what else?—his face carved upon it. With news of his approval, all of Weimar opened to us. It was as if its ancient walls had been breached, not by cannon but by rumors of beauty.

We were invited to court, where the Grand Duke sat beside me at the piano and would surely have turned my pages had he known how to read music. The Town Theater, which we had not even been allowed to rent, was now given us without fee, and I played there to five hundred people and must have been asked by at least that many to sign autographs, which as you can see even now has made my usually perfect handwriting almost as bad—note I say "almost"—as yours. So we left Weimar in total triumph, though not before Papa got in a fight with the Privy Counselor, who refused to give Papa letters of introduction because he claimed Papa took my career more seriously than he took Beethoven's music. But Papa didn't care. He said with Paganini and Goethe behind us, what did we need Privy Counselor Schmidt for anyway. Besides, here in Kassel, where you should not be worried to hear the cholera has also reached, Ludwig Spohr himself introduced me to the court. There, we were seated at the royal dining table, and Herr Spohr turned my pages and allowed me to introduce him and all of Kassel to the Chopin Variations as well as to my own scherzo (for which I have written Herr Spohr a new coda just to keep him happy and also a little letter much shorter than this one to tell him that I once got a new piano because I had learned all his songs) and wrote for Papa an endorsement saying I have such gifts as "might be found only in the greatest of living artists" and then insisted I stay until the very end of the grand ball, though Papa, with the endorsement in hand (in his pocket, actually, and well buttoned up as you might

*Mr. Sweetfoot—the late Frau Goethe's affectionate term for her husband's penis.
**Clara was apparently, in using the word *Fussnote* (footnote), both showing off her new-found love of words to the person who might most appreciate it and, with this play on words, forcing his attention back to the utterly prurient *Schönfuss*.

imagine) kept telling me I need stay no longer and should go to bed, as if he didn't know as you do how much I love to dance.

Your friend,
Clara Wieck

He apparently didn't. In a separate letter, in which Wieck told Robert with much less charm and much more tympany of Clara's various triumphs, he remarked of the grand ball in Kassel that "all such diversions and attentions and invitations to gavotte make no impression on Clara."

Robert knew. He and Clara had danced together often. He had attempted to teach her the steps he had learned from his sister and his mother (his father had not objected to the idea of dance, only to its practice as what he had called "the greatest temptation there can be, since one *can* smoke and read at the same time, to a man at his books") and various forgotten women in various forgotten taverns on various unforgettable but, alas, forgotten nights. The gavotte, certainly, with the lifting of the feet at which Clara became adept only after he had told her to think of stepping over puddles. And the courante in which the feet glide. And the carmagnole that had them marching around her room singing revolutionary songs. And the allemande, savior of German reputation in the dance, much like the Ländler that his sister danced as he had played for her, except Emilie had danced alone and Robert danced with Clara in his arms, astounded at the smallness of her, boned and edgy, every muscle in her back making an impression on his fingertips, and the strength of her, particularly in her hands, as might be expected, one gripping his hand and the other his shirt as far as she could reach toward the crest of his shoulder.

Her brother Alwin, two years almost to the week younger than she, often played the violin for them to dance to. And he played it well, provided his playing was not measured by his sister's, which Robert would never have thought to do—you might as well compare a mallard to a thrush. But Wieck had not long prior to their departure made that mistake himself and thrown poor Alwin to the floor and taken his violin away with one hand and pulled the boy's hair with the other, complaining all the while of how poorly Alwin had been playing. Alwin, like Clara when Wieck forbade her the piano, begged and begged for his instrument back, but his father would not give it to him. Clara sat through all this with a strange smile and finally sat down at the piano and played, a Weber sonata as Robert recalled, trusting she did this to remove the terrible pressure and humiliation being heaped upon her brother and not to shine at Alwin's expense. As for Wieck, Robert felt he was getting to know him as he would prefer not to know him, a man who ranked his children according to their talents and acted like a Jew with his fervent eye on the cash drawer when there was a chance to stick four groschenstück into his own pocket.

In truth, Robert realized, he had left the Wieck home not simply because his reasons for being there—Wieck, his teacher; Clara, his friend—had departed but also to escape from memories like these. He had felt himself too much like Alwin, in a young pianist's frail shadow that eclipsed the light of all on whom it fell. Here she was now, in Paris, being compared to the greatest pianists alive, and here she had been, on Grimmaischestrasse in Leipzig, impossible not to compare oneself to.

It was strange, he thought, that his ambition to become a great pianist, as foolish as it might have proven to be, was never so strong as when she had left.

And so he had moved out of her house and into this anonymous room of his own in this anonymous suburb.

His piano was rented, a ducat a month. It might not have been as fine an instrument as Wieck had provided, and he now had to pay for it. But it was at least a piano that he was convinced had been played by no more proficient hands than his own, whereas every piano in the Wieck household had been tainted by Clara's greater mastery of it and thus, as pianos will, mocked all those of lesser talent who dared lay hands upon it.

He commenced a course of study in composition with Heinrich Dorn, who was the music director of the Leipzig Opera and presumed in his East Prussian way that a musician's bottomless immersion in counterpoint and thoroughbass would make him a composer. Robert knew, however, that it was in the mystery of the unconsciousness of the imagination that its poetry dwelled; this caused him to subscribe, at what distance was allowed by reticence and reclusion, to the growing belief in *Innerlichkeit,* which was the nurturing of the interior being, that inner self made manifest within the material world only on the wings of art. And yet, Dorn's insistence upon the sovereignty of the fugue, together with Friedrich Marpurg's book of theory, brought Robert finally to the Bach of *The Well-Tempered Clavier,* whose fugues he dismembered and analyzed down to every separate note and pause, which he felt gave strength not only to his playing and composing but to his entire moral fiber, the presence of Christel in his bed notwithstanding. In the absence of Clara Wieck and the way her music fed his deteriorating sense of who he was, Bach became his daily bread.

He played the piano for ten hours a day. He had never practiced so much before or experienced such sublime agony. His shoulders seemed to be trying to lock themselves atop his head as they rose ever higher with the increased difficulty of what he was learning. His neck became an inflexible spike driven between his clenched jaw and his spine. His back itself became curved as if lashed by some typhoon of music, that forced his head ever closer to the tidy row of headstones upon the graveyard of his instrument. And his fingers . . . his fingers were in danger of becoming what Weber himself called "those damned piano fingers that through endless practicing become the ignorant and tyrannical enemies of creation." He bloodied his knuckles and left upon the white keys red smears that never had time to dry before he once again attacked the piano and, through the piano, himself.

But if his fingers were damned — and at least one of them certainly seemed anathematized, at least to the extent that it was now anesthetized — it was not because he had been practicing the kind of work that for Weber and Wieck alike would produce mere brilliance at the expense of the truly musical. The sublimity of this experience for him had been precisely in the music, particularly Bach's fugues, this one a gavotte, that one a double fugue in the guise of a prelude that nearly obliterates the true fugue that follows, another a stretto fugue in which the second voice takes up the subject before the first has finished speaking it, to produce an intertwining that for all its formality has the casual quality of human interaction, a conversation between himself and Clara, she always bursting with interruption, this late-speaking child so intent upon expressing herself in every conceivable way, or he and Christel in bed, her limbs like music bending over his, the overlapping of their breath.

He had lost the use of his hand, at least for the purposes of playing the piano in the way the piano must be played if one is to play in and for the public, because he, like Faust, sold his soul to the Devil. The Devil, blessedly, being himself, so that what was loss was also gain. He had destroyed himself as a performer of music so he might become its creator.

It was not Clara alone who had forced him to this monumental decision, though there was no one else to thank. Neither had it exactly been a decision, because he had set out not to ruin his hand but to strengthen it.

Before he'd moved into the Wieck household, he had left Leipzig's law school and joined Heidelberg's, to be closer to Gisbert Rosen, primarily, but also to study with Anton Thibaut, who was nearly as famous for his knowledge of music as for his classes in law. Professor Thibaut was the author of *On Purity in Musical Art,* and it was he who recognized what was pure in Robert, telling him, at the time Robert was required as a Saxon citizen to return to Leipzig University to take his degree, that it was pointless for him to continue the study of law because he had clearly been called not only to music but to the life of music. "The law," Thibaut told him, "is for those who would comfort suffering; music is for those who find comfort in suffering." It was only when Robert repeated these words to his mother that she agreed he might use his inheritance from his father's estate to board and study with Friedrich Wieck and thus abandoned her futile dream that he make a living as one of those who, as she put it, "lives small and earns big."

While studying law in Heidelberg, and finding like all law students that there was time for little else, Robert discovered himself necessarily torn from the piano itself and thus began carrying with him everywhere a miniature dumb keyboard with very stiff springs attached to the keys. It was on this contraption that he would practice wherever he was—in class, at the tavern, sounding the English he studied with the angelically lisping wife of Ferdinand Ries, at home with Rosen until Karl Semmel had arrived and inspired in Robert what he called a more masculine and firm love than the girlish feelings he had for Gisbert, from whom he split to be with Karl. He would sit in his room with his hands working themselves into stiff exhaustion on the silent keyboard as he stared out the window at the Catholic church on his right and the insane asylum on his left, his mind in doubt whether to turn Catholic or go mad.

Perhaps he had gone mad. It had not been so long since he was in the park at Zweinaundorf reading Jean Paul's *Siebenkäs*. He sat enraptured among the trees and actually heard a nightingale. He could scarcely contain his body. His hands and feet were thrashing in the air. He was so happy he wanted to weep. But on the way back into Leipzig, he felt he was losing his mind. He was aware of his mind—of containing it, or of its containing him—but he was also aware of losing it. He may actually have gone mad. If so, it was madness with a purpose, it was madness that had brought him not to despair but to the exaltation he felt now at having been freed from the grip of the piano upon his hands.

Anyone looking at him, with his middle finger sunk to its knuckle in ox shit, might think him mad. Christel surely would, if she ever woke up from the sleep into which she always floated immediately after her crisis, purged of guilt and thus so unlike himself, who could no more fall asleep after his own than he could reclaim his innocence.

Christel had noticed, hanging from the ceiling above his table, the instrument of his torture, which put the dumb keyboard to shame in how it stretched and, finally, tortured the fingers. It was a sling that immobilized his middle finger so that the others on both sides could begin, like children sent off to board at school, to assume their independence.

Christel had climbed up on his chair to get a closer look at it. Smiling and shaking her head, she pulled it down to the extent of its elasticity. "If you want me on the table, fine. But you'll never fit in this."

He laughed. "It's a stretcher, all right, but not for that. It's for my fingers."

"Your fingers are quite big enough as well," she said, releasing the sling and coming toward him with her own fingers wide. He could give her only his left hand. The right was in too much pain.

It was pain that nothing had relieved. Not ice. Not even the best cognac in a fifty-fifty rinse with water, twelve tedious hours at a time. Not an anti-inflammatory paste of butcher's broom or a salve of devil's claw or an emulsion of ergot made from a rye fungus that caused him to feel there were insects crawling down between his fingers or a libation of bilberry juice (which he noticed improved his eyesight and reduced his need to squint), nor one of sarsaparilla, which strangely did seem to stretch his penis, or at least to render it more often swollen to its utmost girth, which he was too embarrassed to mention to Dr. Glock, to whom he was grateful for help with his hand in place of his previously incapacitated penis. And not even Dr. Otto's electrotherapy, which sent chemically produced galvanic currents shooting up and down his arm and hand until he felt like screaming and finally did, though as soon as Dr. Otto turned off his machine, Robert felt in the skin of his arm a desire for it to be turned on again.

So he had been reduced—or was it elevated?—to this: an animal dip in the feces of an ox. Several of his doctors had told him to stick his hand into the thorax of the animal itself and let whatever was there—blood, entrails, this stuff—do its healing. But Robert had been embarrassed to ask the butcher for permission to stand in his shop thus ravishing one of his animals and most likely driving away other customers who might naturally question whether they should buy the meat of an animal into which a strange young man had not only thrust his hand but appeared to be allowing it to set up permanent residence, unless this was his way of showing affection, like a man who rests his hand all afternoon on the stomach of his sleeping dog. Besides, Robert had been almost giddy with the idea of taking the jar of feces home to see how Christel would react. The very thought of it had him giggling as he walked back to his room with his injured hand over the top of the jar so that no heat would be lost and no smell would be wasted on strangers.

It was not an unpleasant sensation, to partake thus of an animal dip— the warmth and softness of this substance soothed, and just as it proved so vital a fertilizer for plants, so it might very well ease the pain and stiffness in his finger. It would not cure his hand, as each of his doctors had made clear.

He had done too much damage, not only to this finger but to those on either side of it. For all this he was grateful. His hands had stood in the way of what the Greeks called his *nous,* the self-expression of his being in the world outside himself. It was not enough to play the piano. It had never been enough. It was not enough even to write poems and stories. Music, he had decided, was poetry raised to a higher power. Spirits might speak the language of poetry, but angels communicated in tones. To have been freed actually to create music—this was indeed an exaltation of the soul.

Yet it was his body with which he was concerned at the moment. He had anticipated this worry and expressed it to Christian Glock: "Is there any danger that, when I dip a part of myself into the very hypostasis of the animal, I shall absorb some of its animality and thus become an animal myself?" Glock had answered, "The only hypo I see is a hypochondriac."

Only Robert knew he had once been a horse, whinnying over his vision of taking Liddy Hempel from behind like an animal. And now that he had, with Christel, whose only inhibition seemed to be mortality itself, realized such an image in his very flesh, he knew he was animal enough and longed for the fulfillment of another vision, one not of the eyes but of the inner ear, to hear flowing from him the music he heard within his head.

"My God, that's the stinkiest cigar I've ever smelled!"

Christel had finally awakened. Her long feet hung out beneath the sheet of his bed and rubbed one another against the chill in the room. She had only to touch herself to arouse him—in any way, with any part of her body on any other part; she had once crossed her eyes to make him laugh and in addition made him desirous.

"Very expensive," he answered. "From Cuba."

"It smells like shit, if you don't mind my saying so." To make her point, she pinched closed her nose.

"Oh, that's not my cigar you're smelling," he teased. "It's this."

He withdrew his finger from the jar and held it up to her.

She gasped. "How dare you!"

"It's only a little bit of oxen—"

"The last man who did that to me, I broke his finger."

"Oh, no, no, no!" She didn't understand what he was showing her. The poor girl thought he was baiting her with the *digitus impudicus,* when all he'd meant to do was make her laugh at the absurdity of his attempt to cure himself of pain and discontent.

"I'm sorry," he said into the anger from her eyes. "I didn't mean to offend you. It's only ox manure."

"On your *finger?*"

"Yes. Nowhere else, I assure you."

"On your *finger*?"

"Yes." He waved it at her before he realized that it did seem a rather obscene gesture.

"And you thought I would find that enticing?"

"No."

"Then why?"

"Doctor's orders."

"A good doctor tells you to wash it off your fingers, not to put it on them."

"It's a *cure*," Robert explained.

"Well, thank God you didn't break your jaw then." Christel smiled. "Or your nose!" Now she laughed.

"Yes, thank God it's only my hand," said Robert ruefully.

"Does it still hurt?" Christel asked in a sympathetic way that Robert realized was the beginning of seduction.

"Yes."

"So much for ox manure, then."

"Yes, so much for ox manure."

"Go wash it off. And I mean *off*. Heat the water."

"That will take time."

"Heat the water. I can wait."

As she waited, she came gradually out into the air from beneath the sheet—narrow shoulders, tiny breasts whose very diminutiveness was for him a comfort and delight, solid ribs, surprisingly large buttocks that had been the first thing about her he had noticed, swelling genially beneath the fabric of her skirt as one day he had come upon her at the Wieck house bent over to retrieve a piece of fallen piano music.*

---

*This he discovered was the very delightful and simple Opus 20 Sonatina by Jan Dussek, who had been so handsome that he could not bear the fact his audiences were unable to see his face and thus he turned his piano to the side and became the first pianist to display his profile, to say nothing of allowing the raised lid of the piano to become a sounding board. However, after the death of his revered patron, Prince Louis Ferdinand of Prussia, Dussek became so fat that his profile completely disappeared and the man whom the French had called *le beau Dussek* became known as *le gros Dussek* and was buried in the bed in which he died in St. Germain-en-Laye, having grown so large that, once rigor mortis set in, he could not have been removed from the bed without the amputation either of his limbs or no small portion of the bed itself. Because he made Christel laugh in telling her this story, it was not long until the two of them were in Robert's bed.

By the time Christel was fully uncovered, her long feet now comple-
mented by her long legs, he had washed his hands under her scrutiny.

She threw to him, from the bed, the small towel she always placed between her legs just before she drifted off to sleep. It was still wet with the
two of them so that when he came to her he was still drying his fingers.

"Enough," she said and took the towel from him.

"Charitas," he said as he lowered himself upon her, because she loved for
him to call her by a name that was his alone for her.

"Now," she said, pulling him within her.

"Careful of the hand," he whispered.

Paris

APRIL 9, 1832

*I really don't know whether there is any place with more pianists
than Paris, or whether you can find more asses and virtuosos anywhere.*
Frédéric Chopin

Her father hated Paris. He complained constantly. Though they both spoke
French, it was not a French that was understood by the French. What good
were all their letters of recommendation when he couldn't make people
understand what they were in the first place? The French looked at these
laudations like menus in a restaurant in which they had no desire to eat.
Even when he explained, "*Un pauvre Allemand ne comprend pas un mot à Paris,*"
people didn't understand that he was telling them he was an unfortunate
German who didn't understand *them,* and so they would go right on bringing him a fly swatter when he'd asked for a chair or dog food when he'd requested watermelon.

Before beginning what turned out to be four uninterruptedly miserable
days and nights in the diligence in order simply to get to Paris, he first had
to pay the driver a bribe so he and Clara might sit inside. Only then did he
discover that the French, as if it were a national obsession to force bodies
upon one another, squeezed in six people to occupy the four seats. Worst of
all, he wasn't allowed to smoke even one of the fifty cigars he had so carefully selected and protectively packed. It was nearly enough to cause him to
draw the pistol he kept in his belt whenever he ventured out of Leipzig—if
you won't let me smoke a cigar, I'll shoot you! Once in Paris, he found he

must not smoke in restaurants or in the salons of the wealthy to which he brought Clara in case she might be invited to perform, because the ladies said cigar smoke made their dresses stink. Thus he smoked only in the little hotel room they shared, where he griped endlessly about the cold because he was unable to get the fireplace to work and because the stone floor sent the chill right up his legs and into his lungs. And he felt dirty all the time, as who would not, he said, when they were given one towel a week to share and one glass of water a day between them for bathing. "The French. *Ce n'est pas dire!*"

Yet for all the filth, he was forced to dress like a popinjay, out nearly every night to publicize her in a blue double-breasted, brass-buttoned, velvet-collared frock coat and black trousers with the silk stripes along their seams in the new style dictated by Nestor Roqueplan and gloves the gaudy yellow of Goethe's house and a neckband as white as the new dress he had to buy for each of her appearances in public, because heaven forbid someone see her wear the same dress twice, though no dress of hers ever became nearly so dirty as his neckband after a single night out among the princes, ambassadors, and ministers in their tapestry-suffocated salons filled with porcelain, ornate vases large enough to contain the body of a faithless lover, which gossip indicated would include everyone they met, and stuffed birds held aloft upon spikes up their derrières. In such places as this, where a mass for the dead was as likely to be sung as a fugue to be fiddled with, of primary concern was whether the ice cream would be served before or after the De Profundis.

Then there were the heavy-actioned pianos, from whose tough bones he continually lamented she could get no expression suitable to her clear and singing style — every note sounded jerked and quivering.

Paris, he said, was a nightmare from which there would be no awakening until they might finally set foot back in Germany.

Clara, on the other hand, adored Paris.

Until now, the most sophisticated city in which she had been was Dresden (the further spread of cholera having kept them out of Berlin on their way to Paris). But what was Dresden compared to Paris? Paris was life; Dresden was merely breath.

And what was life? Life was revolution. So said Herr Schumann, who was referring more to art than to the affairs of man, though he had told her — more than once; perhaps a hundred times if not a thousand — that art has a greater effect upon man than does politics, even if its influence always hovers in the blood as distinguished from spilling it.

Little more than a year before they had arrived, there had been blood flowing in these very streets, as the Bourbon Charles X was pushed aside after the "three glorious days" and with him all his censorship and restraint, not to mention the inquisitorial burden of Catholicism as the state religion.

As a result, Paris seemed to her the first place she had ever been where the air outside her matched the heat within her. It was not a matter of temperature, or fever, but of ardor. The city burned with a passion for passion itself.

There had been riots over performances of Hugo's *Hernani,* though whether for its insurrectionary politics or its botched alexandrines no one seemed to know. Even now, with the Orléanist Louis Philippe in command, the streets (though lighted at night with the gas lamps installed by Napoleon after his 1813 defeat at Leipzig in a futile attempt to be able to see the invading allied armies) were full of a kind of raucous unrest as defeated revolutionaries from other countries streamed into France and gravitated toward the restaurants and brothels and liberal newspapers of Paris, in particular the Poles, whose revolt had been crushed by the czar with the defeat at Ostroleka and the retaking of Warsaw. These Poles were far and away the most popular of the democratic zealots among the Parisians, who admired their unselfconscious swagger, and their ability to hold their liquor, and their beatifying of their General Sowinski's wooden leg by which his corpse was planted upright like a scarecrow over the acres of his dead soldiers, and most of all their utter Polish lunacy in having challenged the very Russians who twenty years before had chopped up Napoleon's French soldiers into an average of six pieces each.

Fearlessly, excitedly, Clara walked everywhere—with her father, of course. He would have preferred to have been left behind as much as she preferred to be allowed to go out alone, which he would not permit her, though she hardly thought she might be mistaken for what she learned was called a lady of the night, for reasons she could not entirely fathom because such women were absolutely multitudinous in broad daylight around the Palais-Royal and on the boulevard Montmartre and between the Hôtel de Ville and the Châtelet and even on small winding streets like the rue de la Vielle Lanterne where they stood in the doorways of doss houses, the images of whose rooms made Clara shudder with fear and excitement. Surrounded always by the ubiquitous posters warning of the terrors of venereal disease, which Clara found peculiarly tantalizing, these audacious women were wrapped in colors so bright that she felt positively drab when she put on her puffy-sleeved white dresses in the evenings. Her father turned up his nose when they came upon these ladies, but then he looked down its long, curving planes right at them, head aswivel, mouth agape. He never mentioned them, and he and she never discussed them, but Clara knew what they were and what they did and stared at them a lot more directly than did he.

There were virtually no sidewalks in Paris, and so they often made their way in the streets themselves, she with her hand in his arm because the large hunks of stone that made up the streets were of unequal height and because she was proud to be out with her Papa even if she would have preferred to be out alone. All around them careened the small calashes, cabriolets, britskas, tilburys, and victorias, which far outnumbered the huge berlins and landaus and barouches, cumbersome traveling beasts next to Lord Brougham's sporty new coupés, in which she longed to ride with her hair loose and unribboned and her face to the wind.

But they walked, not rode, all the way to the western boundary of Paris at the place de la Concorde, where Louis Philippe had ordered trees be planted to shroud those places where the guillotines had stood and where Clara now imagined the hordes screaming as the heads plopped down into their baskets and the dying of an age that Herr Schumann said had brought its death upon itself because of its injustices to people and its rigid adherence to outmoded forms of artistic expression.

She insisted her father take her where few dared go, beyond the place de la Concorde toward the Champs-Elysées and then down to the edge of the forest where workmen climbed like tiny bugs all over a huge arcing framework of canvas and wood that had been begun twenty-five years earlier, and thus even before the birth of Herr Schumann a mere twenty-two years ago come June 8, by Napoleon in honor of his triumphs. Nearly everywhere they went, in fact, there was evidence of Napoleon's influence on the building of this city, from the Bourse to the smaller Arc de Triomphe de l'Etoile to the Chamber of Deputies to the Vendôme column to the Rivoli wing of the Louvre to four of the bridges over the Seine—Beaux-Arts, Austerlitz, Saint-Louis, and Jena—though it didn't matter what bridge she was on, she loved to stop and stare down into the water as if it were her own blood flowing through Paris. Even the finest street in Paris, the rue de la Paix, was still referred to by most as rue Napoleon.

To the south she and her father walked to where the city ended and saw the Tuileries, to which the royal family had moved from the Louvre. In the Latin Quarter they strolled about the monastery of the Feuillantines, where Victor Hugo himself had lived before moving to the rue de Vaugirard, not far from Charles Sainte-Beuve, who was part of a group of young romantics surrounding Hugo in one café or another in the faubourg St.-Germain and whose name she had heard whispered in more than one salon as the lover who had stolen Hugo's wife, Adèle. But the story that most excited her about Sainte-Beuve was one more brayed than whispered and concerned his love for girls her own age, he being in his late twenties already and taking these girls to the Café Brébant, where he was said to have said to one of them, "Listen, my child. I want to satisfy all your desires. Ask of me the finest, the most expensive, the most exquisite thing of which you have ever dreamed," to which the girl was reported to have licked her lips, smiled with delight, and lisped, "I would like to eat some tripe, Monsieur!"

When she dreamed of coming upon these men in one of their cafés, and thought of what she might say to them that didn't involve anything as silly as tripe, or sweetbreads for that matter, she realized she had something more in common with at least one of them than merely her devotion to art and to the revolutionary in art. This was with Gérard de Nerval, who was younger than the rest and at the age of nineteen had become famous for his translation of Goethe's *Faust*. It was said that Nerval had fallen in love with a beautiful young woman he had seen but once, riding past him through the woods near Chantilly, and, not knowing her name, called her Adrienne and wrote about her and discovered only much later that she was a poor English girl who had been won at a game of whist from the duke of Kent by the duc de Bourbon, who upon the recent ascension of Louis Philippe had been found hanging from an espagnolette in his château at Saint-Leu. Nerval had been one of those lucky ones to attend the première of *Hernani,* to which he had gone with his best friend, Théophile Gautier, and Théophile Dondey, who turned his name into Thimothée O'Neddy so as not to be just another Théophile and wore glasses when he slept so he might better see his dreams, and Petrus Borel, who was famous for the orgies at his home in the rue d'Enfer, at which Nerval dressed like — exactly as she would have pictured him — young Werther, drinking rum mixed with ice cream from a skull he said was his mother's and dancing endlessly the fashionable *galop internal,* in which people moshed their bodies together so violently that all eventually ended up unconscious, which she assumed therefore must happen following the orgy part of the evening unless she was misinformed as to exactly what an orgy was.

She actually found herself rehearsing her lines in case she might meet up with Nerval and his pack of rowdies, known as *les bousingos*: "I am Clara Wieck, whose fanny was fondled by Herr Goethe before he gave me this medallion of himself accompanied by a note that says, 'To the greatly gifted artist Clara Wieck.'" The problem was, her father carried the medallion sealed up in its box, and she knew she could never ask him to display it in her favor to these beautiful young men of whom she wanted nothing more than to sit in their presence and be desired by them.

So instead of a glass of wine or a cup of tea at Café Brébant, she had to be satisfied with her father buying her an ice cream from Violet in the faubourg Montmartre or a pastry from Frascati, whose bakery was in the same building in which Balzac had lived and was right across the street from Camille Pleyel's famous piano shop, where Monsieur Pleyel sold the pianos his firm manufactured.

Soon after they arrived in Paris on February 15, her father took her to the Salle Pleyel, which was on the ground floor of that magnificent building, and introduced her by saying, "This is my daughter, Clara. She plays the piano. She plays the piano better, in fact, than does your wife."

Monsieur Pleyel shook his head and laughed and said, "Nobody plays the piano better than my wife. Except perhaps for Chopin."

"Chopin," repeated her father. "Yes, I've seen your advertisements in *La France Musicale*. I tried to call on Chopin, upon the recommendation of another of my pupils, Robert Schumann, but Chopin was too impolite to receive us, though Schumann himself has written a most positive review of Chopin's Variations on "*Là ci darem*" from *Don Giovanni*. Would you care to hear my daughter play them?"

"Thank you, no," said Monsieur Pleyel, much to Clara's relief.

Though she had been, she believed, the first to play Chopin's piece in Germany—at the Town Hall in Weimar two days after she had received Goethe's approbation—she could remember when she and every other pianist had considered it incomprehensible and virtually unplayable. She had been forced to spend eight whole days learning it to the degree that it might satisfy the Weimar audience, if not herself. And the last thing she wanted was to sit down here to play and be interrupted by the arrival of Monsieur Pleyel's wife, the former Marie Moke. It was not that Marie had studied piano with Herz, with Moscheles, with Kalkbrenner himself, and had become the wunderkind against whom all other wunderkinder were measured. It was Marie's renowned beauty that intimidated Clara, filling her with a fear of what would happen should she be playing the piano and get a first glimpse of this famous young woman rising toward her—hair, face, neck, breasts—over the keyboard. As if it weren't enough for her poor assaulted imagination to picture this, she now began to worry that Anna de Belleville might marry Pierre Erard, whose pianos were the first equipped with foot pedals and were said to be Anna's favorites among the French—though their reputation had suffered ever since Hector Berlioz had written a story about how an Erard piano had begun to play Mendelssohn's G-Minor Concerto all by itself and could be made to stop not by the application of holy water, not even by dismemberment, but only by its pieces being set on fire!

And they said Berlioz and Mendelssohn had been friends ever since they'd met in Rome just the prior year and met every morning to sing Gluck's *Armide* together!

If anyone was on fire, it was she. Without waiting for her father, she rushed into the street out of Monsieur Pleyel's vast expanse of threatening instruments.

So it was with no small sense of shame and embarrassment that she found herself back there a few nights later, on February 26, for Chopin's oft-postponed Paris debut, originally scheduled for Christmas day, when Clara wished it had been held so she would not have to be here tonight, hiding her face against her father's blue sleeve as he pointed among the audience that barely began to occupy the three hundred seats of Monsieur Pleyel's large concert hall, saying, "My God, there's Mendelssohn!" "My God, there's Liszt!" "My God, there's—look at that *nose!*—Pixis!" his German the only sound she could understand among what she realized were almost entirely Polish voices, until Chopin himself came out and played upon the smallest piano in the place, a little monochord that belonged to Friedrich Kalkbrenner, his own Variations on "*Là ci darem.*" She thought they were the most beautiful thing she had ever heard, aside from Herr Schumann's improvisations, though her father groused that the Variations were not even recognizable as those she played because of the stiff and obstinate nature of Kalkbrenner's piano.

After the concert, her father wanted to introduce her to all the assembled musicians, so they would know her name and face and prepare one day to tremble before the onslaught of her fingers upon a better keyboard than might be found here in Monsieur Pleyel's emporium; but Clara, still trying to hide against his frock coat, said, "No, I am not ready," and once again slipped into the street.

She felt not ready either when he took her once more to hear Chopin, this time at Abbé Bertin's, where Chopin played his E-Minor Concerto and once again her father sat there criticizing him—*him* and not even his piano this time, accusing the very Paris that had refused to listen to her play the piano of having made Chopin sloppy and careless in his own playing.

"You are wrong about that," she whispered, though the piece had ended and the room crackled with applause.

"I am never wrong," he whispered back.

This time when she left him she headed not for the street but for the artists' room at the side of the stage.

"You were wonderful, Monsieur Chopin," she rehearsed in her mind as she walked, wishing she knew how to address the man in Polish but hoping he would, in his solitude after his performance, forgive her ignorance as that of an inexperienced young woman who was on her first journey into the great world.

By the time she knocked on the door and then opened it herself when there was no response, and discovered that Chopin was hardly alone, it was too late for her to retreat.

There he stood, almost frail without his black coat, hardly larger than she, with a beautiful, delicate face and skin so transparent he seemed, like his music, visibly invisible.

Next to him was a very handsome man whom she recognized even though he appeared to have had a strange new haircut, Felix Mendelssohn.

On the other side of Chopin was someone else she recognized, Ferdinand Hiller, who was a bit older than the other two and was known to have been one of Hummel's finest pupils. But what most intrigued her about Hiller was the story of how he had become the piano teacher of none other than Marie Moke, when she was a student at Madame Daubrée's school for girls, and of course like everybody else fell in love with her and had to find a place to make love to her and persuaded Berlioz to let him use his apartment, where he took her and made love to her and while he was making love to her Marie was said to have imagined it was Berlioz himself making love to her and so she went right out and seduced Berlioz.

It was as if the very air in Paris bred lovers just as it bred pianists, or at least drew them here, to compete with one another and, if she could believe her father's assessment of their predilections, to destroy one another. Liszt was in Paris, and Thalberg, Kalkbrenner, Herz, Pixis, Dreyschock, Chopin, Mendelssohn, Hiller, Marie Pleyel, and herself as well, her little self, so eager to play and love and grow into her years and life.

Yet these men before her now in the artists' room, famous as they were, seemed hardly on the brink of mutual annihilation. They were in their shirtsleeves and appeared to be in the midst of a toast, champagne glasses held high as they turned to stare at her.

"Who have we here?" said Hiller in German-accented French.

"I have never seen such eyes," said Chopin in what she supposed must be Polish-accented French.

"You look familiar," said Mendelssohn in perfect French, the first to address her directly.

"You must have seen her on the stage," said Chopin. "A tear in those eyes would be visible from the last row."

"Gentlemen," said Hiller, drawing them back to their toast.

"Excuse us," Mendelssohn said to her.

{ 109 }

"May his soul rest in peace," said Hiller.

The three young men clinked their glasses and then drank down their champagne with one tilt each of their splendid heads.

Somebody must have died. She couldn't imagine who. She hoped it wasn't a member of any of their immediate families, for that would have made inappropriate the drinking of champagne.

"I'm sorry," she said, testing her French and her nerve with as few words as possible.

Now they all looked at her with the slightly pinched faces of people who have swallowed bubbles too abruptly.

"No need to apologize. We were merely drinking to the passing of Johann Wolfgang von Goethe," said Mendelssohn, in whose own eye a tear was suddenly visible. "Perhaps you have heard of him."

"Goethe's dead!"

"Fetch that girl a chair," said Chopin to no one in particular.

Clara shook her head. She didn't want to sit down, though she wouldn't have minded someone's arm to lean on. If Chopin hadn't looked so fragile, hadn't been renowned not only for his playing but also for the fact that he was cared for by fourteen physicians in Paris alone, she might have clung to him, might even have taken his hand in case some of the power of his playing might pass into her. It was common knowledge that he had left Poland on the eve of the revolution and had been in anguish ever since he had learned in Stuttgart, while on his way to Paris, that Warsaw had fallen to the Russians.

"I played for Herr Goethe just weeks ago," she said.

When they looked at her confusedly, she added, "The piano."

"But you are so young," said Chopin.

"She is *not*," said Mendelssohn. "I played for Goethe when I was twelve. How old are you?"

"Twelve."

"You see!" said Mendelssohn.

"Goethe didn't mention you had played for him, Herr Mendelssohn."

"You see," he said to the others. "She knows who I am."

"Of course I do," she said.

"It's over ten years ago," he said. "I played Bach fugues for him and then I improvised and then I played Mozart. After that, he called me his David and himself my Saul—probably because my teacher had introduced me by saying that while I was the son of a Jew I was no Jew myself. 'I haven't heard you yet today,' Goethe would say to me, 'come cheer me up with your playing,' rather like Count Keyserlingk calling young Goldberg to him to play the variations Papa Bach had written to protect the count from the demons in the mind that are said to rob men of their sleep, though I must say I have no trouble sleeping and never have."

"I would have thought as much," said Chopin, who looked as if he slept as poorly as Herr Schumann.

"Goethe kissed me, once every morning and twice every afternoon," Mendelssohn said to her. "Did he kiss you as well?"

"No," she answered, "but he did put his hand on my fanny."

All three men laughed, Hiller being the first to stop when he said to Mendelssohn, "Watch out for this one. She could be another Delphine."

"Who is Delphine?" she asked.

"Someone much older than you," said Mendelssohn.

"Not much," said Hiller.

"She meant little to me—Delphine von Schauroth"—her name crawling from Mendelssohn's small mouth as if merely to utter it brought pain to his heart.

"I believe you wrote your G-Minor Concerto for her?" Chopin seemed exasperated at the lies love spoke.

"Only because she's a wonderful pianist. And are you a wonderful pianist?" Mendelssohn asked her.

Where was her father when she needed him?

"You might judge for yourself if you could hear me, but I cannot get a hearing in this city."

"Then you must indeed be a wonderful pianist," said Chopin. "What can one expect in a city whose music is controlled by the likes of Cherubini and Lesueur and Paër, who taken together, heaven forbid, are over four thousand years old, and a city that celebrates the operas of Hérold and Auber and Boïeldieu? But tell me your name. I'll get Kalkbrenner to have you play at his house. He owes me a favor."

"You owe that thief yourself more likely," said Mendelssohn, who was known throughout Paris for having accused Kalkbrenner of stealing themes from Hiller and, worse, for writing in what Mendelssohn called the fervidly lachrymose key of F-sharp minor.

"Not true at all!" Chopin seemed indignant. "Kalkbrenner introduced me to Pleyel; I agreed to endorse Pleyel's pianos; Pleyel gave me a piano; only by happenstance is it the most sensitive piano I've ever played. When I told this to Liszt, he said, 'Sensitive! One brings a woman to her climax not by tickling her but by banging her. Pianos and women run with equal haste from men who proclaim their sensitivity.'"

Before he went on, and apparently to silence Mendelssohn, who appeared to have something to say if only he could find words to fill his wide-open mouth, Chopin said to Clara, "I trust you are young enough to have no idea whatsoever Liszt was talking about, though if you do then I apologize for his very insensitivity both to pianos and to women."

Before Clara could respond, as unsure as she was whether she should admit that she felt sure she knew the meaning of a woman's climax though she had never before actually heard it mentioned aloud, Chopin continued with his explanation for the discomfort he felt at the exploitation of his name. "Who is the only one in this whole equation that comes off without an obligation yet with two others in his debt? Kalkbrenner! I am second to none in my admiration for his playing—the rest of you are all zeros next to him, and so am I; he is the only one whose shoelaces I am not worthy of tying. Nonetheless, in this matter, *he* owes *me*. Or do you think I actually enjoy seeing my name used next to the word 'ravishing' in *La France Musicale* in order to help Monsieur Pleyel sell his pianos? I would *never* use the word 'ravishing' about anything! First they prostitute us by tempting us mercilessly to endorse their products, and then they put into our mouths words wholly out of keeping with our manner of discourse in the real world."

"Liszt doesn't seem to mind endorsing Pierre Erard's pianos," said Hiller, referring to Erard's proprietorship that had begun six years earlier when he sent Liszt off to England virtually attached to the Erard newly invented double-escapement piano, upon which the boy played so impressively for George IV that the king, dizzy from trying to follow the flight of Liszt's hands over the full seven octaves, proclaimed the Hungarian wunderkind the superior of the Hebrew Moscheles. But it had been here in Paris, even earlier, when Liszt had been her age, only twelve, that he had been proclaimed by the public itself the ninth wonder of the world. To this day one might buy in music shops replicas of his twelve-year-old head made from the cast fashioned by Franz Joseph Gall himself to further his phrenological study of genius. Clara remembered how the false report of Liszt's death had reached even Leipzig, several years ago, when he had disappeared from public for two years after the father of his lover, Caroline de Saint-Criq, had found Liszt with his daughter and forbidden him ever to see her again. Herr Schumann had helped her read the French in the *Etoile* obituary. Liszt had been fourteen at the time he had been torn from the arms of his love. He "died" two years later, not having been seen in public in all that time of his mourning for his lost Caroline. In two years Clara would be fourteen. It was Liszt's example, she believed, that gave her license to love.

"Liszt would endorse a pessary if the woman to whom it belonged allowed him to test it," said Chopin.

"Hush!" said Mendelssohn. "The child!"

If she had known what a pessary was, she would have protested Mendelssohn's attempt to protect a delicacy in her temperament that she was determined to obliterate. She was not a child any longer. But neither was she wholly a woman. She was caught between the two, full of longing for what as yet could only be imagined.

"You inquired as to my name," she said to Chopin, seeming to change the subject but in fact determined to turn it toward herself. "I am Clara Wieck."

"I knew you looked familiar!" said Mendelssohn. "I have seen your portrait. But where?"

"My father leaves them at the homes we visit."

"You see!" said Chopin.

"See what?" asked Hiller.

"That all we pianists are forced to prostitute ourselves. I endorse pianos. This young woman passes out her likeness."

"I don't do anything like that," said Mendelssohn.

"You don't need to," said Chopin.

"Except kiss Goethe's ass," said Hiller.

"Touché!" called Chopin.

"And get a new haircut," added Hiller at Mendelssohn's expense.

"That's not fair!" Mendelssohn's hands went to his head to cover his hair.

"What do you think of his haircut?" Hiller asked her.

"I'd rather not say," she said.

"If you're as fine a pianist as you are a diplomat, you must play gracefully indeed," said Chopin.

"It's all Meyerbeer's fault," said Mendelssohn, his hands still over his hair.

Chopin called her over to him and pretended to whisper in her ear, though it was clear he meant the others to hear. "Somebody told him he looked like Giacomo Meyerbeer, so he went out and immediately had his hair cut in order to assassinate the resemblance. Are you familiar with Meyerbeer?"

Chopin smelled sweet. He didn't look like a man who would smell sweet, because he was so pale, almost wasted. She wondered if perhaps this fragrance rose in the aftermath of his playing the piano, a kind of efflorescence of his art through his skin.

In answer to his question, she said, "My father took me to visit Monsieur

Meyerbeer in the hope that he would arrange a public concert for me. That he has not done, but he did give us tickets to *Robert le diable*."

"Just like Meyerbeer," said Hiller.

"And what did you think of the opera?" asked Chopin.

"The chorus sang through megaphones," she replied.

"Ever the diplomat," said Chopin.

"Megaphones indeed!" said Mendelssohn. "And you wonder why I had my hair cut!"

"Let us at least see your hair again," said Hiller.

"No!" Mendelssohn pressed his hands more firmly over the top of his head.

"After him!" said Hiller, seeming to direct this call to battle as much to her as to Chopin.

But it was Chopin who was first upon Mendelssohn, moving like the whippet he would have most resembled had lethargy and a kind of physical gloom not appeared to have cleaved him to the floor.

Hiller joined Chopin as the two of them tugged at Mendelssohn's hands until they had succeeded in pulling them from his head, at which point Mendelssohn fell to his hands and knees and Chopin vaulted over his back, and then Hiller did the same, and Mendelssohn rose and vaulted over Hiller, all three of them yelping boyishly and continuing to laugh as Mendelssohn called out, "Your turn, Fräulein Wieck," and she pulled up her white dress from around her ankles and more acrobatically, she thought, than the others leapfrogged over Chopin, wondering if this resembled perhaps an orgy and laughing for the first time in Paris as she had not laughed since she had left home and Herr Schumann had appeared in her room running around like a ghost afraid of his own malevolently invisible shadow.

So it was that Papa found her, playing like the girl she was with the older brothers she did not have, these superb, and in Mendelssohn's case famous, musicians who were no farther out of one end of their teenage years than she was from being received into the other. She knew her father well enough to know that whatever stern reproach might have risen to his throat was immediately softened into flattery when he realized who her playmates were.

As the four of them straightened their clothes and introductions were made, her father said to Chopin, "I might have taken your concerto for something by a pupil of mine back in Germany, Robert Schumann. I found it wonderful myself but could not help noticing that it was much too difficult for the ears of tonight's public audience. It is hardly in the fashion of today's music. And for that, sir, I congratulate you."

It was a perfect display of her father's inability to apply the balm of praise without first inflicting the sting of censure. But at least he had not been so impolitic as to berate Chopin for having failed to receive him and her at home.

In the minutes that remained before he took his daughter back to their hotel, the talk among the four men was of the cholera that was said to be on its way to Paris.

Clara for her part was ready to die. She stood as close to Chopin as she dared, exulting in the sweet smell of his genius and the image in her mind of her leaping over his back.

True to his word, Chopin indeed spoke about her to Friedrich Kalkbrenner, who because of the flawless elegance of his playing was her father's favorite pianist, at least until Clara had played for him at his house. There, her father got into a fight with Monsieur Kalkbrenner after Madame Kalkbrenner had said that Clara would be ruined as a pianist if she continued to study in Germany, and her father had replied that that would never happen because "I shall never let her out of my hands," words that sent a shiver up Clara's spine, as well they might any girl's. Then Kalkbrenner joined the conversation in defense of his beautiful young French wife. (Clara had noticed how common it seemed for rather homely, sometimes downright ugly, musicians to have pretty wives, as if the making of music might by itself create a desire that otherwise would no more have reared its head than the goddess of the moon would bathe in the Dead Sea.) "In Germany," said Kalkbrenner, with the waxy, hardened smile Heine compared to that found on the lips of a mummified Egyptian pharaoh, "all pianists play in that groping, sprawling, scrambling Viennese style, and when they come to Paris"—at this he looked directly at her—"they bring that style with them just as surely as they do the silly ribbons in their hair." Her father turned red as he screamed at Kalkbrenner in his own house that his methods of teaching his daughter were as far from the Viennese as Kalkbrenner's taste in furniture was from the *comme il faut*. Kalkbrenner merely laughed and turned away from his guests without another word.

"Did I use that term incorrectly?" asked her father as he pulled her toward the door.

"I have no idea," she responded.

"I saw him kiss you when you finished playing," he said—"what did he say when he kissed you?"

"He said I had *le plus grand talent.*"

"Even I know what that means. Do you suppose he would write it down for us so it would at least be of some use?"

"No, I do not, Papa," she said, happy to have an excuse to leave anybody's house before midnight.

There was no one to support her but Paganini, who had arrived in Paris without any teeth, which he blamed upon a dentist in Prague, and said he would perform with her, but only, he joked in a strange whispering tone that made him sound as if his larynx were disintegrating, if she would play with his son, Achilles. She joked back that if he would allow her to play with Achilles, she would not require that he, Paganini, appear with her. Her father did not understand her wit and nearly exploded on the spot, but Paganini understood her perfectly and said that he would make two appearances with her for her kindness to his son, if only they could find a hall that would book the two of them. Her father didn't understand Paganini's wit either and actually said, "Oh, you underestimate your fame, sir," to which Paganini replied, giving Clara so large a wink that she could discern it from behind his dark-blue glasses, "No, I don't."

But Paganini was soon thereafter forced to withdraw, which he did with a considerable and sincere expression of regret, for he had become ill, though not, luckily, with the cholera that now pressed upon Paris seemingly from all sides and emptied the city of all those who could afford to flee the way a summer heat wave drives the rich to the breezes off the sea.

She was scheduled finally to appear before the public at large at the Hôtel de Ville on April 9, at six francs a ticket, with many gratis invitations sent out personally by her father proclaiming (with the French approved by the clerk in their hotel): *Mademoiselle Clara Wieck, jeune pianiste allemande, âgée de 12 ans.*

Virtually no one responded. Mendelssohn had fled to England, Hiller to Frankfurt, Liszt to Switzerland, and Chopin into seclusion in his house on the Cité Bergère.

Those Parisians who were left were not the sort who would go to a recital in the least plagued of times, and now they had taken to rioting in the streets and hurting no one but themselves and their compeers in their frustration at being unable to afford to follow the affluent into retreat from the invisible — until it struck — malevolence of this terrible disease.

And so when the management of the Hôtel de Ville canceled her engagement for lack of response, not to mention fear of mingling with whatever fools might actually attend, she was offered by Franz Stöpel the tiny hall at his music school, where, upon a piano munificently provided her by Pierre Erard from his shop on the rue du Mail, she played magnificently for a handful of people, whose names are lost to us but whose departed souls are among the most blessed wherever they may be, for they were present when this young German pianist, aged twelve, for the first time in her life played her entire program from memory and then improvised for them a music that was never written down and never heard again.

Four days later, she and her father escaped from Paris, he still grumbling, she expectant with bliss.

Leipzig

MAY 1, 1832
Now, you are my right hand.
Robert Schumann

The very day she had returned with her father, after seven months away, including an unscheduled fourteen-day cholera quarantine in Saarbruck, Alwin and Gustav had come knocking on Robert's door, screaming, "Clara's home, come quick! Clara's home, come *now!*" He immediately regretted that he had not visited her brothers more often in her absence. He was fond of them and did not understand why they seemed almost to have no meaning, no existence, apart from their sister. He wondered if they could sense the presence of Christel in his room, though she hadn't been there in several days.

He followed them home. Or, more accurately, was dragged behind them, as each had him by a hand and pulled him through the narrow Leipzig streets and the dark little Leipzig alleys that opened finally into the huge cobbled market square, across which the boys ran fast enough to make Robert feel in his lungs the curdled accumulation of the pleasure of his cigars. Goethe, so recently dead—Robert enjoyed the thought that the last musician the master might have heard was Clara and the last wheedling, death-hastening voice her father's—had called Leipzig the "little Paris," wholly appropriate in that Robert should now be running through it toward her who had just returned from its actuality.

He found her in the kitchen, sharpening knives. Her back was to him, as it often was when she played the piano, and he was struck at how there was the same competence in her movement, the knife in her right hand, the whetstone secured by her left, the bones of her shoulders riding rhythmically through the soft fabric of her dress and the wisps of her hair that had come free of their ribbon grazing her neck as the music from the knife opened him up to her.

So intensely did she seem to be performing this most kitchenly, domestic, of tasks that he was afraid to speak to her, for fear she might do injury to herself with the knife whose blade threw the day's fading sunlight back at him each time she turned it over in her hand. He simply stood watching her, engrossed in her movements and wondering how it could be that she could not feel his presence when he felt hers, quite apart from her visibility, so keenly.

It was only when she raised the knife toward her head—a gesture he had practiced playfully, unconsciously, if always knifelessly, as if to slit his throat—that he announced his presence, with a gasp.

She turned around and pressed her sleeve against her forehead, wiping away the perspiration from her effort at honing the knife blade but leaving her arm as a shelter over her eyes as she looked at him.

He found it impossible to say anything to her. She was a stranger to whom he had not been properly introduced. During the seven months of her absence he had withdrawn from the world as he never had before, living alone for the first time, seeing almost no one aside from Christel and Dorn, his teacher, and a woman at a window, and now and then some men he knew in a tavern where he would speak only when drunk and then cease to speak entirely when even drunker, alone with his music and his wrecked hand. Now here she was, returned, and the world with her, opening a door back into existence through which he found himself unable to enter.

Harry Heine, in Paris, had written in an article about her that she might be taken for nothing more than a charming little girl of twelve, but if you looked more closely, you saw in the small, pretty face a peculiarly voracious glance and a wistful mouth that opened into a mocking smile. She excited in Heine a strange feeling, about which he used the word "confess," though he could not, or would not, confess what this feeling was.

Thus was Heine once more linked to him, through this shared desire to possess Clara somehow, to break through the grip that music had upon her and thereby to impose themselves upon the story of her life. It was a story Heine envisioned would be "woven out of joy and pain."

Robert sensed a shyness in her now, this little girl who had always encircled him with her exuberance and teased him with the irony of her childhood. Language, not to mention girlish shrieks and laughter, had poured out of her at any given moment when she was not at the piano, as if her inability to talk had survived until that same moment. But now she could say nothing. The two of them stood there in the kitchen staring at one another, shrinking the half year of their separation into this astounded silence.

When finally she lowered the knife, he could see that the sleeve of her dress was wet and there were tiny beads of sweat on her upper lip, at which she caught him looking. She used her bottom lip to dry the top.

He didn't know where to look and so looked away. As soon as his eyes had left her, she walked off. He was tempted to follow as he might have done months ago before the Paris trip, howling like a ghost and breathing like a demon in pursuit of his giggling prey. But he remained where he had been standing, looking back at the space she had occupied and at the knife on the table that had moments before been in her grip.

He was not surprised when she returned. He felt he had willed her back.

She handed him a narrow package, in which he discovered a silk tie from a shop in Paris whose name meant nothing to him and a note in her hand:

> Dear Herr Schumann:
> Here is something to catch the soup I shall make you.
> Votre amie,
> Clara Wieck

He could say nothing. Her eyes pleaded for him to speak, but he could not.

He turned and, with the tie draped over his wrist, walked away.

He was closing the door of the kitchen when finally she spoke.

"I would like to eat some tripe, Monsieur!"

He was charmed to hear in her German a French accent, which Leipzig would soon enough, he knew, drive out of her.

Leipzig

MAY 28, 1832

"It has pleased or it has not pleased," people say;
as if there were nothing better than to please people.
Robert Schumann

He wore the tie she'd brought him from Paris. Wieck's anger with him over the injury he had done his hand was assuaged at least in part by his Opus 2, the *Papillons*, which had been published during Wieck and Clara's absence and that Wieck proclaimed scintillating and original.

Robert told him the *Papillons* represented the beginning of the destruction of the sonata. The old music had pretended that there was some form to man's existence on this earth, a symmetry in which exposition and development appertain to recapitulation and coda, a structure amid the constant destruction, a neat development where one thing led to another in the progress of the universal soul, and that music sought to mirror this wholly imaginary, ridiculously idealistic, configuration. The fact was that in the world, all things, like all beings, were alone, discrete; and one thing—everything—led to nothing, just as all music led ultimately to the silence out of which it had been born.

The *Papillons* were poems in sound. He had been inspired by the masked ball at the end of Jean Paul's *Time of the Young,* with a bit of Goethe's funeral masque from *Wilhelm Meister,* when Mignon, who insists upon dressing as a boy, is robbed of her energy and her life as a consequence of being stripped of her male clothing. In Jean Paul's work, the brothers attend the ball each dressed as the other so that the outgoing Vult might win the heart of the angelic Vina for the shy Walt, and he does, but he loves her too, and so to avoid betraying his brother, he departs forever, alone. Once the low D in Robert's music has been held beneath meandering harmonies for twenty-six measures, the clock in the tower finally strikes six, the sound of the carnival is silenced, and the single being that Walt and Vult had represented is divided forever against itself.

It was through this music that Wieck inadvertently brought Robert and his daughter back together, for he insisted Clara learn the piece just as he insisted that Robert play it for the guests at his musical soirée on May 28.

The music came slowly into Clara.

"Your hand is too heavy," Robert told her.

"Because of the pianos in Paris," she replied.

"You play like a hussar."

"And you look like one. You should shave that ridiculous mustache."

"It makes me look older."

"Then perhaps I'll grow one."

"It would certainly improve your appearance."

"Then why has it not done so with you?"

He could not teach her the music. She was uncertain of the rhythms, confused by the harmonies, and ignorant of the meaning. All the pieces but the simple third (which he, in his passion to bestow upon the ephemeral the substantiation found in the very act of naming, called "Vult") continued to elude her. She became anxious over her failure and cold as he tried to explain and capricious as he attempted to flatter her and whiny as he showed her how it might be done, "my nine fingers to your ten."

She was, he concluded, too young for his music.

And he was too old, or too injured, or too frightened.

He told her father he would not play at the party.

Wieck shook his head in disgust. "Then Clara will play your *Papillons*."

"How dare you use her to threaten me?"

"How dare you use her to threaten *me*?" Wieck replied, leaving Robert to wonder if between them they might divide Clara forever against herself.

On the night of the soirée, when Clara was about to play, Robert separated himself and his wineglass from a group of men to whose conversation he had been pretending to listen and sat down next to Agnes Carus.

"What an interesting tie." As she fingered the silk, the back of her hand rested against his chest.

"Clara brought it from Paris."

"Look, Ernst," she said to her husband on her other side, "how this tie brings out the blue in Robert's eyes."

Dr. Carus looked first at Robert, then at his wife. "And look how you bring out the red in his cheeks, my dear. Perhaps it is the cut of your dress. As Talleyrand said, it is impossible to show more and reveal less."

Robert wanted to hide his face in the very bosom her husband was so in-accurately maligning, to evade the embarrassment of Dr. Carus's distress-ingly nonchalant acknowledgment of the passion Robert felt for his wife and also to touch in reality, after an infinity of caresses in fantasy, the skin-burstingly perfect breasts of his A-flat spirit, his very Leonore, whom he would like to dress up like a boy so she might steal him, as Beethoven's Leonore does her husband, from the prison of his life.

Clara appeared then, a little girl in white with her hair in Dutch braids, her thin ankles flashing above her long shoes because she had grown too tall for her dress, and her own breasts discernible perhaps only to those who had known her as the almost invisibly thin child who nonetheless drew to her then, as she did now, all the attention in a room.

"I shall play for you the *Papillons,* twelve short pieces written by my friend Robert Schumann, who is sitting among you now unless his fear of hearing me ruin his work has driven him away." As she delivered this strange little speech, she stared directly into his eyes, her expression at once confronta-tional and convivial.

Most of the audience laughed politely, including Agnes, who, just as Clara began to play the rising octave scale in D major of "Larventanz," whispered, "I must see you later, in private." Such promise as was held by this demand, which was accompanied by the blithe touch of the outside of her hand upon the outside of his thigh, was extinguished by the sound of Clara playing his music.

What had been heavy in practice was now mercurially light. What had been slovenly was graceful. What had been ignorant of his intentions was now uncannily divinatory. She played the music as he would have liked to have been able to play it and would never have been able to play it even if he'd managed to stretch his fingers to the width of the keyboard.

And she played it from memory, as she had told him she had played an entire recital in Paris, which was one thing, however novel, to do in France and quite another in Germany, where adherence to the text was expected not only in how a piece was played but also in how one sat while playing it. But he could see that the absence of the score had freed her from the need to lock her eyes upon it no matter how well she might know it and to anticipate the turning of the page, whether by herself or another, with the anxiety that often made pianists raise their arms and shoulders as if they were ducks attempting to rise out of murky waters.

Thus, she closed her eyes, and opened them, and tilted her head slightly side to side, or leaned it back upon her neck so that she exposed her throat to the music rising from her fingers, which he took to be a direct reference to their silent encounter in the kitchen on the day of her return and the knife she had seemed about to bring to bear upon herself. With no text before her, she gave the impression of containing the music actually within herself, and relinquishing it, phrase by phrase, to her grateful Stein, which responded, as pianos will, by attempting to impress her with its tone and touch and finally its surrender. In possessing his music, she possessed him.

When she was finished, and was bowing as deeply as the polite applause would allow, he looked around and saw the others in the room shaking their heads and attempting to catch the eyes of anyone else who might have upon his or her face a similar look of profound stupidity.

"Excuse me," he said to Agnes and rushed to Clara, who stood by the piano surrounded by people whose jabbering ceased the moment he appeared.

He took her hands in his as he had when she was a child and, walking backward, pulled her away.

"I never expected to hear it played like that," he said.

"You mean you still don't like it?"

"Don't like it!"

Clara smiled. "I'm teasing you."

"It's as if you've brought a dead flower to blossom."

"If it was dead, it was only because I killed it. Which of course gave me a chance to bring it back to life."

"I feel you've done the same with me."

Her father approached them. "Well done," he addressed her, "under the circumstances."

"I thought she was magnificent," said Robert. "Better than Anne de Belleville."

"That's very kind of you to say," said Wieck, "but Belleville's technique is better, at least for now."

Clara smiled indulgently at her father.

"Belleville is a poet," said Robert. "Clara is poetry itself."

"Very eloquent," said Wieck. "Now if you would only extend that eloquence to your music."

"I thought you liked my little *Papillons*."

"Tonight they sounded odd. American. Did you see the response? People shaking their heads. Straining to grasp the changes. They weren't ready for this kind of music."

"Yes, I could tell," said Robert. "But I suppose I was ready to write it. And Clara to play it."

"Art to be art must be comprehended," said Wieck.

"Art to be art must only be realized," responded Robert.

He excused himself and went in search of a glass of wine but found Agnes, who said, "I thought you had forgotten me."

"Only in the music," he replied by way of confession.

"I've never heard music like that before."

He smiled. "Good."

"I didn't say I cared for it."

"No, you didn't."

"And I didn't. Care for it, I mean."

"That's all right." Robert smiled. His affection for her had little to do with her critical capacities.

"We have always been honest with one another."

"No, we haven't," he said.

She laughed and took him by the hand and led him into one of the practice rooms, where she lit the lamp and sat him down next to her at the piano.

"What would you like to hear?" he asked. "Of course my poor hand . . ."

She kissed him once, a soft, lovely kiss, full upon the lips. It was the first genuine kiss he had received from Agnes, after so much yearning, so many nights in his twisted sheets dreaming of her, a holy image sleeping chastely in his soul but quite the opposite in his imagination. As her lips left his and her fingers struggled to become disentangled from his thick hair, he felt her disappear forever, though she remained with him until her tears had stopped and she lifted her head from the wet shoulder of his jacket and only then left the little room and closed the door behind her.

He stayed at the piano. Despite the pain in his right hand, he felt as the music poured forth in descending fifths, from A down to D, E down to A, that flowers and gods were flowing out of his fingers.

Zwickau

Clara stood with Robert's mother at the window in the very house in which he had grown up. Below them, in the market square, the merchants shrank into their clothes against the chill wind, which she could see and hear but could not feel in the comforting warmth of this sitting room.

It was most peculiar to be here. Robert had lived in her house in Leipzig, it was true, and had spent many hours up in her room, playing games with her and her brothers. And she had spent even more hours in his room, listening to him make music and watching him breathe and touching his face with the back of one finger. But to be in the house where he had been a child—it confused her. There was too much of him here. There was all the unobtainable evidence of his departed presence in the shapes of the rooms and the drape of the cloth and the seams where walls met clasping their secrets. She did not want him to have a past. She did not want him to have existed before he existed for her.

Yet here was his mother, to whom he displayed a filial devotion that Clara felt put her own to shame. While she loved her absent mother increasingly as she grew to esteem her stepmother less with Clementine's every giggle and gaucherie, Clara didn't write to her mother nearly so often as Robert wrote to his, and Clara had replaced her as the first one in her heart with the very son of this woman who stood next to her now and somehow made her feel it was precisely where she belonged.

"Were you frightened last night?" Frau Schumann asked.

"By my dreams?"

Frau Schumann shook her head but asked nonetheless, "Have you trouble sleeping?"

"Never."

"Robert does."

"Yes."

"It is one of the worst things for a mother. The night has always seemed a prison in which one's children are locked away."

"Sometimes he would play all night," Clara said, to show that she was guarding him faithfully. "The piano," she added.

"Did it keep you awake?"

"Never," said Clara again. "But I heard every note."

Frau Schumann nodded and said, "I meant were you frightened by the riot at the hall?"

Clara laughed. "It wasn't a riot, Frau Schumann. Besides, I am used to it by now. They mistake me for an object of desire."

She had played the night before in the hall at Zwickau, as part of her tour of Saxony, and upon her completing Herz's Bravura Variations, with which her father had insisted she open in order to be sure to please the audience, that audience rose seemingly as one, though she knew it was not, and, applauding and vociferating madly, moved toward her like a river breaching its banks and surged through the orchestra, knocking over the music stands, pushing aside the musicians, the string players futilely trying to defend themselves with their bows, and stopping only when Clara could smell the garlic and beer and eau de cologne rising off the lips and skin of those admirers nearest her. They had no intention of molesting her, she knew, or even of touching the hem of her dress. They merely wanted to see her more clearly. They always want to see you more clearly, some to try to solve and some to try to deepen the mystery of how such music could come from *this,* a frail share of flesh in a white dress.

It was unfortunate that the next piece was what Robert had thus far written of a symphony, in G minor.* This was the first time Zwickau residents had been privileged to be presented with one of his compositions. Yet they seemed to hear little of it and jabbered on as it was being performed and made sour faces at one another when they did bother to listen. Robert later told her jocularly that it was just as well the audience and his symphony had proven to be so antipodean, because the local orchestra had ruined any parts of it that he himself had failed to ruin with his inexperience at orchestration.

———————————

*Lost.

But she knew he was merely disguising his pain: From behind the curtain she had watched him in his seat as his music was being played, and he sank ever more deeply into it.

"This is your town," she told him. "Your symphony, and not the Herz, should have been the first thing played."

"It was not me, or Herz, they came to hear."

She might have taken this as an accusation had he not been looking at her with some of the same wonder in his eyes as other members of the audience had displayed as they had pushed close enough to touch her. But they hadn't, and neither did he, despite her longing. *Do touch me,* she thought while he stood there looking at her as if, had he ever seen her before, it was in another lifetime. *Touch me.*

But she received no more from him than a sweet wash of wine from his breath, which, when he departed to find his way toward another glass, she inhaled and held within her until she felt quite drunk, or at least lightheaded, herself.

Now, the next morning, it was Frau Schumann who was touching her, taking her sleeve as she said, "Mistake? There could be no mistake. I find you very beautiful."

Clara found herself wanting to put her hands over her face. "You are too kind."

"Perhaps," said Frau Schumann. "But not in this regard. And to think you are so young—a woman's beauty never truly manifests itself until..."

"Yes?" demanded Clara, who was desperate to have someone to talk to about these things.

"You are...how old?" asked Robert's mother.

"Thirteen."

Frau Schumann smiled deeply into Clara's face. "Robert was right."

Clara flushed. "I hope he didn't say that I was merely a child—"

"No. He said—"

"—who happens to play the piano well."

Now Frau Schumann frowned. Clara was afraid she had offended her through her interruption. But then, when Frau Schumann spoke, Clara realized it was the gravity of the conversation and not its configuration that caused such solemnity to possess Frau Schumann's kind face.

"When Robert wrote to tell me you would be playing in our little town, and he would be accompanying you and your father on this part of your journey and thus I would have the opportunity to meet you, he said you would give me something to think about."

Something to think about? What, Clara wondered, could that mean? One could think anything about anything. It was just like Robert thus to dwell on private matters of the mind. Some things he himself confessed to thinking about were so excruciatingly morbid that she often wondered why she loved so much to hear of them. Death and doubles, despair and doom—how did he manage to cloak himself in such raiment and yet appear constantly wrapped in radiance? Perhaps, she thought, it was just she who dressed him thus with her eyes.

"And so you have," added Frau Schumann, causing Clara to wonder for a moment if this woman had somehow managed to capture within her own mind the image at that moment in Clara's—her enfolding Robert within the transparent beauty of undissolute light.

"You have given me much to think about," Frau Schumann went on. "I will confess to you that I did not want Robert to become a musician. It was your father who convinced me, by holding up yourself as an example. But after last night . . . I could feel his humiliation."

"Yes," said Clara.

"It was not your fault."

How she would love to be able simply to fling herself into the arms of this woman. How she missed, with a sudden yearning, her own mother. No one had held and comforted her for years, she realized. The closest thing to a true and long embrace were her and Robert's names together for the first time on last night's program. And even that did not envelop her flesh.

"His music is . . ." Frau Schumann could not find the word.

There was no word for it. But if there had been, it wouldn't be the word Frau Schumann was unable or unwilling to say. "Brilliant," Clara provided, as inadequate as it was.

"That too," said Frau Schumann.

Because they were having their first disagreement, however subtle, and it was over something as important as Robert's music, they could not look at one another, and so both were staring self-consciously down into the square and thus both saw Robert at the same time as he walked toward them, upright and seemingly oblivious of the cold, not even wearing his usual leather cap so that it was left to his thick, dark hair to protect his handsome head.

He looked up, squinting, at his house, *as one would when cold and heading home,* thought his mother, and *as one would when one's beloved is inside,* thought Clara, and he waved, though whether at one of them or both neither could tell.

The next moment Frau Schumann did, quite abruptly, take Clara into her arms and, with tears in the eyes that followed her son across the square, said something to this little girl that caused Clara to wonder if she could possibly have heard what she heard.

Leipzig

JULY 4, 1833

A chain of sparks now attracts us to one another.
Robert Schumann

Just as he had feared and—to himself only—had predicted, his little nephew Robert had died, not yet one year into this life and on the very eve of the very eve of Robert's own birthday, his twenty-second.

He had not known that his brother Carl and Carl's wife, Rosalie, would name the baby Robert, and when they had, he had been afraid to tell them of his fear that in creating a double of himself in this way, they were dooming one or the other of them to imminent annihilation.

The relief he had felt upon hearing the news of little Robert's death had been subjugated almost fully beneath the weight of his guilt over this relief. So he had been in a kind of despair ever since, bereaved in particular for, among the living, Rosalie, who had become in his heart nearly the sister that his own sister Emilie had been, and for, among the dead, little Robert himself, who roamed the land of the ex-animate in his own place and who had left him roaming the land of the living, empty and afraid, as happens to any supposedly fortunate survivor when his double has died.

But now, he was convinced, he had found a new double, and one who would not be doomed, or doom him, for they had been born strangers to one another and shared no natural blood.

He had taken her with him in April so that they both might be elucidated by Dr. Karl J. Portius's psychometer, which its inventor and thus far sole trained operant called the Electromagnetic Soul Machine. It was their first time out alone together when they were not simply taking a walk somewhere, anywhere, for the exercise that Wieck insisted all his students get daily to make them equal to the rigors of playing the piano. Before this, he and Clara would spend two or three hours a day walking to Connewitz and back, or round-trip to Zweinaundorf, she skipping and running around like a child when she wasn't tugging on the back of his coat so he wouldn't trip over stones in the middle of the footpath. She talked all the while, and he took increasing pleasure in observing how her gifts of heart and mind kept developing, leaf by leaf, as he described it in a letter to his mother. One particularly dry day, as he and Clara were walking back from Connewitz trailed by the dust they kicked up, she quite absentmindedly chanted to herself, "Oh, how happy I am! How happy!" He, who knew he had never been as happy himself and who had by this time in his life, like so many of his cerebral contemporaries, embraced melancholy as a kind of philosophical imperative, moved closer to her side on the path as though to absorb from without such joy as he was not capable of begetting from within.

He told her she mustn't tell her father they were going to visit Dr. Portius, not as subterfuge but as kindness toward the skeptical if not yet suspicious Wieck. Nonetheless, Clara took this directive as the former and seemed to revel in the intrigue. On their way through the streets, she wore a hood up about her head and face and spoke to him only in excited whispers.

The Electromagnetic Soul Machine itself was a deceptively simple-looking contraption, much like Dr. Portius himself, who was by profession a schoolteacher and shared with many other teachers the expressionless gaze of the person to whom so many stupidities have been uttered over so many years that he has himself been rendered lamebrained.

He was also, as his psychometer itself proved to be, nearly monosyllabic.

"We have an appointment for, or perhaps one should say with, your Electromagnetic Soul Machine," Robert began.

"Ah," said the doctor.

"What do you require of us?" asked Robert.

Doctor Portius held out his hand. "Money."

"I meant—," began Robert.

"Money," repeated Dr. Portius.

This response caused Robert to abandon his plan to engage Dr. Portius in a discussion of just how much he might have been influenced by Johann Lavater's intriguing studies in magnetic-trance conditions. Robert handed over the fees for both himself and Clara, which caused Dr. Portius, once he had extracted the cash, to grasp the same hand and wrap it around the iron rod that protruded out of the small machine. Immediately the magnet caused the arrowed gauge to settle upon the word *hypochondriacal.*

"Silly machine," said Clara.

"No, no!" Robert defended the device. "It is accurate. It is honest. It is forthright and unintimidated. I *am* hypochondriacal! Indeed, I do on occasion imagine myself to be suffering from something with which I am not genuinely afflicted."

"I trust you are not referring to me," teased Clara.

"How could you think such a thing?" Robert responded with utter seriousness, when what she wanted was for him to tease her back and tell her that her afflicting him was quite genuine indeed. Perhaps he was simply too taken with this ridiculous machine, to whose master he turned and said, "As you are no doubt aware, it was the belief of Dr. Isenflamm of Erlangen that hypochondria is in and of itself a fatal disease. What is your machine's alternative to *hypochondriacal*?"

"*Depressed,*" answered Dr. Portius.

"So what your machine is saying is that I am not depressed, merely hypochondriacal?"

"Merely," said Dr. Portius.

"I am most relieved," said Robert. "Lately I have thought myself depressed over the death of my little nephew, who was given my name, you see, and because I have been writing music that no one but this young lady here seems to appreciate. But what your Soul Machine is telling me is that my depression itself is merely a symptom of my hypochondria and is therefore not depression at all. Is that correct?"

Dr. Portius, looking at Robert as if he were quite genuinely and not hypochondriacally insane, found himself finally leached of all language and thus reduced to a puzzled shrug, following the delivery of which he pointed at the metal rod.

Robert grasped it once more, and this time the machine told him he was *sensitive.*

"True," Robert said.

Emotional.

"Absolutely," he said.

Stubborn.

"Alas," he said.

Genial.

He nodded. "Ah, geniality."

Quiet.

After a moment's thought, he said, "Increasingly."

Kindhearted.

"That is not for me to say," he said.

"True," provided Clara.

Shy.

"Oh, very!" he proclaimed.

"You?" She found him, or at least dreamed him, unreserved and confident in the love she secretly bestowed upon him.

"Oh, yes," he answered.

"Then this machine knows you better than I do," she said. "I want no part of it."

"Enough," said Dr. Portius.

"But we are not arguing," said Robert, mistaking the doctor's meaning.

"Enough," he said again and moved Robert's hand from the iron rod.

"It seems to be your turn," Robert said to Clara. "Or else he wants more money."

"Yes." Dr. Portius held out his hand.

"You may have my turn," she offered Robert.

Forgetting his initial goal, he attached himself once more to the Electromagnetic Soul Machine as it probed ever more deeply into his being until there seemed nothing left of him, or nothing left for her to learn except the truth. But if she was unwilling to allow a machine to prove them the double of each other, he became convinced that music would.

Dr. Portius's psychometer filled Robert with hope for himself and for his future. It did not find him, as he had feared it would because he had thus been called by some of his intimates, *covetous, sly, secretive, dissolute, dogmatic, irresolute.* He felt he knew himself now and in that knowledge was more at ease with the mysterious and difficult music he was finally confident enough to set down. He wrote some études, complete with rigorous pedagogical aids, based upon the airy Caprices of Paganini, as much for Clara as for anyone, so successfully had she portrayed that demonic genius as generous, kind, and, most surprising of all, paterfamiliar. Robert also began his first sonatas and was intrigued more than frustrated over the fact that he himself could not play the music he composed. That is to say, he could not play it as he meant it to be played, at tempo and with the kind of passionate accuracy with which, he sometimes imagined as he composed his work inside the mantle of wine and sweat and tobacco smoke that sequestered his gift, the universe had been created. There were times, indeed, when he was not sure he would have been able to play his own music even had he not injured his hand. In this he took a strange delight and sometimes found himself laughing aloud when he devised a passage of such monumental difficulty that he could picture all the pianists in the world curling miserably from their benches, like the leaves from an artichoke, until only one, grasping the heart of his music, was left. Art was created to challenge and charm the best minds and the highest sensibilities, not merely to satisfy those simple souls who begged for something they would call beautiful because they had no notion of the torment in the heart of beauty. And because it was *familiar.* The artist's job was to afford the *unrecognizable,* and to make *that* familiar. The success of any great work should be measured in how small an audience could understand and appreciate it most profoundly. Indeed, it was his desire to reach as few people as deeply as possible. In this he was, he felt, like Chopin, about whom Legouvé had written that he reserved his surpassing genius for an audience of five or six, which number struck Robert as quite a crowd when it came to his own work. He would settle for one, provided he was not required to fill that role himself. Or no one, for there was within a void an infinitude of possibility, and the reverse.

His most recently acquired doctor (for a man could no more have too many doctors than too many books), Franz Hartmann, actually promised Robert he could cure his hand, which Robert felt it was his duty to pursue, though he was not entirely disappointed when Dr. Hartmann proved to be so homeopathically obsessed that rather than tell Robert what he must do to cure his hand and what medicines he must ingest, he gave him nothing more than a powder made from *hyssopus officinalis,* which peasants had been using for centuries to harden their stools and steel their hearts, and otherwise told Robert what not to do and what not to consume: no smoking, no beer, no wine, no coffee, no meat, no eggs, no orgasms, no swimming.

"May I keep just one?" Robert asked him, immediately to discover from the sour shock upon Dr. Hartmann's face that he shared with virtually every other physician on earth so complete an absence of humor that he appeared eager to amputate even a smile.

Robert's hand remained beyond help, regardless of Dr. Hartmann's regime, which, had Robert put it into practice, would have reduced him to such misery he would no longer have wanted to live, never mind play the piano. But then he gave Dr. Hartmann a more palpable affliction with which to earn his fee, for he came down with the malaria that was eating its way through Saxony with nearly the insatiety of the cholera several years before.

Quarantine was demanded of the disease's many victims. Thus was Robert restricted to his new rooms on the quiet edge of town, across the Pleisse in the tranquility of Riedel's Garden. There he lived in a fourth-floor apartment with Karl Günther, a law student, who, during their first nights together, when Robert had suffered from insomnia but could not compose at the piano for fear of waking their neighbors, had stayed awake himself and read to Robert and held his hand and head, until Robert contracted malaria and Karl moved out immediately while attempting to say good-bye without taking a breath.

So now he was alone, wasting away because he had no appetite, describing himself to Clara in a letter as something like the dried-up prickly heart of that leafless artichoke, but forcing himself to compose music at the piano and allowing himself to bang it out all night, with no fear of reprisal from his neighbors because of the sign on his door proclaiming his quarantine. He did not mind the solitude at first and took some comfort from the idea that grew daily larger within his mind that all men, doomed as they were and shut off from one another in their essential unknowableness, lived in quarantine. He saw himself, therefore, the very paradigm of modern man, shut away and shrinking. He realized that Dr. Portius's Electromagnetic Soul Machine had proven unnecessarily prolix and need have but one word for any and all who grasped its iron rod: *Quarantined*.

But he found himself, as the days went by and he encountered no one but the brave Dr. Hartmann, longing for more than the knowledge that he had become the very symbol of the insularity of man. He found himself wanting to unite with another. To leave himself without abandoning himself. Find himself without uprooting himself. Give himself without surrendering himself. This was possible, he believed, only with one's double. And one's double, he had concluded, in moving beyond the simplicities of Jean Paul's *Siebankäs* and Hoffmann's *Devil's Elixirs*, was not literally an invisible replica of oneself or even a sort of complex carnate imposter but was rather the one other human being on earth whose existence did not make one feel one's own was futile.

Having no one else to whom to speak, Robert told Dr. Hartmann, who was with one hand spoon-feeding him tea made from white-willow bark and with the other pressing a cold cloth to his feverish forehead, that he felt an overwhelming longing to be with Clara Wieck and that he must go to her immediately.

"The young pianist?" the doctor asked.

"It's not what you think," replied Robert.

"I think nothing," said the doctor.

"Spoken like a true physician," Robert baited him.

"You are under quarantine, Herr Schumann. I could not permit you to visit the whore of Babylon if she stood on the other side of your door begging for Meister Iste."

"How dare you!" But Robert found his outrage obscured by his laughter as he covered his groin with his large hands.

Dr. Hartmann was not laughing. "Your desire for this girl is not healthy."

"It's I who am not healthy."

"Yearning for what cannot be can only weaken you." Dr. Hartmann removed the cloth and placed the back of his hand against Robert's brow. "Your fever worsens."

"The fire you feel is my desire to be with her."

Dr. Hartmann shook his head. "Children her age are dying everywhere. A girl's strength is claimed by the woman fighting for her being. There's precious little left to blow off this evil air. Go to her, and you'll kill her."

Robert asked Clara, therefore, in a letter Dr. Hartmann himself agreed to deliver, to play at exactly eleven o'clock the next morning the adagio from Chopin's Variations, the piece she had played for Ludwig Spohr in Kassel. And while she played she must think about Robert, think about him and nothing else. He would, at that very moment, do the same—play the Chopin note for note with her and think of her as if she were the only person on earth. In that way, over St. Nicholas's Church, where Bach himself had nearly worked himself to death after twenty-seven years at a job that all others had refused, equidistant between her room and his, their doubles would meet and their spirits would come together as one.

Clara was disappointed only in his insisting upon the spiritual nature of their relationship, for she found Robert troubled her somewhere deep and distant and thus far untouched within her body, and she carried this ache with her wherever she was, whatever she was doing, and if she thought for a moment that the pain might be going away, she drew it back into her by thinking of him.

She wrote him by return that day (the note carried to his room and slipped beneath his door by her faithful Nanny, who had raised her from the age of five while Clementine gossiped and tried to see her eyes in the polished leather of her boots) to say as much. But Clara was unable to state her feelings baldly, not because she feared the words or their possible effect upon either Robert or herself but because she knew her father was now reading her mail just as he had always read, not to mention written in, her diary. So she said to Robert only that her life was not the same now that his illness kept him from visiting her family. But, yes, she would meet him the next day over the portal of the church, wrapped in music.

Above his own signature, Robert had written, "My whole heart is in this letter."

Below hers, insidiously and, he had to admit, excitingly, she wrote, "If this letter arrives without my seal intact, tell me."

What was for him a lame seduction became for her a conspiracy, much the better use to which to put their furtive doubles, who the next morning at eleven o'clock above Bach's old church met and listened and coupled secretly, carried heavenward by the music on which desire thrives.

Leipzig

NOVEMBER 1, 1833
*I often drive self-torture to the point of
sinning against my entire existence.*
Robert Schumann

Robert was spared by malaria, but his sister-in-law Rosalie was not. The mother of little Robert died at twenty-three, his own age almost to the day. Only when she was dead did he allow himself to realize how much he had loved her, that there could have been talk of real love had she not been married to his brother Carl and had Robert not been bound by the conventions of morality and family honor. He became haunted at night with images of her, not dream images, for he could not sleep for days on end, but images that were nonetheless involuntary. He saw her then as he had never seen her in life, naked, aroused, open.

At the same time, he once more withdrew his own body, as it were, from the world. His irregular couplings with Christel ceased entirely. He turned his eyes from prostitutes. He no longer crooned the name of Agnes Carus in the whorl of his bedclothes.

But such abstinence merely increased his anxiety and thus deepened his insomnia, which caused him to experience the sensation of death within eternal wakefulness.

He sought out, in his diploma-encrusted, leather-smelling, ground-hugging office on Marktschreierstrasse, his old friend Dr. Moritz Reuter. Robert confessed everything, for it seemed like a confession to him, the admission of sin, in that he did not know whether his desire to die might be stronger than his fear of death.

"The night I learned Rosalie was gone was the most terrible night of my life. I was seized by an idée fixe: the fear of going mad. It was the most terrible thought a person can have and with which God can punish you—the loss of one's own mind. It's as if you can see and feel yourself leaving yourself. There's nothing left of you but suffering. The pain is real, but it's mental pain. One's mind literally aches. There is no thought, no idea, no concept that can bring you peace, except the very thought of death itself, which is what caused such suffering to begin with. I am caught in a circle of destruction. I want to die."

"Good heavens!" said Dr. Reuter, whose customary expansiveness seemed to close in upon itself so that both he and Robert sat there shrinking further into their respective beings.

"There's nothing good about Heaven when it's the next stop on one's train."

"But if you truly wanted to die, you would not be here talking to me."

"I have raised a hand against my own life."

"But you have not brought it down." Dr. Reuter allowed himself the tiny smile of one who has recovered from the failure to match one metaphor by rallying to the next.

"Oh, but I have," answered Robert. "I threw myself out the window."

Thinking his patient was concocting yet another literary image, Dr. Reuter answered, "And look where you have landed—safely with me."

"I landed in a tree."

"In a tree?"

"The big tree in Riedel's Garden."

"Is that not where you live?"

"No longer. I can't go back to my rooms. They're on the fourth floor. And I'm suddenly terrified of heights. I sometimes think were I to leap into the air, I'd die of fright before I came down. Not that I could get into my rooms even were I to go there—I have thrown away my key. The sight of any key now fills me with the most awful fear. It's as if the only entry I might make would be the entry into the house of death. But death is everywhere, is it not?"

Dr. Reuter allowed his hand to reach halfway across his desk toward Robert. "Look around you. Life is everywhere."

Robert surprised the doctor by leaning forward and grasping his hand, which he could not now very well withdraw without offending his clearly anxious, confused young patient, who seemed to have absorbed the romantic eccentricities that had caused an entire generation of otherwise intelligent youth to replace reason with emotion, love with concupiscence, health with debauchery, respect for the past with lust for the present, answers with questions, and, in his case certainly, reason with madness.

"When I die," said Robert, "my fear of death will be so great that I shall be unable to attend even my own funeral."

Now Dr. Reuter began to fear for himself. He attempted to remove his hand, but his patient's proved too strong, notwithstanding the self-inflicted injury to one of them for which he had prescribed an animal dip some twenty months ago. He knew of course that Robert played the piano, but he had thought that all pianists had delicate hands, the beauty of music being so fragile. In the clutch of Herr Schumann's hands, he could hear only thunder and bedlam. Perhaps, he thought, one's hands can be read as the tangible image of one's mind, as some believe the nose forecasts the schwanz.

"You think I'm joking," said Robert. "But you see, Moritz, I simply don't go to funerals. I had to bury my own father while my mother was off in Karlsbad, and when she returned, though she was positively consumed with grief, I envied her. It was done, you see. He was gone, but for her he'd disappeared into thin air. She didn't have to see him as I did when I found him, freshly dead, and to bury him as I did, coldly, stiffly, stinkingly, endlessly dead. She doesn't know, as I know, that death changed him. He—"

"How did it change him?" Dr. Reuter hoped his interruption would cause Herr Schumann to become irritated and no longer want to hold his hand.

"He no longer existed."

It was Dr. Reuter who became irritated, sufficiently so, in fact, to cause him to be tempted to slap some sense into his incoherent young friend. While he resisted the temptation, he was able to regain possession of the hand with which he would have carried out this discipline had he not, as always, confronted impatience with restraint.

"Of course he no longer existed!" he shouted. "He was dead!"

Robert smiled in perfect agreement. "Then you will understand why I did not attend the funeral of my brother Julius, though he was my favorite brother, who died of consumption not three months ago, nor of my sister-in-law Rosalie, who died of malaria not one month ago, even though by so doing, or not doing, I incurred the wrath of her husband, my brother Carl, who has said he will never forgive me for not coming to say good-bye to her. Carl accused me of not loving Rosalie, when in fact I loved her so much that I cannot rid my mind of the image of taking her."

Dr. Reuter seemed to have awakened from a brief sleep. "Taking her? Taking her where?"

"*Taking* her."

Dr. Reuter not only removed his wire glasses but took the added precaution of closing his eyes. "You can't possibly mean..."

"Yes. I do. I was in love with her. I was in love with her even though I could never forgive her for replacing me."

Dr. Reuter opened his eyes and squinted at Robert. "By marrying your brother, I assume you mean."

"No. By having a baby and giving him my name and then killing him."

"Your sister-in-law murdered your nephew!" As Dr. Reuter spoke, he pushed his chair back from his desk until, had he pushed any more, he might have fallen out the window of his office—which fortunately was on the ground floor, precisely the reason Robert had chosen to visit him in particular and not one of his other doctors whose offices might happen to be up a flight or two.

Robert nodded. "By making doubles of us."

"Doubles! I've had enough of this romantic claptrap, Robert. You suffer from quite concrete symptoms but you seek reasons for them in the most phantasmal corridors of quackery. You would no doubt prefer me to prescribe a cure that was written on a tablet somewhere centuries ago by a wizard in a pointed cap. You have insomnia. You have no outlet for your sexual desires but an occasional whore and fantasies of incest. You live alone and keep alone and bang away at your music to the exclusion of any other activity and any other congress with a world that appears unable or unwilling to listen to the music you make. And if you are, as you claim, suicidal, it is because you have reduced the entire world to yourself and when you stop to look at yourself you realize, to employ your own words, that you no longer exist." Dr. Reuter paused to take a breath and at the same time smiled ever so slightly and moved his chair back until his short legs were under his desk so that once more their inability to reach the floor was obscured. "Am I wrong about all this?" he asked rhetorically as he replaced his glasses on his huge nose.

"You are brilliant," answered Robert. "I do no longer exist."

"And are you ready to hear what you must do if you are to be cured?"

"I am ready." Robert reached out his hand, but he was not fast enough, for Dr. Reuter moved both of his onto his lap beneath his desk.

Dr. Reuter looked past Robert to the small, dark painting of Frau Reuter that, far from the diplomas that seemed to swim around the doctor's head like so many ducks, graced the wall most distant from his desk. "You must get married."

Robert laughed. "I would prefer to take some herbs."

As Dr. Reuter rose from his chair and somewhat warily offered Robert his hand in a gesture of both reconciliation and dismissal, he ordered, "Take a wife."

PART TWO

Before the Wedding

Leipzig

MARCH 13, 1834
I will be irritated with her for the rest of my life.
Friedrich Wieck

"I no longer want my kittens," Clara said.

"Your kittens are no longer kittens." Grimacing, her father watched the three of them—Mittens, Fluffy, and Agnes, thank goodness for the small favor that they were all of one gender—as they clawed at Clara's white nubby bedspread like fretful pianists lacerating chords.

Clementine bent forward to look at them more closely. "If they are not kittens, what are they? Dogs?"

"Cats," said her husband with a patience he bestowed upon no one else.

"I no longer want them," Clara repeated.

"What would you have me do with them? Drown them?"

"Oh, my," said Clementine.

"Do you wish to drown them?" said Clara.

"What is the matter with you?" asked her father.

Clara smiled. "With me?"

She lay beneath her cotton flannel sheets and her thick woolen blanket and her white bedspread, still able to feel upon her thighs and tummy the rise and fall of the cats' paws, from which she took a pleasure that was no longer adequate.

"Do you have any idea what time it is?" her father asked.

"What time is it?" she answered.

"How late do you plan to sleep?"

"How can I sleep if you suddenly appear in my room and talk to me?"

"How can *I* sleep if you persist in behaving this way?"

"Are you having trouble sleeping, my dear?" Clementine reached out to touch him, but he shook his head and caused her hand to retreat back to the knitting in her lap, a winter cap for him that was too late in the season and suspiciously the size and shape of the bald spot that was removing his hair with the precision and the indifference of a scalpel.

"What way?" Clara asked, fully aware, even if he was not, that she responded to every question of his with another question. She had discovered this was the best way both to avoid answering unpleasant questions and to vex the questioner.

"Must you force me to tell you?" he nearly bellowed.

"Why else would you have come here, if not to tell me?"

"We came here to get you out of bed. Do you have any idea what time it is?"

"What time is it then?"

He drew his timepiece out of his waistcoat pocket, making a great show of flicking its cover up with the nail of his thumb, which was the only nail a pianist allowed to grow long enough even for so modest a purpose, and staring at the face as if it had somehow stolen valuable hours from his life. "Well after nine o'clock," he announced.

"In the morning?"

"My God, child!" He rose from the small upholstered (with the most idealized ballerinas and balloons, which Clara felt she had long ago outgrown and the cats had long ago punctured and pitted) chair so abruptly that it fell over backward, causing Clementine to miss a loop. Not pausing to right the chair, her father went to the window and pulled back the heavy curtains, first one side and then the other. "Morning," he announced gravely.

"Can it really be so early?" Clara sank farther beneath her bedclothes.

"So early!" He thumped back toward the center of her room and hesitated at his fallen chair and seemed to decide he would lose his (wholly illusory) upper hand should he stoop to place it upright. So he proceeded on with even greater forte in his feet until he stood pressed against the very footboard of her bed and took the kind of deep and pious breath she knew by now announced a tirade.

"You are an inconsiderate child, arrogant, domineering, contrary, negligent, stubborn, cantankerous, disobedient, rude, nasty, lazy, and, with not the slightest reason to be so, vain. What is to become of you, God only knows. You never get out of bed before nine o'clock. You never appear among the human race before ten-thirty, though what you've done with that time is invisible to any of us with the slightest good taste in clothing and hair styles. And then you spend the rest of what little is left of the morning receiving your visitors, most of whom want nothing from you but the glow of your fame, which I must warn you is barely visible any longer. But still you let one or another take you out to lunch. And when you finally get home from that you complain and complain when I ask you to play the piano because I am interrupting your thoughts about what theater you are going to go to after supper and what men are going to be there. And when I do force you to spend time at the piano, all you come away with are complaints about how hard my instruments are to play, with the result that you are ruining my business not only insofar as it concerns your hopeless career but also my selling my pianos in the first place. You are, in short, thoroughly impossible, and you make me thoroughly sick."

"Oh, my," said Clementine, whose instinctive sympathy for Clara as a female under attack was almost wholly eclipsed by her gratitude that she herself had not, at least as yet, been forced to suffer such a scolding as this from the man she loved and from the man who, she knew, loved his daughter more than he would ever love his wife.

"Now get out of bed and get dressed and go downstairs and play the piano as you did for all the years of your life until now." He leaned forward and took Clara's bedspread in both his hands as if to pull it down.

Clara did the same with her hands, as if to keep it up.

"Are you refusing to leave this bed?"

"Are you unaware that I am naked beneath my covers?"

"Naked!" Clementine shrieked, so it was impossible to tell if Friedrich Wieck's hands flew off the bed in response to his daughter's words or his wife's whoop.

"Don't you sleep naked?" Clara addressed her first words to her stepmother.

"Not since —," began Clementine, when her husband stopped her by saying, "For the love of God, no!"

"—I was your age," Clementine could not help but continue, damn the consequences.

"Shall I get out of bed now?" asked Clara with a feigned innocence she found it absolutely delightful to assume.

As Clara lifted the top half of her body from the bed with the bedspread and blanket falling away and only the sheet locked tightly under the pits of both arms, her father finally retreated and barked, "Let's go!" to his wife, who seemed glued to her chair in anticipation of sharing at least this most superficial of intimacies with her stepdaughter.

"I promise to reform, Papa," Clara called out as her bedroom door was closing. "Please tell Herr Banck to wait for me in Robert's old room."

As soon as they had closed the door behind them, Clara sank back into bed and, laughing, kicked the kittens off.

Leipzig

APRIL 3, 1834

Once you were my feminine beloved,
Now you are my masculine beloved.
Robert Schumann

Though it was the evening of the publication day of the first issue of *New Journal of Music,* and their colleagues in the magazine were no doubt celebrating at The Coffee Tree, Robert was home with no one but Ludwig Schunke for company.

They had moved together to 21 Burgstrasse, on the ground floor in deference to Robert's continuing fear of heights, about which Ludwig had commented only half ironically, "It's not the fear of heights, but the fear of depths, that makes a man tedious."

Schunke had appeared several months before at Krause's Cellar, out of nowhere, "like a star," as Robert was to write in the magazine, though he had arrived, as it were, from everywhere, also like a star to those whose feet are fixed in mundane soil. Plagued by consumption, told to prepare himself to die, he had left Paris, where he was considered a pianist the equal of Liszt and Chopin, at the very end of the cholera scare, only when it was healthy to remain, and then tried Vienna, Prague, Dresden, and finally here, Leipzig, where he fell in with the boys of David and moved in with Robert.

For the first time in his life, Robert had found himself part of a circle of friends, not merely the solitary companion of another solitary dreamer. They met regularly in one tavern or another to discuss art in general and their plans for a new music magazine in particular. They sometimes called themselves Davids, because they agreed they were united against the Philistines and because they were taken, for one reason or another—aesthetic, carnal, or merely metaphysical—with the image of "a goodly-to-look-at boy of beautiful countenance" (so many musicians were homely little men with large ears) who was also a "cunning man with a harp." Perhaps they would agree, should a poll be taken, that a woman's form was most desired; but a man's was most admired.

While a student at Heidelberg, Robert had heard the term *Philister* applied by his fellow academics to the townspeople in the customary way in which those being educated insist upon demeaning those who have the misfortune to abide within earreach of that education. For Robert and his friends, however, the Philistines had become those who did not merely dwell in but ruled the world of music, of art, of everything in which men expressed themselves and sought to win approval by appealing to the admiration for superficial vulgarity that was surely man's greatest failing. Yet Robert was embarrassed by such blatant biblical symbolism. He preferred to think of himself and his group only as simple warriors, not kinged, and if named at all, named something playful and obscure.

He always made it a point to sit next to Johann Lyser, a deaf artist who was convinced that his drawings of their Leipzig meetings in Krause's Cellar or The Coffee Tree would one day assume the eminence of Titian's *Last Supper*; not the painting from the 1540s, in which nearly everyone seems intent upon listening to a pontificating and, to Lyser, mundanely divine Jesus, but the one finished twenty years later in which several discussions are being carried on at once and Jesus, like Robert, is the doomed spiritual leader who comforts with his silence and, as upon Lyser's own back with the hand not holding a glass of beer, the occasional touch.

Robert enjoyed the sensation of watching the chaos of their gatherings become the imperturbation of art. Every once in a while Lyser halted the fricative twitter of his pen on paper and looked sideways into Robert's eyes and directed them toward his drawing.

Here was the pianist Julius Knorr in all his theological, Mephistophelian grandeur, black beard, twisted black cigar, leaning back in his chair so his clubfoot in its peculiar black boot might find room on the table among the dozens of beer glasses and champagne flutes and ale tankards and coffee cups and ashtrays and books and coins and snow-soaked scarves and hats, his pale face as coyly expectant of reward as when he had within the last hour quoted Stendhal on romanticism as the progenitor of art that gives people the most profound pleasure and classicism as the progenitor of art that gives the most profound pleasure to their great-grandfathers. It was Knorr who, Clara's claims notwithstanding, had been the first in Germany to play Chopin's Variations on *"Là ci darem,"* a fact that Robert had bribed Knorr with a box of Caribbean cigars never to reveal to her.

Here, in contrast, was Karl Banck, blond, evilly handsome, who wrote songs and then sang them himself, distressingly well. Banck had been hired by Wieck to work with Clara. For some reason he always seemed to be singing with Clara whenever Robert visited. Robert found this annoying not because he suspected that the love songs they sang together were being sung to one another but because he himself did not sing well at all. He felt shut out by their art, not to mention the fact that they went right on singing even when he popped his head into the room Banck sometimes lodged in, the very room over Reichstrasse that had been Robert's own in those days when Clara would sit beside him silently as he wove the two of them together within the detours of his improvisations.

Here was Joseph Mainzer, who actually had been a priest and then became a revolutionary and finally a teacher of voice.* Robert wished it were Mainzer and not Karl Banck who had been hired to work with Clara, for he was so jovially homely that he claimed to have quit the priesthood because he found he didn't need a vow of chastity in order to be forced to practice it.

Here was Ludwig Böhner, at one time so famous a composer that he was the actual model for Hoffmann's Johannes Kreisler, who by now had been brought so low by drink he could barely dress himself; and yet he had prevailed upon Robert's worship of Hoffmann to have himself named the magazine's "foreign correspondent," prepared to travel, he said, wherever the beer is best and the music impetuous.

And here, among all the rest of these arguing, table-pounding, music-worshipping, iconoclastic, Christmas-fat romantics, was Friedrich Wieck himself, progressive in the ear—he admired the music of Beethoven and Schubert if not quite yet that of Chopin—and retrograde in the heart, with the result that he was that most dangerous of aesthetes, an avant-garde bourgeois.

Yet all of them believed with Schiller that if man were ever to solve the problem of politics in actual practice, he would have to approach it through the problem of the aesthetic, because it was only through beauty that man made his way to freedom. It was not the beauty of the merely decorous or genial. It was the beauty of darkness illuminated. The artist, in Friedrich Hölderlin's words, rejoiced in flinging himself into the night of the unknown, as Hölderlin himself seemed to have done in having entered the insane asylum in Tübingen almost thirty years ago.

---

*Mainzer had been influenced in the schema of his career by that of the French priest Félicité Robert de Lamennais, whose burgeoning liberalism was attacked generally by Pope Gregory XVI's encyclical *Mirari Vos,* which condemned not only freedom of the press but also freedom of individual conscience, and specifically by the encyclical *Singulari Nos,* which pronounced Lamennais's belief in the equality of all men to be "contrary to the word of God, false, calumnious, leading to anarchy." As Mainzer himself commented on this condemnation, which drove Abbé Lamennais from the Church, "Anarchy is the despot's term for liberty."

In the true artist, art and life were one, as in time past and as was their goal for time present, the poet and the priest were one, according to Novalis. This was at the center of their beliefs: the *self*, conscious, creative, munificent to the degree of profligacy, and most of all visible, tangible, inarguably unique, inarguably free, and, in those whose natures had become sufficiently refined, sublimely expressive.

At the end of the last century, a group of men, not unlike themselves, came to be known as *Die Romantik*, among them Novalis and Hölderlin and Eichendorff; Tieck and Wackenroder, the latter of whose death at the age of twenty-four kept the heart of the former shattered for the remaining fifty-five years of his life; and the younger of the Schlegel brothers, Friedrich,* who on the one hand carried forward the Johann Winckelmann tradition in extolling the "smooth, tight, marble-hard" male body and on the other quite betrayed that tradition by seducing Felix Mendelssohn's Aunt Dorothea into leaving her Jewish husband and wrote a novel that described their sexual relations in the most intimate terms, including Dorothea's desire to experience her passion in positions they had not known a woman could imagine, let alone assume. Had not Dorothea herself been so unutterably plain, she and her lover (later wife and husband, after she had "converted") might well have epitomized Théophile Gautier's romantic ideal of the beautiful, the free, and the young.**

---

*Whose brother, August, inspired Madame de Staël to write *Germany*, her study of German culture, which Napoleon felt belittled *French* culture. So in the very year he attended the birth of Robert Schumann in Zwickau, the emperor took the time to ban *Germany*, ordered all 10,000 copies of the French edition destroyed, and was confirmed in his conviction that his having banished Madame de Staël from Paris seven years earlier was evidence of the necessity of political prophylaxis.

**Both Schlegels, like most of their fellow German romantics, inspired by the writings of the mystic seventeenth-century cobbler, Jacob Böhme, believed that true sexual perfection resided in the androgyne. Since, however, a man could not marry himself, nor make true love to himself, or marry another man with or without making love to him, the Schlegels decided the only practical place to locate the androgyne was inside the boundaries of ostensibly normal heterosexual union, where a man could make love to as many men or women as he wanted within the infinite confines of monogamy's multifaceted mirror. Friedrich's androgynous ideal was Caroline Michaelis, whom he compared to Plato's own androgyne, Diotima. And Caroline, with devastating courtesy, satisfied his lust for hermaphroditic dissipation by running off with, and marrying, his brother. Seven years later, however, she left August for Friedrich Schelling, whose pansexual view of the world encompassed the inevitable decline of physical desire in any relationship by promoting in its place the idea that the artist, in engendering art, creates the world itself. Friedrich Schiller

It had been a glorious time, in the aftermath of the French Revolution, when the rights of man and the emancipation of the artist coalesced to produce what Joseph Eichendorff considered an inner regeneration of collective life.

Yet in how short a time did the profundities of self-expression lead to the superficialities of commercialism. What Schubert called "wretched, fashionable stuff" predominated. The great mystery facing mankind was not why all fashionable stuff was wretched but why so much wretched stuff was fashionable. Artistic standards were abandoned, the comfortable cult of the mediocre prevailed, and presentation became confused with substance.

In consequence, society itself was weakened, corrupted, and desolated: When art is trivialized and debased, the resulting devastation makes war and famine and plague and natural catastrophe seem negligible. It is one thing to die individually or to be wiped out en masse. It is another and far more grievous thing entirely to be forced to live in a time of squalid art.

Nowhere was this more evident than among pianists, who allowed themselves to become so celebrated for their technique that they were forced to write their own music simply to find pieces showy and empty enough to play, with the result that those called the greatest musicians of their time were also held to be the greatest composers of all time: Henri Herz, Franz Hünten, even the young Sigismond Thalberg.

It was enough to tempt one to destroy his hand. And Robert was to some of these men—Wieck as his former piano teacher being the primary dissenter, and Dr. Reuter not far behind—a hero for that act. They interpreted his act as a symbolic gesture, but hardly empty, given the pain involved and the ruination of a brilliant career. He had confronted the Philistines and had slung the potent, smooth stone deep within his own brain. Who better to lead them?

Otto Nicolai, back from too long a visit to the Teatro La Fenice in Venice to understand how a magazine might save the world, not to mention accomplish so impossible a task as to exalt a Schubert over a Pixis, asked

---

would have none of this and feuded with the Schlegels before his premature death from outrage over Romantic excess. A poem of unknown authorship popular at the time read:

> Of Schiller and Schlegels and Schelling
> The pronouncing's as hard as the spelling.
> Just to tell them apart
> Demands scholarly art.
> And their love lives are less than compelling.

Robert how he thought music could be written about in the first place, words and music being so antithetical.

"I learned more about counterpoint from Jean Paul than from anyone else," said Robert. "A painter can learn color from a Beethoven symphony, and a musician can learn rhythm from a Goethe poem."

"But how can music be described in words?" said Nicolai.

"Much like this cigar"—Robert waved his—"if you have the capacity to appreciate it." He put the cigar between his beer-washed, chastity-plumped lips and drew from it a huge mouthful of smoke, which he released in a stream through his mouth and drew back into his head through his nose. "Of course, should we find ourselves sucking upon one that's foul, we'll call it such. If you can't attack what's bad about a work, then you can't defend what's good about it. So let us drink to the dawn of a new poetic age."

As they toasted, Ludwig Böhner lost nearly all his drink as he missed bashing his stein against Joseph Mainzer's. But even as he licked what beer he could from his saturated sleeve, he asked Robert, "Surely you have not chosen words over music?"

Robert shook his head. "Literature interprets us, but music defines us."

"Brilliant!" It was an unfamiliar voice, deep and somewhat rasping, as if something had eaten away at it, and to Robert's musician's ear sounding the way he had always imagined Weber's voice after he had swallowed the acid. It had come from a strange young man, a new young man, tall, thin, with huge curls rising from his high forehead to swim back over his raised collar and snow-dusted crimson scarf, a trim mustache atop a wide, smiling mouth, a glorious thin nose hooked like something off an ancient statue, and eyebrows hovering delicately over eyelids almost swollen with intelligence. Who can this be? thought Robert. He must be the one they'd been waiting for.

"Ludwig Schunke from Stuttgart," he softly introduced himself to the table.

From the moment Ludwig had appeared at Krause's Cellar, everyone had admired him.

Some thought he looked like John the Baptist. Others claimed he resembled the kind of idealized Roman emperor who might be dug up at Pompeii.

Robert could not disagree but displayed his erudition in stating that Ludwig most reminded him of Thorwaldsen's bust of Schiller, though privately he saw, when he looked at Ludwig, a man with the beauty of Bernaert van Orley as painted by Dürer, hat cocked, mouth voluptuous, eyes on eternity, and hair of such inviting, shining softness that it tempted one to put one's hands within it, on either side of Ludwig's head, and bring his face so close it could not be distinguished from one's own.

He bestowed upon Ludwig as his Davidite *New Journal of Music* pseudo-nym the name Jonathan, for Ludwig had immediately become his best friend in the world and in becoming his Jonathan had made sense for him finally of the whole notion of the fight against the Philistines and his own assumption of the kingdom of, and as, David.

Robert had joked with Ludwig that as Davidites they lead off the first issue of *New Journal of Music* with a pledge to deliver to its audience the fore-skins of a hundred Philistines.* After they had amused one another in dis-cussing drunkenly (Robert on Rhine wine, Ludwig on the bitter coffee with which he tried to acidify his disease to death) just what the foreskins of Herz and Hünten might look like, they settled more seriously on a message declaring their aim to be to deliver the poetry of art to a place of honor among men.

Robert and Ludwig lived their belief. They immersed themselves com-pletely in their work, and did not drown in the madness of it only because they rescued one another from the abstraction of composition and the aus-terity of the endless repetition necessary for the illusion of spontaneity.

In the beginning, they had lived in two rooms, each in his own with his piano and his bed and his books. But because they were home all day, be-fore going out together most nights to the taverns, and because each worked ceaselessly at his music from dawn to dusk (and in Robert's case sometimes long beyond), they found the sound of one another's piano, as occasionally beautiful as the music from it might be, so distracting that nei-ther could work to his full capacity.

So they moved to new rooms, also on the ground floor, at 21 Burg-strasse, and each still had his own room, but between them they now had a completely empty room, or almost completely empty. The only thing in it was the Turkish rug that had been in Robert's father's office in Zwickau, which Robert had begged his mother to ship to him as soon as he and Lud-wig had signed their lease. The rug was large even for a work produced by the lavish villagers of Ladik and as thick and durable as a Persian Bidjar but

---

*The foreskins of Philistines were routinely cut off by the Jews as an aid in enumerating enemy dead. This method was not completely accurate insofar as the occasional Philistine was, during battle and quite incidentally, circumcised or at least genitally mutilated and thus might as easily and joyously be counted a Jewish casualty by the Philistines as a Philis-tine casualty by the Jews. When King Saul ordered David to deliver a hundred Philistine foreskins in order to win his daughter's hand in marriage, David returned from battle with two hundred, half of them for Michal, whom he married, and half of them for her brother, Jonathan, whom he buried.

wholly floral in its decoration because of the Koran's admonition against the portrayal of either men or beasts. Even now, nearly eight years after Robert had found his father sitting dead with his feet planted lightly but finally upon this very carpet, it smelled of his tobacco and the bindings of his books and the million exhalations of his sweet breath that in the midst of sleepless nights Robert could still feel reach from the Heaven in which he did not believe to his own aggrieved lips.

Sometimes, when he and Ludwig happened to take a break from their work at the same time, they would meet and sit beside one another upon this rug in the middle of this vast, empty room and, like tiny figures alone on the deceivingly flat plane of the earth, talk and sing to one another.

Robert had begun to compose some of what he called dances in honor of his colleagues on the magazine, but he could not maintain a strict dance form in any of them and realized they were beginning to form a conversation not between himself and Ludwig, as he would have wished, or himself and Clara, whose voice he could not yet locate in his music, but between two sides of himself, at least, for he sometimes felt he had been shattered at birth and was made up of an army of different souls, all of whom might be dressed in the same uniform but few of whom fought on the same side. For the very first dance, in G, Robert borrowed a tune he had heard Clara composing at the piano, all in the left hand, a kind of double ascension toward a frolic of higher, sunnier notes. Ludwig was much taken with this theme, as he was with the clash in Robert's music, as in Robert himself, between bliss and anguish. Robert, who, as a man divided between the solidity of the word and the evanescence of sound, loved to bedeck his music with little mottos and epigraphs, penned at the top of this first dance, when he handed it to Ludwig to play, the words from an old German maxim: "Forever and ever, joy and pain* are joined." They punned in English with the word *lust* and punned in German with the similar sounds of *Leid* and the word for song, *Lied*.

Robert was inspired by Ludwig's ability to understand his music and to play it as Robert wrote it at the piano even as he could not quite force his hands to play it. Even more than Clara—which might have been the result merely of her youth and the visible fear in her eyes and hands of confronting the darker, wilder crasis of eternal tones Robert found hidden in the piano— Ludwig grasped the music and in so doing lay hold of its creator. Until Robert heard and saw, awe struck, Ludwig play his *Toccata,* which he came to believe he must have revised in supersensual anticipation of Ludwig's arrival into his life, he had not believed any pianist would achieve his own turbulent

Lust und Leid.

vision of the work and, more prosaically, that its final chord would ever be achieved without arpeggiation, until he saw Ludwig embrace those dilated notes with the ingenerate ease of a hawk's clasp of a rat.

But for Ludwig, there was something unnatural about Robert's work: not the music itself, but how it was made. Robert wrote always at the piano, a cigar clenched in his teeth, a thick pen shoved into the rift of dark hair over the helix of one ear while his spectacles swung from the other, his eyes squinting through the cigar smoke and the haze of indecision, sometimes at his hands upon the keyboard and sometimes at the sheets of music paper covered with what looked like black teeth.

When he worked, he worked within a globe of time that was transparent but imperforate. He didn't lock himself away but was unapproachable until he finished. Robert's insomnia allowed him—forced him, Ludwig sometimes thought—to work all night, and he seemed able to go three days without sleep, nearly without food, certainly without bathing or shaving, producing music like evidence in his defense.

His life hung in the balance. When his work went poorly, or did not go at all, he seemed to have died. If he spoke, his speech was slow and monotonic. If he walked, it was only across the room, the way one would to a gallows, body crushed from the shoulders down, feet flat, head nailed shut. If he breathed, he did so almost secretly, discernible only to someone who loved him, all in the upper chest, almost in the throat itself; panicked breathing. His stomach was in turmoil. Fart he did, from one corner of his room to another. It was a wonder there was not a depression in his piano bench to match that in his mind. Long coils of giddy noise pushed outward from his guts before he'd oboe out the gas, only to have the entire process begin again within the instant. He trembled. He sweated the cold sweat of unaccomplishment. He suffered terribly in the grip of nihility.

But when his work went well, then he became truly worrisome. He might sit at the piano for twenty-four hours straight. He might smile demonically with darting eyes at the notes escaping from his fingers. He might cry out, "Genius! Genius!" This gratification, such as it was, was shadowed always by misery, for he knew not its source and trusted not its return. So utterly was he at the mercy of the ebb and flow of music that he felt engulfed, oblivious to the disgrace of silence. It was an exhilaration he feared he could not bear for long.

When they chanced to discuss this, usually in the empty room, Robert remembered none of it. Upon finishing a piece of music, he knew only exhaustion. He could fall asleep in the middle of a sentence. He could sleep, there upon his father's old rug, for the same twenty-four hours' duration in which he was capable of composing, and Ludwig would throw over him Emilie's strange blanket made of rabbit skins beneath which Robert slept, or tried to, when he dared lie down upon his derisive bed.

As Robert was consumed by his music and compulsive in his composition of it, Ludwig was consumed, literally, by consumption itself. Robert had never before been with someone whose death was so clearly written in his flesh. Emilie might have gone on living for years, if she could have borne the itch that attacked the very part of her body that should have given her the greatest pleasure. His father had died suddenly and unexpectedly, as had little Robert and Rosalie and Julius and as would he himself, he ardently wished, so that he need not have to find in himself the courage he saw in Ludwig, putting one foot after the other as they made their way through Leipzig when Ludwig knew full well that he could count the footsteps left to him and count the meals and count the days and nights and count the hours left for music and for love.

Leipzig

APRIL 3, 1834
Along came Ernestine.
Robert Schumann

Ernestine von Fricken hailed from Asch. But Clara met her in Plauen, the town in which Clara had spent her fourth summer on earth with her mother and her mother's lover before her father had recalled her to Leipzig and her mother and Herr Bargiel had moved to Berlin. It was here that Ernestine and her father approached Clara and her father within moments of Clara's having taken her final bows, the orchestra behind her seemingly as moved by her playing as the audience before her was stunned.

"She was magnificent," said the man who had introduced himself as Baron von Fricken.

Because he addressed her father and not herself, as if she were, like musicians of old, the property of some patron rather than of her own imperious need to make music and of her father's to make money, Clara ignored the man's praise and concentrated on his daughter.

Ernestine was as open a girl as Clara had ever seen. Her face positively beamed with the pleasure of the occasion, and her blonde hair provided her the radiance of an innocent flower at full bloom. Her bosom made up in proud visibility what it lacked in scope.

"How old are you?" asked Clara, not, she hoped, like a child in a schoolyard but like a woman in search of intimacies.

"I'll be eighteen in September." Ernestine had a voice as airy as her face.

"Not the *thirteenth*?" asked Clara more excitedly than she would have wished.

"Is that *your* birthday?"

"Yes."

"We were born in the same *month*." Ernestine found this the occasion for taking Clara's hand, which was something Clara did not customarily encourage in the aftermath of one of her concerts, though she did not object at all in this instance, since she trusted that Ernestine's desire was to touch another woman, not merely a pianist whose corporeality and thus reality could presumably be determined in no other way.

"I'm fourteen," Clara admitted, proud of not feeling the need to boost herself into the next age.

"Everyone knows that," said Ernestine, shaking her program as evidence of Clara's notoriety.

"So you don't think I'm too young?" asked Clara.

"Too young for what?" Ernestine did not giggle as she said this but assumed as much gravity as her blithesome being would allow.

"Too young for—"

Clara's father interrupted. "Baron von Fricken has asked if he might be allowed to enroll his daughter as my pupil. I have accepted her as such. Without the customary audition." Her father nodded at Baron von Fricken to solicit a show of gratitude for what was not, Clara knew, an extraordinary circumstance. The baron smiled gratefully in the midst of a vigorous outnodding of the generous pedagog before him. "She will come to live in our home as soon as he can arrange her removal from Asch."

Without waiting for Ernestine's reaction—either to this news of her change of circumstance or to the fact that neither of the men had directed it to Ernestine personally—Clara exclaimed, "Oh, goody!"

Dresden

JUNE 8, 1834
You were at the parting of the ways between childhood and girlhood.
Robert Schumann

Dear Herr Schumann,

Today, Sunday the 8th of June, on the day when the beneficent Lord
sent from heaven the fire of your music, and you were born, I sit here
all alone and write to you. (Though I need not: for this afternoon alone
I had two invitations and was forced to tell my handsome inviters,
"Sorry, but it is the birthday of a far fairer gentleman than you and I
must write to him or I shall never forgive myself nor he forgive me
either." Is that not so? I mean, could you possibly forgive me if I did
not write? Are you not at this very moment saying to yourself, "I am
so happy that she wrote"?)

The first thing I must say is that I send you my following heartfelt
wishes: that you won't always be contrary; that you drink less Bavarian
beer; that you not turn day into night and vice versa; that you write
your music without fail; that you finish your articles for your
magazine; and most of all that you promise to come to see me in
Dresden.

It is as if Papa has sent me into exile, away from himself, away from
yourself. I am daily studying composition with Herr Reissiger, who you
will be pleased to know is almost as fond of my progress on "Ballet des
Revenants" as you were with its humble beginnings. And I sing every
other day (he stupidly instructs me not to sing or even to speak a single
word on the days we don't meet) for Herr Miksch (who studied with
Caselli, who studied with Barnacchi, who studied with Pistocchi, who
studied with Manelli, who studied with Folignato — in case you aren't
aware, a castrato! — who studied with Apollo for all I know). And I am
perfecting my French with Monsieur Baragouin and my English with
Mr. Edea, because Papa tells me that the more languages I know, the
more money I shall make, as if my music could remain pure while my
voice becomes covetous.

But I am lonely here. Do you think it is to be tolerated, Herr
Schumann, that you take so little notice of your friend that you have

not written to her even once? Every time the mail arrives, I hope to find a little letter from a certain Herr Devotee, but alas I am always disappointed. I comforted myself with the thought that at least you would visit me here, but I have just heard from Papa that you are not coming with him after all because Knorr is ill and you must therefore work even harder to keep the magazine on schedule. Before long you shall have six pages for it from me, and you will so admire them that you will have to pay me a lot.

In the meantime, please send me your new Rondo so I may work on it and have at least a part of you within my hands. And might I not expect also a letter, both original and legible, Herr Schumann? This ingenious, original, and witty epistle commends to you with due deliberation (you who do not like haste) your friend

Clara Wieck
Clara Wieck
(Double)

P.S. There is a pretty girl here (though not as pretty as Ernestine, you will be happy to hear) named Sophie Kaskel who is quite in love with your Impromptus and practices them religiously.

Leipzig

JUNE 9, 1834

By all means play piano duets with Schumann,
but no more.
Baron Ignaz von Fricken

On the day after his twenty-fourth birthday, Robert went with Ludwig and Ernestine to the home of Henriette Voigt, who had, among his married friends, taken the place of Agnes Carus in his heart. But he did not long for Henriette, as he had longed for Agnes. He merely kept her within that compartment in his mind reserved exclusively for women whom he could not, after all, have. This lent her the kind of eternal desirability that never quite managed to adhere to those women he had had.

Henriette was married to Karl Voigt, one of the richest men in Leipzig, who appeared to spend all his money on art and on his wife, in the former

of which he displayed as questionable taste as in the latter he demonstrate
simply for having chosen her to marry, the most discriminating. She was a
most exactly Robert's age and quite boisterously beautiful. She wore he
hair loose in all its wild curliness, never needed to rouge her cheeks because
merriment did it for her, laughed at everything and nothing, though never
obstreperously, and spent her husband's money on clothes that fit her so
well they appeared both superfluous and indispensable.

What freedom Henriette sacrificed in her strict adherence to the vows of
marriage she bestowed upon others in her passion for their coupling. It was
not merely, or even primarily, the carnal sort she advocated, though she
took no small delight in the tingle of the news of concupiscence incited.
What she loved most in life was love itself, preferably between two people
who, if not for her, would not experience their love for each other and thus
would not have her as the avenue down which they walked on what she was
convinced was the only road to earthly paradise. She could not meet someone, or at least someone unattached, without trying to think immediately of
someone else to whom he or she might become attached. Leipzig was full
of young couples who, if not for Henriette Voigt, would not know what she
herself had found with Karl Voigt: comfort, tranquility, asylum.

And while she had not introduced Robert and Ernestine to one another,
she was now offering her home to them as a safe haven, away from the
unreasonable, unnatural restrictions of the Wieck household, where Ernestine lived and was guarded in her virtue by Friedrich Wieck himself, who
had promised her father, the baron, that no kiss, no caress, would pass between his daughter and Schumann, though two things were clear to Henriette: Wieck had promised this only because he believed, particularly after
the devastation of his divorce, that solely if planted in such virtue could the
flower of lifelong love bloom; and Robert and Ernestine had at the very
least both kissed and caressed, if indeed they had not yet surpassed such superficial knowledge of one another's bodies with a true plumbing of the
depths of love's great congress.

Wieck knew as well as Henriette that there was something between
Robert and Ernestine; he wanted to nurture it while at the same time he didn't
want it to become something that would render their wedding night anti-
climactic or her father apoplectic. Wieck himself had told Henriette as much,
and more, in telling her that immediately upon Ernestine's arrival in his
house in April he had arranged for Clara to be sent to Dresden to further her
musical studies. This demonstrated to Henriette that Wieck was her formi-
dable foe as a matchmaker. But it was precisely the privacy Wieck refused to

allow Robert and Ernestine that Henriette was able to give them and thus to assure herself that their union would be achieved through her and not him, his inadvertent introduction of the two of them notwithstanding.

She had met Ernestine several times at the Wieck house and had found her beautiful if, at seventeen, not yet in possession of that beauty, which shone from her but did not illuminate her. Robert himself described her, like someone who'd rehearsed the words in order to convince himself of their truth, as a brilliant jewel with the face of a Madonna and a wondrously pure soul.

When Henriette invited Robert to come visit with Ernestine, he thanked her profusely for this opportunity to be alone with Ernestine, who was, as he put it, passionately attached to him. He explained he could not invite Ernestine to his own modest home because he lived with his best friend there, whom he begged Henriette's permission to take along with him to her house as the friend was not well and was also passionately attached to Robert. Henriette had found this curious but agreed cheerfully because she was always on the lookout for new young men, even those who were delicate or perhaps ailing, given the fact that there seemed to be in Leipzig and she guessed in the world at large approximately a hundred attractive and intelligent young women for every similarly endowed young man, truly one of the great tragedies affecting the human race and an imbalance in nature so grievous as to argue for either the absence or the cruelty of God.

And so, when she opened her door herself (never comfortable with her servants' participation in her arranged trysts) to what she recognized as Robert's curiously rhythmic yanking upon the ancient brass-and-marble bell pull for which Karl had paid some giddy sum, Henriette Voigt saw before her her sturdy Robert, his fetching inamorata, who greeted her with a smile so charmingly guiltless that Henriette wished for a moment something she had never wished before (that she were seventeen again), and a tall young man of strange beauty (he had the tranquil eyes of a religious in the bedazzling head of a serpent) who immediately said to her with a kind of ruined, distant voice, "This is difficult to believe."

She had no idea what he meant, which made her laugh all the more mischievously. "That you are the chaperon?" she asked.

"That *you* are the chaperon," he responded.

"Look what I have for your birthday," Henriette said to Robert as she led the three of them into her home.

He looked first into her hands, then about the sitting room whose doors she opened.

"What?" he inquired.

"Any room of my house you desire—but for this one, where Herr Schunke and I shall sit and talk, and of course the servants' quarters, where I fear Fräulein von Fricken might observe things she is not yet old enough to appreciate."

Ernestine blushed. "You mistake my innocence, Frau Voigt."

"For what?" asked Henriette.

"For its opposite."

"And what might that be, Fräulein von Fricken?"

"Why, guilt, I suppose."

"I should have thought you might say the opposite of innocence is experience."

"Oh, I have so little experience."

"Poor child, you have guilt without experience?"

Ernestine thought for a moment and then seemed to come to what seemed upon her face a very revelation. "I suppose I do."

"Well, then," said Henriette, "you will have either to earn your guilt or expand your experience."

Again, Ernestine needed time to think before she said, "Do those not amount to the same thing?"

"Not in my house!" Henriette laughed merrily. "Never in my house."

She poured sherry for all of them and toasted Robert's birthday. "May you live forever and marry soon."

Again, Ernestine blushed.

"Now, go and enjoy my birthday gift," said Henriette.

Robert left the sitting room with two glasses of sherry and with Ernestine, who, as soon as Henriette had closed the doors behind them, said, "I cannot imagine why you aren't in love with her instead of with me."

"But she's not available." The moment Robert uttered these cruel words he wished he could take them back. He opened his mouth and screwed a cigar into it.

But Ernestine, bless her simple soul, simply said, "And I am available, I suppose?"

"I never meant to imply that," he obfuscated with the truth.

"Well, I am," she said. "And I shall remain so until we marry."

"Available to whom?" He wondered if this is what a woman did: threaten to give herself to others so that the one to whom she really wanted to give herself would claim her.

"To you, of course."

She grasped his arm and led him down a long hallway as if this were Ver-führungstrasse instead of the private home of a woman whose considerable

{ 159 }

charms Robert hoped would somehow miraculously inhabit this sweet young woman who had secretly agreed to be his wife, or whose husband he had secretly agreed to become, he couldn't remember which.

On their way to wherever she was leading him, they passed through the gallery in which Karl Voigt had hung the majority of his most recent acquisitions. There was something new by Carl Blechen, who seemed to have abandoned waterfalls and gorges for a smoke-voiding factory farting poison at the river. The paintings by Peter Cornelius and Friedrich Overbeck put Robert in mind of the music of Otto Nicolai: a German attempting to become Italian succeeded no better than, as Robert remembered from his own youthful trip to Italy, a German attempting to mount an Italian. He spoke to Ernestine of the influence of Perugino, not to mention of the monks of Sant'Isidoro, whose celibacy was reflected in the passionlessness of the paintings and whose disapproval Robert compared to that of the two stern men looking at Ary Scheffer's naked Francesco and Paolo. He was more fond of the tortured and clearly anti-Italian drawing by Géricault of the woman in Paris he had loved with utter hopelessness and of Géricault's faces of madmen that represented his own only to the extent that they portrayed not his features but the repercussions in the mind of unrequited love. (Ernestine, however, seemed more interested in Robert's recounting of Géricault's death, precisely ten years ago, by being thrown from his horse while in exile in London.) And he could not help admiring Julius von Carolsfeld's painting of the strangely haloed king of the elves offering the doomed little boy of Schubert's "Erlkönig" his bountifully comely daughter, one of whose breasts was so perfectly and succulently round that Robert could barely refrain from testing it with his fingertip. But for every Géricault and Prud'hon pencil study of the Empress Josephine's sumptuous, shadow-casting bosom, there was a ridiculously overblown von Kaulbach, which compelled Robert to proclaim that he could imagine no worse fate than to have to live in Düsseldorf, and a Sunday bandstand scene by Oscar Ohrenschmalz and a landscape by Alfred Schlimm and a still life by Josef Kürbis in which a gourd and two grapes were so composed that even Ernestine giggled. "A self-portrait, no doubt," commented Robert, which caused Ernestine, unmindful of the sherry glasses still in his hands, to throw herself into his arms.

"Take me," she said.

"Where?" he asked.

"To show me more funny paintings."

They left the gallery and began to climb the wide, curving stairway, along the wall of which were hung at least a dozen of Heinrich Grundverschieden's portraits of his mother, in each of which she was wearing a different hat and each hat bearing a different bird, looking out at the viewer as if he or she were a worm.

"Have you ever been up here?" asked Ernestine when they had reached the top of the stairs.

"Yes."

She stopped and looked fiercely into his eyes. "When?"

"Never."

"I might answer the same if you were to ask me if I have ever made love."

"You have and you haven't?" he inquired.

"I have only imagined it," she answered.

Now he did love her. She was rich and a virgin and at least intelligent enough to tease him with his own words.

She opened the door to a small bedroom.

"This will do," she said.

Robert looked around. There were no paintings on the walls — this in itself was cause for celebration — nothing but a single melancholy drawing by Moritz von Schwind of Schubert at the piano. Within the room, there were merely a bed and a chair and a relatively simple Jacobean oak chest of drawers on stile feet and a small, well-worn prayer rug with a particularly gentle mihrab, or arch, inspired by a mosque that was particularly welcoming to those pilgrims on life's last journey.

She closed the door behind them and held out her hand. "Now I am ready for my drink."

Robert looked down at the glasses in his hand. There was almost nothing left in either of them. "I seem to have spilled it all," he said.

"I doubt it," she said and took the cigar from his mouth and a glass from his hand and thrust her tongue all the way to its bottom until there was nothing left but an amber drop or two that rolled off her lips onto his.

The longer Henriette Voigt sat with Ludwig Schunke, the more time she wished she might have with him. She tried to distract herself with thoughts of Robert and his Ernestine, wherever they might be lost or hiding in her cavernous house, however they might be exploring each other's considerable charms (his profound, hers generously superficial), but she seemed to have lost her former gift for, and pleasure in, the visualization of others in the act of love. This man before her was robbing her very soul. He was sitting at no small remove from her — she with her feet up on a French walnut duchesse brisée, he having sought the refuge of a far-less-comfortable George I walnut armchair with its narrow shepherd's-crook arms, and between them a hideous giltwood banquette covered in red toile de Jouy over which Karl had wept in presenting it to her—but had entered her as surely as if... It was an amazing thing for a relationship to have been consummated thus. The flesh had not been bypassed. It had been foreclosed upon. She felt they belonged to one another as the sky did to the sea and the sea to the sky at that point beyond which vision failed and only faith was left to imagine the infinite.

He was dying, this man. He was wandering through the house of death and showing her the rooms, not to trap her there but simply to provide the pleasure of an afternoon in which eternity is measured in a gesture, a word, the serenity of silence.

She had not known anyone who was dying. That is to say, she had not known anyone who had known he was dying. She wondered what it was like to live with such knowledge. Did it make you want to hide yourself away or to dance with practically everybody? Did it make life precious or demean it? Did it inspire fear or courage?

It was not that she asked these questions of Herr Schunke—that would be impertinent and intrusive. But she did ask them of herself, even as she sat there watching and listening to a man who seemed, with his very dying, to bring life into her life.

He himself appeared nothing if not comfortable with the entire subject. He treated it as if he were planning someday soon, he wasn't sure just when, to go off by train or carriage to yet another city, as he had, he told her, left Paris for Vienna, Vienna for Prague, Prague for Dresden, Dresden for Leipzig.

"But this will be your final journey," she said, not insensitively, she trusted.

"Let us hope so," he replied, laughing.

Take me with you, she wanted to say, but could not. She hardly knew him, or at least had known him for so short a time, mere hours that love had tricked into seeming an eternity. She had never been able to imagine accompanying a man even to a hotel room, let alone this, through the door of death itself.

"How can you talk of this so breezily?" she asked.

"It's a bigger wind than you might imagine, Frau Voigt." He put his hand upon his frail chest, as if to indicate both the nucleus of its force and the site of the dying going on within him. "My doctor speaks only of illness, and Robert... Robert cannot speak of death at all. We avoid the subject entirely. We live together with it but do not touch it. He has had so much death in his life, as you know."

"And I have had so little."

"Now you have me," he said.

Her whole body became chilled. She feared he would see her trembling and mistake what was love for antipathy.

"Now I have you," she said.

Robert and Ernestine lay upon the bed, his head upon her naked breast, her fingers in his hair, not moving, trapped there in its thickness, strangely unaffectionate.

"Do you suppose this is her bed?" she asked.

"I believe she sleeps with her husband."

"You have not been in this bed before?"

"Never."

"Nor with her?"

"Never."

And yet, this whole short time he had spent with Ernestine—playing with one another, touching, looking, laughing a bit, wishing for more sherry, each undressed to the waist but no more, aside from their shoes kicked off, each aroused but each unspent—Robert had found his thoughts wandering to Henriette, and to Ludwig with her, wishing he were there instead of here; nearer the sherry, of course, but nearer also to his friends, those he loved more than he loved this girl he was to marry, who was beautiful and kind and whose breasts were so incredibly ripe it seemed a crime against nature itself that they not occupy him fully rather than provide a mere resting place for his confusion and distress.

Finally, he said, "We best join the others."

"Are you done with me?" she asked.

"Done? How?" If only, he thought, she might release me now, let me go, banish me forever.

"*Done* with me. Here." She took his hand and placed it upon the middle of her body.

"I could not force myself upon you."

"No force would be involved."

He shook his head. "It is too soon."

"Are those not meant to be my words?"

"And are they not?"

"They are not."

"It is too soon," he said again. "I want to save you."

"For what?"

"Not for. *From.*"

"From what?"

"From me."

"It is too late."

He sat up and took his watch from the pocket of his trousers as he turned to place his feet upon the floor. "Alas, you're right—it is too late."

Ernestine was not at all sure how to present herself when she and Robert joined the others. She knew, from the evidence of her tangled hair and her wrinkled dress and her cheeks red from their contact with Robert's and a certain tightness in her bosom, that it would be assumed he and she had done something they had not done. Wishing, indeed, they had done it, she felt it quite unfair that she provided merely the appearance of having done it. It did not matter whether the others would envy or disdain her for it. She merely wanted to do it. Or, in this sad case, to have done it. Not only to have looked as if she'd done it. One might as well have been arrested for stealing something one had been tempted to steal and was indeed about to steal when suddenly an announcement was made that the shop was closed for the day.

She decided, therefore, that she would act as if they had done it.

And so, after Robert had knocked gently on the door, they walked into the sitting room with her arm in his, her head on his shoulder, the front of her dress pulled even farther down, her hair shaken into even greater turmoil, and a look in her eyes, as near as she could get it, of having devoured or having been devoured. She also, in deciding whether to let her breath come in short spasms or huge gusts, chose the former, which had the advantage of causing her breasts almost to quiver beneath the flush of her neck and the pride of her chin.

Assuming this attitude of the fallen woman, she felt risen. And if it were this easy, through such minor deception, to feel you were ascending to Heaven, she could only imagine what flight her heart would take when finally he made of her a true woman. And a true woman she needed to be: As it was, she was seducing him under false pretenses. She had been born out of a profane passion, and it was the very profanity of the act she wished not to escape but to duplicate.

Yet, from the looks of it, it was Frau Voigt and Herr Schunke who had achieved some union that Ernestine felt would have escaped her and Robert even had they torn every scrap of clothes from one another and ground their sherry glasses to sand beneath their bleeding flesh.

It was a union not of the body. Frau Voigt and Herr Schunke sat quite far apart, she on a strange kind of double-headed bench, he in a chair of monstrous proportions, at least in comparison with his frail bones, its arms as skinny as his own.

Their clothes were in place. So was their hair. But there was between them some kind of concentration it was impossible to breach. How foolish Ernestine felt, having made herself look ravished. They scarcely saw her, and even had they gawked, they would not have cared. Somehow, these two had left the world. And they had left it together.

Robert seemed not to notice. "Might you have more sherry?" he asked Frau Voigt.

She unlocked her gaze from that of Herr Schunke and turned to Robert and looked at him as if she had forgotten he was in her home. She smiled at him in a way that convinced Ernestine she was not, and had never been, his lover. It was the kind of smile a grownup gives a child who has interrupted the most private of reveries: indulgent and dismissive at the same time.

"I have more of everything," Frau Voigt answered and pointed toward the elaborate decanter in which the sherry lay as still and dark as Ernestine's heart.

Leipzig

SEPTEMBER 6, 1834
I desperately wanted a woman to hold on to.
Robert Schumann

Clara was given a reprieve from her exile in Dresden through her commitment to play two charity concerts in Leipzig on September 11 and 12, the same program for each, she had decided, Chopin and Schumann, in particular Robert's brand-new Toccata, which she was still learning. It was strangely sonata-like for so rebellious a composer, and she hoped the audience would appreciate the astounding hush in its final bars, huge chords attenuated into a kind of eerie repose, provided she could achieve cleanly and sedately the final octave-and-a-half in the left hand. But even shut away in her room on the third floor, she was unable to avoid the turmoil in the house, and was finding it very difficult to practice.

The house was filled constantly with people, and not only the usual servants and students and *New Journal of Music* contributors and near-strangers who wanted to ennoble their own lives under the guise of providing some little favor for her own.

Robert was here for Ernestine, and Ludwig Schunke was here for Robert, and perhaps also for Henriette Voigt, who, most peculiarly, was here for him as well as for Ernestine and Robert, for whose union she claimed responsibility and to whom she had apparently opened her own house.

Worse, Baron von Fricken was here. And when he was not playing upon his flute for anyone who would listen some Variations he had written,* he seemed to be carrying on an endless dialogue with Clara's father about possible compromises to Ernestine's virtue. The baron kept asking Herr Wieck if his daughter was still "whole," as he put it, and Herr Wieck kept assuring him she was, calling as his witnesses Ernestine and Robert themselves, who, belying their offended answer to this ridiculous question, gave every evidence that their intimacy knew no bounds.

Ernestine, who upon her arrival in April had befriended Clara, now shunned her or, when she could not avoid talking to her, spoke of things so inane that Clara was tempted to inquire after Robert's talents as a lover. She imagined herself telling Ernestine she had taken lovers of her own in Dresden and had found them to be not as all as skillful as she had found Robert, from what she could remember of their many happy unions. But what she really wanted to tell Ernestine (having no one else to tell) was how lonely she was in Dresden, fourteen years old and all alone in cold, old Dresden, to which she was condemned to return immediately after her final concert, and how she loved Robert more than Ernestine ever could, because she had loved him for what seemed her whole life and knew him better than Ernestine would if Ernestine were to spend her whole life trying to love him as much as Clara did.

Clara tried to picture saying as much to Robert, but it was too difficult even to envision such a scene, out of fear not of her own words but of his. When he had finally written to her in Dresden, he had called Ernestine "the shining jewel whom it is impossible to overestimate," which at the moment she read it brought to mind a precious stone of such proportions that it tore off the finger upon which it had been slipped. This image of mutilation caused her to think of Robert's injured finger and his music lost to the world. Tears fell from her eyes upon his letter as she saw him taken from her by another woman and destroyed by his own hand.

In person he seemed, except with her, perfectly content. He shadowed

---

*These would immortalize the otherwise lamentable Baron von Fricken by providing Schumann the melody of the theme of his Symphonic Etudes.

Ernestine and inquired constantly after her welfare, saying such things as, "How is my little Estrella?" which, whether it was his nickname for all of Ernestine or for a particular part of her body, Clara detested. And Ernestine, if Robert happened to be out, would stand by the window watching for him to appear in view, or as soon as he had left would rush to her room to change into yet another outfit, in which she would appear and only then address Clara, soliciting opinions about the bunch of her dress or the tilt of her shoe or the beribboning of her hair or the pronouncement of her bosom, all of which made Clara want to scream at this betrayal by someone she had been foolish enough to imagine might become her friend.

Clara was in her room practicing Chopin's E-flat Rondo when there was somewhere in the house beneath her a commotion so resonant that her playing was interrupted and her curiosity overwhelmed. She rushed from her room, nearly stepping upon her cats where they stretched out in the usual place and positions they occupied when she was at the piano. Then she ran down the stairs to the ground floor, all the while over the sound of her own breath hearing a kind of multivoiced fugue of accusation, recrimination, explanation, outrage, and woe.

She came upon a large gathering just inside the front door, which was open to the street, on which there was a carriage with its door held wide by the coachman, who appeared nearly bug-eyed at the extravagant words that gushed from this otherwise decorous, even solemn house.

"But I *am* a virgin!" Ernestine proclaimed, her head tilted back so it was impossible for Clara to tell to whom she was addressing this ridiculous falsehood.

"All the more reason for me to take you home," said her father, the baron.

"Do you mean if she were not a virgin, you would allow her to remain?" asked Robert ingenuously.

"Not a virgin!" Clara's father uttered these words with an incredulousness so sudden and profound that Clara felt compromised in her own sad innocence.

"If she were not a virgin, I would cut her off," the baron pronounced.

"Cut her off?" Robert shook his head as if to deny the very possibility, even as he wondered exactly what the baron meant: cut her off from her fortune, or, as he pictured it, dissever her from this very earth to have her float away forever.

"Cut her off." The baron chopped the air with his hand. "And, yes, I would leave her here, for I should certainly not allow her back into my home."

Ernestine reached out and grasped Robert's sleeve. "You see, Robert, he will leave me here if—"

"The only leaving," Robert hurriedly interrupted her, "is your father's leaving you no choice but to go with him."

Again tilting her head back, Ernestine cried out, "But I am not—"

"A virgin." Now it was Henriette Voigt who interrupted the poor girl's apparent willingness to sacrifice her fortune for her love, addressing herself to the baron. "A virgin," she repeated, "is the only sort of young woman I will allow into my home. And, as you know, Baron, your daughter and Herr Schumann have spent many happy and innocent hours chaperoned by none other than myself in my home, listening to me play the piano, the poor things, and educating themselves about art through a continuous viewing of my husband's fine collection of paintings and *objets*."

"And in my believing this, you are not making of me myself an *objet de risée*?" the baron asked her.

"Do you observe me laughing at you, kind sir?" Henriette asked him.

"Not all laughter issues from the mouth," observed the baron.

"I see you are a philosopher as well as a father who cares for nothing so much as the good reputation of his daughter." Henriette did not accompany such ambiguous flattery with her usual laughter, which had not been much in evidence, Clara had noticed, since she had begun to spend so much of her time with Robert's friend Ludwig, whom even now she kept by her side through the clutching of his hand and the continual observation of his gaunt but comely face. It was like some kind of hopeless love, in the face of both death and marriage, and brought to Clara an admiration of Henriette she had not felt before, to say nothing of the fact that it left her no longer jealous of Henriette for the passion she had so clearly inspired in Robert.

Ludwig Schunke had taken Henriette away. Now Baron von Fricken was taking Ernestine away. Clara didn't care that the whole world might be emptied if that was what was necessary for her and Robert to be left standing together.

"You have convinced me, Madame," said the baron to Henriette, "that my daughter is whole." He held out his arm to Ernestine. "Come, my child. Let us go home. You will be safe there. And those who love you will know where to find you."

The next moment, Ernestine was gone. Robert appeared lost. He stood in the open doorway watching the carriage disappear around the corner, holding his arms out before him, as if he had recently been carrying a huge bolt of fabric or a woman had been torn from his embrace.

Clara edged closer to him. Ludwig put a hand on his shoulder. Henriette held Ludwig's other arm with both her hands. Clara let her sleeve touch Robert's. Now they were like two couples, two ordinary couples, two tragic couples, standing at an open door in the late-summer sun, pondering the approach of evening, each with its secrets, nothing need be said, their love forbidden and all the more intense for that.

How nice it would be to walk out the door and stroll through town, deciding where to eat and what to drink. Or to stay at home, and talk, and she could sing to them the songs that Johann Miksch had taught her in Dresden, to which she now would not return, not ever, not with Ernestine away; for why else had her father exiled her if not to keep her from stealing Robert's heart, unless it was to keep Robert from stealing hers (so little did her father know that it had long ago left her sole possession)?

"Won't you stay for supper?" Clara asked Henriette and Ludwig. "I shall make soup and meat if we have any and Robert's favorite potatoes, with butter and pepper, and—"

"I can eat nothing," said Robert.

"You may refuse to make love to a woman," said Henriette. "But you must never refuse her cooking."

"Do you imagine Ernestine is a good cook?" asked Robert.

"Oh, no," said Clara.

"Oh, yes," said Henriette.

"What about you?" Robert asked Ludwig.

"You know very well I can't cook," said Ludwig.

Henriette laughed.

"That's not what I meant," said Robert.

"Of course it's not." Ludwig quite enjoyed his little joke and how it had restored the spirit of his ruthful lover. "But why do you inquire after her ability to cook? She is beautiful. She is rich. And if you marry her she will never cook a single meal for you as long as you live!"

"Thank goodness," said Robert.

"Why do you say that?" asked Henriette, who in her matchmaking had learned that it was as important to recommend to men a woman's ability to cook as it was to recommend to women a man's ability to make love.

"Because she's a terrible cook," answered Robert.

"Did she cook for you?" Clara asked before she could stop herself.

"Why did you ask if we thought she might be a good cook?" said Ludwig at the same time.

"I was hoping for evidence to the contrary of my own experience," Robert answered him.

"She *did* cook for you!" Clara no longer cared if she showed her outrage.

"Fish," said Robert.

Ludwig looked as if he might become even more ill.

"Judge no woman by her fish," said Henriette authoritatively.

"I shall make fish for our supper," said Clara, who had thus far limited her cooking for Robert to the soup she had promised him in the note with which she had accompanied the tie from Paris what seemed so many years ago when she had been a child.

"Oh, but we cannot stay," said Henriette. "Ludwig and I are having supper at my home."

"Where is your husband?" asked Clara.

"Karl is away at the Vatican," said Henriette. "But a word of advice, my dear child: A woman may dine alone with a man, and dessert will remain merely dessert."

"What could you possibly mean by that?" asked Clara, who knew the power innocence held over sophistication.

Wisely, Henriette declined to answer. She said her good-byes and gathered Ludwig unto her, a frail man whose footsteps had grown abbreviated against the weakness in his breath and whose spirit had grown more generous within the foreshortened confines of his life. He went with her because she loved him, and he knew enough to know that this would feed the only hunger he had left. Yet he looked back longingly at Robert and Clara, like someone who wishes he could be in two places at once and would willingly die to effect such fission.

Clara was amused to think she might have driven them away with the threat of her cooking. And she was overjoyed to be alone with Robert. It had been so long. All she could recall was their playing Chopin together and meeting over St. Nicholas's Church. But that had been in spirit only, satisfactory enough at the time but no substitute for the man himself, bedraggled as he was, sad in the eye over the departure of his love, bewildered and cautious and withdrawn, which rendered him all the more precious for being all the less stable. She would put him back together and hold him together. She would cook him fish for dinner and pancakes for breakfast. She would never again leave his side.

"Look," he said.

Automatically, she closed her eyes, as she had done when she was a child and "look" meant "don't look," for he'd be hiding something with which to surprise her and her little brothers.

"Which hand?" she said to show him she remembered.

"You know me too well"—and finally there was mirth in his voice.

She opened her eyes and saw in the open palm of his injured hand a ring, diamond solitaire with three stone shoulders bearing the weight of her world come crashing down. It was not for her. His eyes were not giving it to her, and such events did not happen in the world anyway.

"We have agreed to marry," he said. "We have told no one."

"Why?" Hearing herself say it, she thought it the coldest of words.

"Because I need a wife. Don't laugh at me, Clara—she was prescribed by Dr. Reuter."

Clara did laugh, but not at Robert and his mad doctors. "I didn't mean why are you getting married. I meant why are you telling no one?"

"Because I haven't given her this ring, of course. Had I given her the ring, she would wear it, and then everyone would know."

"And why haven't you given her the ring?"

"She knows nothing of the ring."

"I don't think she need know of it to appreciate its sudden bestowal upon herself. I am told it is a surprise that does not make the hair of most young women stand on end."

He took her hand with the one not holding the ring. "I promise to tell you, and you alone, if her hair does stand on end."

"You will give it to her then?"

"I shall follow her to Asch."

His hand closed around the ring. But Clara could still see it, slipped upon Ernestine's long and slender finger, a shining jewel that tore the finger from the hand.

Leipzig

DECEMBER 4, 1834
I would rather lose all my friends together than this one.
Robert Schumann

With the approval of her husband, Karl, who had observed his wife rescued from the frivolity of her obsession with the coupling of other men and women (for which, in part, he blamed himself), Henriette Voigt moved Ludwig Schunke into their home. It was not so they might dally together, especially with so little left to Ludwig of what it is one dallies away: time. It was to provide Ludwig with a place to die.

He might have died in the room in which he lived one room away from Robert's room, or in that empty room between them upon the Turkish rug that had received the body of his best friend's father. But he did not want to die alone, and to die with Robert was to die alone, because Robert, who could attend life with the utmost dedication and a silent reserve that gave the impression of being of eternal comfort, could not abide death. He could not speak of it, address it, witness it, share its habitat, or clean up after it, and though he could think of it (indeed, could not avoid thinking of it), these thoughts made him want to flee not only the present field of death but the very mind that formed them.

Robert had been paying one of his periodic visits to his fiancée, Ernestine, in Asch, when Schunke had begun to hemorrhage. Fortunately, Henriette had been with him in his room on the Burgstrasse, as she was with him almost every day. She sent for Dr. Reuter while she held towels to the sides of Ludwig's face as he coughed the blood from his mouth. She felt it warm the towels and soak her hands and advance up the thin sleeves of her dress like the fingertips of some distracted paramour.

By the time Robert had returned to Leipzig, Ludwig had been moved to the room in the Voigt house in which Robert had lain half-undressed with Ernestine.

When Robert visited him there, he found Ludwig using the prayer rug as a blanket.

"Are you cold?" he asked, for the approach of winter had sucked the winds in from the mountains.

Ludwig shook his head and smiled. "Flying carpet," he whispered in a voice that was slowly returning to the silence Robert both feared and envied. He had discovered that the more music he wrote, the less inclined he was to speak, unless he had been drinking, in which case he might prattle on interminably until the increasing volume of the music in his head drowned out the sound of his words and sent him scurrying off to write down the notes. He sometimes felt that music resented language and did everything possible to annihilate it. Given music's greater precision, beauty, and expressiveness, Robert thought it would be the other way around. But language paid its humble respects to music by struggling valiantly yet futilely to describe it, the equivalent of trying to sing about mathematics. Music, in the meantime, obliterated words, thoughts, meaning itself. It rolled through one's blood and brain with an ecstatic pitilessness.

Robert touched the rug, massaging with his fingertips a small, threadbare patch where someone's knees had worn away the color, or perhaps a chair had sat for years and shifted with the restless weight of time upon the body of a man who read himself to death.

"Have you not flown far enough already?" he asked.

"I'm better off here." Ludwig grasped Robert's hand as if to disenact his defection.

Robert nodded. "You must promise to return to me when you are better."

Ludwig smiled. "I shall fly to you upon this very rug."

"Beware the lightning."

"A flash for us." Ludwig gazed upward, as he had the summer night four months ago, when they were walking arm in arm beneath the beautiful forebodings of a storm, and there was a sudden flare of lightning, illuminating Ludwig's splendid face, and he whispered then what he had now: "A flash for us."

Robert pressed their clasped hands against Ludwig's flesh beneath the rug. "You seem light enough."

"Not as light as soon I'll be."

"The lighter you get, the heavier is my heart."

Tears came to Ludwig's eyes. "Will you remember me?"

Robert shook his head. "I need not bother to remember whom I can never forget."

He could bear no more. He took back his hand and used it to find his hat in the pocket of his coat. He wished to put it, instead of on his head, over the face of Ludwig. Instead, he bent to kiss him. It was the most frightful kind of kiss he could imagine. It was Judas kissing Jonathan.

Ludwig whispered, "Will you come back to see me?"

"I cannot speak," said Robert, leaving.

He found Henriette approaching Ludwig's door.

"Where are you going?" she asked.

"To Asch."

"Did you not just come from there?"

"No. From there." He pointed back at the door.

"You cannot bear to be away from Ernestine?"

"I cannot bear to be here."

"But all your friends are here. She is merely your betrothed." Henriette smiled. "What pleasure is there in the chase once the quarry's on her knees?"

"You're my only friend here, Henriette. The magazine is all business now. Knorr is a maniac. And the Wiecks are gone for months, to the north, I understand."

"To keep her far from you," she said. "He makes a match."

"Wieck?"

"Clara and Karl Banck. A good match, wouldn't you say?"

"He has a fine voice."

"I've never yet met a woman who measures a man by his voice." Henriette laughed at her little joke.

"You seem in strangely fine spirits."

"I'm at peace," she said. "He will die soon."

"Doesn't that make you sad?"

"It makes me inconsolably sad. But I've never been sad before. He's opened me up like a flower to the moon."

"Flowers don't open to the moon."

"I'm not a flower. I'm a woman. The moon makes me bleed."

"I've bled enough." Robert hoisted his coat over his shoulders. "For God's sake, don't write me when he dies."

She put her arms around him and pulled him to her. His coat fell to the floor. He could feel her as he'd dreamed so many times of feeling her, pressed into him. But she was light. Light like Ludwig. It was as if the two of them, Henriette and Ludwig, had been absorbed into one another and were disappearing from the earth together.

Releasing him, she opened the door to Ludwig's room and stepped inside. Robert stood at the closed door for some time but heard nothing.

Magdeburg

DECEMBER 4, 1834
Two men are fighting over me.
Clara Wieck

When she had played in Brunswick, Clara might have fallen in love with any of the four Müller brothers—Ferdinand, Theodor, August, or Franz— who formed (she told them the name was tedious) the Müller String Quartet. But it was Ferdinand who had fallen in love with her, much to her father's delight, not that he favored Ferdinand over any of his brothers or, for that matter, over Karl Banck. Karl had joined up with them here not only as her itinerant voice teacher, not only as a native Magdeburger, but in particular as her escort and her potential lover, which was to say, from her father's point of view, potential husband. It was as inconceivable to her father as it was not only conceivable but inevitable to Clara that she take a lover, and take him in the full sense of the term, the sooner the better, if only she could manage to choose one and then find some way to disappear with him (not easy when you were famous) into whatever sort of dark and private room lovers disappear into to do whatever lovers do.

Her father was happy that one of the Müllers—it didn't matter which— had fallen in love with her because it allowed him to reduce their usual ap-

pearance fee down to nothing, zero, what Robert would have called an absolute cipher of recompense.

Clara had not been present when her father conducted these negotiations.
But since all four brothers had agreed to it, she could not help imagining that
he had pledged her to all four of them. Otherwise, would not the other three
have protested the bartering of their time and talent—and they were one
of the most renowned string quartets in Germany—for so paltry a reward,
unless, of course, her father had actually offered her *body* to them. But that
was inconceivable. Not unimaginable. Merely inconceivable. Unless all four
of them were in love with her. But whether they were or not, it had been Ferdinand, the cellist (oh, well), who had followed her to Magdeburg.

She had been more taken with the first violinist who gave his name to the
equally renowned Karl Möser Quartet in Berlin. But if Karl Möser was in
love with her, his love had surely been diminished if not completely devas-
tated by her father's insistence that *his* quartet play free because the *Müller*
Quartet had played free in Brunswick. Karl Möser's refusal, as evidence he
did not truly, wholly love her, tempered Clara's love for him, though when
he finally agreed to allow the quartet to play for fifteen free tickets to the
concert in lieu of money, she found her love for him grow stronger than
ever, particularly when he graciously explained, as if to pique her father, that
fifteen such tickets were worth more than the quartet's usual fee anyway because all of Berlin wanted to hear the young genius, Clara Wieck. She was
convinced such overpraise of herself was evidence of his love for her—did
not doting husbands even proclaim their ugly wives beautiful? But whatever
love he may have felt was surely destroyed forever when her father said,
"It's no secret you're a Jew, Herr Möser, and even were it a secret, it would
be a secret no longer after your disgraceful insistence that you be given tickets to a concert in which you are performing yourself. We don't need you.
We have our own quartet—no Jews allowed." Of course they didn't have
their own quartet. Or if they did, it was named the Clara Wieck Quartet, and
it consisted of Clara Wieck, not on the violin, not on the viola, not on the
cello, but alone on the piano, doubled not once but doubled twice, four of
her that did not exist and only one of her that did, and it was that one who
had to play alone in Berlin and fill the entire musical program by herself, all
because a violinist didn't love her enough to play free.

But wasn't it nice that a cellist loved her enough not only to play for
nothing but to travel to Magdeburg on the Elbe, equidistant between the
man she loved in Leipzig and the man who didn't love her in Berlin, and
straight into the lap of the man who did love her in Magdeburg; Karl Banck
himself, so blond, so suave, so handsome, so much the tight German tenor

that when Ferdinand Müller met him, Ferdinand Müller seemed about to turn right around and go back to Brunswick when Clara said, "Your being here is a dream come true."

She didn't mean she had dreamed of his coming, or had dreamed of him at all. What she had dreamed of was that there would be two men in one place who would be in love with her, it didn't really matter who they were (unless she happened to be in love with one or both of them, which she was not).

But Ferdinand Müller didn't know this. He knew only what he wanted to know, heard only what he wanted to hear. Thus, far from turning around and going back to Brunswick, he attached himself to one side of Clara with just as much tenacity and devotion as Karl Banck attached himself to the other.

So it was that the three of them—absent even Papa for once, who seemed to believe that a girl with two men could get in no more than half the trouble she could get in with one—went everywhere together, Clara on one arm of each, while with their other arms the two of them might have pulverized one another had they not been such polite artists that instead they vied for her favors with candy and fanfaronade and flattery.

They took her to dinner and competed over who could spread her Leberpastete most thickly on a triangle of black bread and who might most elegantly place upon her bottom lip the most scrumptious dab of marzipan from the tip of a tiny fork.

They danced with her, first one, then the other. Enjoying neither of them fully when his hand cupped her waist and his other hand her hand, she dreamed of dancing with the two of them at once, one arm around the neck of each, perhaps on the top of a table with her dress flying high and her petticoats flown off and her hair for once as loose as when she went to sleep.

They attempted kisses, not always unsuccessfully and fortunately not together. Once she had yielded a single kiss to each of them, she got more pleasure from observing their attempts to maneuver her into privacy than from the kisses themselves. Having kissed you, men seemed to want to set their seal upon the deed, make a contract, sign a pact: Kiss them again, whenever they might desire; kiss no one else and at the same time praise their kisses above all others'; understand the kiss as prelude rather than as coda, the first step toward the body there below, as if a woman were a mountain to be climbed from the top down. But as interested as she was in making love, she was not interested in making love with either of these men and therefore found it curious how the desire for the act itself could be so wholly separated from the man attempting it. Men were not the same, she suspected: The act supersedes the actors, so a man might touch a woman whom his eyes had otherwise rejected, devour her for whom he had no taste.

Which is not to say she didn't care for either of them. Karl had a lovely voice; Ferdinand drew great sweetness from his cello. Karl was so handsome that he took her breath away (but, alas, did not replace it with any air of passion); Ferdinand was homely, gawky, and like many cellists moved his body tentatively, yet he brought out more arousal in her, perhaps because he wore a mustache and it warmed his face and thus her eyes. Karl protected her from everyone but himself; Ferdinand the same.

Before and after each of her concerts they stood beside her like guards hired by her father, who was therefore free to circulate among the crowd, passing out her picture, seeking out engagements, negotiating on their joint behalf. Karl and Ferdinand appeared to take some sustenance from this proximity to her and to her fame. Self-conscious with reflected pride, they held their chins high, cast their glances toward the ceilings of whatever bedizened room they happened to be in, as if it were beneath them actually to look at the people who were looking at Clara so fervently, and left her to answer the questions that were not so ridiculous that Karl and Ferdinand didn't wish these same questions might be asked of them one day.

Immediately before her final appearance in Magdeburg, at which she would play Chopin's E-Minor Concerto—the same piece she had heard Chopin himself play at Abbé Bertin's in Paris—Clara attended a small party. As was customary at such functions, she found the town's leading citizens, and as many of their children as they could manage to convince to dress up for the occasion, pressing in upon her from all sides. She did not like to take hold of the arms of Karl and Ferdinand under such public circumstances, as much to avoid the inevitable gossip as to maintain the image of her growing independence. But every once in a while she moved her own arms out to the sides just to assure herself of their near presence, as she talked to these people and tried to tell them what they asked of her.

"How old are you?"

"Fifteen."

"How old were you when you began to play the piano?"

"Five."

"Do you still practice?"

"Yes."

"How much?"

"More than I should and less than I like."

"Do your fingers ever hurt?"

"Only when I don't play enough."

"What do you think about when you play?"

"Nothing."

"Does your mind wander?"

"Sometimes my thoughts do, but my mind, never."

"Do you ever make mistakes when you're playing?"

"All the time."

"Wrong notes?"

"Never wrong notes."

"Who is your favorite composer?"

"Robert Schumann."

"Who is that?"

"My favorite composer."

"What is your most private thought?"

"I have no privacy."

"What is it like to be famous?"

"Like this."

"Will you sign my program?"

"If you like."

"Do you have a pen?"

"Karl," she said. "Ferdinand."

Each produced for her a pen.

It was as if the pens were magic lamps, drawing to them, and so to her, everyone in the room. Program after program was thrust into her hands, and she signed each, Clara Wieck, Clara Wieck, Clara Wieck. She noticed now, as she always did when in the midst of this ritual, that people would touch her hand as they gave her their programs and as they retrieved them. But whatever they got from touching her—whatever joy, whatever strength, whatever confirmation—she never got from touching herself.

"I must play now," she said.

"Are you nervous?" asked a girl who was about her own age.

"My heart won't stop beating," she answered.

It was during the finale of the Chopin that the keys began to stick on the square piano recently imported from Alpheus Babcock of Boston, Massachusetts, with whose boldly stamped name Clara's father became infuriatingly intimate when, in the intermission, he found himself virtually embracing the piano as he struggled to remove the keyboard, which, in full sight of the audience—most of whom had remained behind in the hall to watch him as if he were some sort of mad laborer dressed in velvet with a starched collar that threatened to emasculate his sideburns—he massaged and plucked back into suppleness. He came off the stage dripping with perspiration and muttering about foreign pianos and the income he had lost by not having put laborer's wages into their contract.

Knowing no one else could soothe him, Clara told Karl and Ferdinand to remain where they were and took her father aside. "Thank you so much for fixing my piano, Papa. Only you could have done it. You are not only an artist but also a veritable Hercules. I thought you were going to lift that entire piano above your head and smash it to the stage."

"Next time I shall," he averred.

Next time, alas, arrived more quickly than either had anticipated. Soon after the interval, when Clara had returned and was playing the kind of staccato variations that were guaranteed to make audiences experience a pianist's fingers tapping upon their very scalps, not only did the keys begin to stick again but the damper as well, so that her father was forced to return to the stage and in the very midst of her playing stick his velveted derrière toward the paying customers and push the damper down by hand, time after time after time, a hundred times at least, while Clara tapped on and experienced the strange sensation that she was playing her father instead of the piano, that he was her instrument, doing her will, and she whispered as she nodded her head so he might know exactly when to dampen and be encouraged at the same time to continue to dampen, "Oh, good! Oh, good! Oh, good!"

The ovation she received at the end of the piece was the most tumultuous she could remember in all her life. She would not let her father leave the stage but took his hand in hers and pulled him down to join her bows until the two of them rose and fell together and the petals of some flowers somehow brought to life on this December day and thrown at them in celebration settled in their hair.

"Is this not wonderful?" she said to him.

"What is wonderful is you," he answered.

That evening, Ferdinand Müller was required to return to Brunswick, where his best cello and his brothers awaited him. Having kissed him several times previously, Clara found herself unable to kiss him good-bye. She could not understand this in herself but felt it right nonetheless that she withhold her lips and hoped her gloved hand in his bare hand would prove sufficient to inform him that their love affair was done.

Once Ferdinand was gone, her affection for Karl Banck she discovered was not doubled but halved at least, if not entirely diminished. This she could not understand either. Neither could she kiss him, though he seemed to be going nowhere.

Asch

DECEMBER 7, 1834
*He wrote that I should save myself while I was able,
since he ruined everything he touched.*
Ernestine von Fricken

At the moment of Ludwig Schunke's death, Robert felt he was dying himself; not because of the demise of his best friend, of which he was not yet aware, having escaped from the jaws of death in Leipzig to the arms of his affianced in Asch, but because that very same affianced was telling him something that he knew, even as the words were struggling to find their reluctant way out of her kiss-weary mouth, would change his life forever.

As for Ludwig, he did not die alone, as Robert would one day. He was attended by Dr. Reuter and by Henriette Voigt and by Karl Voigt as well, whose presence should be of no surprise since he too had come to love Ludwig Schunke, not so much for himself as for the quiet fervor he had inspired in Henriette. It is a generous man who will rejoice in his wife's love for another and a wise man who will let the passion of this love profit himself. Henriette had become, to put it discreetly, considerably more invigorated with the arrival of Ludwig into her life. Passion, like paint, may seep with benefit into its surroundings. Karl could only imagine to what sublimity of yearning she would be inspired by Ludwig's actual departure. Indeed, so involved had Karl become in preparing Ludwig for the most appropriate journey from this world into the total absence of a next that he had hung upon the walls of the poor man's bare little room such inspiring illustrations as Johann Serge's depicting the embrace of Venus and Anchises and Henry Fuseli's *Wolfram Looking at His Wife, Whom He Has Imprisoned with the Corpse of Her Lover,* which perplexed Ludwig in the haze that a consumptive death breathes over the mind to the extent that he sometimes lay in bed staring at the picture trying to determine whether the Wolfram in question might be Wolfram von Eschenbach, whose great hero, Parzival, was not unlike Herr Voigt in that the latter never once mentioned Ludwig's illness, or perhaps a cruel parody of Saint Wulfram, whose life's work consisted of a vain attempt to end human sacrifice—precisely what Ludwig felt himself to have become.

It was a sacrifice he was prepared to make. His body was no longer in its customary balance between pleasure and pain; when all you're left with is the taste of blood and all you desire is the hardly ambrosial taste of air, the glorious sensuousness of existence is liquidated. As for his mind, it was confused where it should have been emancipated. He had come to Leipzig an infected but free itinerant musician, happiest at the piano like any other vain and lonely man. But he was leaving Leipzig, and the world, both loved and loving, as throttled by the threads of human entanglement as by his disease.

Dr. Reuter approached him with yet another spoonful of calomel, which heretofore had prompted him to empty only his bladder, not his lungs, though it did manage to produce such vast quantities of spit that his gums had stopped aching and his bedclothes had been stained pink from the blood-soused runoff. The doctor appeared even smaller than he had before, as he closed in upon himself with death's approach to one of his patients, shrunken in the sight of God at his failure to prolong a life that God begat.

Ludwig shook his head. "No more." His voice sounded even to himself as if it had traveled from afar to reach his throat.

Dr. Reuter, like all doctors, considered himself immune to the refusal of medication, so he allowed the spoon to continue on its journey to the blood-rouged lips, only to find there the back of Frau Voigt's hand, the bones of which, he noticed, were plicated like the joints of a fan, quite sensuous and causing him the unwelcome arousal he experienced whenever he stared at the hand of a woman.

"No more," she repeated Herr Schunke's words.

"But...," said Dr. Reuter, neither advancing nor withdrawing the spoon. "But...," he said again.

But what? It was a terrible word. It was all that medicine was, in the end: but. But we suffer. But we die. But the doctor loses all his patients but for those he leaves behind when he but dies himself.

He turned the spoon around and thrust it in his mouth and drank the calomel himself.

"Good God!" said Herr Voigt. "Why did you do that?"

"It's quite dreadful," he said, "isn't it?"

Henriette could feel Ludwig's breath upon her palm, with no more force than if wafted by an eyelash. His lips were pink and full, in contrast to the pallid gauntness of his face. She longed to kiss him. She had always longed to kiss him, from the moment he had appeared at her door in what would be exactly one-half year ago tomorrow. But there had been no kisses. He was, she thought, in love with Robert, who was in love with her, of course, which made him, Ludwig, all the more desirable, for Robert also was forbidden to her. But kisses were a husband's, and hers of late had been of a heat and frequency she had not known before with Karl, who in turn was aroused to such a pitch and yet such great endurance that she sometimes felt as Ludwig looked, wasted and serene. Why, then, did she feel she was married to Ludwig and no longer to her husband? She was possessed by both of them, but to only one of them did she belong. She might never lie with Ludwig, but he had entered her and lived within her so deeply and completely that as long as she might live, so would he.

He watched her hand before his eyes. If only she would lower it upon his face, grasp his suffocation and in so doing provide it. But no, she took her hand away, carried it quite beyond the field of his diminished vision, the world obscured and growing dim. He raised his head to follow it, her hand, and when he did he felt his lungs explode and blood come spraying through his teeth.

Dr. Reuter wiped away the blood, secretly clenching his nose against a smell he knew existed only in his imagination and yet a smell that quite upset his tummy. Then, with his giant physician's handkerchief between his hand and his patient's skin, he felt for the pulse in the neck.

"Dead," he pronounced.

Karl Voigt immediately put his arm around his wife's waist for comfort, but she left his embrace even as he closed his hand around the sweet flesh where her waist joined her hip. She approached Ludwig on his bed and bent over him and lowered her face to his and placed her mouth over his and opened his lips with her lips and held her breath so she might feel as he felt, floating off to Paradise. But he could feel nothing, which was a feeling in itself and one so pleasant that he fought against it for its vacancy. In the moment of his death—for, truly, he died now—he felt his spirit yield to her as he disappeared into her mind.

Robert was sitting with Ernestine upon his favorite of all the baron's canapés, a great velvety expanse of Louis XVI giltwood whose oval backrest forced the two of them thigh to thigh. Had they separated even modestly, the twisted ribbon carved into the backrest would have massaged their spines quite irritatingly. Had they sat wholly separated, at either end of the canapé, the acanthus leaves sprouting off the armrests might very well have drawn blood. As it was, they were not particularly comfortable. But it was not comfort that inspired Robert's admiration for this rosette-elevated monstrosity. It was the rarity of the piece, its almost stifling self-centeredness, as it sat growing increasingly ill at ease within a baronial home that seemed gradually to fill with the latest examples of the new Biedermeier style, from pedestals to beds to secretaires, as if the baron felt he might impress his prospective son-in-law, whose music was so modern, with furniture he imagined to be the same. But the baron missed the point: Biedermeier was furniture for the masses, and Robert's music emerged from him in forms and rhythms that appeared to irritate nearly everyone who heard it. Much as this canapé went unsat upon, for all its value and insolent beauty.

It was his and Ernestine's favorite place to huddle, at least publicly, thigh to thigh, often holding hands, her left in his right, so that the ring he had given her, when she clenched him tightly, dug into the finger he had injured when he had attempted either to destroy or enhance his career as a pianist, he still didn't know which, though he knew the happy outcome: He lived for one musical purpose only, and that was to write it.

When he had given her the ring, as soon after her hasty departure from Leipzig as he could catch her, she had almost fainted with delight. The engagement they had hidden — much as they had hidden their gradual explorations of one another's flesh, which by then had progressed to that part of the body bordered by the navel in the north and what Ernestine liked to call Robert's dudelsack in the south — could be secret no longer, not with her diamond putting out, as was every girl's design, the eyes of any other girl who might look at it too closely.

But while she had exulted over the sudden appearance of the ring, with tears in her eyes and passionately short-winded breaths in her throat, he seemed intent on something either just over her head or perhaps having simultaneously landed upon it. She wanted him to look into her eyes, with tears in his own, and then to embrace her to seal this moment with the hot wax of their impending matrimony, but he observed her not like her husband-to-be and thus her inevitable deflowerer but like a hairdresser!

As he wrote that evening to Clara Wieck:

Ernestine's hair did indeed stand on end. The moment I gave her the ring, each golden tress rose from off her neck and ears and forehead like an *hommage* to marriage itself, so that soon she stood before me looking as if she'd seen a ghost, yours truly, I fear, who am of course your very own favorite ghost, should you recall the evenings of your childhood when I would haunt your room.

In truth, Ernestine's hair remained as placid as her heart did not. But even in her excitement, the first words she said to Robert upon her possession of his ring were, "Is there something the matter with my hair?"

He laughed and said, "It is risen," which made her laugh too, because that phrase was their private code for quite another part of the body, not hers but his. She had no idea what this had to do with her hair, or why he might have spoken in code since there were no other people present at this moment when he had given her the ring, but she was delighted to learn she was not alone in her arousal.

Her father was the first to see the ring, after herself. While he was delighted with her delight and even more with this solid evidence that Herr Schumann was dallying with his daughter for a purpose more serious than the liberties the baron was convinced he had taken with her, his pleasure was balanced by a certain gravity that darkened his smiles and caused him to say to her at the first opportunity, "You must tell him the truth."

It was the truth that Ernestine, after several weeks of enjoying the ring with the truth still withheld, was finally prepared (after many horrid rehearsals before her mirror and upon paper at night when she could not sleep for fear of what the truth might do) to tell Robert as they sat thigh to thigh upon the baron's canapé.

"I am not," she said, "who you think I am."

"Thank goodness," said Robert.

"'Thank goodness'! What is that supposed to mean? Do you not think highly of me?"

He squeezed her hand to reassure her and to punish himself for having said the first thing that had come into his mind. Her ring dug agonizingly into his bad finger.

"Quite the opposite," he equivocated. "I think so highly of you that I have longed for you not to be who I think you are, for I want nothing so much as to be worthy of you, and I could never be worthy of who I think you are." He pressed his leg against hers. There was nothing quite so distractingly sensuous as pressure upon the leg. It was like riding a horse. "So who are you, my sweet?"

"It is who I am not that I am here to discuss."

"Who you are not? My goodness, that's a metaphysical subject of the first order. Think of who *I* am not. I'm not Schubert, alas. I'm not Frédéric Chopin. I'm not Shakespeare or Hoffmann. I am not, as the saying goes, myself sometimes. By which I mean, sometimes I feel I've lost my mind. And when the mind is lost, its possessor is, ipso facto, not who he is."

"I have not lost my mind," said Ernestine patiently. "Only my heart," she added tenderly and increased the pressure of her thigh against his. "And my fortune," she added further.

"And your fortune...what? You have given me your heart, dear Ernestine. There is no need for you to give me your fortune. It is something for us merely to share, as husband and wife."

She turned toward him and grasped both his hands. "I would not share my fortune with you but give it to you, wholly and without redress, if I but had a fortune to give."

"But you do," he said.

"If my fortune is myself, then I give it to you." She placed his hand over one of her breasts. "And what I have not yet given, I will give tonight, if you so desire."

"I so desire, but I do not so choose. We must wait until we're wed." In the spirit of his reply, Robert removed his hand.

"Has any man ever been so kind and so cruel at once?"

"I have no idea," said Robert.

"I did not mean for you to answer that question," explained Ernestine.

"Then perhaps you will answer one of mine: When you said, 'If my fortune is myself, then I give it to you,' what exactly did you mean?"

"I meant that my fortune *is* myself."

"Well, of course your fortune is yourself, for you are a fortune. But when you said, 'If I but had a fortune to give,' what did you mean by *that*?"

"I meant what I said: that I would give it to you, wholly and without—"

"Am I losing my mind?" he asked.

"Are you not who you are?" She referred back to what he had said earlier, quite delighted to be able to show him how attentive she was not only to his many silences but to the daunting challenge that his speech, like his frequent silences, often presented to her.

"We are not here to discuss who *I* am not, if I recall, but specifically who *you* are not."

"Who I am not?" she pondered. "I am not the princesse de Clèves, alas. I am not George Sand. I am not—"

"You're making fun of me." It made him adore her, for the first time, truly. "It's not like you," he said.

"Oh, but it is." She put her head on his shoulder. The smell of him was in its customary sublime balance, half man, half cigar. "Remember, I am not who you think I am."

"Whoever you may be," he said, "I am fortunate to have you."

She laughed. "I love your play on words. You are so good with words. You should use them more often."

"The more I love music, the more I distrust words," he said. "There's a perfect example, for I made no play on words."

"But you did." She raised her head and looked at his lips. "You used the word 'fortunate' to describe yourself for having me, right after I had just told you that I have lost my fortune."

"You have lost your fortune? You never said you lost your fortune."

"I most certainly did."

"What do you mean, you lost your fortune?" He looked at her from top to bottom. "You could not possibly mean..." He looked at her from bottom to top. "Wait! Oh, wait, dear Ernestine! Now I understand! Your fortune is yourself. You said it yourself. Your fortune is yourself. And you have lost your fortune. That can mean only one thing: You have given yourself to another man!"

"Don't be ridiculous."

"'Don't be ridiculous' is what people say in response to an accusation they cannot deny. Now I understand the convoluted hesitance of your confession. You are not a virgin. You might have done me the courtesy of simply stating as much in the beginning."

She brought her fists down upon his thighs. "But I *am* a virgin. I have always been a virgin."

"As distinguished from a virgin who has not always been one?" he inquired calmly.

Tears came to her eyes. She seemed utterly defeated, this in itself upon so passionate a woman a mark of provocation. "I am merely a poor virgin."

"'Poor?'" he repeated. "But is not your virtue your fortune? You said as much yourself, and if indeed you retain your virtue, as you claim to, then you could never describe yourself as a 'poor virgin,' could you?"

She pulled her hands out from under his and wiped away her tears with her sleeves and looked him directly in the eye and said, "I have no money."

"You needn't bribe me," he said.

"I am a bastard," she said.

He laughed. "A harlot, maybe, but not—"

"I am not Ernestine von Fricken."

"Who are you?" He laughed again. "George Sand?"

"I will tell you who I am."

She was not, she said, Ernestine von Fricken, at least not by birth. She was the illegitimate daughter of the sister of Baron von Fricken's wife. This woman, Christiane von Zedtwitz, had become pregnant some eighteen years ago by an unscrupulous married wire manufacturer (Ernestine shuddered as if she might forever be raveled by his wares) named Lindauer, who seduced her some several hundred times before his seed took root and never again once he was informed of his mistress's gravidity—an interesting word for Ernestine to use, thought Robert, perhaps an echo of *gravicembalo* deliberately inserted into the conversation to deflect his mind from the horror of her words and direct it toward the supposedly safe confines of the musical. This Erdmann Lindauer, like someone who carves his initials into a tree and forever after avoids the forest, refused to bestow his name upon Ernestine or indeed to acknowledge her existence with so much as a single peep into her eye or cupping of her pudgy knee, not to mention bestowal of even the most minor of expenses. Her mother, far from feeling some special kinship with her daughter as a fellow female abandoned by the one person in the world who should at least have loved the younger of them, blamed Ernestine for her shame as well as for the loss of the one person in the world she would ever love. Thus it was that Ernestine, poor and virtually abandoned by a mother who literally could not bear the sight of her and therefore kept her veiled from head to toe and refused to attend to matters of bath and toilet, came to the attention of Baron von Fricken. Christiane von Zedtwitz asked her sister, the baron's wife, to train the baby to make her ploppers in a pot and while the baroness was at it would she mind raising her until she was old enough to find a rich husband?

"But I am not rich," interjected Robert, who inferred from the tenor of Ernestine's sad tale that he was not about to get rich either.

So the baroness took Ernestine into her own home, over the objection of the baron, who had decided, since he and the baroness had proved unable to have children of their own, that he wanted no children and would devote his free time, rather than to the games of childhood and the dissemination of scholarly discipline, to his music. But the baroness prevailed, and in due course the baron adopted Ernestine as his own. Except, she hastened to point out to Robert, who seemed to have awakened from either a trance or a light sleep when he heard the word 'adoption,' the baron had insisted that Ernestine, who carried no true Fricken blood, would inherit no Fricken money. Even after the baroness had died, and Ernestine was the only person left in the baron's home, he settled nothing upon her but his good will and his protection of her virtue and his ardent desire that she be married before that dreaded moment when a woman exited her teens without a husband and was thus as used up by time as by a hundred Erdmann Lindauers. He did not mind her holding out the unspoken promise of his vast wealth in order for her to become affianced, but before the marriage, as an honorable and honest man, he wanted it understood that none of his money would be coming to her and all of it would eventually settle upon the Ignaz von Fricken Institute of the Flute.

"So you see," concluded Ernestine, who by this time had moved so far to one end of the canapé that the sharp edges of the carved acanthus leaves had nearly shredded the right sleeve of her dress, "I have no fortune. I have no property. I have only what you see before you."

Robert laughed. "And a lot more clothes, if I remember correctly."

For the first time since she had begun her rueful tale, Ernestine smiled. As she spoke, she began to move back toward Robert, her dress whispering against the velvet of the canapé. "I fear that I misled you. I know you thought I would come to you with money. It is not something we have ever discussed, but you did believe that, did you not?"

Robert said nothing. He was thinking.

"You did believe I was rich, did you not?"

Of course he had believed she was rich. Yet, now that this fortune had vanished, he found he didn't care. He had a small inheritance from his father's estate. He had a month's supply of cigars, a fortuitous taste for plonk as well as for champagne, and the wherewithal to rent a piano if not the reputation to acquire one through endorsement. He was an artist. Artists, like everyone else, did their best work when their asses sat on bare wood and gristle made their meals. He did not need or want her money. Or her.

He felt himself dying, not into death but into another life. He might never have loved her, or loved her as much as he did at this moment, as poor as she was, as pretty as she was, as vulnerable as she had made herself in revealing a deceit that seemed to him as natural as the truth. What kind of world was it in which a woman felt she must come accompanied by material worth in order to be of value as a wife? What if the same were asked of men? She had never asked anything of him, except that he talk to her and fondle her and promise to be her husband. And what would he leave her? Music, perhaps,* and some memory he hoped would be better than her memory of this.

"I'm not worthy of you," he said.

"Nor I of you," she answered, throwing herself, for what she could not know was the last time, into his arms.**

---

*Specifically, the piano pieces that comprise *Carnaval,* which Schumann originally called "Jokes on Four Notes" and amended to "Tender Scenes on Four Notes," the four notes being A, S (E-flat in German notation), C, H (B in German notation), which form not only the name of Ernestine's hometown but contribute significantly to Schumann's surname (SCHumAnn). In this way, he was able, in a sense, to remain forever by her side even as he fled from her. He named one of *Carnaval*'s pieces for her, "Estrella," as he named another for Clara, "Chiarina," the latter much superior; which may or may not be the reason Clara omitted "Estrella" whenever she played *Carnaval* in public and in private sang along mockingly to it with the words, "How is your little Estrella?" leaving no doubt that a woman's "estrella" was a part too private to be mentioned in such pedagoguish apparatus as this.
**Ernestine von Fricken recovered sufficiently from her rejection by Robert Schumann to marry Count Wilhelm von Zedtwitz, an elderly member of her mother's family, who survived only eight months beyond their wedding. Ernestine herself, under siege from rickettsiae carried by body lice, died of typhus just short of her twenty-eighth birthday.

Robert returned immediately to Leipzig, where he learned of Ludwig's death. He prepared to attend the funeral, dressed in black even to his cravat and undershorts and spectacles so dark they made Paganini's seem lensless. But when the time came for him to leave his room—or Ludwig's room, actually, where Ludwig had lived but not, thank goodness, died, and into which Robert had wandered on the pretext of enumerating his late friend's possessions, which he knew it would be his responsibility to allocate— Robert froze. He could no more attend this funeral than he had his nephew's or his sister-in-law's or his brother's. Less. For he had loved Ludwig more than he had any of them, or anyone else in his life, except perhaps his father, whose funeral he had attended, the last he would ever, including his own, as he had once warned his physician.

He looked at Ludwig's things. The books. The clothes. The soap. The blanket. The bed out of which he had been lifted and that Henriette had returned to make while Robert watched, and she confessed that it was the first bed she had ever made, that she had spent her whole life waiting for someone to serve. The music paper on which Ludwig had copied Robert's compositions. The piano on which he had learned them. The floor. The ceiling. The walls. The utter absence.

He could bear it no longer. He felt Ludwig being buried deep within himself. He feared he would have no more memory of Ludwig than would the obdurate earth, which was at that very moment receiving the body of his friend. He went into the room between their rooms and knelt on the Turkish rug that had been his father's and raked it with his fingers until some grimy dust flew up and, as if he were Achilles, fouled his handsome countenance.

As he lay in the settled dust, on his back, his fingers now pulling at his hair, he recited a poem by Horace taught him ten years before by Karl Richter at the Lyceum:

> In dreams at night
> I hold you in my arms,
> or follow in your flight
> across the Martian field,
> or pursue through yielding waves
> the boy who will not yield.

Leipzig

APRIL 15, 1835
Oh, I love no one as I love him,
and he did not even look at me!
Clara Wieck

As soon as the carriage had deposited Clara and her father at the door in the old Grimmaischestrasse, she went to her room to wash her face and change her clothes and then made her way down from the top of the house to say hello to her brothers and her stepmother. But before she could find them, she heard her father through the parlor door complaining about the piano in Magdeburg and the food in Halberstadt and the Jews in Schönebeck and the leaking chamber pot in Hanover and the men in Brunswick who had tried to seduce his daughter. She planned to wait for him to finish his tirade, a regular occurrence upon his return to Leipzig, which he never loved so much as when he had forgotten what he hated about it. But in the midst of his recitation, she heard him interrupted with a single word, and not by his wife, who would never dare deny him the satisfaction of letting her know what discomforts he had experienced in order to accompany his daughter while she earned the money that would provide him in old age the luxuries he was forced to sacrifice on her behalf right now, when he would most have enjoyed them.

"Seduce?" said the voice.

It was Robert, from whom she had been apart since before the New Year, their longest separation since she had been in Paris and more, she realized upon hearing his voice, than she should have been able to bear. Than she *could* bear, which is why, as interested as she was in overhearing her father's version of the attempted seduction, she opened the doors into the room, stepped inside, and closed the doors behind her.

There stood Robert and her father, near the fire, each with a cup of coffee and a cigar, standing the way men stand when there are no women about, puffed out a bit in the chest, close enough to listen but not to touch, eyes peering anywhere but into each other's eyes. Neither paid the least attention to her entry. Like peculiar twins, they simultaneously contemplated the ash on their respective cigars and, together, rained the excess down into the fire, looked again at the tips of the cigars, put the cigars into their mouths, drew in with decompressing cheeks, and through pursed lips released their smoke, which coalesced in the air above their heads into a private cloud.

With diminishing strips of smoke still unfolding from his mouth, her father said, "I did not say she *was* seduced. Only that there were many who made the effort. An entire string quartet! I had to bring in Banck as reinforcement."

"Do you mean as a kind of reserve seducer?" Clara could not determine if Robert's tone mocked her father, Karl Banck, or herself.

"As a reserve *protector*! Of course he did so fine a job that he has virtually asked for her hand."

Clara was about to interrupt when Robert seemed to speak for her. "Virtually? What does that mean? He asked for a finger first, or a knuckle, or perhaps the wrist before the hand, since he himself is all wrist at the piano?"

"By hand I mean marriage," replied her father. "It is a symbol of the thing. Can you never have heard the expression?"

"I would have thought," said Robert, "that there would be other parts of the body one would ask for in marriage."

If only he would look at her, she would laugh. He could be such a funny fellow, and was the funnier when he teased her father, who, for all his virtues as a teacher and promoter of her career and guardian of her reputation, had the sense of humor of a gargoyle.

"How dare you!" said her father, with a predictability that was as expected and disappointing as Robert's ignoring of her was unexpected and disappointing.

She felt invisible, unwanted, desolate.

Robert, having imagined her somewhere in the house, felt her presence even before she came into the room. Thus he had assumed the posture of her father, a certain rigid insouciance he had noticed men adopted in their own homes before their own fires while smoking someone else's cigars, a kind of pride of ownership that seemed to protect them from the world and the world's judgment. He didn't care to be seen as he saw himself: no longer to be married to a girl he should not have wanted to marry in the first place. So bereft with the disappearance of Ludwig that he had found himself unable to return to the rooms they shared and had tried to live alone on the Halleschestrasse near the Promenade and failed, so now he had moved yet again, with yet another companion, Wilhelm Ulex, near the university in the false hope that he would be inspired by its ferment and protected by its crowds and obliviated by its countless taverns. Burdened enough by the politics of the magazine that he had purchased control of it and fired Julius

Knorr as its editor and become its sole editor himself, which left him sufficiently little time for writing his music that he was now forced to compose
through the nights at a pitch of creativity so fervid that come morning he
often felt a grandiosity and an emptiness that combined to cause him ex-
cruciating doubt.

Thus, when Robert heard the parlor door open, he saw her in his mind
before he could possibly have seen her in the room, his little friend come to
find him and to help him find himself, as if she might with her presence deliver back the time stolen from them in their absence from one another,
bring Ludwig back to life, restore to him the pleasure of his Ernestine, allow
to him the childishness he knew with her, with Clara, that place within his
being in which, when he was judged, he was judged by her alone and only
in accordance with her laughter and her visible delight.

Yet when she entered, and he glimpsed her as she turned to close the
doors, he felt that she, like him, had taken on the pretense of another. She
came into the room a woman, tall, rounded, full, the movement of her hand
upon the doorknob gently wanton, the stretch of her arm languorous, the
shifting of her shoulders quite incautious, and the slope of her back so very
unexpected that he turned away his eyes. She was not so much a stranger as
strange, so unfamiliar as to have been remade in an image that was drawn
from his own desires but upon which he could not permit himself to gaze.

He could not bear to look at her, for fear of what his eyes would say.

Leipzig

SEPTEMBER 13, 1835
*It always gave Mendelssohn pleasure to take
very lively tempi with Clara.*
Robert Schumann

The first gifts Clara received for her sixteenth birthday came from Robert.
They were delivered at at six-thirty in the morning, by which time she had
been long awake because of her excitement over the day and her desire to
finish her practicing before the festivities began.

There was a beautiful little basket with a porcelain handle, and within
the basket was a gold watch, which she hoped was not from Robert alone,

because it was much too expensive and would mock the mere watch chain she had given him for his birthday in June.

Indeed, his card made clear that the watch was from the entire League of David, while the basket was from him alone. It was a fine basket, something to put on a shelf in her room and admire from afar. But it could not match the letter he had sent two weeks before, in which he had told her she had the face of an angel and had ended by saying, "You know how precious you are to me."

His next gift came in a huge box. With her father standing over her, Clara went down on her knees to open it.

"Books?" he said with disbelief.

They were leatherbound and smelled quite wonderful. "'The complete works of Bulwer-Lytton,'" she read from Robert's card. She picked up one of the books. "*The Last Days of Pompeii.*"

Her father peered over her shoulder. "Volume Three! Why would he think you would ever have time to read all these books? We would need another carriage just to carry these to your performances."

Clara hugged the book to her bosom. "Perhaps he plans to read them aloud to me."

After a splendid morning with all the boys of David—Clara was, delightedly, the only woman—at the crowded and noisy Kuchengarten, where Clara hid behind a giant bouquet of stork's-bill so she wouldn't have to make a speech, everyone went back to the Wieck house for dinner. There she changed from one birthday dress, of merino, into another, of mousseline de soie.

The guest of honor at her birthday dinner was Felix Mendelssohn, who had arrived in Leipzig only two weeks earlier. He had been driven out of Berlin by religious intolerance—"They apparently do not like Lutherans there," he quipped—and into Leipzig by the offer of the directorship of the Gewandhaus orchestra, whose members he won over by immediately securing for them a handsome raise in pay.

Mendelssohn was at this time twenty-six, one year older than Robert and vastly more renowned. At the age of twelve, after a year in which he had written several symphonies, two operas, and some complex fugues for string quartet, he had played for, and virtually been adopted by, Goethe, who agreed to receive him after Felix's teacher had written to say that the boy was not only his best student but, though the son of a Jew, no Jew himself. As Felix had mentioned to Clara in Paris in 1831, Goethe compared himself to King Saul when he said to Felix, "You are my David," having no idea that at the same time in Zwickau there was another David sitting at the piano playing Bach.

When Mendelssohn was fifteen, Ignaz Moscheles had traveled all the way from London to Berlin simply to hear him play the piano. At sixteen, Mendelssohn had written his Octet for strings and the next year his Overture to *A Midsummer Night's Dream.** One month beyond his twentieth birthday, he brought Sebastian Bach back from the dead with his revival of the *St. Matthew Passion* in Berlin.

It was to Berlin that his grandfather, Moses Mendelssohn, had walked the eighty miles from Dessau in 1743, when he was fourteen. As a Jew, he was required to skulk into the capital of Imperial Prussia through a particular portal. On the day Moses Mendelssohn entered Berlin, the guard wrote, "Today through the Rosenthaler Gate passed six oxen, seven pigs, one Jew."

Most Jews in Berlin became beggars or peddlers, for want of any other permissible occupation: they were not allowed to manufacture anything, nor to supply the government or army with anything they might have manufactured had they been allowed to in the first place, nor to own land, nor (even as the peddlers they were allowed to become) to sell anything—food in particular, for obvious reasons—except to other Jews, nor to teach anything, including music, to anyone but other Jews, nor to touch anyone who was not a Jew with so much as a fingertip, let alone so intimate a part of the body as a lip. Only their human waste was allowed to mingle with that of non-Jews, on the theory that Jews made good fertilizer, though curiously they were required to inhabit their own cemeteries.

It was in Berlin that Moses Mendelssohn was befriended by Robert Schumann's distant relative Gotthold Lessing, the man who was for an evening to have the happy experience of forgetting that he was who he was without having to stop being who he was. It was upon Moses Mendelssohn, who practiced one of the most difficult professions to suppress—he was a Thinker—that Lessing based the hero of *Nathan the Wise*.

---

*It was when Mendelssohn was sixteen that Heinrich Dorn, not long thereafter to become Robert's teacher, played for Felix one of Dorn's own compositions. They did not meet again for another sixteen years, at which time Mendelssohn played for Dorn that very same piece, which Dorn did not recognize and had no memory of having written. Mendelssohn, who had not even played it before this moment, knew it perfectly. He absorbed music into his memory the way other men did long-ago moments of love.

Moses' son, Abraham—the self-proclaimed "dash" between Moses and Felix, the man known first as the son of his father and then as the father of his son—eventually settled in Hamburg, where Felix was born in 1809. Three years later, the entire family was forced by the approach of Napoleon's Russia-bound army—under the command of the merciless Marshal Davout, who indeed succeeded in occupying Hamburg—to flee back to Berlin. But if Napoleon had uprooted them, he had also made them rich: In defeating Prussia in 1806, he had blockaded all trade with his remaining enemy, England, which allowed Abraham Mendelssohn, operating out of Hamburg's ungovernable port, to carry on as one of history's most benign if successful smugglers an illicit trade with that country in iron, leather, coffee, and tea, and in particular the English cloth so prized that it was worn, however traitorously if cozily, by French troops.

It was in Berlin in 1816 that the Mendelssohns converted their children to Lutheranism (they themselves would sneak off later to Frankfurt to effect the same inversion). This was by no coincidence whatsoever the same year that the Prussians issued the following *votum*, which means, as does the word *vote*, a *vow*, even a *desire*:

> It would be best not to have any Jews in this country. We must suffer those we presently have, but at the same time we must ceaselessly attempt to make them as inoffensive as possible. Jews must be converted to Christianity, and all their rights as citizens will depend on this conversion. As long as a Jew remains a Jew, he cannot exist in the eyes of the State.

In an attempt to bury once and for all his family's debilitating Jewishness under the protective and ordurous shroud of a Christian name, Felix's father took his four children in great secrecy to the Church of Jerusalem, where they were baptized Bartholdy, the name of a large garden by the river in Berlin, which the family purchased. But the Berliners were not fooled. From then on, proving that it's easier to convert a piece of earth than the soul of man, Bartholdy Garden became known publicly as Jew Garden.

Felix, though he considered himself a Lutheran, preferred the name Mendelssohn to either Bartholdy or Mendelssohn-Bartholdy, particularly because in England, the country that had made his family rich and where he was most lionized as both performer and composer, he was known simply as Mendelssohn, and he knew enough to know that the last people one should confuse are one's best customers.

He was a very handsome young man. George Grove called his face "the most beautiful I ever saw, like what I imagine our Saviour's to have been."

Like his grandfather, Moses, Felix knew German, Italian, English, French, Greek, and Latin. As children, he and his sisters published a newspaper from their home with contributions from the likes of Heinrich Heine and Georg Hegel.* By the time he was eleven, he had written more than sixty pieces of music, which he copied in a hand so precise that those who saw the compositions believed they had been press-printed.

Robert had been introduced to Felix in the Gewandhaus by none other than Henriette Voigt, who had progressed from making sexual matches to those of a wholly musical nature. At that first meeting, Robert said, "I know all your work."

"Good Lord," replied Mendelssohn. "I wrote so many pieces as a child that for anyone to see them now would be the equivalent of my standing here on the Gewandhaus stage with my pants down."

"Exactly as I've imagined myself many times," said Robert.

"With whom?"

"Oh, I couldn't possibly say."

"But you must," said Mendelssohn.

"You really must," said Henriette.

"A young lady," said Robert.

"I had imagined no other," said Mendelssohn. "How young?"

"Almost sixteen, I should imagine," said Henriette.

"That isn't young," said Mendelssohn. "I was in love with Delphine von Schauroth in Munich when she was sixteen. Of course, I was only twenty-two then myself, so there wasn't much distance between our ages."

Feeling instantly that he had met a man who, among all men, would best understand him, Robert said, "I trust I am not imposing upon your good will and the brevity of our acquaintance if I invite you to Clara Wieck's birthday party as our guest of honor."

"Oh, Fräulein Wieck. That would be a great pleasure. I met her in Paris several years ago, though I doubt she'd remember me, for I was suffering at

---

*Not many years hence, Mendelssohn would attend the University of Berlin, where he would hear his former contributor lecture on the aesthetics of music. It is not known whether during those lectures Hegel said what later (not long before the cholera epidemic of 1831 carried him off) he wrote with such authority that his words continue to this day to echo in the minds of all humanity: "The fundamental character of the romantic is the musical."

the time from a most incautious haircut. She was just a child then, as I recall, and certainly had not attained the renown that now attaches to her name. How old will she be at this birthday we shall be celebrating together?"

"Sixteen," said Robert, smiling hugely.

After a dinner of smoked salmon and cold cucumber soup and roast duck with apple-sausage stuffing and potato dumplings and red cabbage braised with vinegar—the entire meal, which lasted the good part of the afternoon, accompanied by and washed down with copious amounts of champagne—all that remained were the toasts and the music.

Her father praised her talent and her yet-to-be-realized stupendous income.

Dr. Reuter proclaimed her now a woman, which made her father look at him as if he wanted to snatch his cigar out of his imprudent mouth.

Wilhelm Ulex admired her dress.

Louis Rakemann, who was a good enough musician to have been rehearsing with Clara for a performance of Bach's D-Minor Concerto and a poor enough judge of character to imagine that she might care for him as much as he cared for her, said, "My desires for you are no less than my desires for myself. Long life. Good music. And a husband worthy of your gifts."

"Thank you for informing us, Louis, that one of your desires is for a husband," said Julius Knorr, inspiring great amusement in all but Rakemann.

Knorr, who by that time had put his foot up on the table, leaned forward to remove it with both hands, rose unsteadily, and made his own toast: "If I played the piano half as well as you, I'd be twice as far away from here than I am," which Clara, kindly, took to mean that since he was here and nowhere else, he was doubly pleased to have been asked to her party and to have been given the opportunity to make peace with Robert, whom Julius had threatened to take to court until Robert had paid him twenty-five thalers for his interest in the magazine.

Some others, however, did not interpret Knorr's words so charitably and told him to sit down, which he did with such haste that he left some of his champagne dancing briefly by itself in the air before it drizzled down quite scrupulously into the glass that had abandoned it.

Felix Mendelssohn said, "I came to Leipzig not to direct the music of the orchestra but to be directed to Heaven by the music in you."

When all had toasted her but Robert, and Clara had excused his silence by reminding herself that when there was music boiling up inside him he sometimes seemed to neglect to speak as a chef forgets to eat, he suddenly pushed back his chair and stood up with a glass of champagne in each hand. "I have known Clara Wieck since she was eight years old, half her life ago. When first I met her, all I could see was her music. Today, all I can hear is her beauty. In the time between, she has grown more charming every day, every hour, within as well as without. She has made me laugh. She has made me weep. But most of all she has made me grateful. To have been put on Earth at the same time as she is to have been given a gift that only God and chance could provide. And it is a gift shared by all of us here today—to live in her time, to live in her company, to live within sight and sound of her. There is no one in the world like her, and no world is like ours in its being blessed by her presence. I drink to her twice: in admiration; in affection."

Robert emptied first one glass of champagne, then the other. She saw that both his hands were trembling, but not enough to match the trilling of her heart and the shiver in her spine.

All the other men at the table drank to her as well with a glass in each hand, except for her father, who leaned against her and whispered, "He is drunk."

"So am I," she replied, though her glasses were full.

From there, all retired to the largest of the music rooms, the men with cigars and brandy, she with her gold watch and what was left of a plum tart she cupped in her hand within a linen napkin. Everyone asked her to play the piano, but she graciously ceded the bench and pride of first place to Mendelssohn, who was not only her distinguished guest but whose piano playing she knew wholly by reputation and preferred to experience by sound before she undertook to perform in his presence. Whether inspired by fear or merely example, a pianist flew higher in the draft of other, earlier birds.

To rid his fingers of both torpidity and the suasions of champagne, Mendelssohn wreathed through some Bach fugues, much to Robert's delight, and then, to the delight of all, through improvisations in the styles first of Chopin and second of Liszt. When Clara begged him to play his own music, Mendelssohn began with what seemed a deliberate echo of his previous beginning, a fugue of his own in E minor, which crescendoed and accelerandoed to a huge false climax before subduing itself in a quiet iteration of the fugue theme with, at the very end, so unexpected a diminuendo on a rising scale that Clara rose from her chair. All the others in the room followed her example, mistaking her powerlessness before this music for mere admiration of it.

Mendelssohn seized the opportunity of her standing to invite her to join him at the piano. He placed before them the piano part of his B-Minor Capriccio, and together they played it, he from memory and she by sight, but he no better than she, because he guided her somehow, with the flow of his body and the occasional pressure of his shoulder against hers and every once in a while a kind of anticipatory hum she knew no one else could hear, a pretty little snatch of song that made her giddy.

He took her hand when they were done and pulled her to her feet. Then he drew her forward so that, from his greater height, she was forced into a mighty bow before her friends and her father, all of whom applauded her and him and called for more.

"You'll get no more from me," Mendelssohn addressed them. "For me to play with her is like a pig in a race with an antelope. While I grunt in the mud, she takes wing like an angel to the heavens. So please, my friends, allow me to join you at the trough while together we feed on such ambrosia as might fall from her fingers."

They all laughed at his exaggerated graciousness, and then again when Julius Knorr shouted, "That doesn't sound terribly kosher to me."

"What will you play?" Mendelssohn asked her.

"What would you like me to play?"

"Something you love." Mendelssohn then turned from her and looked around the room, as if for music floating in the air. "Something by him." He pointed at Robert.

"Something I love," she said, and nearly added, *by someone I love.*

She played Robert's new Sonata in F-sharp minor, which he had sent to her only a few days earlier accompanied by a note saying he had been inspired by a melody of hers* and that at the same time this piece was a cry of his heart *for* her. She had wanted to tell him it was her heart that belonged to him, but her father had insisted upon providing her words of gratitude and had dictated to her the note he insisted she send back: "Thank you for the sonata. I look forward to finding the time to play it someday."

This was the time.

---

*Her "Scène fantastique."

Leipzig

OCTOBER 4, 1835
I do not regard Carnaval *as music.*
Frédéric Chopin

When Clara and her father and Robert returned from a long afternoon walk, during which not a word was spoken because of Friedrich Wieck's insistence that such walks were for exercise and that the tongue was the only part of the body a pianist didn't need to strengthen, they found Felix Mendelssohn sitting in the drawing room of the Wieck house. There was a man beside him, but he didn't get up to greet them when Mendelssohn did.

Clara recognized him immediately. In the three years since she had leapt over his back in Paris, he had become perhaps the most revered pianist in Europe; if Franz Liszt were more renowned, this was owed not entirely to his playing. He had also, she saw, become both more beautiful and more pallid, his eyes weary and yet almost desperately lucent.

He reached out his hand toward her. "*Now* I remember you," he said in his heavily accented French. "Please forgive my not rising both to the occasion and to yourself—I am not as strong as I was when last you saw me and we frolicked."

"Monsieur Chopin," she said. He no longer smelled sweet; perhaps he had not played the piano in a while. His hand felt strangely small. She wondered why the critic Rellstab had said that if you were going to play Chopin's études you'd best have a surgeon by your side. She had played enough of them to know that as long as you were willing to break some chords, you needn't break your hand.

"He came all this way to hear you play," said Mendelssohn.

"Splendid," said Wieck. "I hope you won't mind if we tell others of this honor," he said to Chopin. "And may I assume we are your only stop in Leipzig?"

"Hardly," said Chopin. "First I picked up Mendelssohn and then we went to the Voigts."

"You stopped at the Voigts before—," began her father, who seemed even more offended than he had been in Paris when Chopin had declined to receive the two of them in his home.

Chopin seemed to know instinctively how to deal with her father's anger, for he dared to interrupt him. "And considering the fact that we waited here

{ 200 }

more than an hour for your daughter, we should have gone to see someone else in the meantime. Besides, sir, what does it matter in what order one visits people? In Paris, the one seen last is the one seen longest."

"Then may I assume we are your last stop in Leipzig?"

"If it is, sir, it will be because your daughter proves to be as talented as you are proving to be tedious. And in bad French, no less."

Chopin smiled and seemed to enjoy the sight of her father's reddening face. At the point at which it looked as if it might explode, Chopin looked away toward Robert. "And who is this quiet boy over here?"

Clara was worried Robert might find this condescending. Yet he *was* a boy. Though only two or three months older than Robert, Chopin seemed to bear the weight of both fame and experience; the world and his work had made him weary. Robert was robust with possibility and restlessness. Even his smile at Chopin's notice of him was guileless.

"This is Schumann," said Mendelssohn, in a tone that indicated he had spoken of him to Chopin.

Again, Chopin did not rise. Rather, he seemed to sink back farther into his chair. "Ah, yes. The one who so praised my Mozart variations that I was barely able to compose anything else for months, so intimidated was I by such undigested praise."

"Thank you," said Robert. "It is such an honor—"

"I am not sure you should thank me. I am not sure what I said was intended as a compliment. For your dithyramb struck me, I must say, as remarkably silly. Which is to say, you made of my rather straightforward variations some kind of phantasmagoric tableau. Don Juan does not gambol about with Leporello in my music. Nor does he kiss Zerlina at all, let alone on something so specific as a D-flat. And if you knew me better— which I hope you shall—you would know I have so little experience with women that I wouldn't even know where to find a woman's D-flat."

Robert laughed. "Well, if you need any advice in that regard—I mean where to find the D-flat on a woman, though I strongly recommend you begin with her A-natural—I'm your man." He chuckled again.

Chopin could not resist a smile at encountering this appreciation of his little joke. It was not a broad smile—his face was too contained for that— but it fully brightened his eyes above the hammocks of darkness on which they languidly rested.*

---

*Chopin was either being disingenuous or was not yet aware how inspiring he found Robert's praise of his work—inspiring in his love life, that is. It would not be long before he, as would Balzac and Delacroix and Delaroche, not to mention Beau Brummel and the

"I do not tell stories in my music, Monsieur Schumann," he said with far less exasperation, almost with a kind confessional friendship. "My music relates to nothing but itself. And whatever drama it contains, it is the drama of the next notes first and of all the notes together finally. It is the drama of harmony, in which the villain is dissonance and the hero is most often the same. I don't read books. I certainly don't read magazines. And the only theater I enjoy is the opera, which I attend solely for the music. To hear Pasta in *Otello* or Malibran in the *Barber* or Cinti-Damoreau in my poor Bellini's *Beatrice* is to experience not drama but song. It just happens that I find my own voice in the piano. When I sing—and all I do is sing—it comes out of that wooden box. I only hope I'll still be able to sing when I'm *in* a wooden box."

"So you too think of death?" said Robert.

"How nice to find we have something in common," answered Chopin.

They adjourned to the studio with the largest windows, to let in the light from the street. Clara performed two of Chopin's études and the last movement of his concerto. Chopin, his eyes lowered, sat motionless while she played and even at the end of each étude, so that the others, taking their cue from him, did the same. Robert, even more than he wanted to applaud the brilliance of her playing, wanted to reach out and grasp Chopin by the charmeuse lapels of his beautiful black dress coat and shake him so he might acknowledge the joy he must be feeling, to have someone this young and this beautiful display such love for his music and such mastery of it.

But Robert didn't move from his chair. And Chopin didn't move within his own. He sat as still as someone listening for a rumor of wind on a listless sea.

Finally, when Clara had finished the concerto and dropped her hands to the tops of her thighs and slowly stood up from the bench and walked toward an empty chair, Chopin said in what was almost a whisper, "No."

---

duke of Orléans, fell in love with, and indeed made love to, the magnificent Delfina Potocka. Hippolyte Delaroche may have ended up painting Delfina as the Virgin Mary, but it was Chopin who christened as her "little D-flat" the part of her that served as the door into her body through which all these great men entered. Once having occupied her, however, Chopin was led to question, as he put it, "what ballades, polonaises, perhaps whole concertos, have been forever consumed in your little D-flat." He even perverted poor Plautus in quoting to Delfina a transposition of the Latin poet's *Oleum et operam perdidi,* implying that he, Chopin, had squandered the oil from his lamp within the darkness of her little D-flat.

"No?" said Wieck, much more loudly and with the disbelief of someone for whom any negative expression involving his child's art was intolerable.

"No," said Chopin, now accompanying the word with a slight shaking of his head. "And I am addressing not you, Monsieur Wieck, but your daughter." He looked directly at Clara for the first time. "So if I may impose myself, because after all it is my music you have played: No, you must not leave the piano; no, you must not stop playing; no, I have never heard my work played more beautifully."

"Aha!" exclaimed Wieck, whom Robert, thrilled as he was himself with Chopin's words, was prepared to throttle should he now demand of Chopin a written endorsement.

Clara walked not back to the piano but directly toward Chopin, who rose now as he had not when she had first approached him in the drawing room. "I merely serve the beauty in the music," she said. "If all études were as precious as yours, there would not be a person in the world who did not play the piano. Thank goodness, therefore, yours are unlike any others. But as for whether I will play more of your music, it is I who must say no. I do not yet have it under my fingers. But I do have him."

She turned from Chopin to face Robert, gave him a smile that struck him as complicitous, and immediately marched back to the piano.

"Here are some pieces from his *Carnaval*," she said, "which I am learning even as he writes them."

"So he is under your fingers, and I am not?" said Chopin.

"Not entirely," she said with a smile. "But he knows me well enough to forgive my mistakes. And I know him well enough not to fear his judgment."

Among the pieces of *Carnaval* she played was a brief nocturne that Robert called "Chopin," and if Chopin realized he was being both mimicked and honored, he gave no sign. He was as still listening to Robert's work as he had been listening to his own.

When she finished, she had no hesitation in turning to Chopin to ask, "Well, what do you think?"

"Incredible," he said. He turned to Robert. "Out of this world."

"Play for Frédéric the sonata you played at your birthday," said Mendelssohn. To Chopin he said, "It succeeds marvelously despite the sad burden it carries of having been written in, if my ear does not deceive me, F-sharp minor."

"You have a fine ear," said Robert congenially. He never minded when people criticized his keys. An insult to the ear was the best way to open it. Beauty must inflame as well as comfort; art must challenge before it consoles.

"Your birthday?" Chopin addressed Clara. "How old were you?"

"I am sixteen," answered Clara as she lowered her fingers upon the piece that had been written for her.

As Robert listened to her play his music, he could not, for the first time, remember having composed it. She had obviously practiced it since her birthday and made it enough part of herself that she had taken it from him. All the suffering was gone from it, all the puzzlement and insecurity of form, the endless moments when no music or the wrong music had come to him, the bitterness of the coffee and the dryness of the smoke, the confusion at feeling at one moment he was a genius and the next a bungler, the terrible false joy over whole pages that one day made him swell with pride and the next day he could not bear, the passion he'd felt for her when he'd been writing it and the dread that it was beneath her and thus that he was too. Now, as she played, he embraced himself with a contentment he hadn't known before.

Clara was quite exhausted when she finished, not least from the demands of the accented chords in the finale, and felt no need to ask Chopin's opinion of the piece. He seemed preoccupied now or perhaps simply bored by her playing when, after all, it was he who was perhaps the greatest pianist in the world. It could not be easy to sit for so long and listen to someone else. She could remember those days when she appeared in public with other young pianists and, whether she had performed before them or had yet to perform, felt so strong a desire to play that she often had had to fight a perverse temptation to dash onto the stage and throw the other girl or boy from the bench.

"Now you," she said to him. "Please play one of your pieces for us."

"I cannot."

"Are you ill?" asked Clara.

"I might as well be," he said. "I am in love."

He had been ill, he explained, in the winter, with the influenza that had sent half of Paris to bed and the other half out of town. Because of the weakness of his lungs, he had contracted bronchitis, which caused him to cough so much that his hands would play chords when they had been poised for chromatic runs. But it was only when he began to spew blood from his mouth onto the keyboard that various of his doctors ordered him to leave Paris and go to the spa outside the city at Enghien, to which he went accompanied by Vincenzo Bellini, his great new friend who stayed with him off and on until Chopin left the baths of Enghien for those in Germany, Karlsbad specifically. Bellini died within a month of their separation, a mere ten days ago. Chopin received the news on his way back to

Paris, in Dresden, where the mail coach had let him out and who should be standing there but a man named Wodzinski who had lived with his family in the Chopin boarding house in Warsaw and with whose eldest daughter, Maria, Chopin had played, games at the piano or hide-and-seek in the vast Pszenny mansion; though he was nine years older than she, which made her now exactly your age, he said to Clara, sixteen, and, as he discovered when he met her in Dresden for the first time since she was eleven, very beautiful and also a fine pianist, if not of course the equal of her. To make a long story short, and because he was running out of breath, he had, God help him, lost his heart to her, Maria Wodzinska, whom he had last seen upon his departure from Dresden for Leipzig only yesterday, a separation that seemed an eternity and had rendered him much too weak to play the piano for them now.

"You didn't tell me you're in love," said Mendelssohn, with amused pretense at being wounded.

"Are you going to become her teacher?" asked Wieck suspiciously.

"You must marry her," said Clara, who felt that his sharing of this story was an even greater gift than his playing the piano for them. He and Robert were the same age, and she and Maria Wodzinska were the same age. It was too great a coincidence to be a coincidence.

"You think so?" he asked her.

"Oh, yes."

"Do you think she'd have me?"

"Oh, yes."

He rose from his chair and for the first time stepped away from it, approaching Clara where she sat on the piano bench.

"This is too high for me," he said. "Might you have a stool?"

"Oh, yes!" She went to a corner of the room and brought back an adjustable stool, which Chopin screwed down; when he sat his elbows were level with the white keys.

He stretched out both arms, so that they reached the extremities of the keyboard with a minimum of movement. "As a man I wish to be taller, but as a pianist I do not. Most women are the perfect height for this instrument, like you, Mademoiselle Wieck. It is meant to be embraced but never ravished. Liszt virtually mounts the thing, the keyboard disappears beneath him. Who knows what his hands are doing? For me, each finger is a separate being. Like the children I shall never have. From their voices alone, they can be recognized."

He drew his hands back in toward his body, relaxed his shoulders, and took a deep breath. He seemed about to play when he turned his head slightly and said, "Forgive the simplicity of this piece. My travels and my illness and my passion have combined to make me tired. It's a nocturne in E-flat. It is dedicated to the erstwhile wife of my dealer, Monsieur Pleyel. At the time I made the dedication, perhaps six years ago, she was Marie Moke. Now she calls herself Camilla Pleyel, but not for long. He is divorcing her, poor man."

Clara recalled meeting Monsieur Pleyel in his salon in Paris, and her fear of his young wife, as much for her beauty as for her reputation as a pianist. Now her fears had turned merely to curiosity.

"Why?" she asked.

Chopin misunderstood her question. "My dedication was not out of love. It is another Marie I was destined to love."

"Why is he divorcing her?" she clarified.

"Wantonness." With the word still on his lips, Chopin began to play, as if music might becloud the perfidy of woman.*

Robert was entranced, finally to be hearing this pianist whose work and reputation he had championed. He didn't care whether Chopin appreciated his efforts. What Robert wrote, whether it was words or music, seemed more often misunderstood than embraced. Art was the expression of the self, and its purpose was hardly to make that self appear lovable or even admirable. To make art was to explode within the world; it mattered not if people covered up their ears.

Yet how much easier it is to love someone else's work. He did not mind taking pleasure from Chopin; only being told he must give it himself. He leaned forward to watch Chopin's hands. They were delicate and narrow and yet seemed able to embrace the piano not through breadth but by movement, flying lightly over keys he seemed barely to touch, fingering

---

*Chopin was too fastidious in such matters and not, despite his several years' residence in Paris, an accomplished enough gossip to mention his own regretted if indirect participation in this marital fiasco. His friend Franz Liszt, Chopin discovered by way of the most ghastly and incontrovertible evidence (of sight, of sound, of scent), had used Chopin's Chaussée d'Antin apartment in which to make love to Camilla Pleyel. Though Chopin had heard rumors of Madame Pleyel's multiple infidelities, he blamed himself for the impending divorce by having provided her and Liszt the venue in which to achieve their passionate tryst, which occurred in all its brutish jubilation beneath—at least it was not within!— the grand piano for which Chopin had traded his good name by allowing Monsieur Pleyel to attach that name to the following statement in *La France musicale*: "I know what ravishing effects can be obtained from Pleyel's delightful pianos." What was truly ravished was Madame Pleyel herself, no doubt staring up at the underside of her husband's huge instrument, giggling in its shadow, and hitting all the right notes.

with a kind of perverse logic found precisely in the hand and not in the mind, thumbs on black keys, longer fingers passing over shorter. Chopin gave the impression he was improvising. It was this very illusion of impermanence that provided the music its eternal sway. It flew out of his hands into oblivion.

When Chopin had completed the piece, looking more tired than the playing of so brief a composition would warrant, Clara said, keeping to herself the echo of these words unsaid in their first meeting in Paris, "You were wonderful, Monsieur Chopin."

"Thank you." He stood and turned back toward his chair. There, pressed against the windows behind it, were faces.

"I told you we would not be able to keep your presence in Leipzig a secret," said Mendelssohn.

"Make them go away," said Chopin.

Robert got up and walked past Chopin toward the windows. "They all look in such ecstasy," he said. "When my playing is overheard, I find people at my windows with their tongues stuck out at me."

"You do not!" said Clara.

"In that case, do you suppose it's only my own reflection I see?" He was reminded of what he had written on the very first page of his very first review, of Chopin's Mozart Variations—that he had listened, like these people, pressed against his own self in the embrasure of a window.

Robert closed the curtains, but not before waving at all the people. Only then did Chopin venture farther toward his chair. "I cannot bear it," he said, as if he were addressing his now invisible admirers in the street. "The public frightens me. They hold their breath when I'm about to play, and it's I who am suffocated. They sit motionless and stare at me, and it's I who am paralyzed. They are silent before me, and it is I who am rendered mute. I decided even before I left Paris that I would play no more concerts for strangers. Never. I dream of playing only for myself. I dream impossibly of sound being being captured the way Monsieur Niepce has captured an image of light.* Imagine, sound painted on something other than air. It will never happen, of course. It is imaginable but inconceivable, no? We are fated, we musicians, to be the only artists whose work dies when we do. It is one thing to write music—far too much of that is left behind. But our

---

*Joseph Niepce had, in 1822, produced the first photograph and at the time Chopin invoked his name was, with his son Isidore, working in France with Louis Daguerre to perfect a method of causing light to fall on a suspension of silver salts so as to darken it in part and thus produce an image.

{ 207 }

sound is gone forever. And what is a man but his sound? It is the print of our soul upon eternity. It is the essence of our being. And it ends up, God help us, as silent as the very voices of the dead themselves."

Only now did Chopin turn to face his companions. He did not sit down. "Forgive my morbidity. And also if I take my leave. Do you suppose those people will be gone?"

"You cannot be serious," said Wieck.

"I can assure you, sir, I have spent more time with you than I have or shall with anyone else in Leipzig."

"No, no, no," said Wieck. "You misunderstand. I am satisfied with your visit. I am appreciative of your patience in allowing yourself the good fortune of hearing my daughter play. I meant only to say that I find it difficult to believe that you yourself will never again play for the public. How can this be true? Imagine if Thalberg said this. Or Liszt. To give up the adulation, the profit, the —"

"I told Liszt of my plans. This is not idle talk on my part, Monsieur Wieck. Liszt, of course, was as skeptical as you, at least until I told him I meant to prescribe a course of action — or inaction, as it were — for myself alone, not for him or for any other pianist. What *I* cannot tolerate, I told him, *you,* Franz, are destined to do, for even when you fail to captivate your audience, you still have the power to stun it.* I, on the other hand, depend upon more subtle effects. And subtlety is, when one deals with the public, the equivalent of insult. And now, I trust I shall insult none of you if I say, good day."

Chopin turned to Robert. "I wonder if you would mind seeing me out?"

"But this is *my* house," said Wieck.

"He's bigger than you."

Robert felt Chopin take his arm and did not understand what Chopin had meant until they were at the front door and Chopin said to him, "Please be so kind as to peek out to see if any of those people remain. And if they do, beat them thoroughly until they leave me in peace."

"Beat them?"

Chopin smiled. "Or otherwise distract them while I make my escape."

Robert opened the door. The street before the house was empty. "Gone," he said.

---

*The word Chopin employed in speaking to Liszt, and repeated here, was *assommer,* which means, it is true, *to stun* but in its colloquial usage carries the meaning *to bore to death.* Liszt, who believed Chopin was praising him, failed to grasp this further evidence of Chopin's subtlety, not to mention his wit. Chopin's Polish accent might have rendered his French a bit inelegant, but his use of the language itself was deft.

He hoped, in a way, that Chopin would show some disappointment. But he seemed thoroughly relieved.

"I have never heard such music as yours," said Robert.

"Nor I as yours," responded Chopin as he put his head into his hat and walked away.

When Robert returned to the others, Mendelssohn was discussing Chopin's rubato, that technique by which time was withheld from the beat, only to be restored a moment or two later. "He leans about within the measure," said Mendelssohn, shaking his head. "When he and I play for each other, it's like a Mohican and a Kaffir trying to have a conversation. He carries too much of Paris around with him—all that love of suffering and exaggeration of the emotions. And yet one feels one could listen to him play forever. There is something about his music—even when you see it written down, and you analyze it, it remains beyond comprehension. You can play it and wonder, even as you play, where this sound is coming from. And what about his idea of *capturing* sound! Imaginable but inconceivable, he says. I fear he's right. It is one thing to reproduce an image that one sees. If a painter can do it, why not a scientist? But sound is invisible. We can represent it only by the ugly little symbols that are the tools of our trade. How could a trumpet call from a piece of paper? How could the voice of a soprano rise out of a closed book on someone's piano in the dead of night? But imagine it, my friends! Music in the air and not a musician within smelling distance. Music everywhere and always."

Mendelssohn shook his head but at the same time positively beamed. It was not difficult to imagine what he was thinking about: the sound of an entire orchestra, perhaps even combined with the kind of chorus he had conducted in the *St. Matthew Passion* in Berlin six years before, that historic performance that was now just gossip and in fact had been no more than that the moment after each note had been sung or played . . . sound apprehended, sealed, made immortal.

Mendelssohn lit a cigar, a rare indulgence.

"Imagine it," he said again, clearly continuing to do so himself.

"The world would stop," said Robert, whose own cigar was now not much longer than a finger joint. "If we could listen to music whenever we wanted, the world would stop."

So pleased was he with the thought that he ignited a new cigar from the morsel of the old, which Clara wished she could take from the ashtray and place between her lips.

Leipzig

NOVEMBER 25, 1835

I remember how once when I wanted to kiss you, when you were a little girl,
you said to me, "No, later, when I am older."
Robert Schumann

On the eve of her departure for a series of concerts in Zwickau, Clara stayed up with Robert long after the rest of the Wieck household had gone to sleep. Together, they did what they usually did in the evening, before she went to her room at the top of the house and he went home to write music: drank tea and coffee and Robert the more-than-occasional brandy to accompany his cigars, ate candies and pastries, played the piano for one another, talked. When they talked, it was mostly of music. Mendelssohn's arrival in Leipzig had changed the very texture of the city's air, as any city would be changed when its orchestra obtains a new and brilliant conductor. A city without music is like a meal without food. And a city whose musicians are led by a man of taste and intrepidity is a city whose very breath is sweetened and its sky enlarged. No conquering emancipator with his weapon held triumphantly aloft can bring such liberation as a man of music with his baton poised before the onrush of beauty.

In fact, the Gewandhaus orchestra had never before experienced the emancipating discipline of the baton. Its conductors had sat at the piano, nodding and shrugging and grimacing at the first violinist, who stood at his chair trying simultaneously to play and to dictate rhythm with his bow. But from the moment Mendelssohn arrived, he stood before the entire group, anointing them with the breeze from his slender whalebone baton, which was wrapped in white leather and appeared to be lighted from within.*

---

*The baton had first been used by Danile Türk, who became so excited over his innovative implement of command that he often inadvertently accompanied the music with a shattering of glass in the chandelier that hung without sufficient clearance above his head in the concert hall in Halle. In 1798, Joseph Haydn had used a baton when conducting *The Creation,* and Ludwig Spohr, who turned Clara's pages in Kassel in 1832, had tried unsuccessfully to popularize the baton in 1825. But it was Mendelssohn who succeeded in placing the baton in the hand of virtually every conductor once he had revealed it to his Gewandhaus musicians and their audiences. He and Hector Berlioz exchanged batons, Berlioz's accompanied by a letter so heavily influenced by his enthusiastic reading of *The*

Two weeks earlier, Mendelssohn had conducted the Gewandhaus orchestra as Clara played for the first time her piano concerto, which she had completed almost exactly two years before, when she was fourteen and unsure enough of her ability at orchestration to have asked Robert to help her with it; which he did with the first movement and then left her on her own for the rest, much to her initial annoyance and later gratitude. By the time she felt the timpani rolls at the end of the second movement shake the very bench on which she sat, and continue shaking it at the opening of the third movement as they were joined by the brass fanfares she remembered having had so much amusement writing, she had come to understand the power she possessed. To write for an orchestra was like throwing stars into an empty sky. And then to write, and play, a solo part was to fly among those stars in danger and delight.

Later that same evening, Mendelssohn had removed his white gloves and come down from his conductor's platform to sit at one piano while she sat at another and Louis Rakemann at a third, and the three of them performed Bach's D-Minor Concerto. It was the first time any of the music of Leipzig's greatest composer had been played in the fifty years of Leipzig Gewandhaus concerts and the first time this particular piece had been presented in public in the nearly hundred years since it had been written and played upon harpsichords by Bach himself and his two eldest sons, Wilhelm Friedemann and Karl Philipp Emanuel. Of the three of them performing this November night, Rakemann seemed happiest, playing from memory so that he was able to gaze the whole time over his piano at Clara, united with her through the music as he would never be in the flesh and able this once not only to abide but to glory in such renunciation, a sacrifice he would question only when they were taking their bows and he grasped her right hand (Mendelssohn, more decorous, did not take her left) and once again his desire became almost unbearably corporeal.

Robert had written for *New Journal of Music* a fine review of the whole concert and of her concerto in particular (careful not to mention his own role in orchestrating its first movement), and they had between them now, spread out on a table, a copy of the magazine opened to his review, which both had memorized but neither felt the need to recite; it merely sat there like another voice in the room, unequivocally in support of their own union, such as it was, undefined to either of them, unspoken of by either of them,

Last of the Mohicans that he addressed Mendelssohn as Great Chief, referred to their batons as tomahawks, and denigrated squaws and palefaces for their love of more ornate weapons than Mendelssohn's sleek whalebone rod and Berlioz's own oak stick.

the great mystery at the core of their separate lives, about to become entangled forever.

Robert rose and said the same thing he had said several times earlier in the evening: "I really should be going. You have a long journey ahead of you tomorrow."

"Oh, don't go yet," she said, and somewhat needlessly, because by the time she had finished even so brief a command or wish, whichever it was, Robert was squarely back in his seat.

He had no idea why he kept doing that. He had no desire to leave her, and he trusted her enough to know she had no desire for him to leave. In the past, when he had stayed too long, she had simply fallen asleep even as he spoke to her, the only one since Ludwig to whom he spoke with such ease and at such length, her legs tucked up beneath her on her chair, a posture that was quite modest and yet that utterly captured his attention, amazed as he was at the suppleness of her slender body and its difference from his own; that she could actually sit on her legs struck him as miraculous and so far from his own capabilities as to signal the most profound difference between their bodies.

"Are you not tired?" he asked.

"I'm exhausted."

He rose again.

"Sit down," she said. "Why do you keep getting up?"

"I was wondering that same thing myself."

"Perhaps you're restless. Perhaps I'm boring you."

"*I'm* not the tired one. Perhaps I'm boring *you.*"

"You have never bored me, Robert, not in my entire life. But you have certainly tired me out."

"I know I talk too much," he said. "The more I talk to you, the less I talk to other people."

"It's not your talking," she replied; "if I had my way, you would talk to me and to no one else. It's your *music,* Robert. It's your new sonata."

He had brought to her that evening what he thought was his finished piece in G minor, which he had started working on almost ten years before and had completed but a few weeks ago. She had played it for him for the first time tonight but had stopped during the first movement and, pointing at the music before her on the piano, started to laugh.

"First you give the instruction, 'As fast as possible,' and then you say, 'Faster,' and then you say, 'Faster still.'"

"Quite so."

"But is it not impossible to play faster than 'as fast as possible'?"

"Not for you," he said. "Play on."

So she had, until she reached the finale, a Presto in 6/16 time. "This is just too difficult," she said. "Even those few of us for whom you write will not understand this."

"That's why I've marked it 'Passionato,'" he said, as if this quite explained the music's restrictive idiosyncrasy.

So she had struggled though the final movement. And only when she failed to recognize within it a theme that he had taken from her own writing did he begin to wonder whether the finale might be so obscure as to baffle even her, the one (living) person put on Earth when he'd been put on Earth who could play his music as he heard it in his head.*

They remained together far into the night, until finally she pulled her legs beneath her and closed her eyes. He sat quite still and watched her sleep, not moving even to take a sip of brandy or reach toward the ashtray for his cigar, which went out with that last cunningly sweet gasp of smoke a cigar gave forth before it died.

This, he thought, is how I want to spend my life. To sit before her while she sleeps until I am no more.

Finally, on the brink of peaceful sleep himself, far more peaceful in its approach than he ever found in bed, he rose from his chair and looked at her one last time, full of longing for her life and for her body, before he turned abruptly and walked toward the door, saying silently to himself and to her, "Good-bye, good-bye, good-bye."

"Wait. Robert, wait. Wait, Robert."

He turned around to see her smiling shyly from her chair.

"I fell asleep."

"Yes."

"I won't have you sneaking off as usual before..."

"Yes?"

"Before I show you out."

She stood and picked up the lamp from the table next to her chair and walked him to the stairs. He went down before her on the narrow stairway and when he reached the bottom looked back up at her. She seemed to be floating down to him on the light from her lamp, slowly as he waited until

---

*Three years later he replaced this finale with a Rondo in 2/4. He dedicated the piece to Henriette Voigt, who had recently died at the age of twenty-eight of the same disease, consumption, that had claimed the life of her great love, Ludwig Schunke, exactly two weeks shy of his twenty-fourth birthday.

the light reached him and climbed down his body, causing him to open his arms to receive it and to receive her into them.

He held her for a moment as she stood on the last stair, his cheek against her neck and half his face hidden in her hair, before he lifted her down and put his mouth to hers and felt her lips open as he had never been able to imagine they would. Her hand not holding the lamp came around behind him and, in a fist, pressed into his spine, pulled him against her, as his own hands touched her neck, her shoulders, grasped the halves of her taut and slender back, which rose and fell with the same quick breaths he felt escape into his mouth.

When finally he drew his lips away from hers and looked into her face, her eyes were closed. He could feel her trembling, almost violently, and was afraid she might fall, and so he held her against him until her body ceased to move at all.

There they stood, silent and inseparable, until, without either of them knowing how, he found himself at home sitting at his piano writing the word *innig* on a sheet of music paper with one hand while the other sounded out the music itself, and she found herself with her father beside her in the carriage on the way to Zwickau.*

Dresden

FEBRUARY 7, 1836
Union.
Robert Schumann

When Robert learned from his brother Eduard on February 4 that their mother had died in Zwickau, at the age of seventy, he locked himself in his room. He would speak to no one, not even Wilhelm Ulex, who, while he

---

Innig was a notation Schumann would often thereafter put on his music. It means both *inward* and *intimate*. It was while attaching it to this second of his *Davidbündlertänze* that he had what he described to Clara as "marriage thoughts," which he went on to say "originated in the most joyous excitement I can ever recall. If I was ever happy at the piano, it was while composing these."

could not imagine the reason for his friend's withdrawal, accepted it as further evidence that Robert's genius isolated him from the world and that without such isolation his art would suffer. Why else would Robert make his best friend suffer the humiliation of living with a veritable ghost, unseen and untouched?—if not unheard, for there continued the sound of the piano, interrupted only by the sound of weeping.

It was not until another letter arrived on February 6 that Wilhelm was able to engage Robert in the flesh.

"There's a letter for you," he yelled through Robert's door and, he hoped, over the sound of the piano.

No response.

"It's a letter from Fräulein Wieck."

The piano ceased. The door opened. Robert stood before him with his hand outstretched. He looked, as he often did when he was composing, haggard and almost maniacally distracted. But there seemed, as well, a weight atop him, crushing him in upon himself, whereas his music customarily seemed to shred him into a dozen weightless strips of airy, vulnerable being.

Wilhelm gave him the letter, which Robert placed flat in one hand while with a tip of the index finger of the other he tested the seal.

"Intact," he pronounced. Then he made that same hand into a fist and brought it down with such force that the seal shattered.

"Outtact," he announced.

He read the letter to himself as Wilhelm stood there, witnessing what appeared to be an instantaneous and nearly total transformation of Robert's physical being. The weight was lifted. The red eyes turned blue again. Even his clothes seemed to rearrange themselves into an at least casual presentability.

Robert reached out and pulled Wilhelm into his arms. Wilhelm realized that the letter, whatever its other magical powers, had not succeeded in providing Robert with either a shave or a bath.

"We're off to Dresden," said Robert, which pleased Wilhelm, for Robert, as eager as he appeared to have Wilhelm live with him, had never taken him anywhere beyond the homes and taverns of Leipzig.

But Wilhelm's pleasure was short-lived. Once they reached Dresden, it was into Clara's arms that Robert disappeared and Wilhelm realized he had been, as the term was used to indicate a decoy lover, a beard.

It was not that Robert didn't trust Clara. It was her father whom he doubted. Her letter—her wonderful, liberating, quite possibly life-saving letter—said that her father was leaving Dresden on business the next day. Her unspoken meaning was clear: *Come to me.*

Wieck had taken her to Dresden the moment he became convinced that Robert would not marry Ernestine von Fricken. Once again, Dresden had become his place of her imprisonment. But this time her father was determined to guard her himself. And this is exactly what he had done, without a word passing between his daughter and Schumann, so that when he was called away on business, the lure of increased income overcame the diminishing fear that, should he not be there, Robert Schumann might magically appear and continue to distract his daughter from her music and from a better life than a dissolute lunatic like Schumann could ever provide.

"Now I understand," said Wilhelm as they rode together in the coach toward Dresden. "I had never seen you so distraught. Imagine, to find that your beloved, if that indeed is what she is, has been cruelly torn from—"

"My mother died," Robert interrupted his friend.

"Your dear, sweet mother!" Wilhelm was instantly crestfallen. While he had never been invited to Zwickau to meet Frau Schumann, he was aware of Robert's love for her and hers for him, as evidenced by the money she sent him so he could have his laundry done (not to mention the laundry she did for him when he visited her) and buy good beer. "When?"

"Four days ago."

"Four days? Are you not—"

"No."

"—going to the funeral?"

"No. How could you even ask? Clearly, you don't know me as well as Ludwig did. He would never even imagine I would go to my mother's funeral."

"Your own mother . . . ?"

Robert put his hand on Wilhelm's arm. "That's all right. I wouldn't go to your mother's funeral either."

Nor, he had the kindness not to add, to your own.

He and Wilhelm took a shared room in Dresden, where, before he had unpacked or bathed, Robert wrote a note to Clara and had the hotel deliver it to her at the home of the Reissigers, friends with whom she and her father were staying. He asked that the deliverer wait for a response.

Since he did not trust that Wieck had indeed departed, he felt the need to write in code, should his note be intercepted:

Dear Fräulein Wieck:

A package has arrived for you at the Hotel David. As in the last days of Pompeii, it is ready to erupt. Please be so kind as to attend to its retrieval.

Yours forever,

Herr Einsam*

Too nervous to do anything else as he waited for a reply, Robert finally took a bath, keeping Wilhelm next to him so he might have someone to talk to in his nervousness, though usually he liked to bathe unaccompanied, because he preferred silence to talk and because he was always hearing music in his head; and what better place to hear it and try to remember it than the bath and thus to overcome his humiliating need to be at the piano while composing?

Robert was still bathing when he heard a knocking on a door down the hall.

"That must be the hotel boy with her response," he said to Wilhelm. "Hurry. But if he's gone and has slipped it under the door, be sure to bring it here immediately."

Wilhelm returned empty-handed, shaking his head. Robert looked at him forlornly. "I should have known—her father is still in Dresden. He must have intercepted my note. I should never have made reference to the Bulwer-Lytton. She *told* me he thought it was a most inappropriate gift. He even told her that it was evidence that I understood nothing whatsoever about her. He—"

"It was the hotel *girl*," interrupted Wilhelm.

"What hotel girl?"

"The girl who's come to see you at your hotel."

"Girl?"

"It's Clara herself," Wilhelm finally confessed, at once delighted over his little tease and saddened over his inevitable displacement.

"Well, don't let her stand out in the hallway," said Robert, rising naked and still soap-streaked out of the dirty water. "Take her into the room. And then, if you don't mind, gather your things and go down to the hotel desk to book yourself your own room."

"You are done with me?"

---

*Mr. Lonely

Robert nodded gravely.

"I have served my purpose?"

"Not entirely."

"Shall I seduce her for you, then?" said Wilhelm bitterly.

"A towel, please," answered Robert, stepping out of the bathtub.

When Robert went to Clara, she was sitting at the desk in his room, a pen in her hand and paper before her.

"I trust I did not take so long dressing that you are writing me a note of farewell that had I found it here would have broken my heart."

She did not turn around. She merely went on writing, her back to him, so that he could see her shoulders work against the fabric of her dress. He was reminded of when he had come upon her sharpening knives at her return from Paris nearly four years ago. But then, he remembered, he had felt she was like a stranger. And now, she seemed to belong exactly where she was.

When she had finished her writing with the flourish of a signature, she turned to him, a great smile upon her pretty, joyous face, and said, "Here," holding out to him the sheet of paper.

> Dear Herr Einsamkeit:
>
> In answer to your kind and welcome letter, I offer myself as antidote to your loneliness. Please be so kind as to accept this gift with your customary kindness and passion.
>
> Yours beyond forever,
>
> Fräulein Verloren und Verlobt*

He did not yet dare take her in his arms. He had done so several times after their kiss on the stairway, but only for a moment, for another kiss or two, and never with the depth or meaning of their first kiss, as if they knew that no stolen kiss could be as passionate as the first.

"I can't believe I'm here," she said.

"Here? Dresden? My hotel? My room in my hotel? Or here on Earth?"

"Speaking of your hotel," she said, "I had to follow the boy who brought me Herr Einsamkeit's message. I knew there was no Hotel David, but I knew that David was you and that I would find you wherever you would expect to have my response to your little letter. But I didn't know what hotel that would be."

----

*Miss Lost and Betrothed

"Why didn't you simply ask the boy where he worked? Or better yet, accompany him back?"

"Because then he would know I was here with you. And I want no one to know I'm here with you."

"Wilhelm knows."

"Will he betray us?"

"To your father, you mean?"

"Papa does not want us to be together at all."

"He will."

"Betray us?"

"No one will betray us. I meant your father will want us to be together."

"When?"

"When he knows how I feel about you."

"And how is that?"

"Shall I show you?"

She rose from the chair and came to stand near him. "It took me so long to learn to talk that I perhaps value words overmuch. So rather than—"

"Are you saying you would prefer me to tell you than show you how I feel about you?"

"For the moment, yes." She sat down on the edge of the bed. "So?" she prompted.

"I don't know what to say."

"You might start by telling me that you adore me."

"Oh, I do."

"There," she said, so encouragingly as to give him the impression he had actually said it first.

"And that you have always adored me."

"Always," he emphasized.

"And that you always will adore me."

"Forever."

"And that you like the way I look."

"Of course I do."

"And how do I look?"

"How?"

"Yes, how do I look to you?"

"I think you are the most beautiful creature on earth."

"Creature?"

"Woman. I think you are the most beautiful woman on earth."

He started toward her, and started to open his arms to her.

She held up her hand. "I put the word into your mouth."

"But not into my eyes. My eyes have found you beautiful since the day I first saw you. I thought you were the most beautiful little girl I'd ever seen. And every time I've seen you since then, I've thought you the more beautiful, against the impossibility that you could be more beautiful. And you have never been more beautiful to me than now, tonight, here, with me. I feel we have never been alone together, not truly, and now that we're alone together, and I can see you without the distractions of the world, I can see that you are, for me, the most beautiful woman on earth."

"The most beautiful woman on earth?" She was quite delighted. "No matter that it isn't true, I shall carry those words to the grave."

"Please don't mention the grave," he said, with enough seriousness of tone, he would have thought, to cause her to stop laughing immediately. But this request only intensified her laughter.

"It was merely a figure of speech," she said. "I'm not about to go to my grave, and neither are you."

"But my mother is," he found it necessary to relate.

"Your mother?"

"She's died," he said.

Now, after all this, and on this note, she was finally up and in his arms.

"I loved your mother." She trembled against him.

"And she loved you."

"I believe she did."

"And I love you."

"You love me?"

"I do, Clara. Yes, I do."

She wiped her face hard again his shoulder, which he was surprised to find she reached, and then pulled back so she could gaze upon his face. "And does your love include desire?"

"Yes."

"You desire me?"

"Yes."

"With all your heart?"

"Yes."

"And with all the rest of you as well?"

"Where did you learn to speak like this?"

"Thus far, only to myself."

———

Sometime, in the middle of the night, he truly wanted to sleep. But she would not let him. As he sought refuge from the winter air beneath the thin hotel sheet and the almost-as-thin hotel feather comforter, she sat beside him naked with her legs tucked up beneath her upon the thin hotel feather bed, a posture no longer modest as, he had discovered, neither was she.

So delighted did she seem—with herself, with him, with what they had done and what she clearly wanted to do again—and so almost nervously, ecstatically alive, that, when her mouth was not upon his, she went on talking and talking and talking. There was no stopping her. She chattered away like someone who can subsist on the very words she relinquishes, feasting on her happiness and curiosity.

"You smell good," she said. "Did you bathe just for me?"

"Of course."

"So you suspected we might end up like this?"

"Like what?" he asked, to hear what she might say.

"Doing what we have done."

"And what have we done?"

"You don't know?" she asked with feigned shock. "Have I made so little impression upon you that you're unaware of what has recently passed between us?"

"Did something pass between us? I was under the impression that we left too little space for anything to pass between us."

She bent to plant a kiss upon his cheek. He was, once again, amazed at the suppleness of her body, how she could not only sit upon her own legs but from that position also tilt and swivel, rotate and virtually pirouette, anchored to the earth, the bed, or to himself by her sweet, small backside, which had remained childish, while the rest of her had transformed, as if before his own blind eyes, into womanhood—breasts, mouth, chin, forehead, shoulders, waist.

With her lips still upon his cheek, moving as she spoke, she said softly, "You bathed for me, but you did not shave. Tell me, Robert—did your previous lovers prefer you to shave?"

"Previous lovers?" he said disingenuously.

"Oh, I want to know about them all." She rolled off him and once more sat upon her legs, but now so close to him that her shins pressed against his side and her hair, which she had let fall like some last piece of clothing when she had first undressed before him, sought out the fingers of his raised left hand. "I want to know about Agnes Carus. Did you make love to Agnes?"

He shook his head.

"Oh, I find that hard to believe. From the first moment I saw you two together, which was the first moment I saw you ever in my life, I was sure the two of you were making love. She was my idol, you know. And so it was quite natural that from that moment on, I, too, wanted to make love to you."

So shocked was Robert, he pulled down upon the hair that he had started to weave in his fingers. "But you were only—"

She not only didn't recoil from the pain but laughed. "A girl can want to make love even if she doesn't know what it is. There may be a proper age for the doing of it, though I have no idea what that is, but no age can be dictated for the desiring of it. I desired to possess you. That's all I know. As for what that might mean, I had no real idea of that until this very night. One may dream or look at pictures to the exclusion of all else in life, but there can be no preparation for the thing itself. There can be no rehearsal for the joy of *this*." She slapped her hand down upon the feather bed. "That does not mean, of course, that one might not have had prior experience. In your case, I mean. In my own, I had not progressed beyond kisses, and aside from my kisses with you, not one kiss succeeded in unlocking any part of my body, least of all my heart. But if not with Agnes, then with whom? Where did you gain all your obvious experience, my fine man?"

"Mostly in my head," he answered, a bit distracted by her talk of kisses.

"Mostly, but not wholly. Was it Henriette Voigt, then? What she could not have from poor Ludwig Schunke, did she get from you?"

"No, not Henriette. Henriette is a faithful wife—if one does not count Ludwig, who would test the fidelity of any man or woman. But even Ludwig she did not... they did not...."

Clara understood what Robert was attempting to hide from her sensibilities, whose delicacy she hoped would by now not be in question. "Did they not make love because he was too ill?"

"His illness made her want him all the more. Dying, in our time, has come to seem more an adventure into the unknown than what it really is— delivery into the squalor of emptiness. He made Henriette feel all the more alive, and not merely in her brain. As for me, only once did I hold her in my arms, and so completely did she love Ludwig that it was more like holding him. I did, of course, desire her. Who would not?"

"Who indeed!"

"Have I made you jealous?"

"No longer."

"No longer? I would have thought—"

"By possessing me, you have freed me. By taking me, you have given me to myself. By giving yourself to me, you have unburdened me. So speak not of jealousy. I could no longer suffer that imposter. But curiosity—oh, my God, I'm so curious I could die! What about Ernestine! Surely, you and Ernestine..."

"No."

"No? I imagined it all?"

"Imagined it? How?"

"Oh, I couldn't possibly tell you, Robert. Modesty does not permit it."

He let his eyes travel upon her beside him, so pale and dear and wholly open and uncovered. "Modesty?"

"It's far easier, at least for me, I now find, to display my body than my mind."

"For me as well!" She seemed to have discovered something about him in revealing the same thing about herself, and to have revealed this discovery to him.

She shook her head. "Robert, you wear your mind on your body as if it were your very clothing. I've always felt that everything you think and feel appears upon you instantly for everyone to see."

"Only for you. Everything I've thought and felt has been for you."

"Oh, really? What about Christel Schnabel then?"

"Schnabel! Christel Schnabel!"

"I suppose you're going to deny her too, which is to say, deny that you did not deny giving yourself to her?"

"No...yes...," he sputtered.

"Now there is a useful answer to a question," she teased: "'Yes...no...'"

"That is her surname? Schnabel?"

"Yes," she answered, "if the Christel under discussion is the same Christel who was a pupil of my father and was seen on more than one occasion either going into or coming out of your rooms. And so fitting a surname, too, is it not? That is, if Fräulein Schnabel indeed frolicked with your *Schnabel*."*

"It is the same Christel," he confessed. "I simply never knew her name."

"Well, under the circumstances, I can hardly expect that you might have called her Fräulein Schnabel, any more than you might, now that you have

---

*A *Schnabel* can be both bill or beak and spout or nozzle, so it is not clear whether Clara was punning on Christel's surname in reference to a kiss upon the lips or, more likely, given her mood, the taking of a gambol with the male member.

not denied yourself to me either, call me Fräulein Wieck. But what did you call her?"

"I called her Christel," he said, to spare Clara the pain of learning that he had called her Charitas. He remembered how bitterly Clara had reacted to his having given Ernestine a nickname, and Ernestine had been his fiancée, not merely a girl with whom he had shared an intimacy so shallow (if, at the same time, profound) that he had not until now learned her surname.

"So who was Charitas?" asked Clara immediately. "Yet another of your conquests?"

"I had no other conquests," he answered, to try to evade his lie with what was, he realized, the truth. "How did you learn of her?"

"My father told me."

Robert was shocked. "How did he know?"

"Papa has made it his business to learn of anything he might use to keep me from loving you, and then of telling me of it. But there's nothing he could tell me, or you could tell me, that would succeed in that. So is it true: Christel and Charitas were your only other women?"

"She was," he said.

She nodded at his tacit confession. "And the rest?"

"Only whores."

"Whores?"

"Whores."

"Many whores?"

"Oh, yes, many whores."

"How many whores?"

"I have no idea. One doesn't count whores, after all. One may count lovers, and children, and one certainly counts beats to a measure, but not whores. I mean, a man—a vulgar man, it is true—might boast, 'I have had twelve mistresses.' But I have never heard any man, no matter how vulgar, say, 'I have had a hundred whores, and tonight I'm going to have my hundred-and-first.'"

"A hundred! You have had a hundred whores?"

"Come to me," he said, opening his arms.

She looked at him skeptically before leaning forward, kneeling into him until her head and hair settled on his shoulder.

"I have no idea how many," he said. "I was usually drunk and had no memory in the morning of what I'd done the night before. For all I know, I had no whores. All I meant to say was that whatever and whoever I had before you, it was nothing and no one. As it feels to me now, you are my life, you have always been my life, and you will always be my life."

She let her body go, and slid beneath the thin hotel sheet and comforter, and there she held him as together they fell asleep and left forever the world that had known them as children.

PART THREE

Distant Beloved

Dresden

FEBRUARY 15, 1836

I love you unspeakably.

Robert Schumann

"Give me his letters. Give me all his letters."

How strange, she thought, that in the middle of her father's latest tirade against Robert, and against what he imagined she and Robert had done in his absence (she nearly smiled at remembering what they had done), he should ask for Robert's letters. Unknown to her father, a letter had arrived this very day. It had been written in the coach station at Zwickau, where Robert had gone to pay respects at his mother's grave. As the snow and sleet came down, and Robert was trapped by the closed roads while he waited for the Leipzig express, he was, in his impatient misery, given the opportunity to write of his love for her. She recalled that night and how she had stood at the little window in this same room on the third floor of the Reissigers' house and watched the snow swirl aloft like dancers' arms and listened to the frozen rain tap out a message she imagined was from him. It would not be the first time they had communicated through the air.

But what joy it had been to receive this palpable evidence of their connection and to learn he was indeed writing to her at the very hour she had been at her window looking for his image in the darkness and listening for the sound of his fingers on her skin.

She hid this new letter beneath her even as she refused to take from the desk between them those other letters from Robert, which her father knew were all the letters and little notes Robert had ever sent or slipped to her. She traveled with them always, to have his disembodied voice with her, addressing her from childhood until now, his first letter since he had embodied her wholly, and she him, in such a way as she had never imagined in all her imaginings.

As her father continued to hold out his hand for the letters, he said, "He's not right for you. You may think he's right for you. Corruption is a magnet that attracts the corruptible. You're like your mother in that—drawn to the flesh. But you have art far beyond what she had, and I had thought—mistakenly, I learn—that it would keep you from such wantonness. You disgrace me with your deception and behavior. But most of all, you disgrace yourself. He is not right for you. He drinks too much. He suffers from illnesses and an imagination of illness that's worse than illness itself. He has, by his own hand, crippled his hand and thereby taken from himself his one best chance to earn a living. Is this the act of a sane human being? Or does he suppose he can live on the income from those dissonant, nerve-wracked pieces he composes, that no one in the world but you and I appreciate or understand? His mind is as weak as his will is irresolute. He will betray you with other women with no more thought than a man eating fowl after fish. Or have you forgotten you're not the sole student of mine whose virtue he's transgressed? Tell me—have you?"

"No longer." Now she could not help smiling.

"Then I have told you something that will succeed in keeping you from seeing him ever again?"

"Oh, no," she answered. "He admitted it himself. After I had let him know I knew. And I thank you for having given me that information, Papa. My knowing it allowed him to be unashamed in telling me about his whores."

As she said the word, she remembered how four years before in Paris she and her father had come upon prostitutes in their enviably garish dresses and how at that time she had been too frightened even to comment upon their constant and exciting presence. How interesting, she thought, that my language should now be freed in the aftermath of the liberation of my body. She felt almost giddy with the power of provocation.

"Whores!"

"A hundred whores at least."

Her father could say nothing. He reached out his hand, not to comfort her, she knew, but that she might put his letters into it, as if they were literally Robert and that to give them up would be to give him up.

She recalled what his latest letter said, the one she sat upon, and how hopeless was the wish that he wished within it: "Perhaps your father will not withdraw his hand when I ask his blessing."

She put her own hand, empty, into her father's. If only he would take it, in place of Robert's, and recognize her love for him, her father, who had taken her before she'd learned to speak and set her down on his lap and then before the piano and taught her how to speak through music and how to listen to herself through the music she made so that she grew to love her wordless voice long before her Robert came and read to her and played with her and asked her what she thought of things and finally helped her find the voice within that called out with a woman's pleasure to the world.

Her father took her hand and turned it over and opened it and placed within it, brought up from his belt, the pistol he carried on his travels. He pressed the gun into her palm, not releasing it but, with his other hand beneath hers, in what would otherwise be a gesture of warmth, not allowing her to let it go.

"If I see him near you, I'll shoot him."

For a moment, before he snatched it away, he let the gun lie by itself, heavy and foreboding in her hand.

She trembled at the thought of it, that she might be the one to cause his death, by causing him to come to her, or herself to go to him.

With the same hand that had held the gun, she reached beneath her and withdrew Robert's letter and gazed down within its words, as much to keep from looking at her father as to read again what she had nearly memorized.

A strange desire came over her, that she might ask her father to help her with the letter, to interpret what Robert meant, not when he said that he and she were intended by fate to be together or that he felt her presence in that cold station house so close to him that he could feel her in his arms but when he said he loved her unspeakably. What did that mean? That he could not express his love for her? That the love he felt for her was somehow objectionable, to others if not to themselves? That there were no words available to tell her how he felt? That only silence was left for them?

He must have known, she thought. He must have known that we may never be together again.

She pushed the letter toward where her father had been standing across the desk from her, but when she raised her eyes to meet his, she found him gone.

Leipzig

FEBRUARY 20, 1837
The way it stands now is that either I can never speak with her again or she will be mine entirely.
Robert Schumann

As Robert lay in Anna Laidlaw's arms, he longed for Clara Wieck.

It had been more than a year since he had spoken to her or so much as had a letter from her. He wrote to her but had no way of knowing if she'd received his letters. Her father had most likely intercepted them. All he'd had back from her were his own earlier letters, bundled up and tied with ribbon, not a word of sorrow or explanation to accompany them, merely his words thrown back at him like rain that falls hard from the earth into the clouds. He could not bring himself even to untie them, let alone read them, though when he'd had enough to drink he would hold them to his nose and sometimes found himself awakening in the morning with his head on his desk or piano and the letters there beneath his cheek or forehead. When he slept in his bed, he placed the letters on his bedside table, not to have her near, for she had forsaken her presence in the words he had written to her, but so that he might in his dreams be inspired by her betrayal to dream of her no more.

He knew from Karl Banck that Wieck had thrown him and Clara back together and that Wieck had said he would kill Robert if he came near his daughter. To Robert's face, Banck told him that Clara no longer loved him. To others in the *New Journal of Music* office, Banck spread stories of Robert's dalliances with other women. These stories were not untrue. Robert knew that Banck was telling them to Clara as well. He did not mind that, not merely because they were true and not because he wanted Clara hurt and jealous, though he was jealous of whatever favors Banck might be winning from her, the most painful to contemplate being the mere sight of her, which to him, now, was more precious than the possession of her body. He did not mind her knowing of his love affairs because they only served to increase his longing for her. What he no longer knew was what he preferred: her, or his longing for her.

He had seen her but once since they had left their bed in Dresden, when both were back in Leipzig. And that, upon the unknowing instigation of Frédéric Chopin, was through a window.

Chopin had come to Leipzig for one day in September on his way back to Paris from Marienbad and Dresden, to each of which he had followed Maria Wodzinska in the hope of winning both her love and her hand.

On September 12, Robert heard a faint knock on the door of his newly rented flat in a house near Leipzig's Booksellers' Exchange. He was living alone once more—Wilhelm Ulex having moved out, apparently over jealousy of Clara—and was in the habit of ignoring knocks on his door, because with each potential intrusion he instantly weighed the worth of solitude against the worth of companionship and usually chose the former. Since the death of Ludwig Schunke and the loss of Clara Wieck, he had preferred to be alone, until the demands of the flesh might cause him to seek out a woman, and when he was with people, he found himself even more given to silence than he had been in the past. The sounds he heard now, and preferred, were memories of Clara's voice and the music he was writing for the piano with greater fervor than he had ever written before, including revisions of his F-sharp Minor Sonata, a new Sonata in F Minor, a group of symphonic études, some dances, and a C-Major Fantasie as a possible contribution toward the Beethoven statue to be dedicated in Bonn at a memorial ceremony being organized by Franz Liszt.

He was resting from work on this last piece when, because the knock on his door was so quiet as to be merely a suggestion of desire to enter, he decided to answer it, half expecting to see only a gentle breeze clothed in fairy form, like the ghost of his sister or a whispered, secret greeting from his lost love, borne upon the wind.

But there stood Chopin, alone, pale and small, pristinely elegant in contrast to Robert's ash-dappled dishevelment. They stood in the doorway looking at one another, until Robert finally opened his arms, though he was frightened of crushing this frail man, and Chopin, if for no other reason than to escape the dangerous grasp of so much larger a person, walked right around him and into his home.

Robert had not seen Chopin since their first meeting a year earlier. He had recently written to Chopin in Paris, if only to remind him of his existence, and thus, in a way, to remind himself of the same. Once you have given your love to someone, Robert had discovered, and that love is thwarted, you become lost not only to your beloved but also to yourself. Every gesture, every breath, every written word, every inked-in note of music is an attempt to remain alive in a world from which you have felt yourself begin to disappear. Chopin's presence at his door, before he could possibly have received the letter, was for Robert evidence, however fragile, that he had not wholly lost his power to ruffle the universe.

"You do me great honor," he said.

Chopin did not dispute that. He removed his coat and walked straight to the room with the piano, drawn by its heat in the aftermath of Robert's playing.

He played études, mazurkas, a nocturne, a Ballade in F Major, and finally parts of a sonata still in progress, full of disordered progressions and certain to estrange and mystify the public, a smiling, mocking sphinx of a piece. Robert found Chopin's playing perfect, except for his annoying habit of moving a finger silently over the entire keyboard as he finished each work, as if to dispel some dreaminess of sound and move the music out of hearing.

"Do you approve?" They were Chopin's first words.

Before Robert could answer, Chopin said, "Of course you do. I seem to have come so under your spell that I am writing ballades to Adam Mickiewicz's poetry. I am seeing images in my head and putting to music what I see. Can you guess what my F-Major Ballade represents?"

Robert had no idea. "The agitato toward the finish . . . ," he speculated, hoping Chopin would supply the context.

But when Chopin merely stared at him, Robert added, "And how you move into A minor at the very end . . . It's quite . . ."

"Yes?"

"It's quite . . . no, very . . . it's very . . . beautiful."

"And what do you see?"

"I see salvation," said Robert, who had seen nothing. "I see rescue from the storm."

"Do you see women?" asked Chopin.

"I always see women," answered Robert.

Failing to find this amusing, Chopin rose from the bench of the piano and went to join Robert on his modest blue sofa, sitting as far as he could from Robert's cigar, which gave forth its gauzy smoke to match the common perception of Chopin's music. What Robert found in Chopin, however, was great power, a kind of muscularity of mind that in trying to please itself alone discovered beauty in dissonance and subversion in the only apparently delicate.

Like someone telling a story to an amiable but stupid child, Chopin recited with a kind of deliberate dispassion the tale told in Mickiewicz's poem: "A group of beautiful Polish girls are captured by the Russians and are about to be ravished by them. They beg God to open up the earth and let them be swallowed by it. God hears their prayers and indeed opens up the earth. As the girls sink within, they are turned to beautiful flowers on the shores of the lake of the Willis. Any man who touches them will die."

"I've known women like that," said Robert, resigned to the fact that Chopin would not find this funny either.

"I have just come from one of them," said Chopin, who explained he had gone directly from the coach station to the Wieck house, expecting to find Robert and Clara there together. "With Mendelssohn away, you are the only two I come to see in Leipzig."

"Did she speak of me?"

"Her disagreeable father was in attendance at every moment," Chopin offered. "It was clear when I inquired after you that neither you nor even the sound of your name is welcome in that house."

"But did she speak of me?"

"Perhaps through her music. I have never heard a pianist who so combines audacity with purity of style. Who can improvise as well as she can sight-read. Whose warmth of feeling is always conveyed by beauty of touch. She is, you know, the only woman in Germany who can play my work properly."

"And my work?"

"She played her own for me. I insisted. I particularly liked the A-Minor Concerto and of course her Bellini Variations. She is very gifted, this girl."

"Was I in her music?" asked Robert.

"Perhaps," repeated Chopin.

"She is in mine."

Robert went to the piano and played what he had written of his Fantasie. He wanted the music to draw Chopin to him and in so doing to bring him in contact with Clara, who but hours before had perhaps touched Chopin's hand and been in his eyes and in the breath he swallowed.

When Robert had finished the piece, Chopin said only, "Like Beethoven."

Robert jumped to his feet. "Yes! I'm writing it for the Beethoven memorial. I call it 'Ruins.' It's dedicated to Liszt, who I understand is behind the monument, if you'll pardon the play on words. But it's written for her. The first movement is the most passionate thing I've ever done. A lamentation—because I'm in ruin myself. And the Beethoven within it is one of my messages to her. At the end of that first movement I have woven in one of his 'Songs for the Distant Beloved,' the sixth song, do you know it? It goes, 'Take them, these songs I sing you, songs of passion, songs of pain. Let them like an echo call back our love again.' You see—passion, pain... the distant beloved. That is our story. She will understand that. I have also included these falling five notes of hers"—Robert bent over the piano to play them—"so she may hear herself inside the music, as I hear her inside myself. And I have included some words of Schlegel as an epigraph: 'Through all the notes that sound within the earth's resplendent dream, one whispered note alone sounds for the secret listener.'"

Chopin seemed to give this some thought before he said, "Perhaps it is better for your secret listener to remain both secret and, as you say, your distant beloved. To me, inspiration comes only when I have abstained from a woman for a long time. I find that when I have emptied myself into a woman, I become totally uninspired. Imagine—for a single moment of ecstasy we waste our lives. Not all of us, of course. The average man who tries to live without a woman will simply go mad with frustration. But a genius who suffers unrequited love and unfulfilled passion, made all the worse by the image inside his head of the distant beloved, will discover a great enhancement of his creativity. Men like us must renounce women—only then will the energy in our bodies make its way to our brains in the form of inspiration and and thus we may give birth to a true work of art."

"Maria Wodzinska?" guessed Robert.

Chopin nodded sadly.

"Have you . . . ?"

"I have asked for her hand. If I obtain that, the rest of her will surely follow. In the meantime, I have been told by her mother that I am in a trial period. She warns me to drink gum water and go to bed early every night and to wear warm socks. Maria herself is making me a pair of slippers."

"There's nothing like a pair of warm socks," said Robert, "to enhance one's creativity."

Chopin laughed, finally, until—though with infinite grace—he coughed.*

The next day, Clara turned seventeen. Robert, having been informed by Chopin that Wieck had deliberately scheduled a concert that night for Clara in Naumburg so she would be away from Robert in case he might be tempted to communicate with her on her birthday, went to her house very early that morning, before she would have left. He found her where he thought he might, and heard her first, practicing at the parlor piano for her concert, awake before the household, sitting at her piano as her birthday dawned and no one, he imagined, heard her play but he. He could see her face clearly enough through the window to see she was smiling and wondered why there were no tears, shed because they would not be together on her birthday as they had always been together, shed because they might never again be together. *And yet,* he wondered, *what kind of love is it that wishes the lover to be sad?* If he truly loved her, he would wish her to be happy no matter the circumstance, no matter the loss. So, he thought, she must be

---

*By the time Maria Wodzinska had returned to Poland and sent Chopin the slippers she had embroidered for him (one size too large so he would have room for his warm socks), he had met George Sand, with whom he was to live for many years, the last eight of them chastely. Not two years after they met, Sand carved the date June 19, 1839, into the wall of her bedroom, to mark the last time they had, and would ever, make love. As for Maria, her only response to Chopin's proposal of marriage was to wed a neighbor boy, whom she divorced for nonconsummation. Chopin never saw her again. He tied her letters together with a dried rose and put them into an envelope on which he wrote, "My sorrow."

smiling at her memory of him and at her dreams that they would meet again and at the music she played so wonderfully, imagining with each note that he could hear it but unable to imagine for a moment that he stood there at the window gazing in at her until the very heat of his breath upon the glass caused her to disappear and all he was left with was the sound of her fingers in his flesh.

From that moment on, it really was as if she had disappeared. He heard nothing of her for months, or would allow himself to hear nothing. That winter became the darkest of times, and he tried to make himself forget her. When he learned, much later, that on the very day of her seventeenth birthday the carriage taking her to Naumburg had overturned and she was cut on the head and face and bruised about the arms and legs, and might, it was said, have been killed, he realized that their estrangement had been complete, because otherwise he would have known of her pain and the threat to her life without having been told.

He took up again with Christel in Leipzig. And then, to escape Christel and the vision of Clara that invaded her body when he made love to her, he went to stay with friends in Maxen, where he met Anna Robena Laidlaw, who helped him keep his mind off what his eyes could not avoid—Sonnenstein, the old castle directly on the Elbe that had been turned into an insane asylum, from which the incurable "inmates," as they were called, had for the past several years been transferred out no longer to prison but directly to the Caruses' asylum in Colditz. He sometimes imagined admitting himself to Sonnenstein and behaving incurably mad, so that he too might be transferred to Colditz and thus find his way, finally, into the bed of Agnes Carus, or she into his, so they might make love among the madmen. But this itself was, was it not, the thinking of a madman? How much more sensible to trade Agnes for Anna, if he could not trade all the women in the world for the one he loved.

Anna was sixteen years old, court pianist to the queen of Hanover, heir to a Scottish fortune, and so beautiful in a pale, blond way that Robert believed he might succeed in replacing Clara with her, move her into his mind by fixing upon the image of her physical being and sliding it into his consciousness as one might an unfamiliar key into a consequential lock. He was determined to possess her solely that she might possess him.

In Maxen, all was innocent. Anna was traveling with her mother and the conductor of the Hanover orchestra, but she was remarkably unchaperoned; her guardians might be his as well and determined it would benefit him and Anna equally that they become lovers.

She would come to see him by herself, delighted to catch him in his dressing gown, smoking his cigar. Her grandmother, she said, had been a friend and benefactor of Sir Walter Scott, having come to his aid when his Ballantyne publishing house went bankrupt and he needed money to pay off his debts and to complete work on his, as Anna called it, ostentatious castle, Abbotsford on the Tweed. His father, he replied, had both translated and published Scott in Germany. Instantly, Anna became Scott's village maid who stole through the shade, her shepherd's suit to hear, as Anna sang, and together they sat at the piano and improvised tunes as they tested each other's knowledge of Scott, the reward to both winner and loser being a shared kiss:

> O lovers' eyes are sharp to see,
> And lovers' ears in hearing;
> And love, in life's extremity,
> Can lend an hour of cheering.

It was all Robert wanted, an hour of cheering, hour after hour, to forget his true beloved in the arms of someone who loved him. Anna followed him to Leipzig, and there he took her rowing and smiled up at her as she gave a recital and hosted her postrecital dinner and reviewed her glowingly in his magazine and walked with her through the rose garden and picked a rose that was the best rose he could find but was not, he said, worthy of her, and it was clutching that rose that she went with him for the first time to his bed, and, with Anna in his arms, Robert found himself longing for Clara.

It was truly a longing for what was not there. Perhaps this was the secret Sanskrit of Nature — a longing not for the Infinite but for the body of an absent lover. Clara did not exist. Anna had replaced her. And yet, the closer he became to Anna — the harder he held her and the more deeply he penetrated her — the more he longed for someone he could no longer even see in his mind, hear, feel, smell, touch, remember. She was gone. Annihilated. Reduced to desire alone. She was nothing but his longing. Clara. She filled him completely and left no room for anyone but her immaterial being.

Once, as Anna lay in his arms asleep in the afternoon with the shutters over his windows so that the light was dulled to a kind of twilight promise, he reached across her to his bedside table and seized the bundle of his letters returned by Clara. He pressed them to the bottom sheet and trailed them through the moisture from their bodies.

After Anna had left Leipzig, she sent him a box of cigars and a lock of her hair, and so delighted was he with the former that he immediately misplaced the latter and feared it had been swept up and discarded by the woman who cleaned his rooms.

He dedicated to her his *Fantasiestücke,* taking the title from Hoffmann's hommage to Jacques Callot, the French engraver whose work inspired Robert in his own, with its mad intensity of detail within a space so confined as to threaten a suffocation of delight. In his letter to Anna accompanying his gift of this piece of music, he drew her attention to the section called "In the Night," which he wrote with the story in mind of Hero and Leander, of whom he had first learned from his father's tale of Lord Byron's famous swim. Hero was a virgin princess of Aphrodite, Leander a beautiful young man who every night guided by the light in her tower swam across the Hellespont to make love to her, until one night a storm blew out her light. Leander, unable to find his way to her, drowned. In the daylight, when she saw his body carried on the waves toward her, she threw herself into the sea and died as near to him as she could.*

Leipzig

AUGUST 13, 1837
I could not do it secretly, so I did it in public.
Clara Wieck

Clara had not completely recovered from her injuries when her father took her off to tour Jena, Weimar, Hamburg, Bremen, Hanover, Brunswick, Freiberg, and finally Berlin, where she was able to spend time with her mother for the first time since her father had repossessed her thirteen years earlier. Clara realized immediately there was a warmth in her mother's gaze and embrace she could not obtain from her father or stepmother. Therefore, it did not surprise her to discover that her father wrote in her diary of the visit that her mother had proved to be "impolite, cruel, deceitful, petty, and arrogant."

---

*Robert and Anna never met again. Found among her effects after her death in London in 1904 were Robert's letters and with them the rose she had carried to his room nearly seventy years before.

He ordered Clara, as he had before, to live in Dresden for the summer, to keep her away from any possible contact with Schumann. Robert, however, had no idea where she was; even if he had, he would most likely not have checked once again into his Hotel David. Clara often went out of her way to walk past the hotel and, looking up at its windows, was gripped by a terrible sense of loss combined with the kind of lust she felt had escaped from her forever and that she certainly did not feel for Karl Banck, to whom she knew she was rumored to be engaged to marry, or for any of the men, young and old, who approached her in every city in which she played and as much as offered themselves to her. She was fascinated to find her body responding to a building, whose bricks and wood and glass had no meaning beyond their material selves except for what she gave them by way of memory.

But then her father ordered her back to Leipzig to play a concert at the Börsenhalle. And she, who had played all over northern Germany and been celebrated as a greater virtuoso than Paganini and applauded for so long in Berlin—a full hour and a half—that her back still ached from bowing, refused. She had not played publicly in Leipzig since she and Robert had been apart and she'd returned his letters and had allowed Karl Banck liberties of time if not of flesh with her and had viewed Leipzig as a place in which to hide. There, she felt, she was serving out a kind of exile from desire. To put herself on display, to wrap herself in her music which was at the same time to expose herself, was to place herself in an impossible position. If Robert came to her concert, she would suffer from being in the same room with him; if he did not come, she would suffer from his absence.

When her father told her she must play—the hall was rented, the programs were being set in type, the notion of a triumphant homecoming was firmly planted in the minds of the public—she relented, but only on condition that she be allowed to play several of Robert's new Symphonic Etudes, which had recently been published and that she had learned—in private, she believed, until her father said, "You show them to great advantage. Play them if you must. I'll inform the printer."

But Robert, she learned from mutual acquaintances, did not want her to play them. Her performing them in public would embarrass him and mock the intimacy they had shared and that she had disavowed with her distance from him and her unwillingness to seek him out and her return of his letters.

So she sent him a message of reconciliation that should not have been necessary once she had announced her desire to play his work in public: *I want your letters back.*

And he replied: *You may not have them back. But you may have new ones.*

It was as if, now, she must play the concert in order to receive a letter from him. What recompense that would be! How it would infuriate her father to know that by allowing her to play Robert's music he would have brought them together again, and that she would have traded all the money that her father would take, and covet, from her performance, for that one letter.

When she stepped out onto the Börsenhalle stage to play, she looked for him, in vain.

He sat in the back of the hall, with his face turned away from her, not so she might fail to see him, and not even that he would fail to see her, but because he could not bear the thought that the reunion of their eyes might be shared by the people between them. Their love had become so private a thing, a thing so hidden in himself that he sometimes felt, when he dived within to find it, that he lost himself entirely and was thereby erased not only from the world but also from himself. If to love was to become slightly mad, to lose love was to be wholly touched.

It was only when he heard the piano that he looked toward the stage. There she was, no fog of breath between them now, playing the newly daring young Viennese Henselt's "*Si oiseau j'étais,*" to which he had introduced her, sitting there in her usual posture, thoroughly self-contained, no sheets of music to distract her, nothing, it appeared, to distract her, not even himself. He might as well not be there.

It was the same with the Chopin and her Bellini Variations. She wrapped herself in music the way a girl, to protect her virtue, might hold her sleeves down within her palms, in the hope she might cover every inch of flesh but unaware that she had drawn her dress more tightly on her body and thus was all the more revealed.

But when she played a little piece by Liszt and in the middle of it missed a beat, one beat, a momentary lapse he could see went undetected by the audience, it was for him like an eternal moment that lasted long enough for the two of them to enter and be reunited. She never made mistakes like that. She was flawless as a pianist. It had to be she was someone else just then, her double maybe, cracking up in order to provide him inlet to her soul.

There he stayed, and grew, when she played his études, moving from the simple theme he'd taken from Baron von Fricken into perfect resonances of musicians they had loved together, Paganini, Mendelssohn, Bach, the history of their love in music, which of all the arts provided best a cloister of creation shared.

He didn't care that those around him seemed puzzled by the music. He enjoyed their consternation. The less his art was grasped, the freer he was to write it as he wished. It might be a musician's job to please an audience; a composer's was to please himself.

He left as soon as she was done, turned his back to her and did not applaud so as not to vulgarize his pleasure. Love was not meant to be shared, and the expression of it was not meant to be common.

She looked for him as she bowed and did not see him. She had been told he would be there, and had been told, as she rested backstage before the concert, that he was there. But she had not seen him and wondered, as she searched the congratulatory bouquets of flowers dropped at her feet like slain birds, whether he had been there at all.

As soon as she was able to break away from well-wishers and sycophants and the usual young men who had detected personal messages in her phrasings and the way her dress revealed her shoulders, she left the hall alone and walked the streets and then into the woods, suffering far more than the customary letdown after a performance. She wanted to see him there, in her mind if not, as she fantasized, coming toward her from behind the trees among which he used to hide when she was young, jumping out like a ridiculously large forest sprite to startle and amuse her. She saw no trees, no flowers, no meadowland, even as she walked among them and through them. Her eyes were for him alone. Yet not for him at all, because she'd been told she mustn't see him and had trained herself to see him not at all. He was, as always, wholly with her, and wholly absent.

By the time she arrived home, the bottom of her dress wet with dew and the back of the skirt stained from when she had sat down in the leaves and grass to rest and wait for him who never came, she was convinced she'd made a terrible mistake. She should not have played his music and certainly should not have used it to try to bring him to her. She'd become the siren he had read her of when she was just a little girl, the ocean nymph to match and to destroy his forest sprite, using music to manipulate desire.

She was sitting in despair upon her bed when Nanny knocked and, without waiting for response, entered. Clara thought at first that Nanny's smile signaled news she'd heard of the supposed success of Clara's concert. But the smile grew as Nanny handed her a folded sheet of paper and said, "God bless you, child," as she touched Clara's cheek and then departed.

The sheet was folded in thirds and sealed. On the outside, in Robert's unmistakably muddled hand, was a message:

After endless days of silence, of pain, of hope, of despair, may these words be received with the love that you once felt for me. If you no longer feel it, please return this letter unopened.

If tears could have broken that seal, it would have melted as they fell upon that letter and her fingers that but hours before had let him hear his études for the first time.

The 13th of August, 1837

My dearest Clara,

As you have broken the seal on this letter, so you have repaired my heart. That your eyes might see my words is, to me, after such long silence, as if they were gazing into my own. I can feel you with me even as I sit alone at my desk, imagining this letter in your hands, your breath upon it, your eyes alight, the very scent of you spreading over it and me.

Have you been faithful? As much as I believe in you, my desire for you is restless and perverse. When nothing is heard for so long from the one I love most in the world—and that is who you are—I lose faith in your strength of will and by so doing in my own.

The fidelity I speak of is not to me but to us. One may give oneself to another without, as it were, taking the other to oneself. What I have learned in our time apart, which is a year and a half nearly to the day, is that we are inseparable, no matter how much time or space is put between us, but that, inseparable or not, we cannot survive in separation.

Therefore, will you promise me that on your birthday one month from now you will give your father a letter from me? He would not have put my études in your program were he not somehow disposed toward me. Say you will. Say "yes" to me. I will not rest until I have your vow.

My heart lies on this page. And now my name.
Robert Schumann

Leipzig August 15, 1837

My Robert,

A simple "yes" is all you want? I have spent my whole life saying "yes" to you, whether you have heard it or not.

As for if I have been faithful, I cannot say "yes" to that. I have betrayed you with my tears, which should have been laughter for our time together and the love we made. I have betrayed you with my dreams, which failed to make real their ecstasy. I have betrayed you with my words, whispered to you every night too softly for you to hear. I have betrayed you with my body, which I have yielded time and time again to memory. I have betrayed you with desire, which has used you in your absence as if you were upon me. I have betrayed you with no man, who is yourself when you are gone from me.

I would say "yes" were you to ask me to cut off my hands and send them with your music pouring forth. But when you ask me to give a letter to my father, begging of him whatever it is you might beg (and if it is not me, then do not break the seal on this letter), that strikes me as risky.

It is one thing for him to allow your music played in public by me—he seems to respect your music, at least so long as everyone else finds it incomprehensible. But your person—so long as I find it desirable, which will be for as long as I live, he…I cannot bear to write the words.

But of course I shall give him your letter. If only to be able to say "yes" to you in the one way I may right now.

Your Clara

P.S. It is actually the 14th on which I am writing this letter, but out of fear that you will not receive it until tomorrow, I am putting tomorrow's date upon it, so that we may at least have the illusion that we are somehow together on this day, whichever day it may be, today, tomorrow, even yesterday. Time has been our enemy, in that it provides a measurement of our isolation; in this way we may vanquish it.

The 13th of September, 1837

Dear Herr Wieck:

On your daughter's birthday—the day on which the most cherished being on earth for each of us first heard the breathing of this earth—I write to you for your blessing.

Of your regard for her, there can be no doubt. Her music sounds it to the world.

Of your regard for me, I believe we are both undeserving of it—you for holding it, I for having it held against me.

I know you like my music, quite against the prejudices of the world at large. But why, then, honoring its complexities, can you not honor the complexities in its creator? I know my faults well enough not to have to repeat them to someone who himself has repeated them to anyone who will listen.

But what of my virtues? I work almost endlessly at my music, and what time I might take away from it to spend with your daughter would be time spent happily—I might say relievedly—away from my art, which can only benefit from the happiness she would bring to it and me. (I am not one of those who believes that great suffering produces great art; great suffering produces great lives, except for those who live them.)

I have been left an inheritance by both my poor departed father and mother, so that even if the publication of my compositions does not produce great income for some time, I shall be able to take care of your daughter.

I have known your daughter since her childhood. I have watched her and watched over her and have grown to love her now as a man as once I loved her as a charmed visitor to her sweet and wholesome life, which you provided her and that now I ask your blessing so I might do the same.

I beg of you, be a friend again to one to whose friendship you entrusted your child, and in so doing be the best of fathers to the best of daughters.

Robert Schumann

Leipzig

SEPTEMBER 17, 1837
*If I should give my daughter in marriage to another man,
it would be to keep her from you.*
Friedrich Wieck

To prepare for his interview with the man he desired as his father-in-law only insofar as that man had fathered the woman he loved, Robert spent the night denying himself both sleep and drink, the former because of his mind's rehearsal for the great event, the latter only through the most profound act of will.

And so when, almost immediately upon his arrival at the Wieck home, Wieck offered Robert a sherry, as he was pouring one for himself, Robert accepted, grateful for what he took to be the acknowledgment of his nervousness and Wieck's consequent wish to put him at his ease.

They were meeting in a small parlor of the Grimmaischestrasse house within which Robert had never set foot. It was furnished only with a single chair and table and, against one wall, a closed cupboard. He had not even known of this room's existence, nor noticed the narrow, unglassed door that opened into it. He found this rather unsettling, because he had, after all, lived in this house and had, he thought, investigated every inch of it, not only out of curiosity but also, once he became aware of his attraction toward Clara, because he believed that those we desire leave desire in every room through which they pass in life, emanations of the shadow self that attach to objects and suffuse the very air.

But he could not feel her in this room. In the house at large, yes. He had had only to enter the front door, to come into this home from which he had been exiled for so long, to feel both her presence and his desire for her. He had no idea if she was even at home. He had rehearsed her running down the stairs to greet him, as she had often done as a child, and in one mad version of this as-yet-unlived day she had taken him by the hand and pulled him up the stairs all the way to her room on the third floor. But reality had hidden her away. And now this strange, hitherto unseen parlor had erased her from the house. She, too, had never stepped within, or Robert would know. Her father had found the one place in the house where she could not comfort him nor he covet her.

The fireplace was filled with wood but unlit. While it might be too soon in the season for a fire, with summer gasping its last, cool breaths, this room was chill, as well it might be, given its ghostly nonexistence until now. All the more reason for the warmth of the sherry.

Wieck even offered him a cigar, which was sufficiently unlike him that Robert wondered if his letter might have done the trick entire and Wieck was merely going to raise his glass in a toast and, bypassing this dreaded interview entirely, pronounce his blessing upon the union of his daughter and the only man who loved her more than he did.

"Habano?" Robert let the smoke drift out of his mouth and into his nostrils, which is what a male human being did to show his appreciation for the gift of a cigar, and as further demonstration of his gratitude he also waggled the glistening brown cylinder of tobacco gently between his first two fingers, making sure Wieck could observe the gesture.

"Caribbean," answered Wieck. "That's all I know about it. If there's anything I can't bear, it's a cigar pedant."

"I was merely—"

"How is the sherry?"

"Oh, very good." Robert could not help himself, he now waggled his little glass before Wieck.

"You drink too much." Wieck punctuated his judgment with a long swallow from his own sherry glass, immediately refilling it from the decanter.

When he moved to top off Robert's glass, Robert did not know whether to hide it behind his back or hold it forth in defiance of Wieck's reproof. It seemed safest to imitate Wieck himself; Robert brought the little glass to his lips, slowly raised his head, and drank down the sherry, Wieck be damned.

"More?" Wieck held out the decanter.

"I drink too much." Robert, smiling confidently, could not help mocking his inquisitor.

"I'm glad to hear you admit it. It's one more reason why you must not marry my daughter."

Robert took the decanter from his hand and poured his own drink. "Are you denying us your permission, Friedrich?"

"Have you heard me deny you my permission, Herr Schumann?"

"No, I have not." Robert became nervously optimistic. "May I assume we then have your permission?"

"You may assume anything you want. Assumptions are the very fodder of misconception. For example, suppose I were to assume you have enough money to support my daughter in the style in which I support her. Let us say an income of a thousand thalers. Would that not be a misconception?"

"Yes, it would."

"Aha!" Wieck waved his cigar with such heartiness that its ash flew off and landed whole and corklike—the sign of a good cigar indeed—on Robert's sleeve. Robert was afraid of offending Wieck by brushing it off either onto the floor or into the fireplace or the ashtray on the mantlepiece. So he held his arm out rigidly before him, balancing the ash thereon, as he proceeded to offend Wieck far more grievously than he would have done had he taken a deep breath and blown the ash directly onto Wieck's cravat.

"The misconception is that *you* support her. If I am not mistaken, it is the money she makes from her concerts and recitals that you keep and spend."

Wieck turned his back and walked away. Only when he reached a wall did he turn around. He pushed his cigar almost punishingly between his lips and sucked on it again and again until his cheeks swelled and only then did he release a huge cloud of smoke toward Robert. Wieck's words seemed to Robert to percolate out of that smoke as the Devil's might out of the steam of Hell.

"Unless you've had a child with one of those whores of yours, you have no idea what it means to be responsible for the life of another. She is my daughter. She is not even my only daughter. Nor my son or only son. But she is the child dearest to me and the one who costs me most—my time, my dreams, the sharing of my knowledge, which I tried to share with you, to transfer from my head and my heart to your hands, only to have you disdain me by crippling your hands. *Hands,* yes. A pianist has but one hand, divided in two. We speak of hands, but each hand is, literally, the other hand. So it is with Clara and me. We are one hand. Injure one of us, and the other is destroyed. She is my treasure, and I am her bank. I put her share away for her within. In the meantime, room and board. If you want a metaphor for life — you with all your books and the foolish magazine articles you write in which you pretend to be two people,* as if you were your own two hands — then there it is, the metaphor for life itself: room and board."

"She can live with me free," Robert ventured, attempting to bring Wieck back to the topic at hand.

Wieck returned from across the room. Robert could not tell if he came for the conversation or the sherry. "I see you're using your sleeve as an ashtray," Wieck observed. "There might be the metaphor for yourself: the man who makes a mess of himself for others to clean up."

"This is your ash," Robert informed him. "And I can clean it up myself." He shook his sleeve toward the fireplace. The ash remained intact when it hit the hearth. Then what must have been a wind through the flue blew the ash back toward Robert and onto the rug before the hearth, where it disintegrated.

"She cannot live with a man who drops his ashes on the floor. Imagine what her life would be like. Children running about. Noise. You playing the piano. She playing the piano. No money. The world shrunk down into your tiny rooms in your tiny house somewhere. The *world* must be her world, as it is now. She is wanted everywhere. We are leaving soon for Dresden, Prague, Vienna . . . Vienna! I cannot let you enslave her."

"Enslave! I want to marry her, not—"

Wieck held up his hand. "It's the same thing. Marriage is enslavement."

"Are you enslaved then?"

---

*Wieck was referring to Schumann's going by the names, and sometimes even assuming the characters, of Florestan and Eusebius. Florestan was the hero of Beethoven's *Fidelio,* rescued from certain death in a dungeon by his wife, who was disguised as Fidelio, a man. Eusebius had been a much-persecuted fourth-century Christian priest, and eventually saint. Florestan, at least as embodied by Schumann, was wild, impulsive, even dissolute; Eusebius, gentle, contemplative, abstemious. Schumann did not so much outgrow them as grow beyond them. But while they lasted, they satisfied his desire, shared by so many of his artistic contemporaries, for that elusive double (or, in his case, double double) who, like a parallel universe, may both share and appease the anguish of existence and the equivocacy of art.

"I? Oh, no. Not I. But my wife is." Wieck began to laugh. "My wife certainly is."

"And your daughter?"

"My daughter is free."

"I'm glad to hear you say that. If she's free, then she's free to marry."

"Free of you," Wieck said. "Free of you."

Robert shook his head and sat down in a chair that faced the cold fireplace.

"Herr Wieck, I am a young man of twenty-seven with a restless mind. I am an artist who thrives upon some expression of the world within my being. And yet for eight years I have not set foot out of Saxony. I have remained here, working ever harder on my compositions, falling ever more in love with your daughter, saving my money for what I have known for some time is the life I plan for us to have together. Can it be that all my industry and the austerity to which I have confined my life are lost upon you? Is there nothing about me that would recommend me to yourself and for your daughter?"

Wieck came and stood before him. "Your new études," he said. "Did you think I wouldn't know that if I let her play them at the Börsenhalle they would bring you two together? It was inevitable."

"Then why..."

"I understand you, Schumann. I understand you, and my daughter understands your music. We are together in our understanding of you. But if you come between us, then nobody will understand you. Why can't you leave us all as we are?"

"Because I want her."

"You cannot have her."

"Will nothing change your mind?"

"Nothing. More sherry?"

Robert took his glass from the table and held it out toward Wieck, who filled it. "Do you know what a privilege it is for me to have let you in this room? This is my gun room. I keep my pistol in that cupboard. Except, of course, when Clara and I are traveling. It is my job to protect her."

"Are you going to shoot me?" asked Robert.

Wieck gestured for Robert to stand up. When Robert was on his feet, Wieck put his glass into his hand and then picked up his own and held it out toward Robert. "A toast. To Clara—alone."

His words were like a knife, thrust hilt and all into Robert's heart.

Vienna

APRIL 11, 1838

These visits from my adorers are more than I can bear.

Clara Wieck

Clara was sitting by the open window in her room overlooking the Sonnen-felsgasse, reading the latest of Robert's letters to be smuggled to her, when as though from the sky there fell upon the letter, and from there onto her lap, a small, stiff piece of paper.

She knew it could not have come from Robert's letter; she was reading that letter now for the third time. Robert's letter was addressed, as had been the inner envelope in which it arrived, to Fräulein Entfernt, yet another invented "pseudofundonym" (as he called them) Robert used in case her father might intercept, or come upon, one of his letters. But what, she wondered, would her father make of a letter addressed to a Miss Faraway? How could he not know that it was she, and that her correspondent was the one who shared the torture of the distance between them? Robert must either be insulting or entreating him with the very transparency of the ruse.

Her own name and address on the outer envelope had been written by one or another of Robert's accomplices, most often Dr. Reuter, to hide Robert's own handwriting from her father, who would recognize it instantly and use the occasion both to confiscate the letter and to claim that Robert's terrible penmanship was further evidence of his lack of fitness to be her husband.

The small piece of paper was blank, at least on the side that faced her. Clearly, it was a calling card. While its method of arrival through the open window was unorthodox, she feared it was from another of the seemingly thousands of strangers who, since her arrival in Vienna over six months ago and her triumphant recitals here, wanted now to meet her, either that she might endorse some business of theirs or that they might bathe in or drink in whatever glory they imagined poured forth from her. She had become a prisoner in her own house, unable to walk the streets for fear of being surrounded, stared at, touched, stripped, torn apart, eaten—whatever people might be driven to do to her or with her by the very fame that was, they believed, their gift to her. This was not even in exchange for her gift: Such adoration, such annihilation, came as much from those who had merely heard *of* her as from those who had heard her. Fame, she had discovered, soon becomes divorced from its source, in her case music, the piano, her interpretation of the former and her effect upon the latter. Fame was now attached to her, like skin on beauty. It rendered her both wholly distant and wholly, delectably, devourable. Merely the anticipation of her presence caused mayhem; if it were announced, even erroneously, that she was to perform at the Redoutensaal or the Musikvereinsaal or the Burgtheater or the even larger Winterreitschule, the last two of which held thousands, thousands more than they could ever hold would overrun the box office so the police had to be summoned to turn them away. When her father reported to her with delight that masses of people were seen weeping, he did not seem to question, as she did, whether it was truly because they had been denied tickets for her performance or rather as a result of having been beaten by the truncheons of Metternich's police and trampled by their horses.

A calling card thrown through her window was threatening only in that it was now known beside which window she sat in her banishment. When she turned the card over, however, and read the name upon it, she almost leapt from her seat. She pushed the window open even wider, leaned out, and saw there, on the street below, a man looking up at her with a face so beautiful she did not know what to do with her eyes and so just stared at him.

"I kiss your hand, gracious miss." He employed the traditional Austrian greeting.

Though she was seeing him for the first time, she had seen innumerable renderings of him and would have recognized him on sight; there was, she thought, perhaps no man on earth for whom a calling card would be as superfluous. Even at this distance from her window to the street, viewing him slightly from above, what he most resembled for her still was Franz Joseph Gall's famous casting of his head, some fifteen years ago. His hair remained as long, his green eyes as big (and his nose even larger, from what she could see), and the bones of his face as startling in their aggressive symmetry. He was now twenty-seven; she was eighteen. He was exactly a third older than she, both their ages divisible by nine, by three. It was a kind of symmetry of time. He had come upon her at the moment when they were most in harmony, balanced not only on the scale of time but dangling similarly, now that she had conquered Vienna, over the gaping, devouring mouths of the public.

They looked at one another for a moment more before both, in the same instant, pointed in the direction of the front door. Together, they disappeared from one another's view for the time it took for them walk to the door and her to open it.

He was wearing—with his long, unbelted redingote, black suit, and flowing white shirt—peculiarly green gloves, both of which he removed before he reached for her right hand with his and clasped it gently. Upon his index finger he wore a gold-grounded ring, within which lay, in silver, a death's head. So sure was Clara that Liszt would do as he had promised and kiss her hand that she found herself pushing against the pressure of his own. In the moment before embarrassment would have overtaken her, he yielded to the pressure and to her desire and put his lips to the back of her hand.

As he then motioned with his eyes for them to leave the doorway and proceed into the house, he said softly, almost conspiratorially, his hand grazing the back of her sleeve to guide her, "Forgive my unorthodox means of announcing my presence. As you know, I was urged by Chopin to track you down. As you don't know, I was told by Chopin to avoid the man I believe is your father, at least until you and I have had a chance to size one another up, as it were, and to discuss the subject I believe is the cause of your father's incivility. Is there a place we might sit and talk where, when we are discovered, as inevitably we shall be, your reputation will not be ruined by your proximity in private to the likes of me?"

She couldn't tell if he was boasting of or apologizing for his reputation that accounted him a seducer and those he seduced the most fortunate women on earth. Neither could she think of anywhere to go but back to her own room, into which she led him, all the way to the window through which they had met, as if her showing it to him were the excuse she needed to bring him to what was in fact the most private place for her in all this rather large rented house.

He looked out the window into the street, pretending, she realized, to get his bearings. "Did you know that Sonnenfelsgasse used to be called Johann Sebastian Bachgasse? Note, I say 'used to be.' Sonnenfels was a rabbi, of all things, who worked for Empress Maria Theresa. No one in history, I suspect, has hated Jews as much as Maria Theresa. She borrowed their money to build the little summer place she wanted, Schönbrunn. But when she met with them to negotiate for the loan, she so feared contamination from the odium that had adhered to them ever since they had murdered her Lord that she sat behind a screen and put her hands over her ears much as you did over your eyes.* Not, I trust, because you find me odious."

---

*Maria Theresa's hatred of Jews had, like execration of any group, been inherited, through not the silence of the blood but the ignorant prattle of what passes in family and school

Clara shook her head.

"Thank goodness for that!" Liszt started to walk around the room, gazing at her possessions in a way that provoked in her no more discomfort than she was already feeling. "In any case," he went on, "whether she could bear the sight of him or not, she listened to Rabbi Sonnenfels. He convinced her to stop torturing political prisoners. These included anyone who might upset the public order—thieves, spitters, liars, dissidents, blasphemers, freethinkers, French. He was a good man. Not good enough to displace Sebastian Bach's name on a street sign, perhaps . . . Chopin was so outraged by that he has sworn never to come to Vienna, though I suspect that may have more to do with the presence of Thalberg in the very flesh than with the absence of Bach on a street sign. But the good rabbi, through no fault of his own, managed to get Bach's name removed forever from the streets of Vienna and, such is the cruel congruity of imperial happenstance, what else but a piece of music dedicated to him."

Like an actor hitting his marks, Liszt was at her piano at exactly the moment he might take his cue from himself and begin to play. He moved about twenty measures into the piece, when the opening arpeggio burst, as it had from the beginning been threatening to do, into the beginning of the

---

alike for the teaching of history. As is well known, the teaching of history is to history as the troth of a seducer is to love—fraudulent self-interest in the service of darkness. Jews had been forced to live in their own section of Vienna in the thirteenth century and a hundred years later (in observance of the seemingly eternal Viennese rubric *Die Juden sind an allem schuld*—the Jews are to blame for everything) were blamed for the rising of the Danube, an earthquake, and, despite their ghettoization, for the plague. Such spurious culpability survived for a hundred years (in other words, beyond the lives of all who first invented it), indeed was amplified by the passage of generations as parents said, in essence, to their children, "We want you to have the privilege of hatred to a degree that was denied to us." Thus, in 1421, those Jews not burned at the stake were told to leave Vienna, and those Jews who did not leave Vienna were burned at the stake. Only some rabbis escaped either fate: In the ghetto synagogue that had been built with its back to the rest of Vienna because no Jewish house of worship was allowed to face the street, these rabbis, to avoid the humiliation of forced exodus or the special, horripilating pain of the flames, slit their throats with butcher knives (kosher, of course). When the Jews were allowed back into Vienna a bit more than a century later (were begged, in fact, to return, because the German banks had failed and you-know-who were the only ones who could rescue the economy), the warmth of their welcome was goosefleshed by a strange sartorial requirement: all Jews must wear, sewn prominently upon outer garments, a yellow globe of cloth, yellow being the most visible color from a distance, particularly when worn against black.

tempest that gave the piece its nickname. At that point he simply stopped. None of the flourishes for which he was famous. No tossing of his hair, flinging of his arms, jangling of medals, not even, alas, one of his no doubt hundreds of lace-trimmed handkerchiefs thrown to the floor that she might later retrieve, since he always, it was said, left behind talismans for the ladies, be they such handkerchiefs chastely inseminated with his cologne or what was left of one of his cigars, moist with spittle from his lips and tongue.

"Beethoven," she said.

"Actually, my name is Liszt. Franz Liszt." He laughed at his little joke. "Or, more accurately, Ferenc Liszt, for as such was I born not thirty miles from here, on the Hungarian side of the border, thank Heaven, except for the Ferenc, naturally. I sometimes think had I been named a manly Friedrich, like a million other men, I might never have left Hungary in the first place. And, yes, that was Beethoven, but the D Minor of course, which I prefer to Rabbi Sonnenfels' D Major. And, yes, that was the first and thus far the only word you have spoken to me: 'Beethoven.' A reference, perhaps, to what I understand was your absolutely revolutionary introduction of these fusty old Viennese to the Appassionata?"

"And it was still too much for them!"

She had amused him, and she was glad, and while she watched him take pleasure in her sarcastic little gibe at the expense of the conservative Viennese musical establishment, she realized he'd been right, she'd not said a word until she'd said, 'Beethoven.' That was not like her any longer. Since the day she had met Robert for the first time at the Caruses', when she had not spoken in his presence, she had learned to talk until sometimes she chattered on and could hardly be shut up, while Robert had traveled in the opposite direction, from a kind of boisterous enthusiasm over everything into silences she knew struck others as brooding but were, she understood, almost literally part of his music. And when she played his music, so full of sound, almost unendingly gorged with feeling, containing, like a broken heart, so few rests, she felt she could hear behind the music those silences that had been necessary to its creation, emotional counterpoints to the passions in his sound and as necessary to an understanding of his work as were the very notes that fell from her fingers.

"He told me to give you a smile," she said.

"Beethoven?" Liszt was very good at seeming serious while joking or teasing. He neither smirked nor smiled but looked into her eyes as if it were actually possible she had communed with Beethoven, or at least with his spirit, and that Beethoven might have told her to look at him warmly.

"My Robert," she said, employing the possessive not, she realized, to indicate that he was hers but that she was his and that if Liszt wanted her heart, or a piece of it, he would have to fight for it. I am taken, she thought, and therefore must be taken to be had.

"And did he indicate whether it is to be a smile merely transferred from him to me through you, or truly your own?"

Never before, in all the men who had approached her, in the past for her piano playing and now for her fame, and attempted to seduce her with as much allure as they could gather into stance and speech and silly grin or melancholy cockatrice, had she encountered such a master of flirtation as this. She felt his charm light up her face.

"Oh, that looks like one of your own," he said, causing it to become wholly that.

"Whether it is or not," she replied, hearing her amusement in the lilt of her voice, "Robert was more grateful for your review than you might ever realize. Until you wrote about him as you did, he was, when written about at all, and when spoken about always, maligned."

Liszt's review of two of Robert's sonatas and of his impromptus based on a little theme of her own had appeared in Paris in the *Gazette Musicale* about a month after Clara had left on her tour. Robert had sent it to her, and she felt upon reading it that Liszt had understood as much about Robert as he did about his music, which is to say that each was an expression of the other and therefore the art as difficult and profound as the man, and the man as the art. So had Liszt, who had never before encountered anything by Robert or even heard his name, directed his music toward those of contemplative mind, those who could not be satisfied by the superficial work that was taken as art by the vast majority. Schumann's ideas, he said, must be penetrated to be understood, dug into deeply for the life they held that like all transcendent aspects of life escape one's initial experience of them. Only Chopin, Liszt had written, matched Robert for the individuality and depth of his music. Thus was Liszt's review very like Robert's own about Chopin in *New Journal of Music*, when Robert had announced to the world that a new and unknown genius had arrived and suggested hats be taken off to welcome him. Liszt was not as dramatic a writer as Robert, and so his piece had not caused the same stir, except in Robert, who had asked her to give Liszt one of her sweetest smiles. So she had.

Leipzig

JUNE 8, 1838
I am no longer a moonlight knight.
Robert Schumann

As Clara had ordered, Robert stood in the shadows at exactly nine o'clock in the morning staring at her window. He had been there, as she had not ordered, for at least an hour before that. It made no difference to him what time it was. He had once again been unable to sleep and had spent the night thinking himself more and more deeply into her, her soul, her sleep, her dreams, until he cried out into the darkness, "Clara, I am calling for you!" and waited in the silence until he heard her voice loudly and distinctly, from next to him on his bed, "Robert, I am with you." He reached for her, knowing she was not there. A kind of dread came over him, as he realized how spirits can communicate over great distance and yet never carry with them the small comforts of materialization. He had called for her almost every night and had thought that the nights on which she did not call back were the worse. But so unstrung had he felt himself by the clarity of her voice and the absence of her flesh that he had decided never to call for her again. Such determination, however, had not kept him from standing outside her window calling to her silently.

Having seen nothing but the glass of the window growing opaque in the rising sun, he was surprised, at exactly nine o'clock, to see the signal she had hoped to send, the movement of a small white towel. He looked for her hand upon it, or at least its shape within it, knuckles, fingers, a ring he had given her. But all he could see was the towel, waved, he thought, with a lassitude that did not match his excitement at learning that her stepmother had spent the night with her own mother, Frau Fechner. Clara, who had been ordered to fetch Clementine home, therefore had an excuse to leave the house and could meet him. It was for him such intrigue as is as appealing in a book as it is tedious and demeaning in life.

As she had further ordered, he immediately left his post and walked to the market square, slowly, almost dragging his feet, listening for her footsteps behind him, hoping to be surprised by her, a whisper in his ear, perhaps even a hand thrust between his bicep and his ribs if she dared touch him in public in daylight. But as keenly as he listened for her, and told himself he would judge the depth of her love according to how quickly she came to him, he was taken wholly by surprise when he felt his arms pinned to his sides from behind and her lips against his neck and heard her breathless giggle in his ear.

"Robert, Robert, Robert. Happy birthday, Robert! Here is your gift."

She swung him around, or herself around upon him, so they were face to face, held together by her arms until he put his own around her, though he was unable to bring himself to hold her with as much strength as she held him. Even when they met at night, huddling in doorway darkness for a few minutes, he could not believe they might not be discovered, no matter whether Nanny was along to stand guard. He was not afraid her father would shoot him, but he had never been afraid of that; dead, he was of no use to the suffering the world seemed to need in order to fill its quota of disillusion. He was afraid that if they were discovered together, they would be torn apart forever. To have her, he often felt, he must forsake her. To possess her, displace her. To touch her, touch her never again.

Now she took his arm and pulled him along, not toward Frau Fechner's house but in the opposite direction.

"Where are we going?" He tried to interrupt the flow of her words, which had continued from the moment she had taken her lips from his.

"To Vienna." She laughed. "Papa has now written down his consent. That is what I have been dying to tell you. He says he will never let us live together in Leipzig, where we would forever remind him of what he calls our treachery. 'What is our treachery, Papa?' I ask him. Oh, how angry that makes him. I think it refers to our sin, Robert? Do you?" She squeezed his hand and pressed her arm against his. "He suggests you go on ahead to Vienna and make arrangements to move the magazine there and then, perhaps, to sell it. That way, he says, you may begin to have enough money for us to live. He claims I need two thousand thalers a year to spend. Or at least that's what he seems to take from me. But I can earn hardly three pfennigs from my art in Leipzig. Yet in Vienna I am quite the darling. The public loves me, the court adores me, and the aristocracy treats me precisely like what Liszt calls a conjurer or a clever dog, which he despises for himself but I quite like, so long as they pay me. For a single concert during the winter season in Vienna I can make a thousand thalers. They charge an absolute fortune there! If I didn't know how to play the piano, I wouldn't be able to afford to hear myself. Not that I'd want to, if I didn't know how to play. But still. I can get more there for my music than for my body. Alas. And if I give a single lesson a day, I can make another thousand each year. And you a thousand also. So there! We're almost rich in Vienna, and we haven't even moved there. What do you think, Robert? Please say you'll go."

"Vienna?" Now that the word was out, he took her arm and stopped her from walking, as if he actually believed he was on his way there by foot. "He just wants me out of Leipzig."

"Of course he does," she said with such agreeableness that he felt she somehow represented all that might be good in her father and was able to act as a kind of purifier even of her father's most duplicitous motives.

"And you?"

"And I?" She leaned against him. "They search me, you know. When Dr. Reuter comes, they suspect he has given me a letter from you, and they make me stand with my arms like this"—she moved a step away to show him—"and go through my pockets and she goes through my clothes as I stand there like this, full of anger and humiliation. So, yes, I, too, want you out of Leipzig. But only so that when I leave Leipzig myself I will have someplace to go and someone there to keep me when I arrive."

"And have they found any of my letters in their unholy searches?"

She threw her arms around him. "Not where I have hidden them!"

Her body shook as he held her. "Are you laughing or crying?"

"Neither." She took his arm and pulled him on their way.

"Are we walking to Vienna?"

"Only as far as your house."

He shook his head. "We cannot go there."

"Of course we can."

"What about your stepmother?"

"Oh, I don't think we should invite her."

"Are you making light of my desire?"

"Are you making light of mine?"

"You may walk me home. No farther."

"I want to come in, Robert. I want to be alone with you. At least for your birthday. I want to lock the door and shutter the windows and hold out my arms like this so you can search me for the message I carry to you."

"What does it say?"

"There is only one way to find out."

He shook his head. "If someone sees you coming in, or leaving, or hears you while you're there, or hears me call for you when you have left, or sees the bruises of your kisses on my neck, or catches in my eyes the reflection of my memory of you, and your father learns that you have been with me, he will turn this Hell he's made us live in to whatever Hell becomes when Hell becomes too hellish for itself. You know I want you, but I want you so that in my having you, and you me, we hide as little from others as we do from ourselves."

"Then we should surely be sent straight to Hell anyway."

She argued no further for the satisfaction of her desire but walked him with a kind of resigned merriment to the door of his home, at which his landlady, Frau Devrient, appeared to be standing guard, her arms upon her ample bosom like trees felled by the impish fire in her tiny eyes.

"She suspects," whispered Robert.

"What a shame to have the guilt without the deed," Clara whispered back.

He introduced her to Frau Devrient as his fiancée, though the good woman seemed confused and even disappointed when he then kissed Clara chastely good-bye and she went off across the street.

"Another pianist," said his landlady.

"The only pianist."

Robert hurried into the house and through the door of his ground-floor flat.

He went to the window hoping to see Clara as she walked away but instead saw her standing, as he had stood, in a merchant's doorway, books on shelf displays on either side of her, her eyes searching all the lower windows of his house. She was standing as he had stood, as if waiting for a signal, something from him that might tell her the coast was clear, that they need not hide their love from the world, that their best years need not be spent living without each other.

He put his hand against the glass. His injured finger ached, as it always did, when he spread his hand open, flat. But the pain was nothing, nothing, compared to the lack of all feeling in the rest of him, the stupor into which desire fell in order to protect his mind from heartbreak.

His nails scratched the glass as he closed his hand around her as she walked away.

Vienna

APRIL 6, 1839
There is more applause here than music.
Robert Schumann

Robert lived in one ground-floor room on Schönlaternegasse. Each time he saw the sign for his street, he was reminded of Clara's seeing prostitutes for the first time in Paris when she was twelve and imagining herself in one of their rooms in the squalid little houses on the rue de la Vielle Lanterne. Schönlaternegasse was named for the wrought-iron lantern that lit his last steps home on the nights he chased his plum or apple schnapps with the rich Puntigamer beer from Styria, usually at the Silver Swan, where he drank alone and where Beethoven had drunk alone, Robert was told, on that spring night in 1824 after he had conducted the premiere of his Ninth Symphony and went on conducting even when the piece was over, a short, slovenly, long-haired man seen from behind with his arms paring the silence he could no more hear than he could the music, until finally the contralto, Caroline Ungher, grasped his hands in her own and turned him around, with his arms still raised, so he might see the audience, which, with this absolute evidence of Beethoven's deafness, cheered itself into a state of self-satisfied, tearful compassion, while Beethoven stood there humiliated and longing for the burn of slivowitz down his throat.

It was themselves they were honoring, not Beethoven. Their pride in him was the pride the ignorant always take in genius; they let someone else discover it, foster it, guard it, fight for it. Finally, when it is safe to proclaim one's allegiance, they do it not to the work but to the man. Oh, what a genius! they say. Based on what? you ask. Why, his reputation, they say. They may even have a bust of him in their homes. But their beings remain empty of his work. So the case in Vienna, Robert found, where there was perhaps less Beethoven played than in any other city in the world.

He traveled to the suburb of Heiligenstadt and there purchased a copy of what Beethoven called his Testament. He had written it, for publication after his death, in Heiligenstadt in 1802, upon first realizing he was going deaf. In it, he acknowledged his reputation for behavior that might be considered malevolent, stubborn, misanthropic. Robert imagined Beethoven grasping the handles of Dr. Portius's psychometer, in order to override this misleading syllabus and reveal the truth about himself: desperate, anguished, blessed, immortal.

Beethoven called his reputation his "seeming." You do not know, he wrote to a world that would not read his words until it was too late to make amends, the secret cause of my seeming. I can take no recreation in the society of my fellows, in genteel intercourse, in the shared exchange of ideas. I must live like an exile.

Robert felt the same.

He had arrived in early October and spent his first days sightseeing, as if on the trail of music. He went to the Schönbrunn Palace, where Mozart had played piano at the age of six for the Empress Maria Theresa and her husband and exactly half of their sixteen children, though because the performance took place in the Hall of Mirrors, Mozart received the impression he was playing for hundreds if not thousands of formally attired, musically attentive, sets of octuplets, as well as several dozen reproductions of one very fat empress, who delighted in disguising her pregnancies from her subjects by way of so gargantuan a consumption of kugelhupfs that the emperor, Franz, was suspected of wearing the horns not of the cuckold but of the Devil. The empress's obesity was said to have pullulated out of her unrequited hunger for the castrato Senesino, with whom she sang a duet in Florence when she was twenty-two and he thirty-nine; it was not his subducted body, so ruffly adorned, that attracted her so much as his feminine readiness with tears, which caused him to stop singing and weep, overcome, he explained, by the beauty of her voice. It was on her advice, in fact, that Mozart was to take singing lessons from the castrato Giovanni Manzuoli, who it turned out was not a castrato at all but merely posing as one in order to increase business; like most teachers of voice, he caused more tears than he shed.

Following Mozart's performance, at which he was compelled by imperial command to execute such stunts as to play upon a keyboard draped in black cloth and to improvise a three-voiced fugue with one finger of each hand, Mozart leapt into the expansive lap of the empress and whispered to her that he would one day like to marry her daughter Marie Antoinette, but a few months older than he, who had sat throughout his entire performance with her pretty, doomed head cupped in her palms, her eyes alone moving, following his fingers on the keys and, when it had been summoned, on the black cloth. Mozart was also said to have been taken with one of the portraits of Marie Antoinette, which hung among pictures of her numerous brothers and sisters, though Robert preferred the sculptures by Franz Messerschmidt; not his grand, obsequious rendering in lead of the emperor and empress in their coronation robes but the grotesque faces he was said to have cast after he had gone insane, each of them modeled upon sketches he made of his own face in the mirror, contorted anew each time to match the nuances of his manifest derangement. These heads were like individual variations in a piece of music, a Messerschmidt Fantasie, all coming together in the end to form, as Robert attempted with sound, a likeness of their creator in the throes of ecstatic distraction.

He walked past the Heaven's Gate Cloisters, which had given Himmelpfortgasse its name, to the Hungarian Crown Gasthaus, where Schubert had met with his friends to carouse and play their music and where Carl Maria von Weber had lived shortly after the great triumph of *Der Freischütz,* in which he had virtually invented German romantic opera, and shortly before his death at the age of forty from a consumption that carried in its tormented susurrus a sustained whisper from the nitric acid in which he had indulged as a young man and that Robert felt followed him in the air as he made his way down Himmelpfortgasse to see some of Messerschmidt's less misshapen scuptures on the façade of the Savoy Institute for Gentlewomen, none of whom were drawn to look out their windows despite his attempt to beckon them with the power of his mind and curiosity.

At the Café Mozart, which had opened three years after its namesake had received his pauper's burial in St. Marx's Cemetery, Robert tried his first Sachertorte.* He ate such more serious (both culinarily and politically) fare as Kalbsbrücken Metternich at the Gasthaus zum Grünen Anker because Schubert was said to have eaten there regularly. Also, Robert discovered, Franz Grillparzer had lived above the restaurant when he was young. Though he did not succeed in meeting Grillparzer, he felt close to him not only because like himself Grillparzer had written a poem about Clara at the piano (and had captured the sensuality of her white fingers, which sometimes at night were the only part of Clara Robert was able to visualize with any clarity)** but because it was the same Count Sedlnitzky, head of the Austrian Bureau of Censors, who told Robert he was unlikely to be able to publish *New Journal of Music* in Vienna (because he was a foreigner, a Saxon to boot) and who had in the name of the emperor condemned Grillparzer's poem "Campo Vaccino" and later had banned his play about King Ottocar not because, he said, there was anything wrong with it but because someday

---

*The origin of which has long been a subject of political debate in Vienna: Was it created by Franz Sacher, Metternich's chef, as some sort of apparent pastriological homage to repression but in fact the very emblem (because of its sponginess) of Austrian resilience, or was it concocted as a taunt to the sweet-toothed Emperor Franz Joseph by Anna Sacher, who offended morality by smoking cigars and pimping for the girls in the Vienna Opera Ballet? If it was the latter, then what Robert was served was, by chronological necessity, an anticipatory imposter and an emblem, therefore, of Count Sedlnitzky's innocent child in whom might one day rise the dough of jacquerie.

**In Grillparzer's words, Clara "sinks her white fingers in the flood...her quickened heart beats fast...she leads them with white fingers as she plays." Schumann had another reason to identify with this great Austrian writer: Grillparzer had been engaged to Katherina Frölich for fifteen years! Indeed, Grillparzer remained betrothed to his "eternal bride" for another thirty-five years, at which time he broke off the engagement. Only then did he feel comfortable asking Katherina to live with him, which she and one of her equally ancient sisters did on Singerstrasse, not many doors from where they had grown up and close, too, to the old home of Beethoven's teacher, Johann Albrechtsberger.

it might be determined (given the need for rulers to control not only what people think but what they might have occasion to think in the future) that there had been something wrong with it. "The censor's job," Count Sedl-nitzky told Grillsparzer, "is to kill at birth any children, regardless of their seeming innocence, who might grow up to cause trouble."*

Robert wrote to Clara that he felt he had been banished. Like Beethoven, he found himself unable to take pleasure in communicating with people who did not know the secrets he carried within him: the secret of his music, which for Robert was an expression of a momentary sorrow expanded through art into an imperishable joy, and sometimes the reverse; and the secret of his love, the existence of which he did not hold from proclaiming but the pain of which was so deep and so inexpressible that he wondered if like an aesthetic version of Count Sedlnitzky's innocent child he had been destined to write music because he had been destined to love hopelessly.

He found himself, more than ever, withdrawn into a silence whose comfort he distrusted much as he would opium, a soothing relinquishment of life with others for the sad vacancy at the core of his being, which only she could fill. Silence in oneself, he found, begets silence in others. He might go whole days without speaking to anyone, wondering why no one spoke to him. He came to depend on the silence of others—as a respect not so much for his privacy as for his grief—while at the same time he longed to hear words that could be meant only for him, words that addressed him with such specificity they could have been uttered only by some omniscient narrator of being, who is perhaps the true secret listener, or by the one person on earth who could know the depth of his longing. He entertained himself with the idea of sound being transmitted across space as three years before, he remembered, Chopin had entertained him and Clara and Mendelssohn with the idea of sound being captured. It would be painted on air, still, but it would travel great distances, and thus he might, as he lay on his small bed in his room on Schönlaternegasse, hear her voice enter his head and spread through him the dispassion of an opiate and the warmth of her long, white fingers on his flesh.

Vienna, he decided, where as many people in the streets carried food as in Leipzig carried books, while at the same time no less an authority than the Emperor Joseph himself had proclaimed *Don Giovanni* "divine" but still

---

*While Robert was in Vienna, Grillparzer announced he would publish no more plays in his lifetime. Thirty-four years later, when he died, three of his greatest works were found among his papers.

"not food for the teeth of my Viennese"...Vienna was a graveyard of imagination and ideas. No wonder, then, that where he felt most at home was in an actual graveyard.

He wandered through the Währing Cemetery for several days—arriving in the morning and leaving at twilight—before he could bring himself to visit the two graves he had come all this way to see, all this way not only to Währingerstrasse but also to Vienna itself. With the censors opposing his publishing of *New Journal of Music* and his growing sense that for all its musical fame Vienna was a city that honored music only so long as music did not have to be listened to (it distracted from eating and from the discussion of fornication, something else that was honored so long as it was not actually indulged in), Robert decided he was here to honor the dead.

As much as he hated funerals, he loved cemeteries. One could never be alone at funerals (except one's own), whereas there was perhaps no more natural sight in nature than a solitary man wandering among the graves of strangers. Funerals buried the dead; cemeteries presented them in the only possible resurrection, as vividly alive as imagination could make them. At the graves of infants, he saw children dancing. At the graves of couples, he saw fingers entwined. At the graves of the very old, he saw infants crawling from the earth with smiles on their lips and promise in their eyes. He called silently for his lover, from the world within himself, and out of their fragile graves, girls would rise and congregate.

When he finally allowed himself to approach the graves of Beethoven and Schubert, he found a place he estimated was equidistant between them and lay down on that spot. In case anyone might come upon him, he took from his pocket the notebook in which he wrote ideas and his pen and placed them beside him, like a poet awaiting inspiration. In fact, he was a composer listening with his left ear for Schubert and his right for Beethoven. Hearing nothing, he played their music in his mind, Schubert for his left ear, Beethoven for his right. He chose simple piano melodies— the former's brief F-minor *"Moment musical,"* the latter's variation on Dittersdorf's *"Es war einmal"*—and succeeded in keeping them sufficiently separated so that both melodies played at once and he had not only two ears but four hands and, in a sense, two minds, since it was well known that two things cannot be thought at the same time, two sounds cannot be heard at the same time, and certainly two melodies cannot be thought *and* heard *and* played at the same time.

He heard them clearly. That was perhaps the most amazing thing of all. That he could hear each one with such clarity he might as well be split down the middle, half of him Schubert, half Beethoven, all of him dead and buried here between them.

On Schubert's stone were carved words written by Grillparzer himself: MUSIC HAS BURIED HERE PRECIOUS TREASURE YET EVEN MORE PRECIOUS PROMISE.

As if to say, the music being made within the ground surpasses even that released into the air.

Robert had gone to the opera in Vienna, the ballet, orchestra concerts, three times separately to hear Haydn's *Seasons*. But not a note of Schubert had been played. And, the way a dying Mozart had been upstaged by an emperor's enthronement almost forty years earlier, it had been Schubert's bad luck that on the evening of the only public concert of his work while he was alive, Paganini was appearing elsewhere in the city, drawing both the public and every last music journalist to him. Schubert's only expressed disappointment, however, was in being obliged to attend his own concert and thus to miss Paganini's.

On Beethoven's tomb Robert found a pen, a steel pen, forgotten, no doubt, by someone like himself, a distracted worshipper come to see where gods were buried. If it were his pen, he would want it left there, either that he might retrieve it or that in the dead of night Beethoven might emerge and dip its point in the viscid darkness and with it write the music left in him. Robert closed his hand over the pen and slipped it in his pocket.

He then returned to Schubert's grave and ran his hands over every inch of the stone, hoping to find a similar omen, and dropped to his knees to feel around in the dirt and grass for something he might take away. There was only the common litter left by men and wind — tobacco, death-crisped leaves, shreds of paper greased by pastry. He put his ear to the ground and heard nothing but the revision of music into silence.* Remembering the

---

*While it was Schubert's deathbed wish to be buried next to Beethoven, the closest available plot was four graves distant. It was for this reason that when Schumann lay down between the graves, he hovered above the remains of Baron von Wssehrd. Twenty-four years later, both Schubert and Beethoven were exhumed so their skulls might be measured in yet another futile, belated attempt by scientists to try to explain, and thus explain away, genius. But when they were reinterred, they were still the same four graves apart! Only in 1888 were they once again dug up, this time to be taken to Vienna's Central Cemetery, where indeed they now rest so close that they can, almost as one, share the terrible silence. And what used to be the Währing Cemetery is now, absent both Schubert and his knowledge of the honor, Schubert Park.

night he heard of Schubert's death, and wept, and woke to find himself embraced by friends who said they feared he'd gone insane from grief, he determined he must look for Schubert elsewhere.*

He prepared to leave Vienna when it became finally clear the censors would not allow him to publish his magazine and that his music would not support him and Clara in this city, whose preposterous repression and arrogance he attempted to puncture with some carnaval jokes he wrote. In one of the opening allegros he put, as a message both to Clara in Paris and to Metternich in Vienna, a barely disguised version of the *"Marseillaise,"* which he had also inserted into the masquerade scene in *Carnaval.* Metternich had banned this song in performances both public and so private as to forbid not only the whistling and humming of it but even the listening to it in one's own head. Robert chuckled as he wrote this piece but soon was overcome with hallucinations of disaster as he worked upon another, decaying bodies floating before his eyes, rotting coffins carried through the streets by dying mourners. As he found himself weeping for no reason except that a distant voice kept screaming desperately for God right out of the notes as he put them down, he received a letter telling him his brother Eduard was close to death in Zwickau.

For one more week he remained in Vienna to finish up this piece, which he called "Corpse Fantasy" and through the writing of which he felt he was serving his brother more faithfully and honestly than had he stopped composing and gone to see him. When the piece was finally done, Robert could delay no longer and with great anxiety boarded the coach for Zwickau. In the middle of his first night's travel, he was awakened by the playing of trombones, a sad chorale that made him shiver and attempt to draw the darkness of the night around him for what little heat inhabited such blank invisibility. But the cold, bright moon escaped a cloud and wrapped its light around the trombones' lamentations.

"Do you hear that?" he whispered into the groans of music unnerving the coach.

---

*So it was that he made his way to the Wieden suburb and knocked on the Kettenbrüchengasse door of Schubert's brother Ferdinand, who ended up showing Schumann hundreds of pages of unpublished music by Franz Schubert—whole operas and parts of operas, four huge masses, several symphonies, songs, piano pieces for two hands, four hands, dozens of unfinished chamber works. Before he left Vienna, Schumann was able to present to Ferdinand an offer of 180 florins from Breitkopf and Härtel for publication rights to the C-Major Symphony, not to mention five gratis copies.

"I hear nothing," said the man seated beside him. He looked at his watch in the moonlight.

"What time is it?" asked Robert.

"Three twenty-eight."

As he learned five days later, when he arrived in Zwickau too late for his brother's funeral, it was at precisely that same minute on the morning of April 6 that his brother had died. He was not at all surprised by this coincidence. Whether the music had originated in the air or in his head, or from some outpost in the heavens where trombones never ceased their crying out to those on Earth about to lose a loved one, he knew that music always played when someone died. It was, like death itself, the ultimate expression of life.

Altenburg

AUGUST 18, 1839

*I would like to compare music to love. If
it is too lovely and intimate, it hurts.*
Clara Wieck

"I don't remember this city at all." She stood naked at the window of his hotel room, its curtains held between her forearms so that only her head might be visible to someone looking up out of the darkness of the street. She could feel Robert's eyes on her back, moving as his hands would soon, fingers in the ditch of spine, palms' heels hard against the fan of flesh. As much as she had longed for this moment in the year since she had seen him, and in the months before that when she had last lain with him, the most she could do now was let him look at her across the distance of the room. How strange that what had been frightfully desired, and pictured almost too often in the mind, could become so abstract when finally made real. The passage of time reduced one's lover to a shadow, or a dream; and his advent—his appearance before her with his thick hair and blue eyes and strong fingers and back and his longing manifest—was more than she could bear. She was afraid to touch him. She was afraid he would disappear, or she.

"Why should you remember it?" His breath followed the words, almost in a slow whistle, not the kind he sometimes made when he composed but the long, slow, satisfied exhalation that accompanied his successful lighting of a cigar. She waited until the smoke should reach her, and then she took a deep breath. It was surely one of the most wonderful fragrances put on Earth, released by heat.

"It was in Altenburg that my mother gave me back to my father. When I was five. I've told you that story."

"But only a hundred times. How can you expect me to remember?"

"Robert!" Finally, he'd made her laugh. She nearly turned around.

"I thought it was your father who took you from your mother. Besides, you must have been through Altenburg a dozen times by coach."

"Yes, but I never thought I'd end up here in a hotel room with you. I never thought I'd actually stop here. I never thought I'd..."

"You needn't," he said.

"I needn't?"

"Just because two people are naked doesn't mean they must..."

"It doesn't?"

"Of course not."

"Oh, but I must."

"You must?"

"Yes, I really must."

She released the curtains, paused for a moment in case there might actually be someone in the street who had been waiting to see her, and turned to face Robert.

"Please put that cigar down."

Their meeting had been arranged in secret by Dr. Moritz Reuter, who had summoned Clara from Paris, where she had gone at the beginning of the year to play and teach and otherwise try to expand the influence of her name and achieve more income than outlay. Though she had traveled such distance without her father for the first time, he had been planning to join her and go on with her around Europe, to keep her from Robert once he had returned to Leipzig from Vienna and to keep her earning through her concerts and her teaching what she could not earn in Leipzig. But when her father learned that Robert was not going to be moving to Vienna permanently, he wrote to Clara that unless she gave up Robert completely, he would disown her, would require her to support her brothers, would hold all her earnings (over seven thousand thalers) for five years at four percent interest, would deduct from those earnings the room and board he had supplied her since the age of five as well as the cost of all the lessons he had ever given her, and would never give her another lesson for as long as she lived.

Strangely, she found, it was the final threat that most upset her. The money was phantasmal, perhaps because it had always seemed to flow directly from her fingers into his, which is to say, she would play the piano, and he would pocket the receipts. As for teaching, that was anything but an illusion. Her father had been her only teacher of the piano. In teaching her to play, he had, in essence, taught her to talk, taught her to listen, taught her to feel (not merely with capricious emotion but with the fingers themselves, with her very body, as both a source for, and a medium of, the music). So it was with her body that she reacted to his threat, yearning physically for the presence of her father beside her as she practiced in her hotel room on rue Michadière, where she had two grand pianos, each given her by its maker, Camille Pleyel and Pierre Erard.

She was expected to choose between them. She knew that her choice would bring esteem (and increased sales) to one man and disappointment, perhaps even offense, to the other. In fact, both pianos felt alien to her. Their touch was stiff and their sound thin, cold, elusive, which she suspected was her fault, not theirs. She had been brought up on her father's German and Austrian instruments, supple, beguilingly generous, sometimes almost alive, always seductive in their sound and feel. These French pianos were like French men, arrogant and demanding, as aloof as they were pretty. Of the two, she preferred the Pleyel. But when she moved from the Hôtel Michadière to a larger apartment on rue Navarin, it was the Erard she took, even though she found its keys nearly immovable and wished constantly as she played upon it that her father were there to show her some new way of attack, to place his hands where her forearms met her wrists and press his fingers into her muscles as she played to train them how to redirect their strength.

But her father was at home, not only threatening her with disinheritance and then a lawsuit but also reported by the Mendelssohns to have taken up with Camilla Pleyel, of all people, though it was not really "of all people," it was deliberate on his part to hurt her, his own daughter, by turning his musical attentions to her only female rival as a pianist. Maria Moke had taken the name Camilla after she married Camille Pleyel, a strange act of fidelity considering the fact that she had proven unfaithful in all else and had been divorced by her husband on grounds of adultery so persistent as to be undeviating. Liszt, it was said, had bedded her; Gérard de Nerval was believed to have met her in Austria and based his Pandora upon her. And now her father had championed Camilla in Leipzig, escorting her onto the stage, sitting beside her to turn her pages (for she seemed to have no more memory for music than for the vows of marriage), nodding with great approval all through her recitals, and smiling with the most exaggerated ecstasy when she had completed each piece. It was not fair, Clara knew, to punish Monsieur

Pleyel for his ex-wife's coquetry, but neither could she bear to sit at a piano with the name *Pleyel* emblazoned upon it.

So she had chosen the Erard. Upon it she taught her three students, whose payments were not sufficient to support her in a city as expensive as Paris, as neither were the sums she earned from her concerts. At these she played everything, it seemed, but Robert's music, which she reserved for the occasional private soirée where she hoped at least some of the guests would be of sufficient sophisication to appreciate the challenge of his work, though after she had played some of his *Carnaval* at two in the morning at the home of Countess Perthuis, and the guests had looked quite puzzled when she had finished, she wrote to Robert begging him to send her some new work that would be easy to understand, not too long, not too short, without a confusing title, in short something that might be suitable for the general public, demeaning as it might be for a genius to have to fashion work that was as far beneath him and his abilities as it was accessible to the common ear. It was, she said, simply too painful for her to play his work for people who did not begin to understand it. And while he was at it, would he please change the title of the "Corpse Fantasy" simply to "Nocturne," so that people would not be so bothered by the title that they would never be able to listen to the music. Well, he explained, it was true that each of the pieces in *Carnaval* cancels out the one before, and not everyone can adjust to such aesthetic purification; it is a cleansing, like that of death, that offends. And he *had* changed the title of the "Corpse Fantasy," though in doing so he had warned her that they might be wide apart in their understanding of what it meant to be an artist and expressed his hope that this would not bring them bitter times in the future.

There was no bitterness now between them. They were alone in the world, it seemed, on the first floor of a hotel in Altenburg, and no one but Dr. Reuter knew they were there. He, who had once told Robert to take a wife, had sent them into one another's arms as a way for them to gather strength for the battle before them.

Robert had petitioned the Appeals Court in Leipzig for permission to marry Clara Wieck without her father's consent. Clara, in Paris—trembling as she took the pen from Monsieur Delapalm, her lawyer (that she should need a lawyer! for the purpose of suing her own father!)—had signed the petition. She and Robert had been summoned to appear, together with her father, in court.

How different, she wondered, was this from what marriage would be? To lie awake in the middle of the night in a small hotel room in a small city that would mean nothing to her—she could not imagine being booked to perform here—had it not been the site of her being given over, as she saw it, to music. Her father had recognized her. Not merely her gift, but *her*. It was as if, when she used to climb to her dead sister Adelheid's room to listen to her mother play the piano, her father had been there with her, seeing in her the birth of her great secret, that music could pass through her body on its way from the living to the dead. He had chosen her because he knew her. He was her teacher. Like all great teachers, he was divine: not for his knowledge but for how he spread it through her, expanding it within her from enlightenment to expression. How could she not adore him, who adored her so much that he had lost himself within her? Perhaps he recognized her too well. It was too much to expect him to approve of this. That she was profligate in passion, wholly given over, when she gave herself, to such pleasure as was blinding, such feeling that, when she had mounted it and thrown herself off the very edge of life itself, she ceased feeling entirely and lay here waiting for the feeling to return.

"Robert," she whispered.

He was asleep.

"My husband."

Leipzig

DECEMBER 18, 1839

She is an immoral girl who has been seduced by a miserable wretch.
Friedrich Wieck

We, the undersigned, have for several years harbored a shared and genuine wish to be joined in marriage. But there has always been a hindrance to the fulfillment of our wish. Although it gives us deepest pain, we have no choice but to take measures against this hindrance. The father of Clara Wieck, the cosignatory, in defiance of our repeated and respectful requests, withholds his consent. We are unable to understand his reasons: we are conscious of no failings; we have sufficient means to support ourselves now and in the future. Therefore, Herr Wieck must hold a feeling of personal animosity toward the other signatory, who nonetheless believes that he has fulfilled every duty a man owes to the father of the woman he desires as his companion for the rest of his life. Consequently, we approach the High Court with a most humble request: that your worships will cause Herr Wieck to give his consent to our marriage or, if it better suits the court, that you will give your consent in place of his.

Robert Schumann

Clara Wieck

"I will never give my consent," said Wieck. "Never!"

"Would you care to tell us why."

Friedrich Wieck found the words of Archdeacon Rudolf Fischer, who presided over the court, confusing. He sat up there between his comagistrates, who said nothing but always nodded in perfect synchronism whenever Pastor Fischer said anything, when he so much as cleared his throat, and uttered such equivocal statements as "Would you care to tell us why."

"Are you asking me if I would *care* to or are you asking me if I *will*?"

"As you wish," said Pastor Fischer.

"I do not care to," said Wieck.

"Then you needn't," said Pastor Fischer.

"But I will."

Now it was Pastor Fischer who was confused. He said so, with more impatience than Wieck felt was granted to himself to express in this court. "I am confused, Herr Wieck. Either *tell* the court why you will never give your consent to your daughter's marriage or do *not* tell the court."

"If the court agrees to rule in my favor, then I will not tell the court. I do not, as I said, care to tell the court, for by so doing I shall ruin the life of my daughter when my purpose is to save it. "

"Challenge," said Wilhelm Einert, Clara and Schumann's lawyer, who was so short in stature and shrill in voice that Wieck felt his very attendance in court gave himself, who was his own lawyer, a distinct advantage.

"The opposing attorney is required to stand when issuing a challenge," said Wieck.

"I *am* standing." Einert glanced down at himself and then, having verified this information, rose on tiptoe to further make his point.

"You are not in the ballet," said Wieck.

"I am in court," said Einert.

"I should have thought that would be apparent without your having to say so."

"Your challenge?" Pastor Fischer addressed Einert, his intentions much clearer, noticed Wieck, than when addressing him.

"I challenge the defendant's request that the court rule in his favor without his even explaining why he objects to the marriage of his daughter to Herr Schumann. For the court to so rule would be to reject all evidence and provide summary judgment when nothing has been presented to summarize."

"I agree," said Pastor Fischer, thus inspiring the agreement of his co-magistrates, who bobbed sagely.

"Are you therefore telling me that I *must* tell the court why I will never consent to the marriage of my daughter?" Wieck addressed himself both to Pastor Fischer and to Advocate Einert.

Pastor Fischer, no fool he, looked to Einert for the answer.

"You *must!*" squeaked the lawyer.

"Let it be on record, then, that it is not through my wishes but through those of the advocate for the very two people who have sued me that I read my declaration."

"What declaration?" Einert rose, though he was not required to, as if to get a better view of a document that had thus far not been produced.

"*This* declaration!" Wieck reached into the leather satchel in which he had carried to court the various papers whose disclosure would, once and for all, rescue his daughter from a lifetime of penurious unhappiness with a dissolute madman. From the folder he withdrew the pages, bound by a ribbon, into which he had poured such feelings that, were he a composer and this his magnum opus, he would become immortal for the very unleashed fury of the truth told through his art, much like his old friend Beethoven himself. With one hand he held the pages out before him, toward the court, and with the other he untied the ribbon. The moment the papers were released from their gentle girdle, they began to quiver in his hand, though with his passion or their own no one, including himself, could discern.

"That appears to be quite a lengthy document." Pastor Fischer was watching the pages wave with the look of a man who realizes at the end of a heavy meal that his host is about to read his own poetry.

"It is only as long as it needs to be, your worship. Would that the same could be said for Herr Schumann's compositions."

"Challenge," said Einert. "We are here to discuss people, not music."

"If one could tell the singer from the song," scoffed Wieck. "If you know as little about law as you seem to about music, sir, then perhaps I shall not even have to read my declaration."

"You plan to read all that?" Now Pastor Fischer pointed at the papers, which caused them immediately to stop shaking in Wieck's hand. He used this dramatic turn of events to bring the papers before his eyes.

"I have spent what seems to be a lifetime preparing this document. True, it has been only eleven years since Herr Schumann first appeared at my door and began his seduction of my daughter. But eleven years is a long time in anyone's life these days of railroad trains and magazines from Boston, Massachusetts, and particularly in the life of a girl who is barely past nineteen and thus is, by the law over which you rule with such authority, still under my control. Therefore, while I would, as I told the court, care not to read these pages, I shall, as demanded by my very adversary, read them. I *must* read them. For they contain the truth."

"And what do they say?" asked Pastor Fischer.

Friedrich Wieck put on his spectacles and began to read. "'This is the declaration, for all to hear, of Friedrich Wieck, born on the eighteenth of August, seventeen eighty-five, in Pretzsch, fifty miles from this very—'"

"We know where Pretzsch is, Herr Wieck," Pastor Fischer said with an impatience that could have been born only of prejudice against his case. "I trust you are not about to declare the names and occupations of your parents and the location and curriculum of your gymnasium."

Wieck put his free hand over the text, to shield it from eyes that had apparently already managed to read it. He wondered if Pastor Fischer or, more likely, the lackeys who were his comagistrates had somehow managed to go through his locked desk as he had gone so profitably through Clara's.

"I should think my education would be of extreme importance here since it has resulted in the genius of my daughter."

For the first time in these proceedings, he allowed himself the luxury of looking toward Clara. He expected he would see her smile at this preposterous remark of his. He had told her often enough that he was the custodian of her genius, not its creator. Of all the people in this cold, vast room, she would be the only one to appreciate the wit and cunning of his statement. It was important she realize he was willing to falsify his own beliefs in order to save her from disaster.

Indeed, she was looking at him. But, like the girl he had apparently trained too well to hide an expression of her feelings so that, when she performed, her music alone would express them, she did not now display her amusement or even her understanding of this secret, among all the many secrets they shared. Her huge eyes looked at him deadly, so restrained in their admiration of his guile that he found himself admiring her ability to conceal her feelings even as he resented her for so doing and thus making him feel he had no allies whatsoever in this court. Aside from Clementine, that is, from whom he was always forced to hide the depth of his love for his one daughter not her own, and aside from his two witnesses, whose self-interest was no secret to him and whom he would banish from his life and most assuredly from Clara's once he won his case.

"This court is in no position to argue, or to hear arguments, concerning the origins of genius," said Pastor Fischer. "To do so would be to condemn ourselves to a procedure even more lengthy than that threatened by this declaration of yours. Please move on, Herr Wieck, and do so into some territory of your life that has some relevance to your defense of your position."

"I should think that my marriage—my marriage to the mother of Fräulein Wieck, that is—would meet your requirements of relevance. To continue"—and he moved ahead several pages into the document—" 'On June twenty-third, eighteen sixteen, I married Marianne Tromlitz of Plauen, a town in the southeastern part of Saxony, some sixty miles from...' But let me once more dispense with the geography," he said, as he saw Pastor Fischer about to interrupt him yet again. " 'It was a marriage that began in the bliss of conjugal morn and ended in the nightmare of treachery. Marianne Wieck became the mother of Clara Josephine Wieck on September thirteenth, eighteen nineteen. Less than five years later, after burdening me with three useless sons, she showed herself as wanton and debauched in her behavior as her daughter has proved herself to be in her relations with Herr Schumann.' "

For the first time, Pastor Fischer seemed genuinely interested in this case before him. "I beg your pardon!" he nearly bellowed.

"That is correct, your honor. Wanton and debauched. The woman took up with her own piano teacher and before my very eyes, as it were, in my very home, proceeded to seduce him and to be seduced by him—as you know, it takes two to allemande—with the result that I was betrayed in the most—"

"I was under the impression that you were her only piano teacher," said Pastor Fischer.

"I am referring to my ex-wife, for God's sake, not to my daughter!"

"It is not your ex-wife, Herr Wieck, who has brought this case against you. Confine your remarks to your daughter. And I warn you, sir, do not bring forth such accusations without proof. I have never heard a man speak in such fashion of his own daughter. It would seem to be to bring shame to the entire family, himself included. If these are the kind of statements that continue in this declaration of yours, I must forbid you from reading from it. Proof, sir. Proof."

Wieck slammed his declaration down on the table before him and picked up from it his leather satchel, into which he thrust his hand. "If it is proof you are after, I have documents. And I shall have witnesses as well. Behold."

He removed the letters one by one and placed them on the table before him, until they made quite a stack. This was a much more dramatic approach to the presentation of his evidence than if he had simply dumped the letters out together. The court was completely silent while he did this, all eyes on the letters as they accumulated. He could feel the desire in the room to know what was written on these pieces of paper. He had counted on that desire. What, after all, could be more enticing than the prospect of becoming privy to an intimate correspondence that was intended to be irretrievably private?

"What have we here?" asked Pastor Fischer, as if it were not obvious.

"Letters."

"From whom to whom?"

Wieck pointed over at the table where Schumann and Clara sat with their lawyer. "Him to her."

He thought she had known. He thought she must have recognized them. But, to judge from the paleness that seized her face like a winter fog, she was only now becoming aware of the trouble to which he was willing to go to save her. Not for a moment taking her eyes off the letters, she whispered something to Robert and their lawyer. Even her lips were pale.

"And how do these letters relate to the case?" inquired Pastor Fischer.

"These letters, sir, are so full of intimate revelations that they cause a father the most profound shame over the behavior of his daughter."

"The shame, Herr Wieck, is yours!"

Where, suddenly, had Einert found so deep a voice?

"You are out of order, Herr Einert," warned Pastor Fischer.

"Will the court ask Herr Wieck where he found these letters."

"The court will not. But you may."

Without waiting to be asked, Wieck said, "Where do you think I found these letters? Where do most people keep letters? In her desk!"

"And was that desk locked?" asked Einert.

"Of course it was locked. Do you have any idea what these letters say? What they mean? One would have to be even more immodest than my daughter is proved by these letters to be to leave them lying about unsecured."

"So you admit to unlocking Fräulein Wieck's desk without her knowledge or permission and stealing these letters."

"Stealing? *Stealing!* Does a thief come into court and produce from a pouch what he has stolen? What kind of lawyer are you, Herr Einert, if you cannot distinguish between stolen property and evidence? As for whether I unlocked my daughter's desk, how else would you have me gather my evidence? It is a father's right to have access to his child's property. Are you telling me I cannot read her letters? Her diary? What is a parent for if not to know his child? And still, I will admit, I didn't know her well enough. And I didn't find these letters soon enough. But if they prove to leave any doubt after I have read them to the court that my daughter was seduced—*willingly seduced,* I might add—by that man who sits there so forlornly and inexpressively at her side, then *this* letter will clear up that doubt for all eternity."

"And what letter might that be?" asked Pastor Fischer unnecessarily, for Wieck had it out of the satchel and was unfolding it before his eyes.

"Allow me," he said. "This letter was sent to me from Dresden when news was made public of the present conflict between my daughter and myself. 'Dear Herr Wieck. Having become aware of the painful and completely unjustified lawsuit brought against your good person by your profligate daughter and her insane magazine-editor suitor who even were he not insane would be too old for her, I feel it is my sad duty to inform you of a fact that, as shocking as it will be for you to hear, will allow you to triumph against your persecutors and prevent forever a marriage that would destroy your daughter's life. Approximately three and a half years ago, when your daughter was only sixteen years old and under your protection in my own city of Dresden, you were called away from Dresden on urgent business. No sooner were you gone than your daughter made known your absence to Herr Robert Schumann, the magazine editor in question, who arrived in Dresden posthaste and proceeded to relieve your daughter of her virtue. Allow me to repeat that: to relieve her of her virtue! Far from finding this loss to be shameful, your daughter, it nearly shames *me* to have to say, so reveled in such concupiscence that she repeated such act with Herr Schumann until such time as all four wheels of your coach had crossed the border of the Altstadt upon your return to Dresden. I trust this news will, even if it breaks your heart, secure your victory in the battle you fight for fathers everywhere. Yours in sad sincerity.'"

As if reading this letter for the first time, Wieck, under the burden of its terrible news, sank slowly into his chair. Once seated, he crushed the letter violently in his hand and then brought that hand even more violently down upon the table, once, twice—over and over until Pastor Fischer interrupted this display of grief and justifiable anger.

"Who is the author of this letter, Herr Wieck?"

Wieck unfolded the letter and smoothed it out upon the table and gazed down upon it. "Anonymous," he said.

"Anonymous!" uttered Pastor Fischer and Herr Einert in harmony so synchronous as to appear suspiciously rehearsed.

"Of course Anonymous!" said Wieck. "If you wrote such a letter to a father such as I, would you put *your* name on it? What if you feared the messenger might be killed? What if you feared that you yourself would be called into this very court and be forced to utter such blasphemies aloud, before the world? Merely to *report* such behavior is enough to destroy the reputation of an honorable man. Look what it has done to those whose behavior it actually was."

As once more he crushed the letter in his hand, he turned an accusing eye toward Clara and Schumann and their lawyer. But they were huddled together over another piece of paper, paying no attention to him whatever.

Finally, Einert looked up and said, "May I see that letter, please."

"It is addressed to me."

"Once you have introduced it to the court, it belongs to the court," Pastor Fischer directed. "And consider, sir, that we are not even breaching the privacy of your locked desk in order to obtain it. Show him the letter."

Wieck threw the crumpled letter through the air. It did not reach the table and fell at the feet of Einert, who bent down to retrieve it. This did not entail much of a journey.

Einert smoothed out the letter on the table and placed it next to the piece of paper at which he and his clients had been looking. Now they appraised both papers together, eyes moving from one to the other. Then they nodded in a suspicious common rhythm and looked up at him, the two men smiling, Clara still blank-faced.

Einert rose, addressing the court. "I have in my hand, in addition to the letter that Herr Wieck has attempted to obliterate into unidentifiability, another letter. This is signed by a Herr Lehmann and is addressed to Fräulein Wieck. I will not try the patience of the court or the sensibilities of my clients by reading it aloud. Suffice it to say that this letter is nothing more nor less than a villainous and wholly unjustified attack upon Herr Schumann. It describes him in the most scurrilous terms and warns Fräulein Wieck that her association with him will lead to her destruction. And I would like to ask Herr Wieck, what sort of man would write such a letter?"

"A wise man."

"What sort of man would write such a letter to his own daughter?"

"Do you mean to tell me that this Lehmann also has a daughter who has betrayed and humiliated him? And with this selfsame Schumann?"

"I mean to tell you, sir, that your anonymous correspondent and Herr Lehmann are the same person."

"Extraordinary! The poor man!"

"They are *you*!"

"I?"

"You."

"Impossible! It is one thing for you to ask the court to believe that a man might be two men at once, namely Anonymous and Lehmann. But for you to think any man, let alone a man as busy as I with his teaching and his selling of pianos and the guidance of the career of she who would be the greatest pianist in Europe if only she will give up the idea that she should marry...for you to think that any man might be three men, and one of them Friedrich Wieck, is preposterous. I don't even have time to write my *own* letters, aside from those required by my present wife when I am away in distant cities with my daughter, attempting—unsuccessfully, I am sadly informed by both Anonymous and this Lehmann of yours—to keep her from being seduced. On what basis could you possibly accuse me of being the author of these letters?"

"Handwriting," answered Einert.

"But those letters are not written in the same hand."

"And how would you know that, Herr Wieck? You have not been shown the Lehmann letter."

"I know that because it is one thing for you to accuse me of being the author of both those letters, but it is another for you to accuse me of being stupid enough to have written both letters in the same hand. Therefore, if I am the author of both letters, they cannot be written in the same hand. And if they are not written in the same hand, then neither I nor anyone else can be the author of both letters. Ergo, it is established that I am not the author of both letters."

Wieck sat down but was immediately called upon by Pastor Fischer to stand up. "Bring me your declaration, Herr Wieck. It is, is it not, written in your own hand?"

"It is, your worship. But it is, as I trust you realize by now, a document most intensely and intimately private. I cannot allow any eyes but mine to gaze upon it."

Pastor Fischer rested his face in his hands. "These eyes have seen things even more pitiable than autobiographical ravings and more contemptible than forgery." Now Pastor Fischer let loose his face, those very same eyes inflamed with what Wieck could not distinguish between compassion and scorn. "Bring me your declaration, Herr Wieck. And you, Herr Einert, bring me the two letters that you claim are written not only by the same man but by the same man who wrote the declaration to whose profane accusations this court has lately been subjected. I shall compare the handwriting."

As Einert, with tiny, soundless steps, went to Pastor Fischer and, bowing, handed him the two letters, Wieck gathered up the many pages of his declaration much as a man would fallen leaves when he had no garden implements, stuffing the papers into his arms, compressing them within his hands, squeezing them between his fingers, from which their edges and corners nonetheless extended into the courtroom with accusatory perceivability. When, finally, they were crushed beyond what he hoped was recognizability, he opened his satchel with his teeth and tried to drop the papers in. Some of them did find their mark; others fell to the table and to the floor.

"What are you doing?"

How could it not be apparent to Pastor Fischer what he was doing?

"Handwriting!" he screamed at the same time he walked from behind the table and trod upon those fallen pages of his declaration.

When he was halfway toward the much larger and more imposing table at which sat the magistrates, he stopped and turned to face neither his judges nor his accusers but rather some indeterminate being who might be hanging by his neck from the gilt-metal and cut-glass thirteen-light chandelier that added a touch of frivolous dissipation to the solemnity of injustice. Stamping his foot as he once again roared, "Handwriting!" he discovered he could make it tinkle.

"You want to judge my handwriting when sitting over there with my daughter is the man with the worst handwriting in all of Germany. Have you troubled yourself, Your Worship, to look at the way Herr Schumann writes? If it is true that the eyes are the windows to the soul—and Herr Schumann is a squinter, as is clear for all in this courtroom to observe—then the fingers are surely the signposts of the conscience. With which part of the body, after all, is more intimacy achieved than with the fingers? And Schumann's fingers can barely write a legible word. Small wonder—he crippled his own hand and by so doing destroyed the one career at which he might have been able to earn a sufficient living to begin to support the woman whose own career he would now cripple by marrying her. Nor are his lips much good for anything but such acts as would be unmentionable had he not insisted on my bringing them to the attention of this court. He has withdrawn from society in direct proportion to his pursuit of my daughter. And when he does converse, he mumbles, he whispers, sometimes he even whistles as if he thinks the rest of us are dogs. He is mystical and dreamy. He lives in his own world, this man, and that is where he belongs. He even drinks alone. He drinks so much that he is sometimes carried home by strangers. He drinks so much that he will be of no use to my daughter as she tours the world and he will be expected to accompany her and to converse with kings and queens. She was made Royal and Imperial Chamber Virtuosa to her Imperial Highness Empress of Austria and handed fifty gold ducats by the empress herself, fifty ducats that I shall be happy to produce in this court as evidence. Can you imagine if Herr Schumann had been there to receive these ducats. He would have spent them immediately on drink. He would have mumbled to the empress, 'Why no ducats for *me*, the composer?' Have you heard his music, your worship? Probably not, for it is nearly impossible to perform. I have been its greatest champion, and even I am more perplexed by it than I am by the behavior of those who shake their heads and cover their ears when they hear it. A husband must support a wife, even if the wife is more famous than he. How will he support her with this music of his? Where is his *Freischütz*? Where is his *Don Giovanni*? And how will she, in turn, run their household? A wife must run the household, even if she is more famous than her husband. But my daughter is an artist. She was raised to be an artist. She cannot make the same bed that she is capable of lying in all day long. She cannot bake a fish. She cannot dust a keyboard except by scales. Perhaps if her mother had not abandoned us in shame...But she would still remain an artist, and artists are not meant to keep a house, satisfy a husband's whims, or tie around her waist some apron of children who cause her knees to swell and her precious fingers to go numb with worry. An artist is a flower. An artist needs a gardener who will nourish her, not a husband who will block the sun and finally cut her down. Can you be so blind, Your Worship, that you cannot see that to allow this marriage will be to commit a crime against art, against society, against me, and even against these two impatient consummators, one still a child, the other a seducer of that child?"

"Blind?" said Pastor Fischer. "You call me blind? You are out of order, sir. You stand there staring off into space, stomping your foot like a child, and you dare to call me blind. I am not too blind to be able to judge handwriting. From what I see in my hand, the letters signed by Anonymous and Lehmann have been written by the same hand, despite some effort on the part of the writer to disguise this fact. All that remains is to discover whether that same man is the same man who wrote your declaration. Bring me —"

"Do you mean to say"—Wieck charged toward Pastor Fischer and stopped only when both other magistrates rose and leaned across that worthy's body—"to say that you believe someone *else* wrote my declaration? I am outraged."

"Your rage is as apparent, Herr Wieck, as your sagacity is invisible. Now give me a page from your declaration and sit down!"

Wieck made sure, as he bent to pick up the pages of his declaration, that his backside was in direct address to Pastor Fischer, who, when he finally held the declaration in his hand, proclaimed it to have been written by the same man who had written the two letters.

All that remained was the calling of witnesses. Clara and Schumann had felt the need to parade forth half a dozen in their favor, all of whom Wieck attacked, except for Mendelssohn, who had become too much of a musical power in Leipzig to risk offending. Wieck allowed himself to go so far as to praise Mendelssohn's own marriage two years earlier and to offer it as proof that he was not opposed to the marriage of a musician provided that musician was of the male gender.

"How old is your wife?" Einert asked Mendelssohn.

"Cécile is twenty," answered Mendelssohn.

"And how old was she when you married?"

"Eighteen."

"Too young?" asked Einert.

Mendelssohn looked across the courtroom at his wife and laughed.

Wieck's two witnesses were Karl Banck and Louis Rakemann, each of whom testified to Schumann's lewd behavior with countless women aside from Clara Wieck. So detailed a description of this behavior did Wieck extract from his witnesses that Pastor Fischer on several occasions interrupted their testimony to tell them they had made their point, only to have them go on to make it yet again.

"Whores?" asked Wieck.

"Whores," said each of them.

Einert, after conferring with his clients, confined his examination of these two witnesses to one question each, the same question:

"Are you in love with Clara Wieck?"

"Yes," said Banck.

"Forever," said Rakemann.

Though Wieck called each of them a scoundrel and accused them of betraying him, he realized he would have felt no different had they answered in the negative. It was not that people might have loved his daughter to which he objected but that she might love in return and because of love squander her art. He no more wanted her with Banck or Rakemann than he did with Schumann, though he wanted her less with Schumann than he wanted anything in this world. If only he might persuade her to play the piano in this court, and persuade Pastor Fischer to allow her to play the piano in this court. He had not raised her, and taught her, and toured with her so she might leave his home and be burdened with one of her own. She belonged to the world, not to any man, including himself.

When Einert, the top of whose head Wieck could see entirely like a tiny, ugly island in the vast sad ocean, examined him directly, he asked if Wieck felt Clara was too young to marry Schumann.

"I have made myself clear on that," Wieck answered.

"How old is she?"

"She was twenty on the thirteenth of September past."

"And how old is Herr Schumann?"

"Too old for her."

"Herr Schumann is twenty-nine, your worship," Einert informed the court. "And how old was your wife when you married?"

"Twenty-two," answered Wieck. "Past the age of consent."

"Your *first* wife," said Einert.

"I have no idea," said Wieck. "I do not remember her."

"Marianne Tromlitz was nineteen," said Einert. "And you, sir, were thirty. She was younger than your daughter is now, and you were older than Herr Schumann. As for your second wife, you are, are you not, twenty years older than she?"

"But she is a good wife," said Wieck.

"And your daughter will not be a good wife?"

"My daughter is a *musician*."

Schönefeld

SEPTEMBER 12, 1840
Marriage is happy only before the wedding.
George Sand

He married her with music. Even as they stood silently before his old schoolboy friend from Zwickau, August Wildenhahn, who was now pastor of this tiny village church in Schönefeld, she could feel in Robert music she could not hear. It filled him, and her, and the church, in which an old woman played hopelessly upon an organ, as if she too were aware of what could not be heard but still could not be silenced. He was restless, agitated, like an innocent man about to be released from prison into the arms of the only one of whom he'd dreamed. His hand was hot in hers, trembling; his eyes burned into her neck and shoulders, and when they met her eyes they closed not only upon themselves but upon hers as well, which yielded to his sight of this, their wedding.

Small as the church was, Pastor Wildenhahn's words echoed in its emptiness. Only her mother was there, come from Berlin, and one common friend of theirs, Ernst Becker, who had, three years before, in Nanny's absence (Nanny, whom her father, for her role in their love affair, had recently discharged!), arranged for them to meet in secret so they might hold one another through the kind of blissful night they would never again, from this day forth, have to seize from the terrible geography of separation.

It was, Robert realized, fitting that the church be so sparsely populated. Not that they had no friends, for they did, both shared and separate. And they both owned family, though his had been reduced to a single brother, Carl, his parents gone, his brothers, his sister Laura dead at birth before his own and therefore mourned in shadow, his cherished, unforgotten Emilie, so death itself might have attended in their stead were this not the very antithesis of death, this marriage. Yet he and Clara had been so alone in the four years since they had declared their love—not without others but without themselves together—that the unencumbered benches and the still oak beams and the sweet untasted morning air were appropriate to their forced seclusion. Whenever she had left him, the world had emptied out. There seemed no reason for it to fill back in now that they were being joined forever. If life had abandoned him, let him now abandon life by claiming for his own its fairest flower. He needed no more than what he gained this day. He needed none but her.

But she, he knew, was in need of one who was not there. Her father, who had brought such pain into their lives and whom she had, with his confused approval, invited to their wedding, had stayed away and by his absence hurt her further. How, she wondered, could her father understand her so little and misjudge her so much that he might think there was not room inside her for both music and the only man, aside from him, she had ever loved? Witness my happiness, she called to him, as she pledged to God and those two attending that she would love none other than the man beside her and him forever.

Had her mother and Ernst Becker not accompanied them in the coach on the short ride back to Leipzig, they might have tossed aside their wedding clothes and let the bouncing of the wheels ease them with its rough surprises into married life. Pastor Wildenhahn, who was traveling behind in his own coach, had brought to the wedding a traditional *Lust,* which Robert had declined to wear. But when they arrived at Clara's mother's sister's house, where some friends had gathered to celebrate, Robert donned that garish headpiece and took Clara in his arms and reenacted a far more immodest version of their wedding than had taken place that morning. As he removed the *Lust* from his head and placed it upon Clara's (where he had to hold it so it would not sink down to nose or chin), he gave a little speech in

English just so he might joke about his lust for his new wife, which, given the occasion, was found inoffensive by all present, especially since it could not have been inspired by drink. For only then was the first drink served, champagne, and Robert moved from English into German as he toasted his wife and recalled what he said was already a whole life spent together. With tears in his eyes, he spoke not of those who did not attend but those who could not, the dead, including his old and greatest friend Ludwig Schunke, whose life and death had taught him, as so too had his love for Clara, that forever and ever, *Lust und Leid,* joy and pain, are joined.

"As I shall demonstrate in song," he said.

The evening before, on what is a traditionally raucous Polterabend that celebrates a wedding come the morn but for them had been quiet and private, as if a noisy celebration might provoke the envy of gods, he had given her a book of songs, music for the piano and the voice. Now he had her bring it forth to show their guests and to say the words he had inscribed to her.

"'To my beloved bride, Clara, on the eve of our wedding. I was completely inside you while composing these songs. From your Robert,'" she read with a strange sense that there were too many of her now, too much happiness, the bride, the wife, the woman who the night before had been surprised by such a gift, the woman named whose name she had just read. . . . Before, she had been one thing only: a woman longing with all her being for one man. Now that he was hers, and she his, and she might have expected herself to be reduced to a tiny knot of satisfaction, she found herself split within herself, among her selves, pieces of her flying whole and formed and giddy quite beyond her reach.

It was a beautiful book, bound in red velvet, printed in gold, wreathed by myrtle leaves, from those flowers sacred to Venus and, in a way more earthly, sacred to a German bride, especially his own, who had somewhere, far beyond his teaching, learned to love, the mother of Eros in the body, still, of a girl becoming woman in his arms. As a frontispiece he had inserted an etching of Adam and Eve Created by God in the Earthly Paradise from the doors of the cathedral of Hildesheim, cast in bronze at around the time of the millennium by an artist whose name was lost forever, a fact that purified—indeed, sanctified—his or her effort. While all true art is an expression of the inner being of the artist, and the artist lives in perpetual battle with his work as with himself, death bestows their disengagement; all artists then become anonymous, all art is rescued from the self's seizure. He was Adam; she was Eve. Here they were like children, naked, arms outstretched, vaulting into union. Earth, for once, was Paradise. The artist, unnamed, unknown, was God.

He took the book from her and put it on the piano and opened it to its first song and placed his fingers over the keys and took a breath and... stopped. Clara thought he must want a cigar. He seemed to have forgotten to smoke this whole day, which pleased her now that she thought of it, not because she objected to his smoking—she was virtually addicted to it herself, through him, the sweet, dusty smell of it in his hair and on his skin—but because it meant he had concentrated his pleasure wholly upon herself. Even now, she found, he did not stop to smoke but once again to talk. She had not seen him so wordy in company since the days before her father had forced them apart, before they had proclaimed their love. Once he had told her he loved her, and showed her he loved her, he seemed to have withdrawn from the world in favor of some concentration equally upon his pleasure and the pain it brought him. "When I have you," he had once told her, "I need no others. And when I cannot have you, I need no others even more."

"Before I sing," he told those waiting for him to do precisely as he'd promised, "I should explain two things. One is that I cannot sing. I play the piano better than I sing, and everybody knows through the advertisement of Herr Wieck that I have not played the piano well since the day this hand committed suicide." He held it up and nearly laughed at the passing thought that he might entertain them with his oxshit story. But he was a married man now, and that was the kind of tale told by the boy he hoped he'd put to rest that morning in Schönefeld. "And the other... the other thing I must explain is how I came to write these songs."

She listened as he told them with a strange dispassion how he had begun to write music to words, and thus to abide by the rhythmic constraints of the words themselves and their concourse through each line of the poetry he chose both to unveil and to clothe with the sound beyond sound that was music. All his life he had disdained vocal music. To sing poetry was no better than to recite aloud a piano sonata, note by note. It might be prettier, but it was still an insult to the purity of art, whether it was poetry or instrumental music by itself. Music was meant to be born completely within the soul and not to find its inspiration in something outside the composer, whether it was the poetry of Chamisso or Rückert or even Heine or it was...

"You!"

It was almost like an accusation, the way he seized upon her with his eyes and his open hand held out to her, not that she might grasp it or even approach it but to put her on display, to present her as corporeal evidence of his inspiration.

"You are these songs. That's what happened to me. When I allowed my-self to believe the court would rule in our favor and this very day would ar-rive that was a day so wrapped in darkness and uncertainty it could not even be dreamed, I started to sing to you. Wherever you were, I sang to you. Space and time retreat before the sound of song. I entered you with song. I was ecstatic. I was brimming over with music. I was so utterly at the mercy of melody I thought I might drown in it and take you with me. All the ter-rible things that were said about me, about you, all the disgrace to which we were subjected and the humiliation we were made to feel because we loved each other more than love has loved before . . . oblivion! I wrote so much I felt inhuman. I thought I could die of the pleasure. Please . . . I want to sing myself to death, like the nightingale."

Were not love and death the same, some final, inexpressible lament and celebration of the end of being? And was not music, like the two of them, insult to the grasp of life?

They sat together at the piano. They opened the book he'd given her. They began at the beginning. She played. He sang.

> You are my soul, you are my heart,
> You are my bliss, you are my pain,
> You are the earth on which I live,
> You are the sky in which I soar,
> You are the grave in which
> I have forever buried my sorrows.

Op. 25

No 1

"Widmung"

PART FOUR

Marriage

AN INTERLUDE

A life looked back upon seems to Robert Schumann both endless and compressed. It is, as his father had translated Byron, "where the day joins the past Eternity." Time is melted into one vast iris, blind and sage at once. And he, Robert, lying in bed in Endenich, is the spouseless Adriatic, mourning his lady. The Siebengebirge painted on the windows by the sun in its asylum are his blue Friuli mountains.

He struggles to put on his glasses to see them but cannot see them. He will open his eyes to nothing but memory. What he remembers is putting on the glasses of his beloved friend Johannes and seeing Clara, walking beside him on the Endenich road, indistinguishable from Brahms until he gave the glasses back and Clara disappeared. And so did Brahms—into the train on his way back to her he embodied.

Everything but death is memory. And were death memory, he would be gone and she unseen except in memory, except in death. He would rather die than live but rather see her face than die. He has forgotten her. Except in memory. His mind is gone (the doctors say). Replaced, he knows, by memory.

Two weeks after Emil's birth, he began to write *The Little Book of Memories of Our Children.* After three daughters, a son. He would have liked to have a child a year, to mark for all to see his love for their mother. And to mark, he must admit, his wife as his. Indeed, Emil arrived less than a year after Julie, too soon, perhaps—Robert's fault entirely, not Clara's, though she called him to their bed as often as he found her there awaiting him. Within weeks, another child coming. He knew how it had happened. But when? He began then to place a sign in their marriage diary, each time they made love. A quarter-note, the letter F, an unrequited phallus—he had no idea what it was, only what it meant. It was a secret sign, after all, but secret not from her, only from the children, who now had their own little book of memories.

Clara and he never named the new child. It was lost in the Frisian Island baths at Norderney, washed into eternity on a crimson wave of the mineral water in which Clara bathed. "One can never have enough children," he had written to Mendelssohn. Because death did not allow it, he came to realize. As did Emil, who never recovered from the grief in his mother's body and the relief in his parents' minds. Emil, in his sixteen months on earth, died (as was said of Beethoven's mother) without having smiled. But Ludwig, next, was named for Schunke, not Beethoven. And Ferdinand, hiding in his mother's belly from the warring, revolutionary men who said they'd kill her, was named, in Robert's mind alone, for Schubert's brother.

It was, he remembers, with five children alive, one dead and buried, one never born but bled away at Norderney, that they moved from Dresden to Düsseldorf. There they would have one more at least together and she have two, not counting one more lost, again in the waters, this time at Scheveningen. Out of ten pregnancies in thirteen years, eight children born to her: three in Leipzig, three in Dresden, two in Düsseldorf. He misses most the one he's never seen. Felix. She named him for Mendelssohn, who had been happy but, dead so young, not lucky. *Happy* and *lucky,* the same word. *Glücklich.* There was the German temperament: happiness a happenstance. One might earn one's pain, but bliss was a bestowal. The truth was opposite. If only all grammarians (and philosophers) were musical.

As they were packing for the move to Düsseldorf, he wrote a story in his children's *Book of Memories.*

> The fish were bored with being forever in the water. "Outside," they said, "the hot sun is shining, and everything looks beautiful and green. But we are deprived of all that, here in the water." So they decided to drink the whole pond dry. They drank and drank. The water got lower and lower. Supreme was their joy when they found themselves on dry land with the hot sun shining beautifully down upon them. But their happiness did not last long. They became weaker and more lifeless from moment to moment. There was not a drop of water left in which to live their lives as fish. The sun shone brightly. They died in agony.

"What is the point of this story?" asked Clara.
"That all should keep to their element."
"And what is our element?"
"Wherever we are not."

Dresden was a city stifled by its railway mentality and by its conservative Court, too quiet even for musicians at their work, incapable of enthusiasm, as lifeless as Robert's fish. Clara and he hated it equally (even more important in a marriage to be in antipathetic than commendatory concord) and took refuge in this bond and in their children. Her father gave her up to him and gave his name to the singer Minna Schulz, promoting her as Schulz-

Wieck, calling her his daughter now, that silly girl who tried to sing the operas that so far as Dresdeners were concerned was the only music. The Dresden orchestra would not even play Beethoven's symphonies for fear of alienating those who made donations to their pension fund.

He finished an opera of his own, *Genoveva*. He offered it to the Court Theater. But the Court conductor, Karl Reissiger (from whose home she had stolen fourteen years earlier, when she was only sixteen, to make her way for the first time to Robert's bed in their private Hotel David), pronounced it not merely boring but "exceptionally boring." Clara laughed. "Everything you do is exceptional." He should have learned from Weber. Weber had refused to bring his operas to birth in Dresden, allowing Berlin, Vienna, and London to hear them first. So, for the premiere of *Genoveva*, Robert returned to Leipzig, where at least the citizens themselves subsidized the satisfaction of their cultural appetite and did not depend upon the patronage of the kind of feudal prince who would allow no one to eat what he could not stomach.

Robert conducted the opera himself, for two acts a singularly satisfying experience — to hear voices rise like birds out of the opening of one's arms to the heavens. But then, at a crucial moment in the third act, the tenor singing Golo came onstage having forgotten the letter he was to hand to his master, Siegfried. It was the letter in which Siegfried's wife, Genoveva, was falsely accused of the very adultery that Golo was desperate for her to commit with *him*. "Read it for yourself!" screamed Golo, handing Siegfried . . . *absolutely nothing!* Siegfried stared at the emptiness between him and Golo as if into an abyss. Then, like any sensible man staring into an abyss, he stepped back, and back again, until he was running away from this stark immateriality. And Golo, rather than pursue his benefactor — become, by tragic passion, rival — scurried around the stage. He was clearly determined to keep as much space as possible between him and the man to whom he had just handed the completely invisible and thus unreadable letter into which he had poured a potent mixture of his heart and his cunning. Neither man thought to sing the consequent text, which now made no sense but would surely have stanched the blood of asininity more effectively than the improvised, apologetic squawks they uttered in recitativo.

Robert held his arms aloft for as long as he could, an Atlas bearing the full weight of a failure not his own but wholly on his head. To bring them down, he thought, would be to put an end to music. Not merely his own — all music. But there was no music. The orchestra stopped. The singers merely sputtered. Only the audience sang, mumbling a hum of confusion, trilling forth a kind of stupefied delight.

But then he thought of Clara's eyes upon him, felt them upon his back, holding him up, letting him see not the disaster before him on the stage but herself, behind him, both suffering with him and laughing at so absurd a permutation in his tragically romantic (or was it the other way around?) tale. Those huge, blue-black eyes. He sometimes felt he had no peace except when he could disappear within them and let them take him from a world in which he felt the less at ease the more he lived. Her eyes—which he could see at night even when the bedroom candle or the bedroom lamp was out, a blackness in her eyes that extinguished all the lesser darkness painted on the mind by failure and by fear, drawn across the face of life by death. She was the very opposite of Shelley's witch, for her beauty made the dim world bright. He was within them now, her eyes, which hid him from such accidents of fate as this, a letter lost, forgotten, a marriage doomed on stage, as his own was nourished through misfortune.

Let *Genoveva* turn a comic opera then. He lowered his arms, smiled at the orchestra and singers, shook his head in sympathetic consternation, and sang for them, without the words, the melody that soon enough, his arms upraised again, they played and sang for him.

What he wanted in melody—what he had always wanted in melody—was not something that people would sing so much as what would sing within people. One might come away whistling from an Italian opera; from a German opera one must emerge reborn, into both the silence of awe and the thunder of creation.

It was on one of their walks through the wooded hills along the Elbe that Robert managed to get Richard Wagner to stop talking long enough to say, "The first two chords of Beethoven's Third Symphony have more melody than ten Bellini arias." To which Wagner responded, "Peps, my dog, has more melody than ten Bellini arias."

Wagner had been born three years after Robert. They shared, among many other things that should have made them close, the presence of Napoleon at their births. In Robert's case, the emperor was marching east through Zwickau, though soon enough he would be heading toward the devastation of his Russian campaign, spreading along the way the typhoid that would send Robert into the arms of Frau Ruppius and the infant Wagner's father, Friedrich, into the arms of death. Wagner claimed to remember the sounds of the cannons at Bautzen. He delighted in comparing the vibrations he felt from those distant cannons while still in the amniotic sac with those he experienced five months later as he lay in his crib in Leipzig as what came to be called (with the usual vainglorious striving for slaughter's significance) the Battle of Nations was being fought around him and

Napoleon was finally driven back toward Mainz, back toward Paris itself, where soon enough the city would fall in almost delicate counterpoint to the Empire's annihilation.

"You can hear it in my use of rhythm," explained Wagner. He sang from *Lohengrin,* first "Ye wandering breezes" and then "Too long I stay—I must obey the Grail!"

Lohengrin! Robert had spent a year taking notes on an opera about the Round Table. Then, one day, Wagner called together a group of his friends and read them the entire libretto of his new opera. *Lohengrin!* Robert went home and threw his notes in the fire.

Yet Robert still made the mistake of going to Wagner as his authority on subjects for German opera: "What shall I write about? Faust? The Blacksmith of Gretna Green? Abelard and Héloïse? Tristan and Isolde? *Doge and Dogaresse? The Odyssey? The Tempest? Sakontala?* The Peasants' Revolt of 1525?"

Wagner shook his head at each of these worthy ideas and finally said, "Why don't you write an opera about Minna, my wife."

"You want me to write an opera about your wife!"

"Well, not exactly about my wife. But something you would call *Minna.* She would love to have an opera with the same name as herself. And it would look like marital sycophancy for *me* to come forth with one, not that I could ever call something *Minna*—it is not a grand enough name for what I write. But for you it would be perfect. You will base it on your relative Lessing's *Minna von Barnhelm.* You see, I have thought out the whole thing. You'll call it *Minna.* It will make my wife very happy and it will ease you in your pain for having to move your chair forever from the Round Table."

As it happened, the only thing Robert took from *Minna von Barnhelm* was the idea of a heroine unjustly accused of a crime, which he found in Friedrich Hebbel's *Genoveva.* But when he showed Wagner the libretto for his *Genoveva,* so disappointed was Wagner in not having the name Minna as its title that he attempted to sabotage the whole effort, particularly in his advice that the entire third act be eliminated.

But what could one expect from someone who insisted that Bach's great experiments in counterpoint needed lyrics? To the vivacious Fugue in G, Wagner sang, "Oh, how much like a child, how much like little boy are you, little boy are you," while to the funereally repetitious march of the G-flat Prelude he complained in a kind of anticipation of his Schopenhauerian obsession, "Life holds such pain, yes, life holds such woe, yes, life holds such grief, yes, life holds such hurt, yes, life holds such . . ."

Robert had no use for what Wagner called the "music of the future." They disagreed on almost everything and everyone, Mendelssohn in particular, whom Wagner dismissed as a mere "Jew technician" among the swarming colony of Jewish worms in the dead body of art and whose early death, along with Chopin's, left Robert wondering (until Brahms turned up on his doorstep!) where the true music of the future would come from.

Peps the dog, he has learned from someone who has visited him here in Endenich—probably Bettina von Arnim, who in old age has like many passionate women sought in gossip what she formerly found in concupiscent whisperings—is dead. In his place there is Fips. Fips was a gift from Wagner's young Swiss mistress, Mathilde Wesendonk, whose husband gave in coin what his wife gave in more succulent specie. But Mathilde had also given Wagner a gold pen, which he said had turned him into a calligraphic pedant. This was more troublesome to contemplate even than a replacement for the despicable Peps. Or a replacement for the pitiable Minna. This was a pen! The image of it diminished the value of his own steel pen from Beethoven's grave, which sits now unused on the table by his bed while Wagner in Zurich writes no doubt prolifically with his gold pen of Tristan and Isolde, one more idea they shared and Robert has lost.

Wagner had discovered Schopenhauer and sent him a copy of Gottfried von Strassburg's original Tristan poem, thinking the philosopher would be moved by this tragic tale of love and the gift to love of suicide. But, in splendid irony, Schopenhauer despised the stratagems of love by which a man might sacrifice his life to win a woman. What was a woman compared to a dog? The great love of Schopenhauer's life was his poodle!

Wagner got no acknowledgment from Schopenhauer. But from Schopenhauer's work he received the notion of the final denial of the will to live. Never having enjoyed the true bliss of love himself, he would drown Tristan and Isolde in it, suffuse them with it, give them a satiety so complete it could be achieved not through the act of physical love but only through death. The denial of the will to live was redemptive. Death through desire became a saintly death. The body and the spirit were finally joined. And in the only possible way. Through the denial of the will to live. Through suicide.

Robert has tried to starve himself to death. He was inspired in this, however, less by Wagner than by Nikolay Gogol, of whom he thinks now and then when he gets hungry. Gogol starved himself too, though for the most understandable if stupidest of reasons: In a fit of self-disgust he had thrown his writing, handful by handful, into the fire, only to discover too late that among the pages burned were the only ones he'd meant to save, those to a second volume of *Dead Souls*. All were gone, irrecoverable, either from the fire or from his mind, the latter of which he had expected would be unburdened by the burning of his papers but instead was itself inflamed by discontent, regret, frustration, insanity—many an artist's companions on the path to flitting fulfillment. Gogol is filled with a remorse a thousand times more painful than what Robert felt when burning up his labors toward an opera on the Round Table. Gogol wants to die. Gogol wants to die as slowly as it took a piece of writing to emerge from mind to paper. Gogol wants to die by taking nothing in, the way an artist lives by giving forth. It is the perverse nourishment of the self-forsaken. It is the starvation not of the body but of the body's song; it is the starvation of the voice.

It was Ivan Turgenev who told him about Gogol. And it was that old lecheress Bettina von Arnim who told him during her visit to Endenich that Turgenev had been unfaithful to his great love, the magnificent if ugly mezzo-soprano Pauline Viardot, who just happens to be one of Clara's best friends. And with whom had Turgenev been unfaithful? A pianist, naturally, Bettina had seemed delighted to inform Robert, as if to imply that no man could resist the sight of a woman's bottom on a piano bench.

Sometimes Robert wonders if he loves Clara as much as Turgenev loves Pauline, infidelity notwithstanding—Turgenev's, for Robert could no more have been unfaithful to Clara, once they were married, than a bird could betray its own song by singing another's.

When they were apart, Turgenev begged Pauline to send him the cuttings from her fingernails. And all Robert has requested from Clara are some music paper and newspapers and cigars and pictures of her and of the children and of Johannes and a ribbon from her hair or hat to tie around her letters or to use as a bookmark and perhaps an atlas or two with which to plan his escape.

But, then, there is something about his marriage to Clara that has made her less lovable. Not to himself, no, but to other men. She had been such a beautiful girl, even if she had never in her life considered herself beautiful. But it was not her beauty that had captured him, not solely, but her spirit, her passion, her abandon, her fund of perversity, the ways she had teased and tricked and amused and aroused and seduced him. And now—if he could speak of now, not having seen her in so long and longing so to see her—she had grown into a kind of severity, from her dark dresses to the way she wore her hair stretched back from her face to her condemnation in others what she had enjoyed so much herself.

So many men had loved her when she was young. Clara would play the piano, and the world climbed up her dress. In Vienna they even named a pastry after her, Torte à la Wieck, so they too could eat her. It was described in the *Theaterzeitung* as an ethereally light confection that flew like an angel into one's mouth.

But Pauline Viardot went on inspiring such passion, and not simply among the likes of George Sand's wistful son Maurice. Charles Gounod had loved Pauline. So had Hector Berlioz, but that is to be expected, his heart so easily ripped from his chest and fed to the nearest woman. Harry Heine had probably loved her too, and in the process of mourning her absence from the Opéra Bouffe managed to demean Clara's even better woman friend, Jenny Lind, who has been heard these days to tell Clara not to be seen so much with Brahms, trying to impose upon her a bourgeois respectability at the very moment she is managing to peel it from herself.

Heine has died. He was the greatest poet of Germany. And one of those Jews, like the Mendelssohns, not so much forced into Christian baptism, since no one held a gun to their heads, as flattered into it. As a genius, would you rather be a Jew and obscure or a Christian and celebrated? Would you rather be reality or a dream? For all the good being a Christian had done him, Robert might as well have been a Jew. Then at least he would have been able to excuse his humiliations ("Are you musical too?") not to mention decorate with a Jewish star his many *New Journal of Music* contributions, as Heine's editors anointed his to the *Augsburg Daily*. But conversion in that direction was uncommon in Germany. And those Jews who became Christians could not hide even in their genius, not from the genius of others guilty of the same crime. So it was that when Felix Mendelssohn in merely his twentieth year brought J. S. Bach back from the dead upon conducting the *St. Matthew Passion* from its only existing copy, and he said, "To think that it has been left up to me, a Jewish boy, to revive this greatest of all Christian music," it remained for Harry Heine to say, "If I had had the luck to be the grandson of Moses Mendelssohn, I would certainly not use my talent to set to music the pissing of the lamb."

What Robert would set to music, if he could set anything to music now that music appears to be dead to him except for the tediously disturbing hallucinatory notes he hears in his head, would be what Heine wrote at the end of his life:

> How slowly time, that horrid snail,
> Comes sliding at its snaily pace!
> But I, who cannot move at all,
> Am stuck here in this endless place.
>
> No glint of sun, no ray of hope
> Can pierce this black cell through the gloom.
> I know that it will be the grave
> For which I'll trade this gruesome room.

But what Robert had actually set to music in the first of his many settings from Harry Heine, when he began to write songs in his longing for Clara Wieck, was what he sings now to himself, wholly within his head, sixteen years later in his longing for Clara Wieck Schumann:

> Waking in the morning,
> I ask, Where can she be?
> In the evening I lament
> She hasn't come to me.
> And finally in the dark of night
> With agony I scream
> To realize she won't visit me
> Except within a dream.

In his dreams, she plays for him. He sees her at the piano as a child—as she had been as a child—and himself next to her, not as he had been, a wild young man falling slowly in love with a child, but as a child himself. He had remained something of a child, he knew, though marriage and the births of his own children had forced him to assume the demeanor of the stable bourgeois. There were books to keep, money to attempt to make, servants to be hired, bags to be packed for Clara's tours or for their moves from city to city and, within the cities, from apartment to apartment. But he'd never felt he'd found his way into the center of life itself, or the center of his own life.

She had always played for him—what music she had written, and what he had. And what he had, she played for others. Only she and Liszt, and rarely he. No one else had played what he had written. Mendelssohn had conducted some, but he didn't play the notes himself. He did not become intimate, as much as Robert admired him, loved him, even; he did not, despite his keyboard virtuosity, dirty his fingers with those same pesty and seductive "musical cantharides" in Robert's music that Heine had described in Liszt's.

Chopin did not play him. Moscheles did not play him. Thalberg did not play him. Camilla Pleyel did not play him. Kalkbrenner did not play him. Henselt did not play him. Not even Ludwig Spohr's wife played him, nor could she; as her husband had informed Robert, she could neither execute nor understand his Symphonic Etudes. Who could blame her? Neither could Clara, though Robert hadn't told Spohr *that*. But, referring to her Börsenhalle recital, he had reassured the shaken Clara: *You were right to play them only once, and that once for me; they are not suitable for the public; I would be pitiable should I complain that people had not appreciated music that was not intended to win approval but exists, as art must exist, for its own sake.*

The first time Liszt came to Leipzig, to give a benefit concert for the Gewandhaus orchestra's pension fund, he played Robert's *Carnaval*.

The audience hated it.

Liszt thought they hated *him* and refused to leave his room in the Hotel de Bavière. Robert sat with him there, saying hardly a word as Liszt consumed what he explained (as he offered to share with Robert) was his customary breakfast of raw oysters, which he washed down with black coffee he let cool and drank as other men drank beer, glass after glass of it, from morning, he said, until night, an antidote both to liquor and to the ennui that circumfused his mind no matter how extravagantly he played the piano or agitatedly he made love or repeatedly he scattered the ashes of his resurrected self.

Robert felt they had known one another for twenty years. There became no need to talk. Hours went by. Finally, Robert stood up and said, "There! We've been speaking with open hearts."

How Liszt had laughed! He seemed cheered completely out of his dejection and came to Robert and took his arms in his hands—those famed hands! those lightning-flashing, volcanic, Heaven-storming hands! "You are as strange as your music."

"Thank you."

"And thank *you* again for your dedication of your Fantasie. I shall attempt to learn it to bring you honor and me as little shame as possible. It will be, you know, a very difficult piece for the public to digest."

"I know."

"Not all your work is thus. You're not like Wagner—every piece a masterpiece. Or so intended. He writes nothing small, nothing intimate, nothing to indicate the quiet breaths we take between our cries for justice and eternal recognition. Nothing for the chamber; everything for the vault. But you . . . opaque at one moment, transparent the next. My daughter, Blandine, is but four. She's like you, perhaps. Very silent, sweetly grave, but philosophically gay. Two or three times a week, I play for her your *Kinderscenen*. They enchant her completely. And me as well. How can this be?"

"Perhaps I'm like someone who writes books for children and books for adults. The books for children are for the best of children, which means that all children love them. The books for adults are for the best of adults, which means that almost no one loves them. For children, one writes in their language. For adults, one writes in one's own language. When a language is not understood, it is not the fault of the speaker."

"I have always considered myself a servant of the public."

"And you have the public's love to prove it."

"And you?"

"Oh, I love you too."

"No no no no no." Liszt laughed again. His face was so beautiful, so manly, that it seemed superfluous for him to smile. The very attention he paid was sufficient indication of his concern and even his possible delight. He was one of those fabled seducers who did not choose among his prey. He wanted everyone to love him. Whatever melancholy he suffered was the result both of his success in this and his occasional failure, as in his performance of Robert's music.

"There is only one person's love I want," Robert answered.

A few evenings later she was in attendance, with Robert, at a party the Mendelssohns gave for Liszt.

"I am upset with him," she said.

"Why?"

"He played your *Carnaval* as if he were sight-reading it."

"He *was* sight-reading it."

"And not very well."

"I'm grateful he plays me at all."

"He doesn't play you as I do."

"And I don't play you as he does," he replied, touching her bottom through her dress, an almost ensanguined silk that faded to pink at her breasts, where the fabric ended in a pale palette of flesh.

He had thought she'd returned from Vienna, years before, in love with Liszt, so highly had she praised him, so spirited had she become in discussing his attentions. He'd been at first confused by this: Liszt was famed beyond envy, should one desire fame, and beautiful beyond beauty, his face become a work of art and the worship of that art catechized into adoration. But Liszt was *his* champion. Liszt had written publicly in praise of him and had gone out of his way to play his music—his Sonata and his *Novelletten* in particular, so that Robert had dedicated his Fantasie to Liszt, out of gratitude and the hope he might choose to perform it as well. To the extent that Liszt played Robert's music, he embodied Robert. Therefore, if Clara loved Liszt, it was another way of loving him, Robert. We are all mixed together in each other, he determined, and those we love are made love to by the one who makes love to us. And we make love to whomever our beloved loves.

As if to demonstrate the proof of Robert's theory through an application of its opposite, Clara removed his hand from her bottom while saying, "He doesn't play me at all."

Liszt, who had in his hotel room worn nothing more ornate than black pants and boots and an open white shirt, had come to Mendelssohn's party dressed like a Magyar prince, his colorful waistcoat topped against the March chill by a long, pleated pelisse trimmed at the collar and cuffs with mink. He kept this coat draped over his shoulders until he was persuaded to take to the piano where, in keeping with his outfit, he would play a Hungarian folk song, "prepared especially for you," he said to Mendelssohn as he removed his gloves finger by finger and then with his pale bare hands placed them on the piano so that they hung lifelessly over its edge like a magic fluted carapace from which all energy has been absorbed.

It seemed a simple tune, barely the sort to which one might picture princes dancing with common damsels by the River Tisza. When he'd finished, Liszt nodded modestly toward Mendelssohn, who raised his hands before his breast as if he might applaud. Before Mendelssohn could bring his hands together, Liszt held up one of his own, tossed his hair so that it rose from his shoulders halfway up his head, and began to play, before his hair had fallen back, a variation on his tune so dramatic in its distension of simplicity that Robert heard a single breath sucked in and bled out from the many people in that room. He also heard the clink and clank of medals worn by Liszt around his neck, as he swayed back and forth on the piano bench, nostrils quivering, lips vellicating, eyes going nearly all the way back in his head, which lent his perpetual smile, directed sweepingly and uninterruptedly at his entire audience now, a rather macabre aspect, though most of the women in the room appeared quite entranced by so maniacal a visage, their excitement growing in direct relation to the proportion of white that showed in those eyes that went right on smiling through a full four variations on the original theme, each more complex than the last.

When he was finally done, Liszt brought his quavering body slowly to rest, closed his eyes, and touched, as had become his habit since its bestowal, the Golden Spur given him by Pope Pius IX. Before recovering his gloves, Liszt kissed the finger that had touched the medal, a gesture Robert realizes should have forewarned him of what he has heard of Liszt's growing dissatisfaction with the things of this temporal world with which he has been so munificently and unsatisfyingly rewarded.

"Your turn."

Robert, who was standing with Clara as close as he could get to his dear friend and host, Mendelssohn, feared Liszt was talking to him. All he could think, upon being asked to follow Liszt to the keyboard, was to beg Liszt to kiss *his* finger now, his poor, damaged digit that had pointed his way to where he was, a composer who could not play his own music.

But it was Mendelssohn who responded: "This evening is for *you*. Tonight we honor *you*. I have no plans to play. I have prepared nothing to play."

"What you are not prepared to play is better than what the rest of us play with preparation," Liszt graciously averred. "And if you do play," he added with what was now the gracelessness of a bribe, "I shall pledge to perform once more for your pension fund and for your uncultured, intransigent Leipzigers."

Though most of those in attendance were precisely the Leipzigers to whom Liszt referred, they were nearly as one in urging their host to give in to the blandishments of his guest of honor.

"Very well," Mendelssohn addressed Liszt. "I shall play. But you must promise not to become angry with me. As I said, and as may become clear to you in a moment, what I shall play I have not prepared to play."

Robert was as intrigued by Mendelssohn's puzzling disclaimer as he was relieved to have discovered that it was not he but Mendelssohn to whom Liszt proposed to turn over the piano. As Liszt rose from the bench, seeming to forget to claim his gloves in his haste to make room for Mendelssohn and to light up one of the nasty Roman cigars he favored over the elegant, fragrant Habanos he could easily have afforded, Robert determined that the only music Mendelssohn might play that he had not prepared to play would have to be improvised. Because anything Mendelssohn had played once, he was prepared to play again.

Mendelssohn sat down. He raised his hands above the keyboard and was about to bring them down when his eyes moved slowly toward Liszt's gloves hanging over the edge of the piano. He cowered. The gloves intimidated him. Liszt might as well have let his hands themselves remain on the piano. But the gloves were warning enough: Let no pianist follow Liszt to the piano. What piano? As Heine had written of Liszt's playing, "The piano vanishes...music appears." The lesson of Thalberg should be sufficient: There was only one pianist in the world. (*Then*—Princess Belgiojoso had never been granted the privilege of hearing Clara.)*

---

*The duel between Liszt and Thalberg had taken place in Paris at the instigation, as well as at the grand home, of Princess Cristina Belgiojoso, who seized upon an opportunity not only to raise money for her cherished Italian refugees but to secure her place, as indeed she did, as one of the immortal impresarias. She charged forty francs a seat and, after the *Gazette Musicale* compared the impending confrontation to the battles between Rome and Carthage, filled them not only with society folk, who could afford the tariff and were genetically disposed to appreciate the gladiatorial aspect of such supposedly refined combat, but with the likes of Chopin, Berlioz, and Heine, who reported on the palpitating breasts and impassioned breathing that accompanied Liszt's performance and, more to the point,

Mendelssohn did the unthinkable. He reached out toward Liszt's gloves and touched one of them with the tip of a finger and brought that finger to his lips and kissed it.

Thus did Mendelssohn become Liszt. He smiled broadly. He pushed back the bench to attain the exact angle of Liszt's attack. He raised his chin. He even tried to toss his hair, but it was thick, dark, Jewish hair and could not wave like Liszt's, it hardly moved at all, so that Mendelssohn once more postponed his playing by putting a hand behind his neck and moving his hair up and down, up and down, quite like the classicist attempting one of the signal flourishes of the romantics.

Only then did he play.

He played every note Liszt had played. First the simple Hungarian folk song. Then each variation upon it, not only note for note but gesture for gesture. All that was missing were the sound of Liszt's medals, since Mendelssohn wore nothing more around his neck than a fine cravat, and the undiluted whites of Mendelssohn's eyes.

When Mendelssohn played the final chord of the fourth variation, he managed somehow to cause Liszt's gloves to drop off the piano. They grasped one another as they fell and landed palm to palm.

So did Liszt cause his own hands to meet, again and again, clearly appreciative of, and unoffended by, this masterful parody of his every exaggera-

---

satisfied most everyone's general lust when he wrote, "The keys themselves appeared to bleed." Princess Belgiojoso, called upon to declare the winner, said, "Thalberg is the best pianist in the world." After allowing time for Thalberg and his supporters to absorb this apparently benign judgment, she seemingly expunged them from existence altogether when she appended: "Liszt is the only pianist in the world." (It was no secret that she and Liszt had briefly been lovers. Nor would it have occurred to Thalberg, or anyone else, to assume that so cosmopolitan a saloniste would have allowed such intimacy, whether past or present, to influence her judgment. Art and sex had no such congress; a lover was only a lover, but a great artist was a god.) Clara herself never engaged in such a duel, but they have remained commonplace among musicians, including the "octave Olympics" between Artur Rubinstein and Vladimir Horowitz. But probably the most famous confrontation after Thalberg/Liszt took place a century later in Nightsie Johnson's bar in Harlem, New York, where Billie Holiday egged on Coleman Hawkins by calling her putative lover Lester Young "the only tenor saxophone in the world," inspiring Hawkins to accompany her so passionately as not only to obliterate Young's coincident efforts but to cast into doubt forever whether Pres and Lady Day had indeed ever made together, in the parlance of jazz musicians, such music as puts the bone in the microphone.

tion and, even more intimidating, the perfect recapitulation of his every dazzling note.

Indeed, when all sat down to the dinner in Liszt's honor, Liszt could not stop speaking of Mendelssohn's feat and proclaimed that Mendelssohn played Liszt better than Liszt played Liszt. Mendelssohn then toasted him and told the story of how, years ago, he and Liszt had been in Paris at the same time and he had shown Liszt the manuscript of his piano concerto and Liszt had taken the manuscript immediately to the piano and played the whole piece through, more beautifully than Mendelssohn had imagined it could have been played and more beautifully than it had been played since by anyone. "It was an absolute miracle," said Mendelssohn.

"You are the miracle," said Liszt, who then toasted Mendelssohn.

When he had completed his toast, and all had drunk to their host, who was, without question, the greatest musician among them, Liszt poured more wine from the decanter into his glass, raised high his glass once more, and said, "A toast, as well, to Robert Schumann, as new a friend to me as he is no doubt an old friend to most of you. Of his musical intelligence there can be no doubt—no greater critic writes in any language, or any language I can read. Yet his true and greater genius is to be found not in what he writes of other musicians but in what music he himself writes. I cannot always play it. I cannot always understand it. If for no other reason than those, it must be superior! Let us drink, ladies and gentlemen, to one who says few words and yet expresses himself to a degree that would be shameful in one less gifted and less profound."

Robert felt himself turn blood red as all about the table glasses were raised by his Leipzig friends and his new friend from Paris by way of Hungary and by the woman next to him, his Clara, in whose loving eyes he felt reborn, so easy was it to find redemption in praise.

But she continued not as happy with Liszt as Robert was. "He did not play *Carnaval* to your advantage or to my satisfaction." She rubbed the cuff of his sleeve between her thumb and forefinger, so that her little finger moved against the skin on the back of his hand, splayed around the bottom of his wineglass. "Everything about him is so agitated, so restless. I don't know how anyone could stand to be around him for very long. He doesn't make the same impression upon me that he did in Vienna. And look at him—he flirts outrageously. A man who looks like him should not flirt. It's an insult to the women who are drawn to him against their wills. He seduces the seduced. One might as well hang the dead."

It did not help Liszt in Clara's eyes that he had arrived in Leipzig just in time to rescue her from the aftermath of childbirth, Marie but two months old and Clara restless. As Robert had bestowed upon his wife their first child, Liszt presented her his Hexameron Variations on Bellini's "Suoni la tromba." He had written it for two pianos, one to be his, the other hers. So together they played it at the Gewandhaus, overwhelming, on the same program, the premiere of Robert's own D-Minor Symphony.

"Don't be sad," she consoled him, cradling his head in the crook of her arm, as was her custom when he was, or she imagined him, in pain.

"I'm not."

"Or angry."

"Only with myself. The winds need work. But I do like that trombone phrase I took from the Schubert symphony. I remember seeing it on the floor of his brother's apartment and thinking, *Nice trombone.*"

"*Very* nice trombone."

"You tamed him."

"It's impossible to tame him. I almost hate Liszt as a composer. And I *do* hate him as a pianist. His music is a chaos of dissonance that follows the most tiresome introductions. His bass rumbles, his treble clangors."

"And his eyes . . . they roll like those of Italian singers who cause one to worry whether artistic passions might give way to some other. And then they go white! I could see this as he played his *Lucia* Fantasy. But not when he played with you. When he looked at you, his eyes were where his eyes were meant to be. So perhaps you did tame him after all. With you before him, he could not, for once, look only to himself. You should be flattered. And I jealous."

"Were I flattered, then you might well be jealous. Have you no idea, dear Robert, why he turns up his eyes that way?"

"I thought it was the passion of the moment."

"It's passion, all right." She laughed. "Or his representation of it. He does it for the ladies. It drives them to distraction."

"It is hardly attractive. It makes him look like a *ghoul.*"

"It makes him look like a man at the moment of release."

"Release?"

"Release."

How would she know, unless she'd seen it in himself?

"Do my eyes . . . ?" he asked.

"Do mine?" she asked back.

From the day they were married and moved into their first home together, at 5 Inselstrasse in Leipzig, he had withdrawn into her, leaving the world behind. What need for the world, when he had her? So accustomed had he become to hiding with her for a night or two—in bedrooms in

Dresden, Berlin, Altenburg, Schneeberg—that he is not sure he ever truly accepted the luxury of what would have been her absolutely constant presence had she not begun again to go out on tour. He had so desired to possess her that he'd had no idea how much more he would desire her once he did possess her.

He'd longed for her when they were apart. Once they were together always, and he might satisfy his longing when he wished, his longing only grew. It was a desire not merely to enter her but somehow to envelop her while at the same time to find himself contained, wholly, within her. To confront her flesh was like a confrontation with her music, layer after layer, veils of recondite intoxication, and to lift them one by one was to find revealed something always different from what he had expected. He often could not sleep and did not want to sleep, or at least resisted sleep, hearing music in his head— not yet the music that would torment him—and watching Clara as she slept, placing his face in the way of her breath, studying her closed eyes to read her dreams upon her lids and to feel them in the quickening of her breathing.

It was, he was to learn in time as the father of four daughters, like watching a child sleep. No matter how urgently or cunningly or implacably he and Clara might have made love, her face, in sleep, revealed a renewal of innocence. Indeed, she had been made anew, to him, by marriage itself. He had expected to encounter, suddenly, a woman, a wife, whatever that might be, however tangibly and stalwartly she might assume a posture in his mind and in their home. But as a wife she was, at first, more a girl than she had been as girl. She sat with her legs beneath her, smiling at him for no reason beyond his presence. She wore her hair down even at the piano, as if she meant, in her abandon, to abandon it. She followed him from room to room, from her piano to his, so he was forced either to embrace her or to close the door against her. And still the walls were evilly thin, and he could hear her in the house, her footsteps, her breathing, her fingers in her hair.

Her piano.

Two artists of any kind, in one home, would prove a test, with their selfish hibernations and fragile moods. But when both can be heard, and when the sounds not only interrupt but beckon, the two must love or perish.

Now, when he would give anything to hear her play again, he remembers how he asked her not to play because he could not concentrate. Too often, he confessed in their diary, his songs were bought at the cost of her silence.

But it was Clara herself who urged him toward the symphony. "The piano is too small for you. It limits your fantasy. What you compose for it is orchestral. No wonder people can't fathom your work. It's too complex for one instrument."

He felt like crushing the piano into the floor.

Before a year was out, Marie was born to the late-summer accompaniment of thunder and lightning, sounds that echoed perfectly the symphony, his first, that he had written during a mere four days of her 280 days' gestation. There was always revision to be done of work written at such heat. But the heat itself was a luxury that nearly matched the ecstasy of music born within its flames. He was almost thirty years old, and married, yet he had lost none of his youthful ability to write for several days and nights on end. He sweated out his ink-cuffed shirts, and burned his eyes with the smoke from his cigars and from the wakefulness he forced upon himself, and felt the music sear the portals of his mind. What joy there was in such fluid, quick creation. How miraculous that it should be matched by the consequence of love.

He had taken Clara in his arms and danced her about the room, the moment she told him she was pregnant. But in their diary the next morning, he saw what she had written: *Farewell to the virtuosa.*

It was to him she said farewell. He toured with her as far as Hamburg. In Oldenburg, she had been invited to play for the court, without him. It was as if he didn't exist. Which was to say, it was as if he had produced no work, or no work worth hearing. Most people offered themselves as evidence of their existence, and it was sufficient. An artist, however, was his work. No part of him extruded beyond its boundaries. The work did not merely express the self; it absorbed it. The self, therefore, became the work.

He waited for her in their hotel room. He could neither read books nor write music.

"I've become nothing more than your traveling companion," he said when she'd returned.

"Travel to my arms."

For the first time, he did not.

"I must return home," he said.

"And I must not," she replied.

"I can't very well ask you to give up your music because I am chained to mine."

"You may ask."

"I torture myself with that question."

"Torture *me,* then."

It was added torture even to contemplate such a thing.

"You must go on without me," he said.

"Yes, I must. We need the money."

"You sound like your father."

"We need the money."

She was right. What he earned from the magazine and from the publication rights to his music and from the interest on his investments was not enough to support them. In order to live together, they would have to separate.

"Where will you go?"

"Copenhagen."

"Impossible!"

Dearest Robert,

Stupid me. After we parted in Hamburg, I cried all the way to Kiel. I was so distraught at being apart from you I could not take the stage. So of course I was forced to pay the theater owner what expenses he had incurred on behalf of such a lovesick coward as myself. To think that I left you in order to make money and lost money as a result of having left you.

And then—here is one reason you have not heard from me in so long—a storm came up and postponed for a week the boat to Copenhagen. Having humiliated myself in Kiel, I went to Lübeck and offered my services, which, to my subsequent regret, were accepted. I played, but no one knew I was to play, because there was no time to advertise. But even if there had been time, I would probably have attracted no more of an audience. It turned out that all of Lübeck went to see a visiting opera company that evening. And how can a lonely pianist playing her husband's brilliant music compete against a cackling group of costumed cantatrici? Again, I had to pay out more money than I took in.

And so I returned to Hamburg, weeping all the way because it was where I had last seen you and I would see you this time only in my mind. But it turned out I had forgotten how close it was to Easter. What music people wanted was not the kind I make or you write. But at least I learned this before I'd indebted myself beyond the wasted travel expenses.

Back to Kiel it was with me, poorer, tireder, hungrier for you for all the bouncing of the coaches. The storm had passed, except within myself. As I sailed for Copenhagen, I cried out for you, and for Marie. It was, as you know, my first time at sea. I was convinced I had for the last time touched land.

But here I am, safely in Copenhagen and so busy (particularly in comparison with dreary northern Germany) that I must offer such constant engagement as the other reason why you have not heard from me in so long.

I have performed many times and have been, or will be, paid for all except of course my appearances for charity, which, as you have always said, are profitable for the music if not necessarily for the musician. As enthusiastic as the Copenhageners may be to hear me play, they are musically unrefined. (Which is my kind way of saying they are ignorant.) I was able to play your music but once. You are in good company: they are resistant even to Chopin.

As was the case in Vienna, I am much loved by royalty. (Were I not your Queen, I might well be some other King's.) I play constantly at court and am vied for by the prince of Glücksburg and the prince of Hesse, each of whom attempts to show me parts of the town he has not shown me before, both of whom I allow such liberty provided they perform this apparently enjoyable duty together. They are, together, less in age than you have accomplished by yourself. I tell you this against my huge desire to make you insanely jealous.

The Queen herself took me into her winter garden and cut some flowers for me. She did not kneel but bent at the waist. I had never thought to see a queen in quite that posture. It did not make me envy her throne.

As a visiting artist of what the Danish at least consider world renown, I have been taken up by Johan Heiberg. He seems to be the most famous critic and playwright (both!) in Denmark and is married to an actress who is said to look so much like me that the newspapers here have remarked on our similarity. Since she is held to be among the most beautiful women in Denmark, you can see how such fame as my own creates its own illusions. Our features are similar, and we have the same figure (I trust you are picturing mine and not imagining hers), but she is most certainly pretty, and I am most certainly not.

Herr Heiberg has made certain I've viewed the sculpture of Thorwaldsen, many of whose pieces are indeed the equal of his bust of Schiller so beloved by you. And he has taken the trouble to introduce me to a philosopher named Søren Kierkegaard, who has been championed by Heiberg and might be termed his disciple did not Kierkegaard display such independence in thought and attitude. Heiberg warns me of Kierkegaard's melancholy. But every time we sit down together, Kierkegaard talks to me with great cheerfulness in his eyes, as much inflamed by the expression of ideas as you by the creation of music. It is as if my girlish wish has finally come true and I am sitting in a café with Gérard de Nerval. All that is missing is yourself. You are but two years older than Kierkegaard and even closer than that in temperament. He writes about such matters as the irony of Socrates and the conflict between hedonism and ethics while using pseudonyms like (do not be envious, Florestan!) Johannes Climacus (which certainly suggests hedonism to an innocent girl like me). He asks my advice about marriage —*giftermal* in Danish, he teaches me, so that I say, "What a beautiful word!" and he says, "*Gift* means 'poison.'" Nonetheless, he calls marriage the deepest form of revelation. I told him, "You have no idea how much there is that is revealed." He laughed. Is there any greater pleasure, at least in conversation, than causing a philosopher to laugh? "Shall I be a husband or a priest?" he wants to know. Everything with him is a choice between incompatibles. (He is writing a book called *Either/Or*!) So I answer his question: "Both." This causes him to laugh even harder. "'Both!'" he repeats. Then, with a revelation of his own, he screams, "Neither!" So I suggest he call his new book instead, *Neither/Both*. This time he did not laugh.

But my favorite person in Copenhagen is Hans Andersen. When he and I were first introduced, I told him of our mutual admiration for his work. Never have I seen such genuine delight in an artist praised! He became quite beautiful at that moment. I put it that way because, Robert, Hans Christian Andersen is possibly the ugliest man ever born! It is not merely his face, which is long and narrow and sunken and frettingly dark beneath eyes as cold and small as mice droppings in the snow (crowned by a forehead from which the hair is in retreat and gathers at his ears like furry fists). His entire body is so long and thin that he reminds me of the creaking mast on the ship that brought me here. (And yet it's as if God had made him so inhumanly tall so that his face would be as far as possible from incredulous eyes, particularly those of the children he so dearly loves and honors with his fairy tales.)

Well, I discovered soon enough the reason for his transformation at my modest (but sincere!) compliment. His work is hated here! Like you, he is a prophet who goes unhonored in his own country. He did not tell me this himself, but I first gathered as much from my very protector himself, Johan Heiberg, who one day began to attack Herr Andersen mercilessly. Not to his poor, suffering face. To me alone. But then I learned that Herr Heiberg had said the same things in print. And why? Because Andersen has found a way to tell the truth, the absolute truth. And he tells it in tales that even children can understand. He is seen as one who corrupts an entire society by stripping it of its illusions.

One day we were discussing "The Emperor's New Clothes." I had a sudden insight and inquired if perhaps he had been influenced by Ludwig Tieck's "Puss in Boots." From his reaction, you might have thought I had achieved with one remark the genius as a critic that you have displayed in ten thousand such percipiences. You would have been so proud of me! He said I was the first person ever to have noticed what had indeed held profound sway over his creation. Fearless in my new role as interpreter of literary subtlety (yet how easier to construe writings than music, which makes me admire you all the more), I then asked him if this same "Emperor's New Clothes" might happen to be about Johan Heiberg himself: "Whatever Heiberg says, no matter how ridiculous, everyone believes," I ventured with the naive confidence of a tourist who believes she comprehends an ancient city after one day among its ruins. Yet so delighted was Herr Andersen at my apparent insight into his fable about the power of critics that he seemed about to hug me. Given the extreme disparity in our heights, this might very well have made me intimate with a part of him I would prefer neither to know nor speculate upon. But it turned out I mistook this awkward man's attempt to bow with the beginnings of an encirclement of my own dear little body. It was his respect with which he honored me. That and his willingness to listen to me talk about you. And so he knows you now not as critic but as artist.

And I . . . I cannot wait to remove my emperor's old clothes and know you even better, if such may prove possible about someone known and loved so well by . . .

Your Zilia

"Critics are to art as shit is to food," is the first thing Robert remembers having said to Hans Christian Andersen, who had neither sarcasm nor cynicism to add to Robert's vulgar condemnation of the community of critics from which Robert himself had withdrawn in having recently resigned from his magazine. But Andersen's agreement with the sentiment was apparent in his virtual exile from the country where he had written his greatest work and received his greatest censure.

By the time Andersen visited them in Leipzig, Robert had written songs to four of Andersen's poems, which Livia Frege sang, with Clara accompanying. "I cannot believe you would honor me in this way." Andersen had tears in his eyes. He did not seem homely to Robert. Men never did. They were either beautiful, like Ludwig Schunke, or they were simply men, wearing their bodies as they might an unremarkable suit of clothes.

"In honoring you, I honor my wife. It is you who inspires her, and she who inspires me. The two of you dwell together in these songs. Everything I write, I write out of love for her."

By such sentiment was Andersen himself inspired to confess his own love. It was for Jenny Lind, whose name Robert was then hearing for the first time. She was a singer, and she had come to Copenhagen to perform as Alice in *Robert le Diable*. What a strange coincidence, thought Robert, as Andersen spoke to him in their corner of the parlor, over brandy and cigars, that this should be the same opera about which Clara had written him from Paris so many years ago, when she was away from him for longer than she'd ever been and he missed her for the first of what he did not know would be countless times for countless hours, and he desired her, desired her for the first time, in her absence, as he desires her now, even as he lies within Endenich, in her absence.

"She showed me art in its sanctity," said Andersen.

Robert thought Andersen was referring to Clara until he mentioned her voice, Lind's voice, which was renowned for its expression of chaste maidenhood and which, in Franz Grillparzer's words, rose out of time and space to become the purity of an inculpable soul singing.

"I felt I had seen one of the vestal virgins," said Andersen.

He might, Robert knew, have stopped speaking right there. But driven by what Robert was soon to comprehend was Andersen's need to confess the humiliation of failure (in words of such graceful simplicity that the beauty of the tale itself triumphed over the brutality of its contents), he went on to tell the story of his tragic love.

He had loved Jenny Lind from afar. He had worked up the courage to meet her. He had played upon his reputation (in the rest of the world if not in Denmark) to impress her. He had given her signed copies of his work. He had written *new* work for her, including "The Ugly Duckling" and "The Nightingale"—a tale for each of them. He had followed her wherever she went, first in Copenhagen, then on the Continent. He had proclaimed his love with everything he did and everything he wrote and everything he thought and everything he said except for the words themselves, which he could not say to her, she was too precious for him to wound with words that might offend her ears.

One day, in one of her hotel rooms, where he continued to pretend he was merely a friend who happened to appear in her life out of nowhere and to write such stories for her as would secure immortality for one who, like any musician, would be reduced by death to the mere hearsay of reputation . . . "One day," he leaned over and down and whispered to Robert, "she interrupted whatever words I was spouting in order to hide the words I felt I would have died to say and died if I failed to say. She interrupted not with words of her own but with a gesture. She held out her hand to me, as I had always hoped she might. But I could not have grasped it even had I dared, for in it was a mirror. 'Look at yourself,' she said. 'I prefer to look at you,' I found the courage to say and gazed beyond the mirror at her face as if it were my own reflected back at me. 'Look at yourself,' she repeated, not impatiently, 'and only *then* look at me.' I looked at my face. What is a face, after all? It is the only mask that's not a work of art. But it was as if I had never seen myself before. In order to show me the impossibility of my love for her, she allowed me to possess her for the first time. Her eyes alone, it is true. But they became my eyes. I saw myself as she saw me. '*Now* look at me,' she said—'see me for what I am: as ugly inside as you are outside.' I looked, of course. I knew it was the last time I would ever see her. (But of course it was not.) Never had she been more beautiful. Her cruelty itself had transformed her. To the degree she made me hate myself, she made me love her all the more."

Strange how all these loves connect. Music seems to thread them through the air itself, entangling people against their wills and judgment. Where music was involved, love went wild. It replaced language. It sped through the blood like the Spanish fly that Heine found in Liszt but was far more deeply hidden in Mendelssohn and took a Jenny Lind to animate.

It was Mendelssohn who brought The Lind, as Clara came to call her, into their lives. Clara asked Mendelssohn to obtain tickets for a Lind recital in Leipzig, no small task even for him, who was the city's most renowned musician and most powerful musical politician and was to play that night on Lind's program. Nonetheless, he was, he told Clara, nearly torn apart in securing the tickets. People who had no interest in music, in song, in sopranos, in Swedes, in women, in beauty, in art, in truth, in going out of an April evening—people who had interest in nothing but what other people were interested in created an almost deadly crush in their desire not to hear Lind make music but to be in that place where she did so.

For his courage, Mendelssohn demanded something in return: When Clara arrived from Dresden, he told her he wanted her to play at Lind's recital that night. "But I've brought no concert clothes," she said. "Jenny won't mind," he replied. "Of course she won't mind—how little you know of women, Felix!" He laughed in agreement: "Cécile has taken all I know and applied it to herself."

That evening, when he had finished playing Beethoven's *Moonlight* Sonata, Mendelssohn left the stage, walked into the audience, found Clara, and walked her back to the stage, where she played two of his *Songs without Words*. The audience, despite its impatience for the appearance of Jenny Lind, seemed to delight in Clara's brief return to the city of her birth and her first fame and the great scandal of her love.

It was Clara who then declared to fall in love with Jenny Lind, and not only with the most beautiful coloratura she had ever heard but with a woman of almost peculiar restraint in an art in which exaggeration of gesture, voice, and attitude was customarily rewarded. She was a small thing, dressed almost as simply in her concert clothes as Clara was in one of her traveling outfits. At the reception following the concert, the two women stood off by themselves for a time, unapproachable somehow, not because each was perhaps the most famed practitioner of her art in all the world but because two women who were precisely that were able to huddle together like sisters in possession of the most tender and secret of memories. Only Mendelssohn was able to come between them.

Clara could, she said later, observe the very first spark of the love between Jenny and Mendelssohn, passing through her as they stood on either side of her. It was her they toasted, for lending her fame and virtuosity to their concert; themselves they celebrated. Adultery's early pretense is the taking of pleasure in another for the purpose of diverting attention from oneself. How Jenny and Felix fussed over her and, together, touched their glasses to hers and touched her themselves—her hands, her bare arms beneath the sleeve, even her hair—her body not so much a barrier between them as a conductor of their implicit passion.

It aroused her even, as she exhibited upon her return to Dresden, when she told Robert of her suspicions. In the telling, she became almost hoarse with lust, thick-voiced as she acted out their parts and touched Robert as she had been touched by them. More than with their absence from one another, which always brought them to uncommon ardor, Clara's assumption of the role of these new lovers, and Robert's delight in playing both audience and participant, opened her to what he could only believe was a new experience. In the sixth year of their marriage, she learned for the first time to find a depth of feeling in her own body through a brief conviction that it had become the body of another, as so, too, had his. She became, that night, quite lost to herself. And so he gained yet more of the only woman he had ever loved.

Clara did not judge the others then, merely portrayed them. The time had not yet come, he realizes, for her to shrink within herself, and thereby to shrink her feelings, out of a bitterness whose by-product was almost always envy. And envy's harvest was, in turn, a condemnation of any pleasure taken by others less afflicted by the world. Her pain was his, his pain hers, which is to say, it has been his suffering alone that has caused hers. Her love for him has destroyed the love she had for others and the joy she took in all they did.

What she would not condemn in Jenny, now Jenny condemns in her. Johannes has redeemed her. And him as well. And all Jenny is heard to say is it is shameful Clara be seen with him so much, at all.

Jenny was seen everywhere with Mendelssohn, even in his home. She had no shame before Cécile. Indeed, her admiration for Mendelssohn himself seemed to extend to his wife. Jenny did not hate Cécile; she merely wanted to become her. Cécile, for her part, seemed to take no pleasure in the attention Jenny paid to her. Nor in the fact that she was far more beautiful than Jenny, her skin darker, her hair fuller, her eyes as blue, her nose at least as small and unobtrusively shapely, her bosom capable of bringing, in the deliberately oafish equivoque of one of her Berlin admirers, men's eyes to their knees. What Jenny wanted, Cécile knew, was her life: the home that sang with children; the children who took her out of reach; the excuse to stay put; the husband who was not just any husband but the man with whom she had found herself in love.

The home Jenny envied imprisoned Cécile, who, unlike Robert, was not invited to accompany the musician in the family on tour. So Cécile remained behind while Felix traveled Europe, no small part of it with Jenny, though always, as they say, on business. It was perfectly natural for him to invite her to sing in Aachen at the Lower Rhenish Music Festival; he was the conductor, after all, and there could be no harm in his looking into her eyes and encompassing her small form within his quivering palms and stroking from her throat "A new created world, a new created world springs up, springs up…" Haydn's second *up* rose upon the F-sharp Felix loved so much to hear in Jenny's voice he put it repeatedly for her to sing in his own *Elijah*'s opening bars of "Hear ye, Israel."

So much did the two of them enjoy making music upon the banks of the Rhine that they took two trips down the river itself, on one of which they stood for hours before the Virgin Mary portal on the cathedral of Cologne, watching her life unfold in relief before them, and on the second of which they celebrated more secular pleasure through a visit to Beethoven's birthplace in Bonn, at 20 Bonngasse. But Mendelssohn did not take Jenny to the Beethoven monument in the Münsterplatz, the financing of which he had opposed on principle, believing that money should go first to living orchestras before it was spent on what he called "lumps of stone."

Robert had Brahms walk him to the monument on one of Johannes's first visits to Endenich. He had still wanted to live, then, to eat and drink and smoke and hear music and make music and to dream, at least, of returning to the home in which Clara lived and their children lived and dear, generous Johannes lived with them. He had not yet begun to starve himself. His feet had not yet begun to swell from the ministrations of the young temptress named Edema. Indeed, he was as able to keep up with the swift pace set by Brahms as he had been when they had gone out for their first walks not long after Brahms had appeared at their door in Düsseldorf and by so doing had transformed his life.

In the boy and his music he had found both reason and passion (so often in lethal conflict) to live; it was, he supposes, a measure of his true madness that upon having made this discovery, he began to edge ever closer to the river, this same Rhine that flows outside the window of his madhouse, and finally to take the dive to death that only now, as he lies in wait for Clara, may see him take the waters.

On their sad way back along the Endenich road, when they had stopped talking either in anticipation of their imminent separation or because Beethoven tended to induce silence in other composers,* Robert suddenly said, "May I borrow your spectacles?"

"Where are yours?" asked Johannes.

"In my room."

"Did you forget them?"

"My mind...," he said equivocally and tapped himself just above his ear.

Johannes carried his glasses in his knapsack, which combined peculiarly with the blue Wertherian jacket he wore as emblem less of his esteem for Goethe than of the kind of hopeless love that had passed for love supreme back in 1774. He rarely used his spectacles. They spoiled the beauty of his face, which was made all the more beautiful because he did not realize they spoiled the beauty of his face. He did not wear them because when his long hair fell across his face and he brushed it away with his hand, sometimes he brushed his glasses off and always he managed to cloud them with the oils from his callow skin.

"Why didn't you ask me for them earlier if you couldn't see?"

"I could see all I wanted to."

---

*As had Bach before him. It was Chopin who said, "In my opinion, Beethoven was tormented by the idea of Bach." And it was Brahms himself who was to say, in reference to Beethoven, "You can't imagine how it feels to have to live beneath his giant shadow."

"The trees? The birds? The road before you?"

"I could see you. Beside me, even."

"I have always walked too fast."

"Does Clara still walk every day?"

"Every day we're together."

"In Düsseldorf?"

"Lübeck, Hanover, Hamburg, Rotterdam...wherever we're together. She doesn't care to walk alone."

"She never did."

"Do my glasses help?"

"I can see her," said Robert, staring through the glasses at Brahms.

Her letters from London (burned, as he has burned her earlier letters, though these one by one and not in such a piss-stenched bonfire as books are burned by tyrants), whence she is now returning upon having received from Dr. Richarz the news that he is dead or dying, Robert can't remember which, Clara has described her meetings with Queen Victoria. They are the same age, it has surprised Robert to learn—queens, unlike princesses, are always old, and Clara becomes to him increasingly the girl she was, as he grows old not so much with time as with weakness and the impotence of an artist emptied of his art. She had been invited to England by the Philharmonic Society and told that a brief concert tour would reward her sufficiently to pay his Endenich expenses for an entire year. Johannes, she said, did not want her to go; he rounded up a group of friends and musicians who agreed to pledge an equal amount of money to keep her home and him asylumed. But she would take no such charity and went to England, alone, her parting from Johannes the most painful she had ever experienced, leaving her numb, her body, she said, "lifeless," a word that's haunted Robert, because it is how he feels himself except when he remembers her. She has written from all the cities where she's played—Manchester, Liverpool, Dublin, London. In the last of these, Robert's oratorio, *Paradise and the Peri,* had been performed to great acclaim. This was the story taken from a Thomas Moore poem that Wagner had tried and failed to make into an opera. The Lind was in London to sing in it; Pauline Viardot was in London to see it; she, Clara, astounded all of musical London by appearing in the chorus and joined her voice to Jenny's and her heart and her tears to the music written by a husband so far away and so long unseen, untouched.

It had been nearly a decade since Jenny made her London debut, again as Alice. Queen Victoria had been there, as had Mendelssohn, who that time, at least, needed procure no tickets and thus was spared participation in, if not observation of, the riot at the box office. The English press went so far as to claim that no artist in history—not Farinelli, not Catalani, not Sontag, not Liszt, not even Paganini, not even *Mendelssohn*—had caused such a fever of delirium.

Queen Victoria, at the final curtain of that day in early May, left her box to place a wreath at Jenny's feet. The queen had done this for no one, not even Mendelssohn.

Six months to the day after he had, with unselfish delight, watched the English replace him in their hearts with Jenny, Mendelssohn died. His first stroke came when, at lunch with Cécile, he began to shake uncontrollably and then passed out and then, in his wife's arms, awakened, speaking to her in great haste and agitation in a language in which he had heretofore never addressed her: English. It was as if he were back in London with Jenny.

A few days later, when he seemed to be resting and thus to be recovering, he began to moan through day and night and finally to sing, to sing endlessly, perhaps the kind of music, said Robert, that I hear in my head and am unable to voice, so in that case Felix was fortunate, to the very end his music was heard by others.

Robert packed his best dark Stutzer und Hinter suit for what the Mendelssohn family called the funeral but was not—the burial would be elsewhere. Robert wanted to see Felix one last time but not at that moment when he became irretrievable.

"I will come with you," said Clara.

"Then I would not be able to go."

"Do you not need me?"

"So much that I could not bear for you and death to occupy the same city, or my mind."

He left Clara in Dresden with the children and went to Leipzig. In order to gain entry into the Mendelssohn home in the Königsstrasse, he had to push his way through a huge, grief-purging crowd and then explain to the servant at the door—someone new who must have been hired in order to deal with the horde of mourners and recognized neither Robert's name nor face—that he wrote music too and was married to the pianist Clara Wieck Schumann. "I was told to look for the man who is to do the death mask," said the servant. "He should be along soon," said Robert—"he just finished working on mine." The servant jumped quickly out of the way.

Robert waited until he could be alone to view the body. And then he had to shut the door behind him, a breach of etiquette and contravention of the custom that required corpses never be enclosed within four unbroken walls;

if this had originated in an ancient Teutonic desire to allow the odor to dissipate or the soul an outlet into the rest of the house, perhaps the universe itself, he did not know. He felt he had no choice. The public was being allowed in a few at a time to the flower-choked room, lit only by torches that flickered with an apt approximation of life itself.

From downstairs, he could hear Felix's children playing with their dolls. Their voices were cheerful, blithe. But death would, now, be forever in their throats.

Felix wore a smile of his own. He could not have died with it. Someone had taken the trouble to mold it there. It was not incongruous so much as unnecessary. There was no more need to advertise joy than despair. God help us all if the dead have moods.

What could not have been manipulated were the two prominent veins standing out on his friend's forehead. Robert had envied these in life and accused himself for a moment of having come all this way merely to see that they had not survived death. Brilliance in life, he noted, was often accompanied by tumid veins in the head. Sometimes they were by the temple, sometimes closer to an eye, sometimes behind the ear, sometimes in a bald man visible amid the bumps and gullies of the landscape of the brain.

He had no such demonstrative veins. He had wished for them, the way a boy might wish to be tall or a man might wish for a larger prick. He had held his breath before mirrors, puffing out his cheeks, in search of these worms of genius lounging on the surface of his long-suffering head. Once, when he was exceptionally, unrealistically, angry with Clara because she had written in their diary that the sound of his piano drowned out the sound of hers, which he took to be a frightful metaphor for a more general frustration, he thought he felt veins swell out of the skin above his left eye and ran from the room to search out his image, only to discover that his anger had caused his forehead to become creased and that what looked back at him was a man who was unhappy with the sound of his own music, not his wife's.

He could feel Mendelssohn's veins upon his palm. Should anyone succeed in coming into the room, he would look like a madman feeling for fever in a body so cold it was soothing. He didn't know whether he wished to impart some of his life to Felix or to take Felix's life into himself. The gulf between them was not enlarged by death, merely extended. No one had helped him more than Mendelssohn—hiring him to teach at the Leipzig Conservatory, providing his wife with stage and audience and therefore income, showing him the example of a composer whose every written note (and improvised too!) was praised and loved and therefore he did not become the composer he might have and worked himself into the grave at the age of thirty-eight because he lived with the curse of satisfying everyone but himself. Yet Robert knew that Mendelssohn did not love the music Robert wrote. He praised it, sometimes, but he didn't love it. Nor should he have. "Don't you want to be popular?" Felix had asked, the implication being "popular like me."

"Perhaps," he confessed, by which his friend was pleased, until Robert added, "I just don't want to have to write popular work."

Felix had asked him, "Are you faithful to your wife?" "Without effort," he replied. "I cannot say the same," confessed Felix. "Do you refer to the infidelity or the effort?" asked Robert. "The effort, of course." "The Lind?" "The Lind."

It was as if Jenny had died with Felix. He left nothing more of an opera he was writing for her than a tantalizing fragment; in it she was to have been Lorelei, the nymph of the Rhine who lured men to their doom with her song, as she, Jenny, had lured him to what she knew, if it was doom, was doom rhapsodic. She had long been scheduled to have appeared in his *Elijah* in Vienna. But when it was sung, on schedule, ten days after his death, she had withdrawn from what turned out to be yet another memorial to her greatest love. The singers were dressed in black; the music stands draped in black. On the conductor's stand lay the score and the same kind of laurel wreath that in great profusion surrounded Felix as he lay here in this torch-lit room on the Königstrasse with Robert's hand upon his forehead. Perhaps his ghost conducted that *Elijah*; no one else stood at the conductor's stand. It was as empty as Jenny's place, and her heart.

And Robert's. He was one of six pallbearers who carried the coffin from the Mendelssohn home to St. Paul's Cathedral. Moscheles was among the others, just behind Robert on the right side of the casket. As they were preparing to lift it for the first time, Robert told Moscheles about a program he had kept from a concert he had attended in Karlsbad when he was a little boy, with his father.

Finally, he wept, for his friend, and his father, and himself. He wept as he marched with more than a thousand people surrounding him on the way to the cathedral (hung with black sheets, which applauded hollowly in the brisk November wind), behind a band of clarinets and oboes and bassoons playing a Beethoven funeral march and a second little orchestra that performed Mendelssohn's own march from the fifth book of *Songs without Words,* into the cathedral, where music students from the Conservatory sat separated from Leipzig and Saxon government officials but all were soon embraced equally by the boundless sound of a choir of six hundred singing a chorus from the dead man's *St. Paul* and the final chorus from Bach's *St. Matthew Passion,* this last piece of music causing Robert to picture Felix at the age of twenty, half a life ago, a brilliant boy releasing Bach into the air.

A thousand more people, now carrying torches to light the night and Mendelssohn's way to Heaven, accompanied the coffin to the railroad station. There, a reserved train left at ten o'clock on its way to Berlin and the Mendelssohn family vault in the Alter Dreifaltigkeitsfriedhof, stopping along the way in Koethen, Dessau, and Halle, in each of which, in the middle of the night, crowds had gathered at the railroad station and sang to the dead man songs he had written.

Robert, who had taken the last train home to Dresden, read aloud to Clara, the next night in bed, the Berlin *Staatszeitung* account of the services and journey and funeral. Robert's name, she was appalled to notice, had not been included among those of the pallbearers. "I don't care at all, so long as I might find my name on your lips," he said, discarding at last his fatigue from the trip and the strange hold upon his emotions that death—that emptiness, that absence, that *reductio ad nihilo*—had always maintained.

It was an absence and emptiness fought over by Cécile Mendelssohn and Jenny Lind. "Life lasts so long," said Cécile—"how can I live it alone?" "He was the only person who provided consummation to my being," said Jenny—"and almost as soon as I found him, I lost him."

They competed in their mourning. Jenny did not sing a single note of Mendelssohn for two years. Then, on the anniversary of his death, she finally made up for her withdrawal at Vienna by singing in *Elijah* at Exeter Hall in London, a performance to raise money for the Mendelssohn Foundation established not by his family but by herself. On that evening, she put aside her trills, she subsumed her *fioriture* and her *grupetti* within her grief, indeed she purged her voice of all its operatic furbelow and produced a tone so pure and unornamented that there seemed no barrier between sound and music. Mendelssohn, it seemed, had finally entered her.

Cécile could do little after this but die, which she did at the age of thirty-six, the very same week, Robert told Johannes, that you knocked on our door in Düsseldorf, considerably lightening the burden put upon our minds by thoughts of the Mendelssohn children, in age near our own, suddenly orphaned.

It had been Marie, then twelve, their firstborn, who opened that door on Belkerstrasse in Düsseldorf, where they had moved from Dresden three years earlier to the very month, so Robert might obtain a salary as the city's musical director and whatever prestige would attach to that position. Ferdinand Hiller had been leaving the post and offered it to Robert, who had hesitated only because when he looked up Düsseldorf in a geography text he discovered there was a large insane asylum in the middle of the city.

"Who is it?" called Robert from the dining room, where he sat alone at the smaller of the two tables in the aftermath of the family lunch.

There was no answer. He became concerned. It was not that he believed death actually knocked at one's door. It didn't need to. Therefore, silence was as much a threat as the inner concerts he had begun to hear, the great drumbeating that kept him awake at night and that Clara, awake beside him, stroking him, pretended were being caused by the unending street noises — screeching wagons, yowling children, sardonic barrel organs — when both knew he was hearing things that were as private as insanity.

He dropped his cigar in the ashtray and went to rescue his daughter from the silence.

But it was not death that stood before her and had rendered her mute. It was the most exquisitely charming boy he, and presumably she, had ever seen.

He was short, not much taller than Marie, who looked like her mother, with her mother's large hands and dark hair in the midst of which a pale, eye-inflamed face had been etched. But he was so slender as to appear somehow stretched to a maximum height, a perfection of balance. His hair was golden but not fine, thick with some sort of radiant promise, not particularly clean but all the more exciting for that. His clothes, as well, challenged the bourgeois edifice that Robert felt swelled out of his own backside into the mortgaged circuit of rooms and furniture and closets and curtains and artwork and glassware that floated behind him in cruel mockery of his own lost youth and the fervor of irresponsibility. The boy wore a collarless white shirt, so that his neck had long since dirtied even the dark blue alpaca of his short coat, which was raised from his shoulders by the straps of what must be — Robert could not see it from the front — a knapsack. His gray pants were short enough to perch almost perfectly on the very tops of his boots, whose leather appeared so worn yet burnished that even his feet were enviable, so free were they to march across the surface of the earth. In his hand he held a green felt hat, taken off, no doubt, in courtesy to Marie but that Robert wished back upon his head, to see what the green might do to the blue of his eyes.

"I am Johannes Brahms. Arrived from Hamburg." His voice was soft, and high — soft, perhaps, because it was high.

"Do you have a package?" Robert raised a hand and pointed with a curved finger over the boy's head toward where his knapsack, if that's what it was, might hold whatever it was he was here to deliver.

"No more packages." His answer was enigmatic but his smile wholly unqualified, his teeth white with inexperience aside from one yellowed at the bottom center that marked him for the solace of tobacco. "But I do have a letter."

"From whom to whom?"

"Joseph Joachim to you."

"Oh, you are *Brahms*!"

·Robert now recalled that he and Clara had had an earlier letter from their young violinist friend asking them to receive one Johannes Brahms, "successor to Beethoven." Aside from the fact that the only possible successor to Beethoven could be, and was, in music's serpentine chronology, Bach, Robert had been concerned at how casually Joachim threw around Beethoven's name. He had that very day, and for about ten days previous, been working on a violin concerto requested, if not commissioned, by Joachim for himself. In that request, Joachim had begged Robert to be inspired by Beethoven's example, as he drew a work out of his "deep quarry," which Robert suspected was a great deal deeper—not in profundity but in obscurity and disquiet—than Joachim could ever imagine.

As if he were a dancer and not a musician, Brahms crossed his arms over his head and reached behind with precious flexibility and relieved his body of what indeed proved to be a knapsack. With one hand, he held it by its straps, and with the other, he opened it. Robert gazed within. What secrets, he wondered, might a boy travel with, so lightly as to touch the earth with nothing more than what he carried on his back? A pair of socks? A book? A pen? A pad? An apple? A space of dreams? A future unconfined? He could see nothing but darkness until Brahms's hand emerged.

"Here is Pepi's letter."

"Pepi?"

"Joseph."

"I've had my own letter from . . . you call him 'Pepi'?"

Brahms pushed the letter toward Robert, who opened it only to see whether Joachim might this time have signed off with a "Pepi" for him too.

He had not.

Robert handed the letter back to Brahms.

"Are you not going to read it?"

"Are you not here to play the piano?"

He would rather look at him than listen to him. From the time he had begun years ago to teach at the Leipzig Conservatory, there had been too many auditions by too many young musicians. How fitting that he should have ended up like his father, whom Robert once came upon reading through a pile of manuscripts with tears in his eyes. "Why are you crying?" Robert asked him. "Because," he answered, "there is so little art and so god-damned many artists."

Brahms handed his green hat to Marie, the perfect gesture toward a girl who could not take her eyes from him until she might touch at least a piece of him. She led him to the closest room with a piano—a small parlor with a large Graf. Robert walked behind them, weary and afraid. He did not want to have to lie to this boy. He did not want to have to tell him the truth. Why were they sent to him, who had once lived in a house with a little student named Clara Wieck, younger than any of them, so gifted as to obliterate the future of pianists, like this one, who had not yet been born when she played for Robert and he went out and tried to make his hand as strong as hers?

Brahms sat at the piano. Robert sank into his chair and motioned for Marie to stand next to him. She would kick him if he started to fall asleep. Or perhaps cover his face with Brahms's hat.

"Sonata in C Major," Brahms announced softly.

"C Major?" Robert felt he could hear it already. "Yours?" he forced himself to be polite.

How many notes had the boy played before Robert stopped him? He has never been able to remember that. He sometimes thinks he stopped him before he'd played a single note. Yet he can hear those notes in his head, along with those others now that seem to come from Hell.

He leapt to his feet and went to Brahms and went to put a hand upon his head. But he could not touch him. So his hand hovered over the boy's fair hair like a halo, protection and glorification both.

The boy went on playing. He seemed accustomed to the attention, or oblivious to it.

"Stop."

But he didn't. It was not that he was playing like a maniac, or a Liszt for that matter, letting the notes whip his body, his body assume the music's corporeal form. Nor were his eyes closed. It was concentration in fulfillment of itself, as well as some vast pleasure in the music that he was unwilling to relinquish, for such was youth, drinking until drunk, indulging in the pleasures of the afterlife long ahead of time.

"Please wait a moment." Oh, to touch his head. "Clara must hear this."

Not "my wife"—"Clara," he realized he had said. That it was this name that made the boy stop, or seemed to. Such an intimacy—to say one's wife's name to one who's never met her. She was, of course, famous, though not as famous as she'd been as a child; marriage, and its ever-present conse-quence, motherhood, had seen to that. Nonetheless: In Europe, the name "Clara," by itself, could mean only Clara Wieck Schumann, as she insisted she be called upon her programs, since the fame of Clara Wieck had not ar-rived undiminished upon Clara Schumann.

Brahms smiled, not up at him but over at Marie, who, if she had been confused at her father's strange behavior, was enlightened, literally, by the young man's cheerful discomposure. She beamed and floated halfway off her chair.

Robert rushed from the room to the foot of the stairs. "Clara, Clara, come here at once!"

So she was there at once, running down the stairs, concern for him shad-owing her face. How he had darkened her, in these thirteen years of mar-riage almost to the day; now, when he called her to share his joy, she assumed it was pain to which she traveled.

"Is something the matter?"

It was so incongruous—the meeting of her anxiety with his ecstasy—that he laughed. He was brimming over with amusement and relief. It had been so long since he could announce such pleasure. "My love, you must hear this. You've never heard music like this in your life."

He led her to him. Marie had risen wholly and was standing next to Brahms, looking down at him who looked only at his hands. She was so like her mother, years ago, waiting for the chance to touch his face.

"Please be so kind as to begin your sonata from the beginning, young man."

Brahms played, it seemed, for hours, one piece after another, beginning like Beethoven with the first chord of his first sonata and in his second, in the same F-sharp minor of Robert's first, beginning like Robert himself, with an even grander, more aggressive chord, and continuing like Robert until, in its finale's cadenza of scales and trills, he broke free from such hom-age and, as had been the case in the first sonata's folkish andante, became himself, one, as Clara was to say, who comes as if sent from God.

"Why have you said nothing?" Brahms asked when he had played all that he could, or would, play.

"What is there to say?" asked Robert in return. What, indeed? "You and I understand one another. Won't you join us for lunch?"

"I don't understand," said the boy.

"So long as we understand *each other,*" said Robert.

"I *still* don't understand." There was a petulance to this sweet-faced, broad-shouldered young man, which gave a twist to the winsomeness of his lips and cinched them into a brief snarl of caustic testiness. What a pleasure to find, at an audition, arrogance not the auditor's.

"As Shakespeare said," said Robert, who had lately returned to a reading of Shakespeare he had begun with Clara soon after their wedding for the purpose of copying every word that English master had written about music, 'I understand thy kisses, and thou mine.' "

"I don't understand about *lunch*. Have you not eaten lunch?"

Marie laughed and nodded vigorously, to confirm the young man's genius and at the same time excuse her father's eccentricity.

"I meant *tomorrow*."

Robert touched Brahms finally, putting a hand on his shoulder to guide him to the front door, where they parted without another word, though Robert watched Brahms as he walked away, raising his arms to Heaven, as indeed he should, even if it was only so he might allow his knapsack to descend from his hands down his arms and over his shoulders until finally, just as he turned the corner and disappeared, it settled enviably into the fanned channel of his spine and carried him away.

They could barely wait for his return. They spoke of nothing and no one else. He knew she had understood perfectly why he had sent the boy away. They could not share their pleasure in him were he to remain. The world was always tested first within the shelter of their marriage.

But then he did not come. The table was set, the food cooked, the children bathed and lectured about manners and hospitality with the usual reference to Greek gods coming to Philemon and Baucis in disguise (in this case not much of a disguise), Marie gently teased but put in charge of the others, made into a little mother so that when the boy arrived she might assume the role of woman and flutter slightly less in her display of instant love.

Robert was surprised to find Clara as anxious as he when the time for luncheon passed and still Brahms did not appear. He was accustomed to her soothing him when he could not sleep or a migraine ate his brain or hemorrhoids his anus or when drums beat inside his head and trumpets blew (in what else but C major) behind his eyes and every noise within the world became a musical tone and visions appeared because of what Dr. Helbig identified as labyrinthitis—finally, Robert thought, the perfect diagnosis for a man lost within the confines of his own existence, like a tone within an endless fugue, and saved each day, and night, by the cord played out by his tender Ariadne, who sometimes knelt sadly before him and sucked his fears away.

"You're making me nervous," he told her, as she paced before the front door, now and then stopping in mid-stride to open it violently, as if the boy were some sort of eidolon who might dissolve if not secured within the depths of her great dark eyes.

"*I'm* making *you* nervous!"

They laughed. His nerves had long since become the family joke, whenever the family was in a mood to joke. Brahms seemed to have brought such ease to their household.

"Go look for him. I'll stay here and keep the food cold."

She was out the door before he could see if he'd amused her in return or even wonder why he'd not gone himself. Often, when he went out alone, he questioned if he would come back. Surely this was a question most men occasionally asked. But not men who loved their wives as he loved his. And so he always returned. But never more had he wished for a double, who might be thrown into the river to swim for himself.

It seemed hours she was gone. It *was* hours. He would normally have been filled with images of her in terrible distress—caught in a burning building, crushed beneath carriage wheels, forced to conduct the Düsseldorf Gesangverein in his stead and letting fly the baton into her own heart, as he was known to loose the thing upon his unprotected musicians. These were always mere substitutes for the image of himself in the distress he would suffer should it be she who would disappear from his life, whether through such accident or choice. Perhaps the true cause of madness was the inability to think without oneself at the center of one's thoughts.

But because he imagined her searching for Brahms, he imagined her happy. So she was when she finally returned, as was he, because there with her was Brahms himself, dressed exactly as he had been the day before, if a little dirtier, a bit more worn for being away from home and thus more free. Clara actually had him by the hand as they crossed the threshold, pulling him along into the house, where they stood before Robert, who had himself not sat down since she'd left.

"Where did you find him?"

Brahms did not let her answer. As he put the back of his hand to his forehead, in a gesture of self-mockery, he pulled her hand along with his; she might have been about to wipe his brow, as she did Robert's when he lay in bed cold with terror. "Stupid me! I was still in my squalid little hotel. I didn't think you really wanted me here. I thought I was a sacrifice to diplomacy."

"I had to convince him of the truth of our enthusiasm!" Clara stepped away from Brahms and stared at him exaggeratedly. He was not to be believed.

"For his music?" asked Robert.

"As well as for himself," explained Clara.

"We are hardly diplomatic," said Robert. "Indeed, we are perhaps the strangest couple in all of Düsseldorf. Or I the strangest man, and Clara the sacrifice to *my* diplomacy—or lack thereof. Which is to say, you would not be here if we didn't want you here. And if we didn't want you here, we wouldn't be who you think we are."

"Who I think you are, and who I thought you might be, or were, are no longer the same."

"Have we disappointed you?" asked Robert.

"A long time ago," said Brahms, which for him, barely twenty, turned out to have been three years earlier, when Frau Schumann and Herr Schumann had come to Hamburg and Jenny Lind had sung with them and Robert had conducted Clara in his piano concerto, which only he, Brahms, seemed to have admired—admired so much, indeed, that he left a package for Herr Schumann at his hotel, a package containing his compositions and a letter asking for advice and begging for a chance to obtain this advice in person.

"And what did I say?" Robert had no memory of the music or the boy. He wondered if he might have contained both for these three years and that their secret presence within him would then account for how rapidly and completely he had given himself to the boy, and taken him to him.

"You said nothing." Such anger from so sweet a mouth. "You didn't even look. The package was returned to me unopened."

"Now I understand!" Robert spread wide his arms, not that his wife or their new friend might rush into them, though he would have welcomed both, but because he felt some new crack open into the world of which he believed we are all, at every moment, a reflection.

"That you are not who I thought you might be?"

"'No more packages,'" said Robert. "That's what I understand: 'No more packages.' And so it shall be. Now we understand each other completely. Shall we eat?"

Brahms moved between their table and the children's, as did Marie, who customarily sat within the crowd of siblings and was rewarded for this custodial service with a glass of wine in the evenings, at which she sipped while distracting her three sisters and two brothers from the endless conversation their parents seemed to carry on with one another, in their father's case to the exclusion of conversation with the rest of the world. But this day, when late lunch had become early supper, Marie slipped into a chair directly across from Brahms, who seemed relieved to have such intimate company nearer his own age than were the adults at either side of him. When the other children, absent Marie, began to quarrel, Brahms went to them first, asked them to tell him their names again, and then made up a song using their names so he might celebrate them and memorize them:

> Elise, Elise, I ask you, please,
> Won't you kindly pass the cheese,
> All the way around to me
> By way of tiny Eugenie
> So I may take some with my hand
> And pass it on to Ferdinand,
> Who so as not to be a pig
> Hands the plate on to Ludwig.
> And Ludwig gives it to Marie
> Who's taken such good care of me
> Yet saves the last for pretty Julie —
> Wonderful children, I love you truly!

They loved him in return. It became a happy battle, between the children and the children's parents, for the attention of their young visitor, who came to them every day, for food and music and admiration shared.

He played games with the children on the floor and then, seemingly, in the air itself, as he ran up the front stairway, stood on the landing with his arms aloft like a conductor of the six-piece orchestra gazing up at him, and then grasped the banister, shot his feet into the air, and walked all the way down to the ground floor on his hands. The applause brought Clara and Robert, for whom Johannes was convinced to repeat his performance. Clara held her fingers to her lips as he descended.

He was eager to see every room in the house. "Look at all the books," he said. "Look at all the glasses — my God, you could go for days without washing a single one of them. And a wine cellar! I have always dreamed of having a wine cellar."

"You need a house first," said Clara.

"Oh, a house is the last thing I want."

"Just a wine cellar?" Robert inquired.

"Just a wine cellar."

The two men sat and smoked for hours at a time, Johannes the cigarettes he rolled and the occasional cigar Robert was able to convince him to accept, Robert his cigars and sometimes a pipe, the same pipe Johannes would observe in his mouth the first time he was allowed to visit Robert at Endenich and the doctors had him watch his friend through the little judas in his wall.

They needn't always talk. Robert found in Johannes someone unintimidated by silence, to the same degree he could embrace conversation, with an excitement for words and ideas as yet neither restrained nor corrupted by a knowledge of the limits of words and the failure of ideas. They might sit side by side with books in their laps, smoking, only occasionally reading aloud to one another from their Jean Paul Richter or their E. T. A. Hoffmann.

"Those pieces I sent you in Hamburg," Johannes told him—"I had signed them 'Johannes Kreisler, Junior.'"

"Had I known that, I would have looked at them." Perhaps the obscure mystery was finally to be solved, his wild, mad desire satisfied, not with, but within, his own heart. Johannes was like Emilie to him, except her suffering had been replaced by his joy.

"Well, I couldn't very well have put that name in the return address."

"Are you afraid people will think you're a madman?"

"It's no longer chic to be mad."

"I'm sorry to hear that."

He suffered, he told Johannes, from the *furor divinus* described by Plato in his *Ion,* at least so far as, like Plato's poet, he sang his beautiful melodies in a state of inspiration. But he did not agree with Plato that the spirit by which he was possessed was not his own. It was precisely the fact that everything he did and everything he was came from *within* that rendered his insanity divine. The artist was his own god. And the madness through which Plato said in *Phaedrus* we receive the greatest benefaction comes not as a gift of Heaven but as a kind of blessed curse from the self.

Robert and Johannes toured the shelves of books like travelers who carry flambeaux toward the walls of churches, who try to memorize a sunset. With them, always, was Clara, a memory for Robert and for Johannes a dream of travel yet to come, which sometimes is the best of travel, to sit at home and picture what it will be like to get where you will, though you do not yet know it, finally get to go.

Robert took down *Either/Or* and told the boy how he'd missed his wife the first time she left him as his wife, to go to Copenhagen, where she'd met the author of this book. And how fortunate that had been, for otherwise Robert might never have come upon the story Kierkegaard tells of the Sicilian tyrant Phalaris, who executed his prisoners by putting them in a bronze bull and setting a slow, hot fire beneath the bull, yet when their shrieks of agony reached his ears, they were transformed by having passed over the reeds he'd placed in the bull's nostrils, so that all Phalaris heard was music so sweet he could not bear to have it stop. This, then, was the artist, as he made his way to freedom the only way he could, through beauty, turning anguish into beauty, dying like Saint Eustathius himself as he sacrified his family to his unwilllingness to appease the false gods who tempted every artist into the simplifying subversion of his art.

But the anguish wasn't always quite so veiled, as evidenced by the Bulwer-Lytton shelf, the most weighted in most people's libraries, with such prolificacy of more than symbolic meaning, for here was a man who, like me, said Robert, worked himself through the exhaustion of toil and study into madness, which he called "anxiety and grief." Bulwer-Lytton ended up at a place named Malvern, about which he wrote *Confessions of a Water-Patient,* his copy of which Robert placed in his new friend's hands. "I have had my own hydro-treatments," he explained. "I had gone from Dr. Carus to Dr. Glock to Dr. Reuter to Dr. *Carl* Carus—relative of Dr. Ernst Carus but not so blessed in marriage—to Dr. Walther to Dr. Helbig to Dr. Hasenclever to Dr. Müller, none of whom I ever abandoned for reasons other than geography, and none of whom ever abandoned me, aside from dear Dr. Reuter, who died before his patient, which is always cause for a kind of retroactive concern. Each had his specialty, of which Dr. Müller's seems to be treatment by water. A couple of years ago he had me bathing naked in the Rhine each day for three weeks. When that didn't work, he packed me off to Scheveningen, in Holland, where the water, being of the sea, was even colder, and Clara lost a child. How was I to know, after that, whether I remained sad and anxious because I was merely sad and anxious or because another of our children drowned before birth?" He snatched back *Confessions of a Water-Patient* and in its stead, like a flower for a weed, presented the startled young man with *The Last Days of Pompeii.* "I gave this to Clara for her sixteenth birthday," he said, replacing at least in his own mind the image of the disconsolately relieved wife at Scheveningen with the girl he had not yet corrupted.

Brahms seemed unable to get enough of the books or of their peculiar owners, who saw no error in the equation by which their lives (time, home, children, food, affectionate regard) would be exchanged for his music and his presence. It was so easy to seduce him with their routines and their possessions, and so easy to be seduced in return by his spirit and his physical beauty and the music that was sometimes so difficult to comprehend, not as much for its form as for its source. Robert saw him sprung whole from the head of Zeus. Clara could not help continuing to think he had been sent by a god who spoke German.

He carried around *The Last Days of Pompeii* until he had been presented with so detailed a description of Clara's sixteenth birthday and the parties attending it that he felt, he said, finally, if momentarily, no longer the youngest person in the room. He looked at her as if she were sixteen, and he twenty, as he was, attempting to read the past in her body and in so doing to obliterate those lost years.

They passed him between them like a gift to each other. When he and Robert were alone, they read and talked and smoked and played chess and indulged in the newly popular table-turning, which allowed Robert a chance to communicate with the dead and in the process to introduce his compassionate new friend to his old friends and family passed away. Otherwise, Clara had him to herself.

Robert could hear them at her piano, she instructing, Brahms playing, each time a bit differently, as he was literally absorbing her into his hands.

"Chohannes," she would say, her voice impeded still by the affliction of her childhood, but only when she addressed him privately. She struggled otherwise for a certain propriety in the public represented by the rest of the family, trying to breathe his name correctly.

She had been taking on students for years, even during her concert tours. Such money as she made from this seemed to Robert tainted, because she should not have had to earn it. Yet with such a pupil as Brahms, whose payment came in his mere willingness to be taught by her, her teaching became a gift given back to herself through him.

He played for them each evening—a fantasie he'd written, songs of his own and Hungarian folk songs, both piano and violin parts of a violin sonata—and each evening through his playing moved more deeply within their lives.

"Tell Robert about Liszt," she said, laughing as she said it, full of a kind of private pleasure that made Robert envy not only Brahms and Clara, for what they shared, but himself for having reason to envy them.

"I fell asleep," said Brahms.

"That's the *punch line*!" Clara touched him on the shoulder.

"You fell asleep while Liszt played!"

Clara now turned to Robert. "How did you know?" And to Brahms: "Did you tell Robert this story before you told me?"

"How *did* you know?" Brahms reached out and put his hand on Robert's sleeve.

Robert tapped himself on the forehead.

"Music is not your only supernatural power," Brahms flattered him.

"Robert can see into the past," teased Clara.

Brahms had fallen asleep some four months earlier while visiting Liszt in Weimar at the Altenburg, the grand home of his mistress, Princess Carolyne Sayn-Wittgenstein, who had inherited thirty thousand serfs from her father and from her mother the vastly more commutable strength in her thighs that allowed her to stay in her horse's saddle for eight hours straight and to lock Liszt in place as no woman had before.

"I liked her," said Brahms. "She had black teeth from cigars. She kept them in a box she told me was from Egypt."

"She kept her teeth in an Egyptian box?" asked Clara.

"Her cigars!" The boy's laugh was as high-pitched as his voice; it joined with Clara's and made Robert shiver with delight. He had not seen her so frolicsome since that part of her girlhood she'd spent with him, nor so provocative with a man since she had been so with him.

"The *cigar* box was lined in pearl," Brahms went on. "She would take my hand and put it in and run the tip of my finger along the pearl lining and then close my hand over the biggest, fattest cigar. That one was mine. She smoked small cigars. But she smoked them *all the time!*"

"And Liszt?" insisted Clara. "Is he not still the same insufferable cock?"

"Oh, I don't think he is," said Brahms. "He doesn't wake early."

They were not able to determine, when they discussed this later, whether his naïveté was real or assumed. It hardly mattered, for it flattered him, and it flattered them, that he should be so unashamedly childlike in their presence, when he must know that both saw him as a god.

"He asked me to play for him, and when I wouldn't—I was frightened by his reputation, and I *hated* the room—he took my scherzo from me and put it on the piano and sat down to play. You've seen it—it's scored in my own hand. My own father wouldn't be able to read it. But Liszt—he just sat there and played it. It was even better than I thought—my piece, I mean, though so was his playing."

"And still you fell asleep?" Robert found this hard to believe; Liszt had sight-read Robert's work, and he didn't sleep for three nights after that experience.

"Not when he played *my* work," Brahms answered.

"Oh, no!" said Robert.

"Yes," said Brahms. "He said he was going to play a sonata of his own, in B minor, something new, something revolutionary. Of course it put me right to sleep."

"How terrible." Robert found the story delightful as an anecdote but at the same time distressing when he considered either of its principals, the sleeper or the fallen-asleep-upon. Sometimes it seemed the only place for art was beyond the human capacity to defile it with indifference.

"It was the music that was terrible," said Brahms. "To call that a sonata would be like calling rain wine. That they are both liquid will not make water intoxicating."

"So what did Liszt do?"

"He didn't play my music again. And I didn't play his. But he did give me a gift when I left Weimar. Wait here—I'll show you."

Brahms almost ran from the room, as he almost ran practically everywhere.

"Do you know what it is, darling?"

"Probably an undergarment—though whether Franz's or the princess's I won't hazard a guess."

"Perhaps they share it."

Johannes appeared with his knapsack, hand thrust within. "What are you two laughing at?"

This only amused them further. They would not tell him.

"This is it."

"It's a box," Clara observed.

"A *cigar* box. With my name engraved."

"Are there any cigars inside?" Robert held out his hand.

"No cigars." Brahms put the box into Robert's hand.

Robert looked inside, shook his head, closed the box, and stared at it. "Who is 'Brams'?"

"Aha!" Brahms jumped off the floor.

"Well," said Clara, "if you fell asleep while I played, I would spell your name wrong too."

"As long as you call me Chohannes," he replied.

He did not fall asleep at that moment, but he could without a moment's notice. The great, youthful energy he displayed in everything he did—at the piano, in perilous acrobatics upon virtually any flat or angled surface, in seizing upon ideas and reading books with a zeal that cracked their bindings—he could set aside with no more thought or preparation than a bird bestows upon the stream of air beneath its wings. He glissaded into sleep at any hour, in any place, so that they might come upon him napping in any room, on almost any surface, though he seemed to favor chairs over couches and floors (if carpeted) over tables.

When one of them happened to come upon Brahms sleeping like this, he or she would fetch the other and there they would stand side by side, watching him, as they sometimes watched their own children sleep. But this was not a child, for all they called him boy. This was their young deity, and his sleep protected them as much as they protected him and it, standing over him, able to stare into his features and limn his figure and breathe with the breath they saw migrate through his chest and move the strands of golden hair upon his shoulders like fingers on a piano.

Robert, in particular, tried to learn from Brahms to sleep so simply. He stood and matched him breath for breath and even closed his eyes upon the only thing he now could look upon with unambiguous joy. Sleep had always been his enemy. But when he saw it like this, embracing, and embraced by, a young man whose indisputable genius appeared disconnected entirely from disquietude, it seemed a whole new science, the invention of contentment. He had been insomniac, he guessed, his whole life. It was one thing not to sleep — and when he was young, he had prided himself on spending night after night awake, all fired up and in flames, seething in sweet and fabulous sounds all night, free, light, and blessed as he swam in the pure ether of dangerous emotions while writing music, smoking, drinking, until finally, one morning, the sun would so hurt his vision that he would clamp his lids against it and feel the alcohol paint his brain to rest. But it was another to lie awake and hear what Dr. Helbig called auracular delusions and Robert called his inner concerts.

Dr. Helbig proclaimed hearing the most animate of the senses once night had come, the last to shut down and the first to awaken. It was also, he said, the sense most closely related to the emotions and linked with the forces affecting discretion, aggression, revenge, and the appreciation of music. Imagine — a doctor so percipient that he is able to find a connection between hearing and music!

To draw anxiety from Robert's brain, Dr. Helbig attempted what he called transcranial magnetic stimulation by putting a magnet to Robert's head and moving it gently across his scalp and face and then, in apparent frustration, with enough force against the back of his neck to suggest to his patient the shoeing of a horse.

"You handle that thing like Lavater trying to galvanize the genitals."

"Your brain is impervious to science," complained Dr. Helbig.

"Likewise, I'm sure," said Robert, who was immediately presented with evidence only that Dr. Helbig was impervious to humor.

Robert nonetheless allowed Dr. Helbig to proceed to hypnotize him, which he did by swinging a large key before his eyes, with the result that the fear of keys Robert had confessed years before to Dr. Reuter was reinforced and augmented — the house of death was now on both sides of the door.

Dr. Helbig told him he was working too hard on his music for *Faust,* in which, fittingly enough then, as now, who should arise during the midnight scene but the figure of Anxiety, blinding Faust for his part in the deaths of Philemon and Baucis, whose story, in Ovid, had moved Robert to tears from the early days of his marriage, when he realized he could not imagine life on Earth without his wife.

"Dr. Helbig said he had observed my symptoms of overwork in two professions. Mine and one other. Can you guess what the other was?"

"Prostitution," said Brahms with a wicked smile dancing through his eyes. So long as the children weren't in the room, he seemed eager, always, to allude to his teenage piano-playing days in Hamburg's harborside Kneipen, where the whores worked the sailors and used him as a kind of bait, kissing and fondling him one after the other until such time as she was hired.

"Close."

"Oh, Robert, it's not close at all." Clara knew this story well.

"Tell me!" Brahms retained a child's enthusiasm for information; their lives, to him, seemed a series of riddles, the answers to which were always diverting.

"Accountant."

"No!" The boy leapt to his feet. Whether it was amusement or outrage he could not contain was impossible to tell.

"Accountant," Robert repeated.

"And you let this idiot hypnotize you!" Johannes was practically dancing in place. "What did you see when he hypnotized you?"

"I saw what I see in my dreams. Horrible visions of people I love — distorted into ghosts that stretch from sky to Hell. And dreams themselves. I dream of dreaming. I observe myself both as the creator of and the participant in nightmares."

"And yet you long to sleep." Johannes did not resist the exaggerated effect that words forced on such affliction. He entered sympathetically into the experience without making the mistake of being seduced by it into either imitation or incense. He early on displayed the clemency and curiosity he brings to Endenich.

"Because when I don't, I hear my inner concerts. Hallucinations in sound. Not always beautiful. Sometimes, but not always."

"And so you work all night."

" 'The night cometh when no man can work' "—he quoted the book of John oracularly, before pausing to give his words their utmost bathetic effect—"that's why Clara bought me my *tepee.*"

"Oh, show him your tepee!"

On her second tour to Paris, she had once again had a fantasy that she might sit down with Gérard de Nerval. But she learned Nerval had traveled in reverse direction, from France to Germany, when the woman he loved had left him for a flutist, the news of which made Clara believe that *she* might capture him, until she was further informed that in Austria he had fallen in love with that treacherous Camilla Pleyel. And what did this have to do with a tepee? Johannes might wonder.

"It's such a delight to hear you talk that I'm impatient only that you continue."

"You remind me of myself when I used to try, and fail, to say such things to Agnes Carus."

"He brings her up," said Clara, "to chide me for my mention of Gérard de Nerval. Whom I have never met, let alone *kissed,* by the way."

"And yet adored." He wondered if Brahms was, for her, Nerval come to life, or come into her life—a dream of a youthful lover, whom she had never had. Those we never see remain immortal. Nerval himself was older than Robert and had served his term in the madhouse, out of which had come *Aurélia.* Gautier had described him as *"comme un oiseau,"* in direct reference, once again, to Plato's *Ion,* in which the divinely mad artist is a bird who pulses in the air, ever looking upward, careless of the world below. "*'Il s'en alla disant,'* " Robert quoted his wife's ideal lover: "*'Pourquoi suis-je venu?'* "

"Please," said Brahms.

"'He went away asking: Why did I come?' " he translated. "Is it not the most meaningful line of poetry every written?"

"Perhaps my Nerval did not mean it metaphysically," Clara commented wickedly.

"The tepee?" Brahms surrendered, though whether to inquisitiveness or discomfort was unclear.

She had learned in Paris that Nerval carried a tepee whenever there was the slightest chance he might not sleep at home, which was often indeed. Therefore, no matter that a bed or mattress might be offered him, whether in the aftermath of one of Petrus Borel's orgies or in Théophile Gautier's garret, he would unfold his tepee, set it up, crawl within, and, with the floor beneath him and a mere saucer of ceiling visible above, fall immediately asleep.

"May I try it?" was the first thing Brahms said after Robert had erected his tepee in the middle of the sitting room, where the three of them spent most of their time together when they were not making music.

He was on his knees and halfway through the flap when Robert said to him, "It's impossible to sleep in there," and to Clara, "Forgive me, dar-ling—it *was* the most thoughtful of gifts."

They heard no more from Johannes, who curled up in the shape of the tepee's base. They watched him sleep and collaborated in their love for him.

"He wants what I have," whispered Robert.

"And do you want what he has?"

"I want to be him."

"And he wants to be you."

The month after his arrival the two men's portraits were done by Jean-Joseph Laurens, a fastidious Frenchman who admired Robert's music but had never heard of Brahms and so would not sketch the two of them in a joint portrait. Robert had to persuade him to sketch Brahms at all.

"Sit by me," Robert said to Brahms.

"You confuse my eye," said Laurens.

"I should be so fortunate," said Robert.

He gave Brahms things to read so he would not be bored and saw in his mind a portrait like Filippino Lippi's drawing of St. Sebastian and his book-ish friend.

But what emerged from the silver stylus of Laurens's pen was a truth in contrasts: Johannes in profile, a dream of beauty, his hair like a woman's not in its length but in its careless skew, its embrace of that noble head and its ten-tative touch upon the cheek, to frame his face like a curtain framing a stage; himself dead on, stupefied almost, hair ill-fitting, face bloated, eyes insane.

Was there ever better evidence of Goethe's *draussen/aussen* lines? No part of us is completely inside or outside. The interior determines the exterior. The body is a map of the mind.

"Thank God I didn't let Dr. Helbig make a plaster cast of my head. Re-member, Clara, how he tried to trick me by saying that history would want to compare my skull with Haydn's and Mozart's and Beethoven's, when the entire purpose of the scheme was to subject this poor cephalon to some psychical scrutiny that might reveal the source of its inner tumult. Imagine having to live with a three-dimensional version of *that*." He pointed to the portrait. "Of *this*." He pointed to his head.

"I love to live with it," said Clara, bringing it to her bosom and only then telling him that Laurens had noticed, while drawing Robert's eyes, that his pupils had become enlarged.

"I was just trying to stay awake."

"I thought you could not sleep," said Brahms, at whom Robert looked up from his wife's breast as he looks up at the portrait beside his bed in

Endenich, Brahms's hair glowing in the moonlight, and waits to die to wait for Clara.

He had in the past been separated from her, when she was not touring, only by the revolution, so called, which fizzed into Germany, like so many other inebriate illusions, straight out of France. There, King Louis Philippe was deposed, the Second Republic declared, and Louis Napoleon elected president. Germany had seemed to have been freed from repression either by our marriage, Robert told Clara, or, because it occurred in the same year as their sacred union, by the death of Prussia's King Friedrich William the Third, who had fired the brothers Grimm, of all people, from the Göttingen University faculty (because they would not take a loyalty oath), banned smoking on all but the Charlottenburg highway in Berlin (on which thousands of shameful exiles then appeared at the lunch hour, in so great a cloud of smoke that the king's espions were unable to identify one from the next), and so cozied up to his friend Metternich in Vienna that Germans, as well as Austrians, came to believe that subversion lay in every thought and therefore every thought must remain either spoken or unspoken, the king could never remember which. So when his son, FW IV, assumed the throne, everyone believed it was the dawn of a new era. Or was it the Schumann/ Wieck marriage that brought such hope?

Friedrich William the Fourth did pardon the brothers Grimm, in the process of which he mixed that blessing by making them members of the Berlin Academy, the kind of appointment that for any artist signals an approbation virtually guaranteed to stifle audacity, not to mention the baneful weight with which it burdens one's résumé and the vainglorious gasbags it confers as one's drinking partners. He also tried to do away with the CIA (the Central Investigation Agency, not to be confused with the Federal Bureau of Investigation, its mirror in repression and yet its greatest enemy, spies being the very priests of earthly communion and therefore jealous of both the favors and the strictures of their common god). But the CIA told the king that if it did not exist, the state itself could not exist, for like a religion the state demanded the rooting out of secrets that would not be secrets if there were not someone in authority to name them so and to punish those who tried to hide what were otherwise thoughts unthought and therefore unindictable. The king, realizing that the CIA possessed the *arcanum arcanorum* itself (i.e., freedom is an illusion fostered by the state for the purpose of compassionate subjugation), countenanced its continued operation while pretending to the public that he had dissolved it, a rather delicious secret in itself and one whose revelation, no matter how discreetly whispered—or whose realization, no matter how profoundly masked beneath such quotidian concerns as weather or health or what's-for-supper—was punishable by death or such alternative to death as the state deemed homogeneous.

But the king was confused in his patriotism. He forced the resignation of Professor Hoffmann von Fallersleben not because he didn't love to sing the professor's famous new song—"*Teutschland, Teutschland über Alles,*" in the king's antiquated pronunciation—but because Professor Hoffmann had waited so long to write the song, waited centuries. The king blamed his subject for having been born in the modern age. (Who isn't?) Hoffmann had not, like most people, merely outlived his usefulness—he had outlived, period! So had the king himself, and this drove him mad. He wanted to govern like kings of old, riding his horse (if anything would kill the monarchy, and thus bring an end to civilization, it was the railroad!) through his towns, bowed to by contented peasants, paid his Peter pence by honest landleasers, prayed for by devout and obedient clergy, given hot baths and moist damsels by his princes. It was a romantic vision that left no room for the kind of federal constitution put in writing. The written word was an insult to the ideal of ruling. No sheet of paper would come between God in Heaven and Germany. And if people wanted a parliament, then to hell with the railway between Berlin and Königsberg—pay for it yourselves!

And pay for your own goddamned potatoes. It was one thing for the Irish to begin to starve after the failure of two years' crops. That alone would have been enough to raise potato prices in Germany. But the blight showed no respect for the high seas or the great mountains or boundaries forged by war and language; it attacked the defenseless German potatoes that had heretofore grown with enviable profligacy in Saxony and Thuringia and Hesse. And who ate more potatoes than German peasants? German *pigs*! No more Schweinebraten! No more Ripple mit Linsen and no more salty Bierschinken, and not just because the pigs were perishing. Lentils weren't growing! The gentle female flower of the Humulus was being raped by Nature in the upper valley of the Main, whose phallic cone became the hops in beer. Beer shortage! No wonder there were riots. Starvation and sobriety formed a tragically potent coalition for social change. What did Germans need to keep them docile? Ham and scissors, boots and garters, wool and soap and yarn and beer. Most of all beer!

The king tried to blame the Jews, until it was explained to him that only they would not suffer from an absence of pork on the table, and if Jews could not suffer from their actions, they simply would not act.

But it was, the king declared, a contemptible Jewish clique responsible for the attempt to destroy the natural order between the governed and their spiritual superiors. The Jews wanted to throw all the estates together! The Communist Manifesto was riding into Germany like a sodomite on the backside of French liberal *poules mouillées*. No longer was communism itself vegetating in unheeded attics on wretched straw pallets, as that traitor Heine had observed six years before; though even then he had warned of a new apocalypse to be led by such beasts as would make St. John's seem like gentle doves and amoretti in comparison. Christianity could do nothing against the martial ardor of the Teutons. The cross had rotted away. A drama would be played out in Germany that would make the French Revolution seem like a school play.

How nice of Heine to warn his ex-countrymen! One might have pardoned him if he hadn't turned around and warned the French, "You have more to fear from a liberated Germany than from *all* the Holy Alliance with *all* its Croats and Cossacks put together." France fear Germany? As the old song went: The French invaded; the Germans paraded. Germans would never soil their bloodlines with the polluted offspring that came from foreign irruption and the gift women insisted upon making of themselves to their conquerors.

He hated everyone, Heine. That was the only redeeming thing about him. Nothing disgusted him more than the nobility, particularly the Prussian nobility, unless it was everybody else. What torture it must be to despise oligarchy and democracy both, to have faith in neither men nor Man, to realize that there could be no constitution adopted by no diet—no laws made to assure justice to all men and comfort to all mortals—that would prevent what he called the old frenzied madness from breaking out again and again and again across the landscape of time.

The king was mad. He reminded Robert of his father, who had worshipped the past by writing about it and thus lived his dreams of chivalry and heroism within the smoke (he would have said the mist, as Robert himself would say the veil) of creation; but how much more healthy that was than to try to live such dreams as if one's visions became corporeal through the very act of dreaming. In this, Robert and the king were alike. Music sometimes ate the paper on which he wrote it, and sometimes ate his mind.

The revolution and the Schumann family rode into Dresden at precisely the same moment.

The former came not merely from France but also by way of Vienna— whence Metternich himself was sent into exile, the words "*tout est fini*" spit from his teeth (little did he know how soon the counterrevolution in the form of Croatian mercenaries would evacuate him back into what Clara called the great universal whirlpool)—and from Hungary, where the rebels had recently been annihilated by the imperial armies of the Hapsburgs, who thought to restore order by mass executions, which didn't work, and then by proclaiming all Jews the enemy of the state (and at the same time charging them a special tax for the privilege of having been made pariahs), which did.

The Schumanns came merely from a lunch in the countryside. It was a fine day in early May, the air serene, the sun descending with languid restraint. Clara was brimming over with baby, not merely Ludwig only just learning to walk and laughing as he stood holding her knees and bounced before her off the bumpy floor of the bumpy carriage, but also with the baby bouncing within her, due in two months. Unlike many women, Clara was no more beautiful pregnant than not; but unlike any other woman he had ever seen, she was never not beautiful. He realized this might have less to do with how she looked at any given moment than with how he looked at her. She had never become part of him. Perhaps that was the secret. He always saw her as someone who was so much not himself that he was continually filled with the desire to contain and invade her both.

Across from them, Marie, seven, sat with Elise, five, and Julie, four, sisters all together with their little brother bouncing before them on the floor. They should have had another brother with him, though where would he have sat, Emil? He would, Robert reckoned, be three years, two months, twenty-three days old, were he not locked forever at the age at which he'd died, one year, four months, fourteen days, exactly one year, ten months, eleven days ago, ailing all the time and miserable, from the day of birth, whining and screaming and without a single pleasure in the world, not the breast, not music, nothing ever made him smile, not once in his entire existence, though when he died, finally and mercifully, a new child was alive within his mother. As soon as Robert saw he was a boy (he needed to *see* him; aural evidence was not to be trusted), he named him Ludwig. This was as much in commemoration of pain as of love; almost unendurably, a friend had died and now a son had died. This new being, then, this Ludwig, would, like art itself, embody nature, love, death, despair, and martyrdom. Yet Ludwig—look at him!—was born containing all the laughter in the world and seemed ambitious to give it back. He bounced now with a rhythm not the carriage's.

"Drums." Clara located the source of Ludwig's inspiration.

Robert listened. "They disturb my counting."

"Money?" She smiled, though this was a sore subject, in that it should be a subject at all.

"How old the children are."

"So long as you don't include me in your mathematics."

He closed his ears against the beating of the drums. She was twenty-nine years, seven months . . . never mind how many days, she didn't want him to calculate, and he had tried in his life with her to go against her wishes neither in the world nor in his head, the former having proved the more governable realm, because there are many times when one seems to have more control over distant kingdoms than over one's own mind. Besides, when you love a woman—desire her—when she is a girl, it is always as a girl that you see her, desire her. Like a Raphael Madonna, Clara was half-girl, half-woman. She needn't fight against her aging, which quite escaped his eyes and the passionate regard in which he held her.

"The drums are sounding the alarm." She pulled Ludwig into her lap.

"And bells," noted Julie, whose age more precisely than four he was unable to calculate because of the music in the air. She was the most beautiful of their children, so comely as to be almost frightening. Because he held her less than he did the others, he was always presenting his arms to her, as he did now. But she came into them less than did the others. Thus had they reached an accommodation regarding her beauty.

"And what is that?" asked Marie, who, as the oldest, did not like to hazard guesses about things of which she was unsure.

"Guns," said Robert, covering his ears and smiling at his children.

The next day he and Clara went for a walk, looking for news, as Lamartine had written of the ancient Athenians, only to discover that cannons blasted in reply. What else was news, mostly, but some pale reflection in words of gunpowder's report and the names of the recognizable dead?

They left the children with Henriette, their nanny, who was too sick to get out of bed. This was their excuse to the children—desperate to find out for themselves what all the shouting and shooting were about—for not taking them along: They must stay home to see after Henriette until the doctor arrived.

The farther they walked into the city, the more intense the strife. Robert felt like a seed in the center of a ravened fruit, an inconspicuous pip that could be neither swallowed nor bitten.

Yesterday's gunfire, they learned, had come primarily from the arsenal, which the rebels had tried to seize after having attempted to detain the fleeing king of Saxony by removing the poles from his carriage. This angered and humiliated Friedrich Augustus, who sent his troops to the arsenal with orders to defend it to the death. He then made plans to ride out of town in a less conspicuous carriage, which he did that night, to Königstein, and in the meantime he sent a message to the king of Prussia to send his troops to save him should he fail to save himself.

The rebels, unable to take the arsenal, were armed with such household instruments as knives, hammers, pitchforks, and scythes, the last in greatest number because the scythe afforded the most defensive distance from one's adversary and for psychological protection bestowed upon its proprietor a certain Grim Reaperishness. It was, however, neither long nor bulky enough to offer much protection against bullets, which kept entering and dropping the bodies of men who but a moment before were slicing futilely at the air before them with that stately, sweeping rhythm Robert remembered seeing in the summer fields around Zwickau once the earth had begun to recover from the insults delivered by the feet of Napoleon's vast army.

Because their weapons were proving useless against the superior power of the combined Saxon and Prussian armies, the rebels had erected barricades in the streets, quite in the French tradition and thus a triumph of delusion over design. Indeed, their design was said to be the work of Richard Wagner, who had been preaching for several years that the new Germany was like a bronze statue awaiting a single hammer blow in order to be freed from its mold, as well as from the fungus of Jewification. These ramparts were a collaboration of paving stones, rubble stones, wooden beams, iron rods, rags, broken glass, deranged chairs, vegetable matter, and such humans as were foolish enough to think such a pile of rubbish might have the force of the commandment *Thou Shalt Not Shoot Me* and so stood shakily upon these quavering cumulus displaying the black-red-gold imperial colors appropriated by the democrats in the common misconception that symbolism has meaning in a witless world.

Robert stopped to count fourteen corpses in the courtyard of the hospital. This was no easy task. They were being arranged by Prussian soldiers for public exhibition, and this display was clearly meant to discourage others from challenging authority. To mock these dead and perhaps to indicate the dispersion of the mind as written on the permutability of the body, one man's head was being put on another's neck, another's hands on another's wrists, some were given two left feet, while halves of men, severed latitudinally at the waist, never east/west, were joined in incongruous fusion, though all the resultant carcasses, Robert realized, were almost exactly the same height. Thus at least one point was made: You want democracy, we'll give you democracy!

Robert wanted democracy. He was a republican in theory. But how could he admire wholly and genuinely those to whom his music, when they troubled to hear it, which they never did, was as foreign and distasteful as their unsettled cadavers were to him, if of considerably less interest?

He felt able to stare at them for hours, and might have, had Clara not turned him away from the direction of the Rächnitzer Höhe, from which were rising huge clouds of smoke as evidence that artillery bombardment was coming from that side of Dresden. He had no desire to be blown to bits, especially today, when the expanding chaos of this war gathered inside him into a peculiarly indivisible asylum. His inner peace grew in direct proportion to disorder. He had to be pulled by her strong hands away from the sun-soaked smoke.

As it was, bodies fell even from the shrouded sky. Robert himself saw two of them in midflight, though by the time he turned Clara's attention to this incredible phenomenon—those two men who had been falling into the morning so visibly full of life, mouths in unabridged dilation, eyes biting at the very air—those two men were dead, the breathtaking drama of their departure noted only by himself and by their Prussian executioners leaning out the windows to watch, the way a child does a coin he sacrifices to the physics of his curiosity.

"Cl-*ara!*"

He could not get even her name out fast enough.

The air remained smoky from gunpowder and fires—the opera house was in flames, a mixed blessing—and the shucking of the pavement for the barricades. She offered him a handkerchief, apparently thinking such vapor caused his breathlessness.

He pointed. She saw. "They are throwing people out of windows."

He remembered imagining her at her window ten years before in Leipzig, pressed against the glass, transparent in her desire for him, surrendering to time and space, to the air between them, so he might catch her when she sailed to him. All he'd really seen was her white towel, signaling him, an emblem of surrender then, and now, as men in windows waved the same at soldiers who desired them, for what else was murder but a coupling?

In the Scheffelgasse, there were twenty-six corpses lined up. All students, they were told, unnecessarily, for these were clearly students, long-haired, ink-nailed, thin and mostly handsome, wearing vests and Mayfair scarves and pants too short and shirtsleeves too long and small conformist beards on those mature enough and on the upper lips of others hair so delicate he wished he were breeze to move it. They had all been hiding in one room, which he imagined must have been invigorating until the soldiers actually arrived, bodies warm from fear and warm from sweet propinquity, ideas swarming the way they do among the young, foolish ideas sometimes but ideas whole and unassailable, voices low against discovery but intrepid in the voice they gave to freedom, which now they had. They had not been mutilated like the bodies at the hospital. They lay in strict surrender to the geometry of death, rather like keys on a piano, but he longed to lie down with them as much as to put his hands upon them, to live within the four strong walls of death.

Clara was weeping. Dresden was on fire as it had not been on fire since it had been incinerated in 1681. It was difficult to imagine that a city might actually burn like this, particularly Dresden, which had been rebuilt to spin like a wheel away from such disaster. But who would have known that fire might come from the sky like this, a mockery of rain?

Three tall houses on the Zwingerstrasse burned together, martyrs on stakes, each racing the others toward the fugue of ash while spectators made wagers on which would vanish first. And flames spread horizontally as well, through the holes carved out of buildings so the rebels could move unobserved through such tunnels as now squealed with fire.

The Zwinger Palace itself, on the other hand, was relatively untouched, the Atlantes carved by Balthasar Permoser poised just above the fires, which gave the illusion of having eaten them off right through the genitals, when in fact they had been sculpted cockless, preening on their narrow columns.

He could not distinguish, he found, between the hundreds of prisoners being guarded in the Frauenkirche, where they displayed their great supply of black-red-gold ribbons on the retable shelves above the altar and from all three levels of gallery, and the even greater number of Prussian soldiers who were resting from their feral labors on the great communal straw mattress raked out over the whole of the Altmarkt. He had no feelings of right or wrong, only of a vague contentment at withdrawal into whatever part of him erected barriers against the fouling of his art.

He did not want to go home, and Clara was unable to convince him of danger to themselves. But when she said the children might be in peril, he insisted they hurry back to them, only to discover that the primary threat came from within the house. Carl Helbig, chief among his Dresden doctors, was in attendance upon Henriette, who, he said, was suffering from smallpox.

Disease had no meaning for children. If it had, Marie and Elise, at least, might have taken greater heed of the illness and then the loss of their little brother Emil. It was the war that enthralled them, the sounds of guns and drums and bells and the occasional shudder through the house and the peculiar interruption of household habits, their parents out together in the middle of the day, the absence of music, the vacuum-like pressure of history producing a strange sort of echoing silence in the house until their father filled them in on his grand adventures in the street.

"It is not a fairy tale," said Clara, as much to him as to them.

It remained just that until the next day, when there was a terrific pounding on the front door. It was for Robert quite an interruption, because he was at the piano, having returned to the composition of music for children to play, easy pieces for the fingers that he felt expressed some complexity of mind even he could not fathom. He was not unaware of the turmoil outside the house—how could he be, with tocsins poisoning the air and cannons engulfing the light!—but felt utterly at peace within the music. In the end, when armies finally disengaged, as they always did, what was left, aside from death (which was the very definition of vacuity and thus was indecipherable), but art? It was the only survivor, finally, in the crush of human discord.

"Someone go to the door!" he said as the pounding continued, which is what he always said when there was a noisy interruption in the world outside his room. He knew he was never heard in such disagreeable edict. He would not offer it otherwise.

Finally, he rose and opened his own door and walked into the hallway, from which he could see Clara at the window, peering out from behind the drape.

"Who . . . ?" he began, only to have her wave violently at him, to urge him back.

He retreated into his music room but left the door sufficiently ajar so he could see her. When she opened the front door, a man's fist came toward her. Her own hand went up, to protect herself, he thought, until he saw she merely meant to catch the man's hand, to keep it from crashing once again into the door. So his fist lay for a moment in her palm, held above her head. What pain the man must feel, to have his fingers crushed in such a hand as hers, that humbled pianos, muscular with music.

There were five men in all, with the black-red-gold hanging from their sleeves and weapons.

"Where is your husband?"

She said nothing. The man stared down.

"Whose baby?"

"My husband's."

"We'll have him back to you in time for *that*." He touched her stomach.

"Back from where?"

"The militia. We're fighting for our freedom."

"There can be no freedom when men are required to fight."

"There can be no freedom when men do not fight."

"Then there can be no freedom."

"Did you hear that, men?" he said to the others. "We're fighting for nothing."

They were puzzled. The capacity for irony that makes a man a leader confounds his followers when it's put to use.

"Search the house," he ordered, perhaps to give them something to do.

She stood her ground. "He isn't here."

"Where is he?"

"Not here."

"When will he be here?"

"That will be known only when he arrives."

"When do you expect him?"

"I never expect him."

To do what? thought Robert.

"We shall return," said the man.

"I shall expect you," said Clara.

Robert was surprised, the moment the door closed on his recruiters, to see Clara rush to him.

He came out to meet her. "That was brilliant!"

"We must leave immediately." She held tight to him, as if, against her words, to keep him there.

"Did you not once tell me that you wished to see me save you from the barbarians?"

"It's the barbarians who ask you to join them."

"Who, then, are the kings' soldiers?"

"Barbarians as well."

"And *I*?"

"You're not here. As I said."

She took charge completely of their evacuation. Out the back door and into the garden, taking Marie only, and taking her only because she happened to be close by when they fled.

"The children." Robert had no idea where she was taking him. It was like being led somewhere by your mother, and you cannot bear to be separated from your brother, your dear sister.

"It's you the rebels want." She opened the garden gate, pushed him well behind her so he would not be visible, and slowly leaned forward until her eyes could see the way was clear.

He laughed. "Your head may be invisible, but your stomach is halfway to Maxen."

"Let's hope it makes it all the way."

They had gotten almost to the Bohemian Railway Station when they were stopped by men with scythes.

"Are you armed?"

They were searched despite her answer.

"Why are *you* not armed?" he was asked.

He had perfectly good reasons. In Leipzig, soon after they were married, he was declared, by the Conscription Commission, unfit for military service, for reasons chronicled in written certification that he sometimes feared would outlive his music: Not only was he nearsighted in the extreme and susceptible to vertigo when at an altitude sometimes no greater than his own height, but he had succeeded, through an act of self-mutilation, in wholly paralyzing one finger of his right hand and partially paralyzing another. In other words, he could not see to aim a rifle; he would not be able to squeeze the trigger even at an inappropriate target; and he might very well start spinning dizzily in the midst of firing, should he be able to fire, and as likely cut down friend as foe.

"I cannot play the piano with a gun," he answered.

"How about with one of these?" Someone swept toward his feet with a scythe.

"Listen," he said. "Swing it again. You can hear it in the air. If you all swing your scythes together, at different speeds and through different thicknesses of this smoke, you'll make music."

Soldiers—even an untrained militia—are made uncomfortable by creativity, let alone what might be interpreted as a lunatic form of it. It was true of these men, who suddenly seemed so eager to have Robert neither on their own side nor their enemy's that they formed a virtual path into the Bohemian Station in order to force this man and his female party out of Dresden.

Thus, as if Schiller had written that it were only by railway that man might make his way to freedom, were they able to take the train to the suburb of Mügeln, whence they walked beneath the afternoon spring sun to Dophna, where they caught another train to Maxen, beautiful Maxen on the Elbe. The insane asylum still dominated its landscape but no longer affected him except as architecture, perhaps because the world had turned mad (what with live bodies flying out of windows and dying from coition with the earth). And accompanying the general madness came a smoothing of what distinction there had been between the sane and what in such times could no longer be called their opposite. Now, he found, he could look at Sonnenstein without threat to the very sanity whose loss might have sent him there.

Indeed, he sat by the window in their room in the large estate of their friend Major Serres and stared until dark at the old castle, quite content, calm, in fact, until they were called for supper and celebrated by the gathered gentry as heroes who had gallantly escaped from the revolutionary canaille, whom these people detested as only the rich can detest others for a desire to be like themselves. Clara became more and more agitated at having to listen to such aristocratic froth but held her tongue for fear of offending their host. Robert, who was known for saying almost nothing out of what were assumed to be reasons peculiar to the suffering artist, and probably were, now found that the usual inner agitation had been disengaged from silence and that the calmness he'd experienced staring at the madhouse was transferred precisely into his staring at these idiots gathered around him. And they left off praising his heroics in supposedly having led his wife and daughter to safety precisely when they realized he was staring at them, staring in what must have been a most intense and eccentric way, for they shrank collectively from his gaze and took to coughing and chattering in such discordance that he could not understand a word they said and therefore experienced for the first time profound gratitude at his own inaptness.

When the sound of cannonading, which he discovered was rendered with great clarity by the night air's fornicate acoustics, joined the prattling of Major Serres's patrician refugees, it all became to him a kind of symphony of negligence, incongruent sounds trammeled into bombast.

But to Clara these guns and echoing of guns and abrupt, scuddering scintillations of firelight through the vaulted night clouds drew her into grim reality, her city lit up and blown up with three-quarters of her children (he did not put into the equation the one precisely 77 percent unborn) left behind, trapped within poor fiery Dresden.

She rose from her chair even as the schnapps was being poured. "Please excuse us," she said to Major Serres. "We must return briefly to the city to fetch our children."

"'Fetch!'" said an old woman. "It is dogs one fetches. Children are summoned."

Major Serres shrugged off his guest's discourtesy with the convivial indifference of the perfect host and said to Clara, "Are you out of your mind! It's the middle of the night."

It was, indeed, precisely the middle of the night by the time she was ready to leave, three A.M., Marie asleep in a little room of her own next to theirs, Robert awake at this hour not from his customary insomnia but because he had been granted, he felt, a singular vision of himself, watching himself sit and watch his wife not sit. He made no move to stop her, join her, or replace her on her perilous journey. He knew she would refuse his help because of the same danger that had caused them to flee in the first place: that he be forced into service, to face Prussian guns with a scythe placed in his hands and off he would go from her forever, cutting the air into neat pieces until such time as he could taste his own blood. He would, of course, love to die for a cause, provided the death last no longer than the cause remain just.

But he did not offer his help. He was like a man whose wife cooks (not that he himself was a man whose wife did cook, or who should have cooked when she did, particularly fish) and who watches her day after day, meal after meal, cooking. She keeps him alive with her cooking, and he could no more step across the kitchen to take her place at the stove than he could step across the Rhine. Or he watches her hammer a nail into the wall, to hang a picture. Or empty a chamber pot. Or feed a child. Or climb a tree to fetch, if that is the right word to use for the fetching of a cat, a cat. Or undress herself while he sits watching. Or hide him from barbarians. Or go off into Europe to play the piano. Or play the piano.

He was, like Hölderlin, "poor in deeds and rich in thought." Such passivity canceled obligation. Such consideration of the self canceled the self. He was removed from life. He was as godly in his powers of observation as in his inability to do anything but observe.

He wanted her desperately but could not have her. There was about her an air of absence, provided perhaps by himself, or at least by his desire, which he knew would increase once she had departed for Dresden with the married daughter of Major Serres's steward, who had agreed to accompany her on that part of the journey safe to go by carriage. He remembered singing in this same house with Anna Laidlaw, "O lovers' eyes are sharp to see," realizing only now that what they see best is the lover who's not there.

"Good-bye," she said, kissing him. "Sleep if you can. Don't worry about me. I'll return with the children and we shall have a picnic by the river."

"Enjoy," he said, referring not to the kiss he gave her in return but to their absence from each other. He longed for her but not to go with her. He longed for her to be gone.

In going, Clara ceased to exist. How else could he have borne her absence?

The world itself did not exist. He remained awake the entire time, sitting where he sat when she had left, except when he was forced to get up to relieve himself and took the occasion to look in upon Marie, which he did with Clara's eyes. It was she who customarily visited the children when they slept, for though he slept so little and so poorly and thus need never awaken for the purpose of replacing blankets or pouring water for a dry-mouthed daughter—he was, he could have sworn, *always* awake through *every* night!—he feared such tribulation was contagious, particularly in the cool and thin black air, which always seemed to transport torments with imperceivable ease. Imagine, to touch a child's forehead in the night, to breathe a kiss upon her cheek, and from that night forth she would never sleep the night through.

Marie, in sleep, seemed like himself, lost to the world.

He went back to his seat by the window and wrote songs in his head to Goethe's words and wondered if one makes art to shut out the world or one shuts out the world to make art. A true musician must place himself above human miseries; he must draw his courage from within himself alone.

What anxiety he finally felt was only for his wife, whom he could not separate from her children but whom he separated entirely from the rest of humanity. He could still hear the shelling and see its flashes infuse the clouds and felt as if war were some astronomical thing.

She returned shortly before noon. He was sitting where he'd sat, the only difference being that Marie had awakened and brought him dried figs her mother had left by her bed and sat beside him, a quiet guardian of his isolation. When Clara entered, framed by Elise and Julie, Ludwig in her arms as he must have been for the entire trip back, Robert could move neither his body nor his mind toward her. It was as if he had partaken of death, not on the battlefields she had crossed but because he himself had become one of those products of the reflective faculty he'd read of in Coleridge, who had himself found through alcohol and opium what Robert could glean from the mere passing breath of life itself.

Clara was dirty and tired and exhilarated. She sent the children into the care of one of Major Serres's servants and, standing before Robert as she took off her dusty clothes and unpinned her gunpowdered hair, delivered him aloud an exuberant letter of the sort he had received from her on paper when she was young and they were separated and his longing for her in her absence had been less enigmatic.

"Oh, Robert, it was such a great adventure! We went by carriage to Strehla. The driver dared not take the road. Or perhaps he could not see it. Or was he drunk? He went across fields. He darted among trees. I was frightened not for myself but for the baby. We were bouncing so much my head was hitting the ceiling of the carriage. But poor Frau von Berg's head was hitting it many more times than mine. Of course, she was not weighed down by child. Under normal conditions, to judge from what I could see of her figure, I should have been the one more thrown about. She is what is called a sturdy woman. Physically. Temperamentally, she is, to put it delicately, fragile. She was so frightened by our drive to Strehla and by the unending thunder of the cannons and their explosions of light and the glow of fire rising toward us from Dresden that when the driver would go no farther, neither would she. It was just as well. I preferred to go alone. I had found myself thinking more about her than about you. *Good riddance,* I said to myself—in reference to her, of course—and set out across the field toward the Reitbahngasse. I had walked perhaps four kilometers. And there, coming out of the mist of dawn and that curious smoke from the gunning…I say curious, because it is not like the smoke from the burning buildings, which is bitter and ugly, but it is almost sweet, and it is as fragile as Frau von Berg's mind, rising and falling in the wind like a veil. Or ghosts. And coming out of it, as I was saying, were ghosts! I thought they were ghosts. They were spread across the field, two thick, in a long line of perhaps twenty creatures that as soon as I saw it, and they saw me, began to close in upon itself. And upon me. They were spectral and ragged and after the events of the past days I was hoping they were ghosts, not men. But then I saw they were carrying those damned scythes. Men! What a disappointment. 'Are you going to kill me?' I asked. 'What a stupid question,' one of them answered. 'What a stupid answer,' I said. Instantly, they parted and let me through. I had thought I was going to die. That's why I spoke so provokingly. Instead, my impudent tongue saved my life. Not a good lesson to teach a woman! From there I walked as in a dream to our house. I cannot tell you my joy at seeing it still standing. At finding the children asleep in their beds. It was like finding you here now right where I left you. As if there are two worlds and I am able to protect you and the children from the unendurable one. Waking them up was no easier than ever. They act like sleepy immortals. Poor Henriette was no help. What a time to get smallpox! So I dressed them myself and then we had a merry walk home to you! My safe and cherished husband."

Her hair was at her shoulders. It left deft scrapings of gray ash on her skin. Her belly and her breasts strained against her underclothes. He so much wanted to rise to take her in his arms, to the extent he could encompass her without the usual tittering brought on by the scope of advanced pregnancy, and to smell the smoke in her hair and take it on his skin so he might also reek of war and sacrifice. But he could only sit and watch his wife, who, undressing, told him with conspiratorial fealty that Wagner had given imperious speeches on the steps of town hall, had raised the black-red-gold from the very apices of his barricades, and had been forced to flee as a leader of the visibly failing revolution.

"The true revolutionary in this world is whoever does nothing to anyone."

"Then that cannot be you," she answered, "for look what you do to me."

He looked, instead, at Sonnenstein and was reminded of it when, barely a year later—the revolution crushed even to the extent that regulations had been issued by Berlin's new chief of police regarding the height to which women might lift their skirts in order to avoid dragging them in puddles— he was offered Ferdinand Hiller's job as Düsseldorf's music director and saw on a map of the city that it held a madhouse in its midst. There were three convents as well, and these, in conjunction with the madhouse, reminded him in turn of his youth in Heidelberg, when he would go from loving one boy to loving another and hang between them like a sinner between the redemption of the church and the indulgence of the asylum.

This had been Mendelssohn's job the year before he came to Leipzig. Mendelssohn was dead. Now Chopin was dead, reason enough to flee wherever one was, for death had a way of spooling through a calendar, gathering up lives in order. (Except when it came to one's children.) Mendelssohn had been the oldest by a year—gone. Chopin older by three months—gone. He would be next. Then Hiller, then Liszt, then Wagner, though Wagner was the sort who might escape his turn to die because for all his exhortations on behalf of the rights of the common man, he behaved as if there were never more than one man in the room.

Clara hated Dresden as much as he did. Its musicians "dear colleagued" with a buggering unctuousness but in private husked each other's privates. So did they excise Robert from the list of candidates to succeed Wagner, in exile with Liszt in Switzerland, as Kapellmeister. It was a position he had needed, she convinced him, not merely for the money and prestige but to get him out of the house. In the aftermath of the revolution, as Europe crawled back toward an apparently irresistible despotism and music poured from Robert as it had not since the year of songs in the year that surrounded their wedding, Robert seemed to have left the world in order to inhabit the inside of his own head. He was working himself, as he had before, into a frenzy of accomplishment and melancholy. Still, as easy as it was for him to write a piano concerto, a cello concerto, an opera to Byron's *Manfred,* so did he always seem to slip into grief, with no warning but for the bleeding of music. The more he wrote, and the better he wrote it, the more deeply he suffered for it. As patiently as she tended him when he was ill, he could never make her understand not so much why this happened as how it felt. It was nothing more, or less, than a rehearsal for dying.

He cared less that he had been refused Wagner's job than he did being denied a church in Dresden, any church, in which to hold a memorial service for Chopin. In Paris, there was a huge funeral at the Madeleine, where Mozart's Requiem was sung, over the objections of the archbishop of Paris, who felt that the kind of singing demanded by the piece would require jongleurs of such accomplishment that their vanity would permeate the church itself and deliver unto Christianity the contamination customarily produced by conspicuous virtuosity. The Requiem hadn't been performed in Paris since the return of Napoleon's ashes to Les Invalides, but it was on that day, for Chopin. Luigi Lablache and Pauline Viardot were soloists and in the audience sat Turgenev, who found he desired Pauline even more because of the stark wretched beauty of the composition, which brought death to life and like all great religious music positively inspirited the flesh. Chopin's own dead flesh—verified as such, because a fear of being buried alive had caused him to request that his body be cut open after the pronouncement of death—was taken in a grand procession, said to match that given Mendelssohn, though not nearly as geographically prolonged Robert was gratified to realize, to the Père Lachaise Cemetery in what was said to be the unfashionable east of Paris (how should he know? Clara had always gone to Paris without him, perhaps to quarantine the innocence of her doomed and distant love for the unglimpsed, untouched, eternally untroubling Gérard de Nerval, whose madness had come to make Robert's own seem the mere pout of a passing fish). There it was buried in the Paris earth along with a jar of soil from Poland Chopin had brought with him nineteen years before. In exchange, Poland got his heart: silent, still, empty. It was delivered by train.

Robert did not grieve for Chopin as he had for Schubert. He considered this a measure of his maturity, not to lie crying in bed all night between two friends but to lie awake all night beside his sleeping wife, performing every insomniac's fundamental ritual, which is to keep an eye open for death. And because he felt through Chopin's departure one step closer to his own according to his calculus of chronological eradication, whichever eye remained closed was employed in picturing his own funeral. Try as he might, he was unable to see his body transported by train across Germany to Zwickau or Bonn or Vienna, or carried in a hearse through the streets of this city or that, it didn't matter which because he had never found a city he

loved. All he could see was himself and his wife—not even his children!—
the world empty of mourners but for her, into whom he disappeared so
there was nothing left of him. Only then did he fall asleep.

He might as well have dreamt of what Dresden would do for him if they
wouldn't even permit a church-begirded memorial service for Chopin, who
had done the city the retrospective honor of coming to it even before the
age of twenty and had played here at least three years before he had played
in Paris. *This* was Chopin's Germany city, and it would not even pray for his
soul. What would it do for the soul of Robert Schumann?

What would Düsseldorf do?

He wrote a song:

> Oh, what do they do in Düsseldorf?
> In Düsseldorf what do they do?
> They apportion a ration
> Of Bach's St. John's Passion
> In Düsseldorf that's what they do.
> And because they were French
> Until eighteen fifteen
> They have sex all the time
> With no thought of hygiene,
> While the sound of the choir
> Can keep to no beat
> As it bleats to the heavens like
> Hartebeests in heat.
> They drink upon rising,
> And then they drink more;
> As Mendelssohn said,
> Half the town's drunk by four.
> But the worst thing 'bout Düsseldorf—
> I swear this is true—
> Is no one in Düsseldorf
> Knows what Düsseldorf do.

"'Düsseldorf do?'" As usual, he could not tell how much criticism
dwelled within the charm of her laughter.

"Sometimes one has to bend the syntax," he replied, which was his excuse as well when she questioned something in his music.

But it was he who began to question hers. He had her replaced in a performance of his piano quintet because a woman couldn't understand the complexity of the piano part (and did not all his chamber work give emphasis to

the piano?) and then demanded her withdrawal as accompanist of the Düsseldorf chorus for almost the same reason: A woman was too weak for such banging as was required, especially with this chorus, which made more noise shuffling its feet than singing, and better noise it was too.

"Why do you turn against me?" she asked.

"It's myself I turn against." He was not so crazy that he failed to understand *this*: He did not merely take out his frustrations upon her, which was common enough behavior even for men whose marriages were matters more of contiguity than of enchantment; he deliberately did what he knew would hurt her most, because he never suffered so much as when she suffered. That he should have inflicted the pain caused him all the more anguish.

Still, he saw she tried to help him. She took to the piano during rehearsals of his orchestra and marked time with her head far more accurately than did he with his intractable baton from the conductor's desk. So taken was he with that bobbing movement of her head, mouth open, eyes half-closed, that he looked at her instead of at the score and conducted accordingly, which further distorted his intentions and thus the tempo of whatever music they were jointly, if surreptitiously, conducting together.

But she was not there—not on the stage—when he scandalized all of musical Düsseldorf in conducting Hauptmann's mass at the Maximilian-kirche.

The entire piece went exceedingly well. He conducted brilliantly—even he knew this, and such knowledge was difficult to come by for any conductor, who is as engulfed by the music flying from his hands as a painter is by the colors he no sooner gives off than they assail his eyes and blind him to their worth and thus to his own.

The singers had sung more competently than he might have expected, given their disgraceful behavior during rehearsals, when they would sit down while singing and bang their feet to the music in protest against what they considered his indolent tempos, wholly unappreciative of his informing them that the more slowly God was celebrated, the more likely He was to have time in His busy schedule to hear the music!

And the musicians made their entrances when they ought to have, again contradicting such rehearsals as when he was forced to rebuke the trombone player for performing his solo so softly, only to be informed that the trombone player had missed his cue entirely and played not a single note. "So what was it I heard?" "Silence," came the answer, which brought him great pleasure.

As for himself, he did not once either drop or throw his baton, which had become for him such a commonplace in rehearsals that he had taken to tying it to his wrist with a string, no easy task and performed solo because when he asked Clara to tie it for him, she turned away with tears in her eyes.

Indeed, he believed it was precisely because his performance of Moritz Hauptmann's mass at the Maximiliankirche was as close to perfection as might be achieved with such singers and musicians that he himself missed his own cue — not to conduct but to stop conducting.

Apparently, for all the singers and for all the musicians and for all the members of the audience — for everyone but himself — the mass came to the end that Herr Hauptmann had intended for it. But he went right on conducting.

It had also come to an end for the priest, who, as was his habit, launched immediately into his sermon, which he found himself delivering from his podium while the conductor, still on *his* podium, was moving his arms through the air, hands expressive, baton secure and perfectly in tempo to a music so glorious it shared with silence great exclusivity.

It was interesting to him that what finally obscured the music only he could hear was a combination of censure and laughter. He was cursed by some and enjoyed by others.

Such was the life of the artist, he concluded, in the instant before he realized just what it was he was doing that caused this discordancy.

He stopped his arms in mid-flight. He let his eyes sweep over the chorus and orchestra both, most of whom were staring at him with the kind of disdain he had heretofore felt was reserved to himself against them, for their incompetence. He was a tree stripped bare by winter, two limbs only held aloft against the empty sky, and his musicians were his birds, frozen on the ground.

Clara was somewhere behind him in the church He listened for her laughter, or for some grievous intake of breath in her sympathy with his plight. How to get out of this one, conducting music he alone could hear, while off to his right a priest was intoning with the arrogance of a first violin?

He dropped his baton, purposely this time, and when she did not catch it before it hit the floor, he knew she could save him no longer.

"It was my Beethoven moment," he told Brahms, who had not been in the church, making light of it, "and you," he said to Clara, "were my Caroline Ungher," though she had failed to be. He was affronted when he learned the executive committee of the Düsseldorf Music Society had told Clara that henceforth he would be allowed to conduct his own compositions only, presumably on the theory that he could bring upon them no greater ruin with his conducting than he had in his writing and that should he once again go on conducting after a piece had ended, he might be said this time to be composing, on the spot, a coda that only he, in the privacy of his addled brain, could hear.

"And listen to this, dear one," he wrote to Brahms upon their first separation when he accompanied Clara on a tour of Holland. "A prince in Friedrich's Hohenzollern circle came up to me to praise Clara after one of her performances and said, 'Your wife is a fine musician. Are you musical too?' Am I musical too! Why was I not offended? It was as if that ignorant, uninformed, fatuous clod of aristocratic fluff could see into my soul. How do we know if we're musical? How do we know if we're artists? How do we know if what we hear in our heads and put down on paper is music? All one can express at any moment is himself. What if the self is shattered? What if the self has ceased to exist, long before life has ended? What if I have merely suffered as an artist but, in the end, produced nothing that might be called art? What if all that one's produced amounts to no more than what Hölderlin called 'summer's empty fields'? Not that I raised these questions with my royal interrogator. Oh, no. To him I said, 'Yes, I am musical too.' And he politely replied, 'What instrument do you play?' I held up to him my poor wrecked right hand. 'I play my wife,' I said. Needless to say, that rid me of him long before any talk of art might have produced so desired a result. Am I musical? At least enough to judge that you are, Johannes, my dear new friend."

It became interesting to him, before it became mysterious and then devastating, that he could hear things no one else could hear. This might, after all, define the composer of music, as a unique ability to see things might define the painter or sculptor and the ability to understand (if rarely to explain) things the philosopher and the ability to express things in words the writer.

The first time he tried table-turning, he put the table to the simplest test by asking it to reproduce the rhythm of perhaps the most familiar two bars in all of music: those that opened Beethoven's C-Minor Symphony. After a delay that caused him to wonder if perhaps this table was not musical even in the most elementary sense (in which case, he would allow it the chance at least to deliver messages from those members of his family who were dead, which should give it more than enough to do in living out its useful, four-legged life), the table began to rock and even more clearly than necessary (it was so slow!) beat out, following a retrospectively observable eighth-note rest, the three famous quavers followed by the semibreve.

"Bravo!" he praised the table, as he had learned to do with his children even when they disappointed him, before he added as demand in the form of constructive criticism, "But the tempo really ought to be faster, dear table."

The table did not hesitate this time to reproduce the tempo precisely as Beethoven had intended it; indeed, it slammed out the beats with an almost aggressive display of indignation, much like Marie, who, on the verge of turning twelve, no more took to being corrected than did this table.

No wonder he came to love it almost like a child of his own. It could read his mind, at least to the extent of always knowing what number he was thinking and pounding it out for him (provided it was between one and three), and in time let him talk to the dead, though because it possessed no more talent than an ability to rock and in so doing to produce banging upon the floor, he was limited in his questions to eliciting "yes" (one beat) and "no" (two beats) and "perhaps" (three beats) answers and quickly grew tired of conversations, even with the dead, that lacked the subtlety of anything more than grunts and depended upon him, who had withdrawn as deeply as he was able to dibble into himself, to do virtually all the talking.

"I want to do something for the table," he said, shortly before its first Christmas with them as a tipping-table, and its last, he realizes, as well as his own last Christmas with his family. He has become just such a table himself here in Endenich, beating out answers from beyond the grave, one foot tapping against his coffin, from the inside. As he waits for his wife.

Clara said without hesitating, "How about sending it on a vacation to Russia?" where they had almost ten years earlier nearly frozen to death and Robert had experienced in the droning of the monks of the Simonov Monastery a sound even more nerve-wracking than that of the Düsseldorf choir.

Though she had sat with him and heard the table rock, he noticed she was always peering suspiciously at its nether parts. Skepticism and jealousy had turned her humor bitter.

"Tables know everything," he said. "Unlike your Nerval," whose most bitter lines he quoted at her: "*'Il voulait tout savoir mais il n'a rien connu.'*

"As for my table," he added abruptly so as not to distress her beyond literature's hem, "I thought I might buy it a new dress," and he did, for Christmas, a beautiful white tablecloth, while Clara gave him something considerably darker: a portrait of herself by Karl Sohn. True, her face was the face of his child-love, that of a mischievous Madonna, tilted in humble provocation, her small lips almost tastily pulpal, her eyelids heavy but modestly free of blue shadow, her eyes themselves downcast but because of the tilt of her head suggesting not the humility of a penitent but the curiosity of a sensualist (and the gaze of a Düsseldorfer Düsenputzer checker). Yet her hair, shining so clean he could smell it, trussed her head with a confining rigor that suggested imprisonment. And her dress, voluminous and airy because she was pregnant again as if in fecund celebration of the saving grace of the arrival of Johannes, was black. It was the gift of this painting that caused him to consider that, like himself, all she wore now was black. In daylight, anyway. At night she wore what she wore until he took it off or pushed it up. Perhaps that was black too. If it was, it always yielded to the glow her skin gave back to candlelight. Otherwise, she was in mourning.

It was the arrival of Johannes, too, that freed him both to die and to go mad, in that order, as he liked to say, so as to give evidence of the latter and to forfeit the former. With an energy and excitement he remembered from his own youth, he wrote about Brahms for his old magazine and compared him to Athena springing fully rampant from the head of Zeus and called him as well the true Apostle of the new age and new force in music, thus granting a Greek *and* Roman benediction and replacing, finally, that other Johannes, Ludwig, his John the Baptist. Ludwig Schunke may have been the one they'd been waiting for, but Johannes Brahms even outwardly bore the signs of divinity, proclaiming with his delicate, tensile beauty, "This is the chosen one."

"He could capsize the world in a few days," he wrote of his new angel, and thus he did.

He recorded for all the world to read that he and Clara, standing together before Brahms at the piano, were swept into what he called "circles of ever deeper enchantment."

What a thing it was for them to fall in love with a musician. The body melts into the music; the music saturates the flesh. You cannot separate the beauty of the art from the beauty of the man. Was it any wonder those who made music were in such secular demand? They play, and you are ravaged.

He thought, or at least wished for his whole life, that it would be love that drove him mad. But it was music.

He and Clara went to Hanover, where for almost two weeks he heard more of his own music played than he ever had before. Joseph Joachim was concertmaster there, and he had summoned them, and he had also summoned Brahms, and where Brahms went, they wanted to go. The court orchestra played his Symphony in D Minor, which he had recently revised and had thus moved into the fourth and last position among his symphonies. Joachim gorged on the violin music, playing the Fantasie in public and the three sonatas for invited private audiences, and the new concerto in rehearsal only, thank goodness, for it gave Joachim a great deal of trouble, which allowed Robert the public pleasure of apology to his new young benefactor and a strange sort of private glee over this evidence of the depth of his quarry, what Joachim called a "troubling profundity" so that Robert was able to quip to Clara, "Well, he's half right."

It was with these sounds of his own music, played so joyfully and generously by his youthful inheritors of music's dissident comforts, still in his memory that, back in Düsseldorf, his inner concerts assumed such precedence as to drive all other music away. He could write nothing and hear nothing either in memory or in life itself but what began one night as a single note, repeated and repeated and repeated, in a kind of drone that attained another interval only when he had buried himself in Clara and screamed out his pleasure in the most irreconcilable release of sound, love and terror merged in body and brain. She would not let go of him that whole night, grasping him to her and weeping, so that her tears soaked the Manna on her eyelids, and for the first time he smelled that odor said to have been the cause of the killing of the men of Lemnos by their wives. Rather than repel him, this smell of earth and sex and what he took to be his own decay drove him into her again and finally to a silent release, not that he did not want to call out but that the music in his head had changed, he heard a chord or two and stayed up all night long to listen.

The sounds continued into daylight, when they stopped for two hours during which he found great relief in the sounds of his household — children, dishes, water, the rasping tenor of the fire — and in the utter silence within his head. Yet he longed for the music to return, with the kind of ache that reaches out seditiously for diminishing pain, whether from a wound in the flesh or from the departure of love.

When the music did return, at precisely ten in the morning, which he realized was the time he had most often begun to compose on those mornings when he had not stayed up all night at the piano, it was once again a single, droning, head-crushing, head-exploding note. It was this musical regression as well as the sound itself that caused him to scream out as if to drown it, though he realized as he screamed that he was screaming for help, like a child who is angry not so much at pain as at not having enough experience of the world to be able to understand the pain. He was screaming at life itself.

What he got for his effort was a visit from Dr. Richard Hasenclever, more a friend than doctor; that function was filled in Düsseldorf primarily by Dr. Adolf Böger. But Dr. Hasenclever was much more musical than Dr. Böger, so who better, Clara must have reasoned, than Dr. Hasenclever to interpret the medical meaning of notes sounding within her husband's head?

Robert was not entirely happy to see Dr. Hasenclever. True, he had recently written music to accompany Dr. Hasenclever's version of Ludwig Uhland's *Glück von Edenhall*. He had done this not so much to please Dr. Hasenclever but to pay homage to Uhland himself, about whom it had been written, as Robert wished someone would write of him:

> He says but half what others say
> And thus feels twice as much as they.

What bothered Robert was Dr. Hasenclever's lofty position in the Düsseldorf Music Society. How could he not have been complicit in Robert's dismissal?

Hasenclever was the kind of doctor who, rather than concentrate all his efforts on medical matters and thus nearly bore to death those he saved from it, involved himself so deeply in the arts that he was of little use to his patients except as an unrelenting chronicler of all the concerts, ballets, operas, recitals, dramas, and poetry readings he had attended. As such, he was of little apparent use to a screaming man. He was accustomed to music in the Schumann home, not this. This was terrible. This was the very antithesis of singing. This was as pure a perversion of music as could be imagined.

"Stop screaming!"

"He cannot," said Clara, who held Robert's hand while Dr. Hasenclever tilted his tall frame away from his patient, his own little perversion of the physician's salutary stance. "He screams when he hears the sound."

"What sound?"

"A single note."

"What note?"

What note indeed. Robert could remember when at least what he hallucinated could be named by its pitch. He had once driven his friend Hieronymus Truhn nearly mad by asking him over and over, "Can't you hear that A? Can't you hear that A?"

He was no longer able to sustain the illusion that anyone could share his torment.

Dr. Hasenclever seemed willing to wiggle out of a diagnosis because of his patient's inability to name the note that brought him such pain. And he certainly had nothing to prescribe to end the pain.

But as was often the case upon the termination of an appointment with one's doctor, the pain went away as soon as the doctor went away. He did not so much take it with him as obliterate it with indifference.

Out of that solitary note grew strange music more glorious, played by instruments sounding more exquisite, than any music ever heard before.

Voices, rising above distant background brasses, sang in magnificent harmonization Bach's "*Ein Feste Burg ist Unser Gott.*" Then there were symphonies played from beginning to end by entire orchestras that seemed squeezed into his brain and unlike the lazy Düsseldorf orchestra were indefatigable. Out of the last chord of one piece grew the beginning of the next, none of the music recognizable until nine nights after his first attack he heard angels sing to him and rose from their bed and wrote down the melody.

In the morning, he played it for Clara. "It was given to me by Schubert and Mendelssohn together," he said. "They came to me in the night. They had never met on this earth. But now they are together. 'Is there room for me where you are?' I asked them. 'There is so much room where we are that you would not be able to find us for all eternity.' An equivocal answer, true, but I noted that the 'would' was not a 'will' and so was given hope. And is it not wonderful that they should be joined together inside me? They have chosen me as the medium for their collaboration. I shall put their names together on this piece."

"But that is *your* music, my darling," she said.

"Only that it comes *out* of me. It was put *in* me by them."

"Listen." She played the theme, without looking at what he'd written down. "Do you not recognize it?"

"Music from the dead," he replied.

"Music from your violin concerto. From the slow movement. Listen again."

At the moment she had managed to make clear that the angels had tricked him into believing that a variation of his own theme had come from the souls of two of the composers he most loved (Bach having shown up first with his cantata), those same angels transformed themselves into demons.

They sang to him and then they talked to him. "Sinner," they called him. He could not remember sinning. At worst he had made love to people he did not love as much as the one he loved most. He drank wine and beer more for their ability to dull than to embolden his mind. And he had written some execrable marches because he had felt bad at not having taken up the scythe against the cannons of pseudoconstitutional autocracy. The devils were not creatures of the air, like the angels. They did not fly about his head but circled him like the jungle creatures he used to conjure in order to scare Clara and her little brothers. He could actually see them now, drooling tigers and gum-baring hyenas. They raked him with their claws as they pestered him with comments about the value of his compositions. Alas, he took them more seriously as critics than as ecclesiastics of the damned. He accused them of driving him mad and could offer as defense only such books as he'd read—Lenhossek on the emotions, Karl Heydenreich's *Philosophical Remarks about Human Suffering*—which he launched against them not by reference to their futile content but as missiles. He hit Clara with one of them and was told by his demons to throw another at her. They wanted him to earn his way into Hell.

She brought the book back to him, who had never before struck her or threatened to strike her or harmed her in any way except by filling her piano with children to keep her from playing and leaving her more often than she left him though he never went anywhere without her except into his room to write and to the tavern from which she was compelled to fetch him each evening because, through the fault not of drink but of his incapacity to remember sometimes who he was and thus where he lived, he was no longer able to find his way home.

"Are you angry with me?" she asked.

The devils would not let him say the devils made him do it. "Very," he answered.

"Why?"

"Because I'm not worthy of you."

Beneath all the noise—from the first repeated note to the shrieking of the demons—he could hear, as he realized he had always heard, the hum of time. There was a sound in the world that was always there, beneath speech and beneath music and beneath the wind when it blew and the abrading of the light when it didn't. It was the hum of time, and whether it was time passing or time standing still, it was a disruptive, awful sound. All who heard it would go mad.

"How can you say that?"

"I can say it because if I were worthy of you I could never say it."

"How can I help you, Robert?"

"Pack."

"Pack?"

"Yes, you can help me pack. As you always do. You know I have never been able to pack for myself. Not if I am to have underwear in Altenburg."

"Are we going to Altenburg?"

"I use it as a figure of speech. Do you remember how we met once in Altenburg and I had forgotten my underwear?"

"I did not pack for you then."

"Will you now?"

"For Altenburg?"

"Not for Altenburg."

"Where are we going?"

"Only I."

"Where?"

"I have been banging my head against the wall of insignificance," he answered. "All this time."

"Perhaps it's my mistake to think the wall has suffered more than has your head."

"All my life I've followed you. Now it's time to follow my head."

"Where?"

"I cannot say it. It's hard enough to think it. My demons tell me it's that or Hell. And still I hesitate. You know where."

She disappeared. He had to pack for himself.

When she reappeared, he was in the bedroom.

"I've sent for Dr. Böger."

"To take me there or keep me here?"

"Robert, do you really want to abandon your wife and your children?"

"Until I've recovered."

"Recovered what?"

"I am not an upholsterer!"

"Am I to laugh?"

"You see. Everything has changed. You have never before had to ask my permission to laugh."

"It wasn't your permission I was asking. It was your meaning."

"If it's philosophy you want, go look in your Kierkegaard. I am no longer his town crier of inwardness. Henceforth, I go out, not in. Or I shall if you will only help me pack. Look at what I've done. I have my whole life spread out before me but nothing packed. What is packing? Is it choosing what to pack or packing what you've chosen? What do I really need where I'm going, Zilia? Clothes?—they will probably dress me in a uniform, or how else will they tell me from the others? Money?—I want you to have all the money I have failed to make. Music paper?—oh, certainly—there is no greater cure for madness than to continue along the path of self-destruction. My Beethoven pen?—a knife in my heart. My watch?—but then I shall never be able to ask, 'What time is it?' of those to whom this very question is once and for all beyond necessity. And will I need my hat?—only to hold the poison in my mind. Cigars?—yes! Cigars I need, the little devils. And if I am not permitted to smoke them, I shall hold them to my nose right down to the stub. I know how much you hate that—how I take them so far down. Now you shall be free of me and my cigars. Thank you for helping me pack."

Dr. Böger was sufficiently convinced Robert might do harm to Clara that he not only told them they must sleep in separate bedrooms but put a guard

{ 367 }

in with Robert, a Herr Bremer, who wore a military uniform (Dr. Böger worked primarily in military hospitals in order to be assured of a fresh flow of patients and to avoid having to treat women, because his admiration would not allow him to tinker medically with their delicate natures). Robert enjoyed having Herr Bremer keep him company. He deliberately did not ask Herr Bremer what it was like to wear a uniform, which omission he knew kept Herr Bremer up all night, while he himself, for what felt like the first time in his life, fell asleep and slept until morning.

When he awakened, Herr Bremer was gone. Robert put on his dressing gown, which he would never have worn in front of a man in military uniform, even if he was merely a nurse in a military uniform, because it was covered with green flowers. Then he opened the door that led to Clara's sitting room, and there he saw Marie, sitting at Clara's desk, watching the door he had just opened, guarding him.

He loved his daughter, his oldest child, but he was insulted it might be thought he was so diminished in capacity that so young and thin a person, especially when compared to Herr Bremer, might keep him imprisoned. "Oh, God!" he groaned, so she would realize he was not blaming her.

He closed the door and wrote a note to Clara and left it beneath his hairbrush and put on a coat over his dressing gown. Only then did he look out the window and discover that rain was pouring down. So he put his bare feet into his slippers before he exited the room through another door that went into the hall. On his way out of the house, unashamedly going toward the front door onto Bilkerstrasse, he heard Clara's voice saying his name and Dr. Hasenclever's voice saying his name back to her. Even before he was in the street, he began to weep for having been the cause of such repetition as he would never allow in his music. His name was ruined.

To make matters worse, he had forgotten his hat! If he hadn't been going to need it in the madhouse — and he had decided before walking out in the rain that he wasn't even going to *go* to the madhouse — the hat had become a necessity by virtue of its rescinded expendability. Quite the opposite of life, which was rendered unnecessary by its very essentiality. Not to mention the cold rain, which coursed through his hair and confused his tears and must have made him look, with his hair greasy wet and the flowers of his dressing gown blooming through his coat and his slippers sloshing in the puddles that collected in the cobblestones' arteries, like a madman escaped from the asylum instead of the madman *escaped* from the asylum that he was. Yet all around him, others were the same, or worse, dressed in masks and motley and terrifying capes while drinking beer from hideously ornate tankards that had done more to ruin German reputation in the arts than all of Wagner's bombast.

It was a relief to encounter in the tollgate at the little pontoon bridge off the Rathus Ufer two men in customary uniform.

"Why is everyone so strangely dressed?" he asked.

"Fasching," answered one of them, while the other seemed to express disbelief at Robert's outfit.

"Oh, I am not dressed for Carnival," he explained, which seemed to confuse the man further. Nor had he ever dressed for it. Lent was difficult enough to understand; the idea of preparing for it with excess and debauchery was stupefying.

"Toll, please," said the first man.

They were on the west bank of the ice-bejeweled Rhine. Robert had no intention of reaching the east.

"I'm here for the scenery."

"Toll, please."

"My sister drowned in the Mulde."

"Toll, please."

"I want to give to the river, not take from it."

"Toll, please."

"Here is my wedding ring."

"Toll . . ."

"It is for the river, not for you."

"Toll, please."

"I have no money."

"*Toll,* please."

He took from the pocket of his dressing gown a silk handerchief. He thought to give it to the men and realized he might instead wipe his wet hair and face with it. But that would be redundant.

"A gift from my wife," he said as he handed it over and started to run off across the bridge.

Then he stopped to look back. The men were not following him but had both poked their heads out of their little shelter, into the rain. "A gift to *me,* I mean," he clarified.

He then opened the hand in which he had been clutching his wedding ring, to keep it dry and keep it safe, and threw it off the bridge into the ice-defiled water, noticing it had left a tiny halo in his palm, and threw himself after it.

As he fell to his death, he remembered Harry Heine's Edith Swanthroat, discarded by her lover, the king of England, but alone able to identify his body among the countless bodies on the battlefield of Hastings. But what if King Harold had been swept to sea? A proper death implies a total disappearance.

He also thought he heard a clock strike in some tower, silencing forever the Carnival, and his music, as death would both divide him forever against himself and unite him for the first time with his life if not with its meaning.

The first thing he saw in the water was Clara, swimming toward him, but not seeing him at all. Her mouth was opening and closing, against the laws of survival, but he could hear nothing of what she was telling him. All he heard was music, beautiful music, unheard before on Earth or wherever it was he now inhabited, which he feared was the same place from which he had just leapt to his death.

The second thing he saw was the bottom of a boat and out of it hands, four of them, palm-gloved hands with huge naked fingers that would have made an oboe cringe and a woman too, for they were raw around what should have been the chaste arc of fingernail and cast a nasty red even into the pallid gauze of the brumal, belching Rhine.

It was colder in the air than in the water. They threw him in the bottom of the boat among their fish, some of which seemed more alive than he, dancing themselves to death while he just lay there picking up their smell but none of their will to live.

"Why?" each of the men said, "Why?" as if he hadn't heard the other. They sounded like hysterical Italian tenors.

He was so cold he wanted to die. The rain was drowning the flowers of his dressing gown. His slippers were lost to the river. But when the fishermen came at him with a thick blanket, on which he noticed scales of fish like silk adornments sewn haphazardly into the stubbled wool, he jumped up toward the blanket, not into it, and threw himself back over the side of the boat, or thought he had, until he realized that a man who's frozen to death moves with the swiftness of a distant star and is as easy to clasp if as difficult to understand.

It was in that same blanket he was carried home, through the masked revelers who had gathered on the bridge to watch what, to judge from their lack of revelry, they had hoped would be not the rescue but the recovery of his body. They were all unrecognizable, but one of them was able to identify him even through the mask he wore of ice and grief and failure. "It's Herr Musikdirector Schumann!" No cheer went up among the gaping mummers. But at least those kind enough to carry him home now knew where to carry him. The two fishermen placed themselves at the positions of honor, and as if he were indeed a table, three took to one side of him and three to the other and thus they dined off him as the most unusual and applauded prop in the entire Carnival as the commencement of the holy season was celebrated in the streets of Düsseldorf.

Dr. Hasenclever answered the door. "Sorry," he said, as what doctor would not to two flocculent fishermen and half a dozen dripping men in masks?

"Herr Musikdirector Schumann," said the man who had first identified him.

"Run off," explained Dr. Hasenclever, not unlike Gotthold Lessing's manservant.

"Herr Musikdirector *Schumann*!" The doctor's gaze was directed down toward the blanket, which was then folded open from around its burden to reveal a man who had left his slippers and his wedding ring in the Rhine and his mind in some unfathomable sea of discomposure.

But Dr. Hasenclever took him for a victim of the rain. "He ran off without an umbrella. And look at how he's dressed!"

"He tried to kill himself," said one of the revelers.

"Well, you can certainly catch your death by going out into this weather in such clothes as these."

"We fished him out of the river," said one of the fishermen.

"Him and me," said the other.

"That cannot be!"

"It can. It is," whispered Robert. "I'm cold. Let me in my house."

"Not yet," said Dr. Hasenclever, who fetched Berthe the maid to stand at the door while he went off to get Clara. Or so Robert thought, until Dr. Hasenclever returned alone and said to Berthe, "The coast is clear. Have them take him directly to the bedroom."

And so eight strangers followed Berthe's amplitudinous backside up the stairs, wholly content that the sight of it was payment for their efforts in saving his life, as it was his payment too, for as he raised his head to watch her waddle up the stairs and down the hallway, he thought how good it was to be home and alive.

Berthe had become Clara. He found himself unable to think of Clara, or to picture her, or desire her, except to the extent that he thought of his absence of thought about her. It must be what life is, if there is life after death—an awareness only of what had been, which now was no more and therefore did not exist, for if it did, how did one bear the separation? He had died and had awakened in a vacant Paradise.

Dr. Hasenclever cooperated in this vision. While Robert bathed in the hot water he had prescribed, Dr. Hasenclever sat by him.

"I have sent Frau Schumann away. You must never tell her you tried to take your life."

"Take my life? I was not taking it. I was giving it."

"Suicide is not a gift."

"Or perhaps I simply have no gift for it."

He went directly from the bath to bed and then, shortly, in dry, warm clothes, to his study, where he tried to write down the music he'd heard in the river and, failing that, went back to work on variations of the theme in E-flat major sent to him he had now decided by Schubert alone. Mendelssohn, too, was fading from his mind. As he wrote it, he could hear Clara playing it. He could not see her or feel her or even imagine her, only hear the music rise out of her fingers upon his fingers upon his pen.

His wife had left him, not as a wife leaves a husband but as a person leaves himself, leaking away slowly over time, taking everything.

He kept hold of Dr. Hasenclever's hand in the carriage transporting him to Endenich. In his other hand, he grasped a bouquet of flowers Dr. Hasenclever said had been sent by Frau Schumann for the journey. He gave a flower to Dr. Hasenclever and to each of the two guards who rode with them. He saved a flower for each of the two drivers who alternated shifts over the eight-hour journey. The rest of the flowers he stared at in order to see the faces of his children.

He had last held flowers in a carriage on the night of their wedding, on their way to their new home on Inselstrasse in Leipzig.

It was almost midnight when they arrived, almost September 13, her twenty-first birthday. They could have married on that date without her father's, and thus without the court's, permission. That their wedding day should have been on her final day without legal freedom had not been planned by them—it was the first possible Saturday after the time necessary for the reading of the banns—but this confluence of wedding and birthday, of justice and revenge, was like some happy trick of fate and an augury of future happiness for their marriage.

He rushed her into bed, or tried to, one eye on the clock, the other on her, until she disappeared into what he did not immediately realize was the bathroom, because this apartment was as new to him as marriage. It might be like all other apartments, in that it was made up of separate rooms, but he didn't know how its spaces sat in relation to one another, as he didn't know how the girl he had loved for as long as he remembered loving could possibly be loved any more as his wife.

When she reappeared, she was wearing the frilly peignoir he had placed within the trousseau he'd given her. As a bride, estranged from family, cut off, she had come with nothing but herself. He wanted to give her, as well as be for her, everything.

Her hair was down, brushed, as if she had knowingly given meaning to the garment she hugged against her nakedness, and as she lay down next to him on their bed he saw she was wearing something else that was new. She had painted her eyelids. He had always found them attractive, permissibly so even when she was a little girl and they were, like the lips, the body's conspicuous portents of future happiness, or of whatever happiness is brought by the kind of imperative attraction he felt toward her, that longing for release and capture both.

He brought the candle closer.

"What is that on your eyes?"

"Do you like it?"

He touched his finger to it, one lid, then the next.

"Is it blue? I can't tell in this light."

"A different blue."

"Different from what?" On stage, she sometimes wore liner, but she had never painted her lids, so far as he knew.

"From any other blue."

"What is it?"

"It's called Manna. I bought it for tonight. It's supposed to be...well, is it?"

"Is it what?"

"If it is, I shouldn't have to tell you."

"It's very beautiful on you."

"Thank you. But that's not what it's supposed to be. I mean, it's supposed to do more than look good. Though I'm glad you think it looks good."

"It is a most unusual blue."

"It's made of woad."

"Woad!"

"You know about woad? I should have known. You know about everything."

He put his nose, as he had put his finger, first to one lid, then to the other.

"Why are you sniffing me? Do I smell funny?"

"Woad was used anciently as a dye. It's what the women of Lemnos were said to be wearing that caused their husbands to reject them."

"Everyone knows that the men of Lemnos had no taste!" She laughed; whether at her own pseudopedantry or in mockery of his customary pedagogery, he could not tell. "No eye for beauty whatsoever. Unlike yourself."

"The men of Lemnos may have liked the way their women looked with woad on them, wherever they happened to put it. What they didn't like was how their women smelled."

"I don't smell!" It was a most feminine cry of truth and question all in one.

"Not like the women of Lemnos. Who, by the way, slaughtered their men, each and every one of them, with one exception, Thaos, who—"

"I am wearing Manna to *attract* you. I was told it would arouse you."

"Me?"

"Any man."

"Look at the time." He brought forth his watch from the night-table.

"The women of Leipzig are known to kill their men who look at the time during the making of love."

"Midnight. Your birthday. You are a woman at last."

"You made a woman of me years ago in Dresden, Robert. Now make me your wife."

PART FIVE

The Breakdown Dialogues

Endenich

MARCH 10, 1854
Does he ask for me?
Clara Schumann

"I'm not a psychicist," said Dr. Richarz.

"Nor I," said Schumann.

"Nor a doctor."

"I'd thought you *were.*"

"I meant *you. You* are not a doctor."

"Nor a psychicist. As I stated."

"They are *my* credentials, Herr Schumann, being presented here. Yours are known to me and to all my staff."

"I'd never thought of madness as a credential."

"I was referring to the brilliance of your compositions."

"You flatter me. I think. Are you saying I've come to live in your madhouse because my work is brilliant?"

"You've come to live in my institution because you tried to kill yourself. Your doctors also felt you posed a threat to your wife."

"Who?"

A Brief History of Endenich

Dr. Franz Richarz claimed not to be a psychicist. He did not believe in the talking cure and the old-fashioned imposition of rules of behavior upon the anarchy of a mind gone mad. He belonged to the new school in German psychiatry. He was an organicist. He believed that the mind was part of the body and not some indefinable, unseeable, unknowable, unfathomable, untreatable piece of cloud that floated in our heads and for all we knew when we died floated out our ears into the limitless beyond. The mind was not our soul, which was fortunate, because if it were, we would all be mindless, would we not?

And yet, Dr. Richarz was an adherent also of the progressive ideas concerning psychiatric practice that he had taken from "Romantic Medicine," so conceived and named by Dr. Carl Gustav Carus, who had not only treated Herr Schumann in Dresden but was cousin to Dr. Ernst August Carus, with whose wife, by strange coincidence, Herr Schumann had once, he seemed eager to confess to Dr. Richarz, been in love and, by even greater coincidence, in whose very home he met Clara Wieck ("I remember *her*," he said, "I remember *that moment*") for the first time, at the very instant he was sitting with Frau Carus at the piano, attempting as always to seduce her, she having accomplished the same with him a year before when he was sixteen and he heard from her lips his first Schubert song and things got hot indeed in Colditz.

Romantic Medicine itself would certainly encourage someone like Herr Schumann to remember, for example, such a romance as this, regardless of the fact that it remained—outside the realm of fantasy and fantasy's normal means of expression in young men—unconsummated.

Organicism would not. A patient must be ripped from his past, protected from it, for within the past, with its roots sometimes cruelly wrapped around the patient's heart, lies the source of the patient's agony. Thus, those closest to the patient were often denied access to him. This frequently brought relief to all parties: The patient was refused permission to receive visits from those who exacerbate the terror his body is causing his mind; and those very terrorists were refused permission to visit their victims, who so often were those they had pledged to God they would love and protect.

In this, Dr. Richarz followed the example of Bruno Goergen, as he had in creating Endenich itself. Dr. Goergen had founded his own psychiatric clinic in Vienna at the turn of the century and had benefited enormously from this sudden accessibility to private care for the disproportionately large number of truly insane people spawned by the wealthy. It was Dr. Goergen who had first forbidden relatives to so much as look in on a troubled kinsman, who, he had noticed prior to this prohibition, invariably misinterpreted his relatives' consoling words as criticism, his fiancée's handwringing as gelding, and the tears and sighs of his collective family members not merely as omens of, but also supplications for, doom. In Bruno Goergen's most widely quoted, if controversial, pronouncement, "The patient all too often sees his dear wife as a mixer of poison, his loving children as demons, his charming home as a prison. He hears voices heard by no one else."

As he knew was common for many people who were going deaf, Dr. Richarz also heard voices. But while they came not from the mouths of devils, as Herr Schumann reported his did, they similarly called his work into question. They came from himself, his own voice divided, as he felt himself divided, trapped as a doctor between the Enlightenment of the last century and its emphasis upon reason, and the Romanticism of this century and its emphasis upon passion. It was reasonable to assume that people went mad because of a sickness in the brain; it was also reasonable to assume that people went mad because of, for want of a better word, *life*.

Thus he was torn between a desire to chop open Robert Schumann's head to have a look inside, and to talk to him endlessly for as long as it might take to understand what happens when an artist is attacked by his art.

Dr. Richarz was born in 1812, which made him two years younger than Schumann, though each felt the other was the older, the doctor because Schumann had been the conductor of an orchestra (to say nothing of the indisputable fact that he *was* older), and Schumann because he continued to feel he had leapt from childhood to the doors of death without passing through the house of life. Artists were children, waiting for a plate to be passed, too often finding it empty.

The doctor had turned to psychiatry in general and organicism in particular when, as a medical student in nearby Bonn, he had come under the influence of Friedrich Nasse, arguably the father of organicism, to say nothing of having been a friend of Goethe, which did much for one's credibility. Dr. Nasse believed that all mental disease resulted from a disturbance of the heart and a disruption of the circulation of the blood. Therefore, instead of trying to impose his own morality upon his patients to get them to act the way he thought civilized, sane people should act, he treated them with medication (drugs and herbs both, including, during the period of his belief in autointoxication, cathartics) and physical therapy (saline baths, hydromineralization, climate cures, cupping, blistering, and the strangely pleasant, decidedly sensual bleeding by leeches).

After graduating from medical school and thus leaving the profound and benign influence of Dr. Nasse, young Dr. Richarz interned with Dr. Maximillian Jacobi at Germany's largest asylum for the insane, in Siegburg. Dr. Jacobi, however, believed quite the opposite from Dr. Nasse. He was convinced that in at least 80 percent of the mentally ill, their symptoms were caused by problems with hygiene, discipline, and morality. This resulted in an inordinate amount of scrubbing, screaming, and preaching throughout the many buildings of the Siegberg lunatic facility.

After eight years as Dr. Jacobi's closest assistant, Dr. Richarz quit.

"Not in a huff, I take it," Schumann commented.

"Yes, as matter of fact, in quite a huff," Dr. Richarz contradicted him.

"It took you eight years to work up a huff?"

"I am a doctor, Herr Schumann, not a musician. In my business we neither write nor receive reviews overnight."

"So you earn your huffs?"

"The best huffs are those huffed slowly."

"I should like to write you a Concerto for Huff," Schumann offered. "But—"

"Now you are having fun at my expense, Herr Schumann."

"—but no good piece of music has ever lasted eight years. Including Wagner's."

Dr. Richarz wondered whether this was some sort of veiled reference by his distinguished patient to the fact that a number of his doctors in the past had told him that his mental problems were the result not of his writing his music too slowly but the opposite: His unceasing but obsessively alacritous labor, for example on the epilogue of *Faust,* caused him to display such symptoms as shivering, faintness, pedal frigidity, insomnia, fear of heights, antipathy toward all metal, keys in particular, which meant he kept getting locked out of his own house, just like his famous ancestor Gotthold Lessing, and, of all things, a dread of death. Dr. Helbig, his homeopathic physician at the time, told him these were precisely the symptoms found in mentally ill accountants, which was no surprise to Dr. Helbig, because music and accountancy were sister disciplines, given their governance by numbers. Was it any wonder that doctors, of all professions, most considered their colleagues to be idiots.

Leaving Dr. Jacobi's hugely disillusioning and disillusioningly huge organization, Dr. Richarz did what many idealistic young people do when they discover in a job that they have been violating their own principles at the same time they have been kissing the ass of the megalomaniac who happens to be their boss: He went into business for himself.

In 1844, in Endenich, a suburb of Bonn, he bought a beautiful seven-acre estate that had been owned by the Kaufmann family until during the Napoleonic wars it was taken over by law students from the University of Bonn, which like all good universities must, if it is wise, shut down when the soldiers start following, like a German lecher his German helmet, their bayonets through a city looking for students in whom to matriculate.

Upon his purchase of the asylum, which he came to call, resisting any doctor's natural temptation to give it his own name, Endenich, Dr. Richarz set about remodeling in order to make it the most comfortable, civilized, progressive, expensive, and exclusive private home for the insane in all of Germany. Most of the work his contractor performed was upon the main building, on the ground floor of which were built his examining rooms and living quarters for his nurse. On the first floor, above, was where the patients were to live, fourteen of them, no more. Dr. Richarz had been willing to sacrifice for the intimacy of truly personal care the income to be derived from a larger population of patients as well as the vastly greater amount of autopsy material, which to organicists was a kind of fleshly gold, particularly, of course, the brain.

So it was that when Robert Schumann was admitted on March 4, 1854, he was given a room on the first floor, just over the heavily bolted front door and seemingly cradled by the fanned hands of two adolescent oaks on either side of that door. It should be said, however, that he was one not of fourteen patients but of sixty. Dr. Richarz had either overestimated how much money might come in from so few patients or underestimated how many crazy people were being produced in Germany, particularly in the post-Revolution years, following 1848, a period not unlike that ushered in by Clemens Wenzel Nepomuk Lothar Duke von Metternich after the Vienna Congress of 1815, in its social stagnation, its authoritarianism, its repression, its failure to unify Germany's thirty-nine separate states, and its utter defeat of the humanistic ideals of romantic liberalism.

Herr Schumann himself was a victim of this postrevolutionary trauma. But he didn't seem to realize it, because while people had been destroyed all around him, the composer not only went on composing but was, by his own admission, as contentedly productive as he had ever been. Whether this was madness or sanity, however, Dr. Richarz was happy not to judge. As noble as it may be to defend one's ideals, one's home, one's children, with force, it cannot be done successfully without losing one's mind. But the same might be said, to judge from Robert Schumann, of the writing of music.

But what music it was! Dr. Richarz was convinced Herr Schumann was a genius. But when he had told him so, Herr Schumann looked at him as if *he* were mad.

Not one to let such a look pass by unremarked, Dr. Richarz said, "If someone were to tell me I am a genius, I would certainly not look at him as if he were, if you will pardon the expression, a madman."

"That's not a situation you need worry you may encounter," answered Herr Schumann, in a rhetoric peculiar enough to force Dr. Richarz to ponder just what Herr Schumann might have meant. And by the time he finally captured the meaning of it, his patient was sitting there on the other side of the peculiar double-chair they shared, his hands over his ears, no doubt suffering from one of his aural hallucinations and certainly in no condition to be chastised for his sarcasm. At the same time, Herr Schumann was also staring up with a smile on his face at the stately Siebengebirge behind Königswinter on the far shore of the Rhine from whose waters he had been spared just, perhaps, that he might come here, though Dr. Richarz knew well that neither psychicist nor organicist believed in fate (which is where the Romantic psychiatrists diverted from both and in so doing took him with them down a path that could lead only to further confusion in his quest to understand the workings of at least someone else's mind).

The reason Herr Schumann was forced to stare *up* through his window at the Siebengebirge, and not merely *out* at them, was that he was no longer on the first floor. So great had his fear of heights proved to be that he had had to be moved to the ground floor and thus more construction done, and done quickly, for the nurse's one room was not sufficient as a place for a great composer to live. And so Herr Schumann's living quarters consisted not only of the nurse's old room, which had become his bedroom where he slept and, alas, smoked, in the half-shadow of his narrow French angel bed's canopy, but also of no small portion of Dr. Richarz's old examining rooms, which went into making Herr Schumann's very pleasant sitting room, furnished to his own specifications: with a comfortable fauteuil, in which he seemed able to sit for hours with his smoking stand at his left elbow and an atlas on his lap; this strange dos-à-dos, which had the two of them, and anyone else Herr Schumann might be permitted to see in time to come, sitting with their backs to one another; a delicate teapoy stand, on which, perversely, he insisted only coffee be placed; an ingelnook, in a cranny by the fireplace, on which Dr. Richarz cannot imagine anyone sitting; and in the middle of everything the very same square piano played upon by Franz Liszt on that day, not long after Dr. Richarz had first opened Endenich, when he walked down the road to Bonn and saw unveiled in the Münsterplatz a Beethoven rendered not only immortal in bronze but forever beyond understanding.

Endenich

MARCH 17, 1854
I like to watch Johannes while he plays.
Clara Schumann

"I have been sent to visit my son-in-law," said Frau Bargiel.

"Sent by whom?" asked Dr. Richarz.

"My daughter, of course. His wife."

"Sent for what reason?"

"Sent to visit him."

"No. I meant, sent, *why*? Why were *you* sent? Why did she not come herself?"

"I have been tending to her in Düsseldorf. Young Herr Brahms and I."

"Is she not well?"

"She has six children and another due in three months. Her husband has been taken from her. No, she is not well!"

Dr. Richarz touched her hand. "Such maternal passion."

"May I visit him now?"

"No."

"Is he sleeping?"

"To the contrary, I expect."

"Then when may I see him?"

"You may see him whenever you like. But you may not visit him."

"I don't understand."

"No visitors."

"But why?"

"Agitation."

He led her from his office to Schumann's room. There were several small shutters in an exterior wall that looked like decoration and, but for one of them, were — decoration and deflection both. This exception he pushed aside, to reveal a peephole.

He looked first but quickly surrendered his spot to her.

Her son-in-law walked back and forth, back and forth, across his sitting room, heading each time directly for the piano and stopping just before he would bang into it. Finally, however, he did bang into it and fell to the floor.

She gasped.

"He hit the piano?" said Dr. Richarz.

"Yes."

"And now he is on the floor?"

"Yes."

"He is squeezing his hands together as if to wring blood out of them?"

"Why do you question when you know?" she asked.

"Agitation." It was unclear whether this was an answer to her question.

Endenich

APRIL 20, 1854

Has he closed off his longing within himself?

Clara Schumann

Schumann was held on either side by his attendants, Herr Niemand and Herr Nämlich.

"Herr Nämlich," directed Dr. Richarz.

"Herr Niemand," Herr Nämlich corrected him.

"You always confuse us," said Herr Niemand.

"I *mistake* you. It is *you* who confuse *me.*"

"Perhaps if we were not required to wear the same uniform...," said Herr Nämlich.

"Outfit. Not uniform. Outfit. This is not a prison. And you are no longer in the army."

"Perhaps if we were not required to wear the same... *outfit,*" said Herr Nämlich.

"Perhaps if you were not *twins,* Herr Niemand."

"Herr Nämlich," Herr Niemand corrected him.

"Forgive me," said Dr. Richarz.

"And we are not even brothers."

"Forgive me," Dr. Richarz repeated, this time to Schumann, as he directed the two large, strong, seemingly identical attendants to hold out one of Schumann's arms apiece so he might slip them into the straitjacket.

Endenich

APRIL 21, 1854

The whole time he has not asked after me even once.
Clara Schumann

Schumann was in bed, no longer restrained.

"Am I alive?"

"I *hope* so," replied Dr. Richarz.

"*Hope* so?"

"Can you see me?"

"Of course I can see you. Have you given up organicism for optometry?"

"You make me laugh, Herr Schumann."

"That, I cannot see."

"I said you *make* me laugh."

"Evidence to the contrary."

"Can you see me?"

"Not laughing."

"If you can see me, and you are dead, then what am I?"

"Dead."

"Aha! That is why I say I hope you are *alive*."

"*That* is why?"

"For your own sake, too, of course. But tell me: Why did you ask?"

"About optometry?"

"No. Whether you are alive."

"Because I thought I was dead. I thought I was in Heaven."

"Of course."

"You knew that?"

"Only because you proclaimed it. Screamed it, in fact — deliriously. That you were in Heaven, and you saw your first wife there."

Schumann tried to sit up in bed. He was excited enough almost to succeed. "I *did*!"

"Your *first* wife?"

"Yes!"

"How many wives have you had?"

"I've never had yours."

"Of your *own*."

"None."

"Then how do you account for the fact that you saw your first wife in Heaven?"

"Because she was dead."

"Did you want to kill your wife?"

"No need — she's in Heaven."

"And your second wife?"

"She's in Düsseldorf."

"You *do* remember her."

"Don't be ridiculous. How could I? I've been married but once."

"That much is true, Herr Schumann. And yet you say you've had no wives. How can this be?"

"How can *this* be?" Schumann pounded his fist on his mattress. "Am I still tied up?"

"Can you not tell?"

"I feel tied up. I feel in the grip of something."

"That's the medication. I didn't like you in the jacket. I had it removed. I would prefer to restrain you from within."

"Ah, medication. *Pharmakon*. Did you know it means both *remedy* and *poison*? It's the word Socrates used in *Phaedrus* to describe what writing is. I'd considered being a writer. But I gave up writing for music. And I gave up music for Endenich. Or music gave me up to Endenich. And what have *you* given me? What medication? What remedy? What poison?"

{ 385 }

"Chloral hydrate."

"And here I had mistaken you for Dr. Clitandre."

Dr. Richarz opened Schumann's file in his lap and proceeded to look through its papers. "I have no record of your having been seen by a doctor of that name. If indeed that is his name. Was he your gynecologist?"

Schumann laughed.

"I thought it was pretty funny myself," said Dr. Richarz.

"I'm laughing at the fact that you don't know who Dr. Clitandre is."

"Who is he then?"

"He doesn't exist."

"Then why did you say you had mistaken me for him? Are you trying to tell me *I* don't exist? Just as your wife does not seem to exist for you?"

"Dr. Clitandre is a character in a play by Molière. He says he heals through words while other doctors use leeches and emetics and enemas."

"Oh, I am a great believer in enemas," said Dr. Richarz.

"Don't speak to me of such things," said Schumann. "I am asleep."

"How can you be asleep and talking at the same time?"

He was by then having chloral hydrate dreams.

Endenich

MAY 29, 1854
His case is considered hopeless.
Dwight's Musical Journal

Waving a magazine, Dr. Richarz approached Schumann where he was standing in the Endenich garden with Dr. Richarz's nephew, Herr Oebeke, himself a medical student. They were supposed to be walking. The nephew enjoyed the fresh air much more than did the attendants, who usually ended up sitting with patients in a nearby tavern, proudly sedating them with drink while complaining that their salaries weren't half that of the doctors. And Herr Oebeke walked them for free. But unlike the other patients, who always seemed grateful to be taken out for a relaxing stroll along the paths that produced an illusion of tranquility in the midst of a nature that had abandoned these ramblers to their minds' caprices, Herr Schumann wasn't walking. He was standing completely still, carrying on a conversation not with Herr Oebeke, who would have loved to talk to him about music and the famous wife he seemed unable to remember he had, but with himself.

"That is not true!" Herr Schumann remonstrated. "That is a lie!"

Herr Oebeke seemed delighted to see his uncle. He fairly fled across the grass, from the side of his ward.

"Herr Schumann is having a terrible argument with himself, Uncle Franz."

"He hears things."

"Music, I was led to understand. I had thought, when he stood still in the garden, to lean toward his head to listen. Imagine — to hear music in the making!"

"And did you?"

"Hear it?"

"Did you *attempt* to hear it? Did you listen?"

"I did," Herr Oebeke confessed.

"That is wrong," lectured his uncle. "You know I insist we respect our patients' privacy."

"You inject them with drugs, uncle. You feed them with tubes when they will not eat. And then you give them enemas when they will not . . . reimburse what they have eaten. Are these not invasions of privacy?"

"We do not put our heads up against theirs in order to hear their private music."

"Only because you know you *can't* hear it, uncle. It would seem to me that your very job is to invade your patients' privacy. They are all privately mad, after all. They are all suffering in the terrible isolation of the insular self."

Dr. Richarz put an absolving hand on his nephew's shoulder. "And to think we are told that romanticism is dying."

"Besides," challenged Herr Oebeke, "how would you know Herr Schumann is hearing things if you didn't listen to him yourself?"

"Oh, I do listen. But I listen to what he actually says rather than to what is said inside him. I listen to his voice when he talks to himself, and I listen to his voice when he talks to me. He hears things, it's true. The music of life, he calls it, to which he says he dances a wild dance within himself. He hears voices no one else can hear. But *I* hear his rendition of these voices. And this is more important than hearing these voices themselves. For they are phantom voices. But his voice, reporting what they've said, is real."

"And what do they say?"

"They say the worst thing a man could hear."

"Oh, no!" said Herr Oebeke.

"Yes," said Dr. Richarz gravely.

"How humiliating!"

"Do you have any idea what his voices say?"

"I can only imagine." Herr Oebeke cringed.

"No, I don't think you can." Dr. Richarz moved away from his nephew and onto the grass toward Schumann, who stood rigidly in the middle of the garden path, only his head moving, as if slapped on either cheek successively, while he berated his invisible adversary. And then, whispering so that his nephew had to run up to him in order to hear, Dr. Richarz said, "The voices tell him that his work is not his own."

"Whose do they say it is?"

"That's hardly the point."

"Then what is the point, uncle?"

"The point is that you should have to ask what the point is. What kind of world does he live in?"

"What kind of world *do* I live in?" Schumann bellowed.

"Herr Schumann?"

"He heard you, uncle."

"What *kind* of world?" he asked argumentatively.

"*This* kind of world." Dr. Richarz waved the magazine. "This is what I've come to show you. *Dwight's*. All the way from Boston. An article about you. Of course it's last month's issue. So it is old news to you if new news to the world."

"Does it review my *Faust*?"

"No, it does not."

"My *Faust* begins in a garden such as this. Gretchen picked a flower such as that. She tried to read Faust's love in the petals of the flower. Faust destroyed the flower with the power of his love for her."

"I love a good allegory," said Herr Oebeke.

"Quiet, you idiot," said his uncle.

"Symbolism," insisted the nephew.

"Precisely," said Schumann, inspiring a smile of delight or perhaps of reprisal from Herr Oebeke.

"Not that Faust actually destroyed the flower," Schumann conceded to Dr. Richarz. "He destroyed its *meaning*. And in so doing, of course, he destroyed its symbolism. As for my *Faust*, it was performed in three cities — Leipzig, Dresden, and Weimar — on the same day. It was the hundredth anniversary of Goethe's birth. And all I wished was that I could have been like Faust himself for that one day, everywhere at once, hearing everything there was to hear. I wonder if I would have recognized the music. It had been in my desk for five years. I had even forgotten I'd written it."

"We often forget what most we love," said Dr. Richarz.

"Symbolism," accused Schumann.

"Thank you," said Herr Oebeke.

"Idiot," said his uncle.

"The magazine." Schumann pointed.

"It's not about *Faust*. It's about you. It's not about what you've produced. It's about your life. Imagine, having such fame as you have that as far away as Boston, Massachusetts, your deeds are reported. Does that not in itself give you reason to live? That what you have created is considered of such importance that what you have done is reported to all the world?"

"Deeds? What deeds? What *have* I done?"

"This article is about your miraculous brush with death. About how you were saved from the river. But that's not why I have brought it to your attention. I have brought it to your attention because it says..." Dr. Richarz opened *Dwight's* and read, "'The overexcitement of an active brain, always intensely occupied with the creation and execution of new musical creations was the true secret...' So you see. There it is—just as you and I have been discussing."

"The true secret of *what*?" Schumann reached for the magazine.

Dr. Richarz closed it hastily and put it behind his back with one hand while with the other he gestured for his nephew to move closer to his patient.

"The true secret of why you felt it necessary to enter the river in the first place."

"Oh, they know about how I jumped in to retrieve my wedding ring?"

"Your wedding ring? What is this about your wedding ring?"

"So they don't have that in the magazine." Schumann reached for it again. Herr Oebeke grasped his hand.

"So you are married, Herr Schumann?"

Schumann removed his hand from Herr Oebeke's and held it and the other up before Dr. Richarz. "How can I be? Look, no wedding ring."

"I thought you said it fell into the river."

"So I did. And so I did. And do I not stand here before you?"

"Yes, you do."

"And do I not not have a wedding ring upon these fingers?"

"You do not."

"I do not not, or I do not?"

"You do not."

"And I do not not as well. Have a wife, that is."

"Then you do!" said Herr Oebeke, who had followed the logic of this conversation with all his might.

"Then where is my wedding ring?"

He held up both hands again before surrendering them to Herr Oebeke, who walked backward along the garden path with Schumann in tow.

He asked Dr. Richarz to let him read the article in the magazine from Boston, but the doctor demurred.* Schumann inspected the flower beds through his lorgnette.

Endenich

SEPTEMBER 12, 1854

Now I want to play with you, the way angels do,
from eternity to eternity.

Robert Schumann

"Come. Sit down. Have a glass of wine."

Schumann didn't wait for a response. He pointed Dr. Richarz into his usual place on the dos-à-dos and poured each of them a glass of a Riesling from the Bacharach vineyards in the Rheinburgengau, not far from the Rhine gorge.

"Too young," said Schumann.

"You are too kind," replied Dr. Richarz.

"I was referring to the wine."

"But we haven't tasted it yet."

"Too young for it to taste of me. The soil in which these grapes are grown is nourished by the waters of the Rhine. These, of course, were picked before I took my fatal plunge. Perhaps next year's wine will embody my flavors."

"In that case we shall have to keep it as a sacramental wine."

"You are too kind."

"Are you mocking me?"

"Oh, not at all. I don't take you seriously enough to mock you."

---

*The actual "true secret" that the April 22, 1854, issue of *Dwight's* claimed to divulge was of what it called Schumann's "lamentable state." Dr. Richarz saw no good to come of revealing this uninformed opinion to his patient.

Schumann raised his glass in expiatory appreciation. He motioned for Dr. Richarz to do the same. "A toast."

"What is the occasion?"

"Do you know what today would be?"

"Whatever it would be, it is. It's in the nature of time to be unconditional."

Schumann laughed. "If I'd wanted a philosopher instead of a psychiatrist, I'd have leapt into the fire of the sun rather than the ice of the river."

"Well, if I were a philosopher—which, as you know, neither I nor anyone else can be, because, as Schlegel says, one can only become a philosopher, not be one, for as soon as one thinks he is one, he stops becoming one—but if I *were* one, I would ask of you the same question I find myself asking as a psychiatrist: What would today be if today were not what it is?"

"My wedding anniversary. So let us drink to the memory of my wife and of the children we had."

"Memory?"

"Aren't they dead?"

"How can you imagine such a thing?"

"I haven't heard from my wife in so long I can assume only that she and the children have died. Why, otherwise, would I have no word from her in all this time?"

"You have denied her existence, Herr Schumann. You have dealt with the terrible pain of separation from your loved ones by disavowing them. But *this*...but *now*...this is a sign of health. This is a sign of recovery. Your wife is alive again—in you. Let us drink, then, to your anniversary. But let us also drink to this redemption of your mind."

Because of the strange configuration of the dos-à-dos, they had each to take a quarter-swivel in order to look one another in the eye and to touch glasses. This they did. Dr. Richarz then took a good long swallow of the young white wine to Schumann's quick sip. Schumann rose immediately to his feet with his glass raised over his head. Dr. Richarz was halfway to his own feet and his glass slightly above his hair and heading higher and the words, "To your health!" dripping from his teeth when Schumann turned his glass upside down. The wine disappeared into the small, worn prayer rug that Schumann had obtained, he claimed, from the widowed husband of the woman who was the lover of the man he himself had most loved before Herr Brahms.

"There's poison in my wine."

It was said as a statement of fact, not an accusation.

Beloved Clara,

How happy I was in your note dated but yesterday (you see I continue to compose at white-hot speed) with your very handwriting, which put me in mind not only of the many letters I had had from you in the Past (I emphasize that word to distinguish my real Past from the time I have spent in this prison) but of your hands themselves, which brought forth music from my passion and passion from my being. Happy too to learn that you still think of me affectionately and so do the children. Hug them for me. I wish I could see you all and talk to you, but we are too far apart. There's so much I want to know—how you are, where you live, whether you still play gloriously, whether Marie and Elise are progressing in their music, where my scores and manuscripts and letters are being kept.

Speaking of which, I need some music paper, because sometimes I want to write down some music. And perhaps you can find and send the variations of that theme in E-flat major I heard howling through my head in my sleep. (Nothing like that here; here all hallucinations are in minor keys.) New clothes too. Washed and ironed, I mean, not literally new. Though new clothes might be called for since I have gotten fat despite occasional walks into Bonn and strolls through the garden here that are so boring I end up talking to myself. It may be, in the words of Hölderlin, "the season of the ripening vines," but what I see now in Nature is what he saw in the midst of plentitude: "summer's empty fields."

Trips to Bad Godesberg too; endless hydrotherapy in the very place where I had those seizures you'll remember well in heat not unlike this past summer's, though I did not notice the heat when it descended, only in retrospect, when everybody said, "Hot enough for you?" In fact, I wore wool and a vest all summer and everyone looked at me the way I have always looked at village idiots in overcoats hovering around our picnics at the solstice. "Looky, looky, here comes the kooky"— remember how those words that were chanted by the children in Würzburg at patients who had just been released from the Würzburg asylum became a chant we heard everywhere? Like a popular song. "Looky, looky, there goes the kooky."

And send me cigars. I very much want you to know this. Cigars. I lead a very simple life here and take great delight in the views of the Siebengebirge out my window. There's so much I want to know and so many things I need. If only I could ask you for them in person. But if you want to draw a veil over some of them (but not the cigars—danger of fire!) I've asked you for, fine. I don't know what I'm doing here. That must be why they keep me.

Do you still have all the letters with the words of love I wrote you from Vienna to Paris? Oh, how I long to hear your wonderful playing once more.

I bid you farewell, my beloved Clara. You and the children. Including the new one. I appreciate your having postponed the christening in the hope that I might attend and participate in the naming. Felix! May he be both happy and lucky! And do thank Johannes for standing in for me as your son's godfather.* I wonder if you would be so kind as to send me his portrait (Johannes's). That and the cigars!

Your old and faithful,

Robert

December 15, 1854

Dear One!

First, I thank you for your tenderness and goodness to my Clara. Now that she communicates with me once again (I believed she was dead! I should have known she could not be dead with you to care for her as you do) she writes about little else but you.

This splendid wife of mine has sent me your portrait. Upon my request. Now I may look upon your familiar features whenever I like. I have memorized its place in my room, which is not the room I am now in writing to you but is the room where I sleep. I have put you under my mirror by the bed. How kind you are to let me see yourself when I might otherwise see someone who looks no better (to put it mildly) than he did on that day our portraits were finished, you so beautiful and I with insane, popping eyes and fatted cheeks.

If only I could come to you, to see you and to hear you. I am gravely shaken by your variations on my theme. Clara, too, has worked from this same theme (which I stole from my dear friend Mendelssohn's

---

*Joseph Joachim had been invited by Clara to join Brahms in becoming godparent to her new son. He was forbidden by Düsseldorf authorities because he was a Jew. Out of this personal insult, and in order to gain what he called a "privileged position" in the Royal Hanoverian Orchestra, he fed the hand that bit him and converted to Christianity soon thereafter.

Andante) but not to the troubling degree that you have. I say "troubling" because you have taken a simple thing of mine and put it out of reach. Transcendence is a bitter gift, however that word ("gift") might be used.

If only I could come to you. If only you might come to me.

Robert

Endenich

DECEMBER 31, 1854

*All my thoughts and dreams are of the glorious time when
I shall be able to live with you two.*

Johannes Brahms

It was New Year's Eve. Dr. Richarz held a party in his own home for his doctors, nurses, and those of his patients who could be trusted with the cutlery. Schumann was surprised to recognize Alfred Rethels, an artist from Düsseldorf.

"How long have you been here?" he asked.

"Ten minutes. And still no drink!"

"I meant in the asylum."

"What asylum?"

"Do you know who I am?"

Rethels shook his head sadly and edged away from Schumann. "I wish I could help you."*

---

*Schumann had several times visited Rethels in his Düsseldorf studio and had purchased woodcuts from both the *This, Too, Is a Dance of Death* and the *Another Dance of Death* series. His favorite was *Death the Rider* from the latter, dated 1849: Death is on a horse, carrying his scythe, as he approaches a walled city with two large church spires and smoke coming from two chimneys. He bought it because it reminded him how the horror of the revolution had rendered him exuberant with music. Alfred Rethels had been driven mad by having had to wait eight years for an official decision concerning whether the south windows in the Aachen town hall would be filled in to allow sufficient space for him to paint his commissioned frescoes of scenes from the life of Charlemagne. He was so unhinged by the delay that he was able to finish only four of eight; the rest were painted from his cartoons by one of his students. Soon after his conversation with Schumann in Endenich, he was released into the care of his mother and sister and died in Düsseldorf three years later.

While such attendants as Herren Niemand and Nämlich were in attendance, their part in the festivities was purely "vigilant," as Dr. Richarz did not hesitate to inform even those who did not ask why the attendants were ringed around the large sitting room in which the Biedermeier clashed with such romanticism as was represented by the collective madness of his patients.

"Vigilance," said Dr. Richarz, "is a medical term for insomnia. And this is, after all, New Year's Eve."

"What difference does that make?" said Schumann. "With insomnia the criterion, every night in Endenich is New Year's Eve."

He was dressed in his usual dark wool suit. His vest pockets were stuffed with cigars, of sufficient number that he looked as if he were greeting everyone with an extra pair of dark, fat-fingered hands.

"Christmas gifts?" questioned Dr. Richarz.

"Why should I? I received nothing from you."

"*I'm* not asking for a cigar, Herr Schumann. I'm asking where *you* got them."

"My wife."

"Wasn't that thoughtful of her."

"*She* didn't send them to me. They were brought to me last week by Herr Joachim. Christmas Eve. My very first visitor. Why?"

"He must know how much you love to smoke."

"I enjoyed his visit. My very *first* visitor. Months, then, of having lost what might have been enjoyed. But he says Brahms will come. I gave him a letter to give to Brahms. I called Brahms *du*. What do you think of that?"

"I make it a policy not to get involved in discussions concerning *du* and *Sie*. I've seen too many lives wasted in consideration of *that* distinction."

"She calls him *du*."

"And I've read too many novels with that line in them. I'm quite serious, Herr Schumann—no *du* and *Sie*."

"But she won't let *him* call *her du*."

"Do you think that would be proper?"

"What business is that of yours?"

"Do you deliberately make my point for me, Herr Schumann?"

"Somebody must."

"But I did so myself. Several times."

"This is Endenich, doctor. What's said here has no reality until it's confirmed by others."

"Endenich is no different from the world."

"That must be why I'm here."

"You *asked* to come, if I'm not mistaken."

"All the more reason, then, for me to be here."

"What you say makes no sense, Herr Schumann."

"To ears that will not hear it."

"I make no secret of the fact that I am losing my hearing. Nonetheless—"

"I make no secret of the fact that what I said about hearing has nothing to do with one's ability to hear."

"What you say continues to make no sense, Herr Schumann."

"Let's drink to that."

Schumann raised his glass like a baton, its stem pinched between thumb and forefinger, his arm so far extended that he nearly touched Dr. Richarz's nose, and his wrist upheld at such a degree that wine spilled over the rim of the glass and onto the cuff of his shirt, which, like most cuffs in most asylums, was a bit soiled; the white wine cleansed it.

"No poison in there this time," Dr. Richarz joked as he touched his glass to Schumann's.

"To the contrary."

Schumann conducted the glass to his lips and drank down all that was in it. He then reached into one of his vest pockets.

"But you *have* a cigar in your hand," said Dr. Richarz casually; he was accustomed to redundancy in the behavior of his patients, though usually it was in actions by which they inflicted distress upon themselves.

But Schumann reached behind his row of cigars and brought forth tightly folded papers.

Slightly changing the subject, Dr. Richarz said, "In the matter of cigars, when a moment ago I asked you where you had obtained them, and you said, 'My wife,' but you then said it was *not* your wife from whom you had obtained them, why did you say it *was* your wife from whom you had obtained them?"

"Are you asking me for a cigar?"

"I don't smoke," said Dr. Richarz wearily.

"You really should. It soothes the nerves."

"What have you there?" Dr. Richarz changed the subject decisively.

"Letters from Johannes Brahms."

"Ah, yes."

"Have you been reading my mail?"

"Of course not, Herr Schumann! But we are aware of what mail our patients get. We deliver it to them, after all."

"I *want* you to read it. That's why I'm showing it to you."

"I would not be comfortable reading your mail. Besides, it's New Year's Eve."

"Have I spent my whole life unaware of a New Year's Eve rule that prohibits the reading of mail?"

"I meant, it's a time for celebration."

"In other words, you wish a respite from your labors."

"Exactly!" Dr. Richarz signaled for wine to be poured into his and Schumann's glasses.

"As I wish a respite from my suffering."

"I see." Dr. Richarz now waved off the servant carrying the tapered green bottle, before a drop of wine was poured.

"I shall read them to you myself." Schumann held his lorgnette to his eyes. He started to read the letters, but he read them silently, nodding here, smiling there, shaking his head ferociously while laughing and ceasing these contradictory activities at the same instant.

"Now I *am* curious," said Dr. Richarz.

Schumann immediately folded up the letters and forced them back into his vest pocket.

"I said 'my wife' because these letters concern her."

"It was your wife you wished to discuss, then? To the exclusion of all else?"

"But not of all others. I addressed my first letter to Johannes in Düsseldorf. He didn't answer it until December 2. Why? Because it was forwarded to him in Hamburg, 'whither,' he said, 'I had gone to visit my parents.' What do you think of that?"

"I think it's very nice when children visit their parents. Only my nephew visits me, and he is not comfortable at Endenich."

"Then what do you think of *this*? 'I should have preferred to receive it from the hands of your wife.'"

"Have you these letters memorized, Herr Schumann?"

"'I expect to be back in Düsseldorf in a few days. I long for it.' He *longs* to be back in Düsseldorf. What could that mean?"

"Anyone who has been in Hamburg and Düsseldorf must prefer the latter."

"Only if you prefer French whores to German."

"Who doesn't!"

"Dr. Richarz!"

"It's New Year's Eve, Herr Schumann!"

"One night a year you are granted a sense of humor?"

"It would appear to be the same night that you are made cruel."

"It was only tonight that I received his next letter. He didn't write it for a week after he'd returned to Düsseldorf. He waited until he'd had my own next letter, delivered by Joachim. The one in which I took fate in my hands and called him *du*. He thanked me for calling him *du*. And my calling him *du* allowed him to confess that the woman he calls my 'kind wife' had brightened his heart by using this same word to him, this word he calls 'intimate.' There, doctor—my wife, as promised. As I am intimate with him, she is intimate with him. 'How long,' he writes to me, 'the separation from your wife seemed to me! I had grown so accustomed to her and had spent such a glorious summer with her. I had grown to admire and love her so much that all else seemed empty to me and I could only long to see her again.' Note—the theme of longing. In every letter, he writes of longing. 'I brought many beautiful things back with me from Hamburg. From Herr Avé the 1779 Italian edition of the score of Gluck's *Alceste*.' Very nice, very nice. 'In addition, your first cherished letter to me and many from your beloved wife.' One from me, many from her. Do you know what this means, Doctor Richarz?"

"You received this letter only tonight? Your powers of memorization are miraculous, Herr Schumann."

"It means that she must love him more than I." Schumann wept.

"Herr Nämlich! Herr Niemand!" called Dr. Richarz.

The attendants came and rescued Dr. Richarz.

Endenich

JANUARY 11, 1855

I should by rights put by my best melodies, 'Really by Clara Schumann,'
for with only myself for inspiration nothing profound or beautiful can
possibly occur to me.
Johannes Brahms

The boy wore a plaid shawl. It was frayed at its edges as if he had sat upon every inch of its fringe and even while sitting fidgeted. It was held together upon his right shoulder by a safety pin, which became visible only when he moved his head and his long blond hair melted off the metal. His left shoulder had, upon his arrival, been occupied by his knapsack, which was as full to bursting as Schumann's heart.

He was a boy. He was so young as almost not to exist. The gods did not age, and their beauty never faded.

He sprawled in the upholstered fauteuil, while Schumann paced before him, stopping only to stare down at him in disbelief. Almost a year since he had seen him last in Düsseldorf.

But it was not his first visit, Johannes was firm in declaring. He had come once before, at the end of the summer on his way back to Düsseldorf from a walking tour of Swabia (Heilbron, Ulm, Heidelberg...).

Heidelberg! When Schumann had been a student at Heidelberg, even younger than Johannes was now, he played the piano everywhere, he was quite a success, and one night when he was playing at a ball, a beautiful young Frenchwoman whose name he still remembered, Charlotte, came up to him at the piano and said something like *Oh, Monsieur Schumann, si vous jouez, vous pouvez me mener où vous voulez.*

Johannes laughed but then asked timidly in his high voice please for a translation. *Oh, Herr Schumann, if you'll play, you may have me any way you like.* Well, not *have me,* exactly, more like *take me,* but, then, she was not referring to a trip to Saarbrücken.

Johannes did not find the German as amusing as the French.

On his way back to Düsseldorf from Swabia, he had been allowed by the doctors only to view Robert through a hole in his wall. He apologized; he had wanted to embrace his master.

Hole in the wall!

The boy blushed as if he had given up the secret of the cepionidus.

But Schumann immediately set him at his ease by confessing that he knew all about the hole in the wall. This was an insane asylum, after all, much as it resembled a valley chalet. People were being paid to look at him through a hole in the wall. Sometimes he looked through the hole in the wall himself. Not out. In. He always expected to see himself, as one was said to be able to see one's image reflected in the cepionidus, and never did. This made him feel invulnerable to the spying of others.

Johannes, nonetheless, had seen him smoking his pipe.

Speaking of which, were there any cigars in that knapsack?

There were! Look at that thing—mightn't they be crushed?

His beloved wife, Johannes told Schumann, had packed the cigars.

Indeed, they were not crushed.

They sat and smoked. Johannes chewed as much as sucked on his cigar, until its end was soaked with his saliva and was frayed and had him picking shreds of dark tobacco off his tongue and twirling them between his thumb and forefinger until they were dry enough to drop into the ashtray on the smoking stand. But the smoke from his cigar was fragrant with spice and an earth that could not be found in the gardens of Endenich, the way another's cigar always smelled sweeter than one's own, and Schumann pulled the smoke into him as he paced before the reclining Brahms, danced through the smoke the boy breathed out into the room that sheltered them.

He was living in a small apartment above her, still, yes, on Bilkerstrasse. His mother had advised him against it. Here was her letter. Was he wrong in what he had done: rushing to Düsseldorf at the first news of Robert's illness, moving into the house, taking care of things?

What things?

Was he wrong? Johannes insisted upon knowing.

Schumann read the letter the boy had received from his mother. She was like all mothers, like his own mother, who had wanted him to go to law school, refusing to believe he could make a living with music. She was right! Even his father-in-law had been right!

Johannes's mother wrote of him, "Schumann" (strange to read one's name in someone's letter, even when accustomed to reading it in reviews of his work, and to see himself as "Schumann" and not "the master," which is what the letter's recipient called him sometimes, or "Robert," which is what he loved to be called by a young man twenty-five years his junior—it was a form of immortality!). She wrote of this Schumann that he had opened doors but that Johannes must expand his own possibilities. He could not live on his compositions—even the great masters had been unable to do that. She hoped he would have gotten a job if Schumann had not taken ill. On a temporary basis, it was allowable for him to help out. But he could not stay there forever. He was losing time. He was losing money. He might not like hearing it, but respect came only to men with money.

What was it with mothers? A genius emerged from the womb, and the mother feared he would suffer more from lack of funds than from the sti-fling of his art.

Schumann offered to burn her letter. He touched the tip of his cigar to its corner. But either his cigar had gone out or the letter was as indestructible as any mother's admonition.

He hadn't answered Johannes's question: Was he wrong?

Of course he wasn't wrong.

And Johannes hadn't answered his question: *What things?* What did he do there all day? It was no longer for Schumann an enduring house, as neither was any of the other places he'd lived with Clara. Everything before his vision was cerebral, conceptual, frozen in the brain. What did he *do* there all day?

Johannes was in charge of all household expenses and kept track of everything in the household diary: mortgage payments, school tuition, servants' wages, food, wine, medicines, piano tuning, postage stamps, firewood, coal. When the beloved wife had gone on tour four months after the birth of little Felix, he supervised the children's studies and music lessons and helped out the housekeeper, Berthe, and the other servants in taking care of the youngest children, including Felix, who was small enough to sit in his hand and often did as he danced around the room to amuse the other children, so that Felix had learned to laugh heartily at a very early age, and the other children had learned something they ought not do with a mere infant. He gave the little ones sugarloaf to encourage them to learn the alphabet. He brought Ludwig to his bed when the child missed his mother and was afraid to fall asleep out of fear that Ludwig would need him and dreamed his dreams awake and when Ludwig awakened at dawn they wrestled and the little boy won. He taught Marie and Elise to play *Pictures from the East* for the beloved wife's birthday, for which he had given her a four-hand arrangement of the master's quintet. In return, for Christmas, she gave him the complete works of Jean Paul. And when Frau Schumann needed clothes sent to her in Ostend, Leipzig, Weimar, Frankfurt, Hamburg, Bremen, Breslau, Berlin, she asked him to search her bedroom for them and send them on. Sometimes he succeeded, and sometimes he failed. How did a woman arrange her clothes? What was the difference between a chemise and a blouse, between *Hemden* and *Blusen*? Why were some buttons buttoned and some not? Why was it more difficult to fold cotton than to write a sonata? What was the purpose of an undergarment that looked in a drawer to be no bigger than to fit an autumn gourd? When was a heel high and when was it merely pitched?

You are asking, Schumann said, the wrong person.

How can her husband be the wrong person?

Schumann had no answer.

Johannes was her husband.

This was a comfort, as well as an excitation, and a grief.

What did the boy make of the marriage diary, Schumann wondered, with its intimacies recorded, night after night, sometimes night after night after night, the cold mathematics of the most heated passion Schumann had known or could imagine? He took a virile pride in being measured by so young a man, if indeed Johannes read and understood the symbols of their fornications and varieties thereof, and he took into him a great sadness that it should be over, and he be replaced, not by this boy he loved but by his own absence. The only place he could be two places at once was within himself.

There was always music. Music, within, was as vagrant as love. But out in the world it was, like love, manifest and gladsome.

The beloved wife had been the first to perform Johannes's work, the andante and scherzo from his third sonata, in F minor. In Leipzig. So she was with both of them the first to perform their work. And for each in Leipzig. And they had both written early sonatas in F-sharp minor, the boy's a kind of homage to his master's, perhaps a lonely cry of his own heart for someone he, too, loved.

In Weimar, with Liszt conducting the orchestra, she played the boy's D-Minor Concerto. He had been writing it first as a sonata for two pianos, and Schumann remembered and reminded him of how he would sit and listen to Johannes and Clara play it together in the house on Bilkerstrasse and each time they began it, he, Schumann, would leap from his seat when Clara played the B-flat chord over the D-minor triad in the bass, and he would shout ... he could not remember what he shouted, could not remember even whether what he shouted was in the form of words. He remembered only breathing something uncontrollably out of the confines of his being where he stored all his knowledge of music as well as that uncommon generosity that allowed an artist to hosanna his humiliation before superior genius. When he heard such chords as Johannes had written, logic fled the world, and in its place came the agitated serenity instilled by beauty.

Because even in the madhouse he received issues of his old magazine — the one in which he had introduced Johannes to the world, God help him!—Schumann had seen Liszt's piece about Clara's appearance in Weimar. Liszt wrote that she had once been a delightful plaything of the Muses (no doubt during their tryst in Vienna), which was a wonderful description of her as Schumann had known her, but that she had become a stern priestess who gazed at men with unhappy, penetrating eyes.

It was he, Schumann, who had caused her such sadness. He had been sick for years, and Clara had grown pinched within the crevice of his sufferings. But when Johannes had arrived ... plaything of the Muses did not do justice to her delight. No little girl as he had known in Leipzig, enchanting and brilliant and provocative of visions of a whole life lived within her spell, should be *stern,* should be *priestly.* Little wonder he'd forgotten her for months and remembered her through remembering Johannes. He could not see one of them without seeing the other.

Johannes assured him he would continue to care for the beloved wife.

He then put down his cigar to play for him.

He played his variations on Schumann's *Bunte Blätter* theme. As he played, and Schumann followed with the manuscript in his lap as finally he sat by taking Johannes's place on the fauteuil and even smoked the boy's discarded cigar, he heard Mendelssohn in the piece and Clara and himself, all put together for what would surely be forever by this boy, this angel, this master, who had written on the title page:

VARIATIONS FOR THE PIANO
ON A THEME BY ROBERT SCHUMANN
DEDICATED TO CLARA SCHUMANN
BY JOHANNES BRAHMS

Endenich

JANUARY 29, 1855
I am dying of love for you.
Johannes Brahms

Dr. Richarz, as was his custom, kept the patient's file in his lap during any discussion. The presence of the file in so distinguished a precinct signaled to the patient conscious of such distinction that he or she was not going to be subject to the shame and inconvenience of such physical treatment as force-feeding, enema, pupillary scrutinization, or the measuring of the cranium, and instead was expected to approach madness autocathartically.

"What is it you are asking?" asked Schumann. He was on his bed but not in it. He had been dozing. He was wearing his usual suit, though when he napped he loosened his cravat. This was his signal to his doctors and attendants that he was not dead.

"A bit of medical history." Dr. Richarz tapped the file. "I need you to fill in the blanks."

Schumann tapped his head. "I need *you* to fill in the blanks."

"The mind has no blanks, Herr Schumann. It is never empty; always full. Sometimes too full. Anxiety manifests itself in the body, and in behavior, but it enters the body from the mind. When the mind can no longer contain itself, it bursts into the body. It insinuates itself into the flesh. It causes such symptoms as you have suffered over the years. The trembling, the itching, the cold feet, the insomnia, the indigestion, the weeping, the screaming, the drinking, the—"

"I hope you're not going to say 'smoking.'"

"Of course not."

"And yet you do not smoke yourself."

"Oh, I would love to. But it makes me sick."

"Have a cigar."

Dr. Richarz declined. Schumann lit his own.

"What is it you're really after?"

"The true secret."

"Of why I went for my swim?"

"Much more than that. I want to know why you're here."

"I'm here because I went for my swim?"

"You're here because you're ill. But I don't know what you're ill with."

"You know perfectly well what I'm ill with! Surely you're not as nosologically deficient as that. What you don't know is why I remain ill."

"I am, I can assure you, a nosologist not to be trifled with. Which is precisely why I can say that you would not remain ill if I knew what you were ill with."

"You have a cure for everything?"

"I have a cure for what I know I can cure."

"Mind or body?"

"I hate that question."

"And I hate enemas."

"I'm not asking you to have an enema, Herr Schumann!"

"Wrong!"

"I merely want your history. All of it."

"All of it?"

"So I may plot the trajectory of your suffering."

"Down." Yet Schumann seemed so delighted with this answer that he pointed his cigar straight up.

"Were you never happy?"

"I was always happy."

"And your misery? Your—?"

"What do you think, doctor, we are vessels filled at one moment with joy and the next with despair? I was *always* happy. Who would not be?—with music and so many children and a wife like mine, who made desire seem a sacrament. And I was *always* wretched, aware of great dis-ease within myself, for the same reasons—music, children, woman. I feared to lose them. And look at me—I have!"

"Why do you proclaim this with such glee, Herr Schumann?"

"Glee? You're right! There it is! My point exactly!"

"But what *caused* this confusion in yourself?"

Schumann sat up in his bed, leaning toward Dr. Richarz. "What a fine way to state it. This confusion in myself. You are not saying *I'm* confused; only that I contain confusion."

Dr. Richarz did not respond. The long ash on Schumann's cigar fell between his legs onto the bed; he scooped it carefully from one hand into the other and deposited it whole into the ashtray that sat beneath the portrait of Johannes Brahms on his night table.

Endenich

FEBRUARY 23, 1855
I can no longer love an unmarried girl.
Johannes Brahms

"You look like young Werther."

Brahms had been admitted to Schumann's sitting room and was approaching the master with an inkstand under one arm and a box of cigars and a painting under the other. He wore yellow pants, a blue jacket, and high boots.

"All the fashion," said Brahms.

"Eighty years ago!"

"Well, what kind of fool would want to wear the fashion of his own time!"

"A fashionable one?"

Brahms blushed unashamedly.

"I had a Werther love once," Schumann said, reaching for the box of cigars. "Agnes Carus was my Lotte. In Colditz. Her husband was one of my doctors. Yet it never occurred to me she was married. Her husband was a prop in the play of my life. I merely had to watch out not to knock into him in my haste to get to her. Not that I ever did. Get to her, that is. By the time she offered herself to me, I was in love with someone else."

Brahms proffered the painting, around which was wrapped the shawl he would have worn had he not been dressed as the quintessential unrequited lover.

Schumann balanced the painting on his new inkstand and unfolded the shawl. Tears filled his eyes as the image held beneath his friend's familiar wrap was revealed. He picked up the painting in both hands and brought it close to his face. "How long I've waited for this."

"She's been afraid you've forgotten her."

"I could no longer see her. Now I can see her."

"I shall tell her of your tears, though they'll bring the same to her."

Schumann put down his wife's portrait and wrapped it carefully in the boy's shawl.

"What else at home?"

"Felix has his first tooth. It's come in on the bottom, in the front. He feels it with his tongue and tries to see it. He goes quite cross-eyed in the effort."

Schumann smiled but said, pointing at the hidden woman, "What else of *her*?"

"She travels. She performs and teaches. She plays my music now in public. She says it reminds her of playing yours—no one likes it!" Brahms in delighted solidarity grasped Schumann by both shoulders. "Verhulst hated it in Holland. Jenny Lind in Hanover. Everyone else everywhere else."

"Everywhere else *where*?"

"I have been with her to Hamburg. My mother and father were happy to meet her. They have agreed to let us stay with them in April when we are there for your *Manfred*. But first we are going to Cologne for the *Missa Solemnis*."

"All the better to prepare for *Manfred*."

"All the better to prepare for *Manfred*," Johannes generously agreed.

"But more of where you've *been*. I am far better able to imagine what hasn't yet happened than to picture what has. "

"I was with her as well in Hanover. And Lübeck. Then it was time for her to make that trip to Holland. I was filled with terrible pain while I watched her pack. You must be able to remember for yourself. Each piece of clothes, each shoe, each ribbon, each sheet of music is like something stolen from oneself. I couldn't bear to say good-bye. So I went with her on the river steamer as far as Emmerich. Then I returned home to see to your children in their mother's absence. But after two days I could no longer bear it. I spent almost all my money to get to Rotterdam. But it was worth it! I was able to keep her company for six days until she left for Utrecht. And I to wait for her in Düsseldorf. But no sooner was she back than off she went again, to Berlin and Danzig and Pomerania, and I to you here to bring you news of her and her picture and cigars and the inkstand you wanted. And now that you have them, you should write to her! There is nothing more I should love to carry back from you than your love in a letter I might give to her with my own hand."

Schumann looked about him in a panic. "But I have no paper!"

"No paper?" It was impossible from Brahms's tone to determine what subtle difference there might be between incredulity and disbelief.

"No paper!" Schumann had seated himself aside his new inkstand, pen in one hand, forehead in the other, eyes on the paperless surface before him.

Brahms went to the door and opened it and called out, "Herr Nämlich! Herr Niemand!"

"What is it?" said whichever one of them it was, and with such haste it seemed superfluous to answer him.

"Herr Schumann says he has no paper."

"More fugues?"

"*Stationery.*"

"Ah, a letter. To you?"

"What would be the sense of that? To his *wife.*"

"Of course." He turned to go. "Paper," he announced his commission.

"Thank you, Herr Niemand."

He returned with but one sheet. Schumann remained poised to write, ink dripping off his pen onto the table, which Herr Niemand wiped clean before putting the sheet before him.

"Shall I wait?"

"I think you make him nervous," said Brahms.

"The moon lightening the sky at full noon," said Herr Niemand.

"Enough poetry, Herr Nämlich," said Schumann, waving him off and in so doing sowing beads of ink like bullets across the gray frontage of his uniform.

As soon as Herr Niemand closed the door behind him, but even before he could resume his place at the window in the wall, Schumann attacked the paper before him, bringing his pen down toward it, letting it hover there above the paper without touching it, and then bringing it back, looking at the full quota of ink upon its nib, nodding in agreement with himself that he needed no more ink, and once again stabbing toward the paper, without so much as writing a word or even depositing a dab of ink within the chaste silence.

Brahms took the pen from his hand. "You are overwhelmed with feeling. You have too much to say to say it. Come, let's play together."

Schumann resisted for a moment his friend's hand hooked into his elbow to take him from the paper he stared at quite as if it were the woman herself to whom he could not move the words he held within. Were it not for the portrait wrapped up in the shawl, he would not see her at all.

"What shall we play?" asked Brahms as they walked arm in arm to the piano.

"Do you recall my *Julius Caesar* arrangement for four hands?"

Brahms grinned. "After you." He motioned for Schumann to sit at the bench where he would take the lead.

Schumann pushed away and took the left side of the bench. "I am the bass."
They began together but soon diverted.

Brahms laughed. "We need to practice. I should move in with *you*."

"Out of tune," said Schumann.

"Oh, I should think we'd get along just fine."

"The piano!"

Brahms rested his head for a moment on Schumann's shoulder. "I knew what you meant."

Brahms signaled the time of his departure by retrieving his shawl from around the painting.

"I shall walk you to the station," said Schumann.

"Are you allowed?"

"Of course. I may go anywhere I like."

"With the likes of me?"

"I doubt it."

"Let me get my coat."

Johannes found Herr Niemand outside the door.

"May Herr Schumann walk me to the station?"

"Ask the doctor."

"Where is he?"

"Herr Nämlich!"

Herr Nämlich led Brahms to Dr. Richarz.

"May Herr Schumann walk me to the station?"

"Your idea or his?"

"Mine."

"Tell me the truth, Herr Brahms."

"His."

"It doesn't matter which. Of course he may walk you. Discreetly attended, needless to say."

"Why did you ask me whose idea it was?"

"How better to learn about someone than to study someone he loves?"

"Why, then, won't you permit his wife to visit him?"

"She's never asked to visit him."

"Only because she's frightened of what she might see."

"What she would see would frighten her even more should she come here to see it."

"It would be worse than she imagines?"

"Her presence would *make* it worse than she imagines. One step at a time, Herr Brahms."

"Do you refer to my visits?"

"I refer to the exchange of correspondence between them. No one more than I wishes that they be back together."

"Except for me."

Brahms and Schumann walked past the station and all the way into Bonn. They visited the cathedral and the Beethoven monument in the Münsterplatz and then had a glass of wine each at the Star Family Hotel, while Herr Nämlich or Niemand was forced to wait outside in order not to upset his patient.

On the way back to the station, along the Endenich Road, Schumann borrowed Brahms's spectacles and, until the time at the station itself when he hugged Brahms and kissed him tenderly and reluctantly returned these spectacles, saw himself see himself see the world as Brahms saw it.*

Endenich

MARCH 12, 1855

I can't stay here any longer; they don't understand me.

Robert Schumann

"What happened last night? Herren Nämlich and Niemand were most horribly disturbed by your—"

"It was I who was disturbed. They were inconvenienced."

"By your anoesis."

"Speak German, doctor."

---

*While it was not to Schumann but in a June 1854 letter to Joseph Joachim that Brahms confessed he "could no longer love an unmarried girl" (in the same letter in which he told their mutual friend, "I often have to restrain myself violently from just slipping my arm around Clara"), he and Schumann had discussed the idea in Düsseldorf. Schumann, in urging Brahms to borrow from his bookshelves Ivan Turgenev's "Diary of a Superfluous Man," reminisced about the spring of 1847 when Turgenev's married mistress and Clara's great friend, Pauline Viardot, appeared in Dresden in Meyerbeer's *Les Huguenots*. Turgenev was with her, as was her husband and their daughter, and while the Schumann children played with Louise Viardot, Turgenev spoke man to man, artist to artist, to Schumann, in the first regard telling him he had never understood passion for a young girl and much preferred a married woman and in the second proclaiming, "It is never good for an artist to marry." It was too late for Schumann (who certainly did understand passion for a young girl) to heed such advice; but Brahms, perhaps because it came from Robert, seemed to take it to heart.

"By your delirium."

"I was pursued by Nemesis."

"In what form?"

"Female."

"I meant, was it in your mind, or did it actually appear?"

"*She*. Nemesis is a woman."

"My question stands."

"In the form of a woman, then. A goddess. And she did actually appear. Whether it was in my mind or in the world itself is a question no man can answer."

"Of course not. Only you can answer that."

"I meant, whatever happens in anyone's mind is indistinguishable from what happens in the world. One's mind is the world. Those who give expression to it are what we call artists."

"You needn't condescend to me, Herr Schumann. I am a champion of artists."

"Is that why you have so many of us here in Endenich?"

"There are so many here in Endenich because they believe what you do."

"I believe I was pursued by the goddess who allots to mortals a precise balance of happiness and sorrow. 'The weight of fortune's smile upon you has been too great,' she said to me. 'Wife. Children. Music. Brahms. It's time for you to suffer.' You, too, I think, doctor, would attempt to vanquish such a woman. I was frightened. I asked my attendants to lie down with me. They did, on either side, curled up against me. But while both fell asleep, I wept the whole night long in fear and sorrow. I was reminded of the night I learned Schubert died—embraced by sleeping men and yet unshielded from desolation. Nemesis continued to pursue me. I was defenseless."

"Yet Herr Nämlich complains of a bite upon the hand."

"How strange. It tasted like Herr Niemand."

"That's not funny, Herr Schumann."

"When you weep, do you say, 'That's not sad'?"

"What I find sad is your dream of Nemesis. Haven't you suffered enough? Isn't the balance in your life already toward sorrow? Come. Tell me. Fill in the blanks."

"I was born."

"I'm not of the school that equates existence with pain."

"I lived."

"I'm not of the school that equates experience with anguish."

"I died."

"In the river?"

"Here. In this bed."

"When?"

"I'm not of the school that equates time with experience."

"Are you mocking me?"

"I take you too seriously to mock you, Doctor Richarz."

"Is this not the ultimate mockery—to mock and disavow mockery and in the disavowal to mock further?"

"You drive me insane with the curlicues of your mind."

"I merely express what's in yours."

"Well, then, why don't *you* fill in the blanks?"

"Because they would be *my* blanks, Herr Schumann. And you would be bored to death. Doctors are forever students and suffer from the disposition of students, which is to learn partial truths and to impart them as whole truths. But you—you made music, sir. And now, for the most part, you make music no more. Music's what exalted you, and music's what cast you down. So let me hear the notes between the notes."

"We call those rests."

"Fill in the blanks, Herr Schumann. Or, if you would, the rests."

"I was born in 1810. I was removed from my father and my mother by illness and war in 1812. I met Agnes Carus in 1824. I was taught by her, without her knowledge but not beyond her suspicion and delight, the perishable pleasures of self-abuse, in case that might be of interest to your investigation. My sister killed herself in 1826. I went quite mad. So did my father—mad enough to die within the year. Schubert died in 1828. I went quite mad. As who wouldn't? The world should have stopped. But it didn't. So I went quite mad over that as well. That same year, I met Clara Wieck. She was eight years old. That I didn't have the sense to fall in love with her immediately, and save myself drunken nights in the arms of people who may not even have existed, has driven me quite mad in retrospect. I became a nine-fingered pianist in 1832. That did not so much drive me mad as result from a madness of which I was not aware. In 1833 I met Ludwig Schunke and in 1834 I lost him. The combination, which itself was entangled within my engagement to, and then my disengagement from, Ernestine von Fricken, if I remember her name correctly, drove me mad. Two years later my mother died. This did not drive me mad. Perhaps that was because at the very same time, my love for Clara Wieck, and hers for me, was acknowledged in the most blissful possible manner. Indeed, I sought life in her arms on my way toward the embrace of the death of my mother. I was madly in love and thus believed that my mind had been freed forever from madness itself. But I hadn't reckoned with her father. His opposition to our love drove me as mad as did his concurrent approval of my compositions. I'm sure you read about us in the newspapers. We married when she was one day shy of legal age. I surrounded the marriage, on both sides, with music, huge outpourings of music that so long as I was writing it seemed to hold off madness. That and the love of my wife. Who could have guessed that such legal and religious sanction as is granted by state and church would prove so aphrodisiac. And yet, the very avidity of my music- and love-making drove me mad again. Overworked in the former, I accelerated the latter. We had our first child. I wrote my chamber works for strings. I stopped writing. This produced in me a different kind of frenzy—it remained within and ate away at me from the inside out. An artist at work is merely mad; an artist not at work is wholly mad. At the end of 1843, I couldn't sleep and yet awoke each morning swallowing my tears in great draughts trailing from my eyes. I accompanied her tour of Russia—four months in Russia! It was winter. We froze—where was the eiderdown! I stopped speaking there. People would ask me questions, and I would pull my hair over my eyes and whistle. She answered for me—I loved to hear her French. When one's lover speaks in a language not her own, she embodies an unorthodoxy quite alluring. She became pregnant for the third time in Russia. Three times in three years! By now we should have sixteen children. If Russia did not make me mad, and it did, returning to Germany should have. And it did. I was dragged around like a disease in search of a cure. We went up the Ramberg, and when I looked down I went mad. We waltzed along the River Bode before descending into the Baummannshöle. I thought of the stalactites as alive, giving forth resounding snorts of endless troubled sleep in which I heard the sounds of Faust's Walpurgis Night. I was hypnotized and magnetized and hydroized and Dresdenized. But it was only through the study of fugues that I became better. Counterpoint demands a concentration worthy of the dead. But in 1846 I went mad again— there was a singing, humming, ringing in my ears as I wrote my second symphony. The bassoon in the adagio became a woeful sound that trailed me like a tail. I itched all over but could not reach to scratch because of vertigo. I took the cure at Norderney and stood with Clara in the baths as the water turned red between her legs and our child swam away invisible. I went quite mad all over again. In Vienna too, that year, where she played my piano concerto, and the orchestra my symphony. The reception was very cold. To my music. Not to her playing of it. But she was bitter. I had never heard her so bitter. Finally I shushed her indignation and said, 'Be calm, dear Clara—in ten years it will all be different.' It is ten years now, and it is not different at all. I am still sick, and she still plays the piano beautifully. Or does she? Or am I mad to ask? They measured my head that year. Dr. Helbig wanted to make a plaster cast of it. I would not let him but caused him great jealousy when I allowed Dr. Noël to perform a phrenological examination in which he read my head like someone looking for crab lice. Every furrow traced, every fissure tracked, every burgschrund skied and burrowed, every mole and pimple squirmed, every invisible worm sought in vain. And when it was all over ... when I had been measured and fractionalized and proportionated, Dr. Noël came to the conclusion, upon the evidence of my very own head, that I am ridden with music and with anxiety. Music and anxiety! Anxiety and music! Dr. Richard Noël must be a genius! Who would have guessed! Music and anxiety. Then came the war. I loved the war. The worse the world, the better I. If that were true for everyone, we'd have no war and I'd be miserable all the time instead of every other year. Have you noticed, doctor? I went mad almost every even-numbered year. Until the war. The revolution saved me. We moved to Düsseldorf, and then I wasn't mad again until 1851. We lost another unborn child in 1852. I went quite mad. I lost my job. I went quite mad. Brahms arrived. I recovered completely. You see, doctor, I didn't want to die. I tried to kill myself precisely because I wanted to live. Doctor? Doctor Richarz? Are you awake?"

"If I told you I had gone to sleep in order to listen to you, what would you say?"

"I'd say you'd gone mad."

"And yet you expect me to accept that you tried to kill yourself because you wanted to live?"

"Suicide is always a great crying out for life."

"Such is the madness of madness."

April 7, 1855

Beloved Clara,

I have been reading in my magazines of the death in January of Gérard de Nerval. I sit up in my bed surrounded by innumerable magazines. They swim across and flop upon my legs like stingrays, begging for attention at the price of pain. One ignores magazines at his peril—they multiply with suffocating regularity. (Johannes even sends me back issues of the Signale.) The most recent issue (at least that I have received) of Dwight's Musical Journal from America says—I have it open to the very insult—"Joachim is injuring himself with the amount of study he accords to the work of Schumann." When you next speak to Pepi (I am allowed to call him that in the privacy of the nuthouse), please express in a single breath my regrets and my gratitude. Remind him how often people said of you, 'What is she doing with Schumann?' when the reference was not even to the man.

When I read of Nerval, I wept. Not for him. For you. I have always thought of him as your lover, "my Nerval," as you called him, and so did I tease you with him for all our years since first you went to Paris. La Revue de Paris prints his letters of love to Jenny Colon, which I could not read without imagining they were to you. In this sense, I am Nerval.

Our lives are parallel. The year I married you was the year he first went mad. Perhaps he knew somehow he'd lost the chance at you forever. He was put into the madhouse of a doctor named Esprit Blance. But it was Nerval who became the esprit, like Plato's bird I told you of. Heine called him "pure soul."

And then, the year we moved to Düsseldorf (which proved that a city can be worse than an insane asylum), Nerval moved back into Esprit Blance's. And then two years later, when I went truly mad, so did he yet again, so that as I was coming here, he was going back again to his own Endenich.

But they let him out for good! He put a blue ribbon round the neck of his pet lobster and walked him through the gardens of the Palais-Royal. He put his hat on the head of a hippo in the Jardin des Plantes and said he would have provided his pants too if there were room for the hippo's ass. He kept around his neck like a cravat an old apron-tie he insisted had been the corset-string of Madame de Maintenon. He threw away what little money he had—literally; into the air, in public, all of it. He slept in the streets without his tepee.

It was that apron-tie with which he hanged himself off the grating of a flophouse on that same street in Paris where you first saw prostitutes, rue de la Vielle Lanterne. Do you not see the parallel with my own flophouse in Vienna? On Schön*laterne*gasse!

A raven, I read, hovered above his corpse. It was not Nerval's raven. But his lobster had run off somewhere. The hippo was in the zoo, no doubt, unaware of the fact that the man who had given him his hat was dead. But there was the raven, floating just off the hair of Nerval's hanging head, saying the only words it had apparently been taught: "J'ai soif. J'ai soif."

The same words I taught you when you were a little girl! Is it not amazing. That I should have been your Nerval all along.

I see Heine has written to him, beyond the grave, "Poor child, you deserve every tear shed on your behalf."

So do we all.

Tell our Brahms—your Brahms, my Brahms—that I shall not forget his twenty-second birthday a month hence.

Comme un oiseau,

Gérobert

From the Daily Endenich Log of Dr. Franz Richarz, May 7, 1855

All day Robert was unsettled. He spouted nonsense loudly and rapidly. When he walked in the garden, such drivel was accompanied by fierce gesticulations. It was not his usual talking to himself. He looked to be trying to fly away. Or to tear away that impenetrable veil that secretes reality from such fanciful notions of beneficent retribution as are entertained by the insane. Back in his rooms, he played the piano for nearly two hours, banging at it crazily and screaming all the while. It made no difference whether we observed him privately through the window in his wall or entered the room and stood by him like a normal audience at a musical soirée. He seemed as unaware of us as of himself or of the sounds he was producing. I cannot call it music. It was the destruction of music. In it I hear the destruction of its maker. (These notes are no place for such sentiment, but I am compelled to add that I am heartsick at the contemplation of this loss. Of music! Of him! Lost! I know no other way to put it.) If music itself could commit suicide, so would it sound. After dinner (which I should record he ate with unruly passion and in amounts unusual even for man who no longer seems to care about his size), he was violent with one of his attendants—he forced him from the room by threatening him with a chair. Feeling that neither the usual copper levigation nor even choloform would sedate him, I gave him an injection of morphine. If only his will to live remained as strong as his will to remain awake. His pattern of insomnia is such that he is touched by sleep at night as often as the rest of us (if I may be unscientific for a moment) are touched by an archangel in daylight. For he did not sleep despite so powerful a drug. He ranted and raved without interruption, in words that could not be understood. Not one of them. Yet they did not sound like nonsense syllables. He sounded drunk, though he was not or we would not have introduced within him the morphine to the wine he'd taken with his huge dinner. Once again, he threatened his attendants when they tried to calm and then to restrain him. I did not want to jacket him. So I withdrew, only to stare at him through the window in the wall until I fell asleep.

Bruhl

JUNE 4, 1855
I had been longing for Johannes.
Clara Schumann

"It's good to meet you finally, Frau Schumann."

"And you, Doctor Richarz."

"Why Brühl?"

"I don't understand."

"Why not Endenich?"

"You don't want me at Endenich."

"Why did you express no *desire* to come to Endenich?"

"Let me repeat what I said, Dr. Richarz: You don't want me at Endenich. Is that not so?"

"Madam, a woman of your renown and, I am told through the world but sadly not through my own experience, your musical abilities would be welcome at Endenich any time. I've never tried to persuade you not to come to Endenich. I've merely said I've not been able to permit you to visit your husband at Endenich."

"And why would I want to visit Endenich if not to see my husband?"

"To see where he lives, perhaps. To see how he lives. It is a beautiful setting. It is not at all—"

"My friend tells me."

"Herr Brahms?"

"Herr Brahms. He and my husband . . ."

"I know. It is very good for your husband to have such a friend. He's the only person your husband seems genuinely to want to see. Others have come, you know." He consulted his papers. "Your own mother, of course, though that was over a year ago. And she has not returned."

"You would not allow her to see him!"

"Oh, she saw him."

"She did?"

"*Saw* him. Saw him only. I couldn't permit her to spend time in his presence."

"She never spoke of seeing him."

Dr. Richarz waved Schumann's file as if to dispell both truth and falsehood.

"Perhaps what she saw was not worthy of mention."

"This is my husband you're speaking of!"

"I meant, Frau Schumann, his actions. Not his person."

"Who else?"

"I beg your pardon."

"Who else has seen him ... *visited* him?"

"Herr Joachim. Herr Grimm, whose name belies his cordiality, though he seems neither the musician nor the intimate to your husband that Herr Brahms is. And there was just last month that old woman who is renowned for her affair with Goethe perhaps two hundred years ago. She called me—"

"Bettina von Arnim."

"A shame that her name should be so well known. She called me—"

"That she is allowed to visit, and I am not!"

"Her effect upon your husband is negligible. Which is evidenced by the fact that she called me—"

"My derrière was more intimate with Goethe than her entire body."

"I beg your pardon."

"Goethe touched me when I was very young."

"Where?"

"Need I be more specific? Is there a medical term that might help you to—"

"What *city*? Where did you *meet* so great a man? He is one of those whose death casts into doubt his ever having actually lived."

"Weimar."

"Charming place."

"Until Liszt moved there."

"You know Liszt as well! I saw him at the dedication of—"

"Herr Brahms told me he walked there with my husband."

"Yes. It's our principal form of recreation at Endenich—to walk into Bonn to pay homage to Beethoven."

"That's not Beethoven. It's a lump of stone, as Mendelssohn called it ... you needn't ask ... yes, he was our friend as well. If you want to pay homage to a musician, do so with Robert Schumann."

"I do."

"How? By keeping me from him?"

"By keeping him from you, perhaps."

"You won't let him come home. Do you also keep his letters from reaching me?"

"How could you imagine such a thing!"

"I haven't heard from him since May fifth." She produced the letter from her handbag and put it on the table between them. It remained in its envelope.* "He writes of being ill at ease but does not explain. He says there will be another letter to follow in two days. That would make it the birthday of our friend. He thought he'd missed the birthday. But he hadn't. He would have been right on time. But the letter never came."

"May seventh, then?"

"The birthday, yes."

He looked at his file.

"He was not well on May seventh. Perhaps this explains why."

"The birthday of our friend should bring him joy, not trouble. He sent Chohannes himself a happy note, together with the gift of the manuscript of *Bride of Messina*."

"And what did you give Herr Brahms for his birthday?"

"What one always gives—books. Some Dante. Some Ariosto. He may look too beautiful to be bookish. Too exuberant to be imagined in repose with a book on his lap and a cigarette in his hand. But he adores our library. If he weren't so busy with the children and household matters, I'm sure he would spend more time there than at the piano. Though I did write him for his birthday a Romance in B Minor.** When he plays it, I . . ."

"Yes?"

"I don't find longing as thrilling as he does. I told him so. He's not too young to understand me, but he's too young to understand himself. Longing brings me nothing but pain. So when I hear him play my own piece, it makes my heart tremble with almost unspeakable sadness. I can't imagine going through that again."

"Then he shouldn't play it for you."

"Oh, doctor, it's not his playing it; it's my writing it. There's a luxury in hearing one's music that quite overtakes the melancholy."

"I should like to ask you more about Herr Brahms."

---

*The last letter she would receive from her husband.

**The last piece for solo piano she would write.

{ 418 }

"More than what I might have given him for his birthday? Didn't you think I might find that question presumptuous?"

"And yet you answered it with such easiness."

"I have nothing to hide."

"And you hide nothing?"

"That's not the same thing. But what I hide, I hide in plain sight. Do I not? He lives with us. He cares for us. I travel with him when I can and miss him terribly when I can't. We see people together. What they make of us is not my concern. My friends lecture me about him. They tell me to pray and read the Bible. I prefer to read his letters — they contain more solace and virtue than any bible. Jenny Lind tells me she hates his music; it's full, she says, of what she calls mistaken tendencies. But it's *my* mistaken tendencies she means to cite. And I have a very good blind friend, who says she cannot stand the sight of him. Rosalie may have a greater sense of humor than Jenny, but she's just as rigid in her orthodoxy and the condemnation of me and of him that it incites. Yet it's he, who turns my friends against me, who is the best friend I've ever had. And my husband's too."

"As I said, no one who comes to your husband is welcomed like Herr Brahms. They are like father and son, with the young one the father. And the son, as sons will, adoring the father with unashamed reverence and need."

"He loves him."

"It is very good of him to visit. When—?"

"I meant that my husband loves my friend."

"He also understands that you love him too."

"I have loved my husband since the first moment I laid eyes on him."

"I meant that your husband understands that you love the same man he loves."

"I love him as I've never loved any man."

Dr. Richarz leaned toward her across the table. He was trembling quite as if he were the topic of conversation.

"And your husband?"

"I love him as I've never loved any man."

"I see."

"If you do, then you ought to be wise enough to cure my husband."

"When I say I see what you're saying, I merely mean I hear what you say. I make no claims to wisdom in the matter. It's hard enough for me to attempt to understand how body and mind relate; the heart, if I may use so primitive a term for the emotions, is quite beyond me. Or anyone else, I suspect. We have no doctors of the heart. For its troubles and its tempests,

{ 419 }

there are no cures and no fit counsel. So, yes, I might cure your husband one day, but never you."

"Cure him, and you'll cure me."

"Only of your suffering. But who will cure you of your joy?"

"What I suffer from is joy."

"It's a wonder you aren't mad as well."

"Yes, isn't it?"

She prepared to leave. They said nothing more until Dr. Richarz, opening the door for her, slowly completed a question he had begun to ask: "Your husband has taken a turn for the worse ever since what I now realize was the young man's birthday. Birthdays are strange occasions in an asylum. They mark a sense of life's end as much as its beginning. Every birth foretells a death, but to the insane such prescience is immediate. Life can become so precious that one throws it away for fear of losing it. I think it would benefit your husband to have a visit from Herr Brahms, if only so he not miss him so much. When do you suppose that might be?"

"He and I are leaving soon to walk the Rhine."

"Perhaps your husband will be able to spot you through his window."

"My answer to such sarcasm, doctor, would be to throw myself through his window, should you only permit me that or any other visit. But we are not coming up the river in this direction. We are heading for the Neckar Valley. And on to Heidelberg."

"I hope you have a wonderful trip."

"By the way, doctor—I know what Frau von Arnim called you. She writes to me. Everyone who visits my husband writes to me. You have no secrets from me when it comes to my husband."

"She called me a hypochondriac. I don't think she knows what it means."

"Whatever she meant by it, she was referring to your failure to cure my husband."

"If so, then there is a secret."

"And what might that be?"

He said nothing more and headed back to Endenich, twenty-three kilometers distant, while she rode off in the opposite direction.

September 4, 1855

Dearest Robert,

Our anniversary approaches yet again, and I anticipate, in fear, the silence I have experienced from you for the past four months. Please do not let the day go by without some word. I know a date by itself is of mere symbolic importance, but to me the day we were joined in marriage is the day my life began.

Do not forget our new address, which I have sent you before to no avail: 135 Poststrasse, where Johannes has a room of his own on the first floor and makes such music there as to reach all the way to you (if only you could hear it).

A week or two ago we had a terrible thunderstorm that seemed to last all night (worse than the night Marie was born or, I wager, the one when Beethoven died).* The children were so frightened they went right to Johannes. First the little ones, then the big girls. He took Ferdinand and Ludwig on his knees, and the baby in his arms, but soon everyone wanted such comfort and courage. He made room for us all.

I am leaving next month to play in various cities but will return home briefly for Christmas and can only wish you will too. Before New Year's I shall have to leave again, this time for Vienna. It will be nearly ten years since we went with Marie and Elise. I shall play your music and Beethoven's, and if the Viennese still cannot appreciate it I shall never play there again.

Please, I beg of you, write back to me even if it's only one word. It matters not what the word is, so long as the word is yours, addressed to me,

Your beloved wife,
Clara

September 10, 1855

Dear Frau Schumann,

Your husband is unable to answer your letter of September 4. Far from showing improvement, he has been declining in health. We do all we can to keep him comfortable, and we continue to try to understand what is causing his illness. But I can no longer hold out any hope whatsoever of a full recovery. You would be wise to begin to come to terms with this difficult prognosis and its meaning to your life.

Yours sincerely,
Franz Richarz

---

*On March 26, 1827, during a violent storm, Beethoven shook his fist at the sky in the midst of a peal of thunder so great it pierced even his deafness. Having thus conducted the music of heaven, he fell back dead.

January 6, 1856

Dear Pepi,

It is three years exactly since our debacle in Hanover. As I am not one to let an anniversary pass without celebration, allow me to thank you again for canceling my string quartet and saving us both the embarrassment we suffered over my Fantasie. What a shame the critics were as deaf as King George was blind.

I have written you before with sympathetic ink and am doing so now between these visible lines. Be sure to hold this letter over heat in order to find those words I want no one else to see.

I understand from the doctors that you have suggested I be galvanized. I appreciate your concern for my health. My fear, however, is that these quacks will hook me up to the electrostimulation machine at the same time they are giving me one of their endless enemas ("endless" repetitive, not "endless" continuous). That's all I need—dynamized turds. That's all *they* need!

As it is, I am fed the selfsame calomel given at the end of *his* life to my much adored and much mourned Schunke. It is both diuretic and sialogogue, so that I am the very model of a baroque fountain, albeit one perpetually in the wind, spraying from distant latitudes. It's a remedy for whores, I suppose, but whores' *what*?

I am also now and then threatened with the application of mustard plasters as a form of counterirritation. Imagine—to attack pain with pain. They might as well cut off one's head to put an end to doubt and misgiving.

I have been working on several pieces. A reduction of your Heinrich overture and piano accompaniment for the Paganini Caprices. My dream is that the two of you arrive together to play for me. My own music is now silent—at least outwardly.

Where is Johannes? Is he with you now? Is he flying high or only under flowers? I should dearly love to be at his side on his flight over the world. Does he still allow no trumpets or timpani to resound? Tell him to remember how Beethoven begins his symphonies and then do the same thing. He must *begin*—that's the main thing. Once you've begun, the end arrives to meet you. Just like life itself.

Where is Johannes? (Forgive me. I didn't mean to repeat that in visible ink but am too weary to write this whole thing over in order to hide it.)

Yours,

Robert Schumann

Endenich

JANUARY 11, 1856
*I could spend a whole day calling you beloved
and still not have said enough.*
Johannes Brahms

Schumann sat at the square piano. With his vest unbuttoned and his sleeves rolled up and ashes from his smoldering cigar flecked upon his shirt front, he looked like a student again. His hair, unwashed and oily enough to ignite from his cigar, was wholly black still, unusual for a man of forty-five and almost freakish for a man of forty-five in an institution like this, where hair went gray as if it were required in the regimen of cure. Indeed, Dr. Richarz considered it a bad sign when hair did not go gray, for it meant the patient was fighting mightily against the dispersion of stress. Stress did not literally rise up out of the head, but, as a consequence of the intransigent intimacy of mind and body, it seemed to, turning the hair gray, or even white, on its way out. Antonio Vivaldi's red hair, Schumann had told him, had not gone gray either, and he was in his sixties when he died, disordered from his prodigality, far away from home, in Vienna, where Clara was at this very moment and so was Vivaldi, but no one knew where, because his grave, like Mozart's, was unmarked, and why not, for we are all walking tombstones and might perhaps prefer a little anonymity once we've pitched.

Schumann's hands flew over the keys of the piano, as the saying went, but in truth they flew across the keys, upon the keys, *into* the keys, and therein lay the problem. What he played was unbearable, as if the mind from which it issued were totally paralyzed.

"Bravo," interrupted Dr. Richarz.

Schumann ceased in what seemed mid-note.

"Fugues. Shall I take up where I left off?"

"How could you?"

"That is one of the magic properties of fugues. They seem unstructured to the ear but to the mind are structured to the breaking point. I can prove it. Shall I take up where I left off?"

"Please."

Schumann poised his hands over the keyboard.

Dr. Richarz locked open his mouth as a way to reduce his hearing.

"So where did I leave off?"

"*I'm* to tell you that?"

"Of course. You're the one who heard it."

"I'm to tell you what *note*?"

"Not what note. What difference does the note make? I want the sound. Sing it for me up to where I stopped. I'll take it from there."

"I couldn't possibly."

"Embarrassed to sing in public?"

"I sing in church."

"That's not singing. That's conforming. Here, this is singing. This is how you sing a fugue: *da da da da, dadadadadadada, da da da da, dadadadadadada, da dadadadadadada, da dadadadadadada, da da, da da, da da, dadadada.* There. You see. A fugue. Fugues are my therapy. I've told you how when I was young I copied out every note of the *Art of the Fugue* and when I was finished I was purged of all madness. Fugues offer a vision of perfection with none of perfection's perfection. They are the ideal parent, strict and forgiving at once. Elastic and secure. And they come with many voices, just like me!"

"Yes, I remember—*Fugenpassion.*"

"Forget *Fugenpassion—Fugenwut!*"*

"But perhaps it's when passions become frenzies that the mind becomes ill. Think of politics."

"Yes, but think of love."

"Frenzy?"

"The mind must match the body in the idiom of love. It must *explode!*"

"But Endenich is where people come when their minds *have* exploded."

---

*Fugal passion; fugal frenzy. Schumann had learned that the study of counterpoint, so demanding in its formality, might ease the informality of madness, its, literally, derangement. And so he studied both the influential theoretical work of Friedrich Marpurg (who when he was not theorizing upon fugues was, as if to balance inevitability with improbability, director of the Prussian State Lottery) and what Schumann called his "grammar," Bach's *Well-Tempered Clavier,* whose fugues he claimed could strengthen one's very morality (by which he meant not behavior but the purity of one's relationship to art). In 1845, when terrifying thoughts had brought him to the "verge of despair," he was advised by Clara to write fugues of his own. This he did for both the piano and the pedal-piano, which had an extra set of strings and hammers and which Schumann, in the midst of his *Fugenwut,* believed would become a standard in the catalog of indispensable musical instruments. As much as he valued the study of the fugue, Schumann was also fond of quoting the following anonymous definition of same: a composition in which one voice races away from the others—and the listener from them all.

"Or when their minds have . . . what is the opposite of 'explosion'?"

"Implode, I suppose."

"No . . . *recoil*—that's what I mean! Do you have any idea what it feels like to go mad?"

"Yes, I have some idea."

"Do you have any knowledge?"

"I know the symptoms, certainly."

"But the feeling?"

"No, not the feeling, I'm happy to say."

"Shall I tell you?"

"Of course."

"It feels like this."

Schumann brought both fists down violently upon the keys of the piano, knuckles first. He held them there so the sound was sustained in his small sitting room and then removed one finger at a time so the absonant chord he made was decomposed note by note until there was a tiny sound in the air that finally, though he kept that one finger down upon the key, dissolved.

"Look at your hands!"

His knuckles were bloodied. There was also a smear of red visible upon the white keys.

"You ask me to look, and I ask you to hear. We remain far apart in our approach to my madness. Now bring me some paper. Music paper. There's something small I want to write down."

"I know what it is."

"What?"

"What you just played."

"My fugue?"

"No. That chord. That chord you say represents your madness."

Schumann stared at the end of his cigar. He shook his head. He touched the end of a finger to it. He shook his head again.

"Don't worry. I have the chord memorized. You can't think much of my future as a composer if you think I would ask for music paper in order to write down a single chord."

"For what, then?"

"I'm writing songs again. Songs for my distant beloved."

"Ah, Beethoven." Dr. Richarz smiled the proud little smile of the allusion-savvy.

"Well, these are really my own. Shall I sing you one? Don't worry—I won't smear the blood all over the piano. I'll just sing. Listen."

Oh, won't you come to Endenich
Or would that not be politic
For you to come to Endenich
To see your favorite lunatic?

I beg you come to Endenich
And I suggest you get here quick
So that you'll be here in the nick
Of time left me in Endenich.

It's not a place that you might pick
To come to whether well or sick
But judge me not a heretic...
We all end up in Endenich!

Schumann found a match in his pocket and lit his cigar with it, nodding all the time at Dr. Richarz as if simultaneously to solicit and to influence his opinion of the song.

Dr. Richarz touched the index finger of each hand to the meatus of each ear. "As you know, my hearing—"

"That's no excuse! Don't you know the old saying that musicians love to quote after performances by their rivals?—Never blame the hearing for what the heart detests."

"Detests? I didn't detest it. I merely thought..."

"Thought? I ask you to listen, and you *think*!"

"I thought it was not true—we do not all end up in Endenich."

Schumann laughed. "Oh, I don't mean *here*." He swept his arm around to take in the entire institution, leaving a trail of smoke and ashes floating in the air. "I meant...*Endenich*. Not your Endenich. Not *my* Endenich. But Endenich. Who can deny *that*? 'We all end up in Endenich,'" he sang the last sentence.

"But will she like it? Will she not be terribly disturbed by it?"

"Who?"

"Your distant beloved."

"And who might that be?"

"She...her...your wife."

"And you think this song is addressed to her?"

"Is it not?"

"'Beloved' is not singular, sir. I address it to everyone. After all, we all end up in Endenich."

Dr. Richarz rose, shaking his head. "I hesitate to bring you paper on which to write down such a song."

"Oh, I'm not planning to write out this song. I'm still composing this song. In my mind. You remember my mind. You used to visit it with some regularity. Before you became more enraptured by my poor body. No, it's not this song. It's another. Shall I sing it to you?"

"Absolutely not!"

"It's not mine. It's nearly three hundred years old. I'm merely harmonizing it. I'm doing my own little setting. Bach did three of this same piece. I told you it was just something small. My Endenich piece is not small. It's less than small. But this piece is merely small."

"What is it?"

"A hymn."

"I like hymns."

"I should think you would. Shall I play it?"

"I don't trust you, Herr Schumann."

"I should think you wouldn't."

Schumann turned his back on Dr. Richarz and placed his hands on the keyboard. His knuckles were now more raw than bloody, but the blood on the keys themselves seemed somehow not to have dried, and he moved it with the tips of his fingers to whatever note he played, as he sang,

> When my final hour is at hand
> To leave this blessed earth
> I beg Thee Lord Jesus Christ
> To comfort me in my suffering.
> Lord, my heart at the end
> I entrust into Thy hands.
> Thou well knowest how to protect it.

Endenich

APRIL 15, 1856
If only Johannes had been with me,
he would have provided comfort.
Clara Schumann

Schumann bent his weak, thin frame slowly toward the floor and touched the bright gold-red end of his cigar to a corner of the gauzy paper on which his wife's hand lay. The paper quickly caught and gathered to a fist, consuming her hand and all the words it spoke. From it, other papers caught, and more from them, until even the prayer rug beneath them began to burn, and he screamed, "Fire!"

Herren Nämlich and Niemand burst into his sitting room. They, too, screamed, "Fire!" but to each other, as if they needed to confirm such madness before they could act to douse its consequences.

Together they went into the bedroom and emerged with two vessels, one filled with water and the other with urine.

"Wait!"—they hesitated only because this was one order no human being could ignore, however briefly. "Let them burn."

Herr Nämlich poured on the water and Herr Niemand the urine. The smoke of the burning paper and wool of the rug, which had been sweet, immediately became bitter, sour, with the smell not of flesh but of its waste.

Schumann puffed on his cigar. Nothing issued from it but a slight sprinkling of ash that fell into the fire and disappeared into its greater ash.

"I merely wanted time to light up. Either of you have a match?"

They grasped him and held him until they seemed to realize together that in this posture they were unable to summon aid.

Herr Niemand let go only after he had put both his hands over Herr Nämlich's and squeezed them even harder into their grip upon Schumann's arms.

When Herr Niemand returned to Schumann's suite, he had Dr. Richarz by the arm, pulling him into the room as he might a surgeon into surgery.

"What have you done!"

"Fire," said Schumann.

"You might have..." Dr. Richarz thrust his hand up and out from his body until he held all of Endenich in his mindful palm.

Schumann shook his head. "It was I who called, 'Fire!' "

"And you who started it."

"Actually, it was my cigar."

"What have you done here?"

"I will confess it, then: Started a fire."

"For what purpose?"

"To burn my papers."

"So these were not for conflagration only? They were not incendiaries toward a graver purpose?"

"Grave enough, this."

"What papers were they?"

"Music. Unfinished music. But unlike Gogol, I—"

"What else?"

"What else is there?"

Dr. Richarz kneeled by the fire. He blew on his fingers before raking them through the corona of ash.

"This appears to be your wife's stationery."

"Impossible!"

"You haven't burned your wife's letters, then?"

"How could I?"

"How could you, indeed. And the prayer rug?"

"Because this was a sacred holocaust. Also, it was so very beautiful. The rug, I mean. Not the fire. The fire smells like piss."

"Your music . . . your wife's letters . . . what does this mean?"

"Nothing. It means nothing."

"Then why would you do it?"

"I told you—it means nothing."

"You did it because it means nothing, or it means nothing that you did it?"

"Clearly, doctor, we differ about the meaning of *nothing*."

"What does it mean to you?"

"It means nothing. Therefore, it means everything. Otherwise, why would I do this?"

"Destroy your past? Is that it?"

"I was thinking more of the future."

Endenich

APRIL 16, 1856

Can I wish him back to me in this state?

Clara Schumann

The sitting room still smelled of smoke and wet ash and urine. This odor had spread to the bedroom, where Schumann was being administered an enema by Herren Nämlich and Niemand. They permitted him to kneel with his head in his pillow, which eased the insertion of the tube and allowed them, at the proper time (if such an expression may be used), to swing him back like a pendulum and hold him over the bedpan, which they had stationed at the end of the mattress.

Dr. Richarz waited at the foot of the bed for his specimen.

"This is the last shit you're getting from me," said Schumann.

"I beg your pardon."

"Is it that you can't hear me or you distrust what you've heard?"

"Your voice is muffled by the pillow. And my hearing isn't at its best today after yesterday's tumult. Why don't you just wait till you've gone to speak to me."

"Gone where?"

"You know perfectly well what I mean."

"This is the last shit you're getting from me!"

"That's what I thought you said."

"Half the time you study my shit, and half the time you study my brain. What kind of life is that?"

"I'm a doctor. I do what's—"

"I meant for *me*. What kind of life is that for *me*?"

"I'm only trying to help you, Herr Schumann. After two years, I still have no idea where your illness originates."

"Well, if it's in my ass, you can stop looking. No more enemas."

"There's no need for vulgarity."

"Tell that to *them*. They're the ones sniffing around my ass."

Without his usual warning, which consisted of the involuntary moans and groans and grunts of the enemaed, Schumann let go.

Herren Nämlich and Niemand were taken aback, literally.

Dr. Richarz, far more experienced in the subterfuges of the involuntarily invaded, merely commented rhetorically, "What have you been eating?"

{ 430 }

"Nothing."

"Why?"

"Heinrich Heine is dead in Paris."

"When did you learn of this?"

"Yesterday. But he died—"

"I know when he died."

"And you've kept the news from me? For two months?"

"Not long enough, clearly. Is that why you've burned your papers?"

"No. But it's why I'm not eating."

"Did he stop eating?"

"The opposite. He said the only way he was able to kill himself was to starve himself to death, and that was against his principles. He was too weak to do anything else. But I'm not too weak to do something else. So I choose to do the one thing he could do but would not."

"I fail to follow the logic of that. It's madness."

"What's mad is to look for logic in suicide."

"There's always logic in suicide, Herr Schumann. Only death itself is illogical.

"Clean him up!" he ordered Herren Nämlich and Niemand.*

----

*Heinrich Heine had died in Paris on February 17, after eight years in bed, so paralyzed in the end that starvation remained the only possible means for him to hasten his death. (Even his eyelids were paralyzed; he had them propped open with matchstick fragments in order to read.) Earlier he had contemplated hanging, poison, defenestration, gunshot, and an overdose of the morphine, of which he already was administered seven grains every twenty-four hours, for which purpose moxas were burned along his spine for cauterization and the morphine rubbed into the open wounds. This was painful, but its after-effect was the opposite, which is to say he felt not pleasure but nothing. This Jewish convert to Christianity, who was accused by his critics of having no religion whatsoever and offended everyone by saying that when he died God would pardon him because that was God's job, proclaimed he did indeed have one: opium. Lying in bed, he relinquished his dark fantasy of escaping to America, where, he wrote, "there are no lords and no aristocracy, where all men are equal, that is to say, equally brutish, except of course for several million people with black or brown skin who are treated like dogs." He even gave up his fantasy of walking again on avenue Matignon when one day his wife had pushed his bed near the window and he looked down at a dog pissing on a tree and realized he envied the dog. It was the last time he looked out the window at anything, even the sky. His wife, who would leave Paris before his funeral and not return for several months, left more and more of his care to the young and beautiful Camille Selden, whom Heine called, as if she were some mark of beauty on the ugly face of humanity, La Mouche, and for whom at the end of his life he wrote a poem called "La Mouche" that reminded Schumann of his own

Endenich

APRIL 30, 1856
Your letters are like kisses.
Johannes Brahms

Dr. Richarz and Brahms sat back to back in the dos-à-dos, while Schumann lounged in the fauteuil with an atlas on one thigh and a large notebook on the other. He was dressed in his bedclothes, which hung loosely from his shoulders and his knees, though the slimness of a middle-aged man that emerged out of evaporated fat was visibly orbed and quaggy. As he bent over writing in the notebook, he chanted, "*Babababababababadadadadadada, babababababababadadadadadada.*"

"You see what I mean," whispered Dr. Richarz directly into Brahms's ear.

For once, the strange configuration of the dos-à-dos was of some use, as it allowed discreet conversation without forcing the confabulators to engage in any direct visual intercourse, though Dr. Richarz, when he moved his lips back from Brahms's ear, tried to wrap his gaze around the delicate maiden-like profile of this exceptionally beautiful young man.

"Does he say nothing else?"

"He eats almost nothing and says almost nothing."

"What is it he suffers from?"

"What is gone from his life—you, when you are not here; his wife; his music; the children; pleasure from the body; pleasure from—"

"Forgive me, doctor. I meant, what disease does he have?"

"As I told you when I summoned you, we feel he's become incurable. Of what, we have no idea. What cannot be diagnosed cannot be cured. As you can observe, his brain is unquestionably exhausted, but we have no evidence that it has softened. His body is exhausted. But that's because he won't eat. One day he says his food is poisoned, and the next he claims

---

desire for Clara to appear before he died, as Heine's image of La Mouche reminded Schumann of Clara as a girl, for whom he had been paralyzed in his desire:

> I waited for you yesterday in vain
> Until darkness became kind
> And hid your absence in my pain
> And my pain in the loss of my mind.

we're feeding him the excrement of other patients. From time to time, he takes some wine, and some jellied consommé, but they don't sustain him. He'd die if we weren't able to nourish him gastrically."

"What other way is there to be nourished?"

"Permit me to spare you the details."

"Shall I ask him myself?"

Now Dr. Richarz turned even from the beauty of Brahms's face and whispered toward the open window that brought in spring breezes from the greening of the distant Siebengebirge. "Through a gastric tube we introduce food into his stomach."

"What kind of food?"

"Decoctions of meat, which are very healthy and energizing, though he won't keep them down. Milk, of course. Saltwater for the sodium. Sometimes even wine. Though, as I said, he takes wine on his own, quite a bit of it, he calls it save, a word from Chaucer, so he claims, though he makes no claims it saves him, merely produces oblivion, which sometimes seems to me in my darkest moments the only salvation there might be for all of us. Usually he takes it—the wine, I mean—with tobacco, though I worry he will set himself on fire even before he manages to starve himself to death. He purports to be one Erysichthon and gnaws on his toenails as if to mock me with such spurious nutrition."

"He professes Erysichthon to be sacred—the god of artists," said Brahms lightly, proud to be unburdened of a bit of scholarship that also demonstrated more than a little intimacy with the professor himself. "But tell me—where does this tube go?"

"To the stomach."

"I meant—"

"Oh, in the mouth. When, that is, he allows it. The jaw is very strong, Herr Brahms. When we cannot breach it, we must enter through the nostrils."

Brahms brought his hands protectively to his face. Dr. Richarz turned now to look at him directly, to stare at those eyes covered by those long fingers.

"There are experiments being done with rectal feeding tubes. I have so far resisted that temptation here. But if I must—"

Brahms left the dos-à-dos and walked toward Schumann, who had been silent for a time and now as Brahms approached began to speak again, not in nonsense syllables but in rhythm to the words he copied from his atlas into his notebook.

"Cologne ... Emmerich ... Frankfurt ... Hanover ... Heidelberg ... Lorelei ... Lübeck ... Neckar ... Rotterdam ... St. Goarshausen ..."

Dr. Richarz, who had cupped his ear in his hand, said, "He sits with his atlases and makes lists of places. In alphabetical order, which in its precision is confounding. He says they're places to which he wants to escape from here."

"These places he's named now are places I have described to him from my visits to them with his beloved wife."

Brahms sat down on the end of the fauteuil at Schumann's feet.

"She's in England now," he told his friend. "I took her myself to the night train for Calais. She stays in London, in Hanover Square. She's scheduled to play in Liverpool and Manchester and Dublin, but for now she's in London. I get a letter from her almost every day. She's most homesick. She says her whole heart is in Germany and that only her lifeless body is in England. She's met the queen and likes her very much but says that playing in her presence is difficult because the queen takes all attention from the music upon herself, though she doesn't mean to. Your wife says it's not easy to be the queen but it's easier to be the queen than to be someone else in the presence of the queen. Oh, good—I found that funny as well. As you will this perhaps as well: Clara was playing one night in the private home of Lord and Lady Overstone, but the guests wouldn't stop talking when she played—it must have been one of my pieces, though she was too kind to say so—so they wouldn't be quiet, as I said, and so she just stopped playing, she put her hands in her lap and just stopped playing, and soon all the talk died away and there was silence and she looked at them with that look she has that makes you feel at once ashamed of yourself and grateful to be observed with such concern. And when she got back to Hanover Square, there had arrived there already a letter from Lady Overstone herself, who apologized not only for herself and her guests but for all the English, who she said had not gained the sophistication necessary for an appreciation of German music. She also wrote me of some gossip she heard that night at the Overstones': Charles Dickens has boarded up the door between his dressing room and his wife's bedroom to help him resist the temptation to visit her. He has too many children as it is, he says. Ten, she writes me, though one died. And she would have had ten with you, she says, had not one died and two been lost before birth. And so imagine how she feels for Catherine Hogarth—that's the name of Dickens's wife—whose husband builds a wall between them. What a thing to do for love, she says. What a terrible contradiction. She says they say all London speaks of it and no one understands the ..."

As Johannes spoke of Clara, Robert began to see her, for the first time since he had left her in Düsseldorf, and to hear her voice as if she herself were reading aloud the letters the boy described, and to sense not her presence in his room but her absence from it, and from his life, his arms, his mind. Even her own letters to him had been no more than words on paper. They had not brought her back but had served to cast her farther out, in that he could read what she had written and touch the paper she had touched and because he felt nothing feel that with each passing day there was less of her in him. So he had burned her letters, to keep what little of her he had left. But still she'd fled until now, when through the tales and telling by this boy they loved her spirit returned to him, her flesh as well, because he could see her real in front of him, sense her shape in the air, her smell off his own hands, hear her voice in the boy's voice, feel her in him as he sat at his feet and gave her to him as he had given her to him. She was memory, he knew, but memory was all he had and all he'd have until he died. He was overtaken by memory, driven quite mad by it so that for the first time he felt mad, mad from within and no longer dependent on others' descriptions of his being mad. He saw her as a girl, and as a woman, and was unable to distinguish between these visions of her young and grown, and she came quite together in him then. And bitterness was replaced by knowledge.

"'Il voulait tout savoir mais il n'a rien connu.'"

"Oh, my God, now he's speaking French!" said Dr. Richarz.

"Please," Brahms whispered to Schumann.

"'He wished to know all things but discovered nothing,'" he translated her imaginary lover for the one who loved her most.

Endenich

JULY 27, 1856
My beloved, as soon as you are here again the sun will come out.
Johannes Brahms

She was in London when the news first came, and sent him lilies. They're surely dead by now, almost a month. Mercy they're called, their insides like a woman's. Like a woman's flower where Mr. Sweetfoot finds his nectar. She hasn't doubted he would note the likeness or consider it a cruelty for his memory thus to be requited. Robert is her husband and the father of her children, all of them, alive and dead and never born, and each was conceived in passion. She has feared to see him sick and shrunken as much to preserve the memory of him bonny, as they said in England, vigorous, copious, as out of fear that his diminishment will diminish her. Two years and four months and more they've been apart. Their eyes will couple like strangers'. How can they not? Intimacy, even such as they had shared that made the intimate seem merely proximate, cannot survive such distance. Time is real, it is a fence that grows, and they both fenceposts on opposing ends, each day uprooted further, pushed by now beyond their invisible horizons. She counts days as he had their ages, though not as accurately, and with loss alone to match the growth he'd so delightedly, if annoyingly, charted. Nine hundred days and nights almost, since she has seen him. If he had merely moved around the corner, she would be afraid to glimpse him in the street. But Robert is in Endenich.

She'd grown tired of London and England and Ireland when Johannes once more saved her. If it could be considered saving to summon her home for what might be the death of her husband. In the past, she had come home from her tours for the comfort of home life. There was no home life among the musicians of England. They tried to earn livings all day long, snatching a mouthful of their dreadful food whenever they could find a moment, and didn't meet to make music until late at night, when they were half dead, worn out from the burden of what passed for their lives, and what life passed them by. Their music suffered and so no doubt did their copulations. The men were limp and the women pallid.

She had been invited to England by William Sterndale Bennett, who had been the same age as Johannes when first he came into their lives twenty years ago in Leipzig and stole Robert's heart as much from Robert's cast-off Ernestine as from her. Now he was the supreme English man of music (which was saying little), married and a father, who, when he had not been conducting the orchestra accompanying her at her New Philharmonic Society concerts in London, reminisced for her and anyone else who would listen about his wild youthful days in Leipzig with Robert Schumann, drinking all night and making music all day. Whenever there was a piano nearby in someone's drawing room, he would sit at it and sing the song he'd written about Robert at the time:

> Herr Schumann is a handsome gent.
> He smoked cigars where'er he went.
> Three decades old, I would suppose,
> With short-cropped hair and a cute little nose.

She hadn't loved Sterndale Bennett young or old. Or Ludwig Schunke. Or any of the other boys or men who were handsome and talented and caused Robert to worship them as much for some ideal of manhood as for their visible energy and dissolute eyes. It is only in Johannes that their love has met in anyone aside from themselves and their children. And he had arrived at almost the last moment in which he might save them. He carries them back and forth to one another between Endenich and the world. He preserves their love over time and distance, through sickness and, soon, she knows, beyond death.

When she saw Johannes, who had come to meet her in Antwerp, she was confused. It had been their longest time apart, as every day added to the longest time she'd been apart from Robert since the day they'd met when she was eight years old. Even the ill will of her father had not been able to separate them for as long as had Endenich.

Her confusion was not between Johannes and Robert. It never had been. It was between her utter pleasure at seeing Johannes and the preparation in her body for the pain of what message he would deliver concerning Robert. They both love Robert. Robert loves both of them. She loves the two men. The two men love her. It would be a peculiarly perfect round of love were not one of them suffering and the others suffering for him.

Parting from Johannes had been the most painful yet. She'd felt stunned. When she'd written him that her body was lifeless in England, it was not merely to allude to her fidelity but to present him with an image of her wrung out, torpid, dead, so he would think of nothing but bringing her back to life. Away from him, she was like Robert, living, it would seem, for no other reason than to see him.

The news from Endenich continued bad. Johannes held her as he told her more of what he'd hinted in his letters. She could not help contrasting the warm reality of his embrace with the image he presented of her husband, whom Johannes had paid a birthday visit on June 8 and found confined to his bed, thin but for some swelling in the feet, unembarrassedly incontinent, quiet except when he coughed and trembled and said thank you for the atlas Johannes had brought to celebrate the day and because he'd asked for it, thank you and little more, recognizing him, Johannes was sure, because he smiled at him with runny eyes before he turned away to open his large new book and continue his search for some escape into the cold colors of the maps and the rigid sprinklings of tiny names. *Should I go to him?* she wondered, but not aloud, because she feared Johannes would say she should. Even Düsseldorf was too close too soon, so when she heard

Johannes say that all he'd ever seen of the sea was the closed-off sea from harbors like this one and like that of his hometown Hamburg, she insisted they go to Ostend, where they spent two nights and a day and he ran across the warm July sand of the North Sea beach like a boy, while she sat on his plaid shawl.

He is two years younger than she than she is younger than Robert. But she never thinks of him as younger than she, because she feels she has grown young with him. He quite frightened her at first, but she learned to give herself up to the truest joy in his presence. Her friends complained that he was too young for her, though they never said what they meant when they said *for her*. He isn't too young to take care of her or her children. He isn't too young to handle the finances or the help or the heat in the two winters and three autumns past or to hold together her breaking heart. She never thinks of his youth, only of his power, which stirs her and instructs her both. It is Robert who had always seemed young, almost childish, perhaps because his passions overpowered his ability to control them.

They returned to Düsseldorf together on July 6, and eight days later, at her insistence, Dr. Richarz met her in Bonn, where she begged him to escort her in his carriage or hers down the road to Endenich so she might see her husband. He refused. Doctor, she told him, no matter how bad her husband is, he could be no worse than she imagines him. Nor, to judge from what their friend told her, could his—Dr. Richarz inquired whether the friend was Herr Brahms—could his seeing her make *him* worse. And, yes, of course the friend is Herr Brahms!

Dr. Richarz seemed as confused as the rest of the world about Herr Brahms. Only she and her husband appeared to understand that Herr Brahms was no intruder between them but in fact the very mortar squeezed into the crack that had opened in their lives when Robert could no longer live at home and fled to Endenich. Johannes brought her more than news of Robert; he brought Robert himself, in his eyes and between his fingers and in the compassion of his grasp. And he took to Robert more of her than she could send in letters or any longer with her mind the way they once played music when apart and sent it to one another so it might join in the air in what she had come to realize, once Robert had truly joined himself to her, was quite a lovely facsimile of intercourse but a mere understudy in the actual role.

Even when she and Johannes had been apart, he would tell Robert they had been together. He had asked her not to be shocked at his brazen lying to her husband about seeing her when he had not. He believed, as he had written her in one of his countless letters when they actually were apart, that by telling Robert about her, and nothing but her, he could cause Robert to become filled with a longing to be hers again. He told her he would write to Robert about their summer trip together along the Rhine and describe it to him in such a way that he would be neither hurt nor distressed.

They had walked nearly a hundred miles, accompanied only by Berthe the maid, and she only because Johannes exaggerated Clara's celebrity and told her there was a danger that whatever they did together would "get into the papers," as he put it, and be regarded as improper. He was like her prudent friends in that, while she was confident enough in the strength of her love for her husband to know that her love for Johannes took nothing from that husband or anyone else, including the children, but gave them all whatever cheer there was to be gotten from her life. She had been gossiped about all her life and was aware when she performed in public that forms of gossip often took up the space of music in the minds of the people, who speculated to themselves about her clothes and her skin and her hair and those parts of her body and mind invisible to the eye and mind and the nature of her passion.

Berthe had her own bag, but she and Johannes lived out of his knapsack, which they emptied of their clothes in inns along the way and packed with food and drink for their hikes along the Lorelei cliff and up from the old gate of St. Goarshausen to the Katz Castle and into woods along the river in which they would stop for lunch and she would tell him the things that occupied her mind. As they drifted in a little flat-bottomed boat at the base of the Lorelei cliff, she held him so that if he heard the nymph sing to him, he would not, however tempted, be able to run to her. There in the tranquil valley, leaning against each other in the mass of rocks, they heard only the wind blowing lightly over grief and suffering, silencing them, there where the primrose dreamed.

Johannes himself dreamed of living with Clara and Robert and told her so at the same time he wrote that he wished to God he were allowed that day instead of writing this letter to tell her with his own lips that he was dying of love for her.

They are all dying of love. That's what love does. Requited love is no less painful than love unreturned or even unacknowledged. The more deeply two beings bore into each other, the greater the pain, not from the penetration itself but from the wound it leaves.

Dr. Richarz would not understand. He sent her away "for the good of the chidren," no longer concerned, it seemed, with what she might do to Robert or he to her. He'd given her up for lost now, lost to her husband, who had been lost to her.

But nine days later, he finally summoned her to Endenich itself, at such time as she could do no harm. The end was near, he said in his telegram. If she wished to see her husband before he died, come now.

And so she went, with Johannes, and saw Endenich for the first time. Saw Endenich but not her husband. He had improved since the telegram. Dr. Richarz apologized for the inconvenience, but he felt it best she not see him now. She was finally there, and she could not see him because he was getting better! It was only when Johannes emerged from Robert's rooms and agreed with the doctor that she left. It would not, Johannes said, kill her beloved husband to see her, as she had feared everyone there thought. And while it would not kill her to see him, it would upset her terribly. Johannes alone had been allowed to see him. He had been, for some time, the only person allowed to see him. Johannes bore all the terror of that sight, for her, for the world, and whatever she saw of her husband she must see in him.

Before returning to Düsseldorf, they walked through the Endenich garden, profuse with flowers and insects and leafy shade in the summer heat. She was tired from the trip and from the preparation in her mind to see her husband and the terrible combination of disappointment and relief that she was not to see him. All she wanted to do was leave the garden path and lie down on the grass beneath a tree with Johannes—those two trees, she pointed out the very trees and told him the story of Philemon and Baucis as Robert had always told it to the children, Philemon and Baucis who were visited by Zeus and Hermes disguised as beggars and were the only human beings who gave them food and shelter and in return were offered by these gods anything they wanted, and they said what they wanted most was to die at the same time so they would never be apart, in life or death, and their wish was granted and they were turned into trees, two trees, side by side; like your mother and me, Robert told the children, never to be apart, because we are kind to strangers and we shall love each other eternally. Johannes did not lie down with her beneath those trees but led her instead back toward the main building and showed her Robert's windows and then took her by the shoulders and turned her around so she might see what Robert saw from the other side of those windows, the river and the mountains and the arrows of the sun.

Four days after that, unsummoned by anyone but Robert himself, and by him silently, within her mind, she returned to Endenich. When she demanded one final reunion with him, and it was granted without hesitation by Dr. Richarz, she wished to flee and whispered to Johannes that perhaps so long as she did not see Robert, and he not see her, he would live. But Johannes told her that someday Robert would die, whether he saw her or not, and to die without seeing her would be to die without grace or salvation.

It is dusk when she enters his bedroom, candles lit and shadows from the half-drawn, wind-stroked drapes purling through the room and gathering her toward him. The others wait in the darker shadows by the door to his sitting room while she approaches him where he lies in bed, covered, clearly thin, almost nothing left of him but his face, which, as if he has been waiting for her all this time, since he'd been torn from her without so much as a farewell, smiles. He takes her to his eyes and smiles.

She is afraid to touch him. Afraid for both of them. But he raises a twitching, shaky arm, tangled in his sheet, until he frees it and motions for her to come closer and puts it around her as she bends to him. She cannot tell his trembling from her own. When she feels his arm weaken, she keeps it around her with her hand on his wrist, unwilling to surrender that embrace for all the treasure in the world. His breath washes across her face, uncorrupted, cleansed, and with her eyes on his she traces his features with the first finger of each hand and feels she is painting a picture of pain. Pulsing in the candlelight beside her face is the Laurens portrait of Johannes.

He tries to speak and does speak, but she cannot understand a word. He babbles, ever more loudly, until he becomes agitated and thrashes beneath the sheets. Dr. Richarz approaches and motions for the two men with him to do something to Robert, she can't imagine what, but she waves them all away and withdraws herself but only so far as the foot of the bed, upon which she lies and from which she stares up at him, scarcely daring to breathe, waiting for the silence that finally comes, so that all she can hear is his breathing and the softening sounds he makes out of which she finally understands only this: "Clara."

The next morning she and Johannes return early from the Star Family Hotel in Bonn and do not leave until dark. Most of the day they take turns looking through the window in his wall, as he lies on his bed twitching and tossing his head and ranting argumentatively and without satisfaction. Because she loves him so dearly, she prays for him to be released.

Only when she is permitted into the room and insists on feeding him does he calm down. She dips her fingers repeatedly into a jar of cold calves'-foot jelly, which, as it warms upon her fingers and in the breath she breathes upon it, reminds her of the warmth that spread from him to her, from man to woman, as they passed the nights of marriage. He sucks it off each time as if he's not eaten since last they were together at their table at home. His mouth is warm inside, his eyes ecstatic.

The day after that, July 29, Tuesday, at four in the afternoon, while she and Johannes are at the train station in Bonn to pick up Joseph Joachim so he too may be there at the end, Robert dies. A half hour later, a half hour too late, she kneels beside his bed and feels a magnificent spirit hover above her and fly off, too soon for her to be taken along.

Johannes brings her flowers from the Endenich garden. She lays them on her husband's head. As for her love, he has taken it with him.

Epilogue

Where are our lovers, our girls? They are in their tomb.
Gérard de Nerval

There were more people buried in the tiny churchyard of Bonn's Alter Friedhof than attended Schumann's funeral two days following his death. Joseph Joachim had indeed been on the train the time of whose arrival prevented Clara from being at her husband's bedside when he died; he and Brahms walked before the coffin. Clara walked behind, as did Ferdinand Hiller, who had journeyed from Cologne and who, though he was separated by nearly sixty years from his renown as a child prodigy, Clara imagined in her mind as young as Johannes was now and making love to her rival Maria Moke in Berlioz's apartment and pictured him watching her in Paris with her white dress flying high as she vaulted over Chopin. But what, she wondered, did he envision when he saw her now, thirty-seven years old with eight children torn from her belly and two more bled from between her legs and grief at war inside her with release?

Robert's coffin was borne by even younger men than Brahms and Joachim, members of the Düsseldorf Concordia male choir, a few of whom had endured his distracted conducting and a few more of whom he would have found beautiful had he been alive to see them.

On what would have been Schumann's forty-seventh birthday, a headstone was erected on his grave, as much the work of Brahms as the Beethoven monument had been that of Liszt and for this reason vastly more simple and obscure. It would be another twenty-five years before Schumann received a monument in his likeness on that site, so cold in its resemblance to him that Clara could not bear to look at it. At its unveiling, on May 2, 1880, Joachim played and Brahms conducted. Money had begun to be raised for the statue seven years earlier, at a concert where Brahms conducted and Clara played, described by her daughter Eugenie as looking like a young girl, a bride; when she finished, at least a hundred and fifty bouquets came flying at her.

Friedrich Wieck was sentenced to eighteen days in prison for what were taken to be his libelous accusations against his son-in-law, who of course went on to live a life that proved some of them to be accurate. By the time he died in 1873 at the age of eighty-eight, Wieck had reconciled with Clara and felt safe, with her husband long dead, in leaving her a small fortune, his pride at this bequest unpricked by any sense that this money had been hers to begin with.

A statue of Felix Mendelssohn was sculpted by Erwin Stein and placed before the Gewandhaus in Leipzig in 1892. There it stood until November 10, 1936. On that date, Sir Thomas Beecham arrived in Leipzig with his London Philharmonic Orchestra and requested of the city's mayor, Karl Goerderler, permission to place a wreath upon the statue. Goerderler said such a gesture would honor both the city of Leipzig and the memory of Mendelssohn. But the statue was not to be found in its place before the Gewandhaus. It had the night before been taken away and smashed to pieces. This was done under directive from the government in Berlin, which had demanded the destruction of the "monument to the one-hundred-percent Jew" (so much for the asylum of conversion) in order, in the words of the *Leipziger Tageszeitung,* "to exterminate the damage done to our cultural heritage by Judaism." So embarrassed was Mayor Goerderler by the confusion caused the delegates of the London Philharmonic, not to mention the shame to his city, that he eventually joined the 1944 plot against Adolf Hitler, for which he was executed in 1945.

Mendelssohn, on pedestal, had lasted longer than Heine, on paper. All Heine's writings were burned countrywide in festively public autos-da-fé in March 1933. Because he had written in "Almansor," "where books are burned, they end up burning people," there were Germans after the war who blamed Heine for the incinerator camps, arguing that prophecy is as much the cause as the forecasting of event and that had Heine not written such words, no Jews, Gypsies, homosexuals, communists, vegetarians, nudists, pickpockets, herbalists, evangelists, mimes, stutterers, journalists, dentists, dwarves, or any other undesirables would have burned. Thus, because Heine himself had been a Jew (or why else would it have been necessary to burn his work?), it was a Jew who by his very prophecy had caused the holycost, whatever that was.

Heine, after nearly eight years lying on his mattress tomb, embraced his Judaism. Where he had once been, he said, a life-engulfing, pleasure-devouring Hellene who smiled condescendingly upon austere Nazarenes, he was now nothing more than a poor, doomed Jew, an emaciated image of anguish. Prophecy in the flesh.

The marches Schumann had written around the time of the 1849 revolution, including those for male chorus and military band, he had either never published or were so bad that even the Nazis couldn't march to them. But there were parts of *Paradise and the Peri* so rousingly martial that they were played in the sacred service of patriotism and by coincidence were used to inspire German pilots on their way to bomb London, where Clara had sung in the *Peri* chorus as her husband lay dying in Endenich.

The large house in Zwickau at Number 2 Amtsgasse, to which the Schumann family moved in 1817, as much to gain space for August's growing business as for the six children to run around in (particularly with Emilie spending more and more time alone in her room on the third floor), was destroyed in an Allied air raid in early 1945.

One of Felix Mendelssohn's favorite quotations (Seneca's *Verum gaudium res severa est*) was chiseled into the façade of the site of his greatest triumphs, the Leipzig Gewandhaus, and together with the rest of the building was reduced to incoherence by bombs in World War II. True enjoyment is serious business, say Seneca's words, now dust in the cosmos.

In the dark of the night of February 13, 1945, Dresden was firebombed by the Allies and 80 percent of the city destroyed. Many of the Schumann family papers (letters, diaries, etc.) were ruined, not by fire but by water meant to extinguish the fire. Their content, however, had been preserved on microfilm in 1938, and survives.

Endenich, the suburb, became incorporated into the city of Bonn as Bonn expanded. Endenich, the insane asylum, was hit by bombs during the aforementioned war. There were still small pieces of Robert Schumann lying here and there.

But not his head. It, together with the rest of his body, had been opened by Dr. Richarz on the day after Schumann's death, for the purpose of autopsy. This autopsy achieved no definitive explanation for the physical deterioration and eventual death of Robert Schumann, which has resulted in numerous posthumous explanations: hypertension; pneumonia; *Osteitis Deformans* (Paget's disease); meningitis; pituitary apoplexy; syphilis; Korsakoff's encephalopathy; a manic-depression so powerful it might have eaten away at Schumann's brain, which was found to be considerably atrophied and to weigh approximately seven ounces less than was normal in a male of his years; cumulative concussive marasmus as a consequence of repeated drunken gravitations; self-starvation; overwork.

It was the last that Dr. Richarz determined was the cause of what he could only vaguely name the progressive organic disease that claimed his patient's life. In short, he concluded, Schumann was killed by his music.

So frustrated were later Schumann votaries (death and time, in their sneering complicity, drew to his music people the likes of whom it had repelled in his lifetime) at not knowing why he had left them for no apparent reason at so reasonably young an age (and with so accomplished a wife; with so many charming children, few of them able to remember him) that they dug up his head.

Actually, they exhumed all of him, but appropriated only the head. It was examined in 1885 by Professor Hermann Schaaffhausen, a medical anthropologist, who declared on the basis of his examination of the skull (everything packed back into the skull after the 1856 autopsy had by that time dematerialized, to put a kindly term upon it) that it was normal. How it might have compared with Haydn's and Mozart's and Beethoven's was left unstudied.

Yet so rare was this head (unless it was merely inconsequential) that it was never returned to its body in the tiny churchyard of Bonn's Alter Friedhof and has been missing ever since.

Thus, when Clara was buried next to Robert on May 24, 1896, her eyes, could they see, would have seen through the wood and soil and leaves and bugs that her beloved husband, whose troubled, beautiful head she had cradled so often to her bosom, had no head and thus was not, in essence, her husband.

She had died of a stroke four days earlier. Johannes was vacationing in Ischl and rushed to be at her funeral. In his weary grief, he missed his connection in Attnang and rode endlessly in the wrong direction, spent an entire night in the Linz station, journeyed to Frankfurt, where she lived and he assumed she would be buried, only to discover that the funeral was in Bonn, where he arrived the next day in time to see the funeral procession moving away from him as if in perfect imitation of death.

In his exhaustion, he caught a cold while standing there shivering and seeing through his tears the refracted image of his one great love floating briefly on the very skin of the world. He never regained his strength and died less than a year later.

Out of fear that their relationship would never be understood, Clara and Johannes late in their lives returned their letters to one another and, as agreed, destroyed them. Clara, many years earlier—almost immediately after Robert's death—had anticipated not only lack of understanding but hostility and wrote in her diary a letter to her children about her relationship with Brahms. In it, she told them that only Johannes, as she called him in the letter, was able to comfort her through the illness and the death of their father. He shared her sorrow. He fortified her heart. He enriched her mind. He lifted her spirits. He was her friend in the fullest sense of the word. They shared an exquisite harmony of soul, and her dear children should never listen to those parochial and envious souls who begrudged him her love and friendship and therefore tried to reproach him or even to decry their relations, which they could not, and never would, understand.

When Clara's safe was opened after her death, this letter was found, as well as the little box and its letter in praise of her given her by Goethe, and Robert's favorite cigar case with several cadaverous, exfoliating cigars within, and the note she had found beneath his hairbrush on the day he disappeared from their house in Düsseldorf and she never saw him again until she saw him at Endenich. "Dear Clara," it said, "I will throw my wedding ring into the Rhine. Do the same and both rings will then be united."

The idea that Brahms might have fathered Felix Schumann was not merely the idle speculation of Robert Schumann's damaged imagination as he lay in bed in Endenich. His grandson, Alfred Schumann, wrote a little book called *Johannes Brahms: The Father of Felix Schumann*. Most copies were burned by the Nazis because such a notion as the book asserted was deemed to dishonor all Germans.

Joseph Joachim married the contralto Ursi Schneeweiss in 1863. Their first child they named Johannes. Their second, Clara.